Archie's® CAMPFIRE STORIES

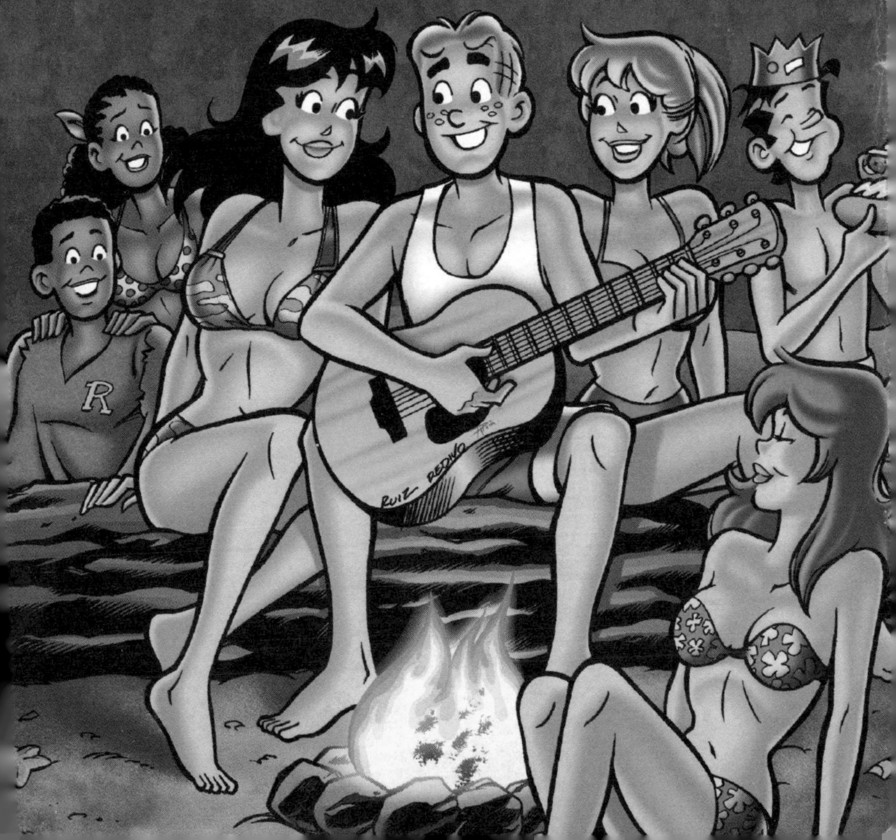

Archie's

CAMPFIRE STORIES

Archie & Friends All-Stars Series: Volume 25
ARCHIE'S CAMPFIRE STORIES
Published by Archie Comic Publications, Inc.
629 Fifth Avenue, Pelham, New York 10803-1242.
www.ArchieComics.com

Printed in U.S.A. First Printing.

ISBN: 978-1-62738-942-6

PUBLISHER/CO-CEO: Jon Goldwater
CO-CEO: Nancy Silberkleit
PRESIDENT: Mike Pellerito
CO-PRESIDENT/EDITOR-IN-CHIEF: Victor Gorelick
CHIEF CREATIVE OFFICER: Roberto Aguirre-Sacasa
CHIEF OPERATING OFFICER: William Mooar
CHIEF FINANCIAL OFFICER: Robert Wintle
SENIOR VICE PRESIDENT,
PUBLISHING & OPERATIONS: Harold Buchholz
SENIOR VICE PRESIDENT,
PUBLICITY & MARKETING: Alex Segura
DIRECTOR, BOOK SALES & OPERATIONS:
Jon Betancourt
PRODUCTION MANAGER:
Stephen Oswald
PROJECT COORDINATOR/
BOOK DESIGN:
Duncan McLachlan
EDITORIAL ASSISTANT/
PROOFREADER:
Jamie Lee Rotante

FEATURING THE TALENTS OF:

Frank Doyle, Joe Edwards, Dan DeCarlo, Alison Flood, Henry Scarpelli, Al Hartley, Joe Sinott, John Lowe, George Gladir, Jon D'Agostino, Barry Grossman, Chic Stone, Bill Yoshida, Jim DeCarlo, Mike Esposito, Fernando Ruiz, Al Nickerson, Mike Pellowski, Angelo DeCesare, Stan Goldberg, Vickie Williams, Dan Parent, John Wilcox, Dexter Taylor, Samm Schwartz, John Rose, Tim Kennedy, Jack Morelli, Jeff Shultz, Al Milgrom, Rex Lindsey, Rudy Lapick, Ken Selig, Bob Bolling, Bill Vigoda, Mario Acquaviva, Victor Gorelick, Bob Smith, Dan DeCarlo, Jr.

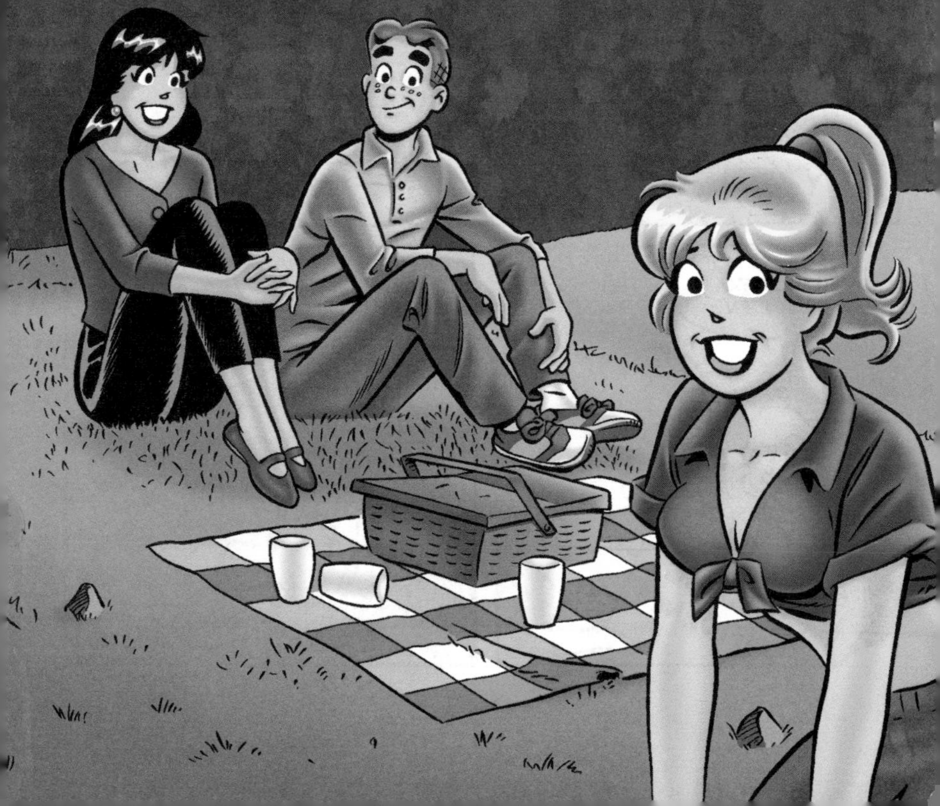

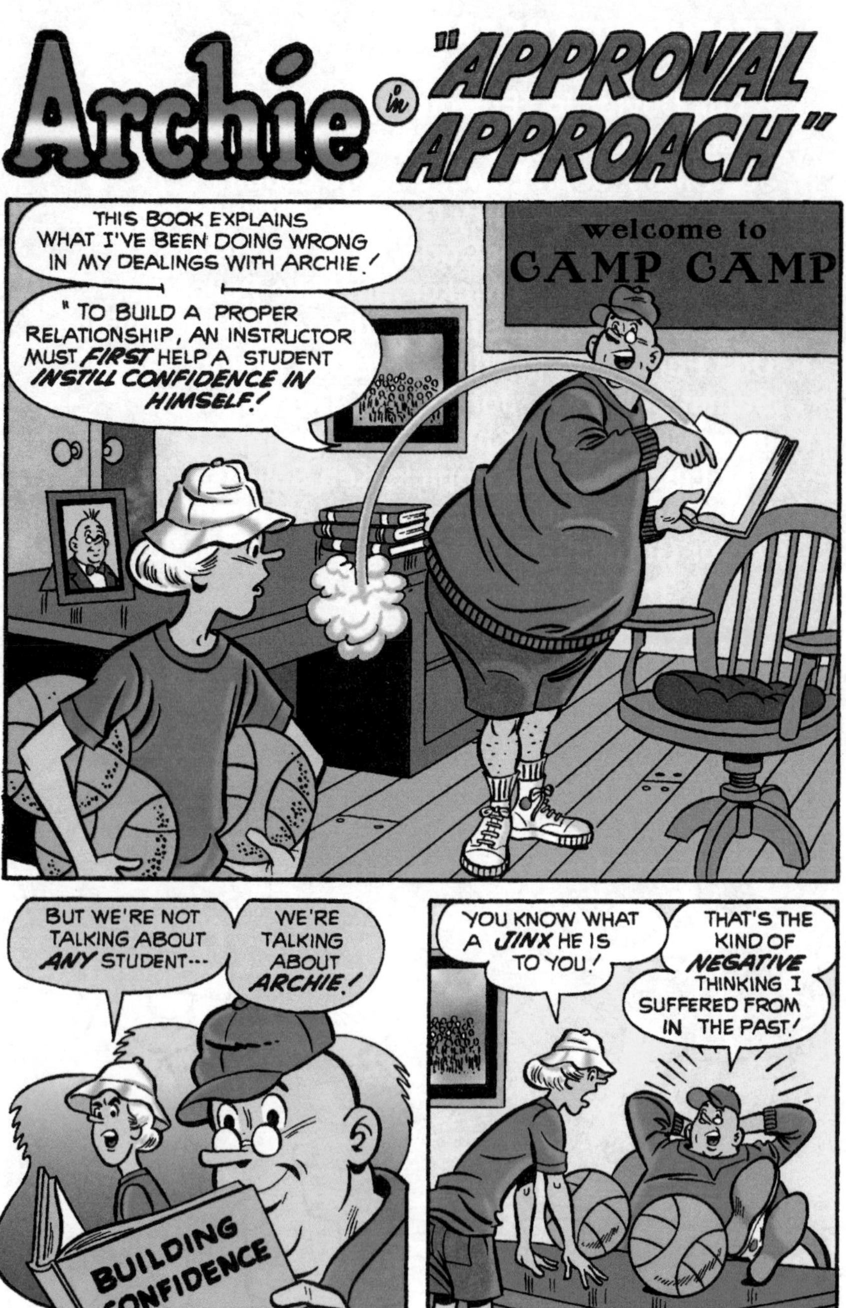
Archie in "APPROVAL APPROACH"
welcome to CAMP CAMP
THIS BOOK EXPLAINS WHAT I'VE BEEN DOING WRONG IN MY DEALINGS WITH ARCHIE!
"TO BUILD A PROPER RELATIONSHIP, AN INSTRUCTOR MUST FIRST HELP A STUDENT INSTILL CONFIDENCE IN HIMSELF!
BUT WE'RE NOT TALKING ABOUT ANY STUDENT---
WE'RE TALKING ABOUT ARCHIE!
BUILDING CONFIDENCE
YOU KNOW WHAT A JINX HE IS TO YOU!
THAT'S THE KIND OF NEGATIVE THINKING I SUFFERED FROM IN THE PAST!

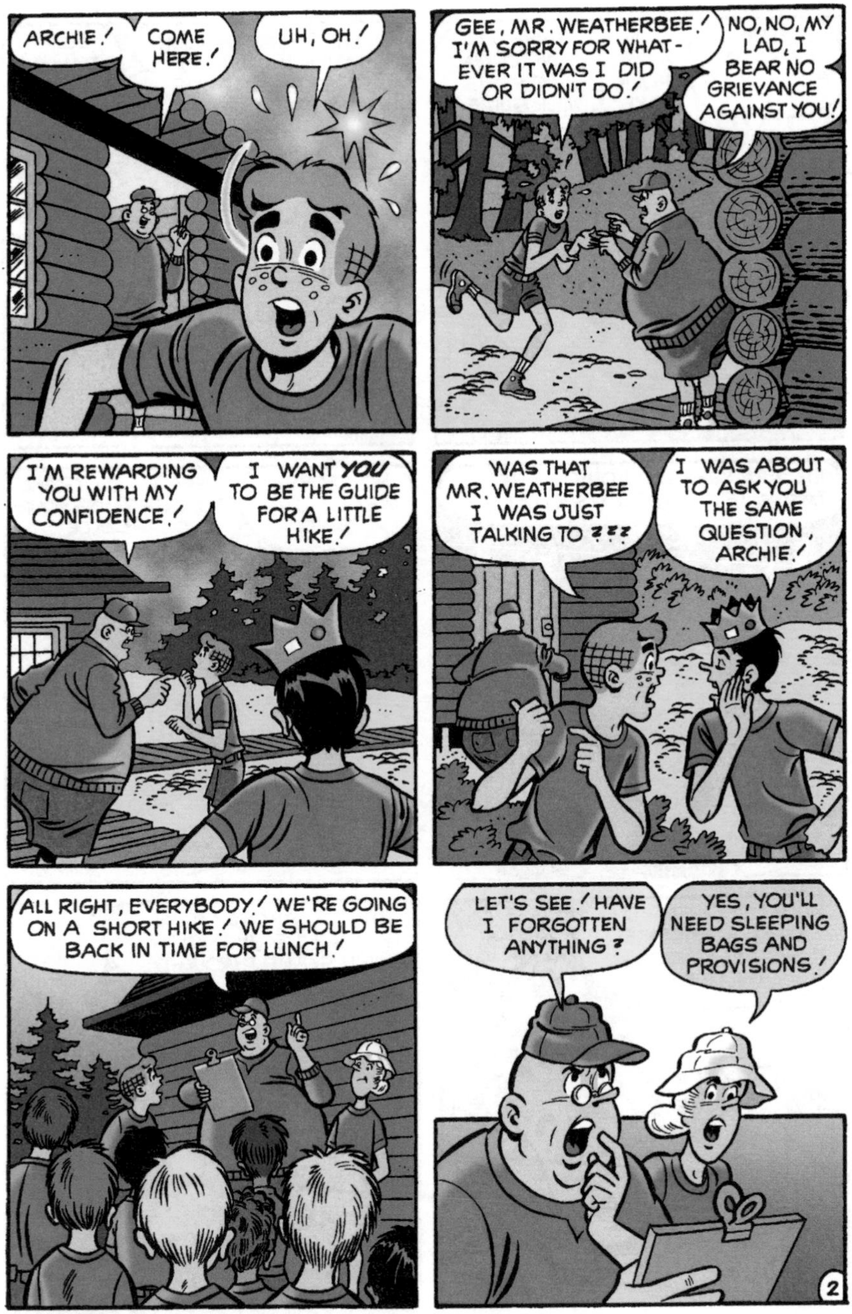

ARCHIE!
COME HERE!
UH, OH!
GEE, MR. WEATHERBEE! I'M SORRY FOR WHAT-EVER IT WAS I DID OR DIDN'T DO!
NO, NO, MY LAD, I BEAR NO GRIEVANCE AGAINST YOU!
I'M REWARDING YOU WITH MY CONFIDENCE!
I WANT YOU TO BE THE GUIDE FOR A LITTLE HIKE!
WAS THAT MR. WEATHERBEE I WAS JUST TALKING TO ???
I WAS ABOUT TO ASK YOU THE SAME QUESTION, ARCHIE!
ALL RIGHT, EVERYBODY! WE'RE GOING ON A SHORT HIKE! WE SHOULD BE BACK IN TIME FOR LUNCH!
LET'S SEE! HAVE I FORGOTTEN ANYTHING?
YES, YOU'LL NEED SLEEPING BAGS AND PROVISIONS!
2

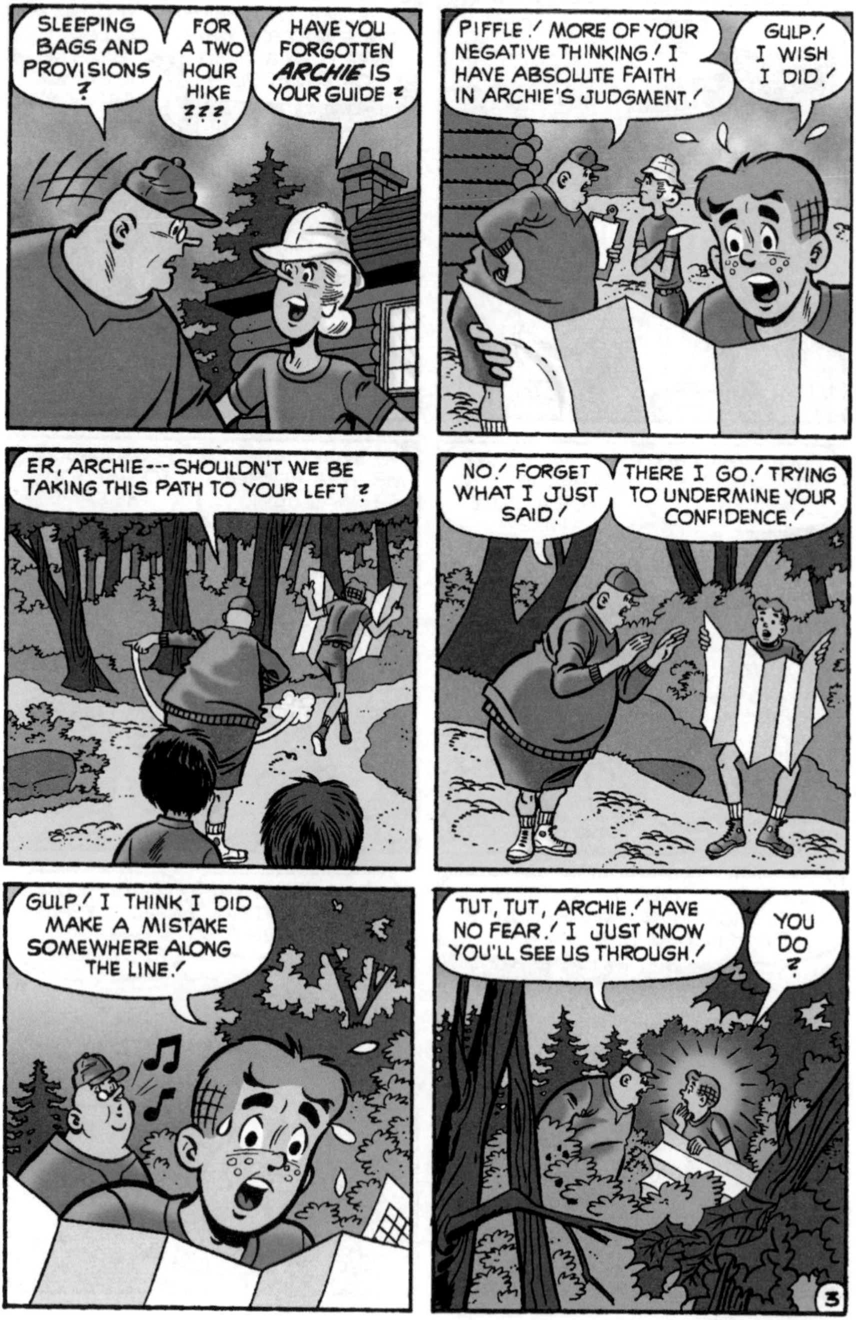
SLEEPING BAGS AND PROVISIONS ?
FOR A TWO HOUR HIKE ???
HAVE YOU FORGOTTEN ARCHIE IS YOUR GUIDE ?
PIFFLE! MORE OF YOUR NEGATIVE THINKING! I HAVE ABSOLUTE FAITH IN ARCHIE'S JUDGMENT!
GULP! I WISH I DID!
ER, ARCHIE--- SHOULDN'T WE BE TAKING THIS PATH TO YOUR LEFT ?
NO! FORGET WHAT I JUST SAID!
THERE I GO! TRYING TO UNDERMINE YOUR CONFIDENCE!
GULP! I THINK I DID MAKE A MISTAKE SOMEWHERE ALONG THE LINE!
TUT, TUT, ARCHIE! HAVE NO FEAR! I JUST KNOW YOU'LL SEE US THROUGH!
YOU DO ?
3

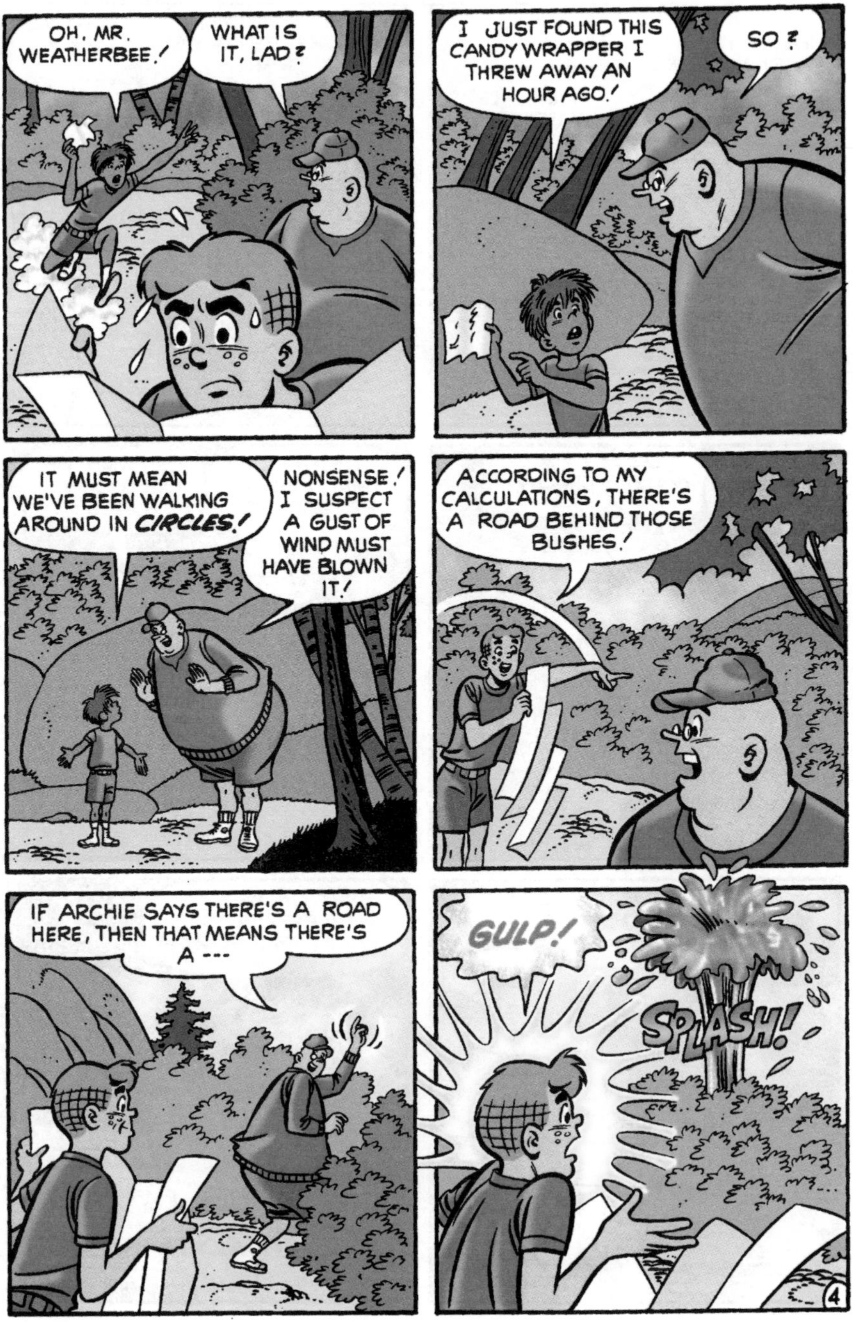

OH, MR. WEATHERBEE!
WHAT IS IT, LAD?
I JUST FOUND THIS CANDY WRAPPER I THREW AWAY AN HOUR AGO!
SO?
IT MUST MEAN WE'VE BEEN WALKING AROUND IN *CIRCLES!*
NONSENSE! I SUSPECT A GUST OF WIND MUST HAVE BLOWN IT!
ACCORDING TO MY CALCULATIONS, THERE'S A ROAD BEHIND THOSE BUSHES!
IF ARCHIE SAYS THERE'S A ROAD HERE, THEN THAT MEANS THERE'S A ---
GULP!
SPLASH!
4

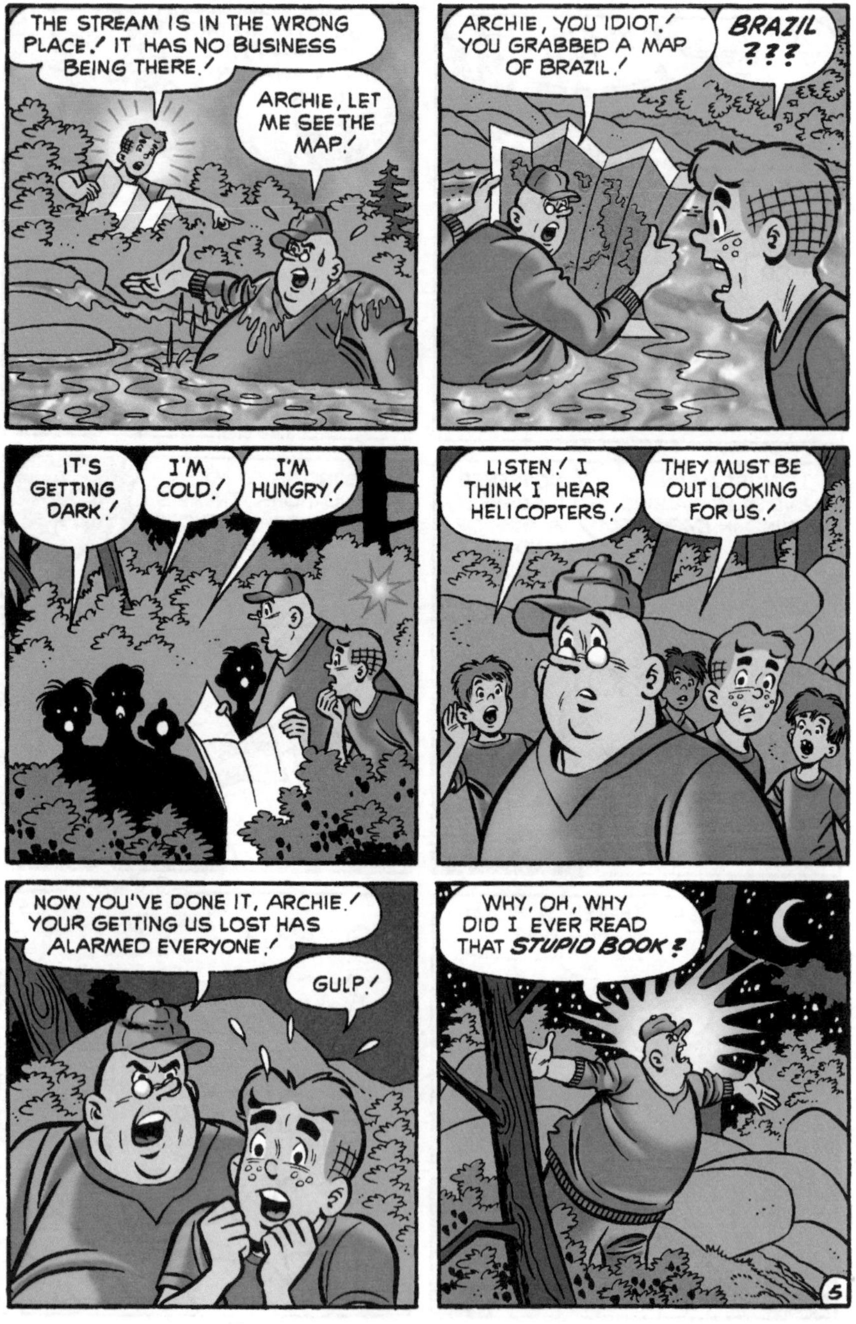
THE STREAM IS IN THE WRONG PLACE! IT HAS NO BUSINESS BEING THERE!
ARCHIE, LET ME SEE THE MAP!
ARCHIE, YOU IDIOT! YOU GRABBED A MAP OF BRAZIL!
BRAZIL ???
IT'S GETTING DARK!
I'M COLD!
I'M HUNGRY!
LISTEN! I THINK I HEAR HELICOPTERS!
THEY MUST BE OUT LOOKING FOR US!
NOW YOU'VE DONE IT, ARCHIE! YOUR GETTING US LOST HAS ALARMED EVERYONE!
GULP!
WHY, OH, WHY DID I EVER READ THAT STUPID BOOK?
5

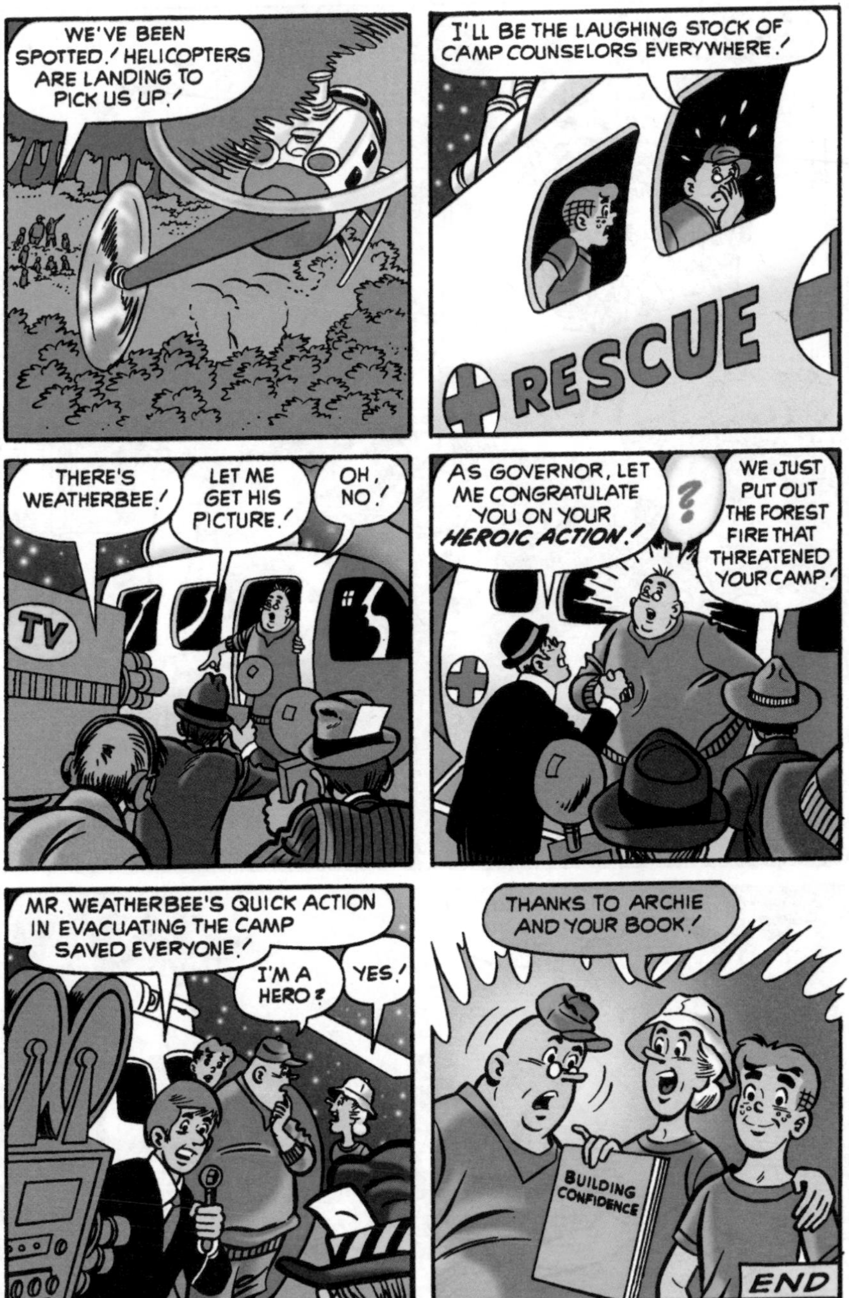
WE'VE BEEN SPOTTED! HELICOPTERS ARE LANDING TO PICK US UP!
I'LL BE THE LAUGHING STOCK OF CAMP COUNSELORS EVERYWHERE!
RESCUE
THERE'S WEATHERBEE!
LET ME GET HIS PICTURE!
OH, NO!
TV
AS GOVERNOR, LET ME CONGRATULATE YOU ON YOUR HEROIC ACTION!
?
WE JUST PUT OUT THE FOREST FIRE THAT THREATENED YOUR CAMP!
MR. WEATHERBEE'S QUICK ACTION IN EVACUATING THE CAMP SAVED EVERYONE!
I'M A HERO?
YES!
THANKS TO ARCHIE AND YOUR BOOK!
BUILDING CONFIDENCE
END

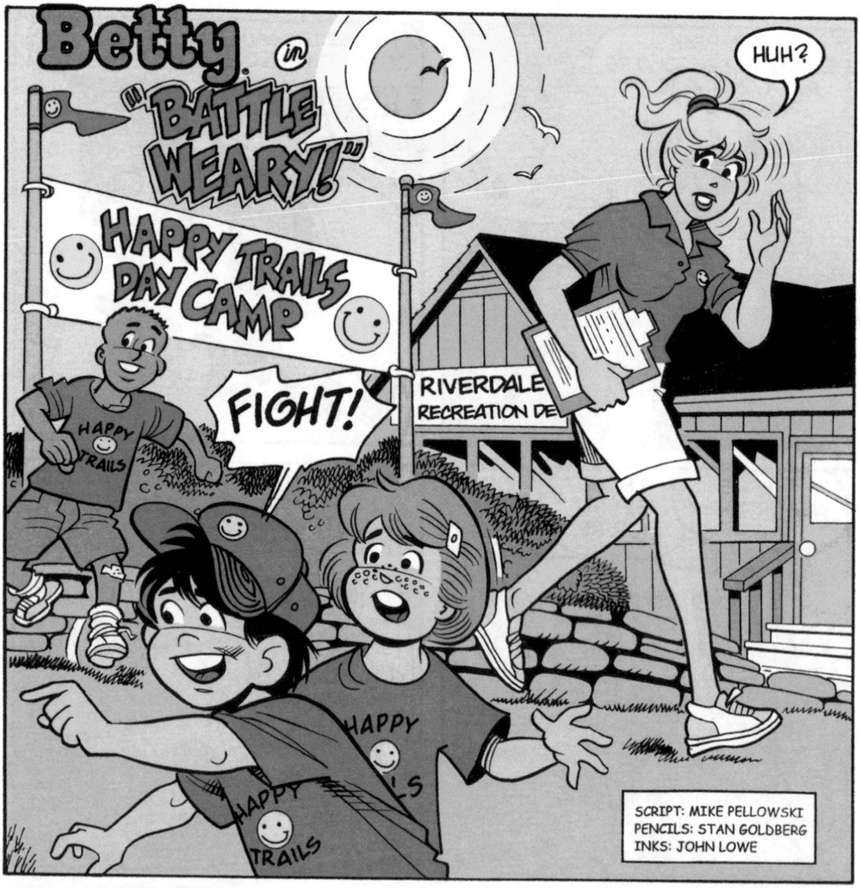
Betty in
"BATTLE WEARY!"
HAPPY TRAILS DAY CAMP
RIVERDALE RECREATION DE
HUH?
FIGHT!
HAPPY TRAILS
SCRIPT: MIKE PELLOWSKI
PENCILS: STAN GOLDBERG
INKS: JOHN LOWE

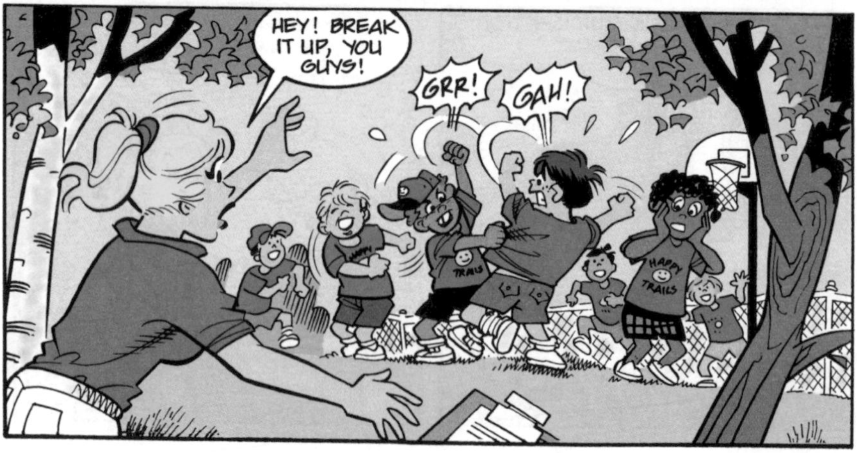
HEY! BREAK IT UP, YOU GUYS!
GRR!
GAH!
HAPPY TRAILS

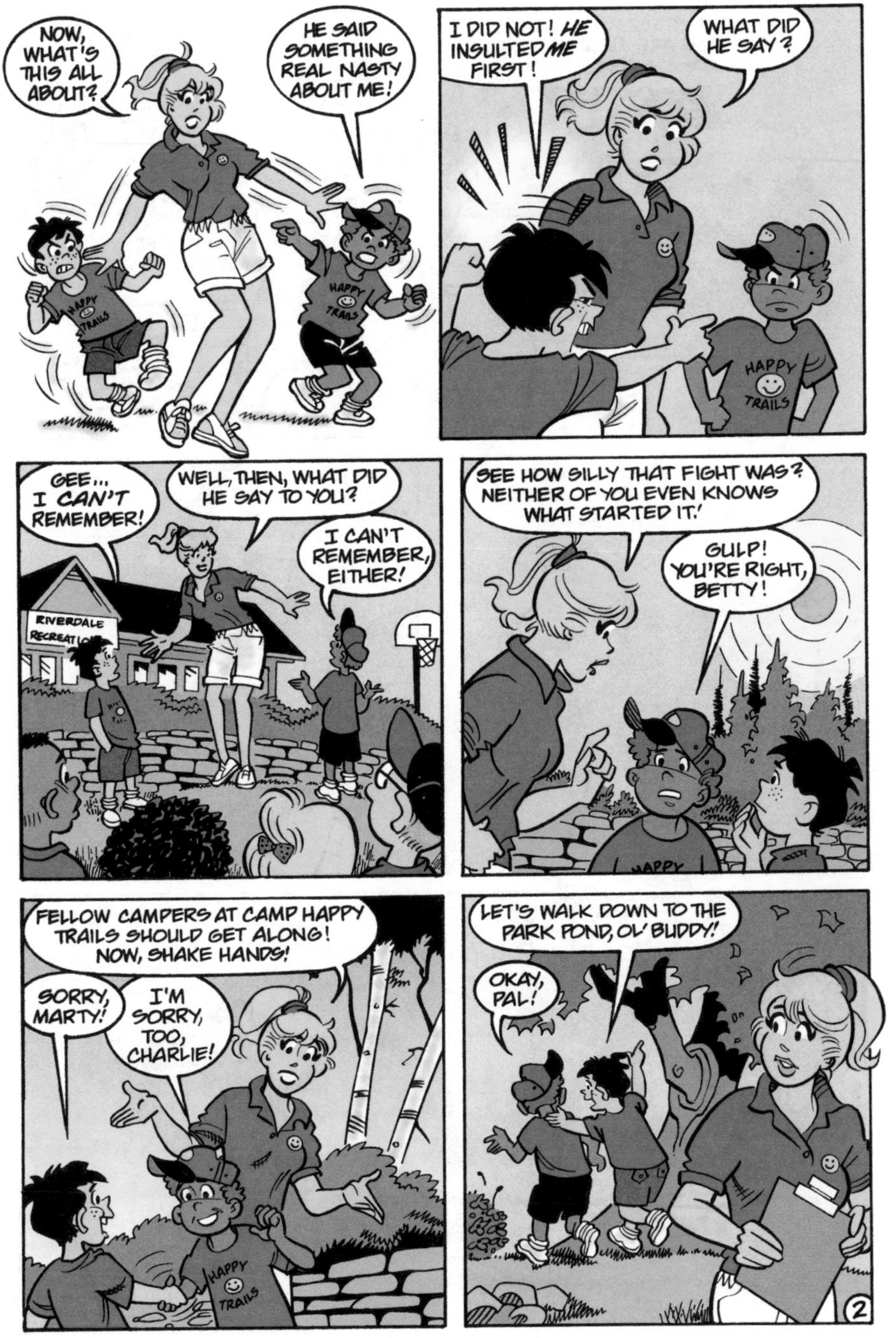
NOW, WHAT'S THIS ALL ABOUT?
HE SAID SOMETHING REAL NASTY ABOUT ME!
I DID NOT! *HE* INSULTED *ME* FIRST!
WHAT DID HE SAY?
GEE... I *CAN'T* REMEMBER!
WELL, THEN, WHAT DID HE SAY TO YOU?
I CAN'T REMEMBER, EITHER!
RIVERDALE
SEE HOW SILLY THAT FIGHT WAS? NEITHER OF YOU EVEN KNOWS WHAT STARTED IT!
GULP! YOU'RE RIGHT, BETTY!
FELLOW CAMPERS AT CAMP HAPPY TRAILS SHOULD GET ALONG! NOW, SHAKE HANDS!
SORRY, MARTY!
I'M SORRY, TOO, CHARLIE!
LET'S WALK DOWN TO THE PARK POND, OL' BUDDY!
OKAY, PAL!

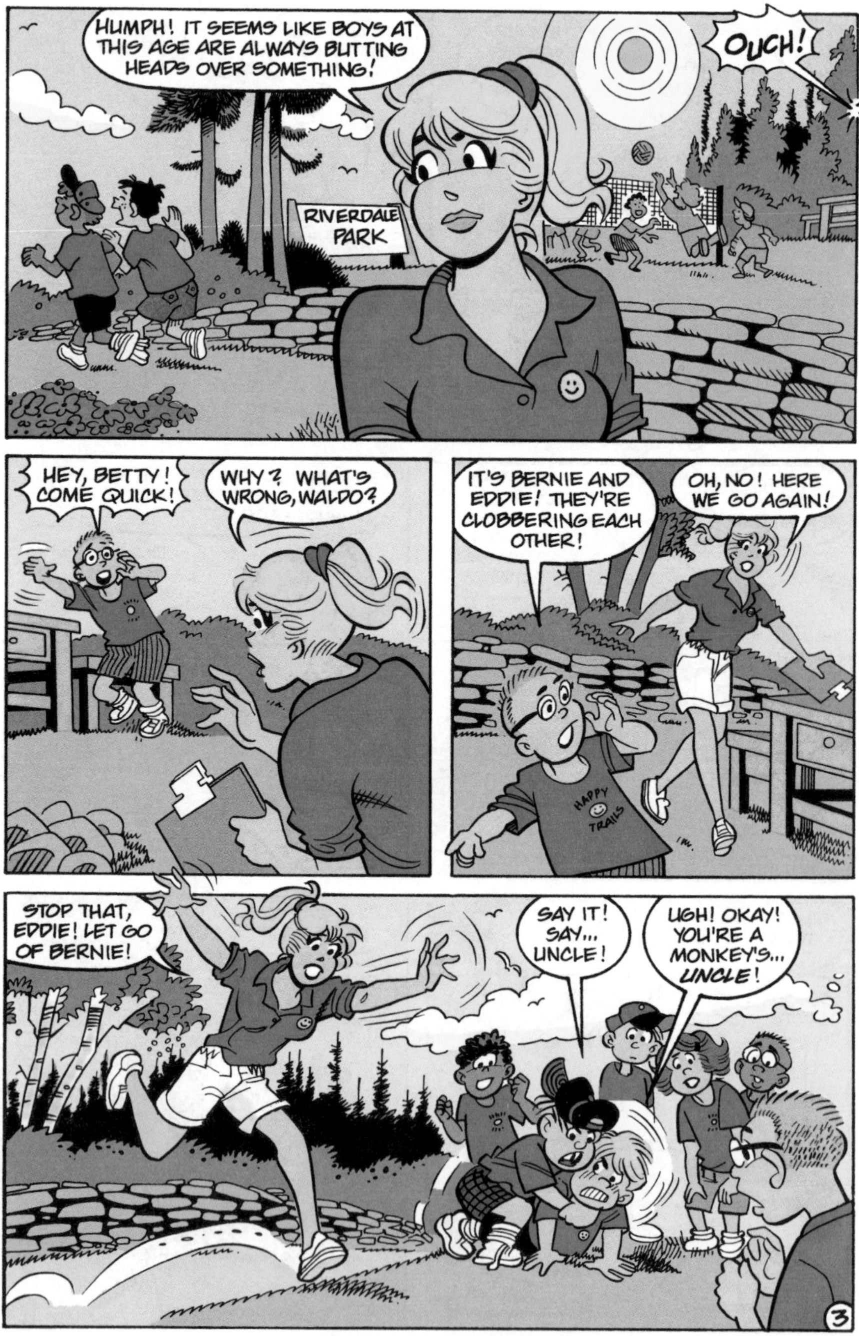
HUMPH! IT SEEMS LIKE BOYS AT THIS AGE ARE ALWAYS BUTTING HEADS OVER SOMETHING!
OUCH!
RIVERDALE PARK
HEY, BETTY! COME QUICK!
WHY? WHAT'S WRONG, WALDO?
IT'S BERNIE AND EDDIE! THEY'RE CLOBBERING EACH OTHER!
HAPPY TRAILS
OH, NO! HERE WE GO AGAIN!
STOP THAT, EDDIE! LET GO OF BERNIE!
SAY IT! SAY... UNCLE!
UGH! OKAY! YOU'RE A MONKEY'S... UNCLE!
3

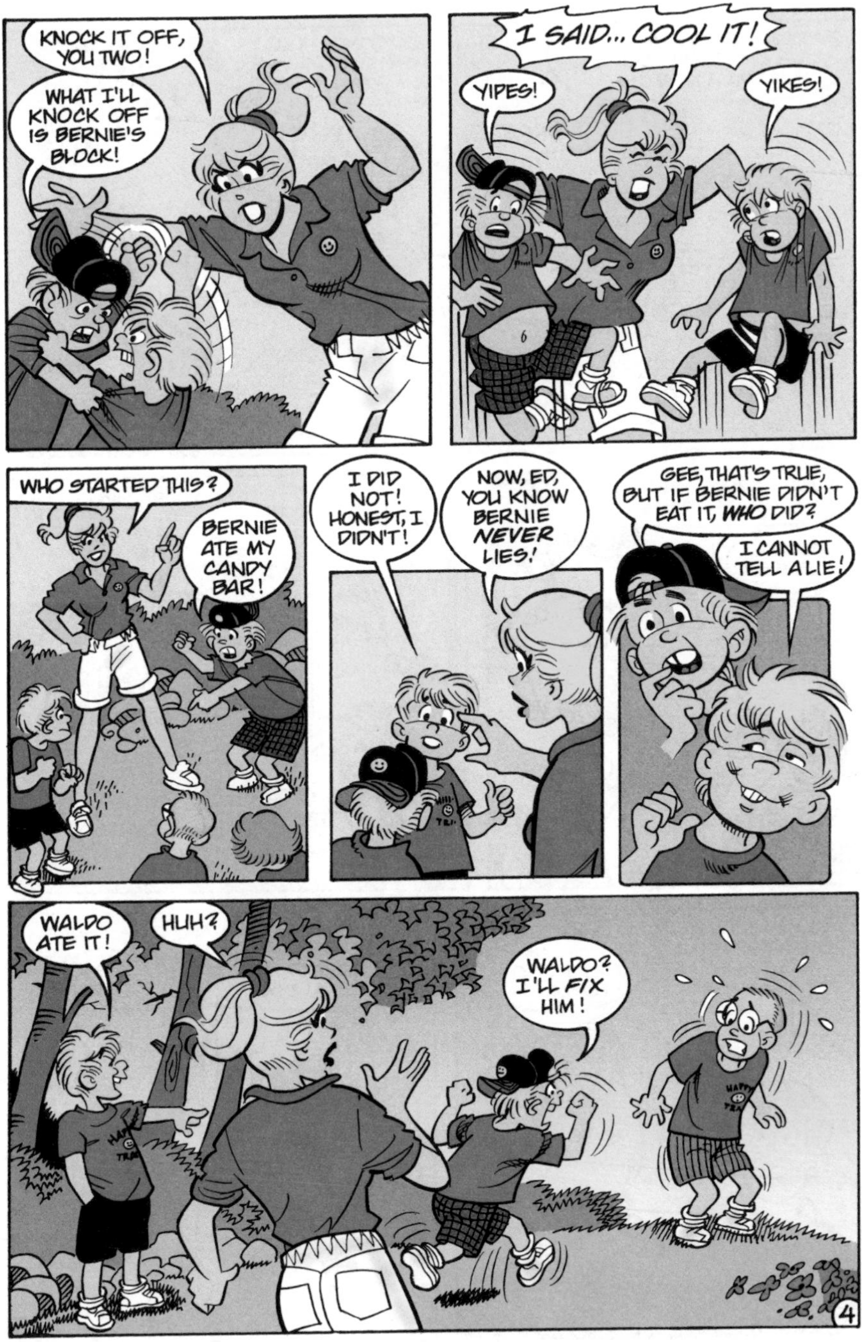
KNOCK IT OFF, YOU TWO!
WHAT I'LL KNOCK OFF IS BERNIE'S BLOCK!
I SAID... COOL IT!
YIPES!
YIKES!
WHO STARTED THIS?
BERNIE ATE MY CANDY BAR!
I DID NOT! HONEST, I DIDN'T!
NOW, ED, YOU KNOW BERNIE NEVER LIES!
GEE, THAT'S TRUE, BUT IF BERNIE DIDN'T EAT IT, WHO DID?
I CANNOT TELL A LIE!
WALDO ATE IT!
HUH?
WALDO? I'LL FIX HIM!

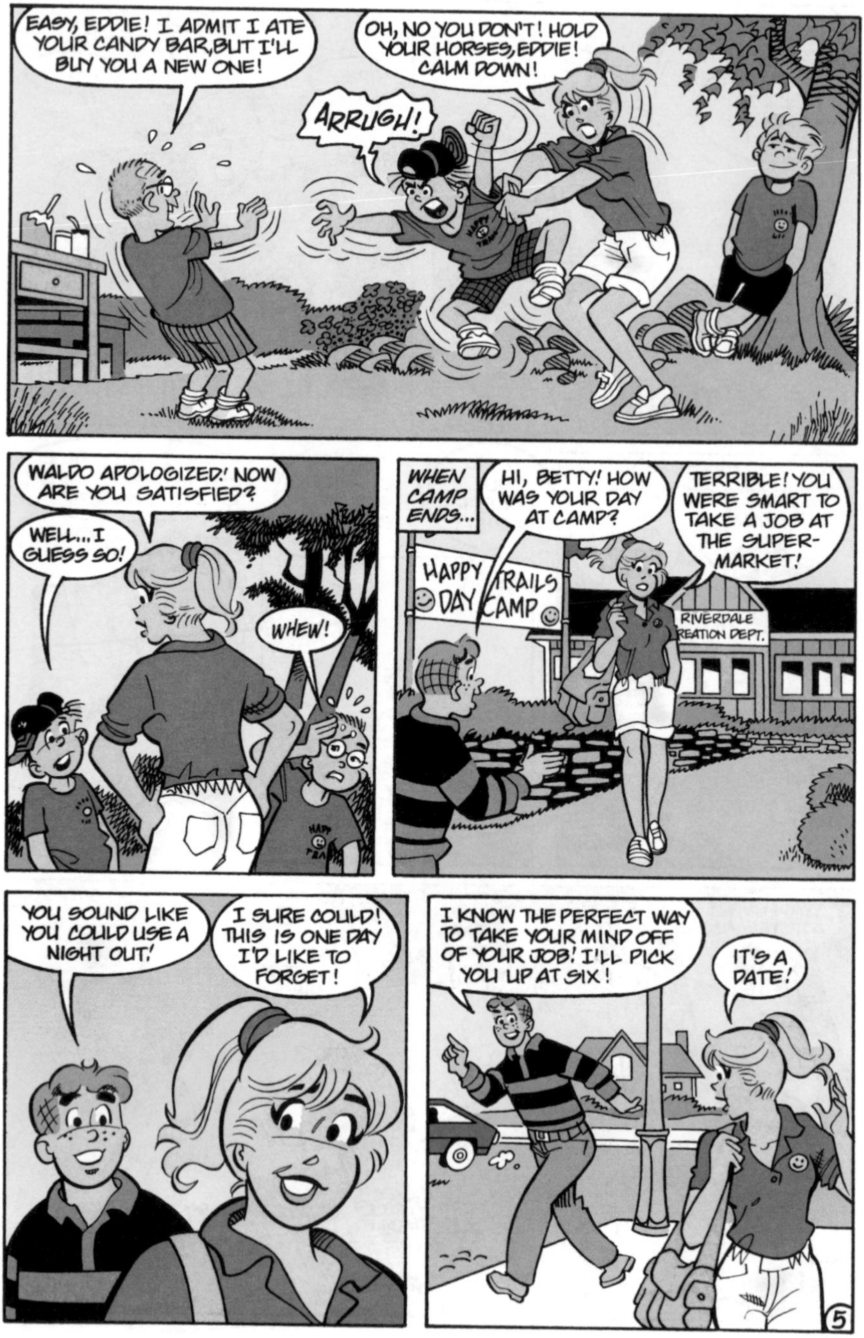

EASY, EDDIE! I ADMIT I ATE YOUR CANDY BAR, BUT I'LL BUY YOU A NEW ONE!
OH, NO YOU DON'T! HOLD YOUR HORSES, EDDIE! CALM DOWN!
ARRUGH!
WALDO APOLOGIZED! NOW ARE YOU SATISFIED?
WELL... I GUESS SO!
WHEW!
WHEN CAMP ENDS...
HAPPY DAY TRAILS CAMP
HI, BETTY! HOW WAS YOUR DAY AT CAMP?
TERRIBLE! YOU WERE SMART TO TAKE A JOB AT THE SUPER-MARKET!
RIVERDALE REATION DEPT.
YOU SOUND LIKE YOU COULD USE A NIGHT OUT!
I SURE COULD! THIS IS ONE DAY I'D LIKE TO FORGET!
I KNOW THE PERFECT WAY TO TAKE YOUR MIND OFF OF YOUR JOB! I'LL PICK YOU UP AT SIX!
IT'S A DATE!

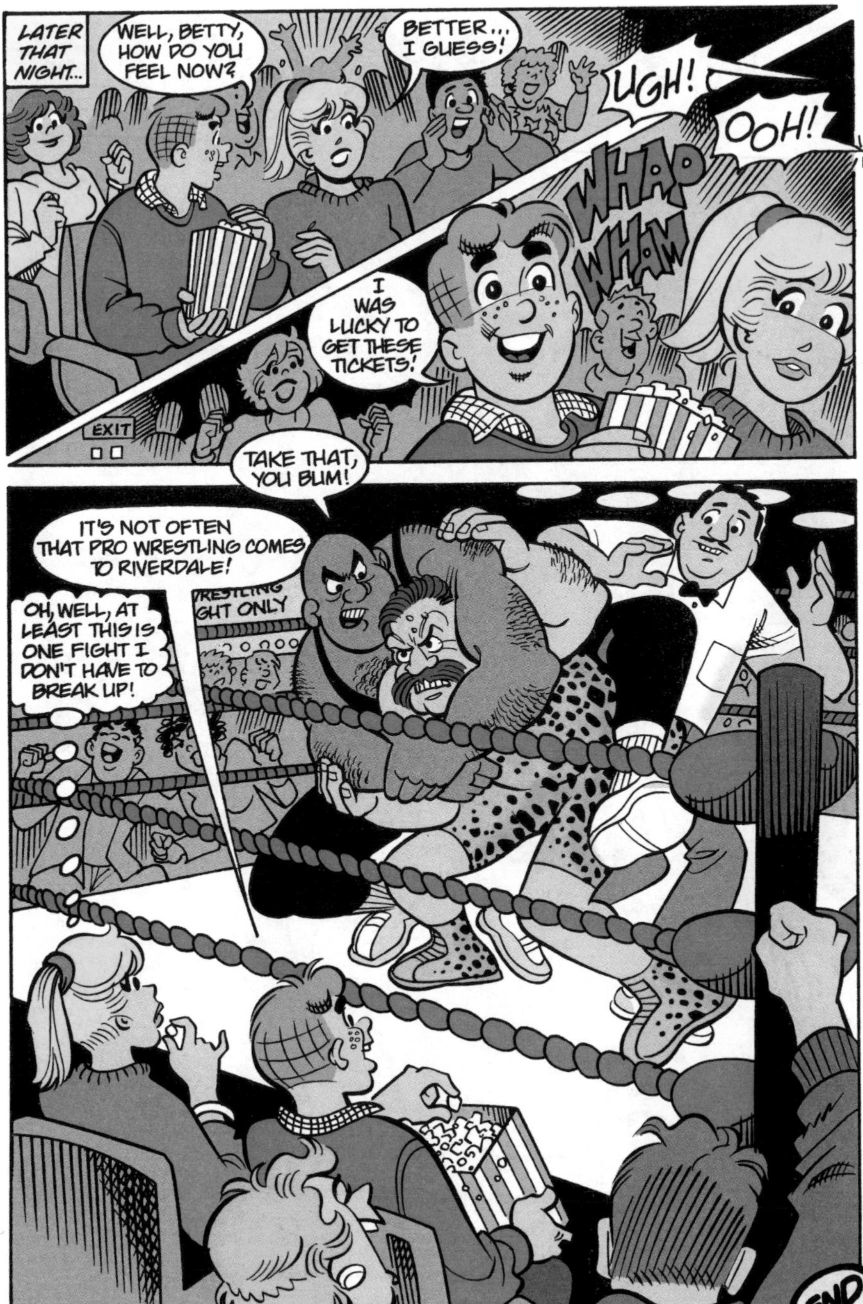
LATER THAT NIGHT...
WELL, BETTY, HOW DO YOU FEEL NOW?
BETTER... I GUESS!
UGH!
OOH!
WHAP
WHAM
I WAS LUCKY TO GET THESE TICKETS!
EXIT
TAKE THAT, YOU BUM!
IT'S NOT OFTEN THAT PRO WRESTLING COMES TO RIVERDALE!
OH, WELL, AT LEAST THIS IS ONE FIGHT I DON'T HAVE TO BREAK UP!
END

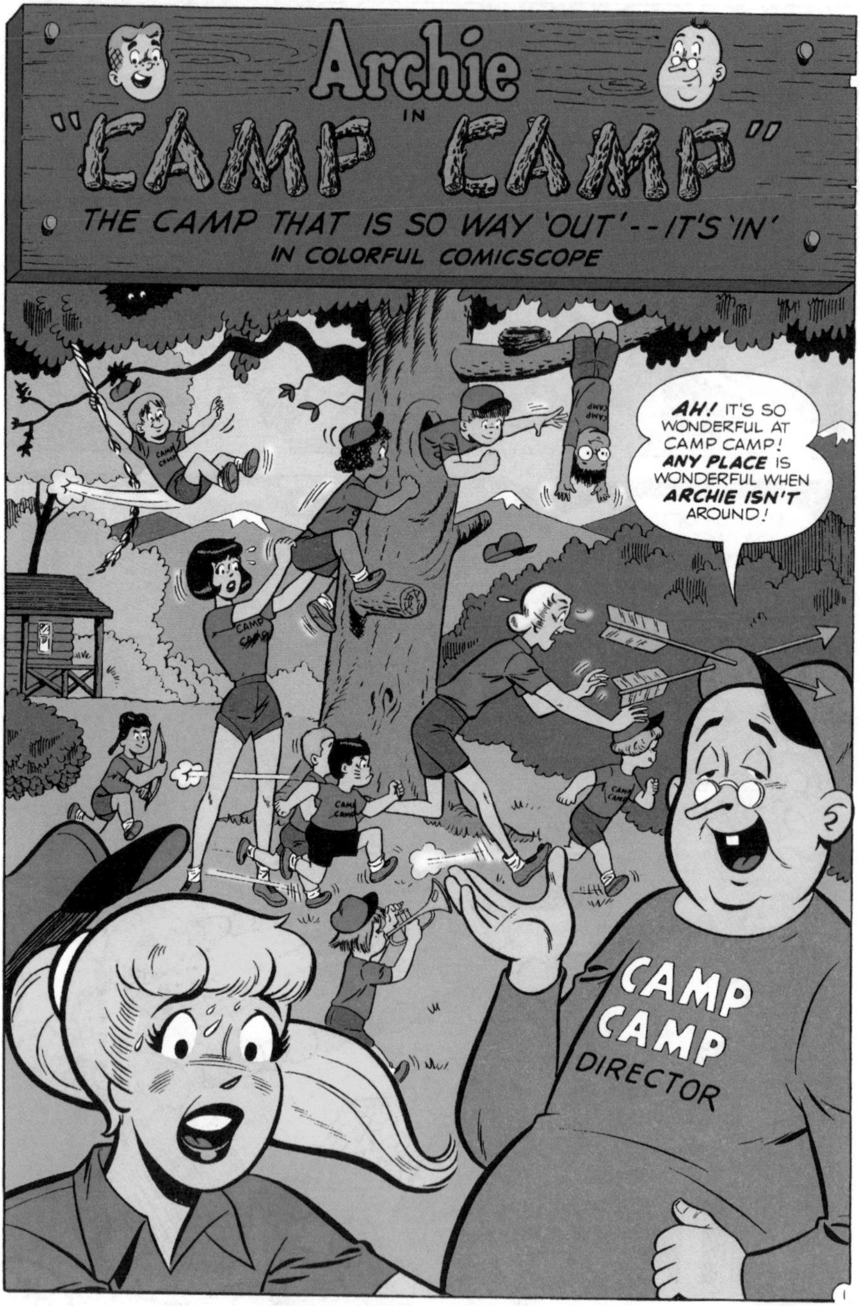
Archie
IN
"CAMP CAMP"
THE CAMP THAT IS SO WAY 'OUT'--IT'S 'IN'
IN COLORFUL COMICSCOPE
AH! IT'S SO WONDERFUL AT CAMP CAMP! ANY PLACE IS WONDERFUL WHEN ARCHIE ISN'T AROUND!
CAMP CAMP DIRECTOR

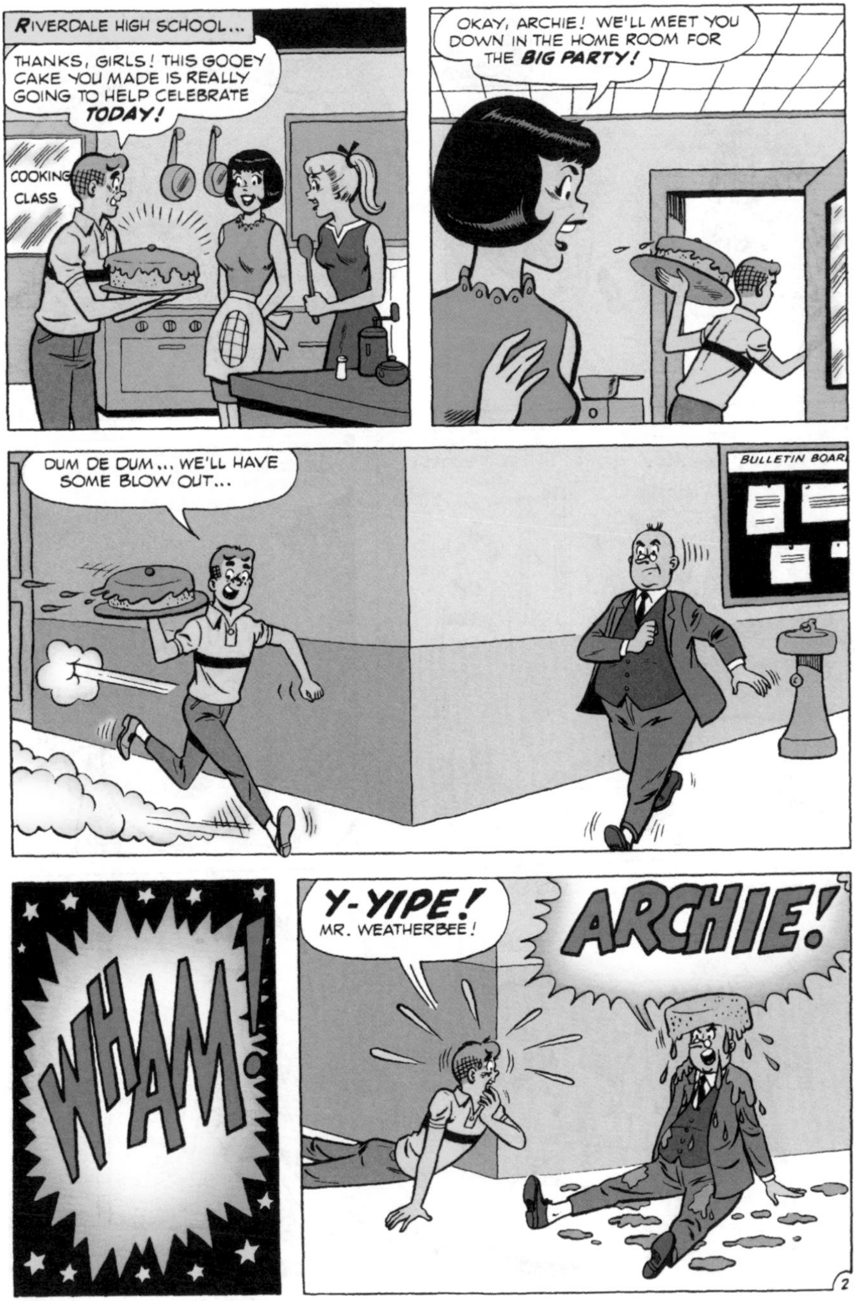
RIVERDALE HIGH SCHOOL...
THANKS, GIRLS! THIS GOOEY CAKE YOU MADE IS REALLY GOING TO HELP CELEBRATE TODAY!
COOKING CLASS
OKAY, ARCHIE! WE'LL MEET YOU DOWN IN THE HOME ROOM FOR THE BIG PARTY!
DUM DE DUM... WE'LL HAVE SOME BLOW OUT...
BULLETIN BOAR
WHAM!
Y-YIPE! MR. WEATHERBEE!
ARCHIE!
2

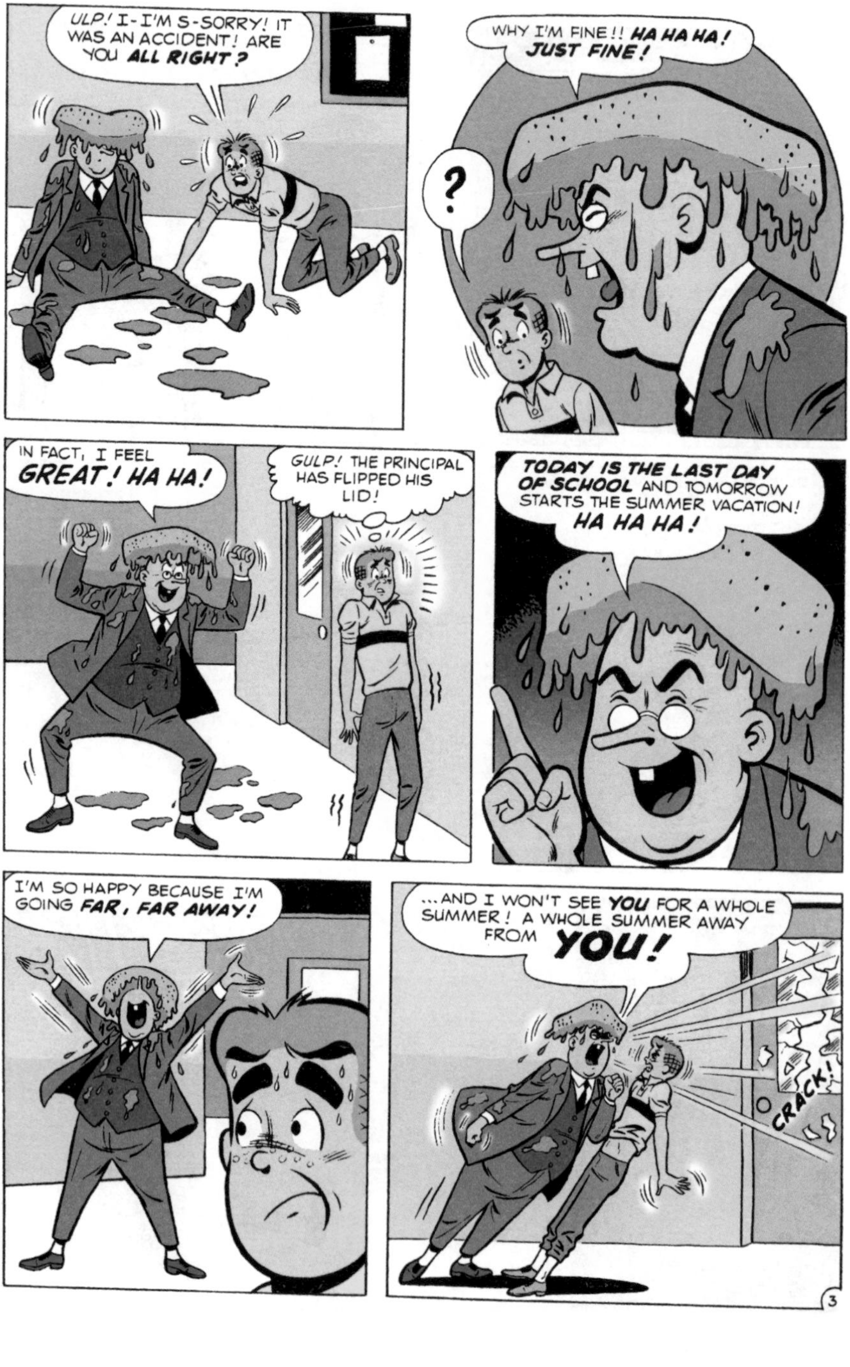
ULP! I-I'M S-SORRY! IT WAS AN ACCIDENT! ARE YOU ALL RIGHT?
WHY I'M FINE!! HA HA HA! JUST FINE!
?
IN FACT, I FEEL GREAT! HA HA!
GULP! THE PRINCIPAL HAS FLIPPED HIS LID!
TODAY IS THE LAST DAY OF SCHOOL AND TOMORROW STARTS THE SUMMER VACATION! HA HA HA!
I'M SO HAPPY BECAUSE I'M GOING FAR, FAR AWAY!
...AND I WON'T SEE YOU FOR A WHOLE SUMMER! A WHOLE SUMMER AWAY FROM YOU!
CRACK!

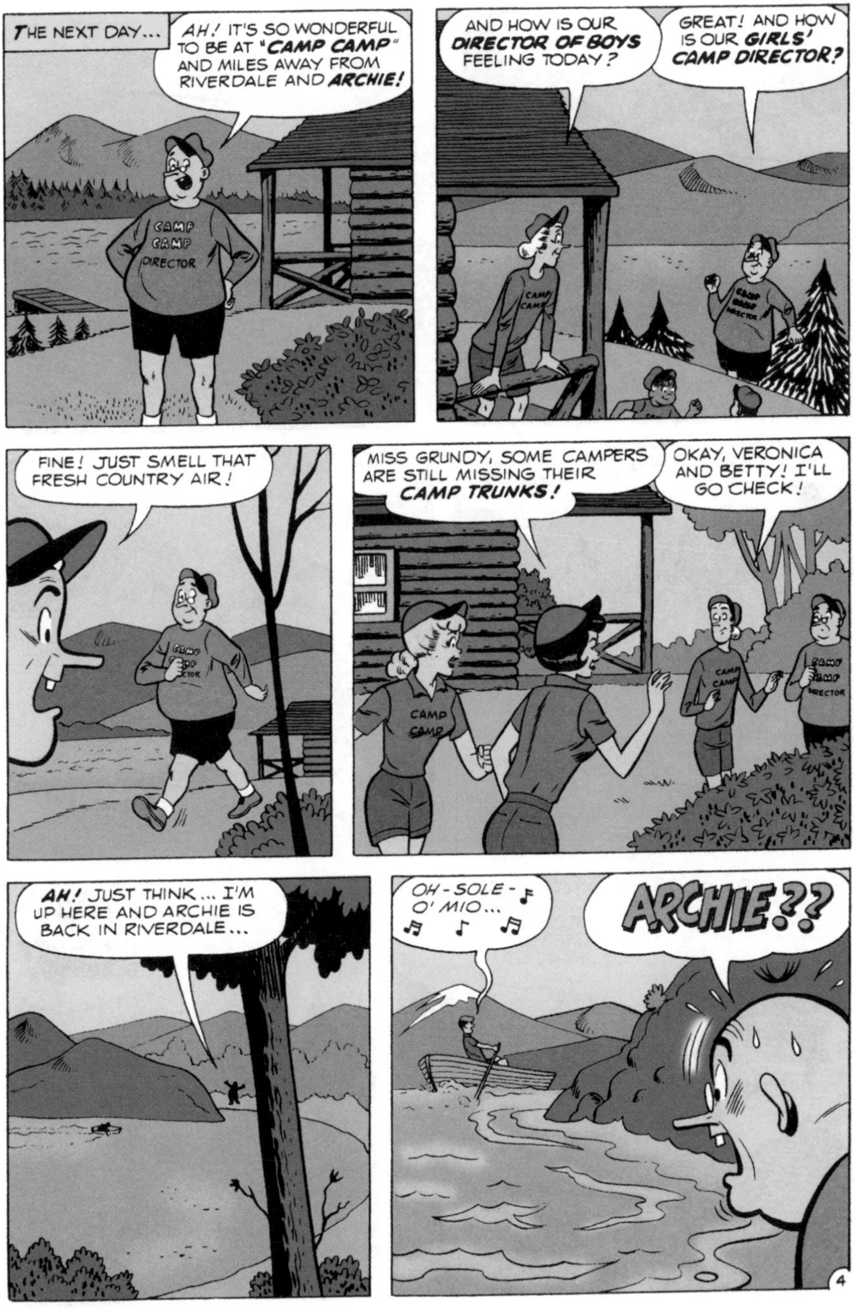
THE NEXT DAY...
AH! IT'S SO WONDERFUL TO BE AT "CAMP CAMP" AND MILES AWAY FROM RIVERDALE AND ARCHIE!
CAMP CAMP DIRECTOR
AND HOW IS OUR DIRECTOR OF BOYS FEELING TODAY?
GREAT! AND HOW IS OUR GIRLS' CAMP DIRECTOR?
CAMP CAMP
FINE! JUST SMELL THAT FRESH COUNTRY AIR!
MISS GRUNDY, SOME CAMPERS ARE STILL MISSING THEIR CAMP TRUNKS!
OKAY, VERONICA AND BETTY! I'LL GO CHECK!
CAMP CAMP
CAMP CAMP DIRECTOR
AH! JUST THINK... I'M UP HERE AND ARCHIE IS BACK IN RIVERDALE...
OH-SOLE-O' MIO...
ARCHIE??

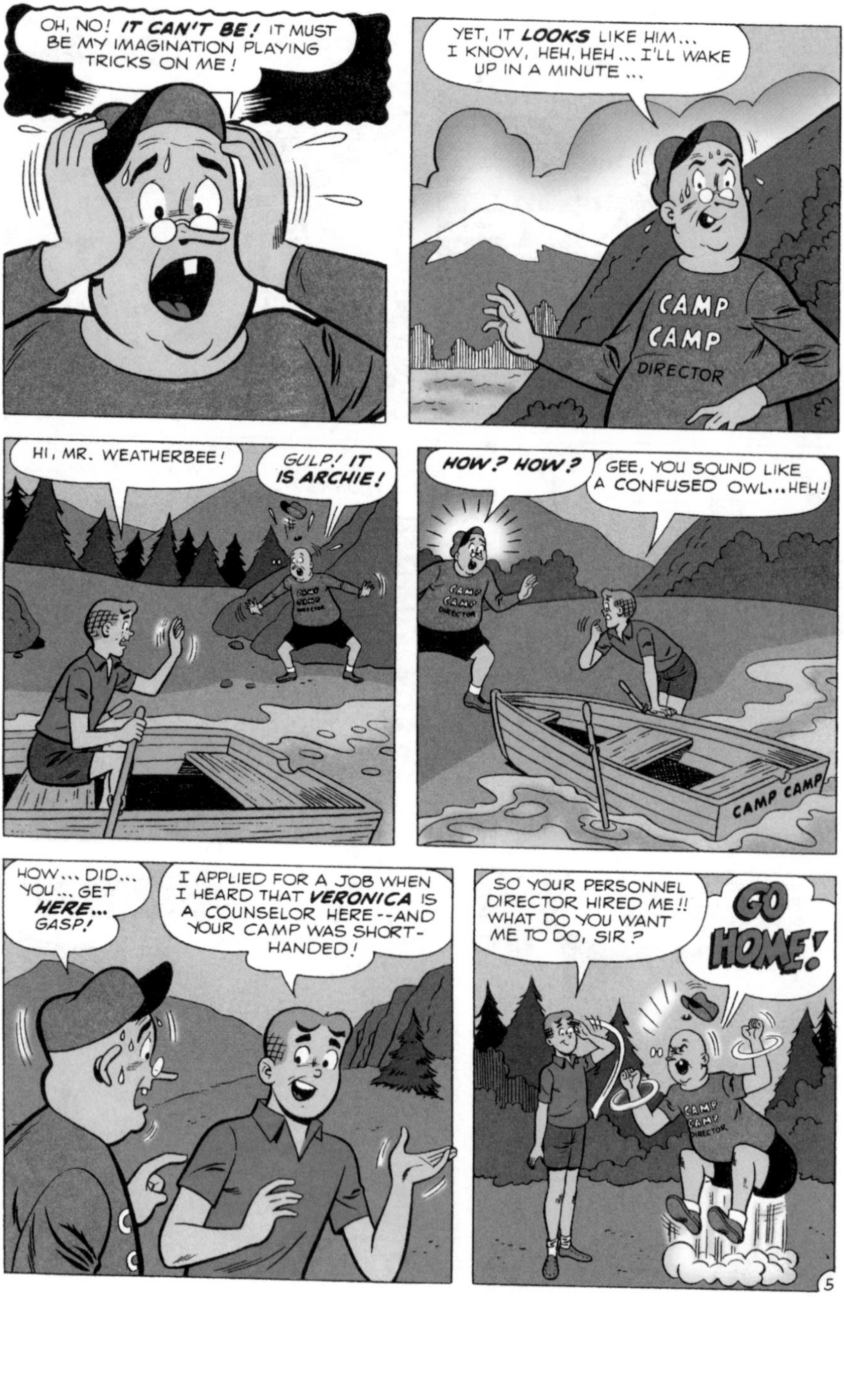
OH, NO! IT CAN'T BE! IT MUST BE MY IMAGINATION PLAYING TRICKS ON ME!
YET, IT LOOKS LIKE HIM... I KNOW, HEH, HEH... I'LL WAKE UP IN A MINUTE...
CAMP CAMP DIRECTOR
HI, MR. WEATHERBEE!
GULP! IT IS ARCHIE!
HOW? HOW?
GEE, YOU SOUND LIKE A CONFUSED OWL...HEH!
CAMP CAMP
HOW... DID... YOU... GET HERE... GASP!
I APPLIED FOR A JOB WHEN I HEARD THAT VERONICA IS A COUNSELOR HERE--AND YOUR CAMP WAS SHORT-HANDED!
SO YOUR PERSONNEL DIRECTOR HIRED ME!! WHAT DO YOU WANT ME TO DO, SIR?
GO HOME!

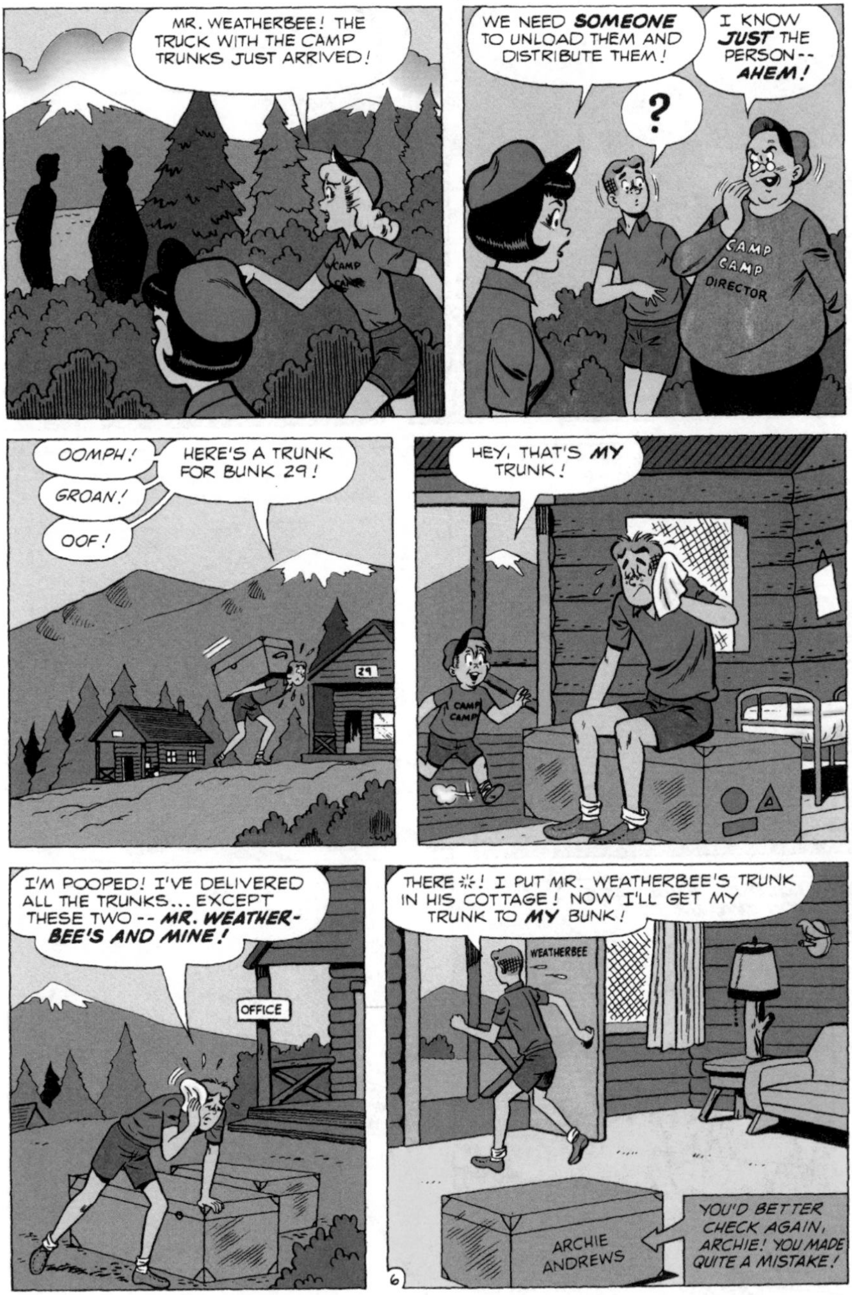

MR. WEATHERBEE! THE TRUCK WITH THE CAMP TRUNKS JUST ARRIVED!
WE NEED **SOMEONE** TO UNLOAD THEM AND DISTRIBUTE THEM!
?
I KNOW **JUST** THE PERSON-- **AHEM!**
CAMP CAMP DIRECTOR
OOMPH!
GROAN!
OOF!
HERE'S A TRUNK FOR BUNK 29!
29
HEY, THAT'S **MY** TRUNK!
CAMP CAMP
I'M POOPED! I'VE DELIVERED ALL THE TRUNKS... EXCEPT THESE TWO -- **MR. WEATHERBEE'S AND MINE!**
OFFICE
THERE! I PUT MR. WEATHERBEE'S TRUNK IN HIS COTTAGE! NOW I'LL GET MY TRUNK TO **MY** BUNK!
WEATHERBEE
ARCHIE ANDREWS
YOU'D BETTER CHECK AGAIN, ARCHIE! YOU MADE QUITE A MISTAKE!
6

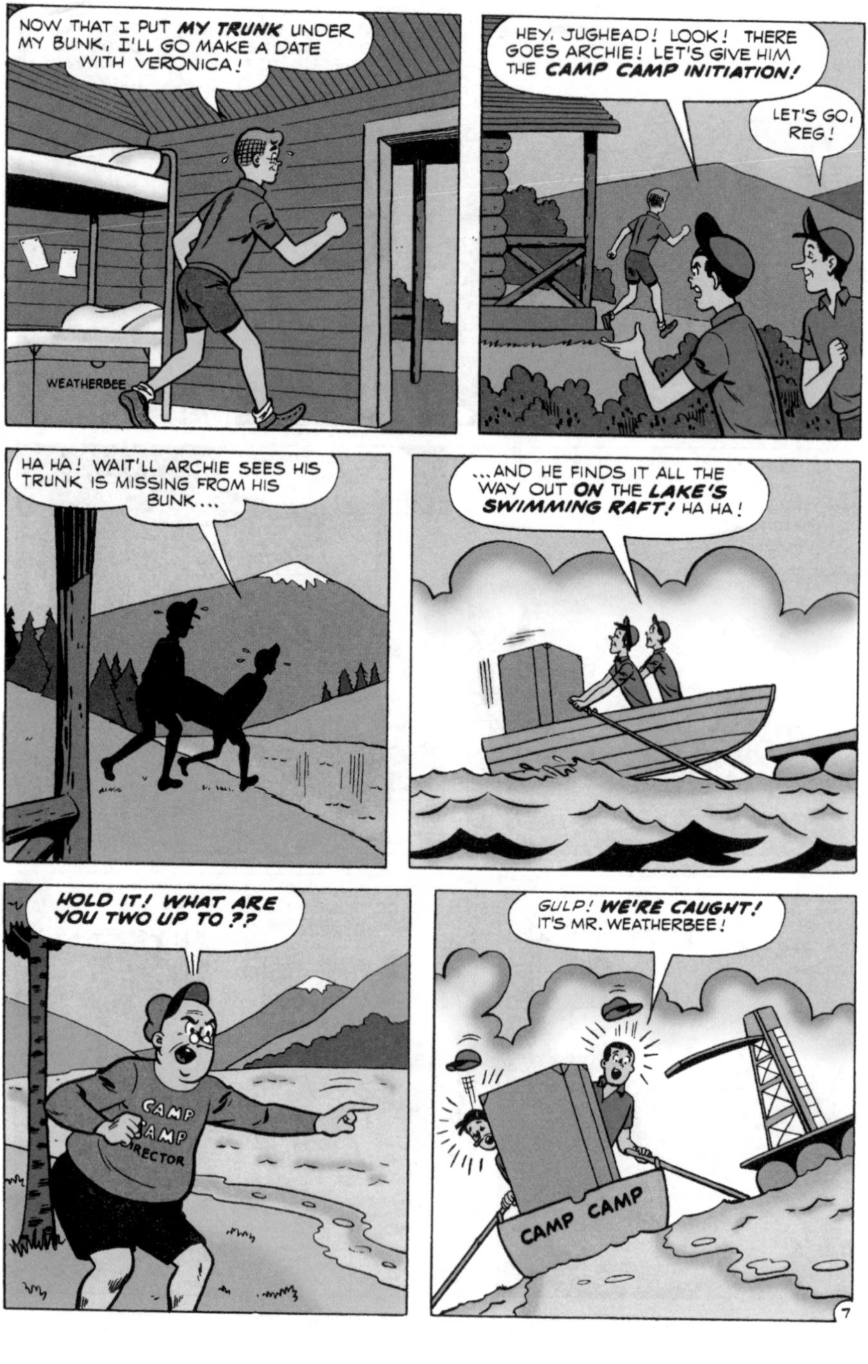

NOW THAT I PUT MY TRUNK UNDER MY BUNK, I'LL GO MAKE A DATE WITH VERONICA!
WEATHERBEE
HEY, JUGHEAD! LOOK! THERE GOES ARCHIE! LET'S GIVE HIM THE CAMP CAMP INITIATION!
LET'S GO, REG!
HA HA! WAIT'LL ARCHIE SEES HIS TRUNK IS MISSING FROM HIS BUNK...
...AND HE FINDS IT ALL THE WAY OUT ON THE LAKE'S SWIMMING RAFT! HA HA!
HOLD IT! WHAT ARE YOU TWO UP TO??
CAMP CAMP DIRECTOR
GULP! WE'RE CAUGHT! IT'S MR. WEATHERBEE!
CAMP CAMP

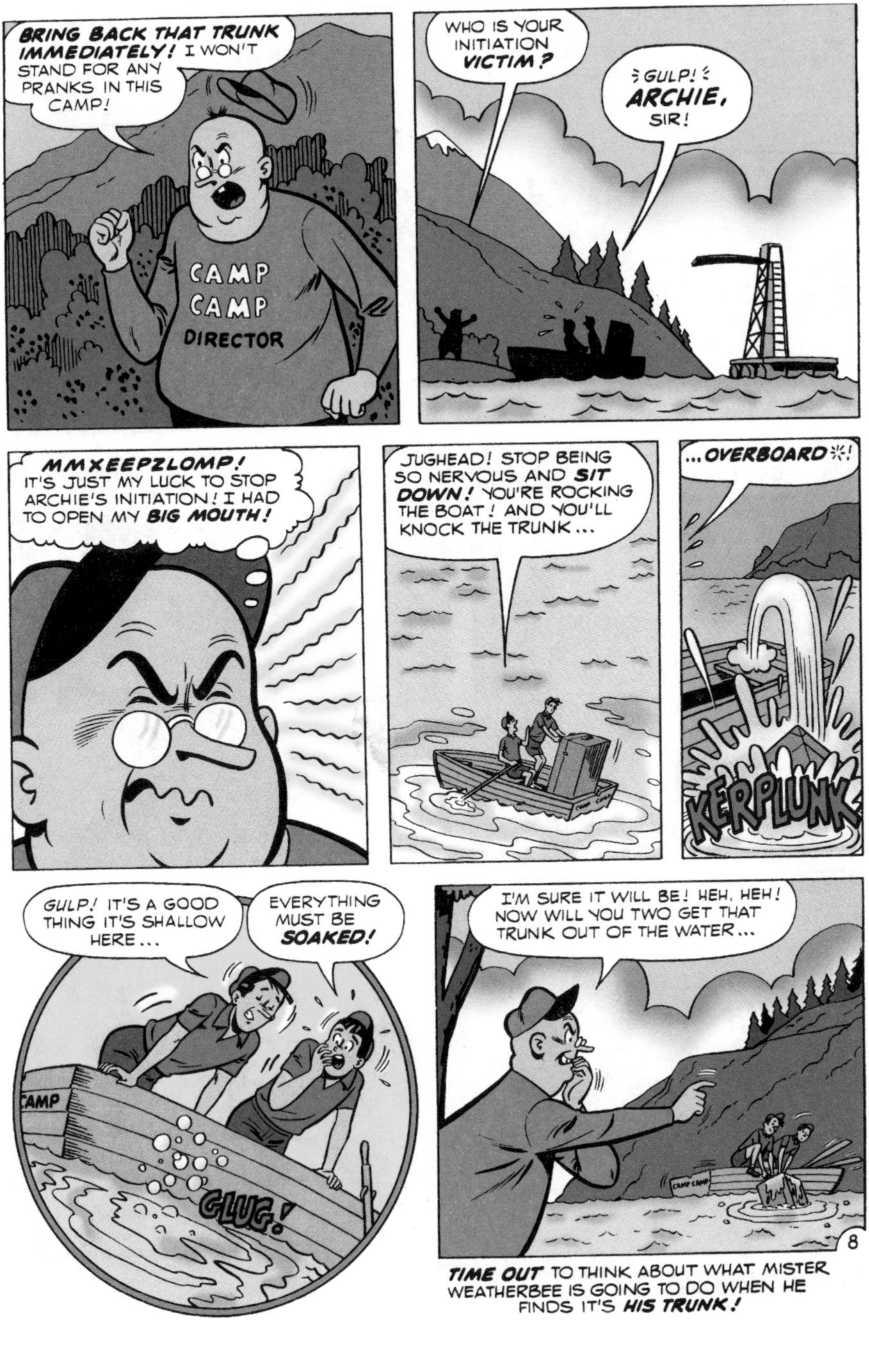

BRING BACK THAT TRUNK IMMEDIATELY! I WON'T STAND FOR ANY PRANKS IN THIS CAMP!
CAMP CAMP DIRECTOR
WHO IS YOUR INITIATION VICTIM?
GULP! ARCHIE, SIR!
MMXEEPZLOMP! IT'S JUST MY LUCK TO STOP ARCHIE'S INITIATION! I HAD TO OPEN MY BIG MOUTH!
JUGHEAD! STOP BEING SO NERVOUS AND SIT DOWN! YOU'RE ROCKING THE BOAT! AND YOU'LL KNOCK THE TRUNK...
...OVERBOARD!
KERPLUNK
GULP! IT'S A GOOD THING IT'S SHALLOW HERE...
EVERYTHING MUST BE SOAKED!
CAMP
GLUG!
I'M SURE IT WILL BE! HEH, HEH! NOW WILL YOU TWO GET THAT TRUNK OUT OF THE WATER...
TIME OUT TO THINK ABOUT WHAT MISTER WEATHERBEE IS GOING TO DO WHEN HE FINDS IT'S HIS TRUNK!

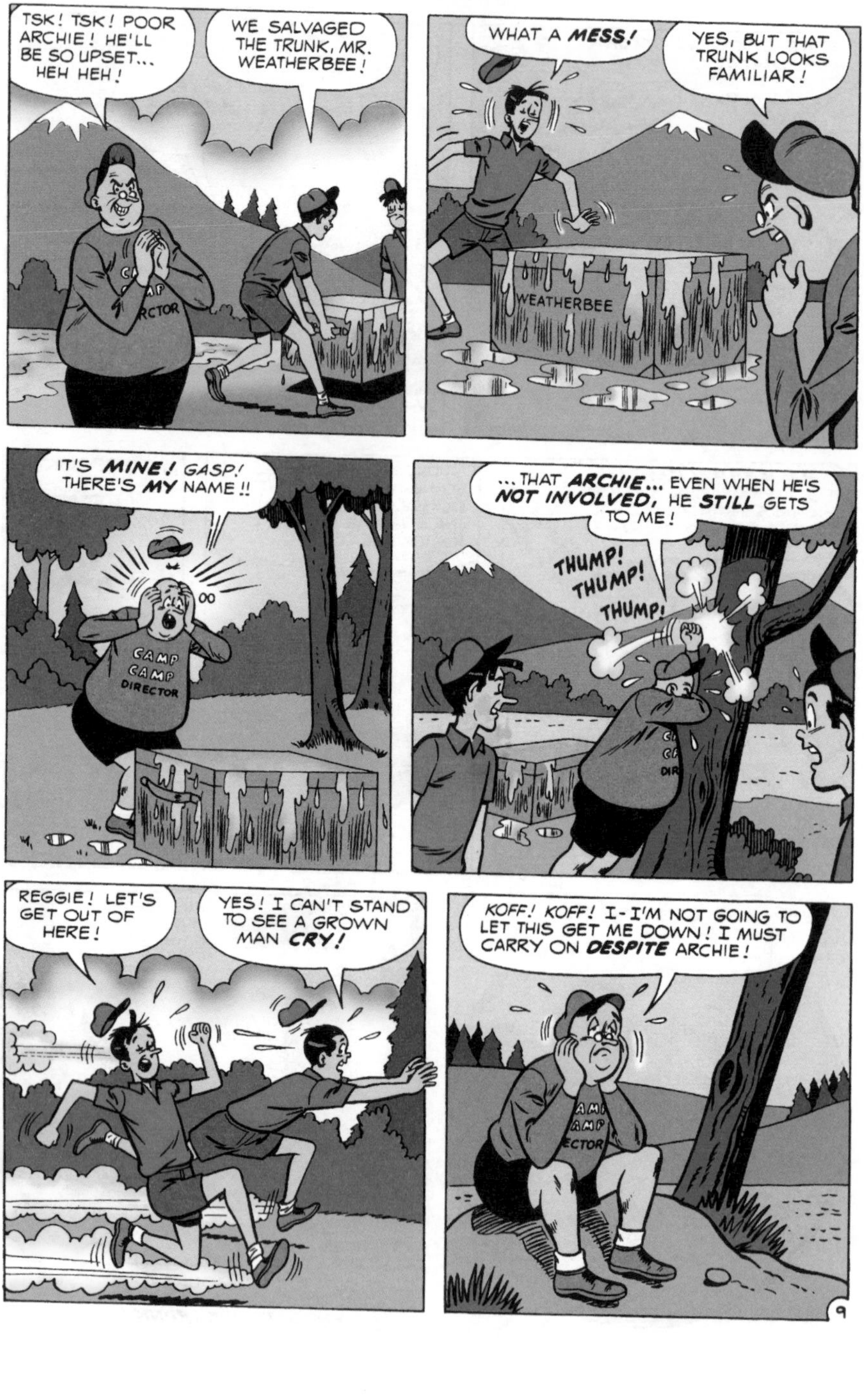
TSK! TSK! POOR ARCHIE! HE'LL BE SO UPSET... HEH HEH!
WE SALVAGED THE TRUNK, MR. WEATHERBEE!
WHAT A MESS!
YES, BUT THAT TRUNK LOOKS FAMILIAR!
WEATHERBEE
IT'S MINE! GASP! THERE'S MY NAME!!
CAMP CAMP DIRECTOR
...THAT ARCHIE... EVEN WHEN HE'S NOT INVOLVED, HE STILL GETS TO ME!
THUMP! THUMP! THUMP!
REGGIE! LET'S GET OUT OF HERE!
YES! I CAN'T STAND TO SEE A GROWN MAN CRY!
KOFF! KOFF! I-I'M NOT GOING TO LET THIS GET ME DOWN! I MUST CARRY ON DESPITE ARCHIE!

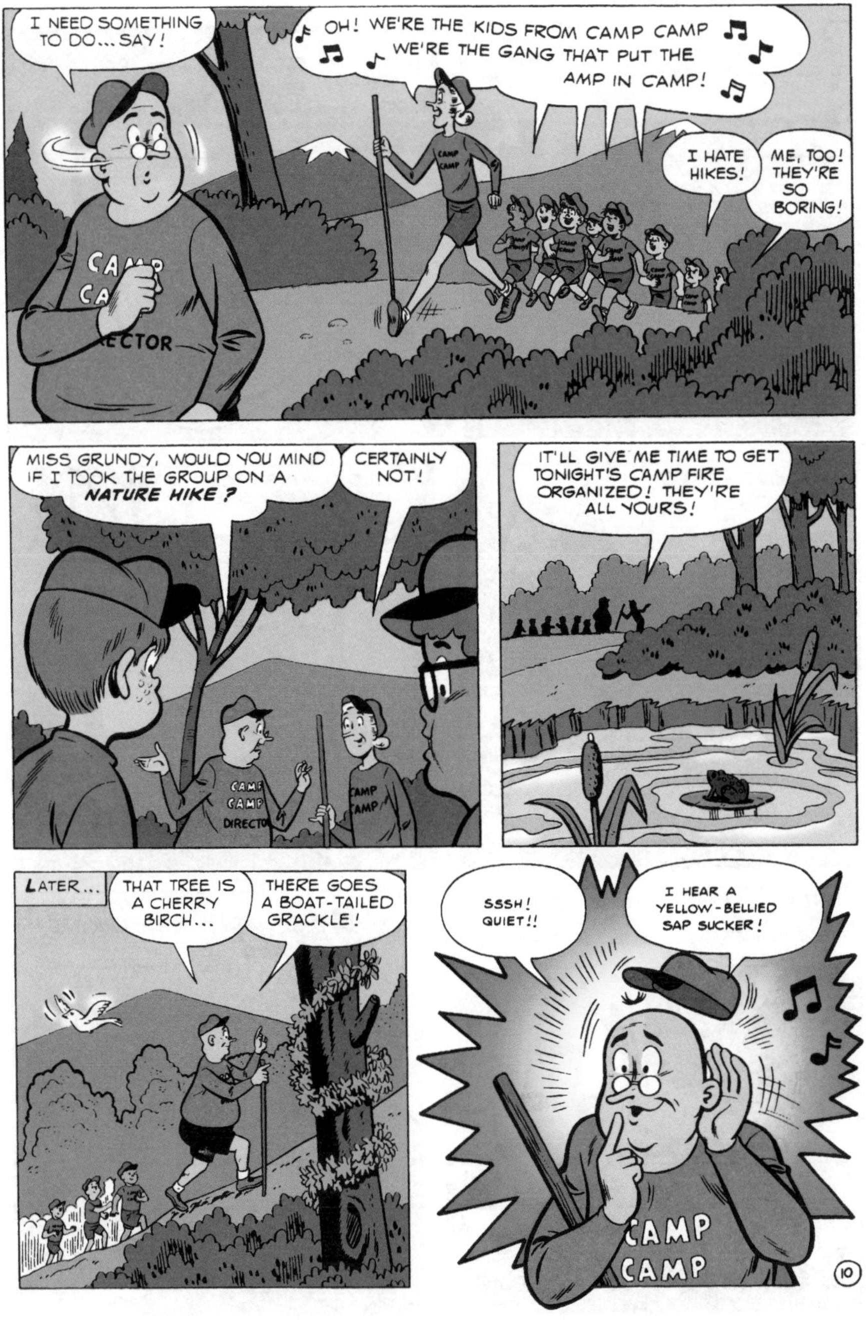
I NEED SOMETHING TO DO... SAY!
OH! WE'RE THE KIDS FROM CAMP CAMP WE'RE THE GANG THAT PUT THE AMP IN CAMP!
I HATE HIKES!
ME, TOO! THEY'RE SO BORING!
MISS GRUNDY, WOULD YOU MIND IF I TOOK THE GROUP ON A NATURE HIKE?
CERTAINLY NOT!
IT'LL GIVE ME TIME TO GET TONIGHT'S CAMP FIRE ORGANIZED! THEY'RE ALL YOURS!
LATER...
THAT TREE IS A CHERRY BIRCH...
THERE GOES A BOAT-TAILED GRACKLE!
SSSH! QUIET!!
I HEAR A YELLOW-BELLIED SAP SUCKER!

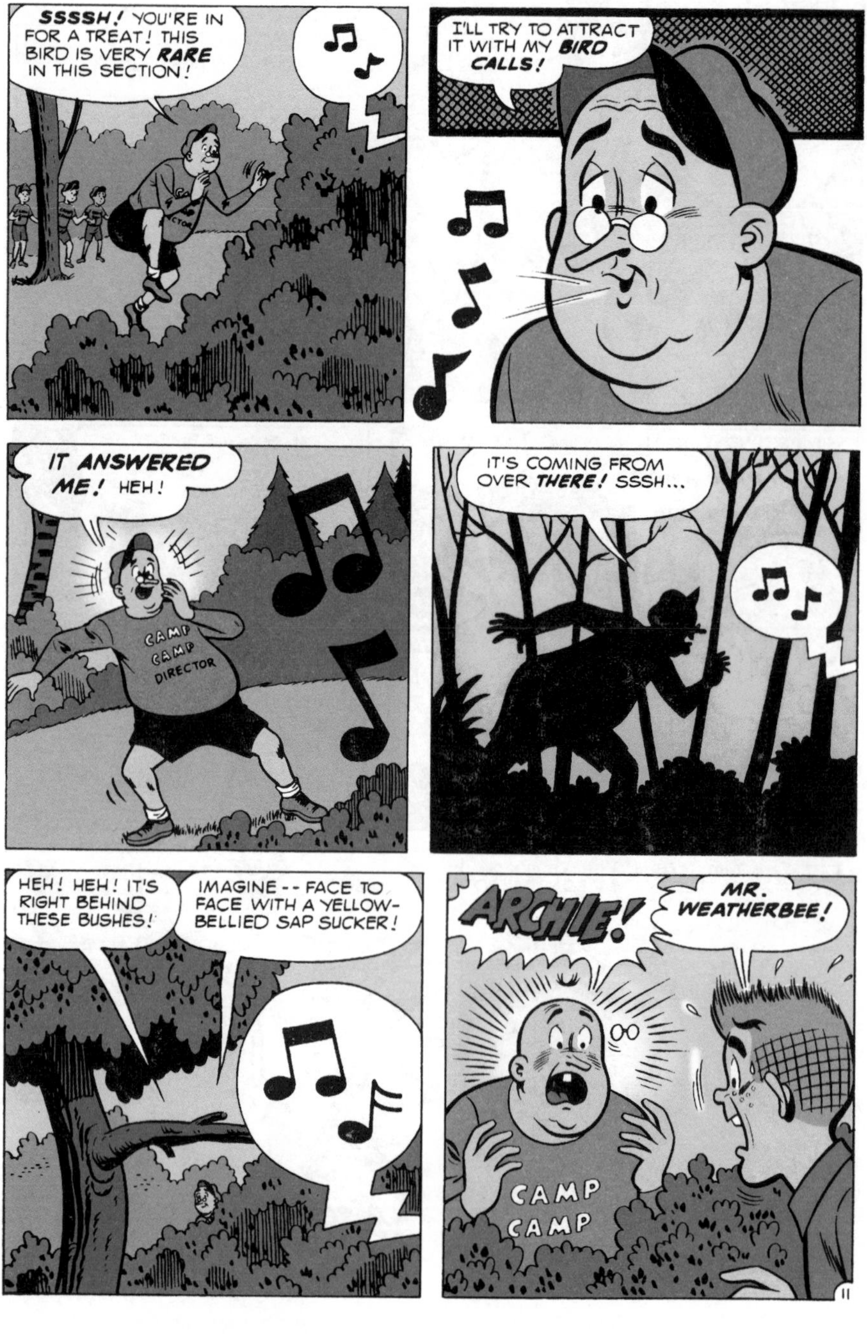
SSSSH! YOU'RE IN FOR A TREAT! THIS BIRD IS VERY RARE IN THIS SECTION!
I'LL TRY TO ATTRACT IT WITH MY BIRD CALLS!
IT ANSWERED ME! HEH!
CAMP CAMP DIRECTOR
IT'S COMING FROM OVER THERE! SSSH...
HEH! HEH! IT'S RIGHT BEHIND THESE BUSHES!
IMAGINE -- FACE TO FACE WITH A YELLOW-BELLIED SAP SUCKER!
ARCHIE!
MR. WEATHERBEE!
CAMP CAMP

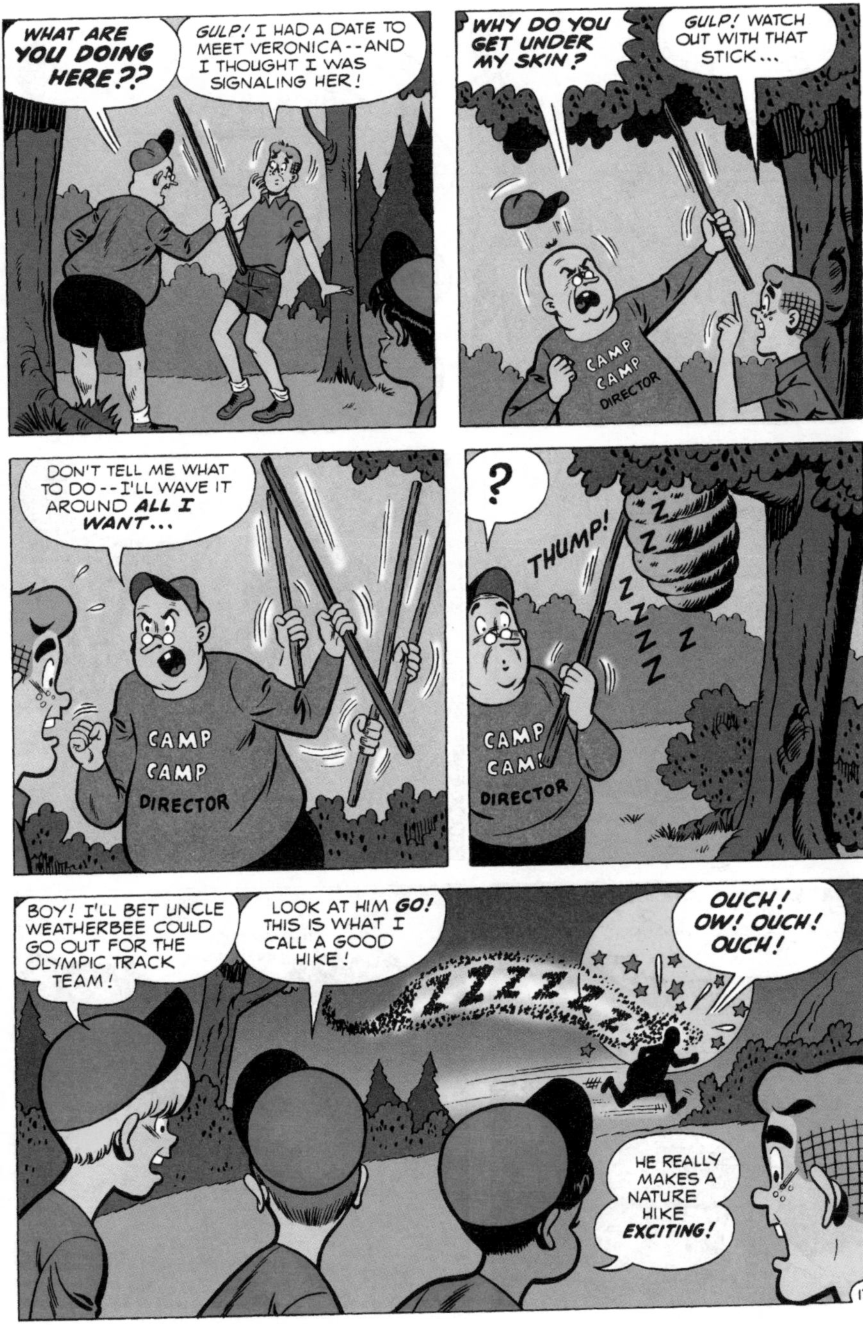
WHAT ARE YOU DOING HERE??
GULP! I HAD A DATE TO MEET VERONICA--AND I THOUGHT I WAS SIGNALING HER!
WHY DO YOU GET UNDER MY SKIN?
GULP! WATCH OUT WITH THAT STICK...
CAMP CAMP DIRECTOR
DON'T TELL ME WHAT TO DO--I'LL WAVE IT AROUND ALL I WANT...
CAMP CAMP DIRECTOR
?
THUMP!
BOY! I'LL BET UNCLE WEATHERBEE COULD GO OUT FOR THE OLYMPIC TRACK TEAM!
LOOK AT HIM GO! THIS IS WHAT I CALL A GOOD HIKE!
OUCH! OW! OUCH! OUCH!
HE REALLY MAKES A NATURE HIKE EXCITING!

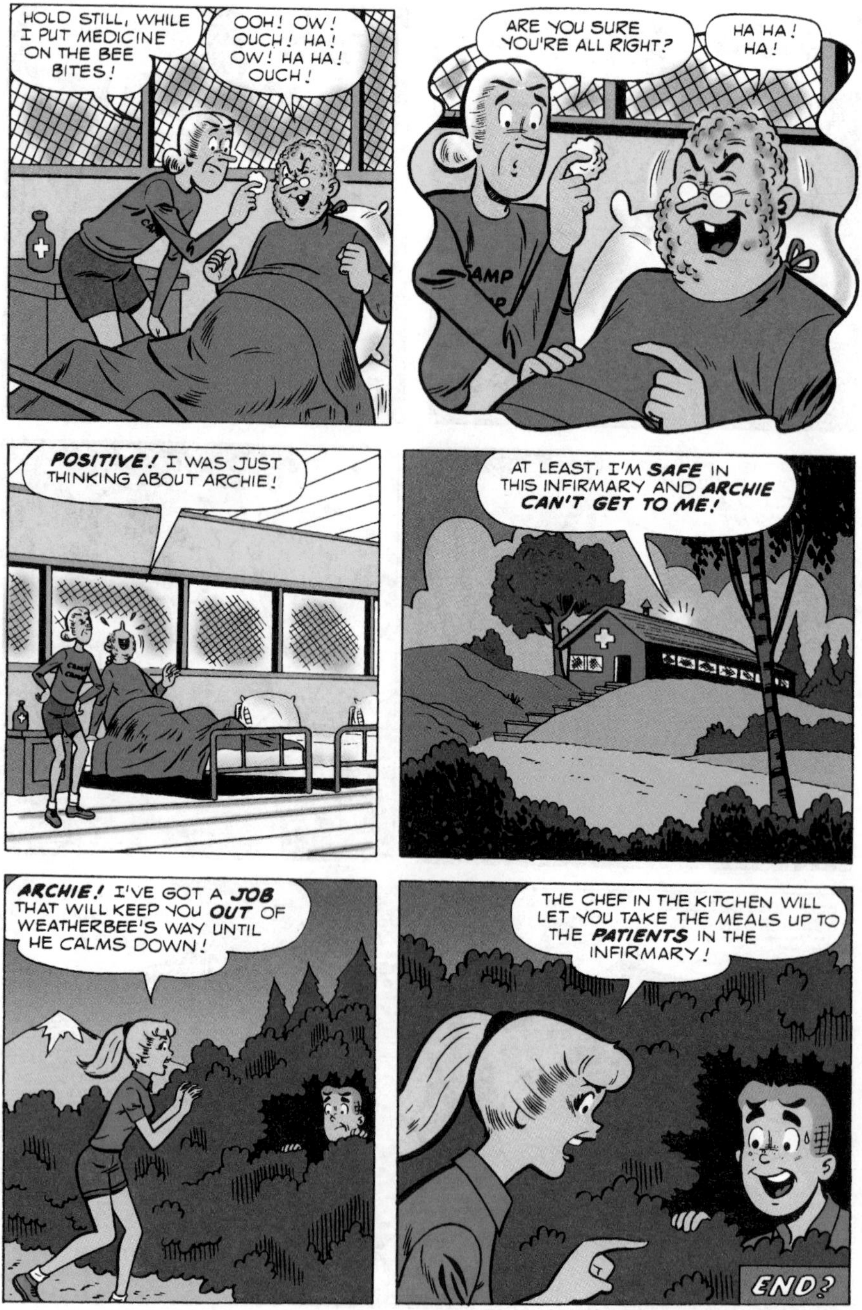
HOLD STILL, WHILE I PUT MEDICINE ON THE BEE BITES!
OOH! OW! OUCH! HA! OW! HA HA! OUCH!
ARE YOU SURE YOU'RE ALL RIGHT?
HA HA! HA!
POSITIVE! I WAS JUST THINKING ABOUT ARCHIE!
AT LEAST, I'M SAFE IN THIS INFIRMARY AND ARCHIE CAN'T GET TO ME!
ARCHIE! I'VE GOT A JOB THAT WILL KEEP YOU OUT OF WEATHERBEE'S WAY UNTIL HE CALMS DOWN!
THE CHEF IN THE KITCHEN WILL LET YOU TAKE THE MEALS UP TO THE PATIENTS IN THE INFIRMARY!
END?

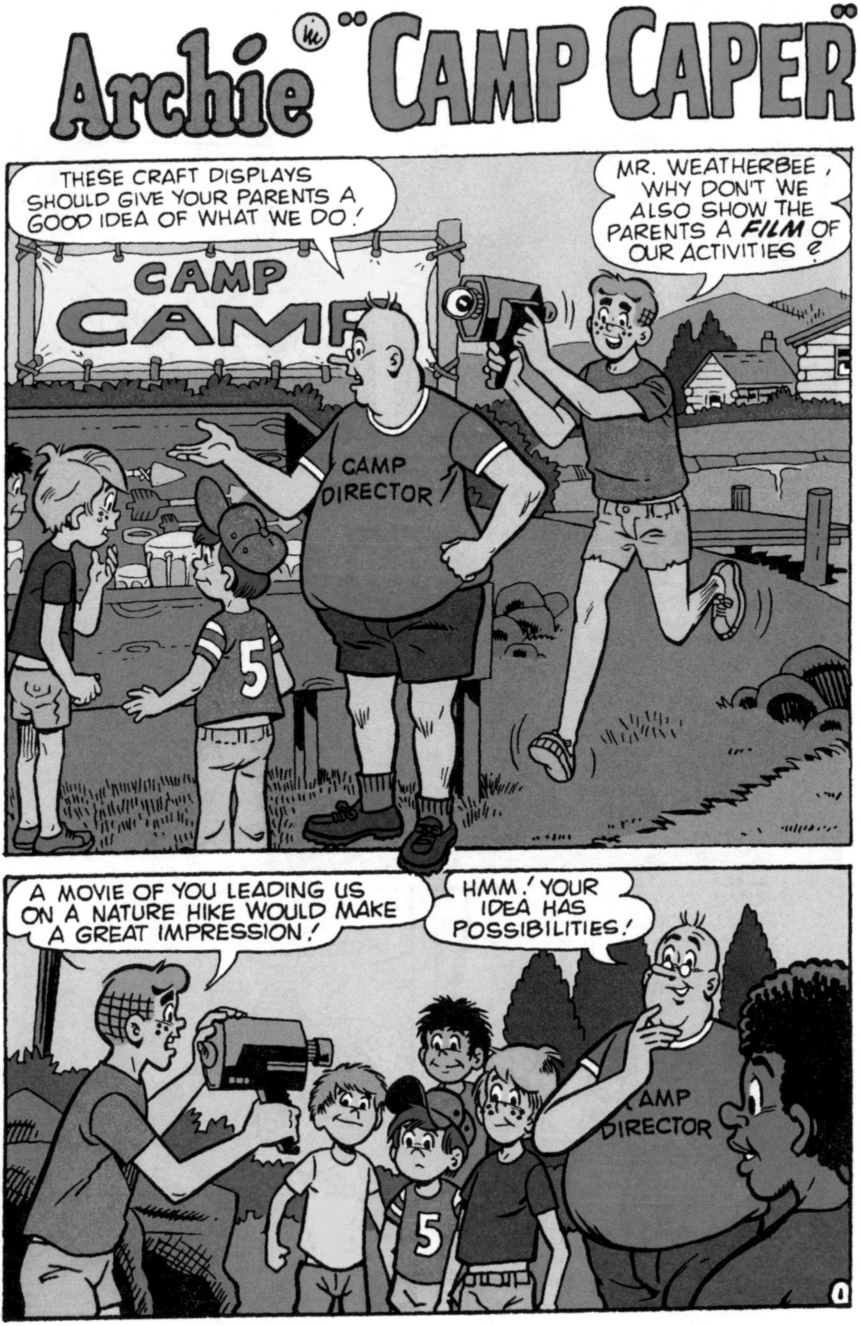
Archie in "CAMP CAPER"
THESE CRAFT DISPLAYS SHOULD GIVE YOUR PARENTS A GOOD IDEA OF WHAT WE DO!
MR. WEATHERBEE, WHY DON'T WE ALSO SHOW THE PARENTS A FILM OF OUR ACTIVITIES?
CAMP
CAMP DIRECTOR
A MOVIE OF YOU LEADING US ON A NATURE HIKE WOULD MAKE A GREAT IMPRESSION!
HMM! YOUR IDEA HAS POSSIBILITIES!
1

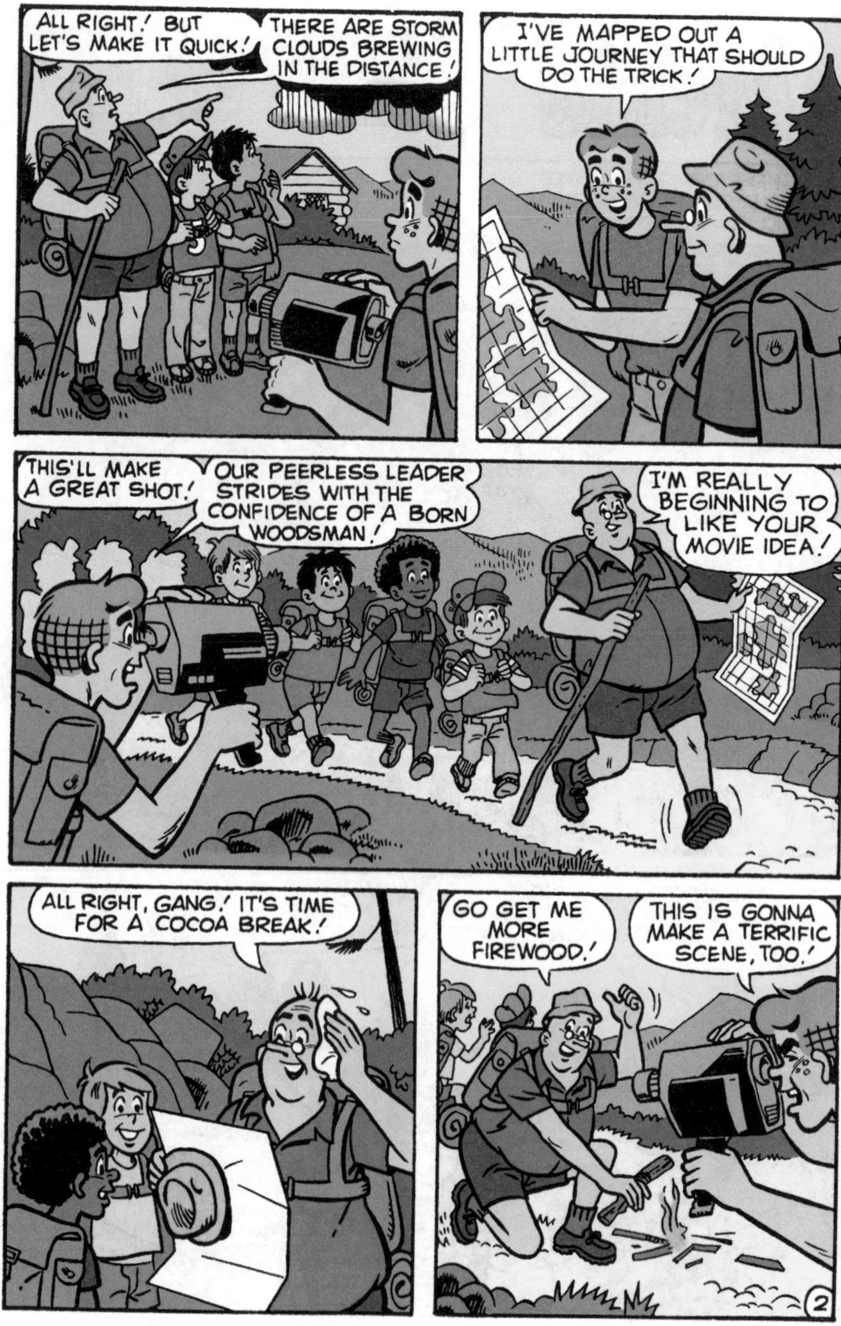
ALL RIGHT! BUT LET'S MAKE IT QUICK!
THERE ARE STORM CLOUDS BREWING IN THE DISTANCE!
I'VE MAPPED OUT A LITTLE JOURNEY THAT SHOULD DO THE TRICK!
THIS'LL MAKE A GREAT SHOT!
OUR PEERLESS LEADER STRIDES WITH THE CONFIDENCE OF A BORN WOODSMAN!
I'M REALLY BEGINNING TO LIKE YOUR MOVIE IDEA!
ALL RIGHT, GANG! IT'S TIME FOR A COCOA BREAK!
GO GET ME MORE FIREWOOD!
THIS IS GONNA MAKE A TERRIFIC SCENE, TOO!
2

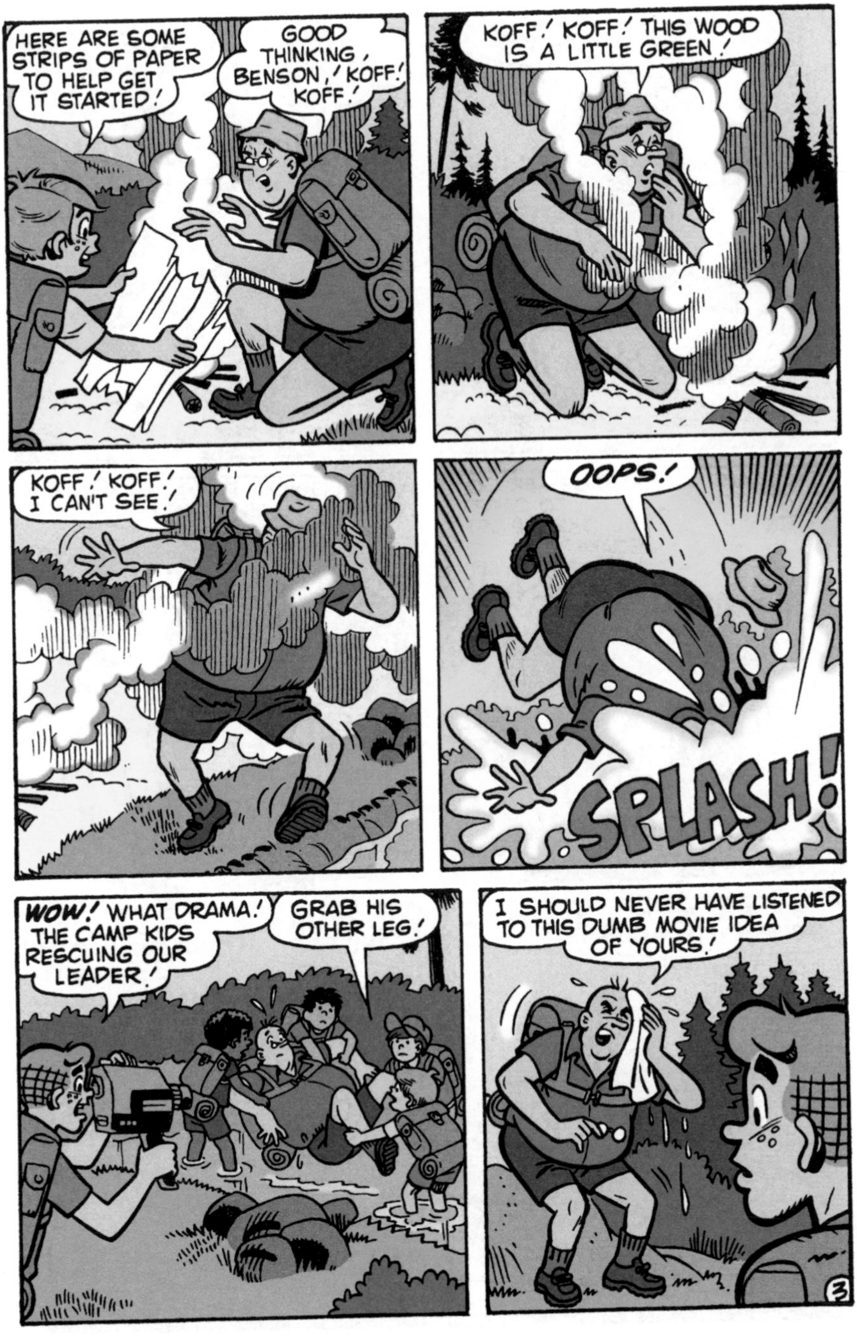
HERE ARE SOME STRIPS OF PAPER TO HELP GET IT STARTED!
GOOD THINKING, BENSON! KOFF! KOFF!
KOFF! KOFF! THIS WOOD IS A LITTLE GREEN!
KOFF! KOFF! I CAN'T SEE!
OOPS!
SPLASH!
WOW! WHAT DRAMA! THE CAMP KIDS RESCUING OUR LEADER!
GRAB HIS OTHER LEG!
I SHOULD NEVER HAVE LISTENED TO THIS DUMB MOVIE IDEA OF YOURS!
3

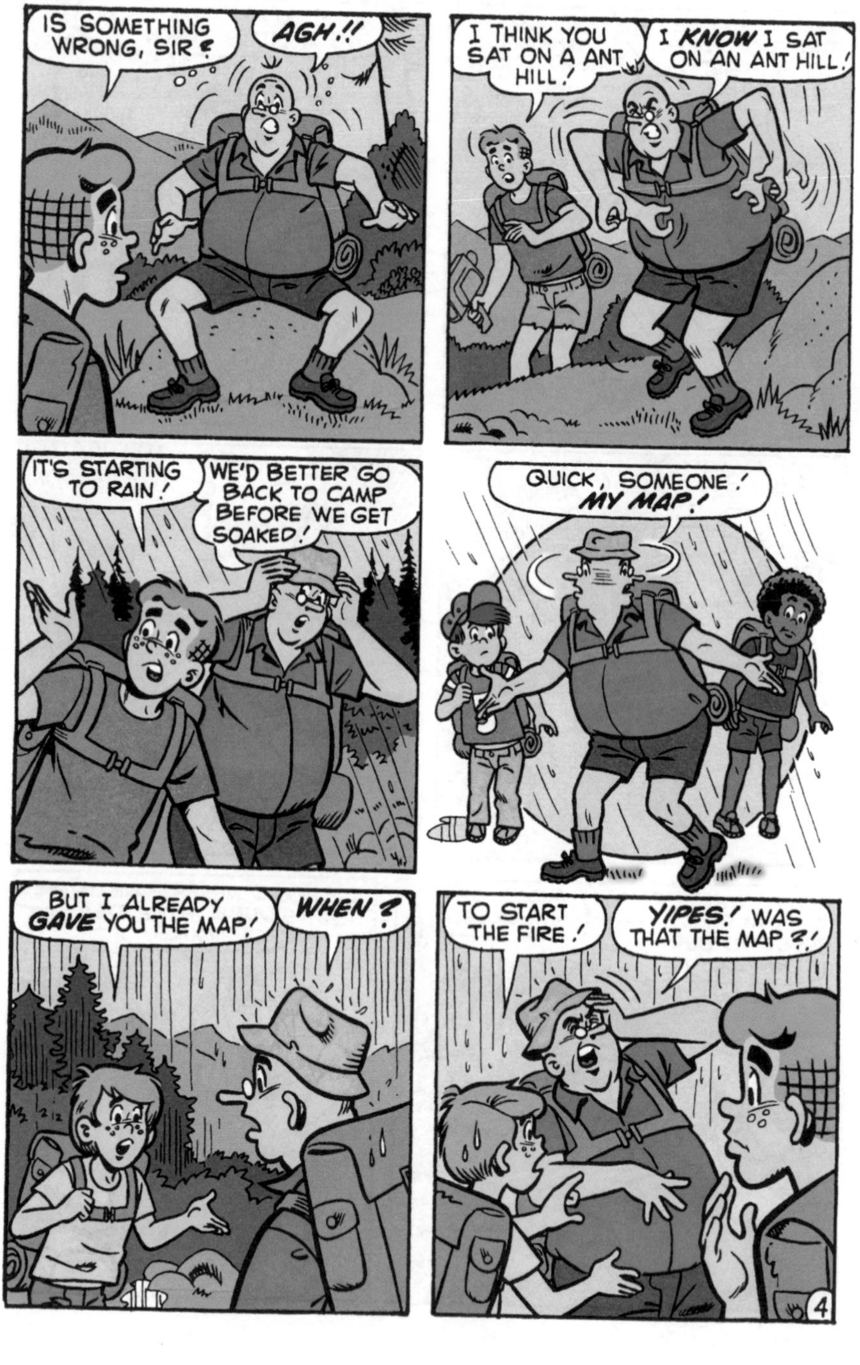

IS SOMETHING WRONG, SIR?
AGH!!
I THINK YOU SAT ON A ANT HILL!
I KNOW I SAT ON AN ANT HILL!
IT'S STARTING TO RAIN!
WE'D BETTER GO BACK TO CAMP BEFORE WE GET SOAKED!
QUICK, SOMEONE! MY MAP!
BUT I ALREADY GAVE YOU THE MAP!
WHEN?
TO START THE FIRE!
YIPES! WAS THAT THE MAP?!
4

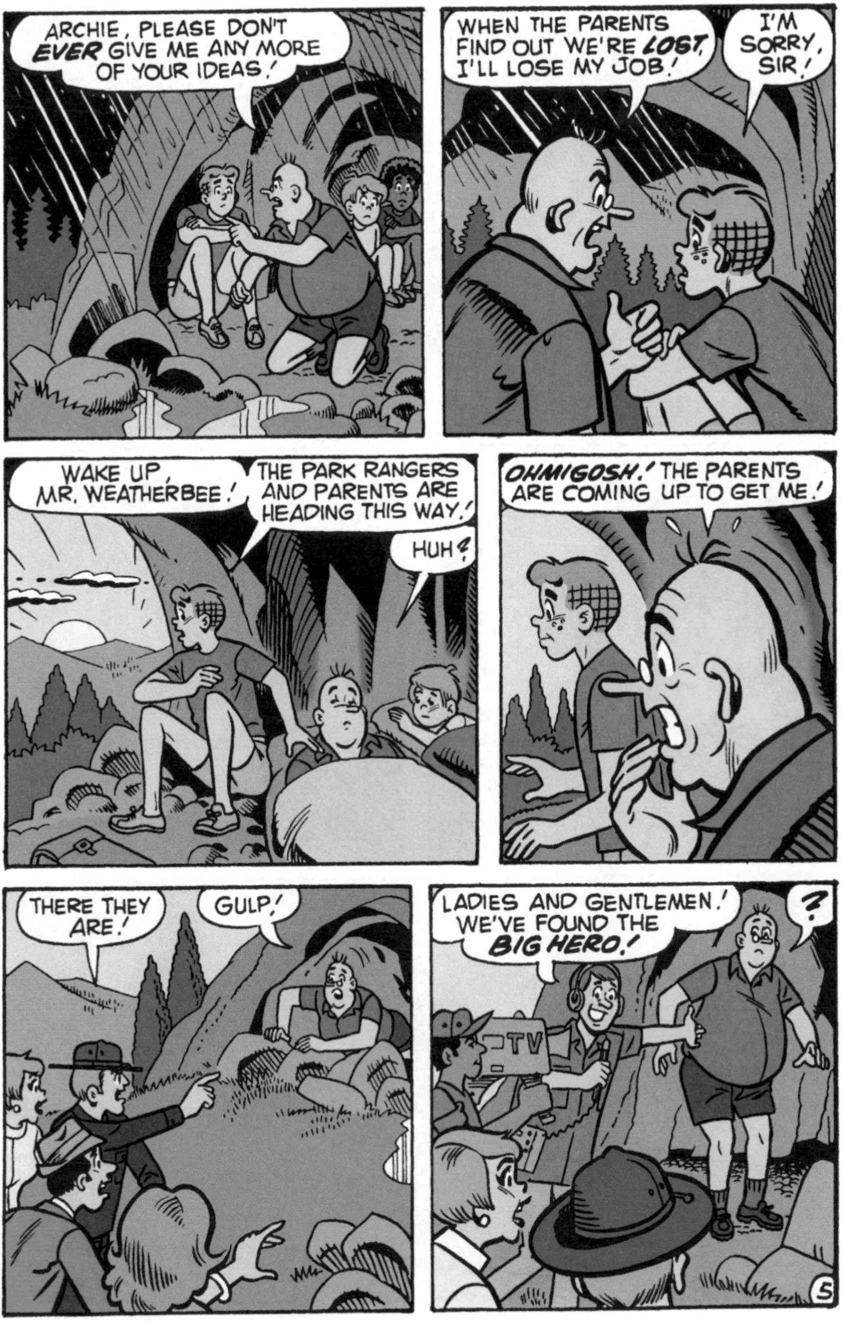
ARCHIE, PLEASE DON'T EVER GIVE ME ANY MORE OF YOUR IDEAS!
WHEN THE PARENTS FIND OUT WE'RE LOST, I'LL LOSE MY JOB!
I'M SORRY, SIR!
WAKE UP, MR. WEATHERBEE!
THE PARK RANGERS AND PARENTS ARE HEADING THIS WAY!
HUH?
OHMIGOSH! THE PARENTS ARE COMING UP TO GET ME!
THERE THEY ARE!
GULP!
LADIES AND GENTLEMEN! WE'VE FOUND THE BIG HERO!
?
TV
5

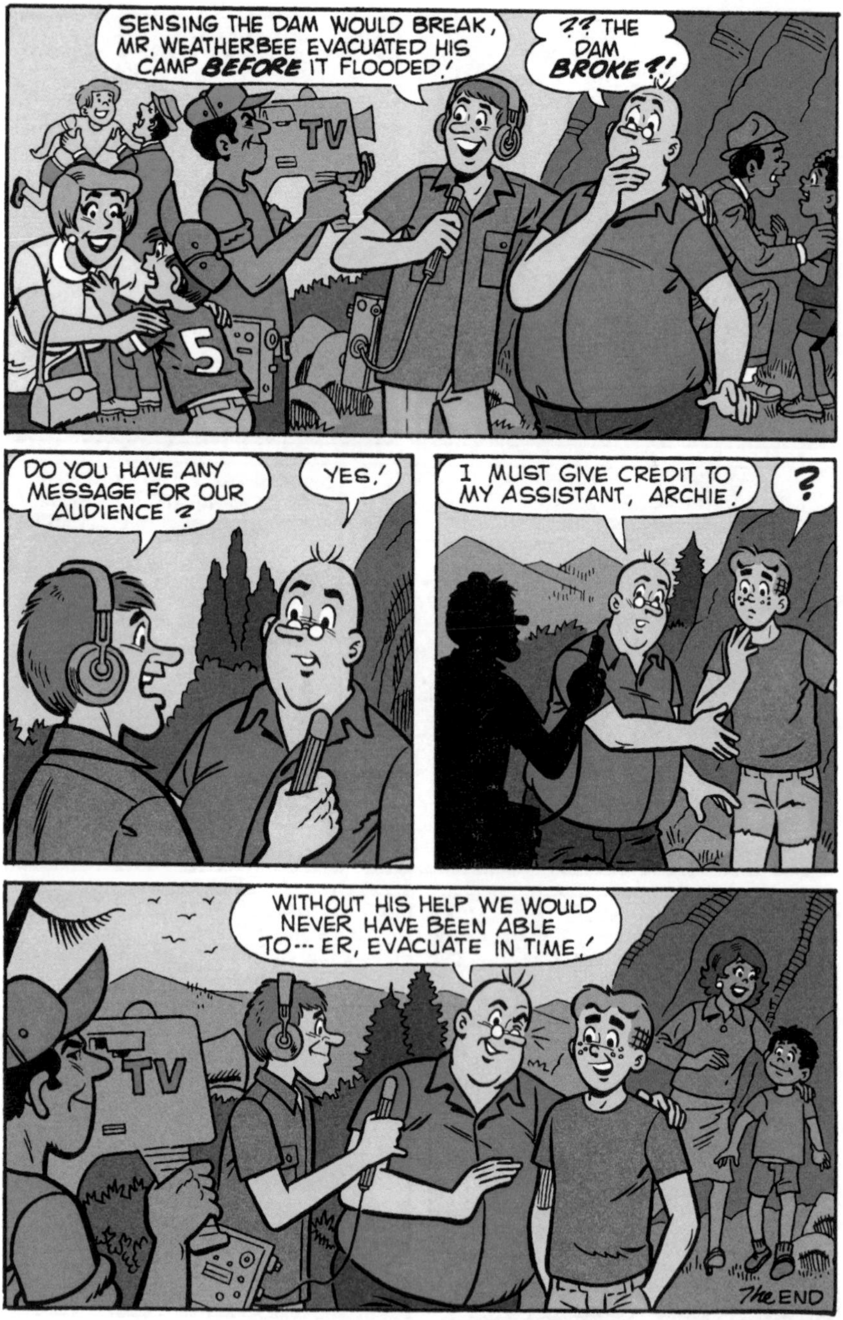
SENSING THE DAM WOULD BREAK, MR. WEATHERBEE EVACUATED HIS CAMP **BEFORE** IT FLOODED!
?? THE DAM **BROKE** ?!
TV
5
DO YOU HAVE ANY MESSAGE FOR OUR AUDIENCE ?
YES!
I MUST GIVE CREDIT TO MY ASSISTANT, ARCHIE!
?
WITHOUT HIS HELP WE WOULD NEVER HAVE BEEN ABLE TO--- ER, EVACUATE IN TIME!
TV
The END

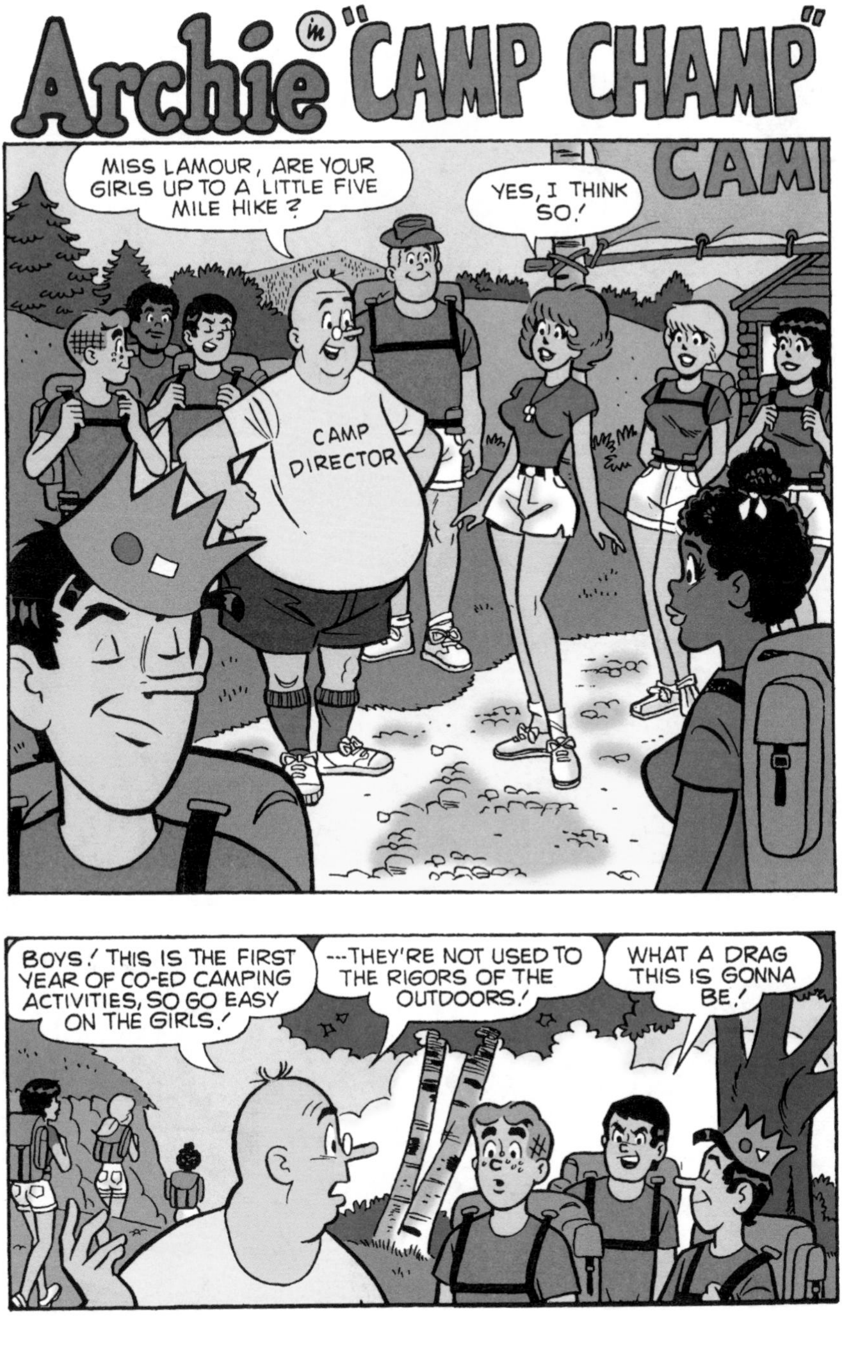
Archie in "CAMP CHAMP"
CAMP
MISS LAMOUR, ARE YOUR GIRLS UP TO A LITTLE FIVE MILE HIKE?
YES, I THINK SO!
CAMP DIRECTOR
BOYS! THIS IS THE FIRST YEAR OF CO-ED CAMPING ACTIVITIES, SO GO EASY ON THE GIRLS!
---THEY'RE NOT USED TO THE RIGORS OF THE OUTDOORS!
WHAT A DRAG THIS IS GONNA BE!

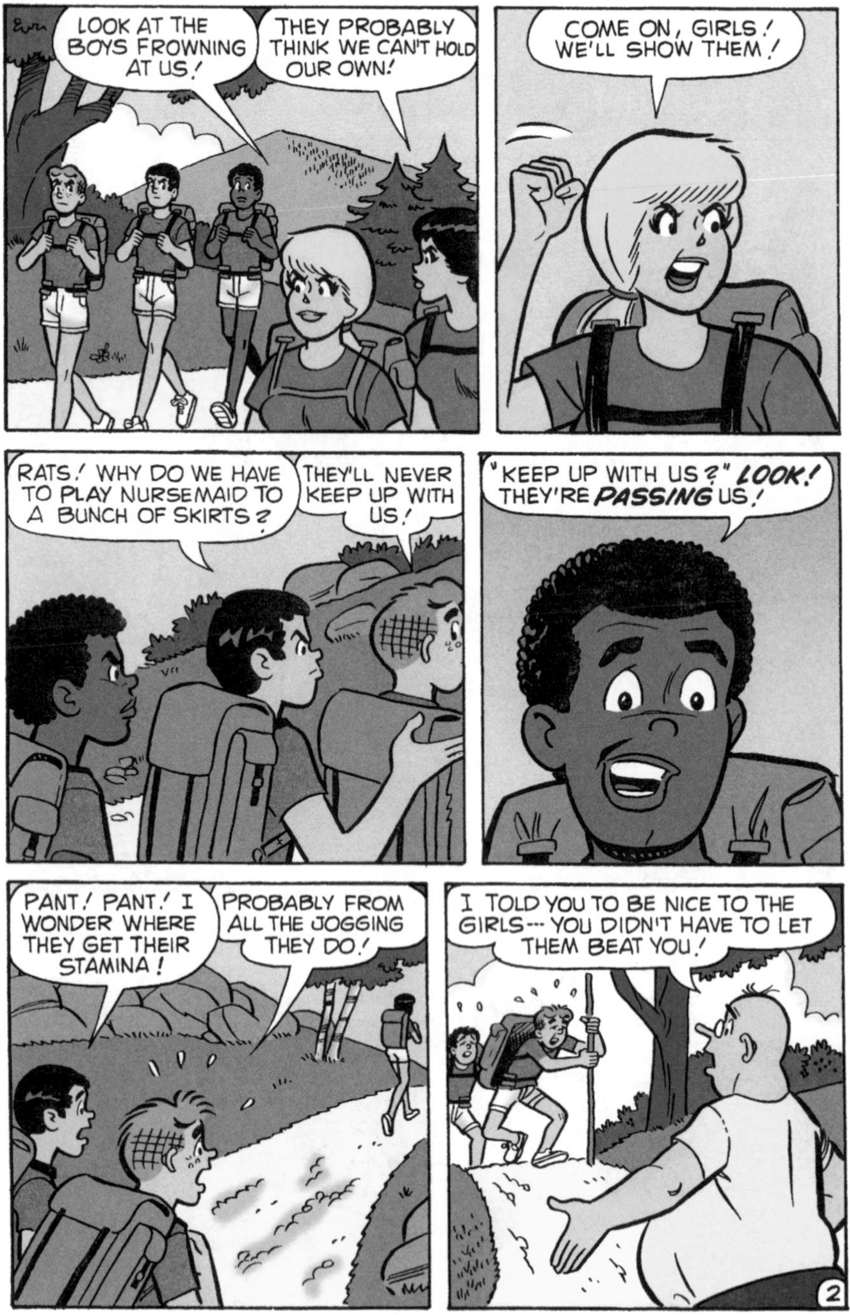
LOOK AT THE BOYS FROWNING AT US!
THEY PROBABLY THINK WE CAN'T HOLD OUR OWN!
COME ON, GIRLS! WE'LL SHOW THEM!
RATS! WHY DO WE HAVE TO PLAY NURSEMAID TO A BUNCH OF SKIRTS?
THEY'LL NEVER KEEP UP WITH US!
"KEEP UP WITH US?" LOOK! THEY'RE PASSING US!
PANT! PANT! I WONDER WHERE THEY GET THEIR STAMINA!
PROBABLY FROM ALL THE JOGGING THEY DO!
I TOLD YOU TO BE NICE TO THE GIRLS--- YOU DIDN'T HAVE TO LET THEM BEAT YOU!

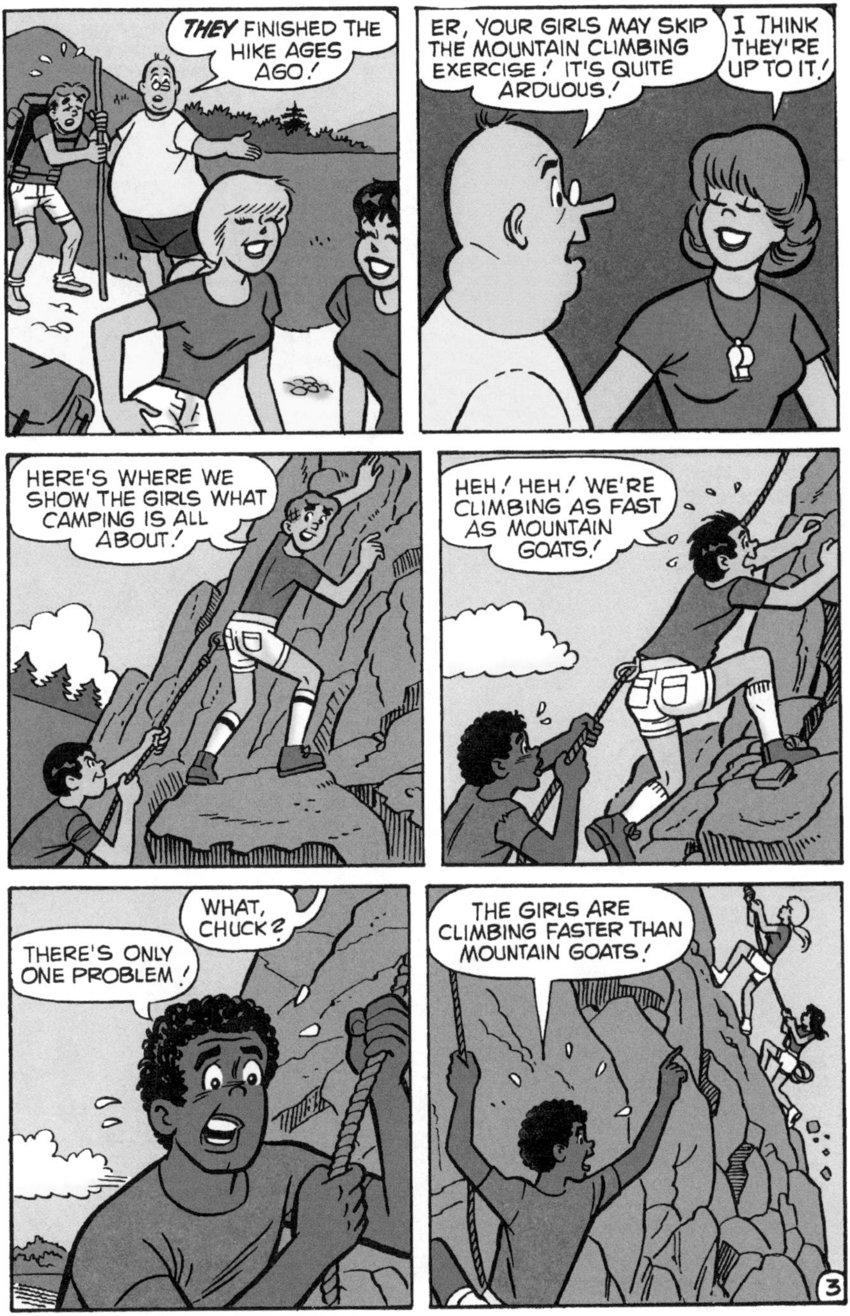
THEY FINISHED THE HIKE AGES AGO!
ER, YOUR GIRLS MAY SKIP THE MOUNTAIN CLIMBING EXERCISE! IT'S QUITE ARDUOUS!
I THINK THEY'RE UP TO IT!
HERE'S WHERE WE SHOW THE GIRLS WHAT CAMPING IS ALL ABOUT!
HEH! HEH! WE'RE CLIMBING AS FAST AS MOUNTAIN GOATS!
THERE'S ONLY ONE PROBLEM!
WHAT, CHUCK?
THE GIRLS ARE CLIMBING FASTER THAN MOUNTAIN GOATS!
3

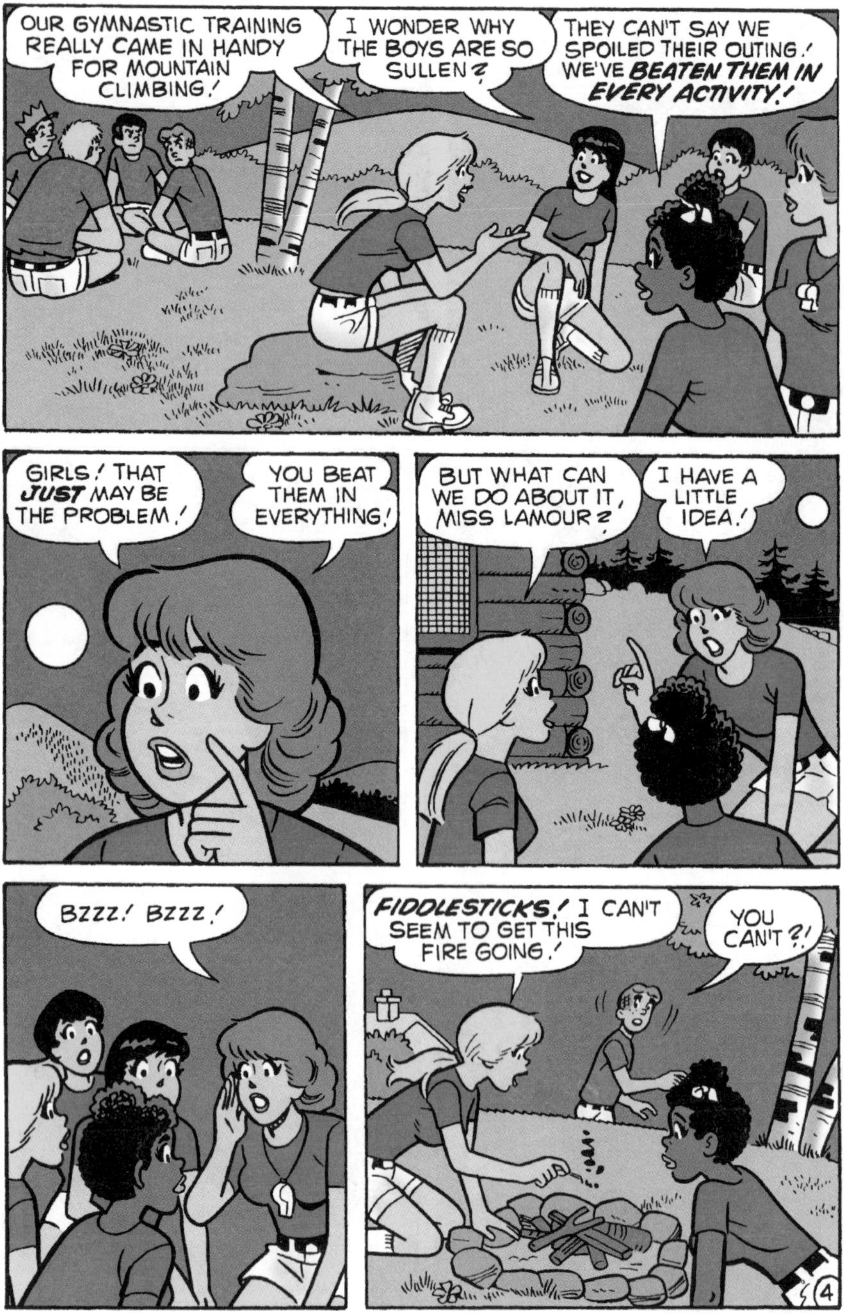
OUR GYMNASTIC TRAINING REALLY CAME IN HANDY FOR MOUNTAIN CLIMBING!
I WONDER WHY THE BOYS ARE SO SULLEN?
THEY CAN'T SAY WE SPOILED THEIR OUTING! WE'VE BEATEN THEM IN EVERY ACTIVITY!
GIRLS! THAT JUST MAY BE THE PROBLEM!
YOU BEAT THEM IN EVERYTHING!
BUT WHAT CAN WE DO ABOUT IT, MISS LAMOUR?
I HAVE A LITTLE IDEA!
BZZZ! BZZZ!
FIDDLESTICKS! I CAN'T SEEM TO GET THIS FIRE GOING!
YOU CAN'T?!
4

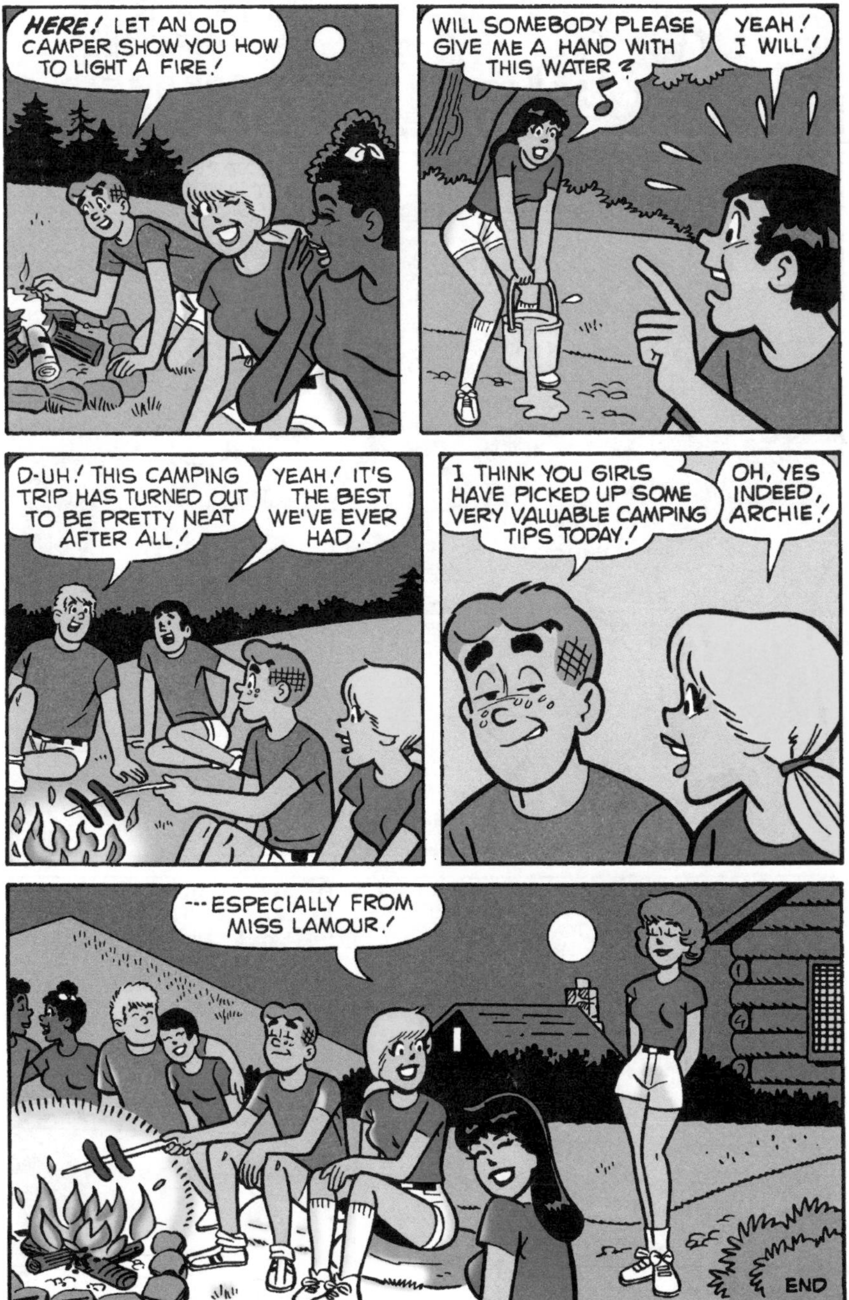
HERE! LET AN OLD CAMPER SHOW YOU HOW TO LIGHT A FIRE!
WILL SOMEBODY PLEASE GIVE ME A HAND WITH THIS WATER?
YEAH! I WILL!
D-UH! THIS CAMPING TRIP HAS TURNED OUT TO BE PRETTY NEAT AFTER ALL!
YEAH! IT'S THE BEST WE'VE EVER HAD!
I THINK YOU GIRLS HAVE PICKED UP SOME VERY VALUABLE CAMPING TIPS TODAY!
OH, YES INDEED, ARCHIE!
--- ESPECIALLY FROM MISS LAMOUR!
END

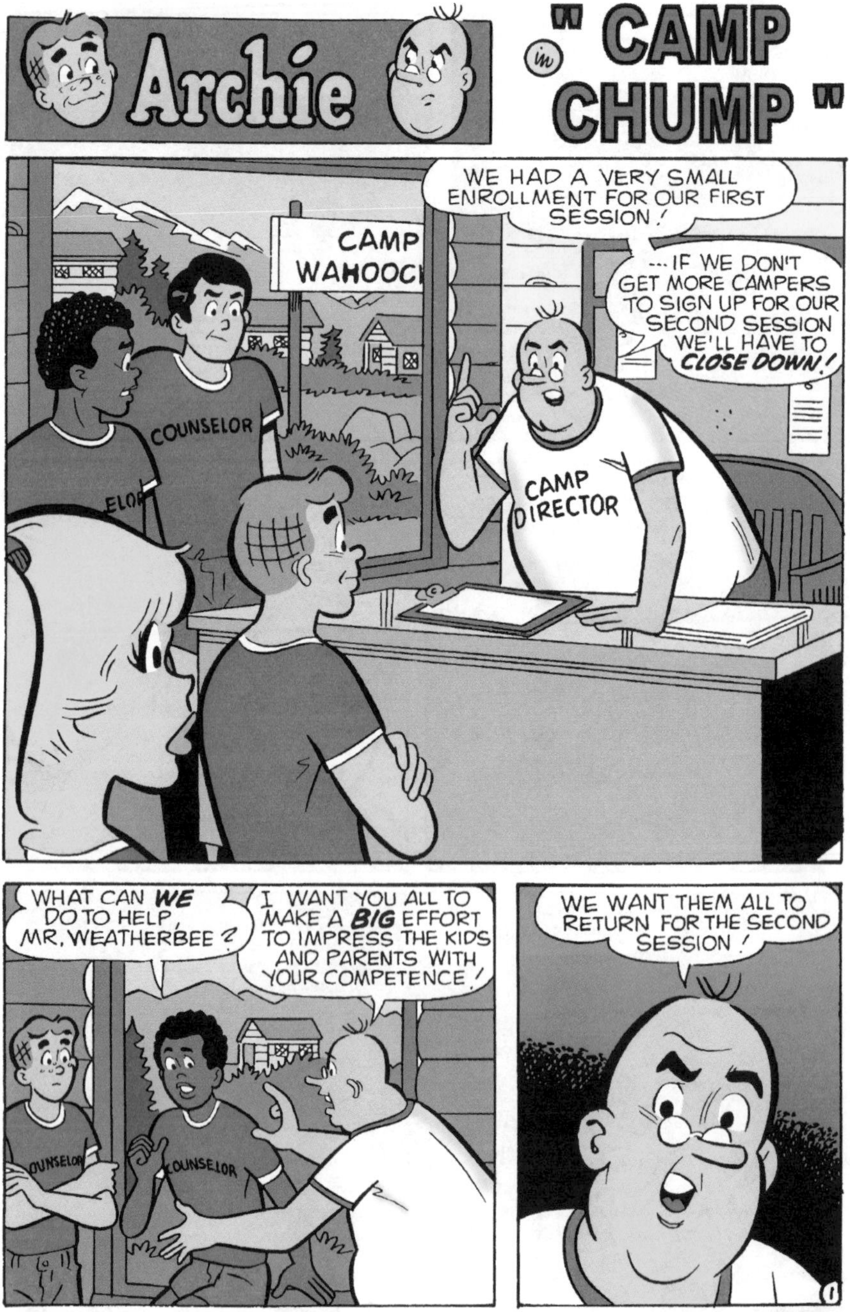
Archie
in "CAMP CHUMP"
CAMP WAHOOC
COUNSELOR
WE HAD A VERY SMALL ENROLLMENT FOR OUR FIRST SESSION!
...IF WE DON'T GET MORE CAMPERS TO SIGN UP FOR OUR SECOND SESSION WE'LL HAVE TO CLOSE DOWN!
CAMP DIRECTOR
WHAT CAN WE DO TO HELP, MR. WEATHERBEE?
I WANT YOU ALL TO MAKE A BIG EFFORT TO IMPRESS THE KIDS AND PARENTS WITH YOUR COMPETENCE!
COUNSELOR
COUNSELOR
WE WANT THEM ALL TO RETURN FOR THE SECOND SESSION!
1

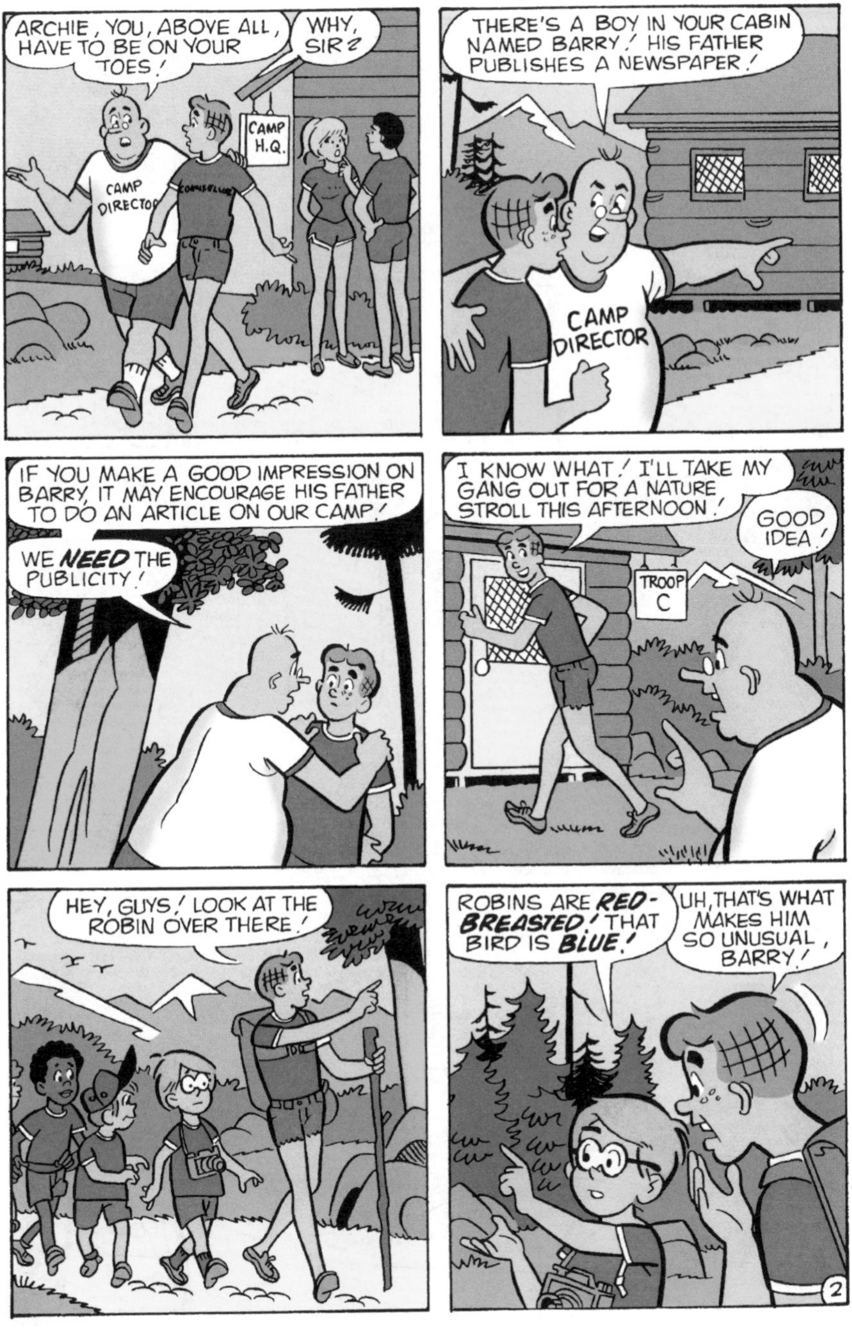
ARCHIE, YOU, ABOVE ALL, HAVE TO BE ON YOUR TOES!
WHY, SIR?
CAMP H.Q.
CAMP DIRECTOR
COUNSELLOR
THERE'S A BOY IN YOUR CABIN NAMED BARRY! HIS FATHER PUBLISHES A NEWSPAPER!
CAMP DIRECTOR
IF YOU MAKE A GOOD IMPRESSION ON BARRY, IT MAY ENCOURAGE HIS FATHER TO DO AN ARTICLE ON OUR CAMP!
WE NEED THE PUBLICITY!
I KNOW WHAT! I'LL TAKE MY GANG OUT FOR A NATURE STROLL THIS AFTERNOON!
GOOD IDEA!
TROOP C
HEY, GUYS! LOOK AT THE ROBIN OVER THERE!
ROBINS ARE RED-BREASTED! THAT BIRD IS BLUE!
UH, THAT'S WHAT MAKES HIM SO UNUSUAL, BARRY!
2

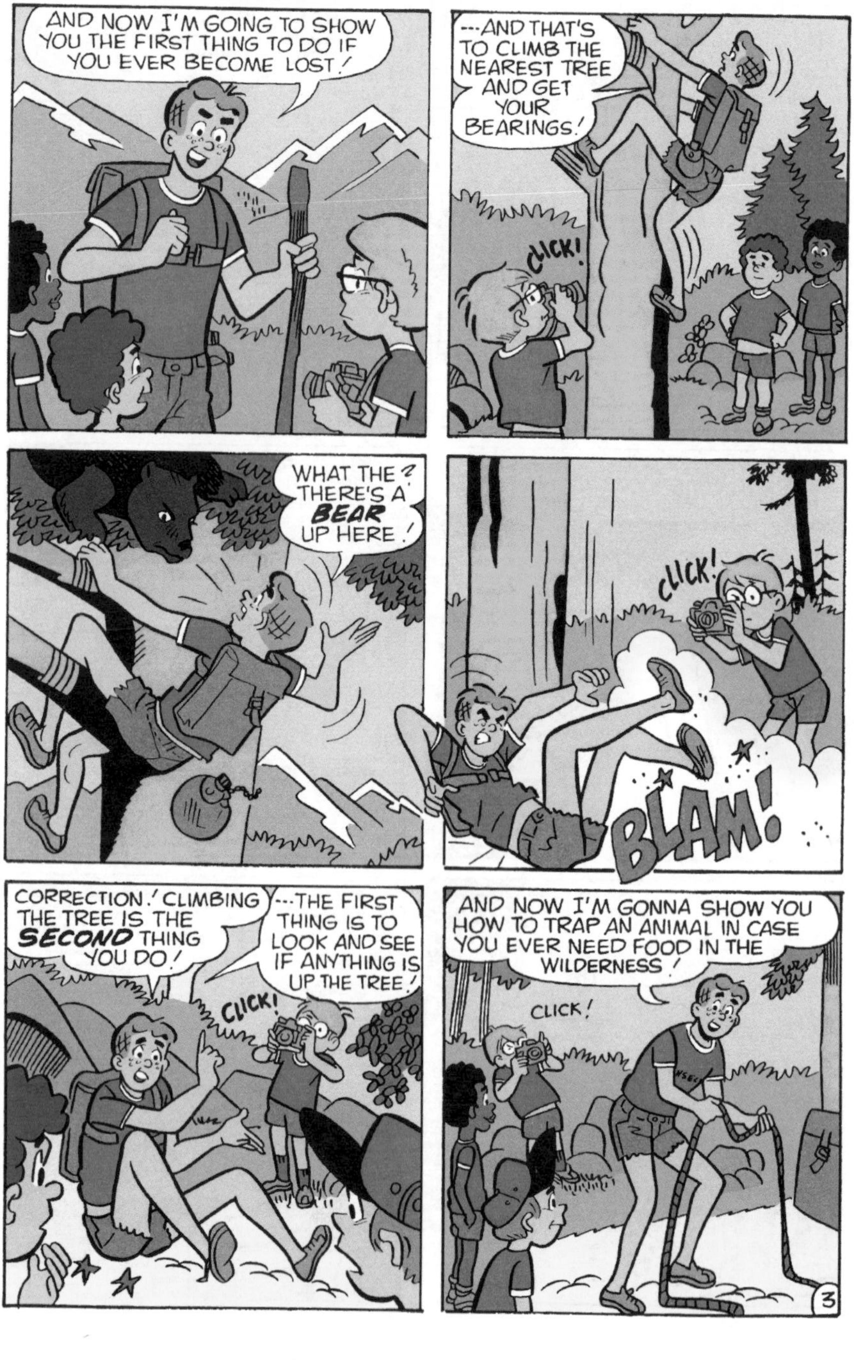
AND NOW I'M GOING TO SHOW YOU THE FIRST THING TO DO IF YOU EVER BECOME LOST!
---AND THAT'S TO CLIMB THE NEAREST TREE AND GET YOUR BEARINGS!
CLICK!
WHAT THE? THERE'S A BEAR UP HERE!
CLICK!
BLAM!
CORRECTION! CLIMBING THE TREE IS THE SECOND THING YOU DO!
---THE FIRST THING IS TO LOOK AND SEE IF ANYTHING IS UP THE TREE!
CLICK!
AND NOW I'M GONNA SHOW YOU HOW TO TRAP AN ANIMAL IN CASE YOU EVER NEED FOOD IN THE WILDERNESS!
CLICK!
3

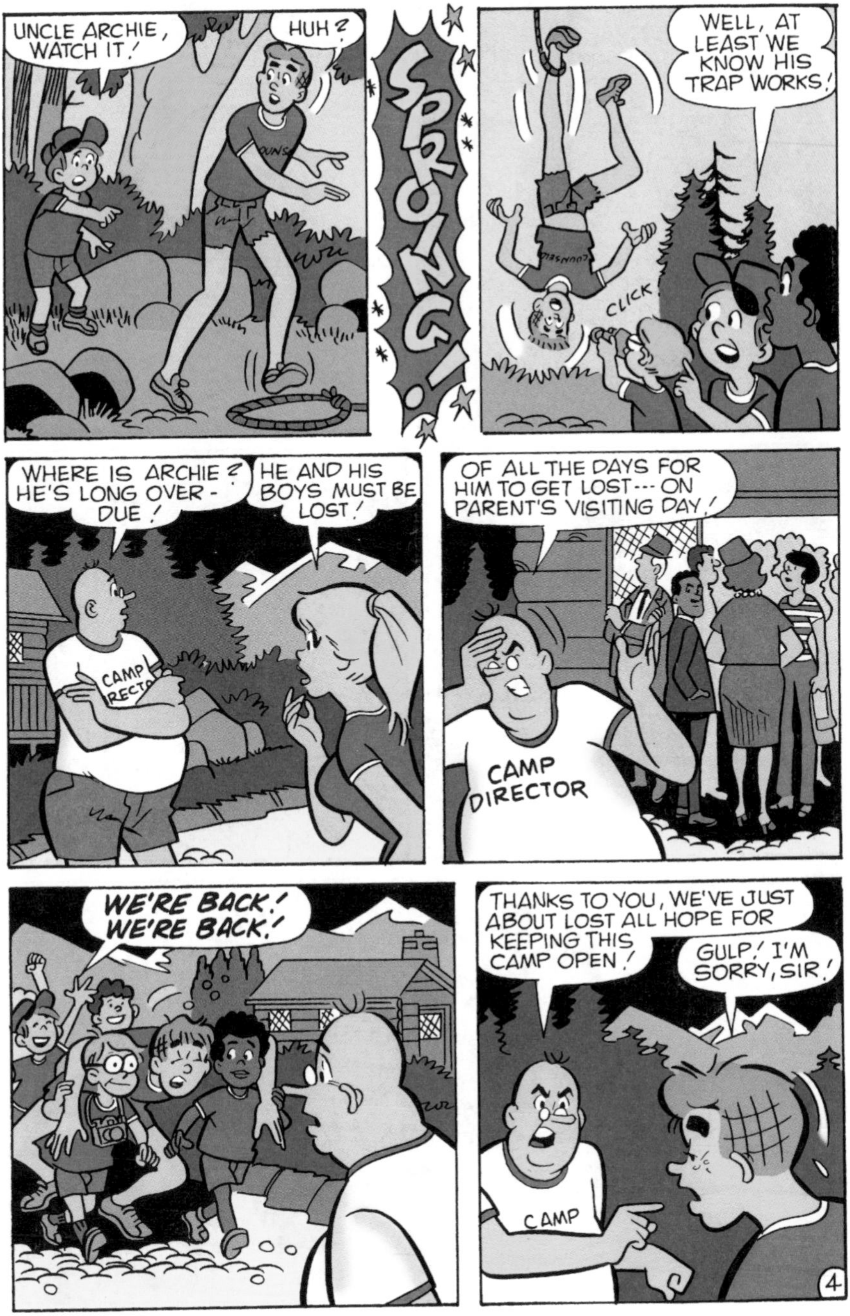
UNCLE ARCHIE, WATCH IT!
HUH?
SPROING!
WELL, AT LEAST WE KNOW HIS TRAP WORKS!
CLICK
WHERE IS ARCHIE? HE'S LONG OVER-DUE!
HE AND HIS BOYS MUST BE LOST!
OF ALL THE DAYS FOR HIM TO GET LOST--- ON PARENT'S VISITING DAY!
CAMP DIRECTOR
WE'RE BACK! WE'RE BACK!
THANKS TO YOU, WE'VE JUST ABOUT LOST ALL HOPE FOR KEEPING THIS CAMP OPEN!
GULP! I'M SORRY, SIR!
CAMP
4

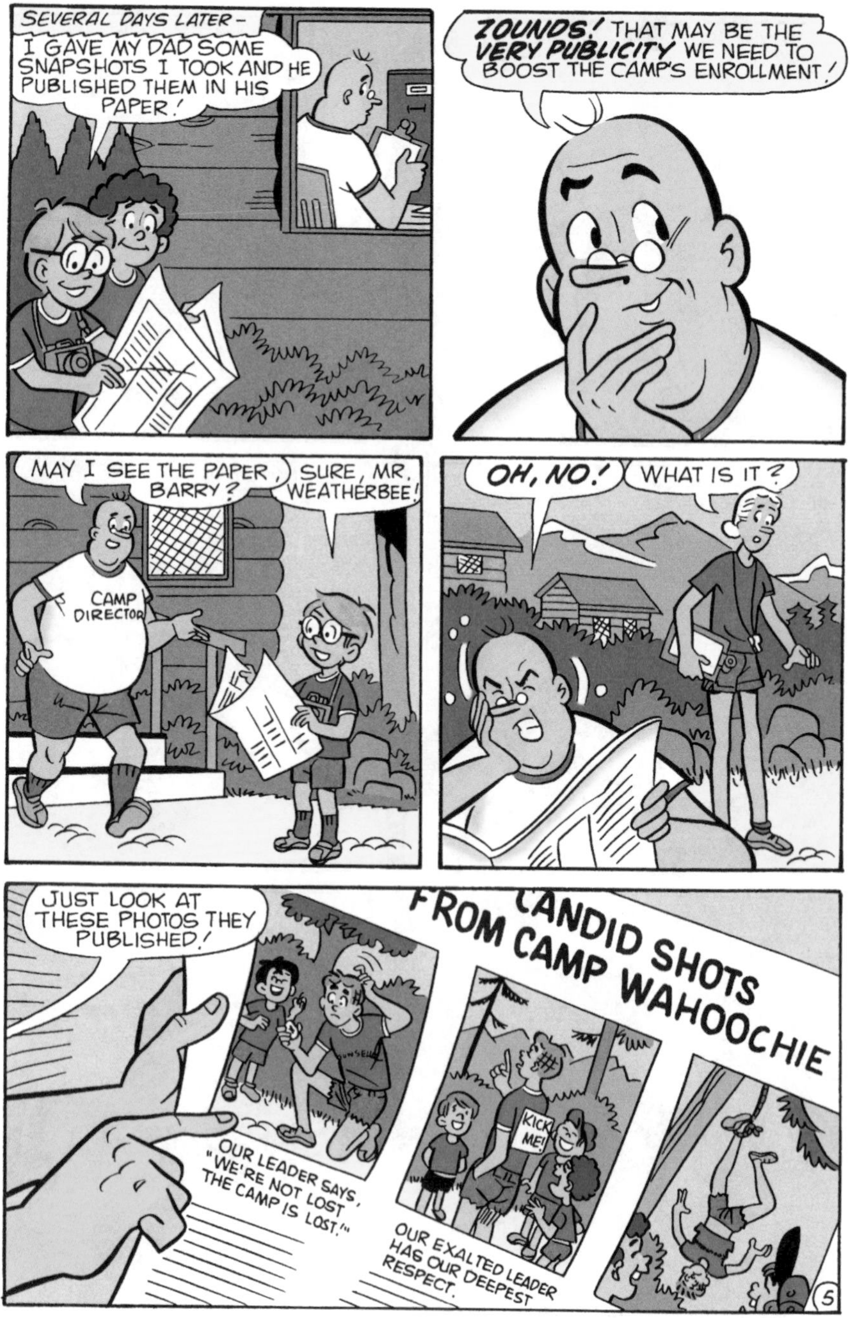

SEVERAL DAYS LATER—
I GAVE MY DAD SOME SNAPSHOTS I TOOK AND HE PUBLISHED THEM IN HIS PAPER!
ZOUNDS! THAT MAY BE THE VERY PUBLICITY WE NEED TO BOOST THE CAMP'S ENROLLMENT!
MAY I SEE THE PAPER, BARRY?
SURE, MR. WEATHERBEE!
CAMP DIRECTOR
OH, NO!
WHAT IS IT?
JUST LOOK AT THESE PHOTOS THEY PUBLISHED!
CANDID SHOTS FROM CAMP WAHOOCHIE
OUR LEADER SAYS, "WE'RE NOT LOST THE CAMP IS LOST."
KICK ME!
OUR EXALTED LEADER HAS OUR DEEPEST RESPECT.

WE'LL BE THE LAUGHING STOCK OF THE COUNTRY!

WE MAY AS WELL CLOSE DOWN RIGHT NOW!

MR. WEATHERBEE! LOOK AT ALL THIS MAIL WE RECEIVED!

HUH?

MAIL

THE MAIL IS FROM PARENTS WHO WANT TO ENROLL THEIR CHILDREN IN OUR CAMP!

WHY WOULD THEY WANT TO DO THAT?

CAMP

THE PARENTS NOTICED IN THE NEWS PHOTOS THAT ALL OUR CAMPERS WERE SMILING AND LAUGHING!

---THEY ALL WANT TO SEND THEIR KIDS TO A CAMP WHERE THE COUNSELORS HAVE A SENSE OF HUMOR!

CAMP DIRECTOR

THANKS TO ARCHIE, CAMP WAHOOCHIE IS *SAVED!*

COUNSELOR COUNSELOR COUNSELOR CAMP DIRECT.

ACTUALLY, I NEVER ONCE DOUBTED THIS REMARKABLE LAD'S ABILITY TO PULL US THROUGH!

END

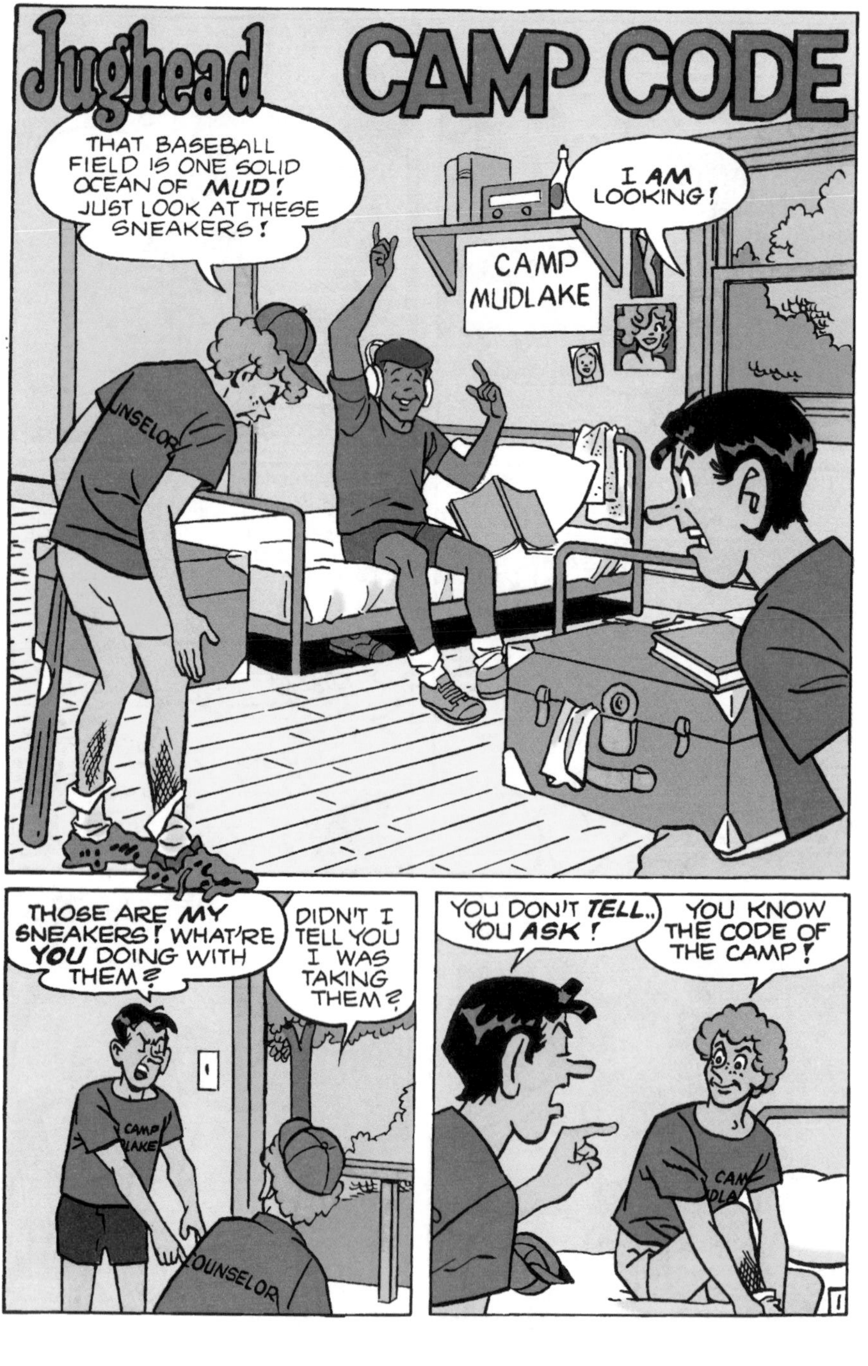

Jughead
CAMP CODE
THAT BASEBALL FIELD IS ONE SOLID OCEAN OF MUD! JUST LOOK AT THESE SNEAKERS!
I AM LOOKING!
CAMP MUDLAKE
UNSELOR
THOSE ARE MY SNEAKERS! WHAT'RE YOU DOING WITH THEM?
DIDN'T I TELL YOU I WAS TAKING THEM?
CAMP
LAKE
COUNSELOR
YOU DON'T TELL.. YOU ASK!
YOU KNOW THE CODE OF THE CAMP!
CAM
DLA

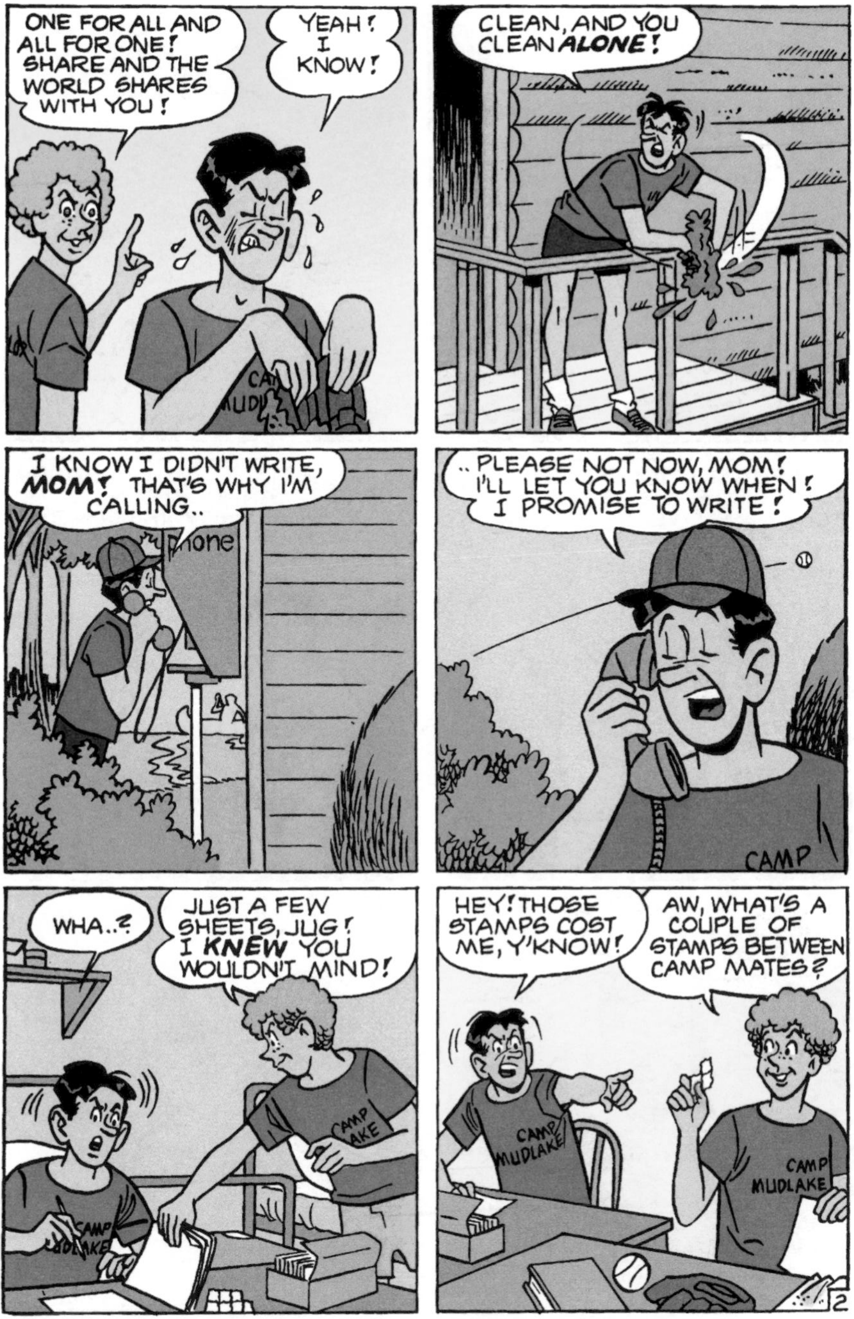

ONE FOR ALL AND ALL FOR ONE! SHARE AND THE WORLD SHARES WITH YOU!
YEAH! I KNOW!
CLEAN, AND YOU CLEAN **ALONE**!
I KNOW I DIDN'T WRITE, **MOM**! THAT'S WHY I'M CALLING..
Phone
..PLEASE NOT NOW, MOM! I'LL LET YOU KNOW WHEN I PROMISE TO WRITE!
CAMP
WHA..?
JUST A FEW SHEETS, JUG! I **KNEW** YOU WOULDN'T MIND!
HEY! THOSE STAMPS COST ME, Y'KNOW!
AW, WHAT'S A COUPLE OF STAMPS BETWEEN CAMP MATES?
CAMP MUDLAKE
CAMP MUDLAKE

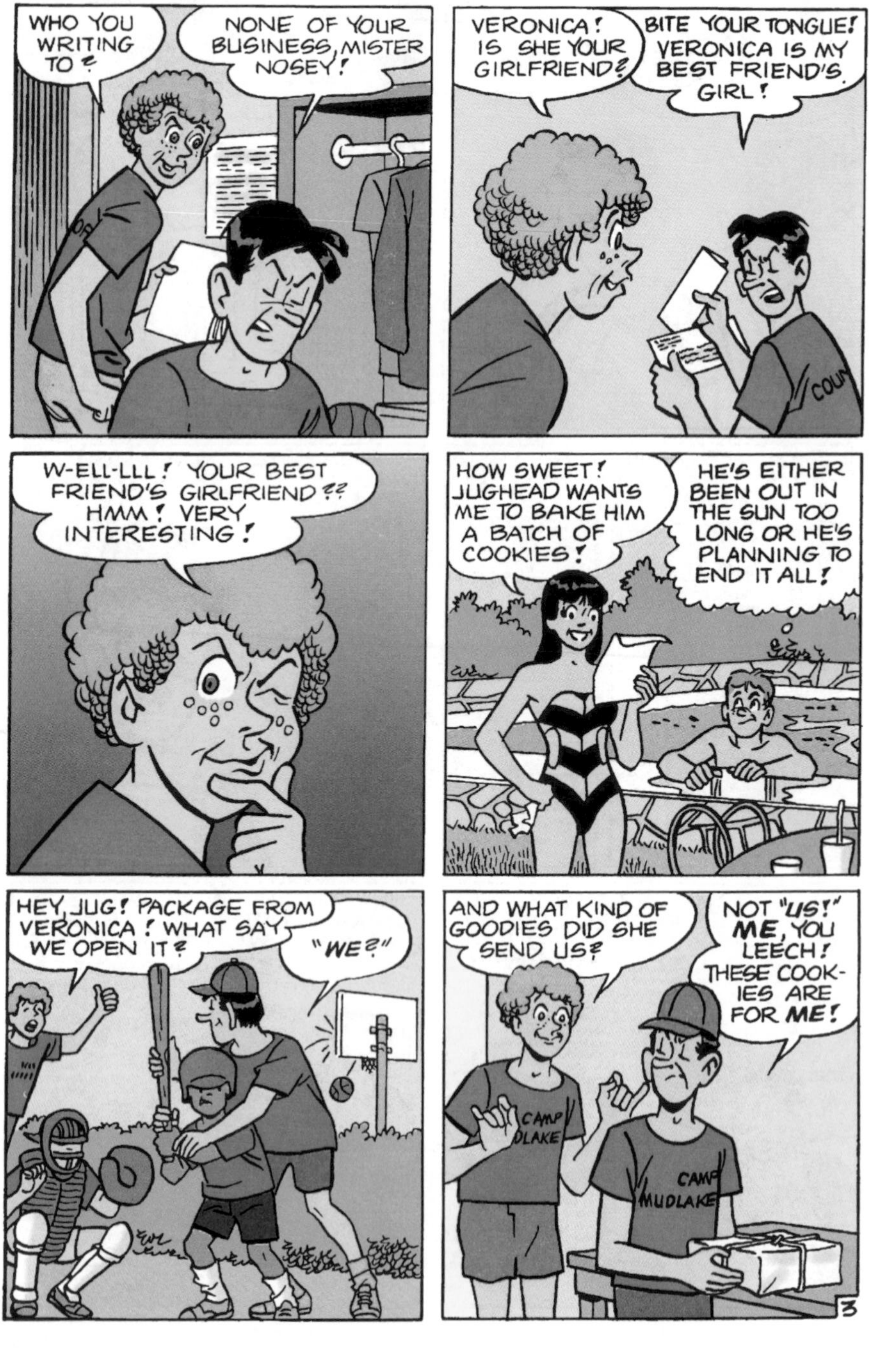
WHO YOU WRITING TO?
NONE OF YOUR BUSINESS, MISTER NOSEY!
VERONICA! IS SHE YOUR GIRLFRIEND?
BITE YOUR TONGUE! VERONICA IS MY BEST FRIEND'S GIRL!
W-ELL-LLL! YOUR BEST FRIEND'S GIRLFRIEND?? HMM! VERY INTERESTING!
HOW SWEET! JUGHEAD WANTS ME TO BAKE HIM A BATCH OF COOKIES!
HE'S EITHER BEEN OUT IN THE SUN TOO LONG OR HE'S PLANNING TO END IT ALL!
HEY, JUG! PACKAGE FROM VERONICA! WHAT SAY WE OPEN IT?
"WE?"
AND WHAT KIND OF GOODIES DID SHE SEND US?
NOT "US!" ME, YOU LEECH! THESE COOKIES ARE FOR ME!
CAMP MUDLAKE
3

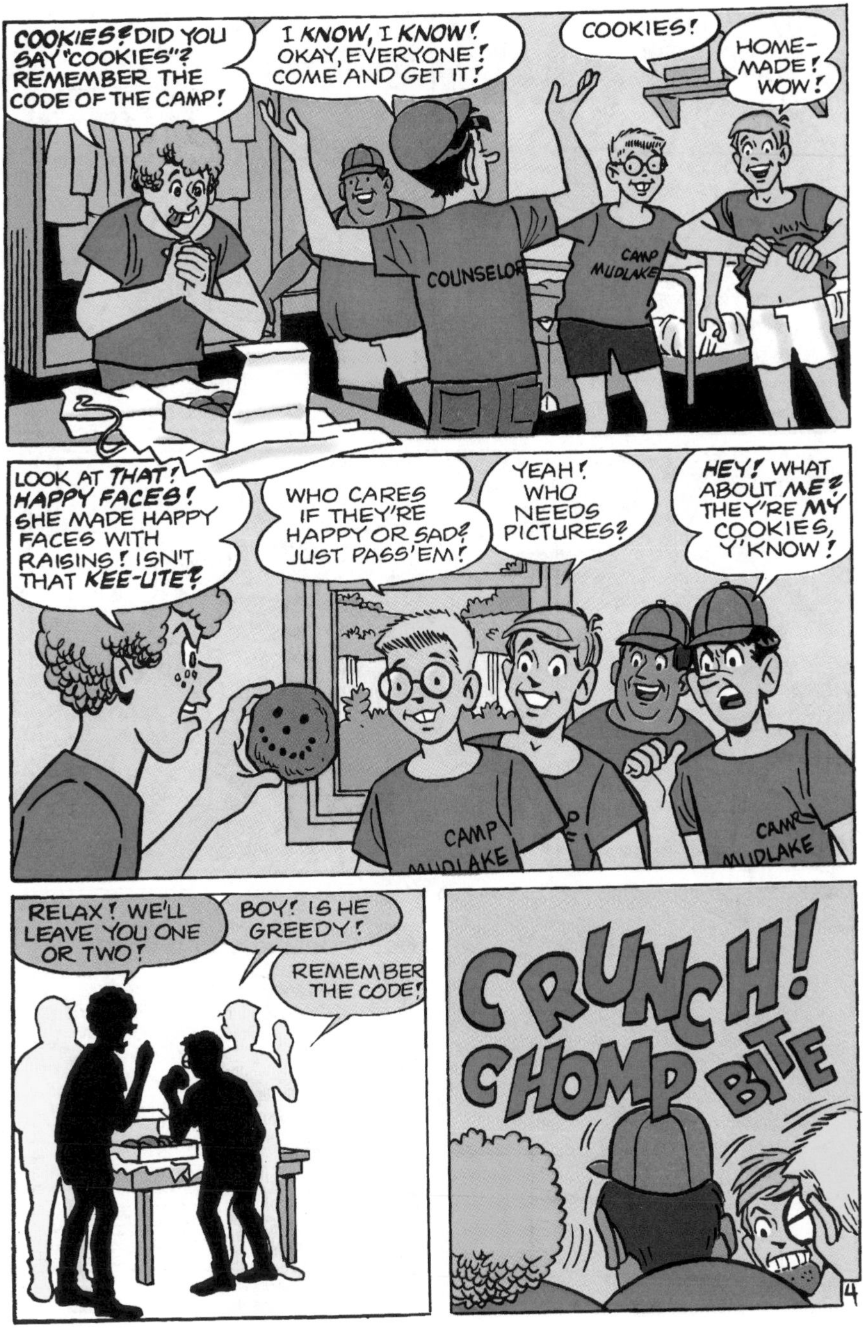
COOKIES? DID YOU SAY "COOKIES"? REMEMBER THE CODE OF THE CAMP!
I KNOW, I KNOW! OKAY, EVERYONE! COME AND GET IT!
COOKIES!
HOME-MADE! WOW!
COUNSELOR
CAMP MUDLAKE
LOOK AT THAT! HAPPY FACES! SHE MADE HAPPY FACES WITH RAISINS! ISN'T THAT KEE-UTE?
WHO CARES IF THEY'RE HAPPY OR SAD? JUST PASS 'EM!
YEAH! WHO NEEDS PICTURES?
HEY! WHAT ABOUT ME? THEY'RE MY COOKIES, Y'KNOW!
CAMP MUDLAKE
CAMP MUDLAKE
RELAX! WE'LL LEAVE YOU ONE OR TWO!
BOY! IS HE GREEDY!
REMEMBER THE CODE!
CRUNCH!
CHOMP
BITE
4

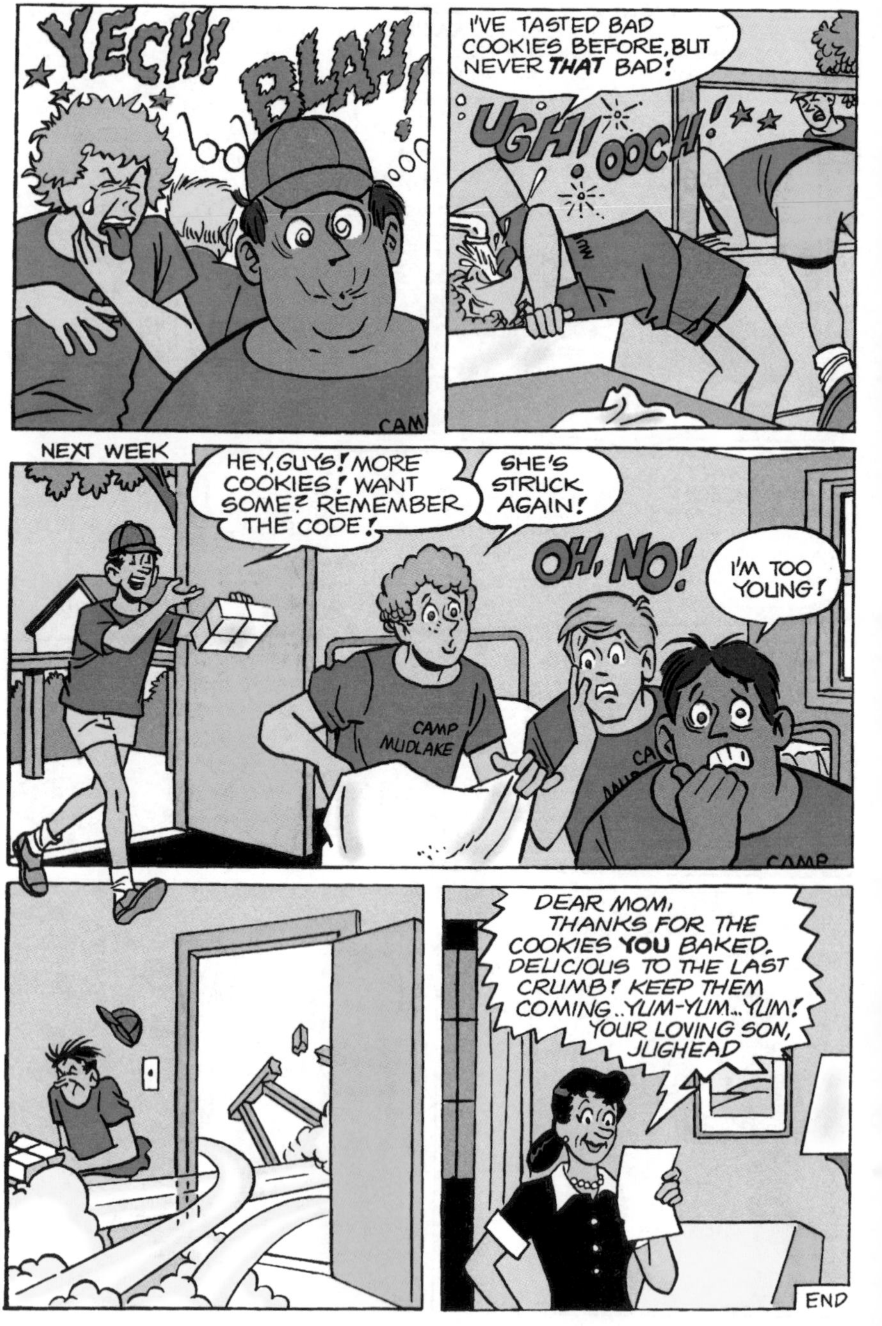
YECH!
BLAH!
CAM
I'VE TASTED BAD COOKIES BEFORE, BUT NEVER THAT BAD!
UGH!
OOCH!
NEXT WEEK
HEY, GUYS! MORE COOKIES! WANT SOME? REMEMBER THE CODE!
SHE'S STRUCK AGAIN!
OH, NO!
I'M TOO YOUNG!
CAMP MUDLAKE
CAMP
DEAR MOM, THANKS FOR THE COOKIES YOU BAKED. DELICIOUS TO THE LAST CRUMB! KEEP THEM COMING..YUM-YUM..YUM! YOUR LOVING SON, JUGHEAD
END

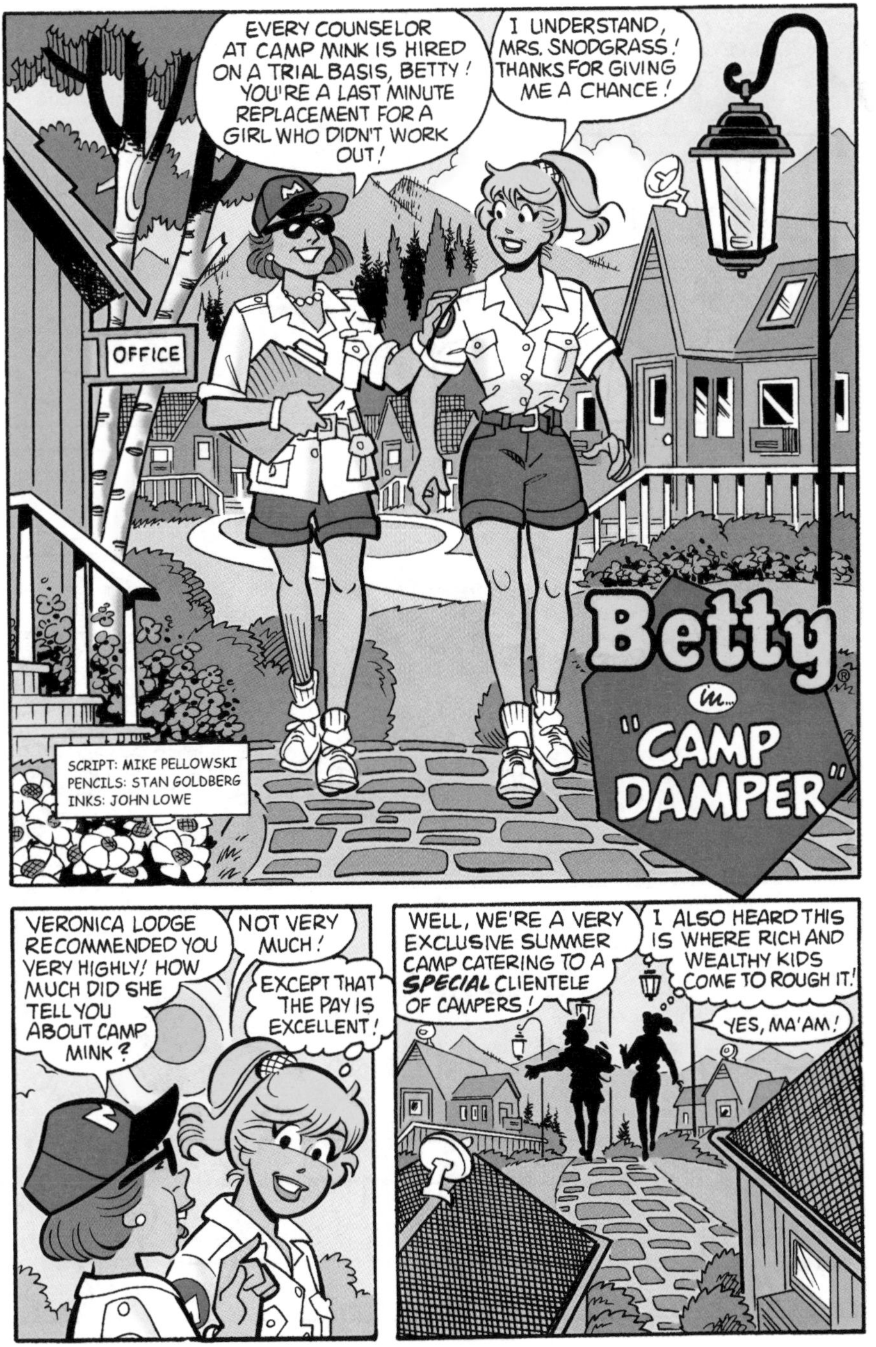
EVERY COUNSELOR AT CAMP MINK IS HIRED ON A TRIAL BASIS, BETTY! YOU'RE A LAST MINUTE REPLACEMENT FOR A GIRL WHO DIDN'T WORK OUT!
I UNDERSTAND, MRS. SNODGRASS! THANKS FOR GIVING ME A CHANCE!
OFFICE
Betty®
in...
"CAMP DAMPER"
SCRIPT: MIKE PELLOWSKI
PENCILS: STAN GOLDBERG
INKS: JOHN LOWE
VERONICA LODGE RECOMMENDED YOU VERY HIGHLY! HOW MUCH DID SHE TELL YOU ABOUT CAMP MINK?
NOT VERY MUCH!
EXCEPT THAT THE PAY IS EXCELLENT!
WELL, WE'RE A VERY EXCLUSIVE SUMMER CAMP CATERING TO A SPECIAL CLIENTELE OF CAMPERS!
I ALSO HEARD THIS IS WHERE RICH AND WEALTHY KIDS COME TO ROUGH IT!
YES, MA'AM!

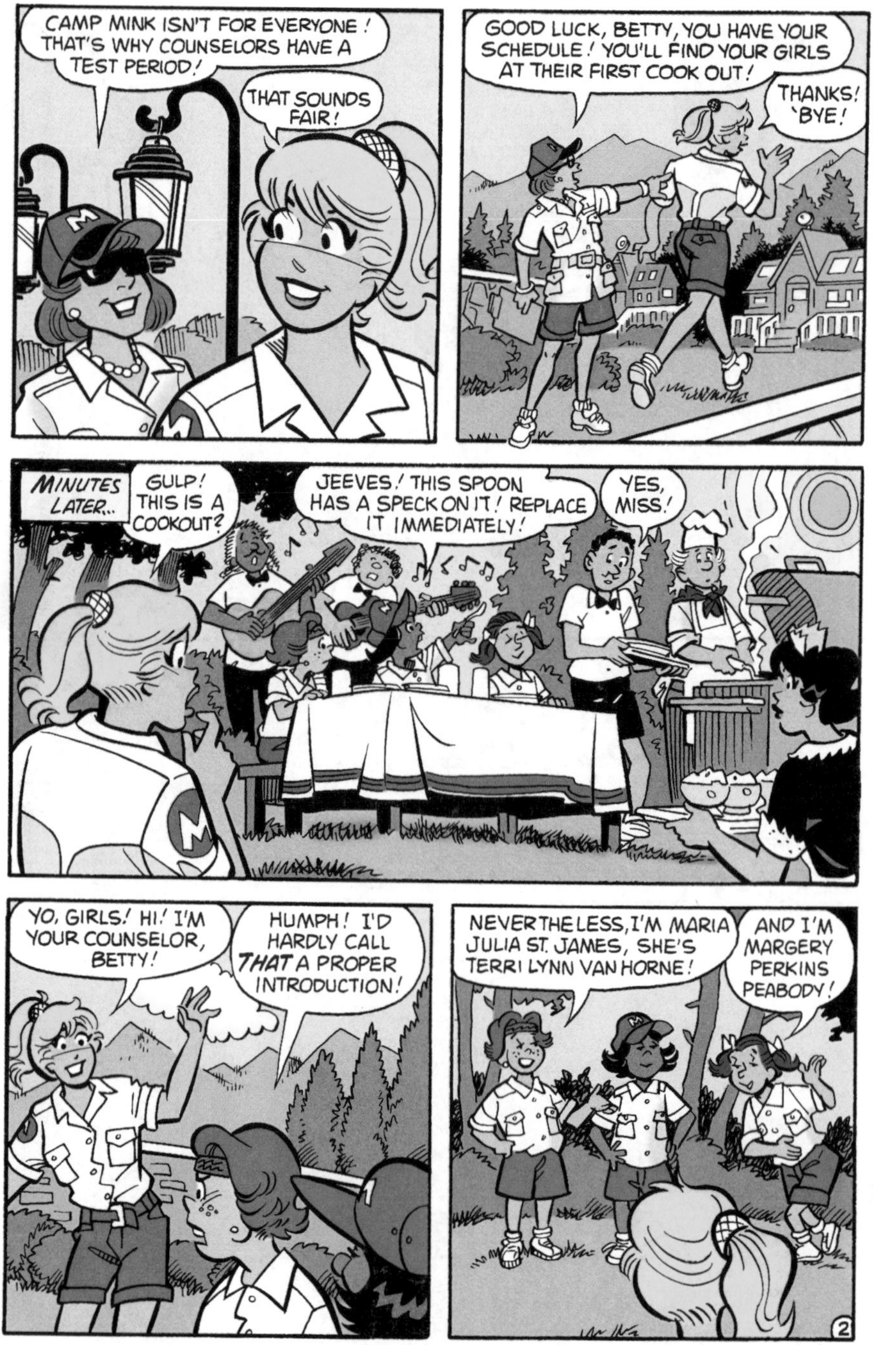
CAMP MINK ISN'T FOR EVERYONE! THAT'S WHY COUNSELORS HAVE A TEST PERIOD!
THAT SOUNDS FAIR!
GOOD LUCK, BETTY, YOU HAVE YOUR SCHEDULE! YOU'LL FIND YOUR GIRLS AT THEIR FIRST COOK OUT!
THANKS! 'BYE!
MINUTES LATER...
GULP! THIS IS A COOKOUT?
JEEVES! THIS SPOON HAS A SPECK ON IT! REPLACE IT IMMEDIATELY!
YES, MISS!
YO, GIRLS! HI! I'M YOUR COUNSELOR, BETTY!
HUMPH! I'D HARDLY CALL THAT A PROPER INTRODUCTION!
NEVERTHELESS, I'M MARIA JULIA ST. JAMES, SHE'S TERRI LYNN VAN HORNE!
AND I'M MARGERY PERKINS PEABODY!
2

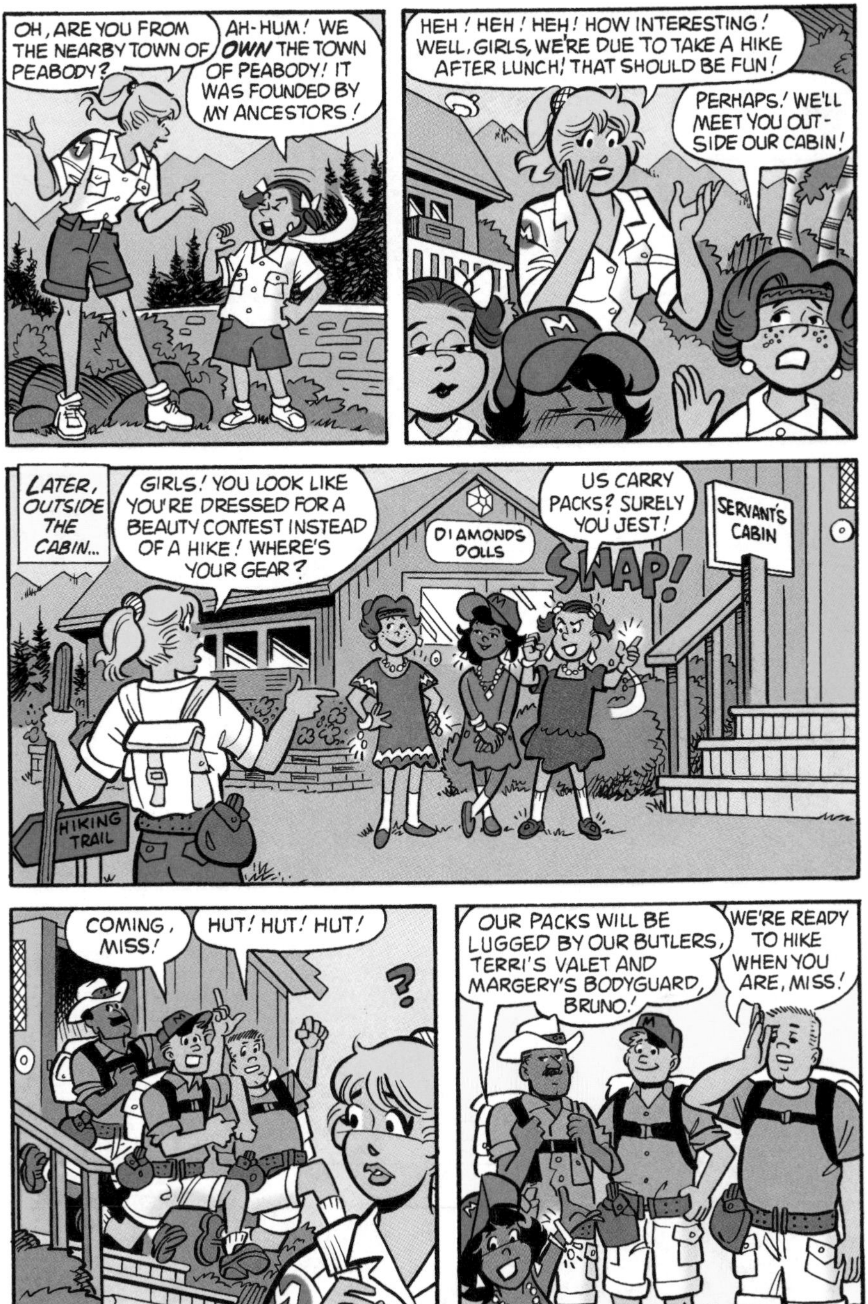
OH, ARE YOU FROM THE NEARBY TOWN OF PEABODY?
AH-HUM! WE OWN THE TOWN OF PEABODY! IT WAS FOUNDED BY MY ANCESTORS!
HEH! HEH! HEH! HOW INTERESTING! WELL, GIRLS, WE'RE DUE TO TAKE A HIKE AFTER LUNCH! THAT SHOULD BE FUN!
PERHAPS! WE'LL MEET YOU OUTSIDE OUR CABIN!
LATER, OUTSIDE THE CABIN...
GIRLS! YOU LOOK LIKE YOU'RE DRESSED FOR A BEAUTY CONTEST INSTEAD OF A HIKE! WHERE'S YOUR GEAR?
DIAMONDS DOLLS
US CARRY PACKS? SURELY YOU JEST!
SNAP!
SERVANT'S CABIN
HIKING TRAIL
COMING, MISS!
HUT! HUT! HUT!
?
OUR PACKS WILL BE LUGGED BY OUR BUTLERS, TERRI'S VALET AND MARGERY'S BODYGUARD, BRUNO!
WE'RE READY TO HIKE WHEN YOU ARE, MISS!
3

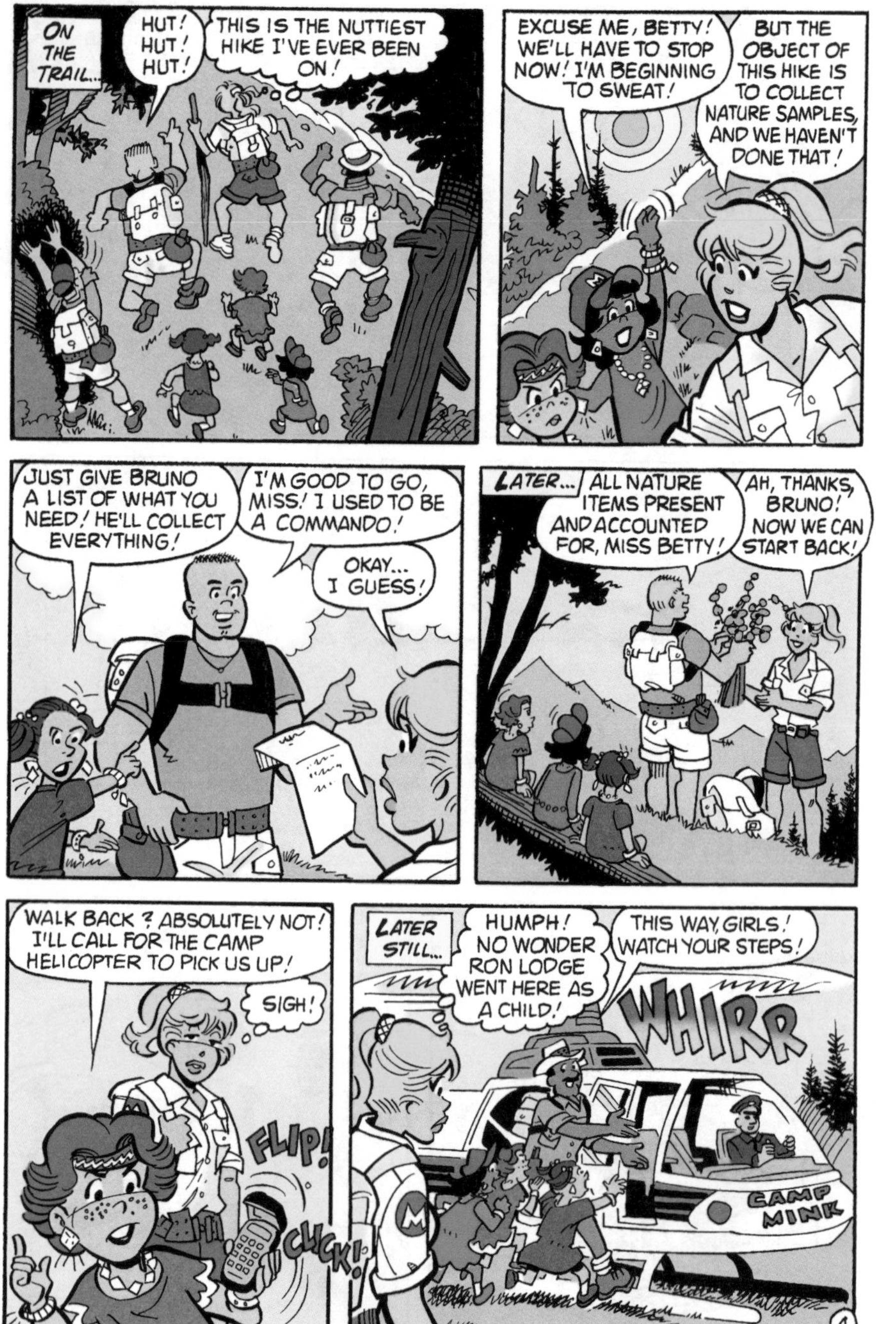

ON THE TRAIL...
HUT! HUT! HUT!
THIS IS THE NUTTIEST HIKE I'VE EVER BEEN ON!
EXCUSE ME, BETTY! WE'LL HAVE TO STOP NOW! I'M BEGINNING TO SWEAT!
BUT THE OBJECT OF THIS HIKE IS TO COLLECT NATURE SAMPLES, AND WE HAVEN'T DONE THAT!
JUST GIVE BRUNO A LIST OF WHAT YOU NEED! HE'LL COLLECT EVERYTHING!
I'M GOOD TO GO, MISS! I USED TO BE A COMMANDO!
OKAY... I GUESS!
LATER...
ALL NATURE ITEMS PRESENT AND ACCOUNTED FOR, MISS BETTY!
AH, THANKS, BRUNO! NOW WE CAN START BACK!
WALK BACK ? ABSOLUTELY NOT! I'LL CALL FOR THE CAMP HELICOPTER TO PICK US UP!
SIGH!
FLIP!
CLICK!
LATER STILL...
HUMPH! NO WONDER RON LODGE WENT HERE AS A CHILD!
THIS WAY, GIRLS! WATCH YOUR STEPS!
WHIRR
CAMP MINK

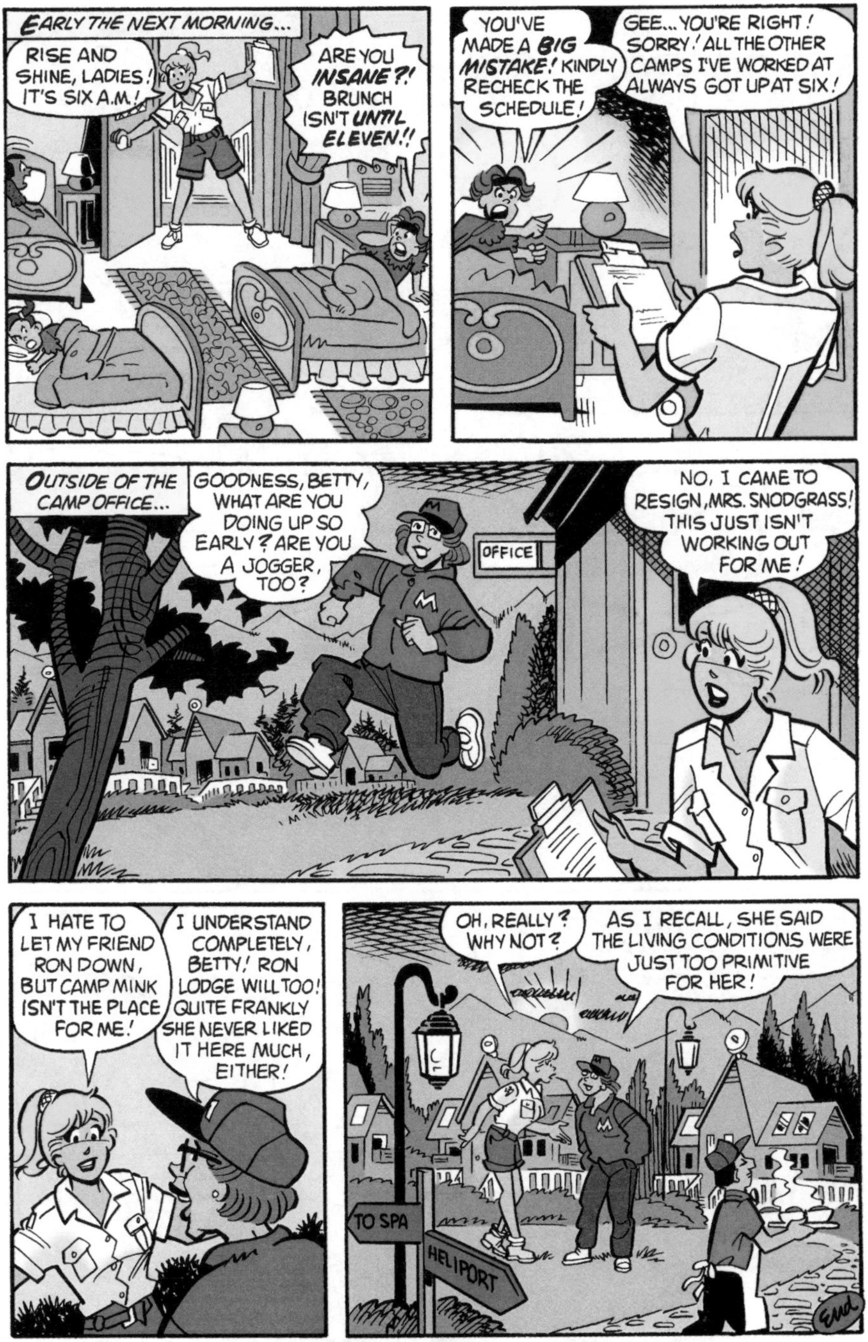

EARLY THE NEXT MORNING...
RISE AND SHINE, LADIES! IT'S SIX A.M.!
ARE YOU INSANE?! BRUNCH ISN'T UNTIL ELEVEN!!
YOU'VE MADE A BIG MISTAKE! KINDLY RECHECK THE SCHEDULE!
GEE... YOU'RE RIGHT! SORRY! ALL THE OTHER CAMPS I'VE WORKED AT ALWAYS GOT UP AT SIX!
OUTSIDE OF THE CAMP OFFICE...
GOODNESS, BETTY, WHAT ARE YOU DOING UP SO EARLY? ARE YOU A JOGGER, TOO?
OFFICE
NO, I CAME TO RESIGN, MRS. SNODGRASS! THIS JUST ISN'T WORKING OUT FOR ME!
I HATE TO LET MY FRIEND RON DOWN, BUT CAMP MINK ISN'T THE PLACE FOR ME!
I UNDERSTAND COMPLETELY, BETTY! RON LODGE WILL TOO! QUITE FRANKLY SHE NEVER LIKED IT HERE MUCH, EITHER!
OH, REALLY? WHY NOT?
AS I RECALL, SHE SAID THE LIVING CONDITIONS WERE JUST TOO PRIMITIVE FOR HER!
TO SPA
HELIPORT
End

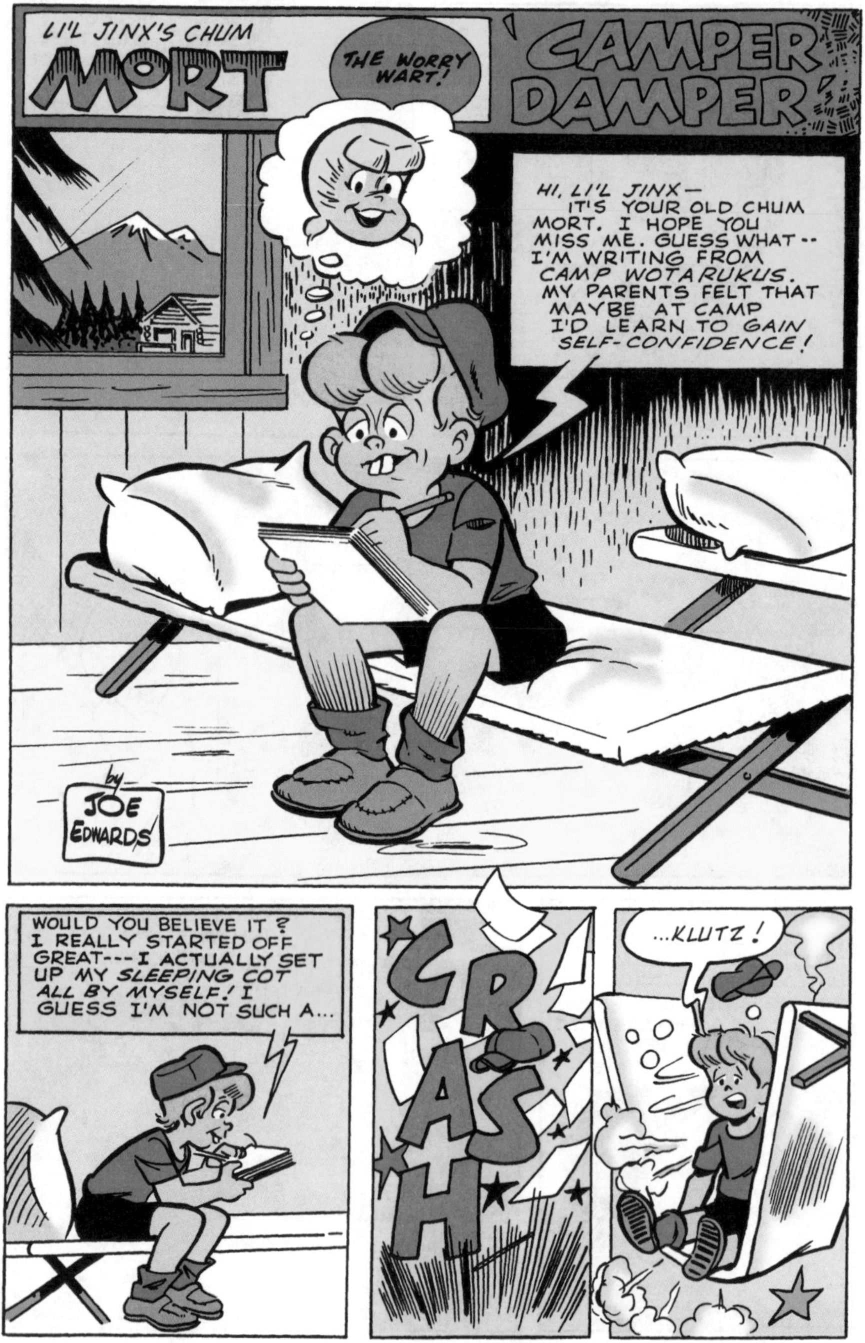
LI'L JINX'S CHUM
MORT
THE WORRY WART!
'CAMPER DAMPER'
HI, LI'L JINX— IT'S YOUR OLD CHUM MORT. I HOPE YOU MISS ME. GUESS WHAT -- I'M WRITING FROM CAMP WOTARUKUS. MY PARENTS FELT THAT MAYBE AT CAMP I'D LEARN TO GAIN SELF-CONFIDENCE!
by JOE EDWARDS
WOULD YOU BELIEVE IT? I REALLY STARTED OFF GREAT--- I ACTUALLY SET UP MY SLEEPING COT ALL BY MYSELF! I GUESS I'M NOT SUCH A...
CRASH
...KLUTZ!

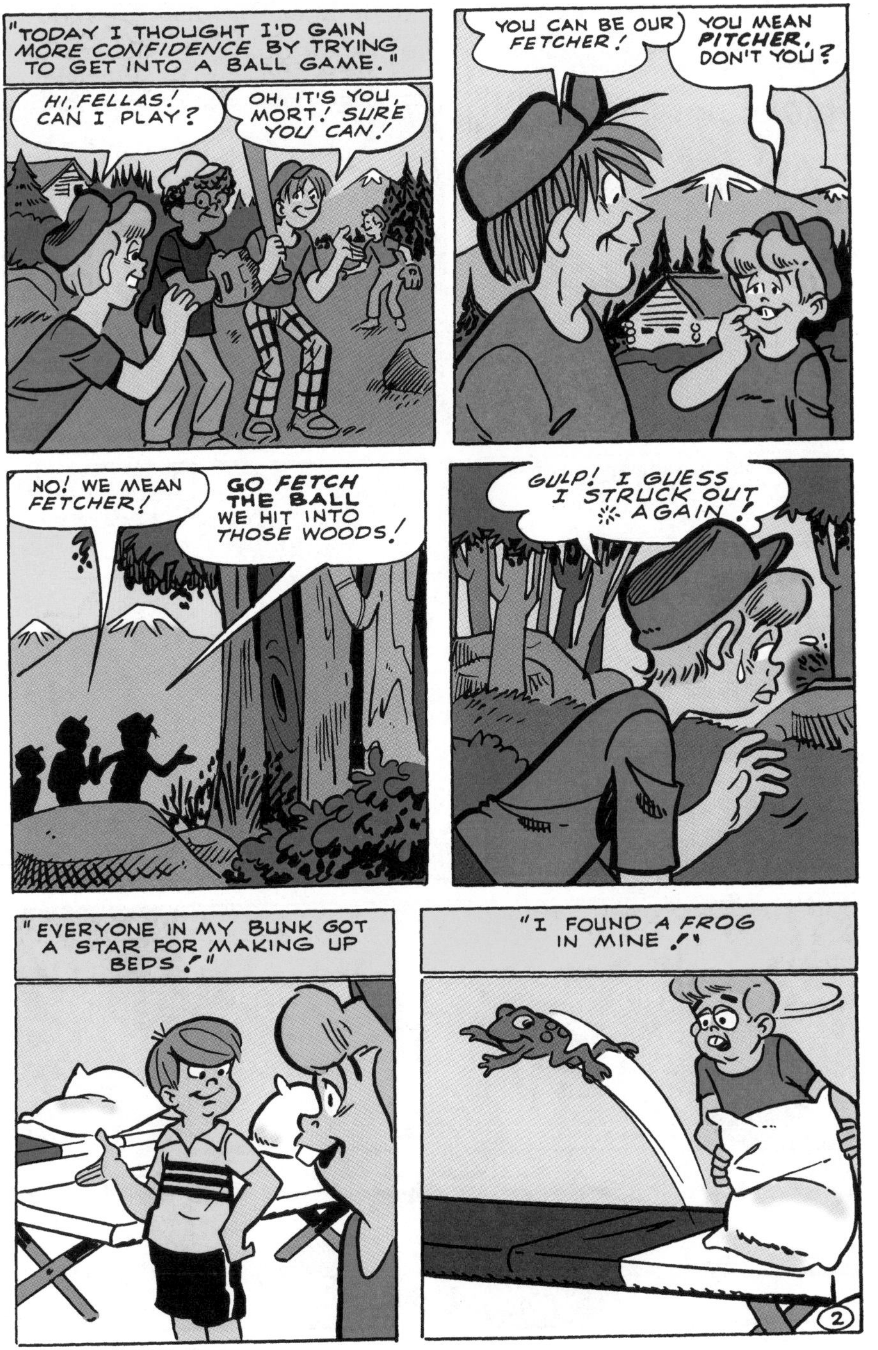
"TODAY I THOUGHT I'D GAIN MORE CONFIDENCE BY TRYING TO GET INTO A BALL GAME."
HI, FELLAS! CAN I PLAY?
OH, IT'S YOU, MORT! SURE YOU CAN!
YOU CAN BE OUR FETCHER!
YOU MEAN PITCHER, DON'T YOU?
NO! WE MEAN FETCHER!
GO FETCH THE BALL WE HIT INTO THOSE WOODS!
GULP! I GUESS I STRUCK OUT AGAIN!
"EVERYONE IN MY BUNK GOT A STAR FOR MAKING UP BEDS!"
"I FOUND A FROG IN MINE!"
2

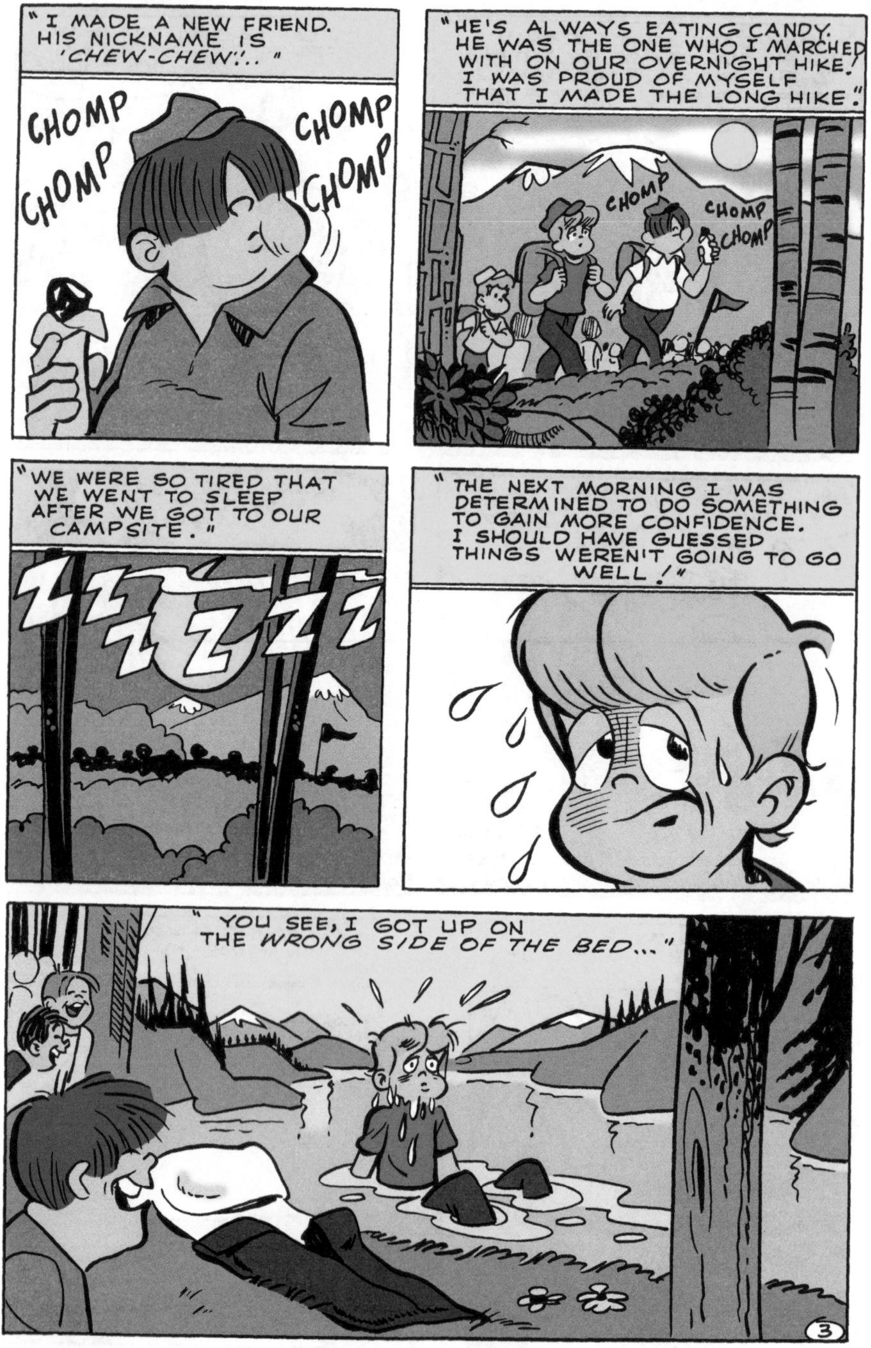
"I MADE A NEW FRIEND. HIS NICKNAME IS 'CHEW-CHEW'!.. "
CHOMP
CHOMP
CHOMP
CHOMP
"HE'S ALWAYS EATING CANDY. HE WAS THE ONE WHO I MARCHED WITH ON OUR OVERNIGHT HIKE! I WAS PROUD OF MYSELF THAT I MADE THE LONG HIKE."
CHOMP
CHOMP
CHOMP
"WE WERE SO TIRED THAT WE WENT TO SLEEP AFTER WE GOT TO OUR CAMPSITE."
ZZZZZZZ
"THE NEXT MORNING I WAS DETERMINED TO DO SOMETHING TO GAIN MORE CONFIDENCE. I SHOULD HAVE GUESSED THINGS WEREN'T GOING TO GO WELL!"
"YOU SEE, I GOT UP ON THE *WRONG SIDE OF THE BED*..."
3

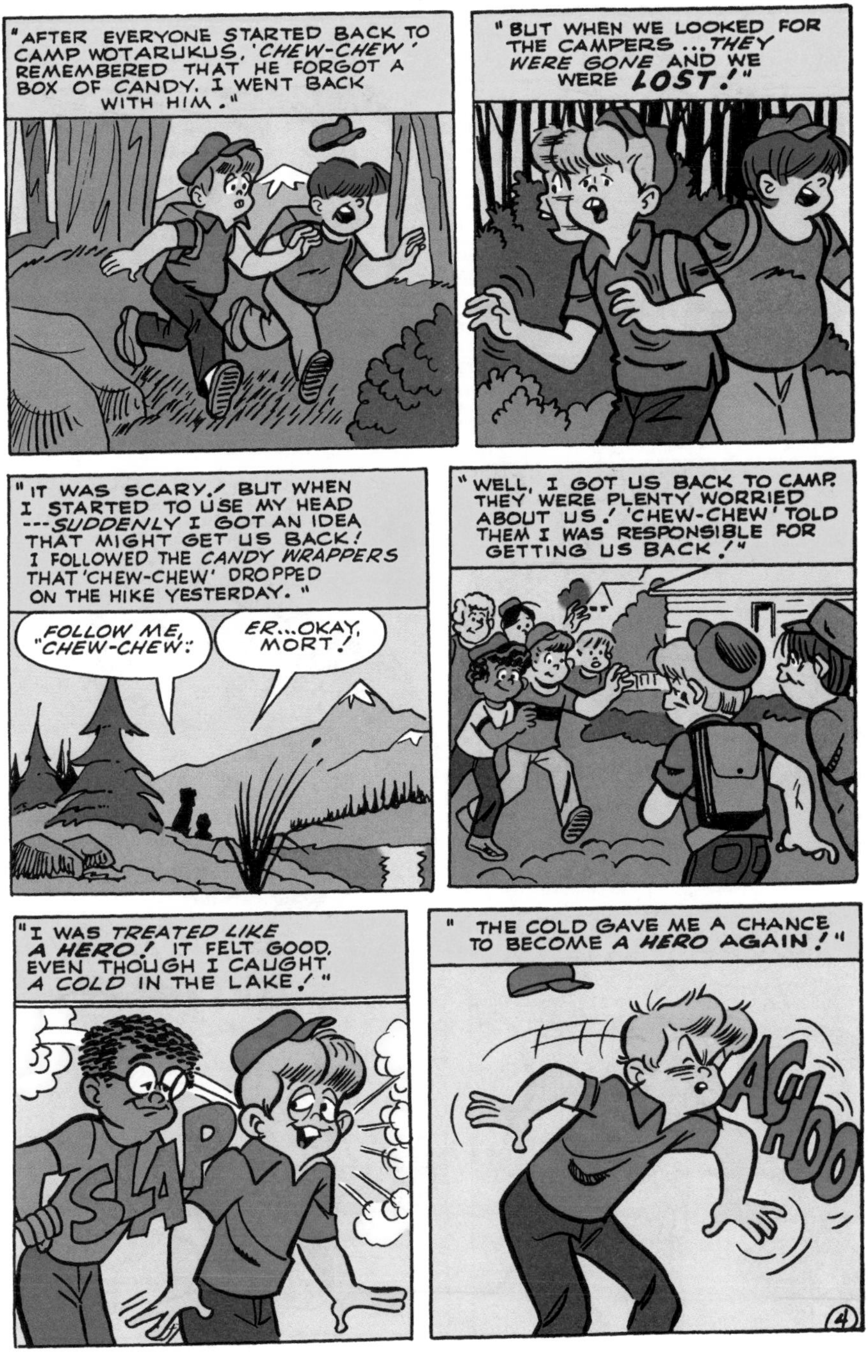
"AFTER EVERYONE STARTED BACK TO CAMP WOTARUKUS, 'CHEW-CHEW' REMEMBERED THAT HE FORGOT A BOX OF CANDY. I WENT BACK WITH HIM."
"BUT WHEN WE LOOKED FOR THE CAMPERS ...THEY WERE GONE AND WE WERE LOST!"
"IT WAS SCARY! BUT WHEN I STARTED TO USE MY HEAD ---SUDDENLY I GOT AN IDEA THAT MIGHT GET US BACK! I FOLLOWED THE CANDY WRAPPERS THAT 'CHEW-CHEW' DROPPED ON THE HIKE YESTERDAY."
FOLLOW ME, "CHEW-CHEW."
ER...OKAY, MORT!
"WELL, I GOT US BACK TO CAMP. THEY WERE PLENTY WORRIED ABOUT US! 'CHEW-CHEW' TOLD THEM I WAS RESPONSIBLE FOR GETTING US BACK!"
"I WAS TREATED LIKE A HERO! IT FELT GOOD, EVEN THOUGH I CAUGHT A COLD IN THE LAKE!"
SLAP
" THE COLD GAVE ME A CHANCE TO BECOME A HERO AGAIN!"
ACHOO
4

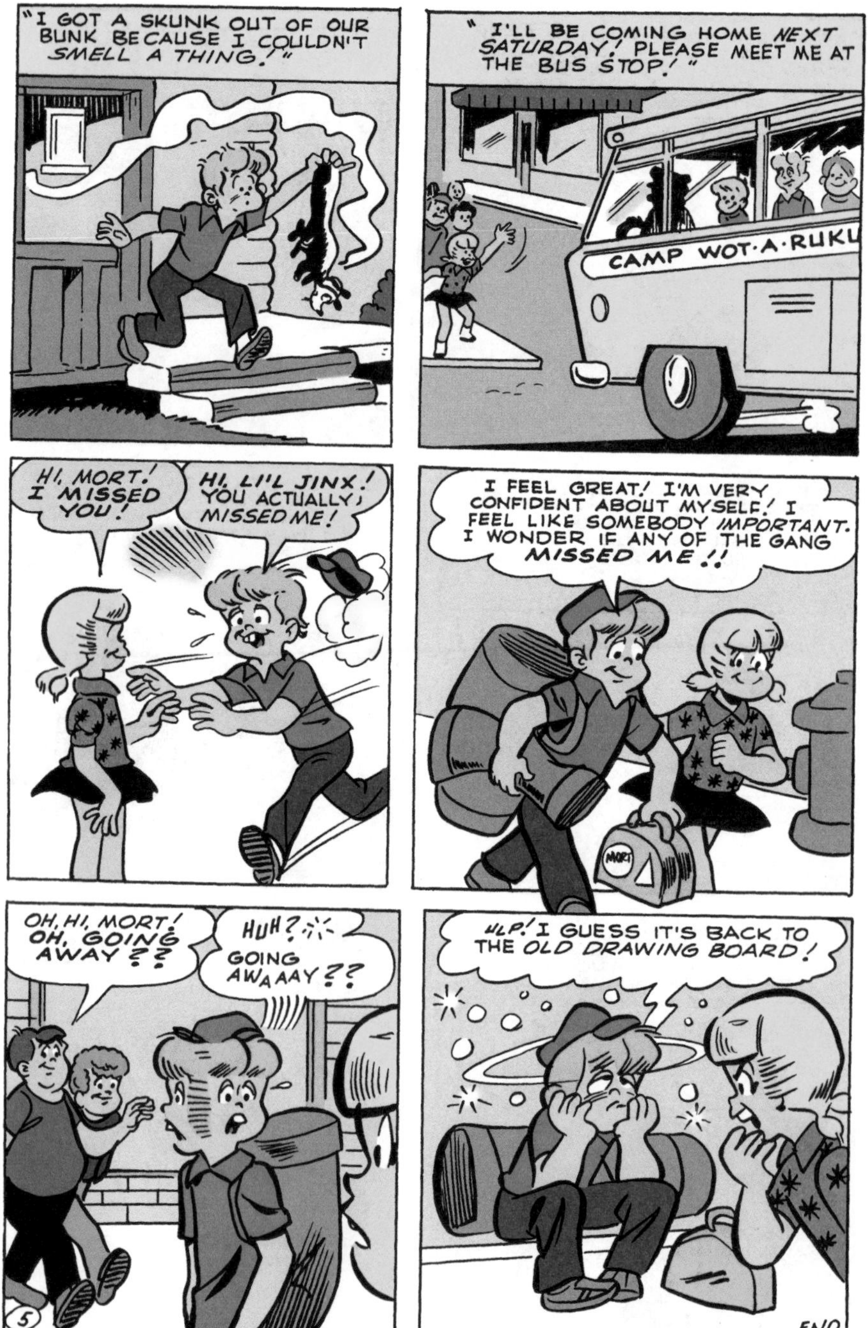
"I GOT A SKUNK OUT OF OUR BUNK BECAUSE I COULDN'T SMELL A THING!"
" I'LL BE COMING HOME NEXT SATURDAY! PLEASE MEET ME AT THE BUS STOP! "
CAMP WOT·A·RUKU
HI, MORT! I MISSED YOU!
HI, LI'L JINX! YOU ACTUALLY MISSED ME!
I FEEL GREAT! I'M VERY CONFIDENT ABOUT MYSELF! I FEEL LIKE SOMEBODY IMPORTANT. I WONDER IF ANY OF THE GANG MISSED ME!!
MORT
OH, HI, MORT! OH, GOING AWAY??
HUH?
GOING AWAAAY??
5
ULP! I GUESS IT'S BACK TO THE OLD DRAWING BOARD!
END

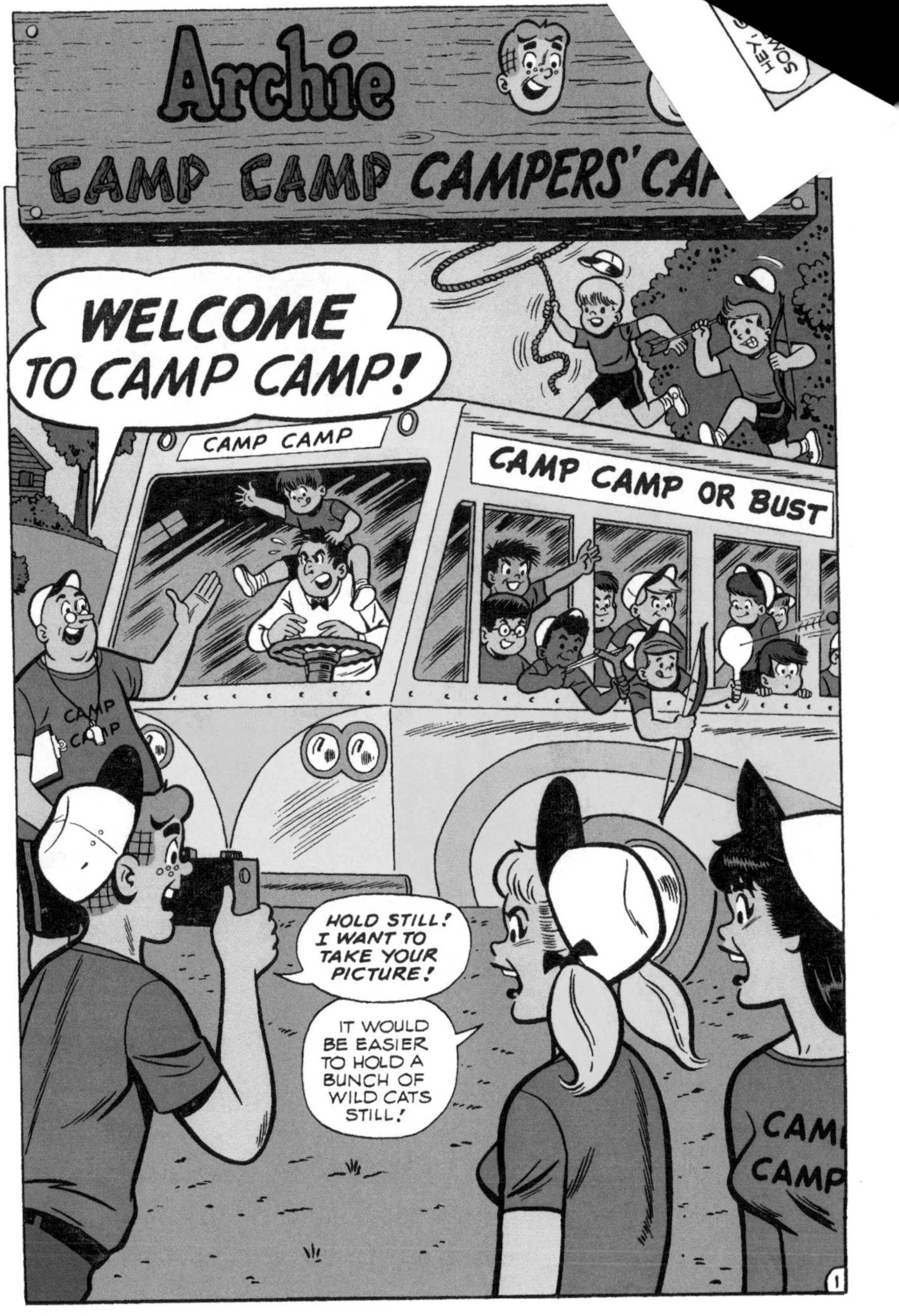
Archie
CAMP CAMP CAMPERS'
WELCOME TO CAMP CAMP!
CAMP CAMP
CAMP CAMP OR BUST
CAMP CAMP
HOLD STILL! I WANT TO TAKE YOUR PICTURE!
IT WOULD BE EASIER TO HOLD A BUNCH OF WILD CATS STILL!
1

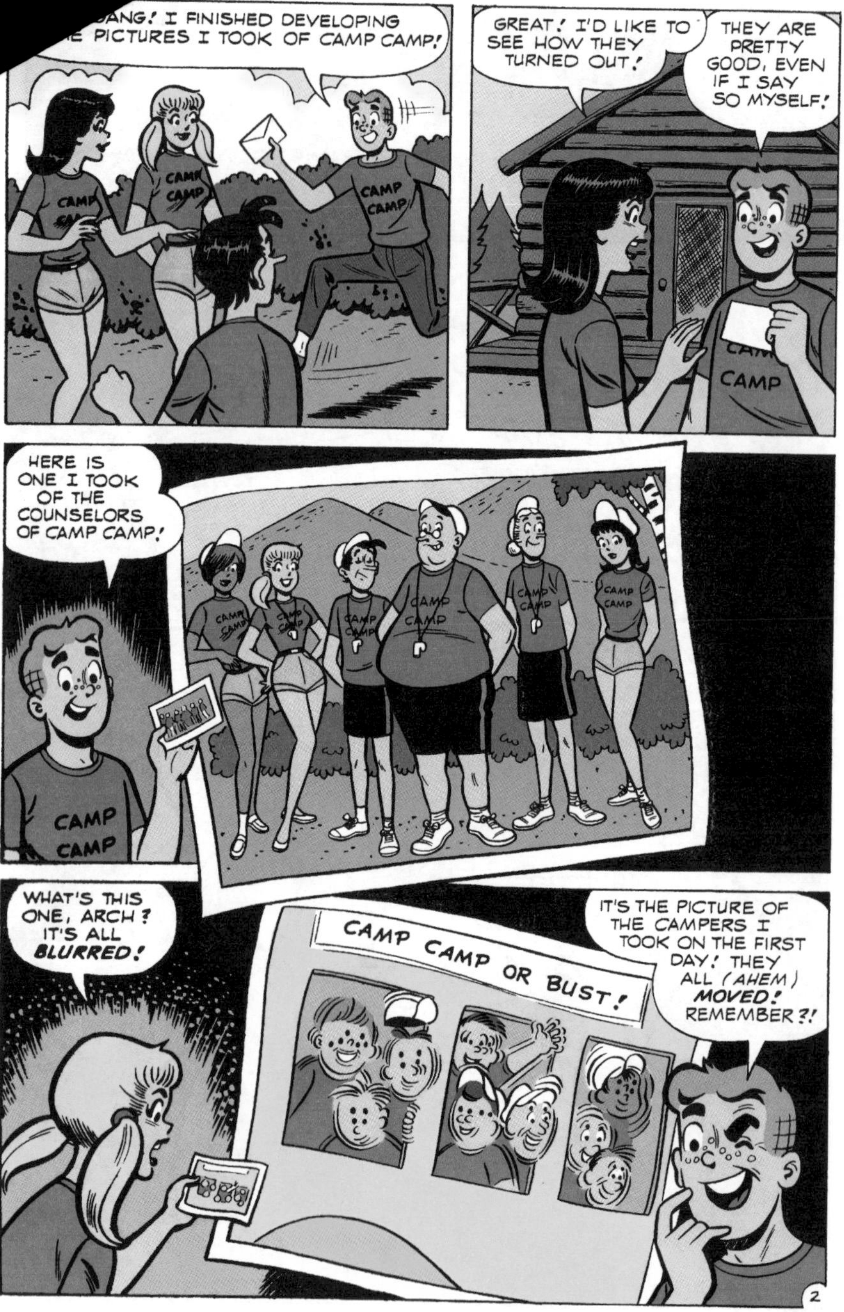

GANG! I FINISHED DEVELOPING
E PICTURES I TOOK OF CAMP CAMP!
GREAT! I'D LIKE TO SEE HOW THEY TURNED OUT!
THEY ARE PRETTY GOOD, EVEN IF I SAY SO MYSELF!
HERE IS ONE I TOOK OF THE COUNSELORS OF CAMP CAMP!
WHAT'S THIS ONE, ARCH? IT'S ALL **BLURRED!**
CAMP CAMP OR BUST!
IT'S THE PICTURE OF THE CAMPERS I TOOK ON THE FIRST DAY! THEY ALL (AHEM) **MOVED!** REMEMBER?!

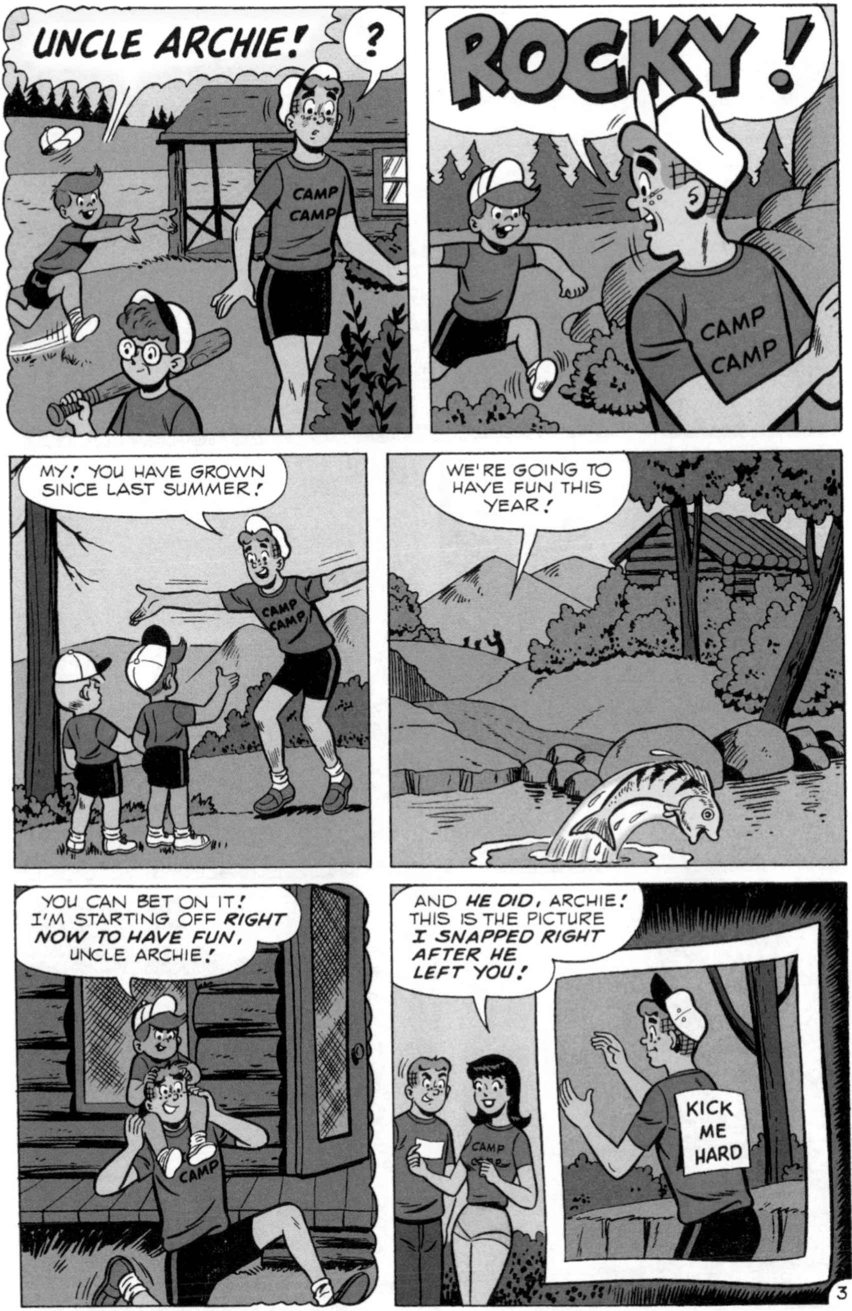

UNCLE ARCHIE!
?
CAMP CAMP
ROCKY!
CAMP CAMP
MY! YOU HAVE GROWN SINCE LAST SUMMER!
CAMP CAMP
WE'RE GOING TO HAVE FUN THIS YEAR!
YOU CAN BET ON IT! I'M STARTING OFF RIGHT NOW TO HAVE FUN, UNCLE ARCHIE!
CAMP
AND HE DID, ARCHIE! THIS IS THE PICTURE I SNAPPED RIGHT AFTER HE LEFT YOU!
KICK ME HARD

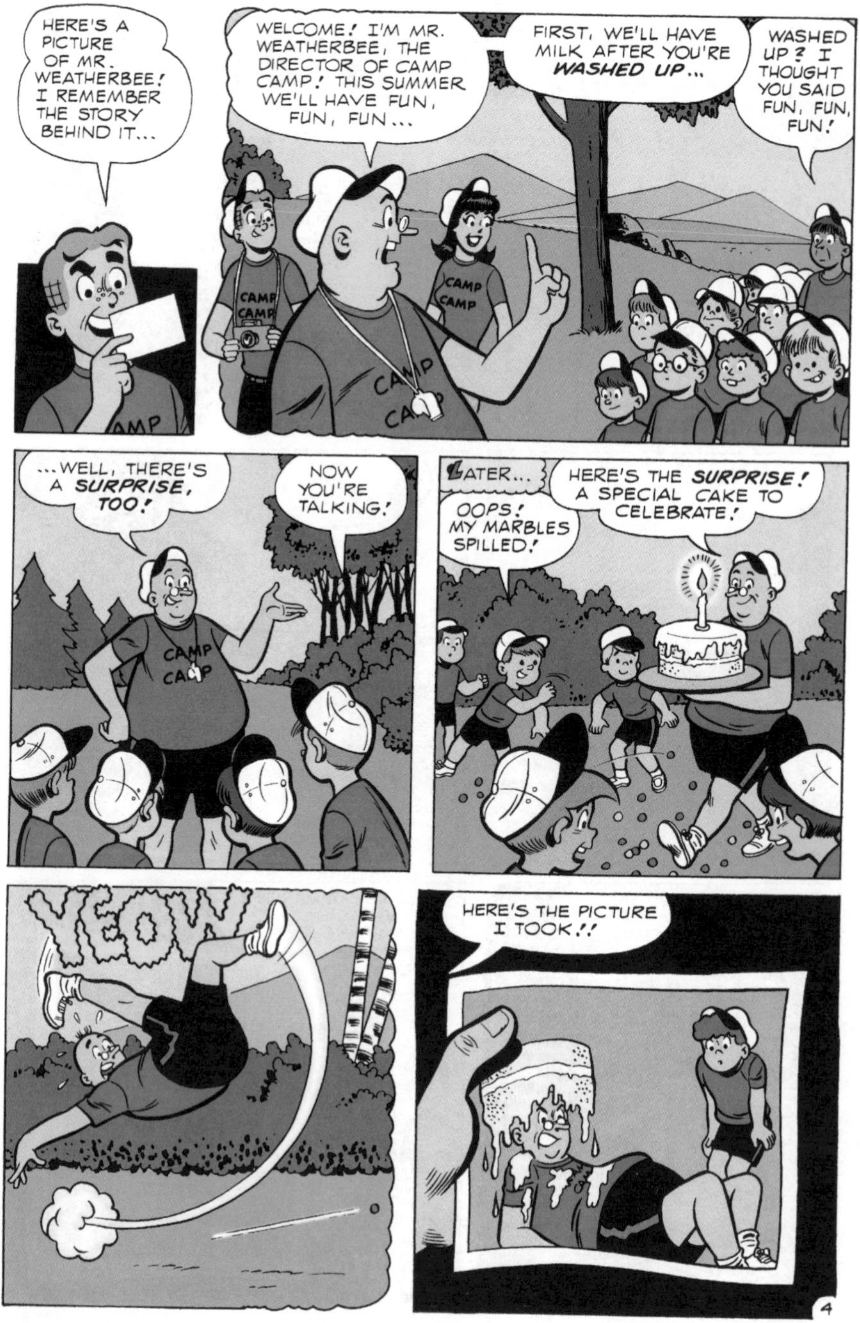

HERE'S A PICTURE OF MR. WEATHERBEE! I REMEMBER THE STORY BEHIND IT...
CAMP
WELCOME! I'M MR. WEATHERBEE, THE DIRECTOR OF CAMP CAMP! THIS SUMMER WE'LL HAVE FUN, FUN, FUN...
FIRST, WE'LL HAVE MILK AFTER YOU'RE WASHED UP...
WASHED UP? I THOUGHT YOU SAID FUN, FUN, FUN!
CAMP CAMP
...WELL, THERE'S A SURPRISE, TOO!
NOW YOU'RE TALKING!
CAMP CAMP
LATER...
HERE'S THE SURPRISE! A SPECIAL CAKE TO CELEBRATE!
OOPS! MY MARBLES SPILLED!
YEOW
HERE'S THE PICTURE I TOOK!!

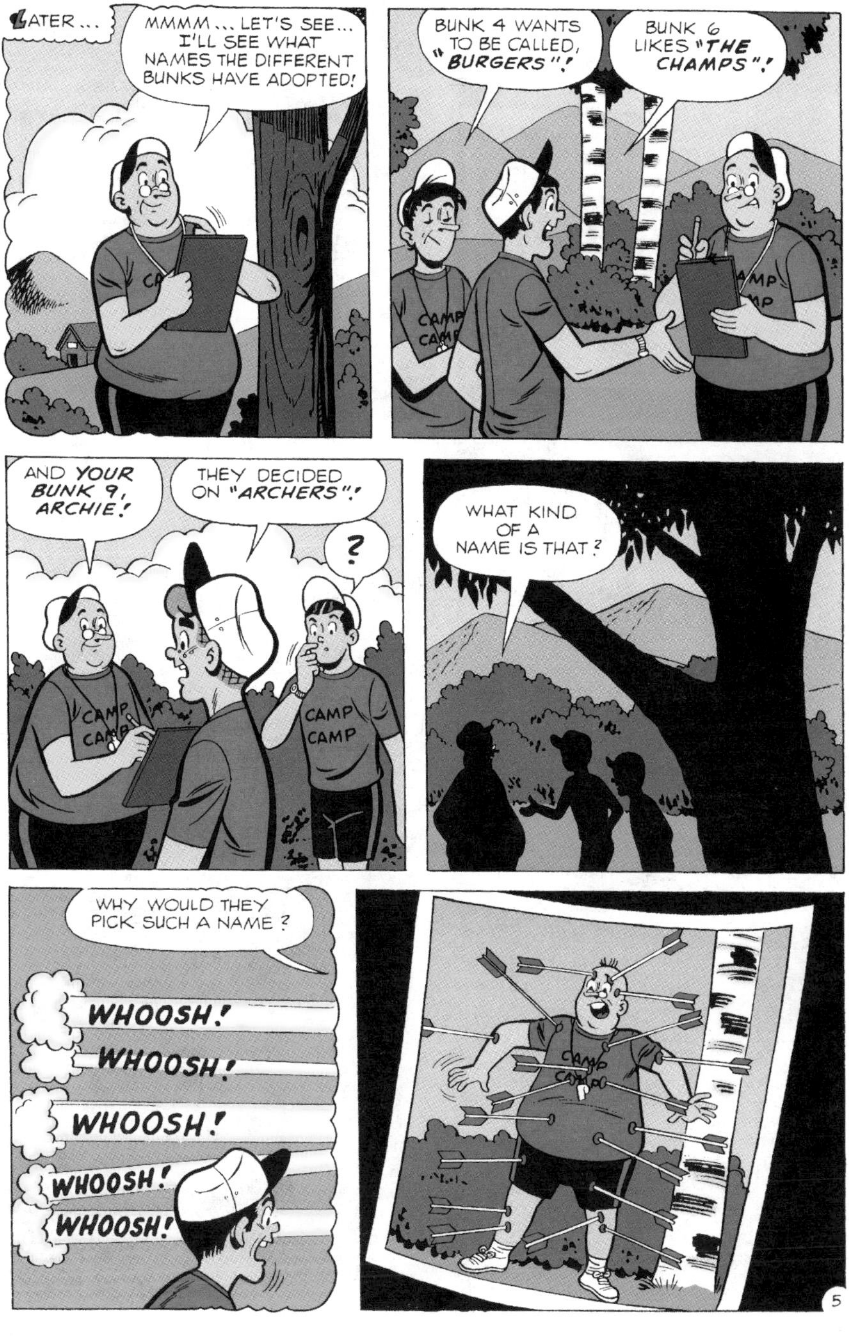
LATER...
MMMM... LET'S SEE... I'LL SEE WHAT NAMES THE DIFFERENT BUNKS HAVE ADOPTED!
BUNK 4 WANTS TO BE CALLED, "BURGERS"!
BUNK 6 LIKES "THE CHAMPS"!
CAMP CAMP
AND YOUR BUNK 9, ARCHIE!
THEY DECIDED ON "ARCHERS"!
?
CAMP CAMP
WHAT KIND OF A NAME IS THAT?
WHY WOULD THEY PICK SUCH A NAME?
WHOOSH!
WHOOSH!
WHOOSH!
WHOOSH!
WHOOSH!

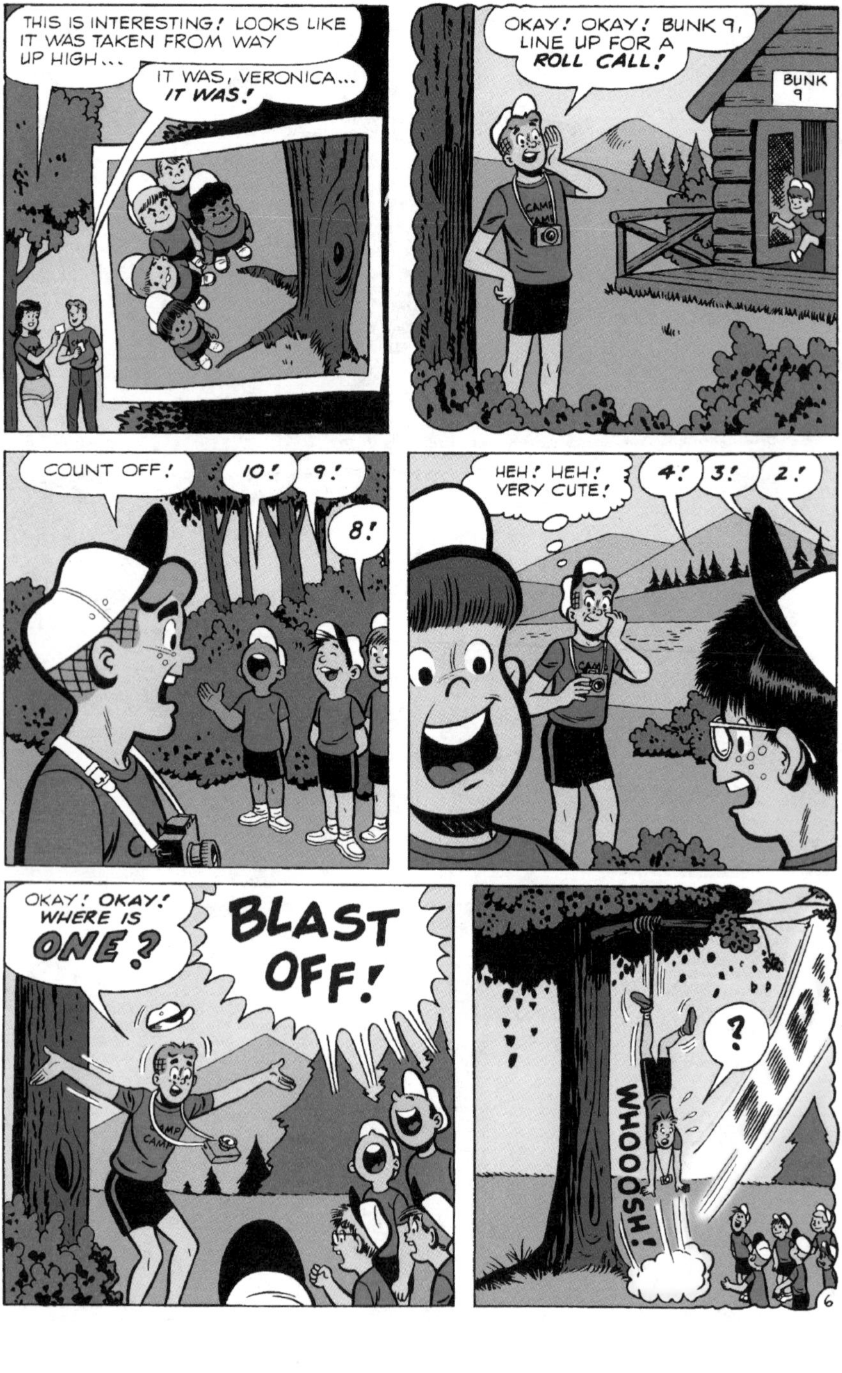
THIS IS INTERESTING! LOOKS LIKE IT WAS TAKEN FROM WAY UP HIGH...
IT WAS, VERONICA... IT WAS!
OKAY! OKAY! BUNK 9, LINE UP FOR A ROLL CALL!
BUNK 9
COUNT OFF!
10!
9!
8!
HEH! HEH! VERY CUTE!
4!
3!
2!
OKAY! OKAY! WHERE IS ONE?
BLAST OFF!
?
WHOOOOSH!

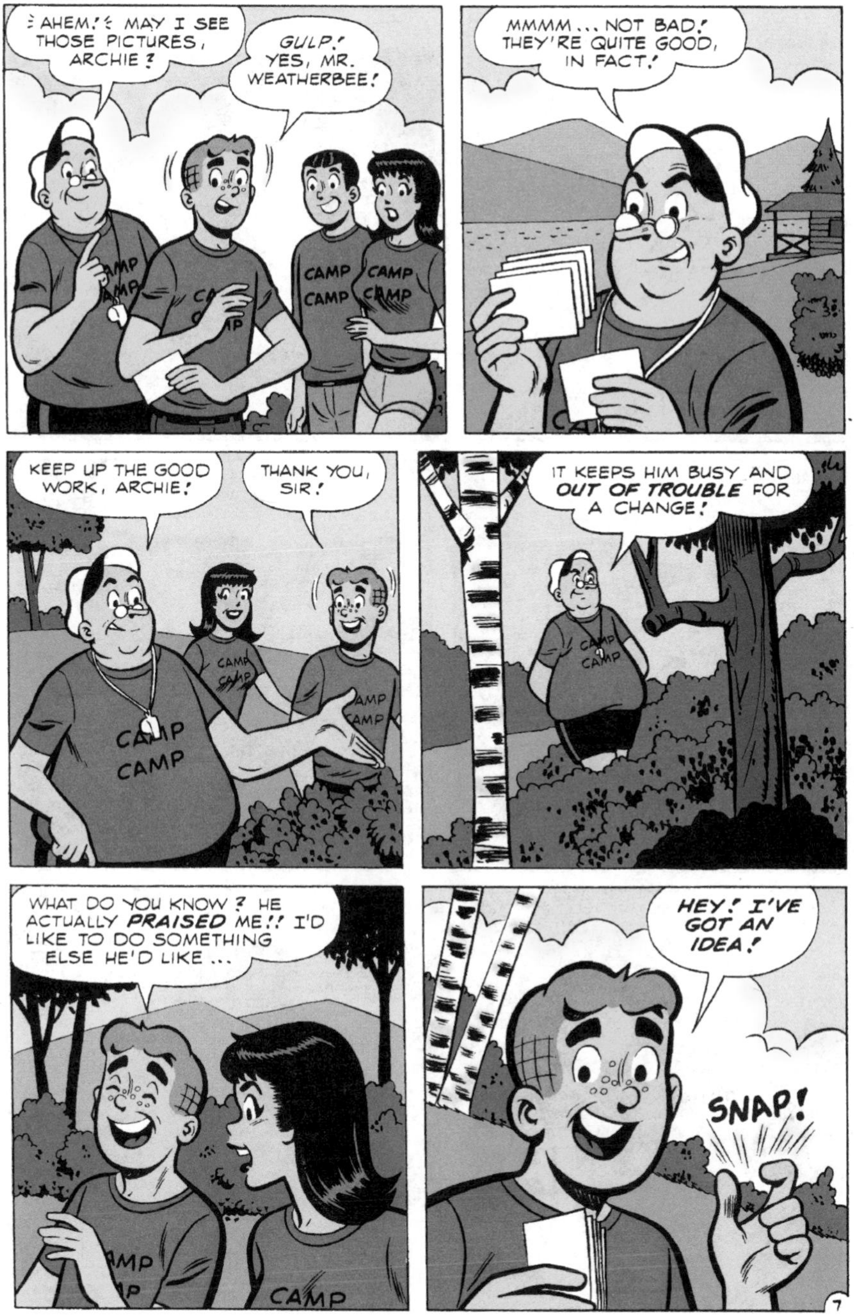

AHEM! MAY I SEE THOSE PICTURES, ARCHIE?
GULP! YES, MR. WEATHERBEE!
CAMP CAMP
MMMM... NOT BAD! THEY'RE QUITE GOOD, IN FACT!
KEEP UP THE GOOD WORK, ARCHIE!
THANK YOU, SIR!
CAMP CAMP
IT KEEPS HIM BUSY AND OUT OF TROUBLE FOR A CHANGE!
WHAT DO YOU KNOW? HE ACTUALLY PRAISED ME!! I'D LIKE TO DO SOMETHING ELSE HE'D LIKE...
HEY! I'VE GOT AN IDEA!
SNAP!

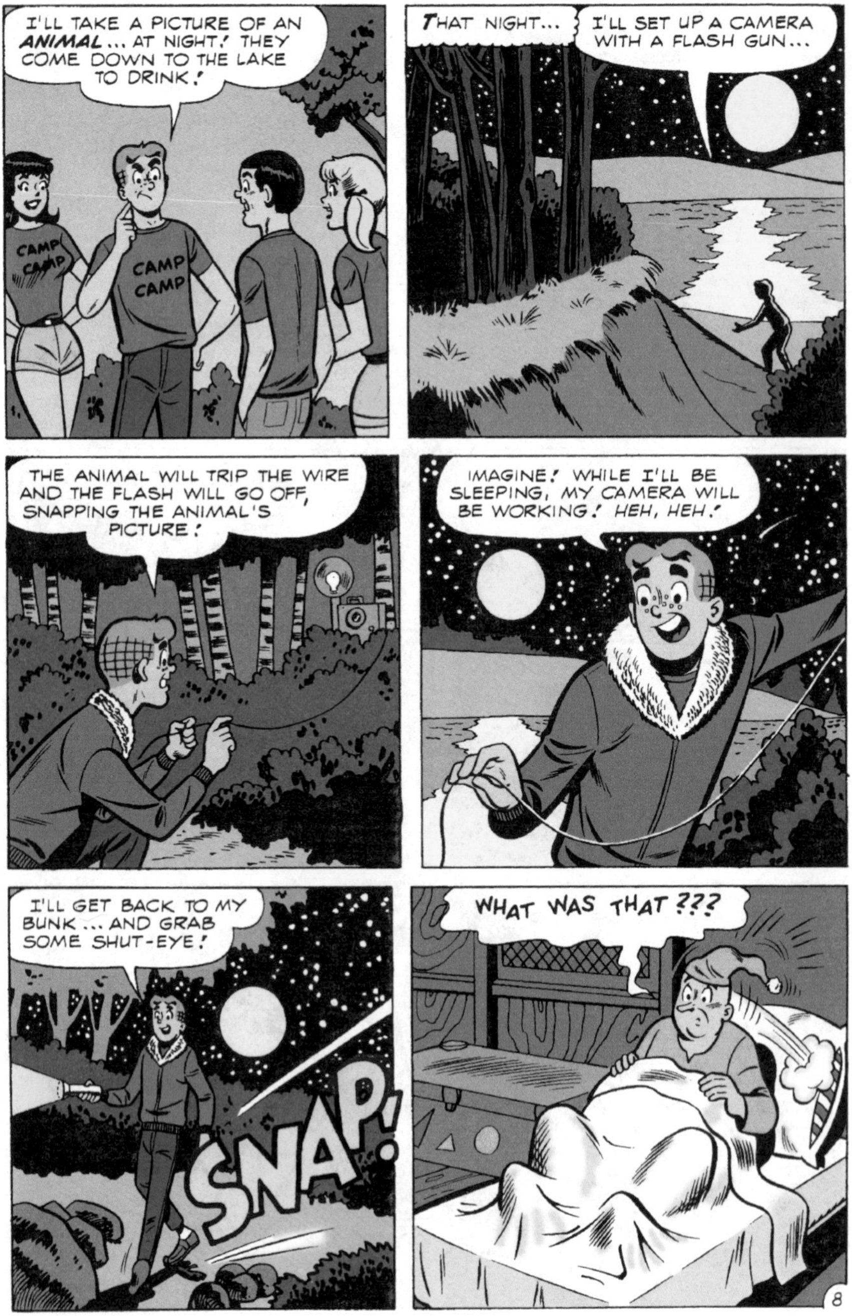
I'LL TAKE A PICTURE OF AN ANIMAL ... AT NIGHT! THEY COME DOWN TO THE LAKE TO DRINK!
CAMP CAMP
CAMP CAMP
THAT NIGHT...
I'LL SET UP A CAMERA WITH A FLASH GUN...
THE ANIMAL WILL TRIP THE WIRE AND THE FLASH WILL GO OFF, SNAPPING THE ANIMAL'S PICTURE!
IMAGINE! WHILE I'LL BE SLEEPING, MY CAMERA WILL BE WORKING! HEH, HEH!
I'LL GET BACK TO MY BUNK ... AND GRAB SOME SHUT-EYE!
SNAP!
WHAT WAS THAT???
8

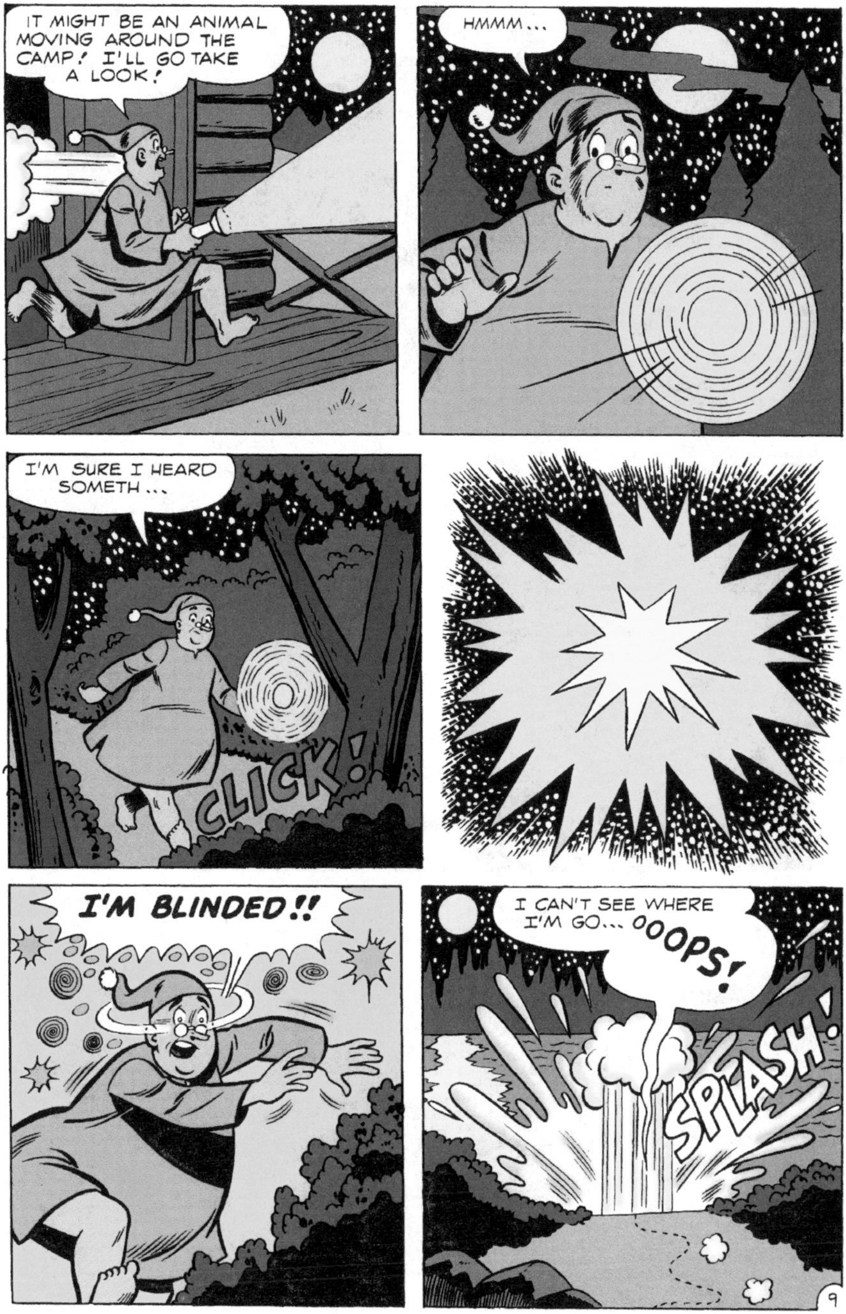
IT MIGHT BE AN ANIMAL MOVING AROUND THE CAMP! I'LL GO TAKE A LOOK!
HMMM...
I'M SURE I HEARD SOMETH...
CLICK!
I'M BLINDED!!
I CAN'T SEE WHERE I'M GO... OOOPS!
SPLASH!

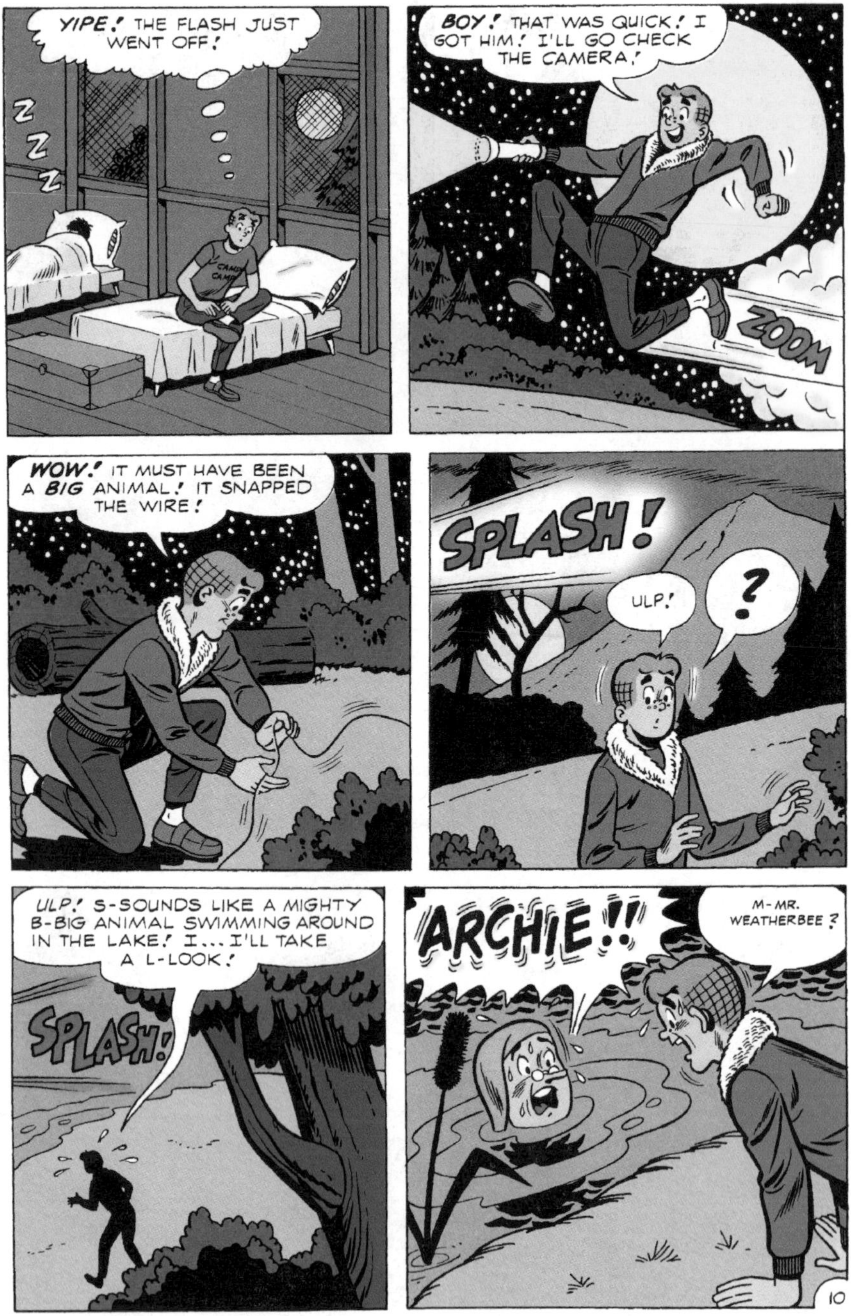
Z
Z
Z
YIPE! THE FLASH JUST WENT OFF!
BOY! THAT WAS QUICK! I GOT HIM! I'LL GO CHECK THE CAMERA!
ZOOM
WOW! IT MUST HAVE BEEN A BIG ANIMAL! IT SNAPPED THE WIRE!
SPLASH!
ULP!
?
ULP! S-SOUNDS LIKE A MIGHTY B-BIG ANIMAL SWIMMING AROUND IN THE LAKE! I... I'LL TAKE A L-LOOK!
SPLASH!
ARCHIE!!
M-MR. WEATHERBEE?

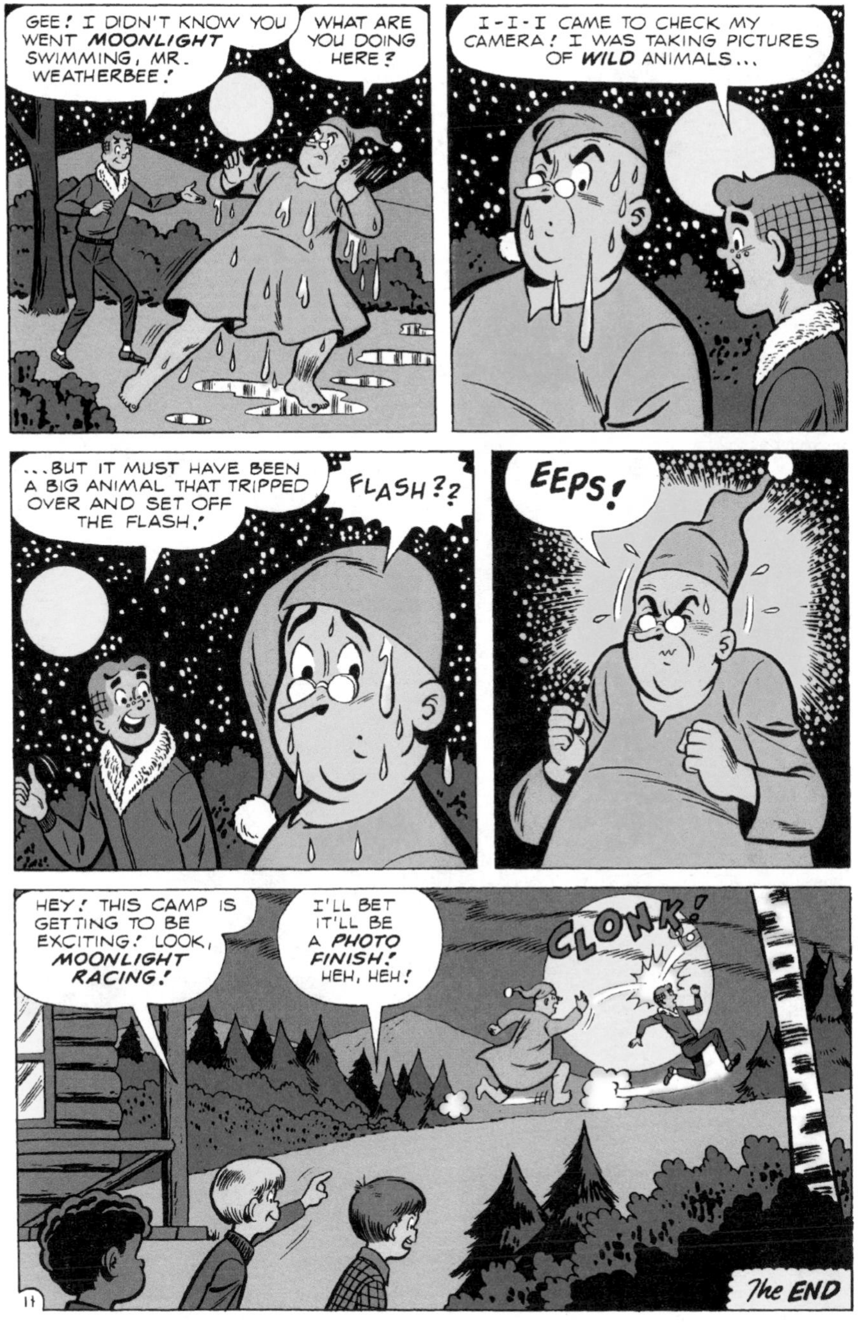
GEE! I DIDN'T KNOW YOU WENT MOONLIGHT SWIMMING, MR. WEATHERBEE!
WHAT ARE YOU DOING HERE?
I-I-I CAME TO CHECK MY CAMERA! I WAS TAKING PICTURES OF WILD ANIMALS...
...BUT IT MUST HAVE BEEN A BIG ANIMAL THAT TRIPPED OVER AND SET OFF THE FLASH!
FLASH??
EEPS!
HEY! THIS CAMP IS GETTING TO BE EXCITING! LOOK, MOONLIGHT RACING!
I'LL BET IT'LL BE A PHOTO FINISH! HEH, HEH!
CLONK!
The END

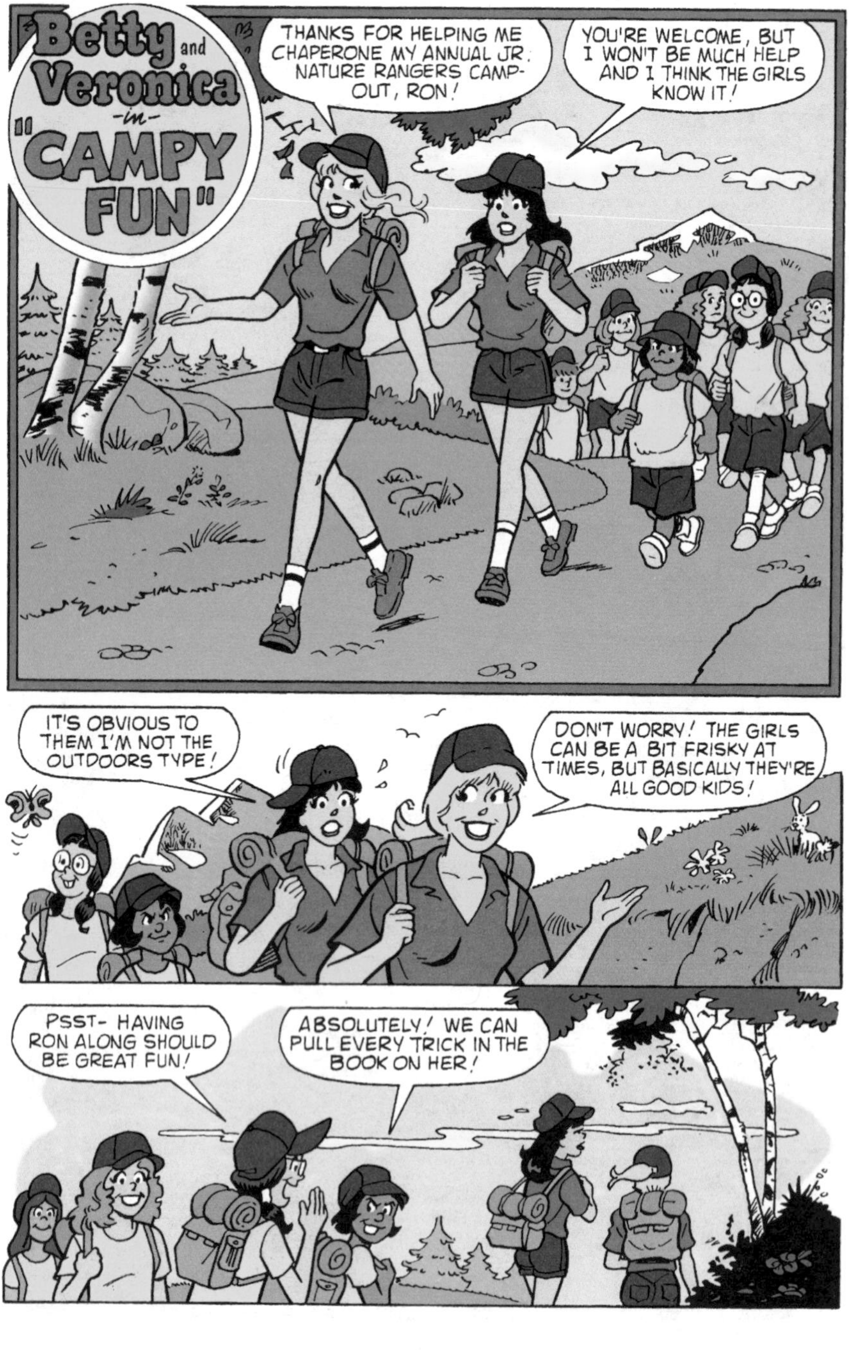
Betty and Veronica -in- "CAMPY FUN"
THANKS FOR HELPING ME CHAPERONE MY ANNUAL JR. NATURE RANGERS CAMP-OUT, RON!
YOU'RE WELCOME, BUT I WON'T BE MUCH HELP AND I THINK THE GIRLS KNOW IT!
IT'S OBVIOUS TO THEM I'M NOT THE OUTDOORS TYPE!
DON'T WORRY! THE GIRLS CAN BE A BIT FRISKY AT TIMES, BUT BASICALLY THEY'RE ALL GOOD KIDS!
PSST- HAVING RON ALONG SHOULD BE GREAT FUN!
ABSOLUTELY! WE CAN PULL EVERY TRICK IN THE BOOK ON HER!

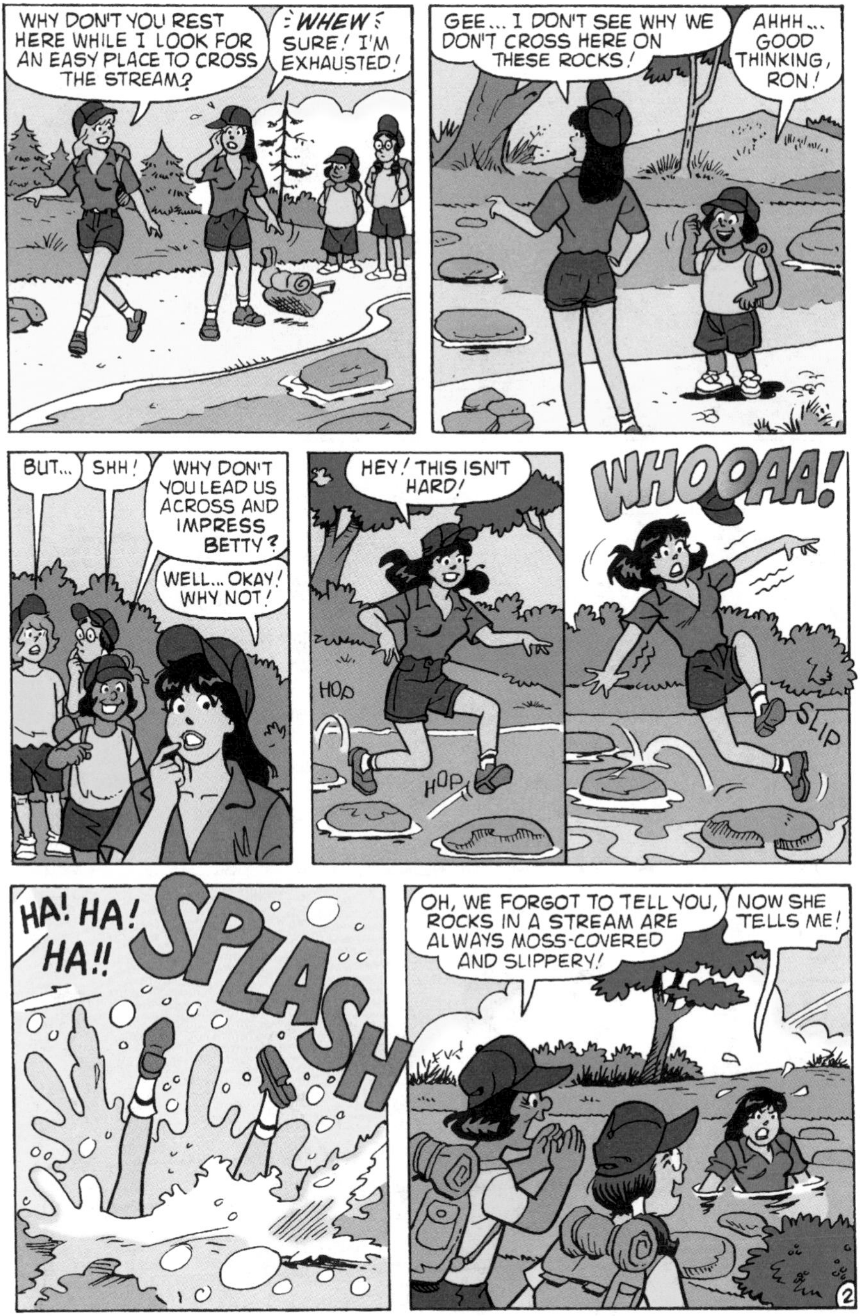
WHY DON'T YOU REST HERE WHILE I LOOK FOR AN EASY PLACE TO CROSS THE STREAM?
WHEW SURE! I'M EXHAUSTED!
GEE... I DON'T SEE WHY WE DON'T CROSS HERE ON THESE ROCKS!
AHHH... GOOD THINKING, RON!
BUT...
SHH!
WHY DON'T YOU LEAD US ACROSS AND IMPRESS BETTY?
WELL... OKAY! WHY NOT!
HEY! THIS ISN'T HARD!
HOP
HOP
WHOOAA!
SLIP
HA! HA! HA!!
SPLASH
OH, WE FORGOT TO TELL YOU, ROCKS IN A STREAM ARE ALWAYS MOSS-COVERED AND SLIPPERY!
NOW SHE TELLS ME!
2

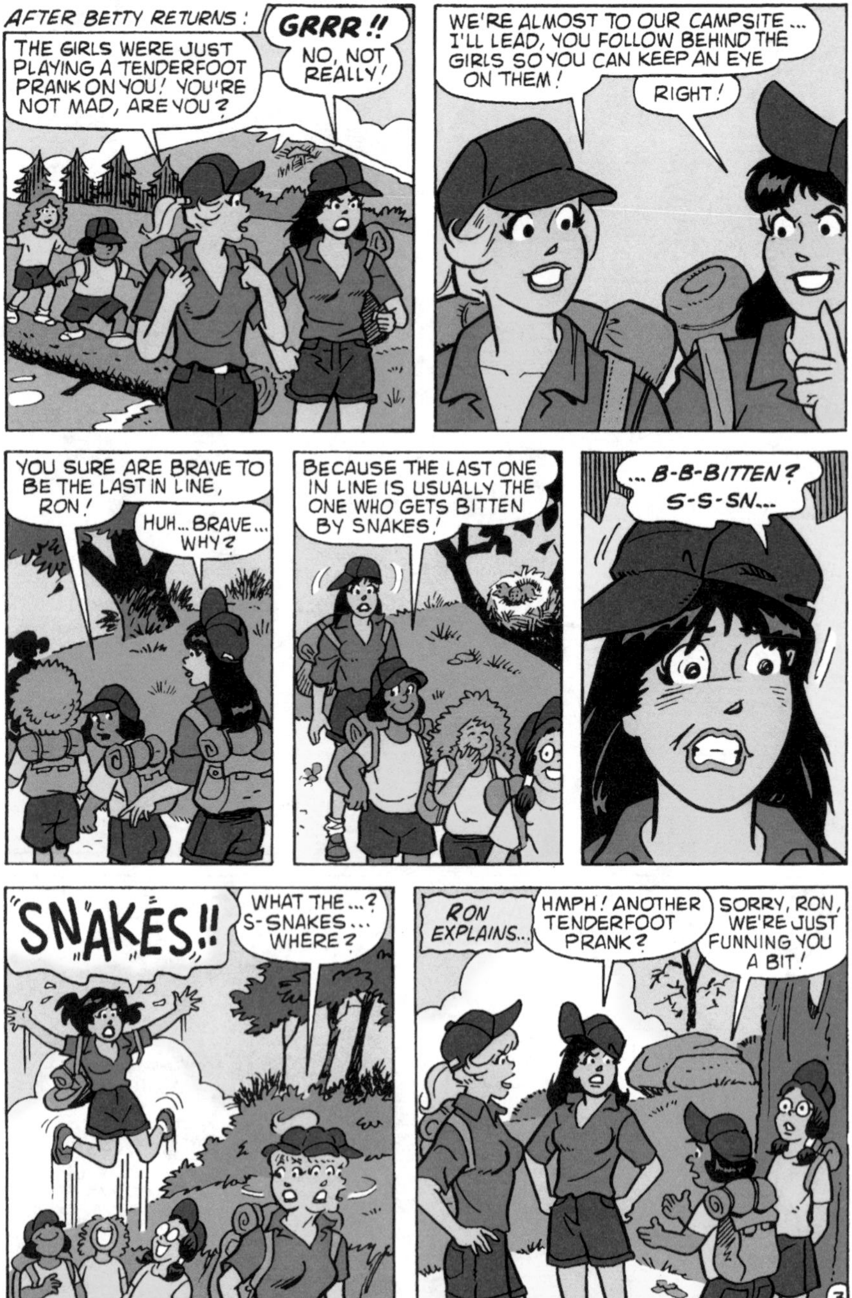

AFTER BETTY RETURNS:
THE GIRLS WERE JUST PLAYING A TENDERFOOT PRANK ON YOU! YOU'RE NOT MAD, ARE YOU?
GRRR!! NO, NOT REALLY!
WE'RE ALMOST TO OUR CAMPSITE... I'LL LEAD, YOU FOLLOW BEHIND THE GIRLS SO YOU CAN KEEP AN EYE ON THEM!
RIGHT!
YOU SURE ARE BRAVE TO BE THE LAST IN LINE, RON!
HUH... BRAVE... WHY?
BECAUSE THE LAST ONE IN LINE IS USUALLY THE ONE WHO GETS BITTEN BY SNAKES!
...B-B-BITTEN? S-S-SN...
SNAKES!!
WHAT THE...? S-SNAKES... WHERE?
RON EXPLAINS...
HMPH! ANOTHER TENDERFOOT PRANK?
SORRY, RON, WE'RE JUST FUNNING YOU A BIT!
3

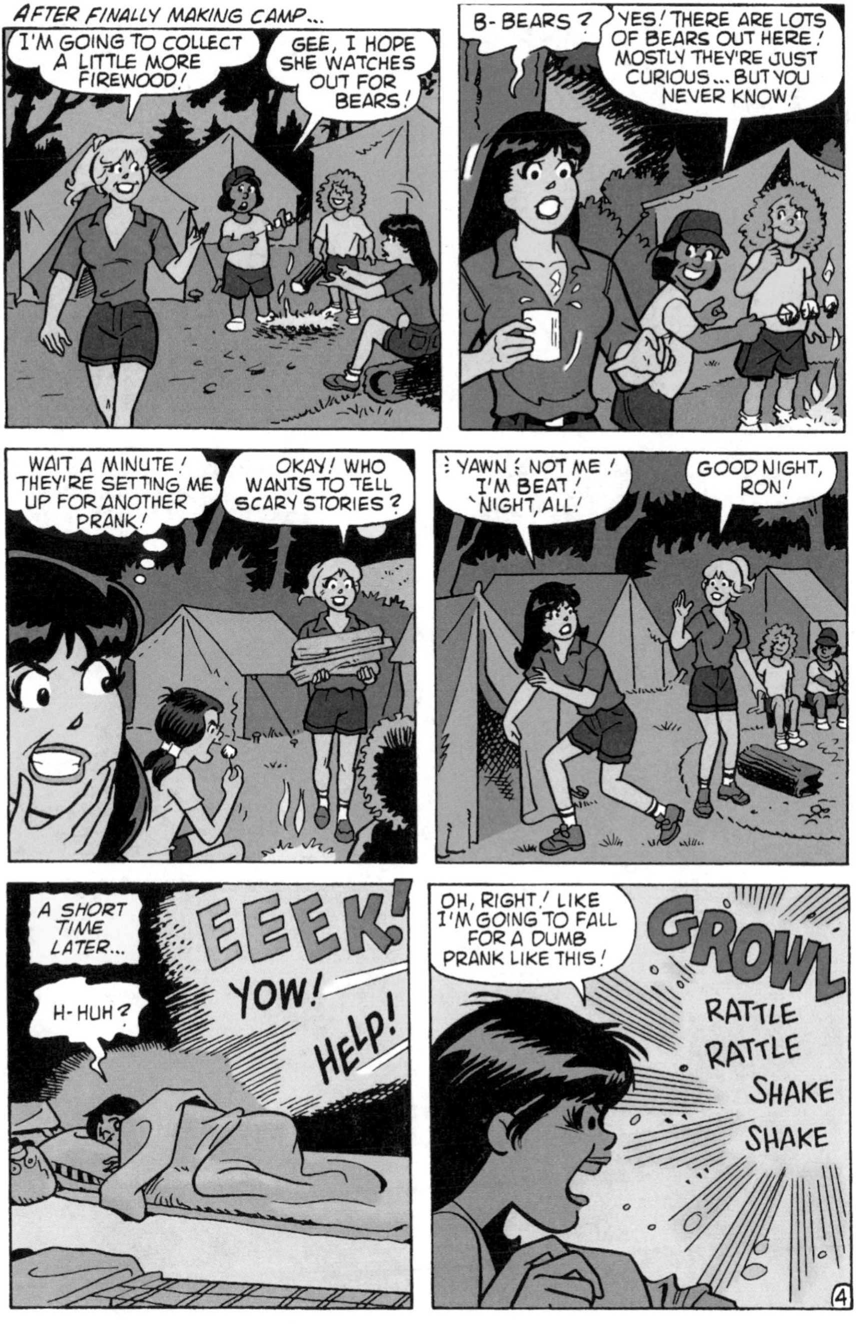
AFTER FINALLY MAKING CAMP...
I'M GOING TO COLLECT A LITTLE MORE FIREWOOD!
GEE, I HOPE SHE WATCHES OUT FOR BEARS!
B-BEARS?
YES! THERE ARE LOTS OF BEARS OUT HERE! MOSTLY THEY'RE JUST CURIOUS... BUT YOU NEVER KNOW!
WAIT A MINUTE! THEY'RE SETTING ME UP FOR ANOTHER PRANK!
OKAY! WHO WANTS TO TELL SCARY STORIES?
: YAWN : NOT ME! I'M BEAT! 'NIGHT, ALL!
GOOD NIGHT, RON!
A SHORT TIME LATER...
EEEK!
YOW!
HELP!
H-HUH?
OH, RIGHT! LIKE I'M GOING TO FALL FOR A DUMB PRANK LIKE THIS!
GROWL
RATTLE
RATTLE
SHAKE
SHAKE
4

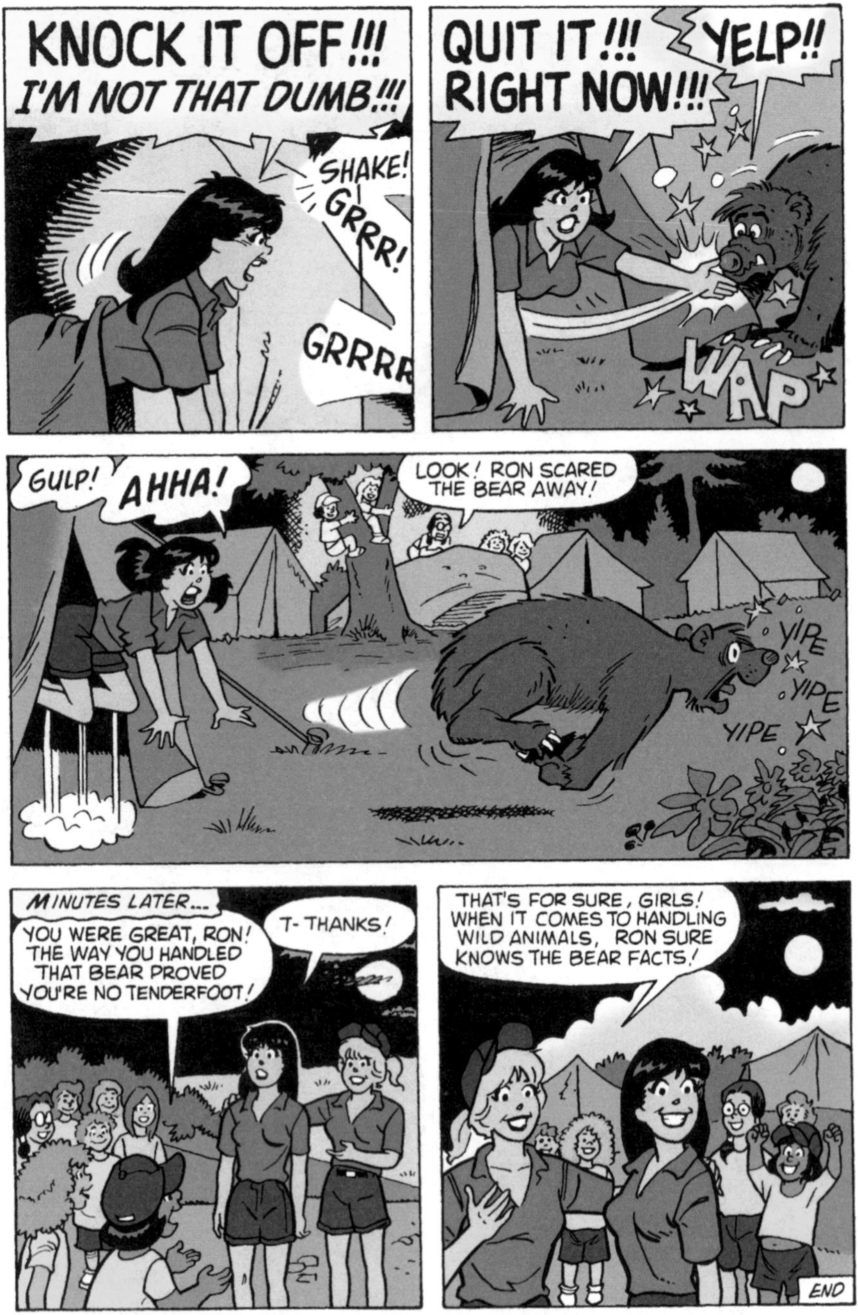
KNOCK IT OFF!!!
I'M NOT THAT DUMB!!!
SHAKE!
G! GRRRR!
GRRRR
QUIT IT!!! RIGHT NOW!!!
YELP!!
WAP
GULP!
AHHA!
LOOK! RON SCARED THE BEAR AWAY!
YIPE
YIPE
YIPE
MINUTES LATER...
YOU WERE GREAT, RON! THE WAY YOU HANDLED THAT BEAR PROVED YOU'RE NO TENDERFOOT!
T- THANKS!
THAT'S FOR SURE, GIRLS! WHEN IT COMES TO HANDLING WILD ANIMALS, RON SURE KNOWS THE BEAR FACTS!
END

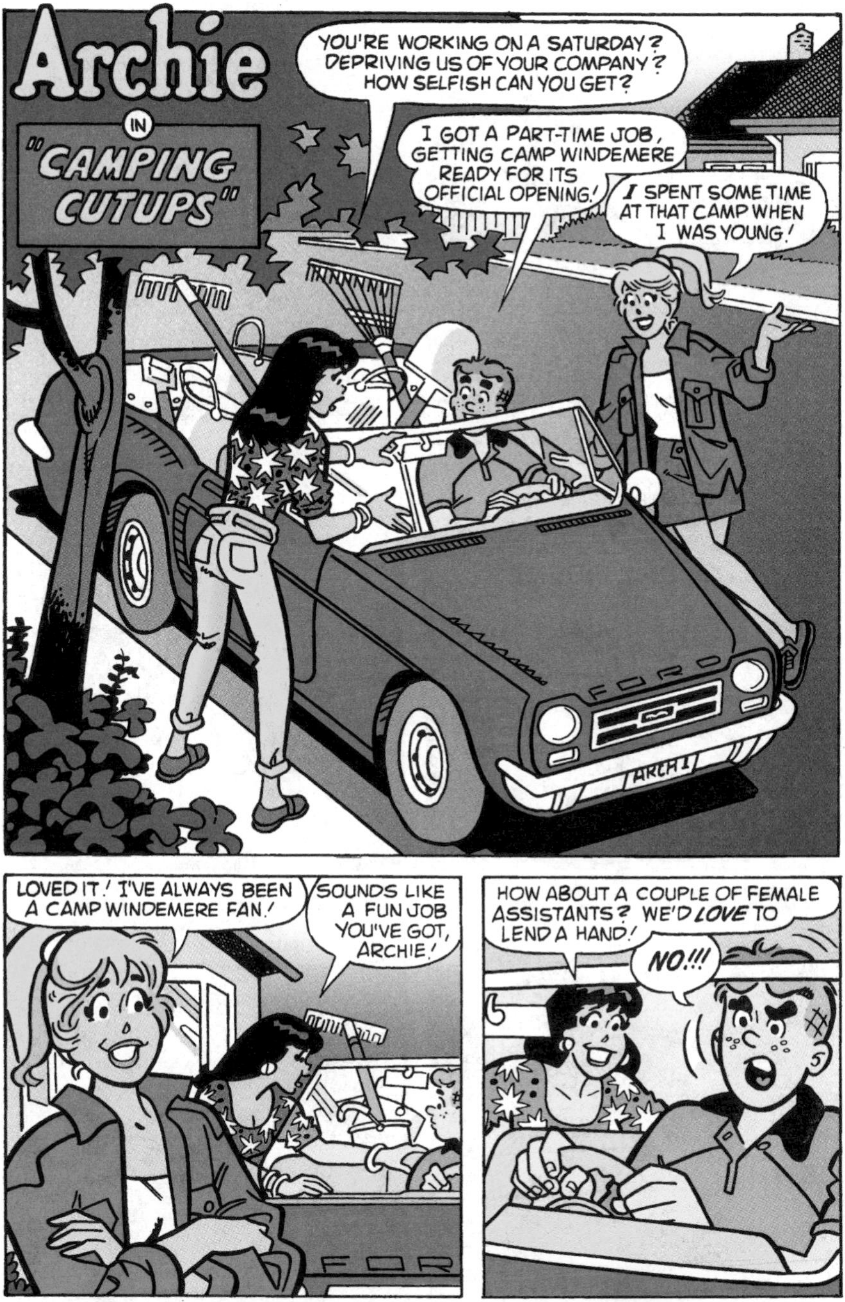
Archie
IN
"CAMPING CUTUPS"
YOU'RE WORKING ON A SATURDAY? DEPRIVING US OF YOUR COMPANY? HOW SELFISH CAN YOU GET?
I GOT A PART-TIME JOB, GETTING CAMP WINDEMERE READY FOR ITS OFFICIAL OPENING!
I SPENT SOME TIME AT THAT CAMP WHEN I WAS YOUNG!
FORD
ARCH 1
LOVED IT! I'VE ALWAYS BEEN A CAMP WINDEMERE FAN!
SOUNDS LIKE A FUN JOB YOU'VE GOT, ARCHIE!
HOW ABOUT A COUPLE OF FEMALE ASSISTANTS? WE'D LOVE TO LEND A HAND!
NO!!!

Gladir / Goldberg / Scarpelli / Yoshida / Grossman

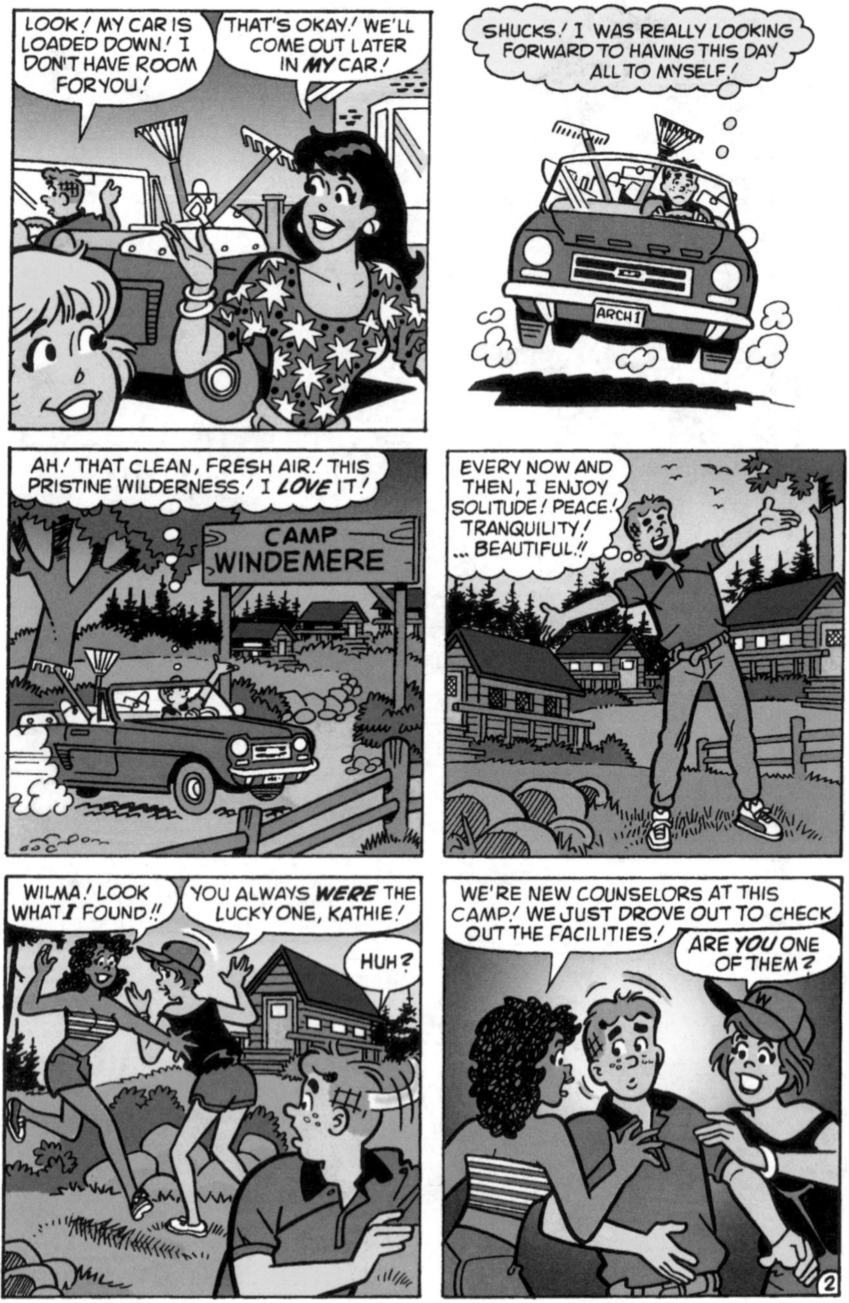
LOOK! MY CAR IS LOADED DOWN! I DON'T HAVE ROOM FOR YOU!
THAT'S OKAY! WE'LL COME OUT LATER IN MY CAR!
SHUCKS! I WAS REALLY LOOKING FORWARD TO HAVING THIS DAY ALL TO MYSELF!
ARCH 1
AH! THAT CLEAN, FRESH AIR! THIS PRISTINE WILDERNESS! I LOVE IT!
CAMP WINDEMERE
EVERY NOW AND THEN, I ENJOY SOLITUDE! PEACE! TRANQUILITY! ... BEAUTIFUL!!
WILMA! LOOK WHAT I FOUND!!
YOU ALWAYS WERE THE LUCKY ONE, KATHIE!
HUH?
WE'RE NEW COUNSELORS AT THIS CAMP! WE JUST DROVE OUT TO CHECK OUT THE FACILITIES!
ARE YOU ONE OF THEM?
2

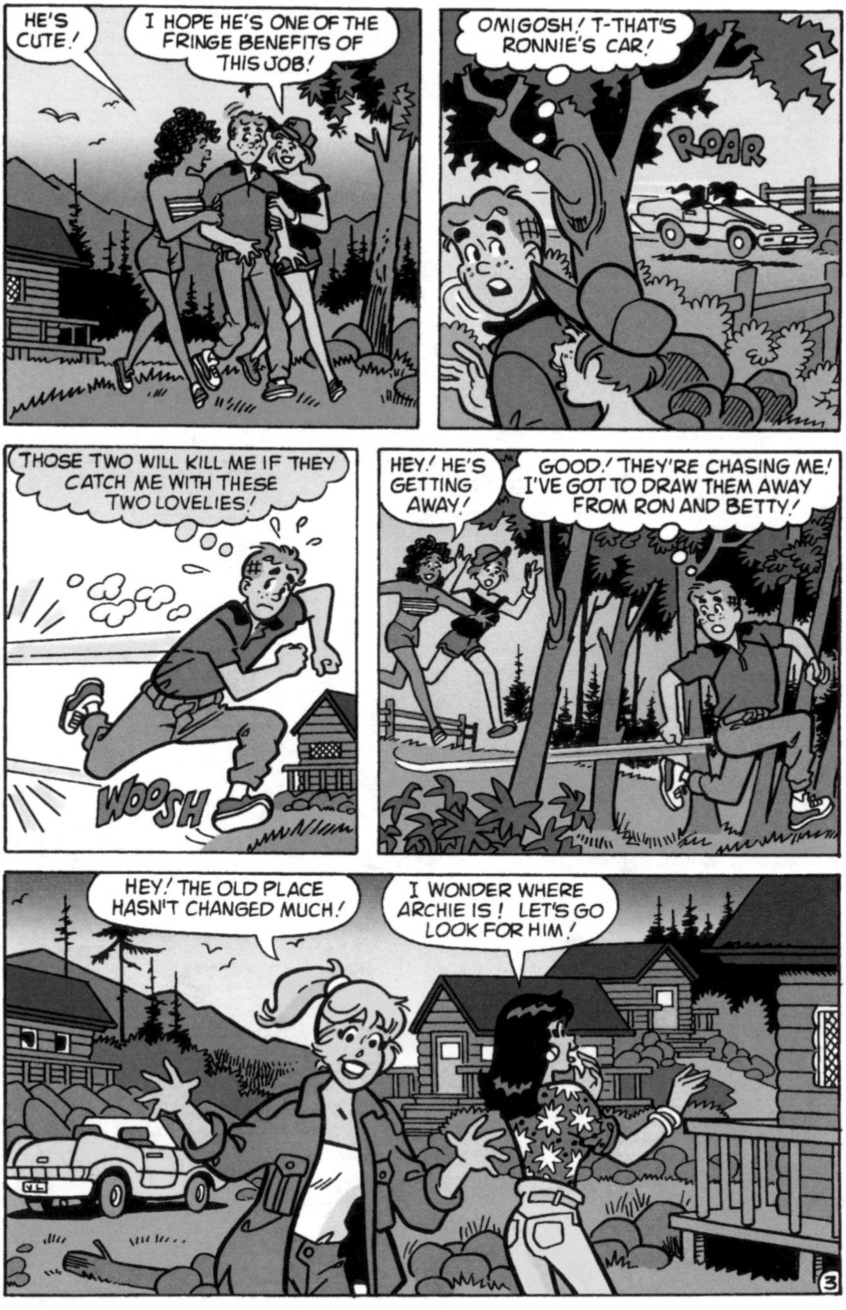
HE'S CUTE!
I HOPE HE'S ONE OF THE FRINGE BENEFITS OF THIS JOB!
OMIGOSH! T-THAT'S RONNIE'S CAR!
ROAR
THOSE TWO WILL KILL ME IF THEY CATCH ME WITH THESE TWO LOVELIES!
WOOSH
HEY! HE'S GETTING AWAY!
GOOD! THEY'RE CHASING ME! I'VE GOT TO DRAW THEM AWAY FROM RON AND BETTY!
HEY! THE OLD PLACE HASN'T CHANGED MUCH!
I WONDER WHERE ARCHIE IS! LET'S GO LOOK FOR HIM!
3

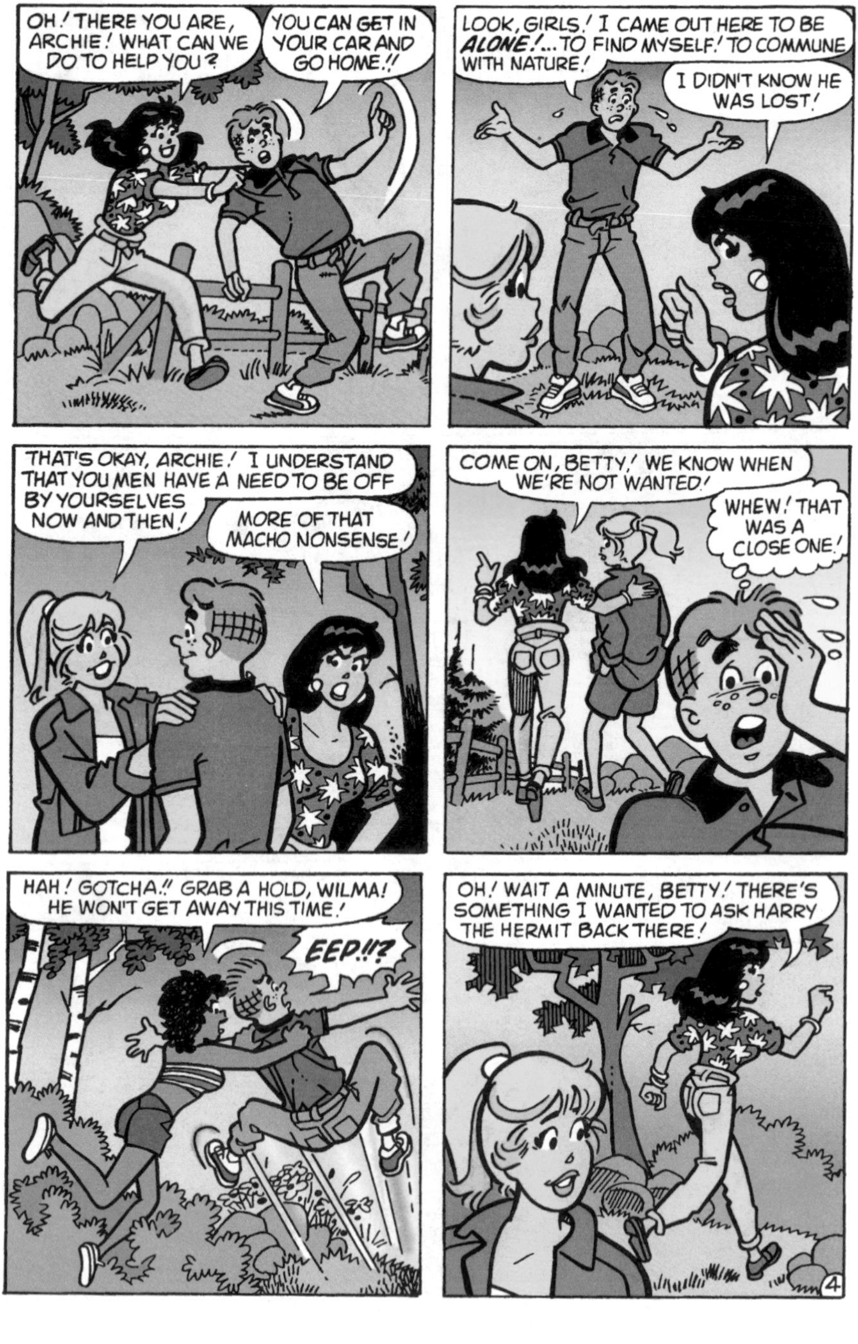
OH! THERE YOU ARE, ARCHIE! WHAT CAN WE DO TO HELP YOU?
YOU CAN GET IN YOUR CAR AND GO HOME!!
LOOK, GIRLS! I CAME OUT HERE TO BE ALONE!... TO FIND MYSELF! TO COMMUNE WITH NATURE!
I DIDN'T KNOW HE WAS LOST!
THAT'S OKAY, ARCHIE! I UNDERSTAND THAT YOU MEN HAVE A NEED TO BE OFF BY YOURSELVES NOW AND THEN!
MORE OF THAT MACHO NONSENSE!
COME ON, BETTY! WE KNOW WHEN WE'RE NOT WANTED!
WHEW! THAT WAS A CLOSE ONE!
HAH! GOTCHA!! GRAB A HOLD, WILMA! HE WON'T GET AWAY THIS TIME!
EEP!!?
OH! WAIT A MINUTE, BETTY! THERE'S SOMETHING I WANTED TO ASK HARRY THE HERMIT BACK THERE!
4

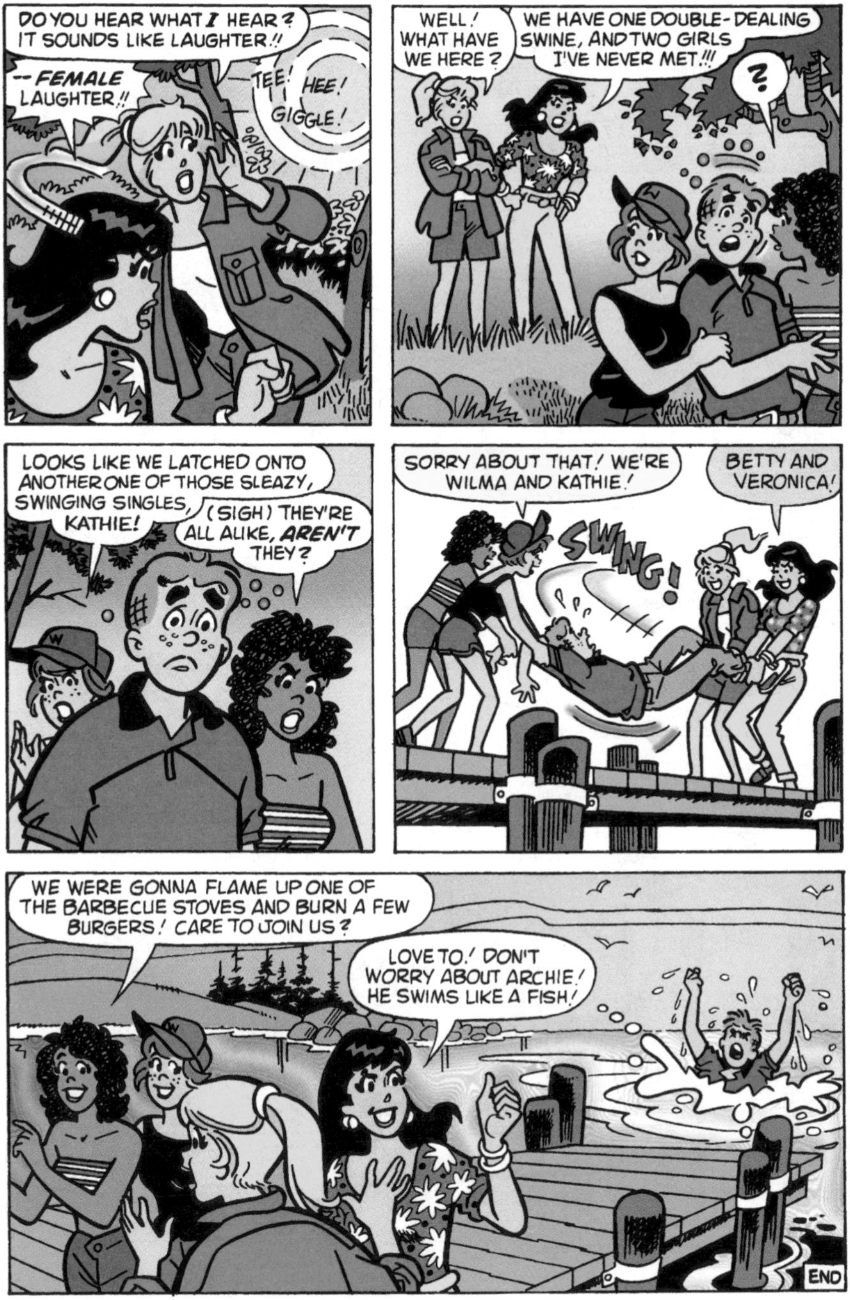

DO YOU HEAR WHAT *I* HEAR? IT SOUNDS LIKE LAUGHTER!!
-- *FEMALE* LAUGHTER!!
TEE! HEE! GIGGLE!
WELL! WHAT HAVE WE HERE?
WE HAVE ONE DOUBLE-DEALING SWINE, AND TWO GIRLS I'VE NEVER MET!!!
?
LOOKS LIKE WE LATCHED ONTO ANOTHER ONE OF THOSE SLEAZY, SWINGING SINGLES, KATHIE!
(SIGH) THEY'RE ALL ALIKE, *AREN'T* THEY?
SORRY ABOUT THAT! WE'RE WILMA AND KATHIE!
BETTY AND VERONICA!
SWING!
WE WERE GONNA FLAME UP ONE OF THE BARBECUE STOVES AND BURN A FEW BURGERS! CARE TO JOIN US?
LOVE TO! DON'T WORRY ABOUT ARCHIE! HE SWIMS LIKE A FISH!
END

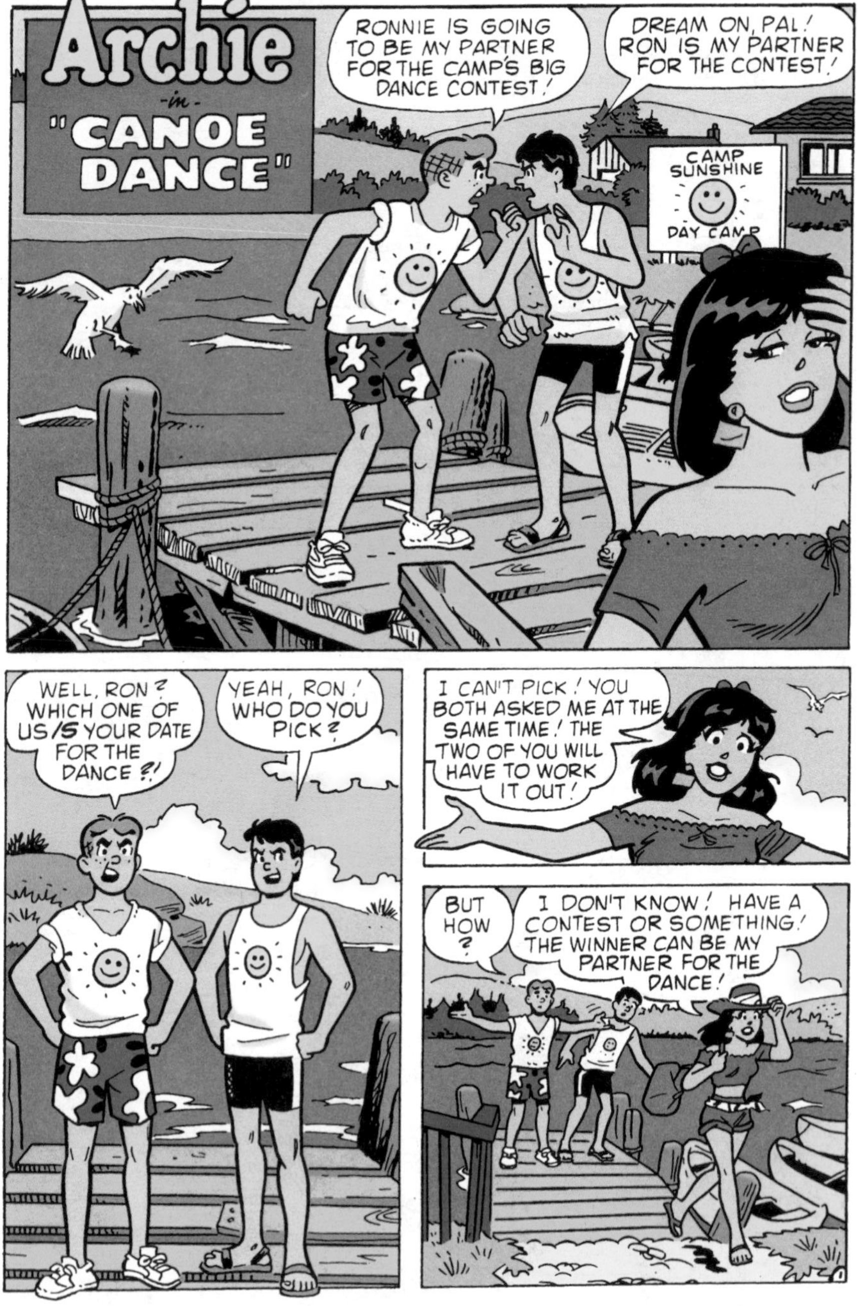
Archie
-in-
"CANOE DANCE"
RONNIE IS GOING TO BE MY PARTNER FOR THE CAMP'S BIG DANCE CONTEST!
DREAM ON, PAL! RON IS MY PARTNER FOR THE CONTEST!
CAMP SUNSHINE DAY CAMP
WELL, RON? WHICH ONE OF US IS YOUR DATE FOR THE DANCE?!
YEAH, RON! WHO DO YOU PICK?
I CAN'T PICK! YOU BOTH ASKED ME AT THE SAME TIME! THE TWO OF YOU WILL HAVE TO WORK IT OUT!
BUT HOW?
I DON'T KNOW! HAVE A CONTEST OR SOMETHING! THE WINNER CAN BE MY PARTNER FOR THE DANCE!
1

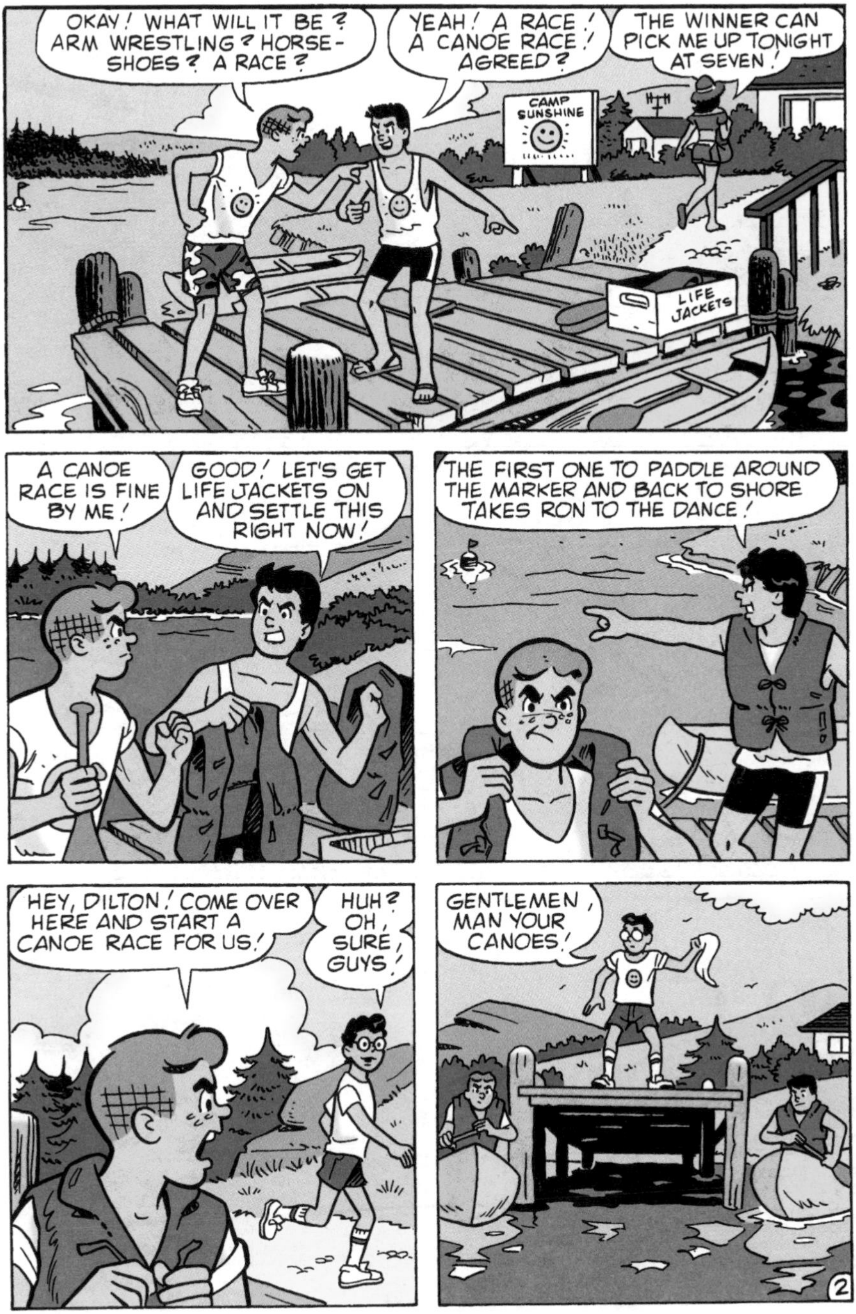
OKAY! WHAT WILL IT BE? ARM WRESTLING? HORSE-SHOES? A RACE?
YEAH! A RACE! A CANOE RACE! AGREED?
THE WINNER CAN PICK ME UP TONIGHT AT SEVEN!
CAMP SUNSHINE
LIFE JACKETS
A CANOE RACE IS FINE BY ME!
GOOD! LET'S GET LIFE JACKETS ON AND SETTLE THIS RIGHT NOW!
THE FIRST ONE TO PADDLE AROUND THE MARKER AND BACK TO SHORE TAKES RON TO THE DANCE!
HEY, DILTON! COME OVER HERE AND START A CANOE RACE FOR US!
HUH? OH, SURE, GUYS!
GENTLEMEN, MAN YOUR CANOES!
2

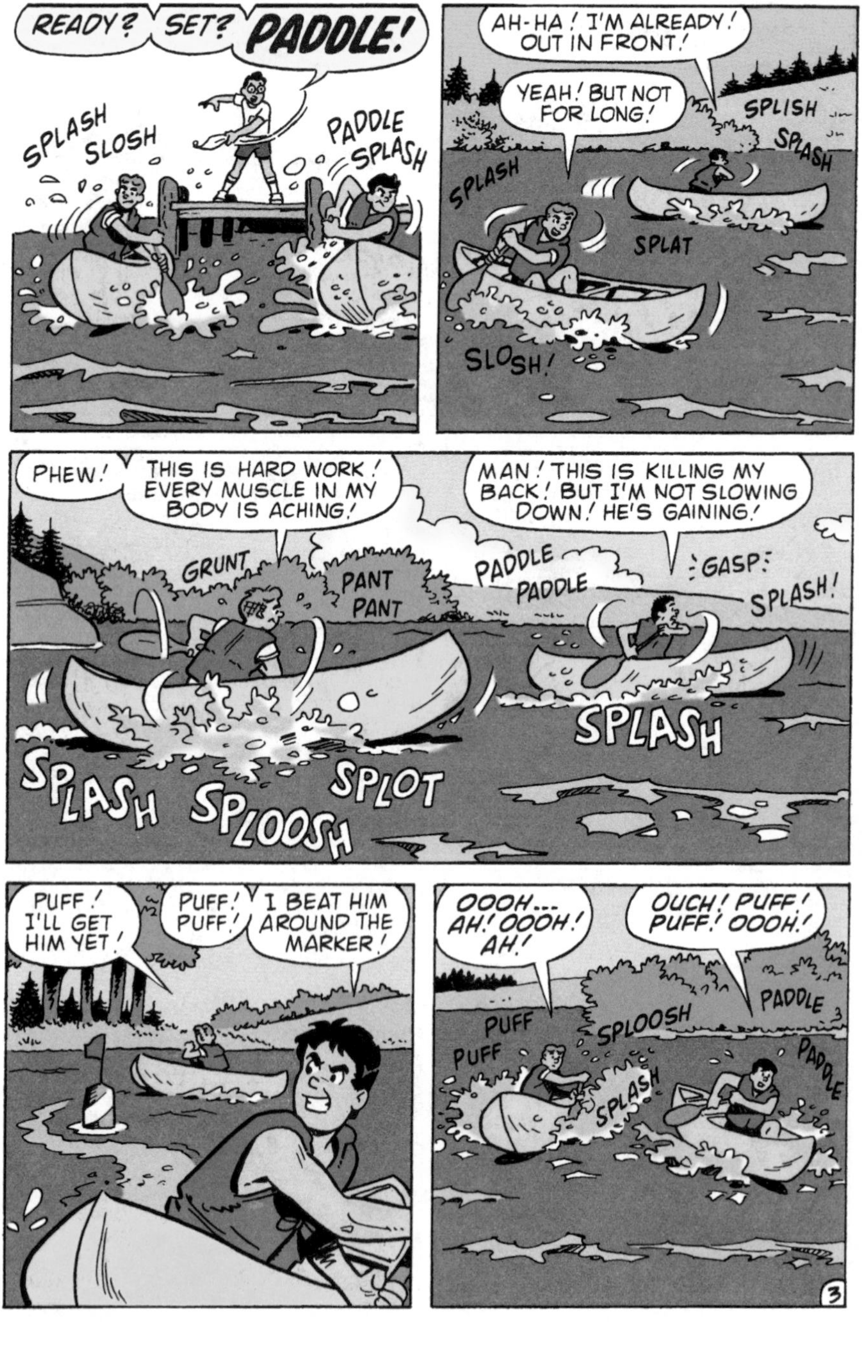

READY?
SET?
PADDLE!
SPLASH
SLOSH
PADDLE
SPLASH
AH-HA! I'M ALREADY! OUT IN FRONT!
YEAH! BUT NOT FOR LONG!
SPLISH
SPLASH
SPLASH
SPLAT
SLOSH!
PHEW!
THIS IS HARD WORK! EVERY MUSCLE IN MY BODY IS ACHING!
MAN! THIS IS KILLING MY BACK! BUT I'M NOT SLOWING DOWN! HE'S GAINING!
GRUNT
PANT PANT
PADDLE
PADDLE
GASP
SPLASH!
SPLASH
SPLASH
SPLOOSH
SPLOT
PUFF! I'LL GET HIM YET!
PUFF! PUFF!
I BEAT HIM AROUND THE MARKER!
OOOH... AH! OOOH! AH!
OUCH! PUFF! PUFF! OOOH!
PUFF
PUFF
SPLOOSH
SPLASH
PADDLE
PADDLE

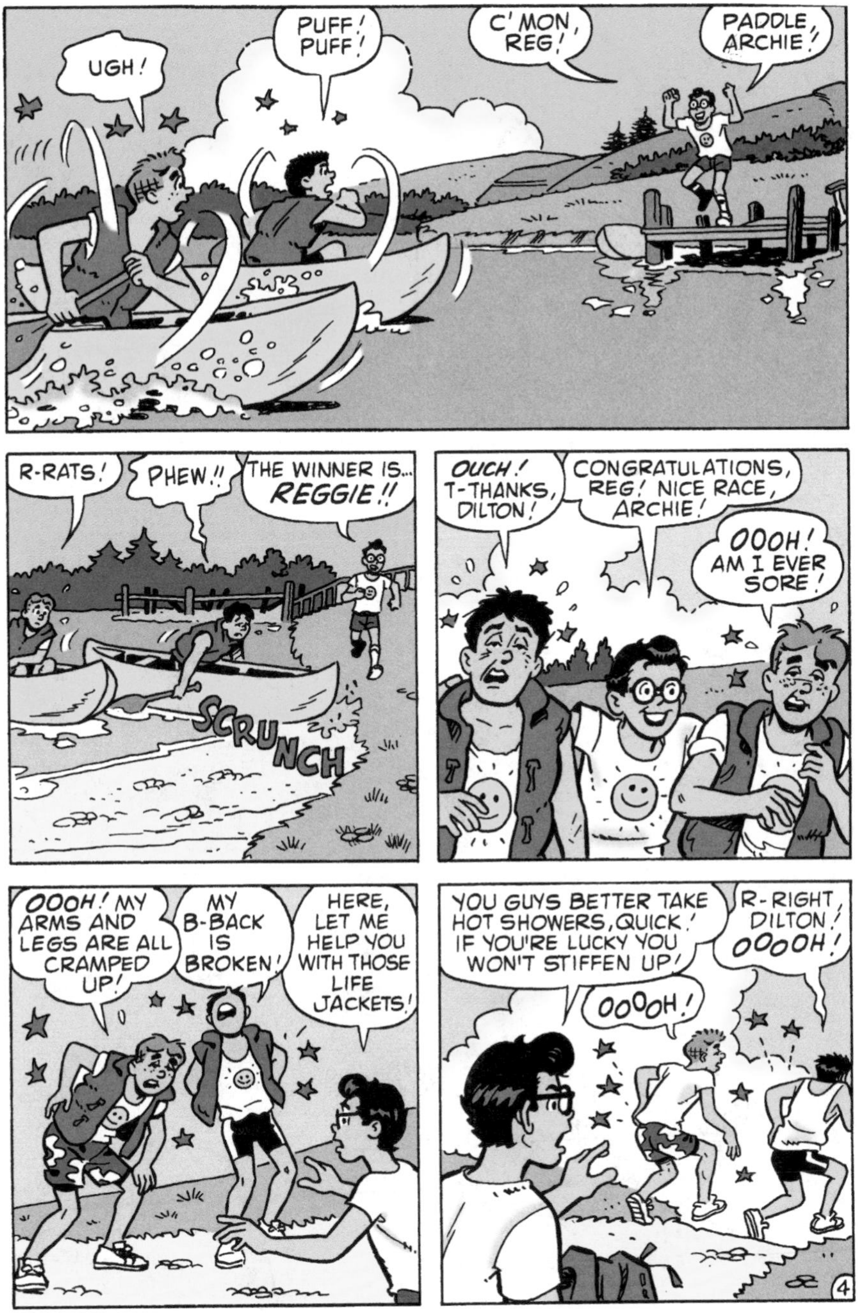
UGH!
PUFF! PUFF!
C'MON, REG!
PADDLE, ARCHIE!
R-RATS!
PHEW!!
THE WINNER IS... REGGIE!!
SCRUNCH
OUCH! T-THANKS, DILTON!
CONGRATULATIONS, REG! NICE RACE, ARCHIE!
OOOH! AM I EVER SORE!
OOOH! MY ARMS AND LEGS ARE ALL CRAMPED UP!
MY B-BACK IS BROKEN!
HERE, LET ME HELP YOU WITH THOSE LIFE JACKETS!
YOU GUYS BETTER TAKE HOT SHOWERS, QUICK! IF YOU'RE LUCKY YOU WON'T STIFFEN UP!
OOOOH!
R-RIGHT, DILTON! OOOOH!
4

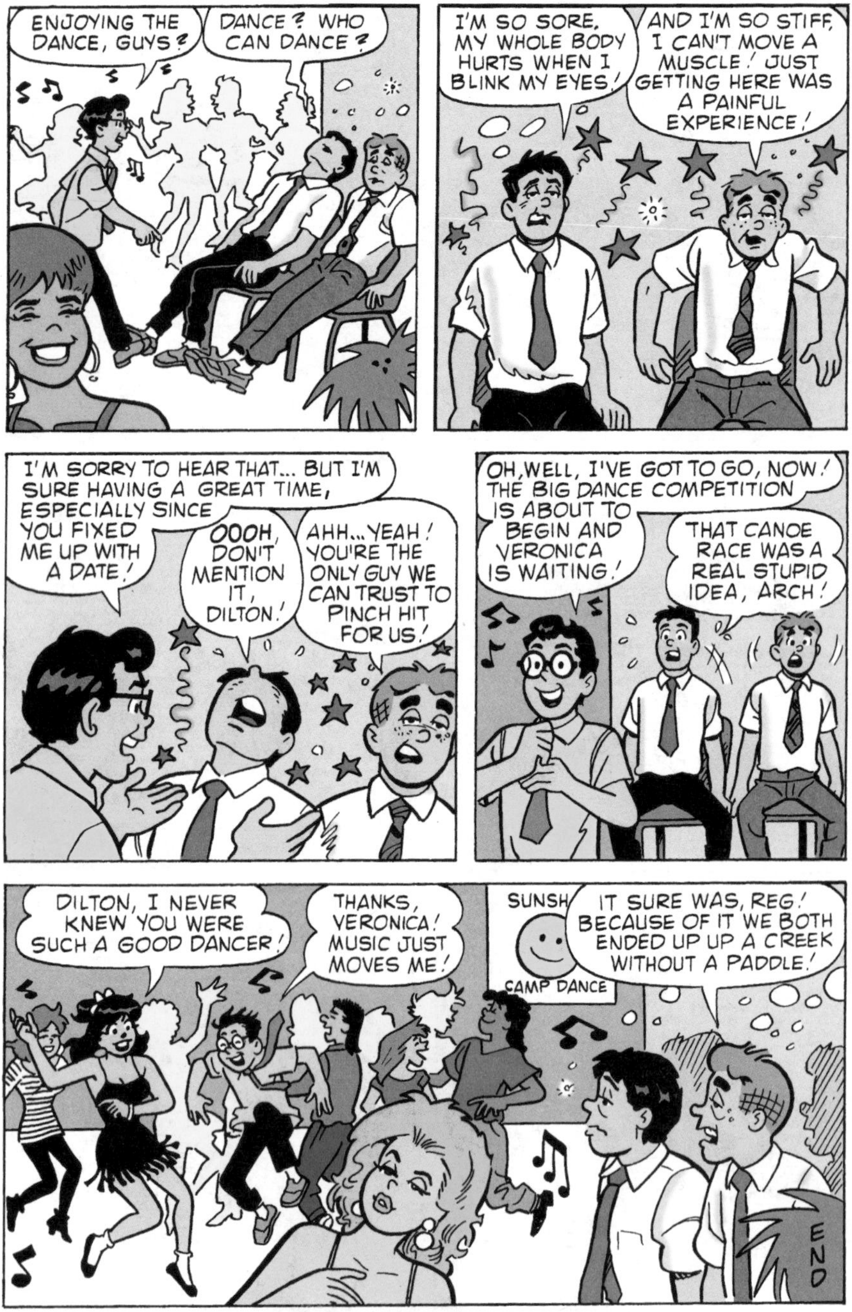
ENJOYING THE DANCE, GUYS?
DANCE? WHO CAN DANCE?
I'M SO SORE, MY WHOLE BODY HURTS WHEN I BLINK MY EYES!
AND I'M SO STIFF, I CAN'T MOVE A MUSCLE! JUST GETTING HERE WAS A PAINFUL EXPERIENCE!
I'M SORRY TO HEAR THAT... BUT I'M SURE HAVING A GREAT TIME, ESPECIALLY SINCE YOU FIXED ME UP WITH A DATE!
OOOH, DON'T MENTION IT, DILTON!
AHH...YEAH! YOU'RE THE ONLY GUY WE CAN TRUST TO PINCH HIT FOR US!
OH, WELL, I'VE GOT TO GO, NOW! THE BIG DANCE COMPETITION IS ABOUT TO BEGIN AND VERONICA IS WAITING!
THAT CANOE RACE WAS A REAL STUPID IDEA, ARCH!
DILTON, I NEVER KNEW YOU WERE SUCH A GOOD DANCER!
THANKS, VERONICA! MUSIC JUST MOVES ME!
SUNSH
CAMP DANCE
IT SURE WAS, REG! BECAUSE OF IT WE BOTH ENDED UP UP A CREEK WITHOUT A PADDLE!
END

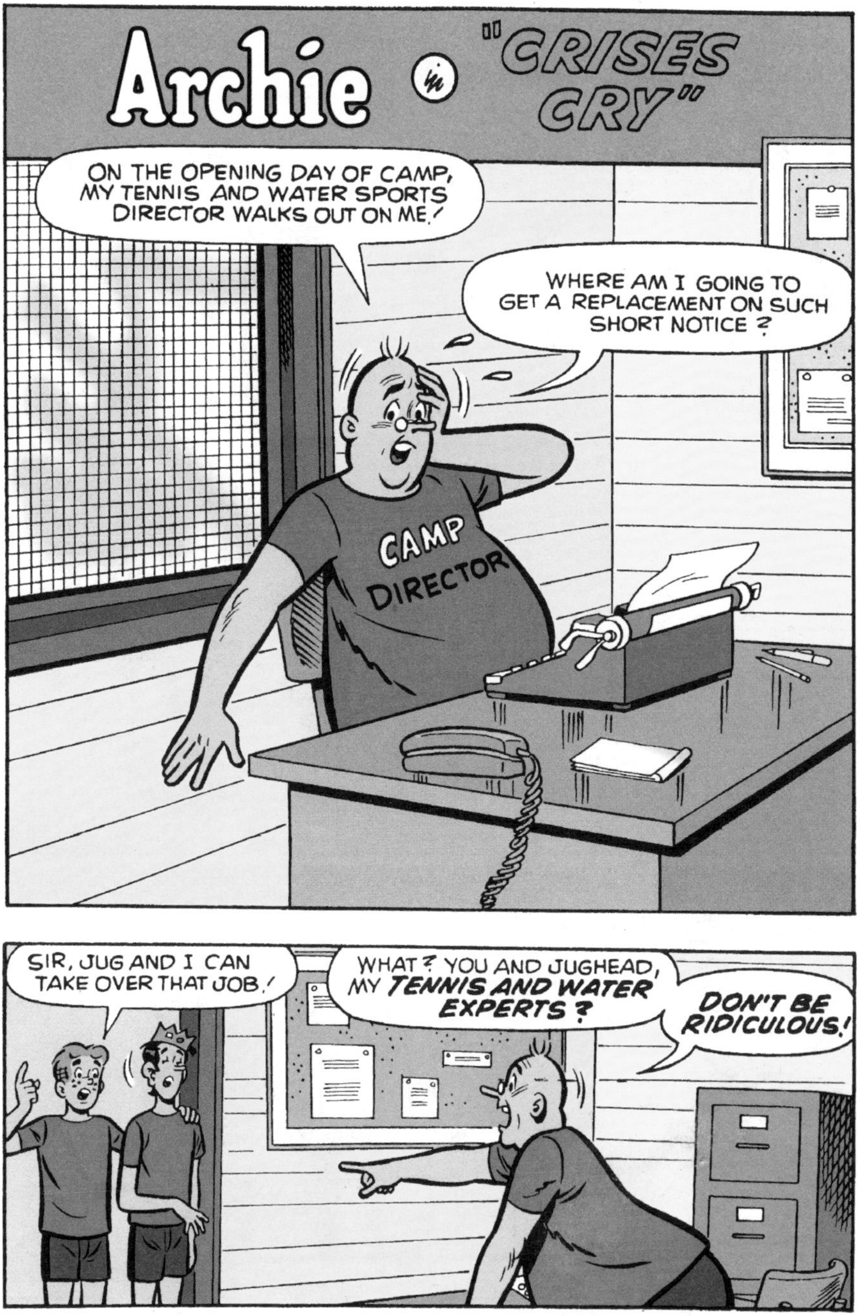

Archie in "CRISES CRY"
ON THE OPENING DAY OF CAMP, MY TENNIS AND WATER SPORTS DIRECTOR WALKS OUT ON ME!
WHERE AM I GOING TO GET A REPLACEMENT ON SUCH SHORT NOTICE?
CAMP DIRECTOR
SIR, JUG AND I CAN TAKE OVER THAT JOB!
WHAT? YOU AND JUGHEAD, MY TENNIS AND WATER EXPERTS?
DON'T BE RIDICULOUS!

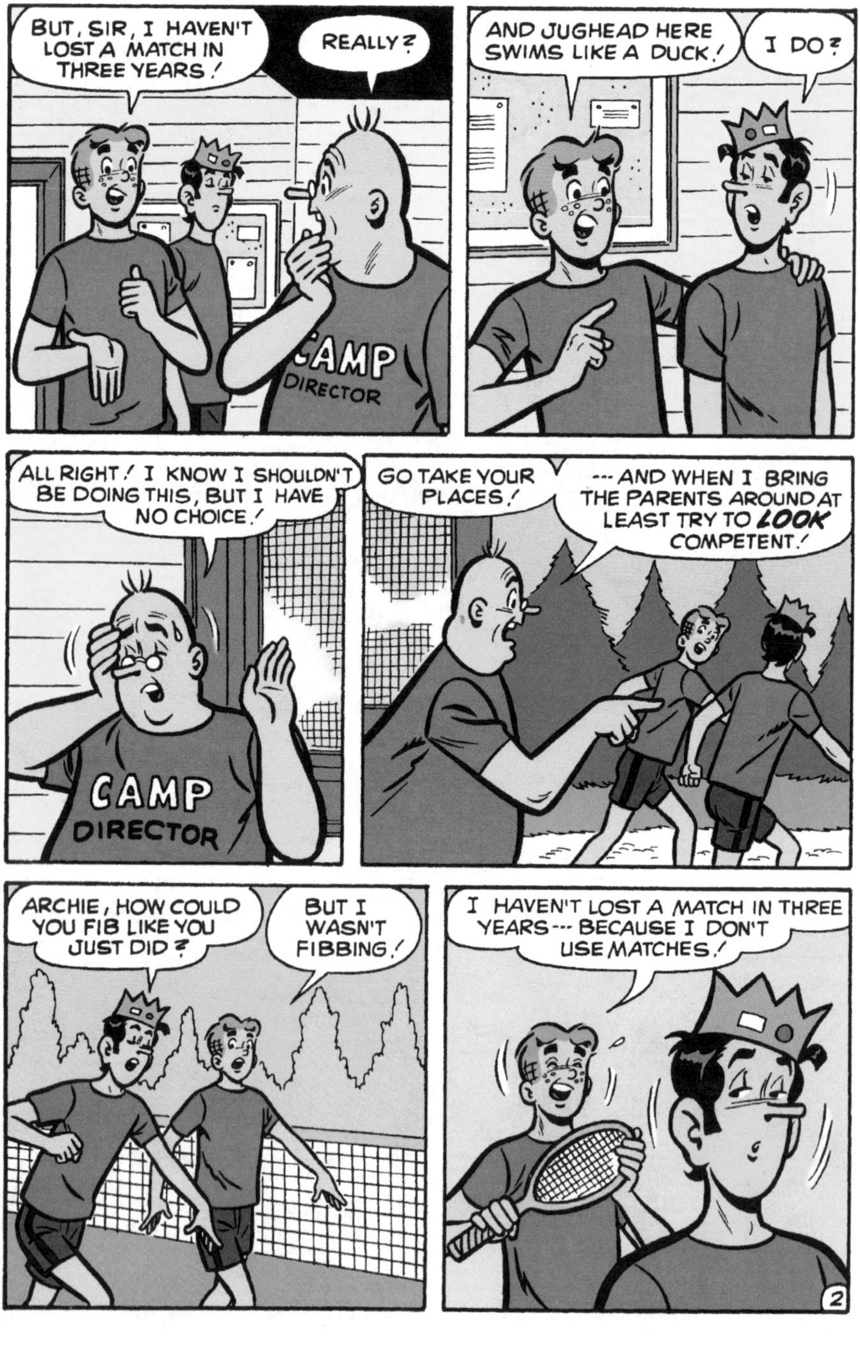
BUT, SIR, I HAVEN'T LOST A MATCH IN THREE YEARS!
REALLY?
CAMP DIRECTOR
AND JUGHEAD HERE SWIMS LIKE A DUCK!
I DO?
ALL RIGHT! I KNOW I SHOULDN'T BE DOING THIS, BUT I HAVE NO CHOICE!
CAMP DIRECTOR
GO TAKE YOUR PLACES!
--- AND WHEN I BRING THE PARENTS AROUND AT LEAST TRY TO LOOK COMPETENT!
ARCHIE, HOW COULD YOU FIB LIKE YOU JUST DID?
BUT I WASN'T FIBBING!
I HAVEN'T LOST A MATCH IN THREE YEARS--- BECAUSE I DON'T USE MATCHES!
2

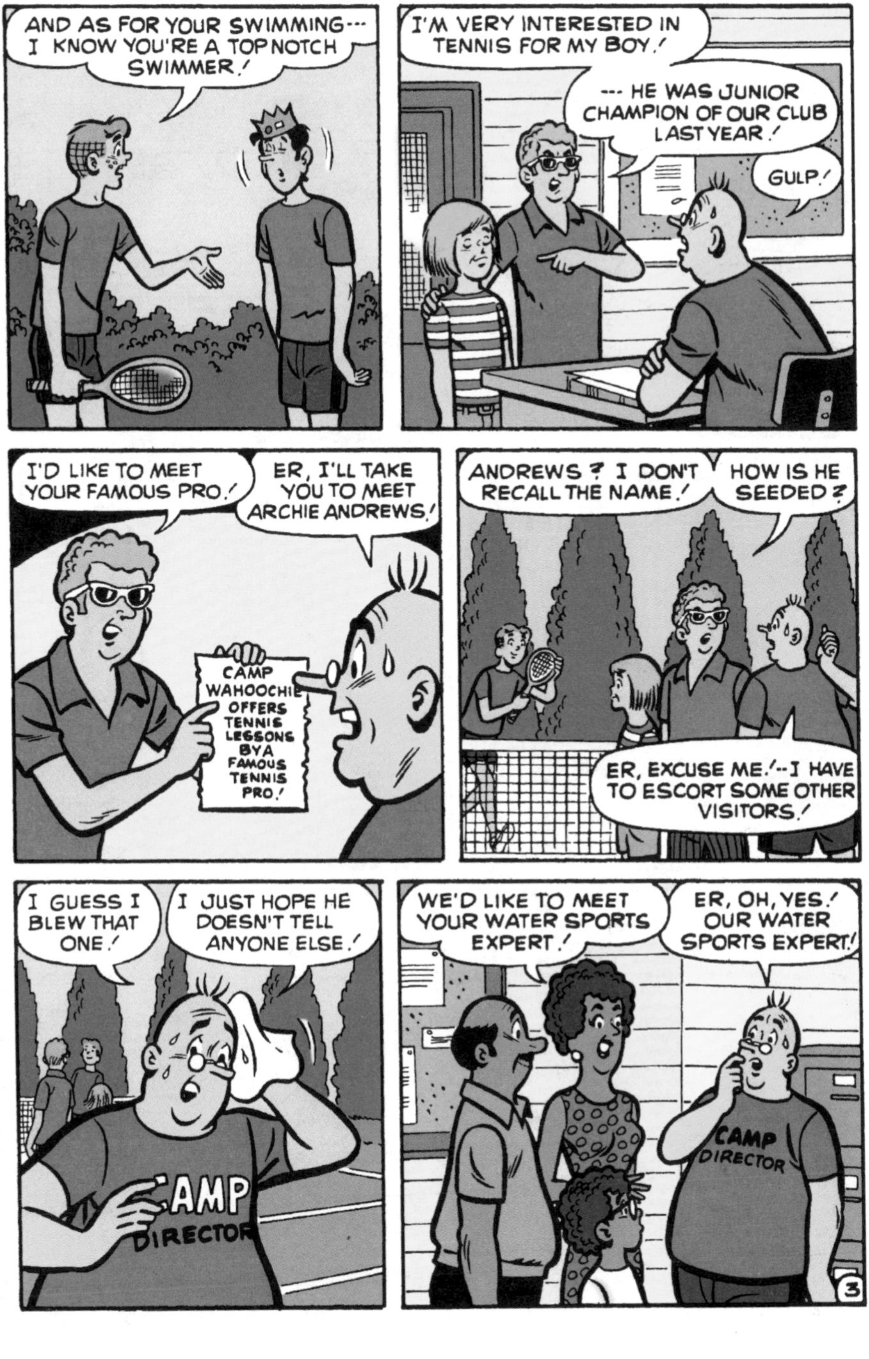
AND AS FOR YOUR SWIMMING--- I KNOW YOU'RE A TOP NOTCH SWIMMER!
I'M VERY INTERESTED IN TENNIS FOR MY BOY!
--- HE WAS JUNIOR CHAMPION OF OUR CLUB LAST YEAR!
GULP!
I'D LIKE TO MEET YOUR FAMOUS PRO!
ER, I'LL TAKE YOU TO MEET ARCHIE ANDREWS!
CAMP WAHOOCHIE OFFERS TENNIS LESSONS BY A FAMOUS TENNIS PRO!
ANDREWS? I DON'T RECALL THE NAME!
HOW IS HE SEEDED?
ER, EXCUSE ME!--I HAVE TO ESCORT SOME OTHER VISITORS!
I GUESS I BLEW THAT ONE!
I JUST HOPE HE DOESN'T TELL ANYONE ELSE!
CAMP DIRECTOR
WE'D LIKE TO MEET YOUR WATER SPORTS EXPERT!
ER, OH, YES! OUR WATER SPORTS EXPERT!
CAMP DIRECTOR
3

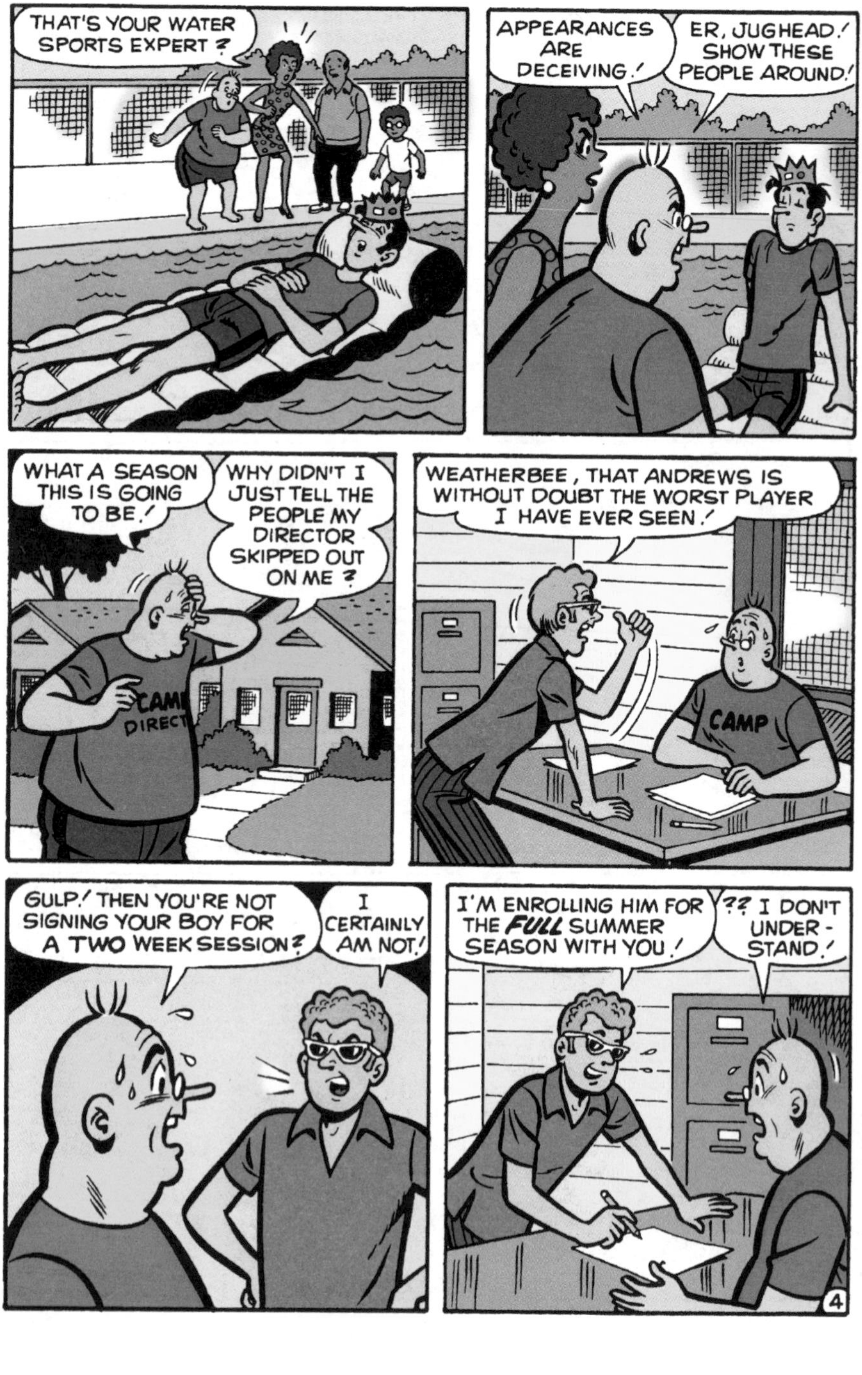
THAT'S YOUR WATER SPORTS EXPERT ?
APPEARANCES ARE DECEIVING!
ER, JUGHEAD! SHOW THESE PEOPLE AROUND!
WHAT A SEASON THIS IS GOING TO BE!
WHY DIDN'T I JUST TELL THE PEOPLE MY DIRECTOR SKIPPED OUT ON ME ?
CAMP DIRECT
WEATHERBEE, THAT ANDREWS IS WITHOUT DOUBT THE WORST PLAYER I HAVE EVER SEEN!
CAMP
GULP! THEN YOU'RE NOT SIGNING YOUR BOY FOR A TWO WEEK SESSION?
I CERTAINLY AM NOT!
I'M ENROLLING HIM FOR THE FULL SUMMER SEASON WITH YOU!
?? I DON'T UNDER-STAND!
4

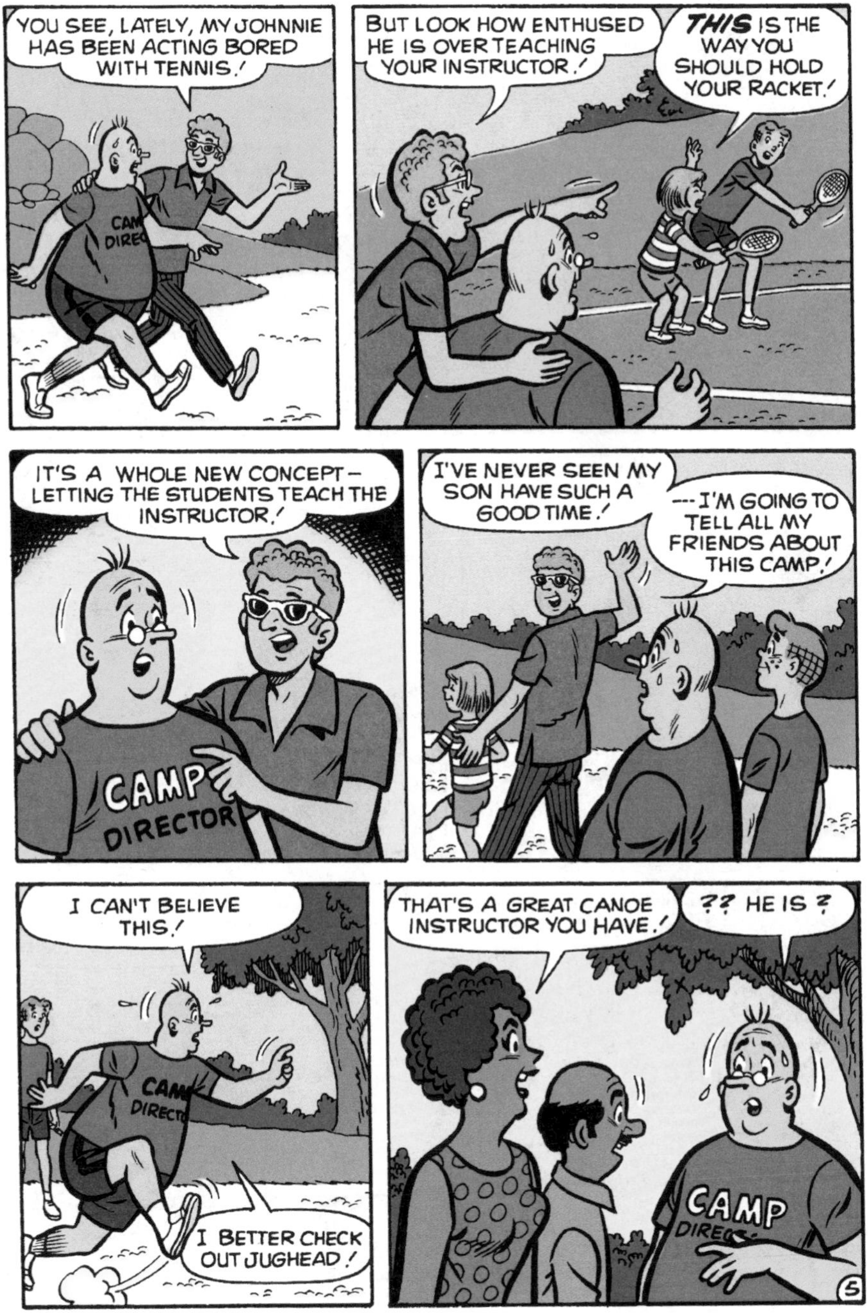
YOU SEE, LATELY, MY JOHNNIE HAS BEEN ACTING BORED WITH TENNIS!
BUT LOOK HOW ENTHUSED HE IS OVER TEACHING YOUR INSTRUCTOR!
THIS IS THE WAY YOU SHOULD HOLD YOUR RACKET!
CAMP DIRECTOR
IT'S A WHOLE NEW CONCEPT – LETTING THE STUDENTS TEACH THE INSTRUCTOR!
I'VE NEVER SEEN MY SON HAVE SUCH A GOOD TIME!
---I'M GOING TO TELL ALL MY FRIENDS ABOUT THIS CAMP!
I CAN'T BELIEVE THIS!
I BETTER CHECK OUT JUGHEAD!
THAT'S A GREAT CANOE INSTRUCTOR YOU HAVE!
?? HE IS ?
CAMP

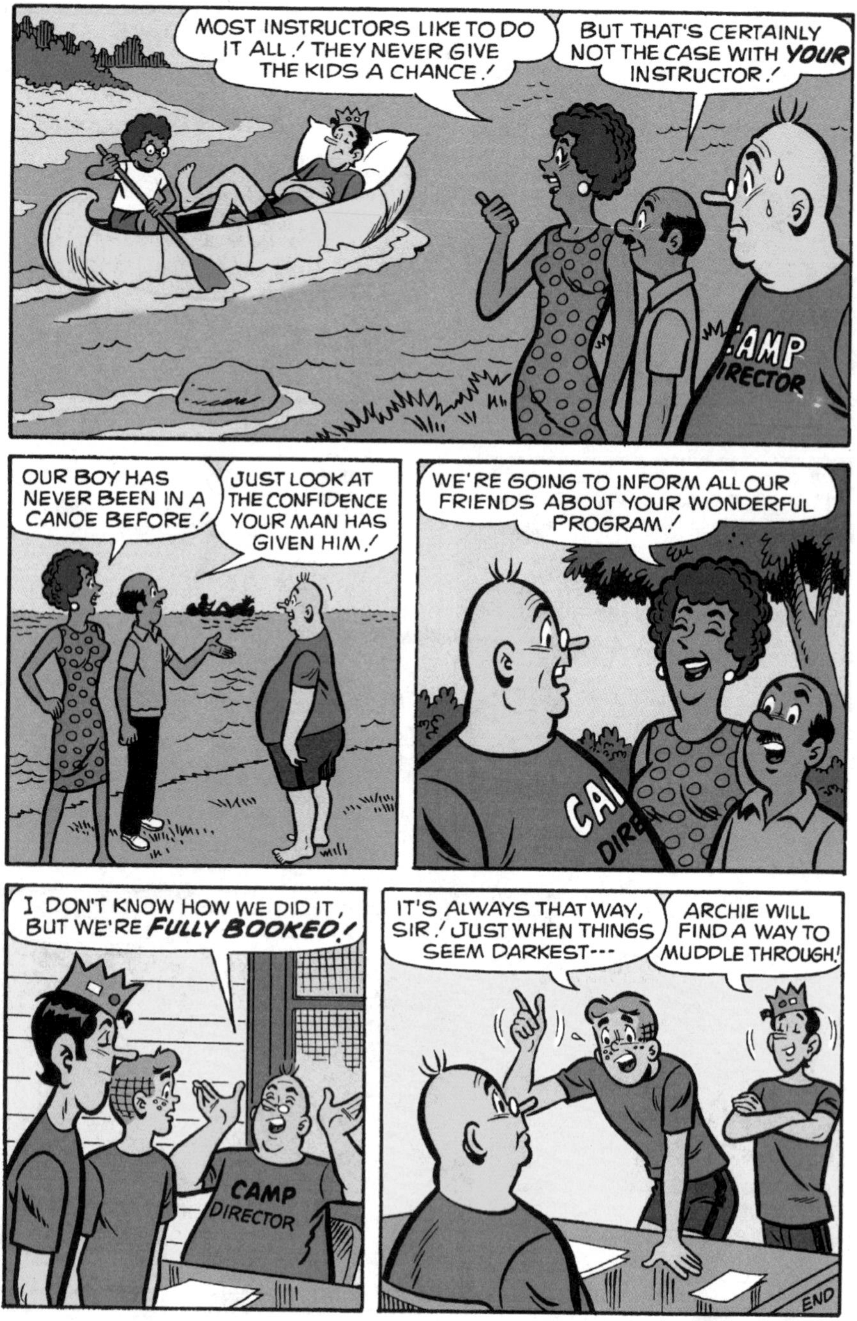
MOST INSTRUCTORS LIKE TO DO IT ALL! THEY NEVER GIVE THE KIDS A CHANCE!
BUT THAT'S CERTAINLY NOT THE CASE WITH YOUR INSTRUCTOR!
CAMP DIRECTOR
OUR BOY HAS NEVER BEEN IN A CANOE BEFORE!
JUST LOOK AT THE CONFIDENCE YOUR MAN HAS GIVEN HIM!
WE'RE GOING TO INFORM ALL OUR FRIENDS ABOUT YOUR WONDERFUL PROGRAM!
I DON'T KNOW HOW WE DID IT, BUT WE'RE FULLY BOOKED!
CAMP DIRECTOR
IT'S ALWAYS THAT WAY, SIR! JUST WHEN THINGS SEEM DARKEST---
ARCHIE WILL FIND A WAY TO MUDDLE THROUGH!
END

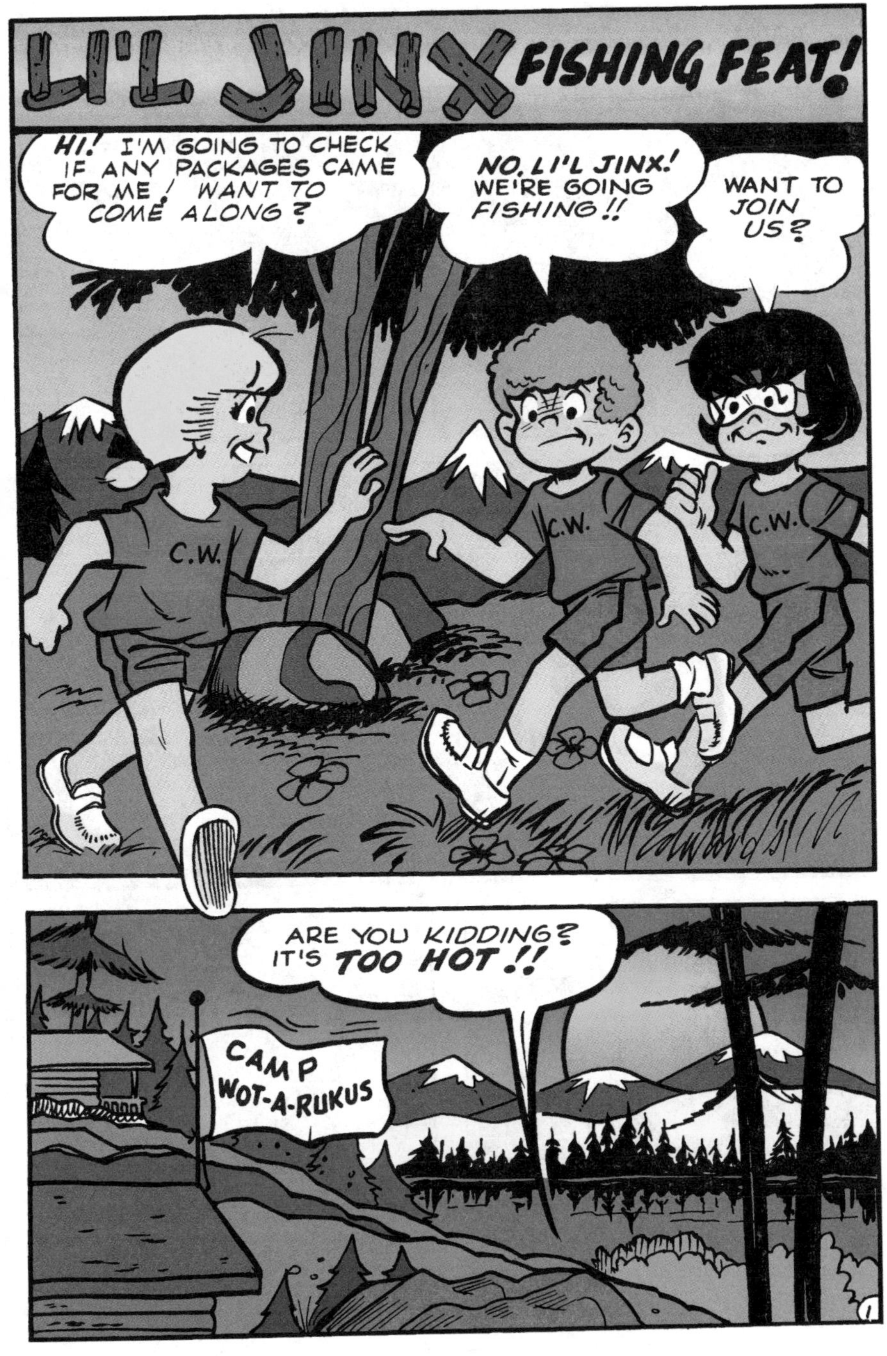

LI'L JINX
FISHING FEAT!
HI! I'M GOING TO CHECK IF ANY PACKAGES CAME FOR ME! WANT TO COME ALONG?
NO, LI'L JINX! WE'RE GOING FISHING!!
WANT TO JOIN US?
C.W.
C.W.
C.W.
ARE YOU KIDDING? IT'S TOO HOT!!
CAMP WOT-A-RUKUS
1

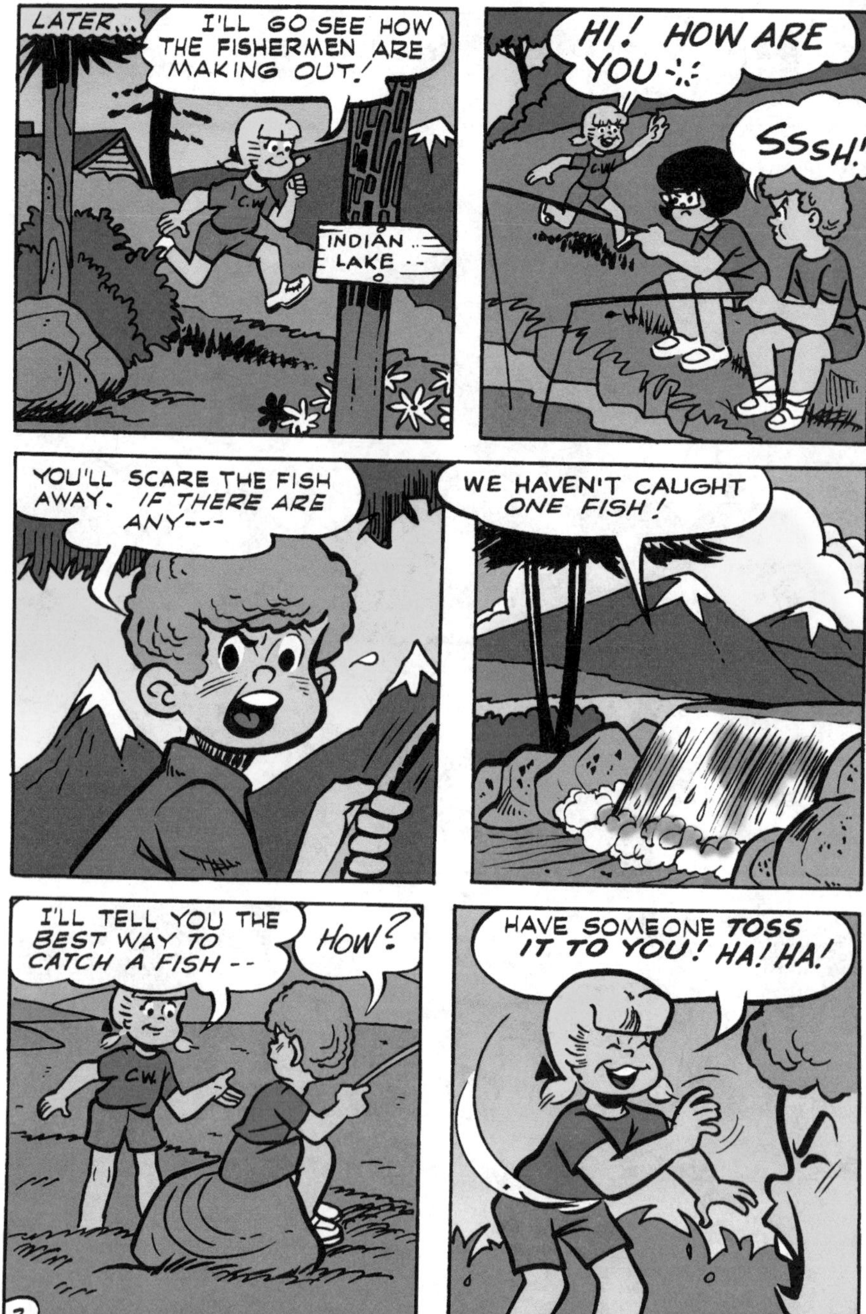

LATER...
I'LL GO SEE HOW THE FISHERMEN ARE MAKING OUT!
INDIAN LAKE
HI! HOW ARE YOU
SSSH!
YOU'LL SCARE THE FISH AWAY. IF THERE ARE ANY---
WE HAVEN'T CAUGHT ONE FISH!
I'LL TELL YOU THE BEST WAY TO CATCH A FISH --
HOW?
HAVE SOMEONE TOSS IT TO YOU! HA! HA!
2

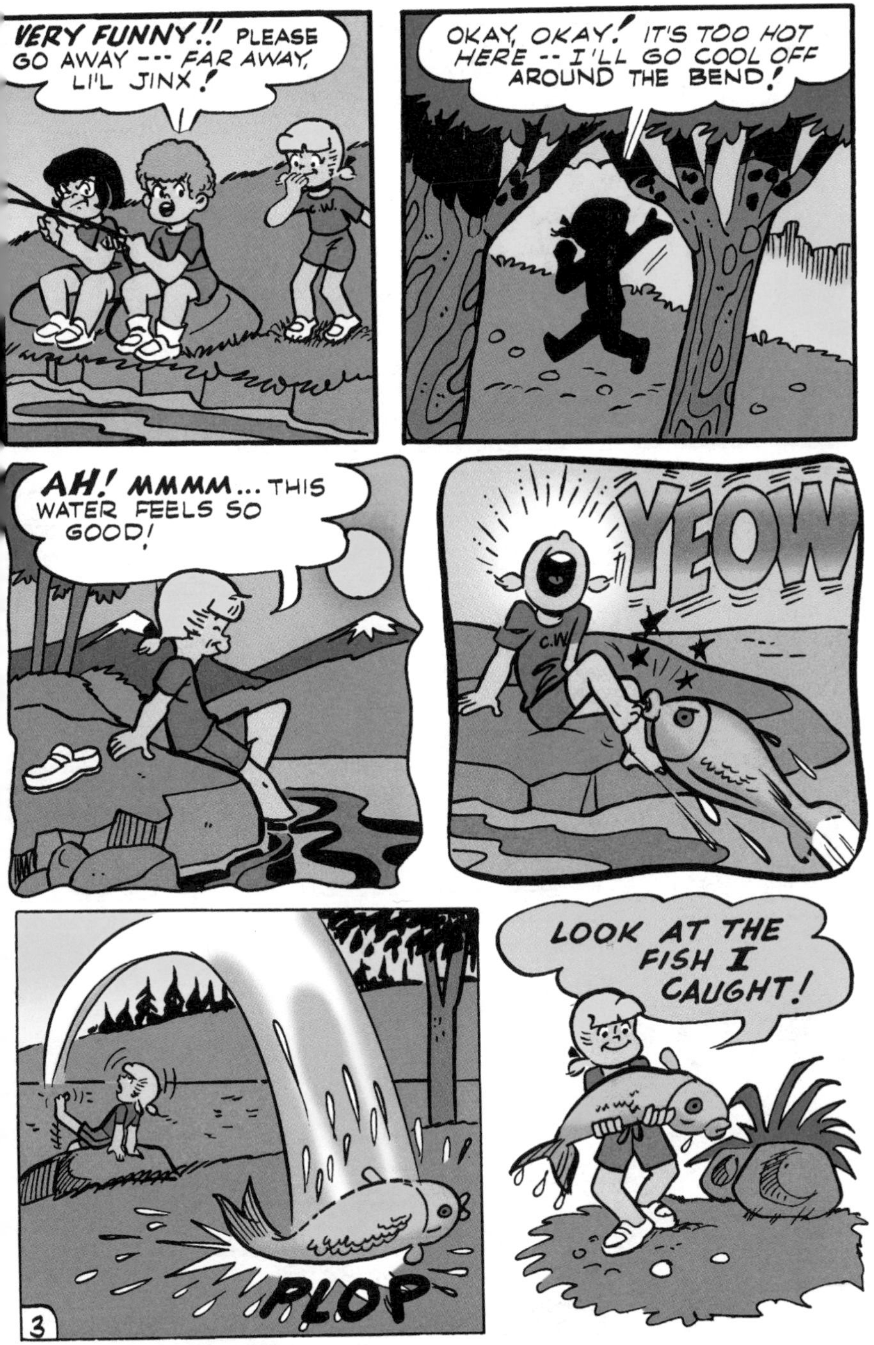

VERY FUNNY!! PLEASE GO AWAY --- FAR AWAY, LI'L JINX!
OKAY, OKAY! IT'S TOO HOT HERE -- I'LL GO COOL OFF AROUND THE BEND!
AH! MMMM... THIS WATER FEELS SO GOOD!
YEOW
PLOP
3
LOOK AT THE FISH I CAUGHT!

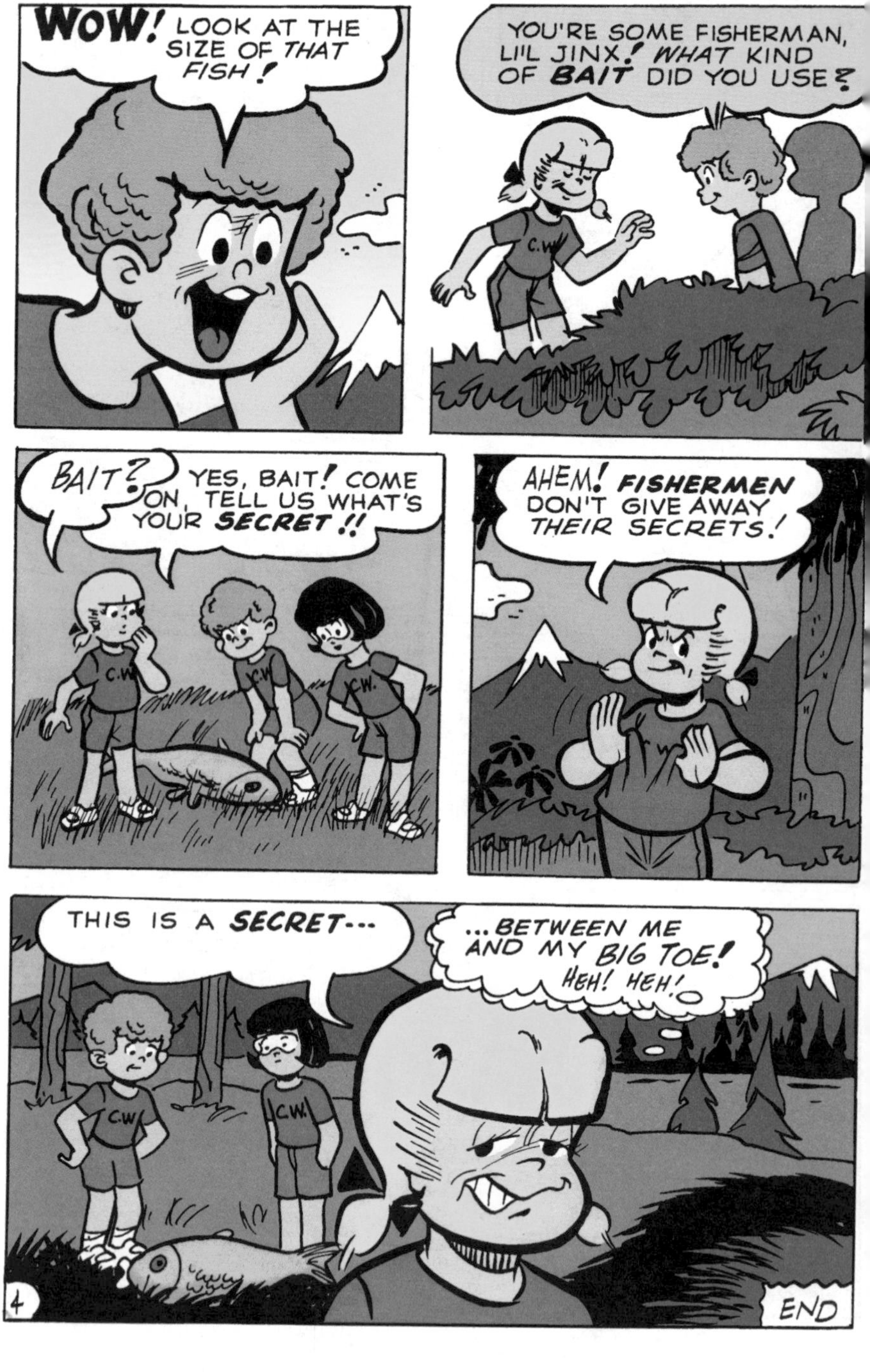

WOW! LOOK AT THE SIZE OF THAT FISH!
YOU'RE SOME FISHERMAN, LI'L JINX! WHAT KIND OF BAIT DID YOU USE?
BAIT?
YES, BAIT! COME ON, TELL US WHAT'S YOUR SECRET!!
AHEM! FISHERMEN DON'T GIVE AWAY THEIR SECRETS!
THIS IS A SECRET---
...BETWEEN ME AND MY BIG TOE! HEH! HEH!
END

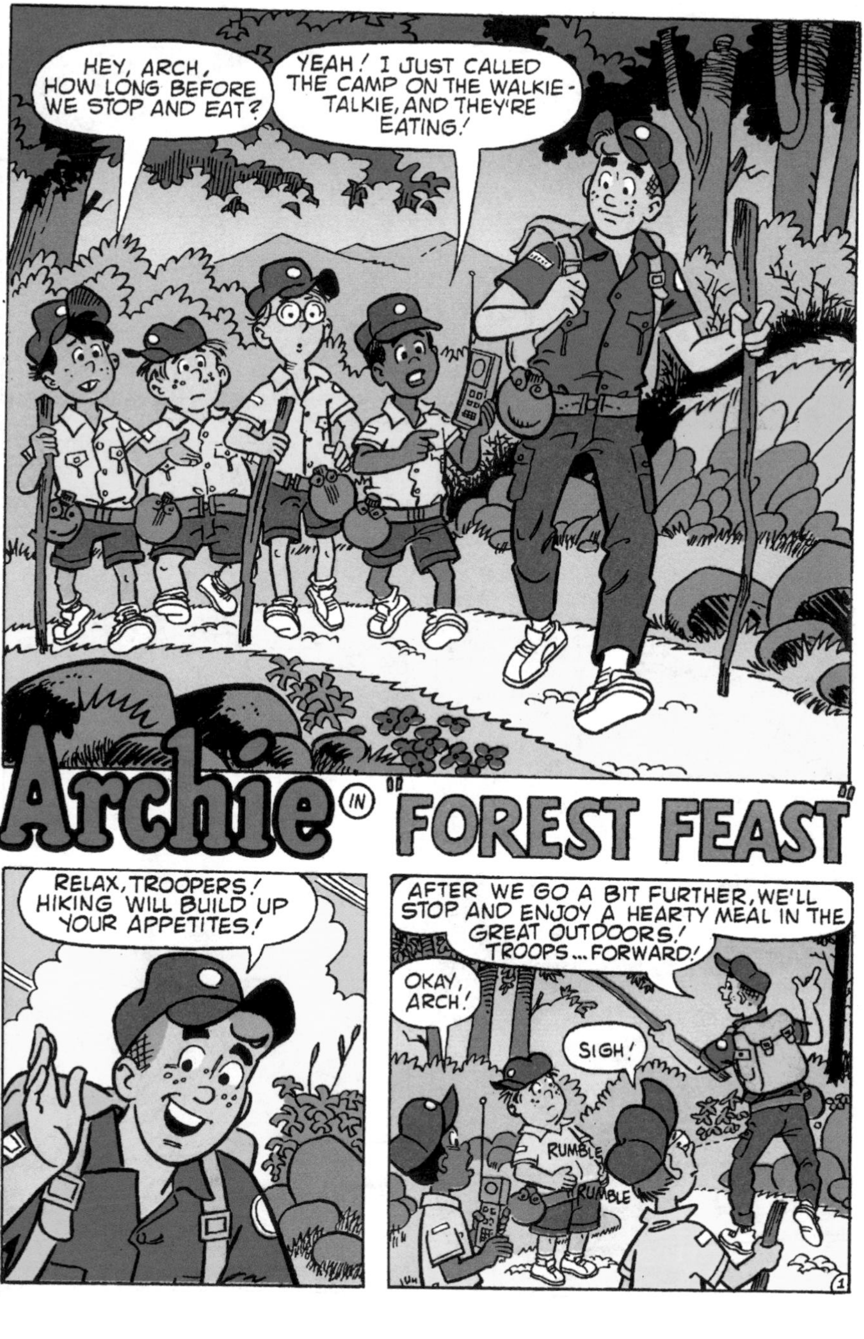
HEY, ARCH, HOW LONG BEFORE WE STOP AND EAT?
YEAH! I JUST CALLED THE CAMP ON THE WALKIE-TALKIE, AND THEY'RE EATING!
Archie IN "FOREST FEAST"
RELAX, TROOPERS! HIKING WILL BUILD UP YOUR APPETITES!
AFTER WE GO A BIT FURTHER, WE'LL STOP AND ENJOY A HEARTY MEAL IN THE GREAT OUTDOORS! TROOPS... FORWARD!
OKAY, ARCH!
SIGH!
RUMBLE
RUMBLE
1

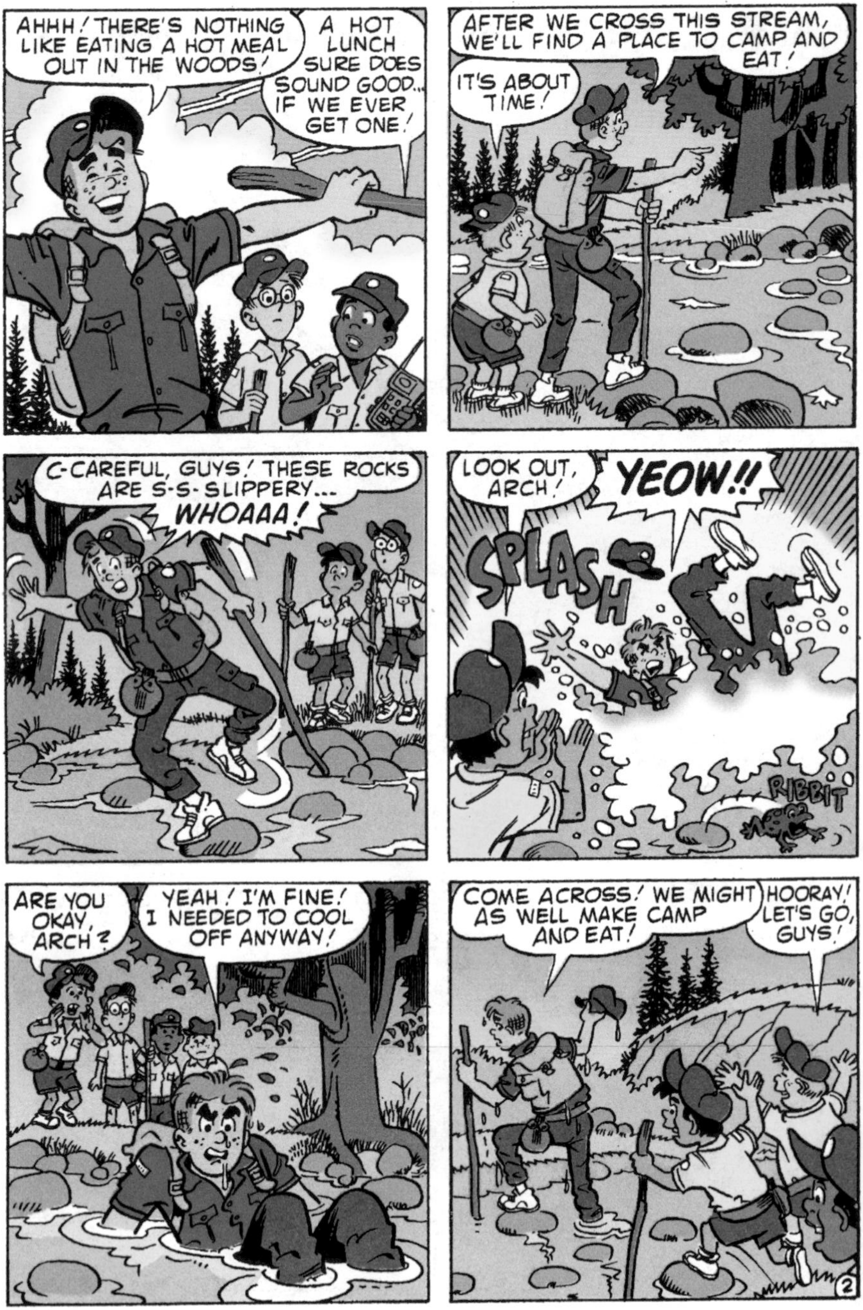
AHHH! THERE'S NOTHING LIKE EATING A HOT MEAL OUT IN THE WOODS!
A HOT LUNCH SURE DOES SOUND GOOD.. IF WE EVER GET ONE!
AFTER WE CROSS THIS STREAM, WE'LL FIND A PLACE TO CAMP AND EAT!
IT'S ABOUT TIME!
C-CAREFUL, GUYS! THESE ROCKS ARE S-S-SLIPPERY...
WHOAAA!
LOOK OUT, ARCH!
YEOW!!
SPLASH
RIBBIT
ARE YOU OKAY, ARCH?
YEAH! I'M FINE! I NEEDED TO COOL OFF ANYWAY!
COME ACROSS! WE MIGHT AS WELL MAKE CAMP AND EAT!
HOORAY! LET'S GO, GUYS!
2

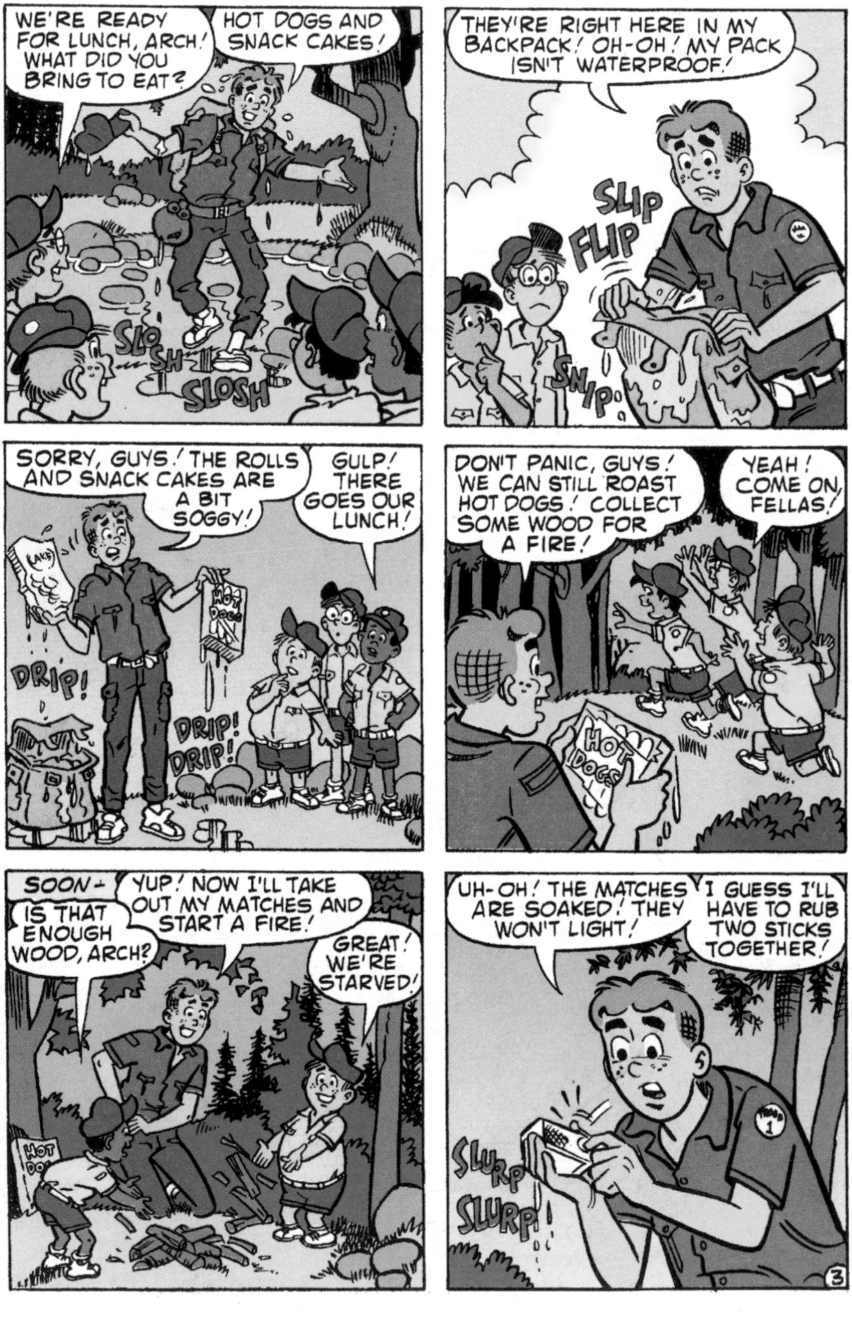

WE'RE READY FOR LUNCH, ARCH! WHAT DID YOU BRING TO EAT?
HOT DOGS AND SNACK CAKES!
SLOSH
SLOSH
THEY'RE RIGHT HERE IN MY BACKPACK! OH-OH! MY PACK ISN'T WATERPROOF!
SLIP
FLIP
SNIP
SORRY, GUYS! THE ROLLS AND SNACK CAKES ARE A BIT SOGGY!
GULP! THERE GOES OUR LUNCH!
DRIP!
DRIP! DRIP!
DON'T PANIC, GUYS! WE CAN STILL ROAST HOT DOGS! COLLECT SOME WOOD FOR A FIRE!
YEAH! COME ON, FELLAS!
SOON-
IS THAT ENOUGH WOOD, ARCH?
YUP! NOW I'LL TAKE OUT MY MATCHES AND START A FIRE!
GREAT! WE'RE STARVED!
UH-OH! THE MATCHES ARE SOAKED! THEY WON'T LIGHT!
I GUESS I'LL HAVE TO RUB TWO STICKS TOGETHER!
SLURP
SLURP

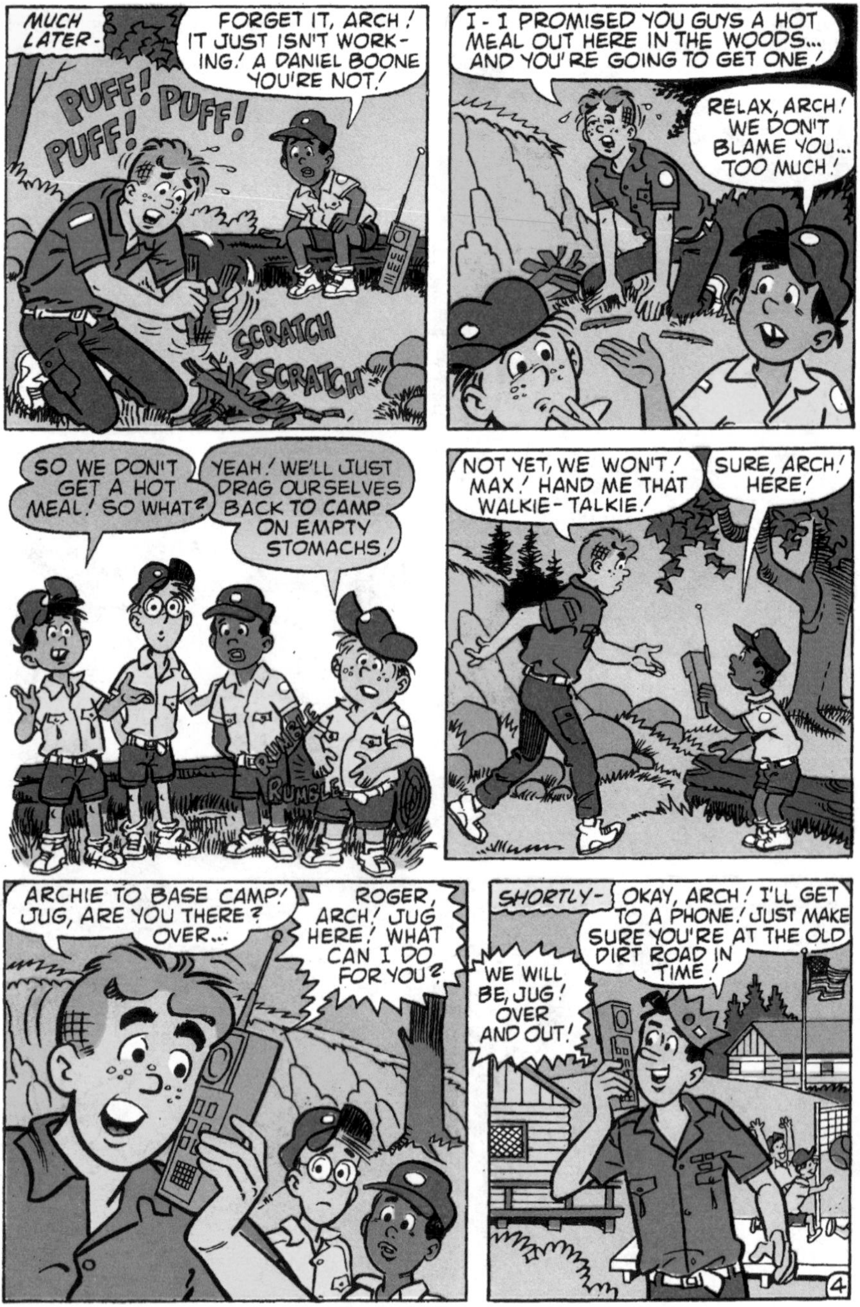
MUCH LATER-
FORGET IT, ARCH! IT JUST ISN'T WORK-ING! A DANIEL BOONE YOU'RE NOT!
PUFF! PUFF! PUFF!
SCRATCH SCRATCH
I - I PROMISED YOU GUYS A HOT MEAL OUT HERE IN THE WOODS... AND YOU'RE GOING TO GET ONE!
RELAX, ARCH! WE DON'T BLAME YOU... TOO MUCH!
SO WE DON'T GET A HOT MEAL! SO WHAT?
YEAH! WE'LL JUST DRAG OURSELVES BACK TO CAMP ON EMPTY STOMACHS!
RUMBLE RUMBLE
NOT YET, WE WON'T! MAX! HAND ME THAT WALKIE-TALKIE!
SURE, ARCH! HERE!
ARCHIE TO BASE CAMP! JUG, ARE YOU THERE? OVER...
ROGER, ARCH! JUG HERE! WHAT CAN I DO FOR YOU?
SHORTLY-
OKAY, ARCH! I'LL GET TO A PHONE! JUST MAKE SURE YOU'RE AT THE OLD DIRT ROAD IN TIME!
WE WILL BE, JUG! OVER AND OUT!
4

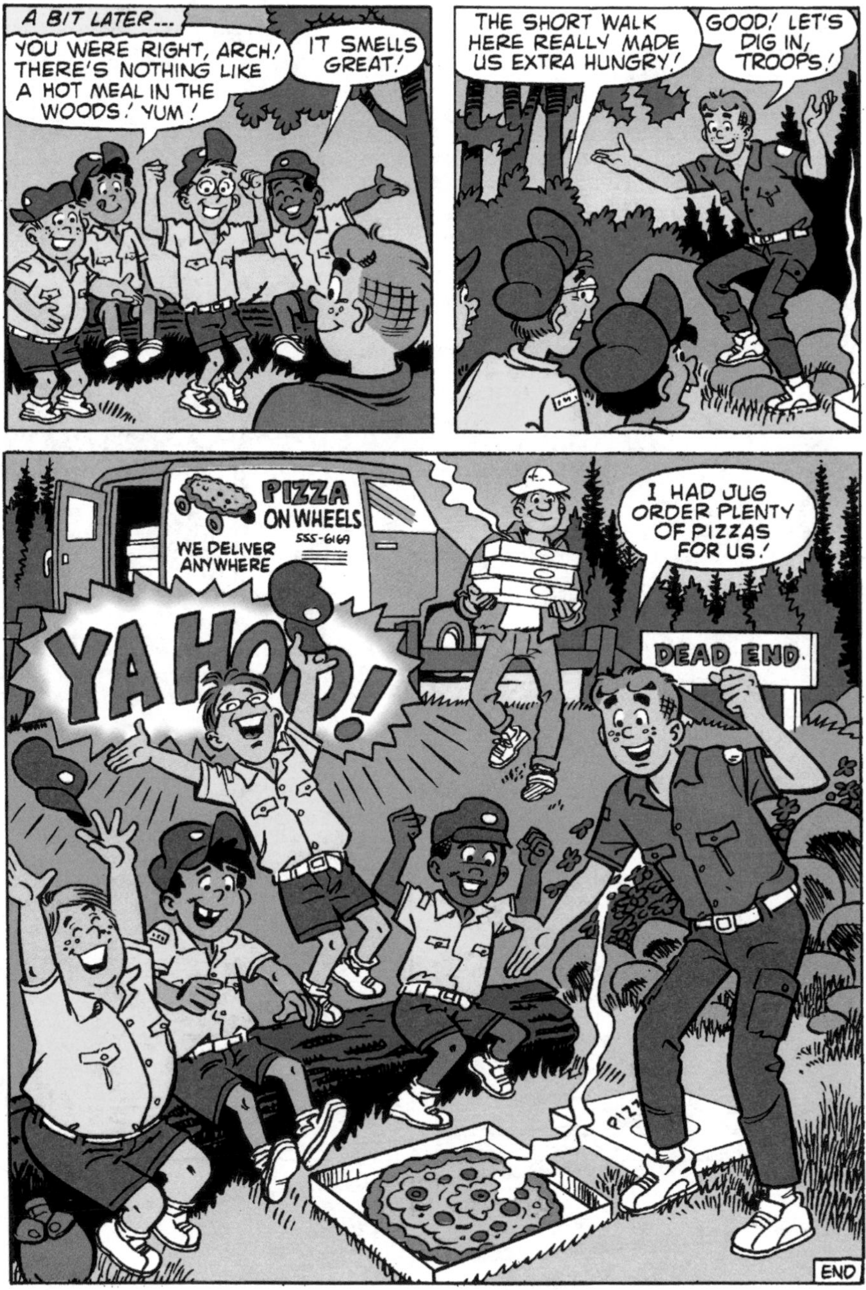
A BIT LATER...
YOU WERE RIGHT, ARCH! THERE'S NOTHING LIKE A HOT MEAL IN THE WOODS! YUM!
IT SMELLS GREAT!
THE SHORT WALK HERE REALLY MADE US EXTRA HUNGRY!
GOOD! LET'S DIG IN, TROOPS!
PIZZA ON WHEELS
555-6169
WE DELIVER ANYWHERE
YAHOO!
I HAD JUG ORDER PLENTY OF PIZZAS FOR US!
DEAD END
END

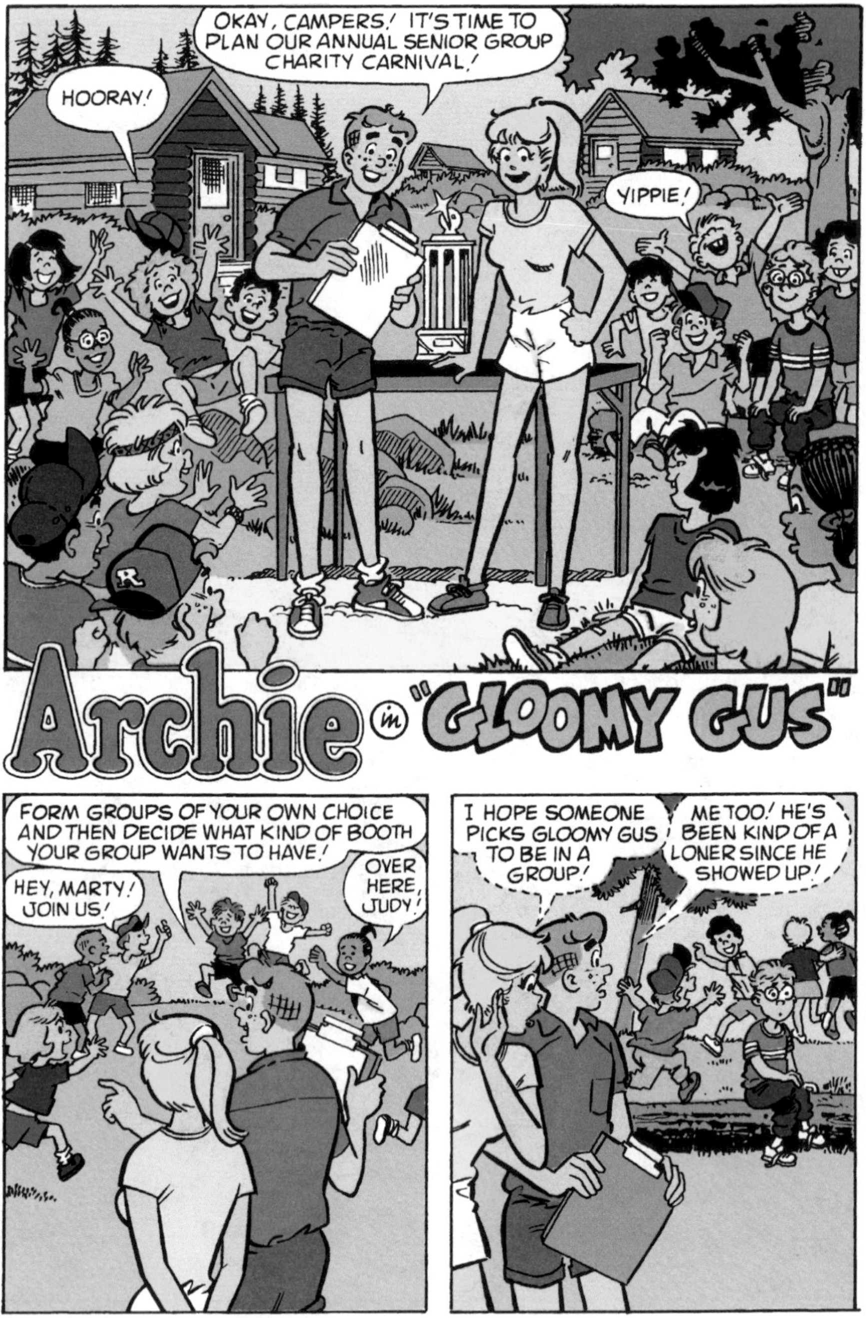

OKAY, CAMPERS! IT'S TIME TO PLAN OUR ANNUAL SENIOR GROUP CHARITY CARNIVAL!
HOORAY!
YIPPIE!
Archie in "GLOOMY GUS"
FORM GROUPS OF YOUR OWN CHOICE AND THEN DECIDE WHAT KIND OF BOOTH YOUR GROUP WANTS TO HAVE!
HEY, MARTY! JOIN US!
OVER HERE, JUDY!
I HOPE SOMEONE PICKS GLOOMY GUS TO BE IN A GROUP!
ME TOO! HE'S BEEN KIND OF A LONER SINCE HE SHOWED UP!

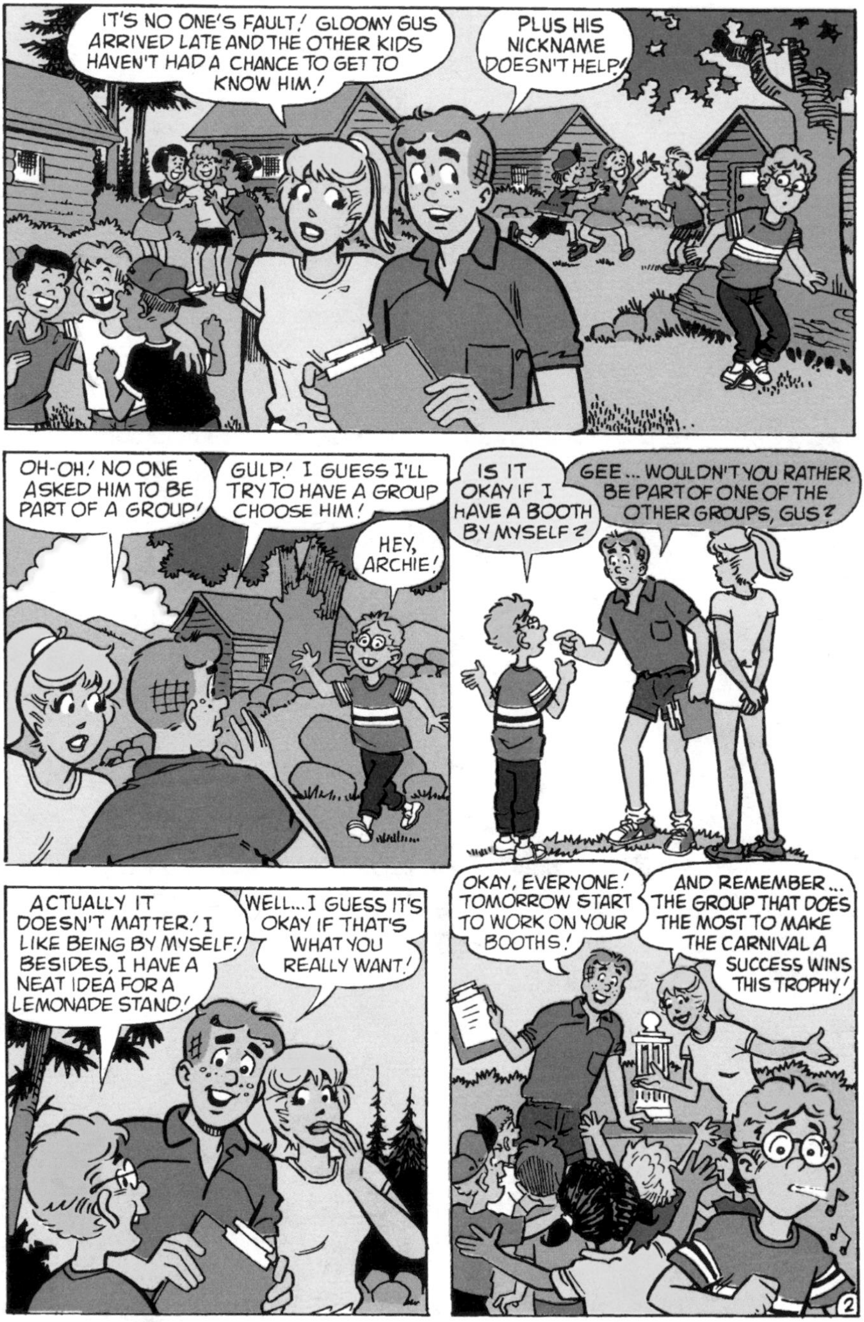
IT'S NO ONE'S FAULT! GLOOMY GUS ARRIVED LATE AND THE OTHER KIDS HAVEN'T HAD A CHANCE TO GET TO KNOW HIM!
PLUS HIS NICKNAME DOESN'T HELP!
OH-OH! NO ONE ASKED HIM TO BE PART OF A GROUP!
GULP! I GUESS I'LL TRY TO HAVE A GROUP CHOOSE HIM!
HEY, ARCHIE!
IS IT OKAY IF I HAVE A BOOTH BY MYSELF?
GEE... WOULDN'T YOU RATHER BE PART OF ONE OF THE OTHER GROUPS, GUS?
ACTUALLY IT DOESN'T MATTER! I LIKE BEING BY MYSELF! BESIDES, I HAVE A NEAT IDEA FOR A LEMONADE STAND!
WELL... I GUESS IT'S OKAY IF THAT'S WHAT YOU REALLY WANT!
OKAY, EVERYONE! TOMORROW START TO WORK ON YOUR BOOTHS!
AND REMEMBER... THE GROUP THAT DOES THE MOST TO MAKE THE CARNIVAL A SUCCESS WINS THIS TROPHY!
2

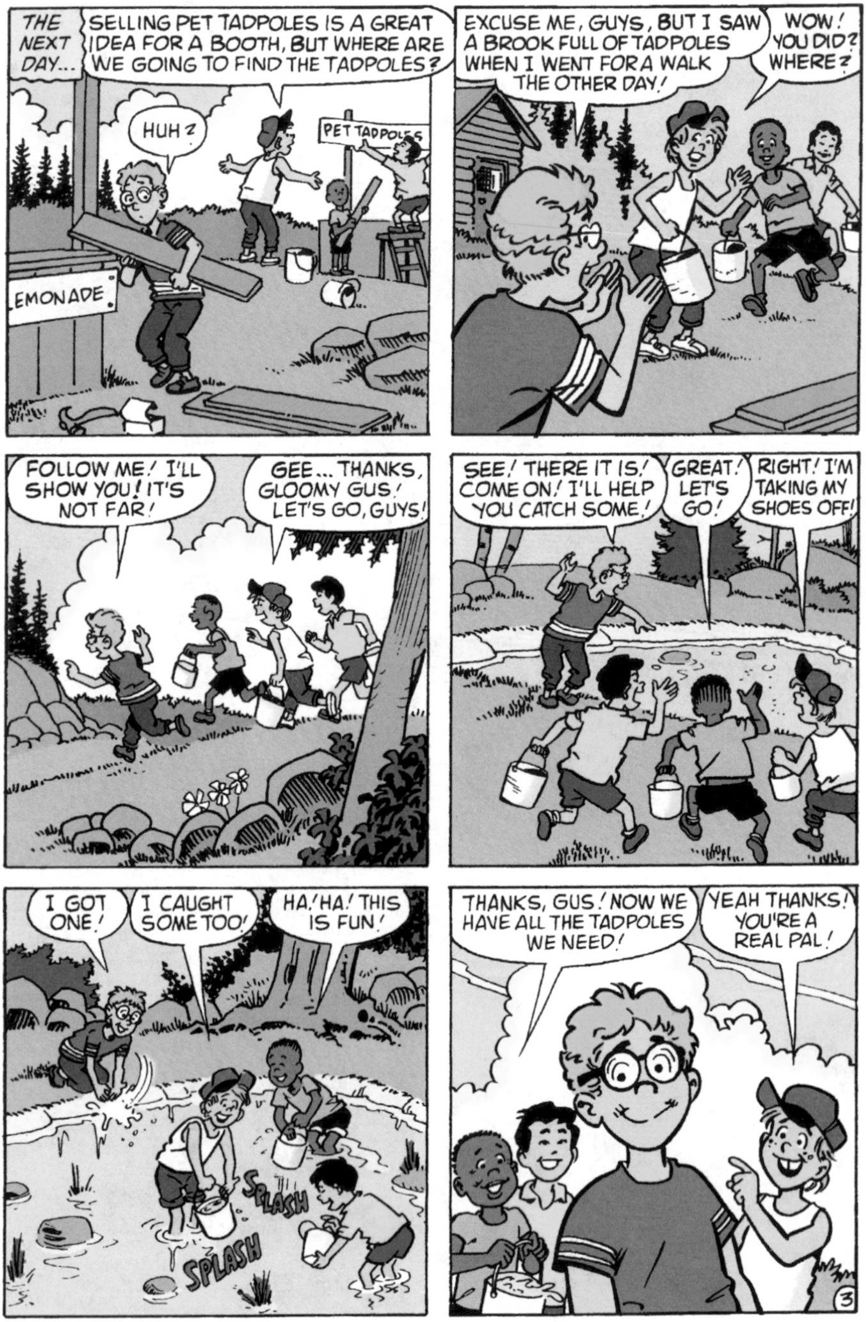
THE NEXT DAY...
SELLING PET TADPOLES IS A GREAT IDEA FOR A BOOTH, BUT WHERE ARE WE GOING TO FIND THE TADPOLES?
HUH?
PET TADPOLES
LEMONADE
EXCUSE ME, GUYS, BUT I SAW A BROOK FULL OF TADPOLES WHEN I WENT FOR A WALK THE OTHER DAY!
WOW! YOU DID? WHERE?
FOLLOW ME! I'LL SHOW YOU! IT'S NOT FAR!
GEE... THANKS, GLOOMY GUS! LET'S GO, GUYS!
SEE! THERE IT IS! COME ON! I'LL HELP YOU CATCH SOME!
GREAT! LET'S GO!
RIGHT! I'M TAKING MY SHOES OFF!
I GOT ONE!
I CAUGHT SOME TOO!
HA! HA! THIS IS FUN!
SPLASH
SPLASH
THANKS, GUS! NOW WE HAVE ALL THE TADPOLES WE NEED!
YEAH THANKS! YOU'RE A REAL PAL!

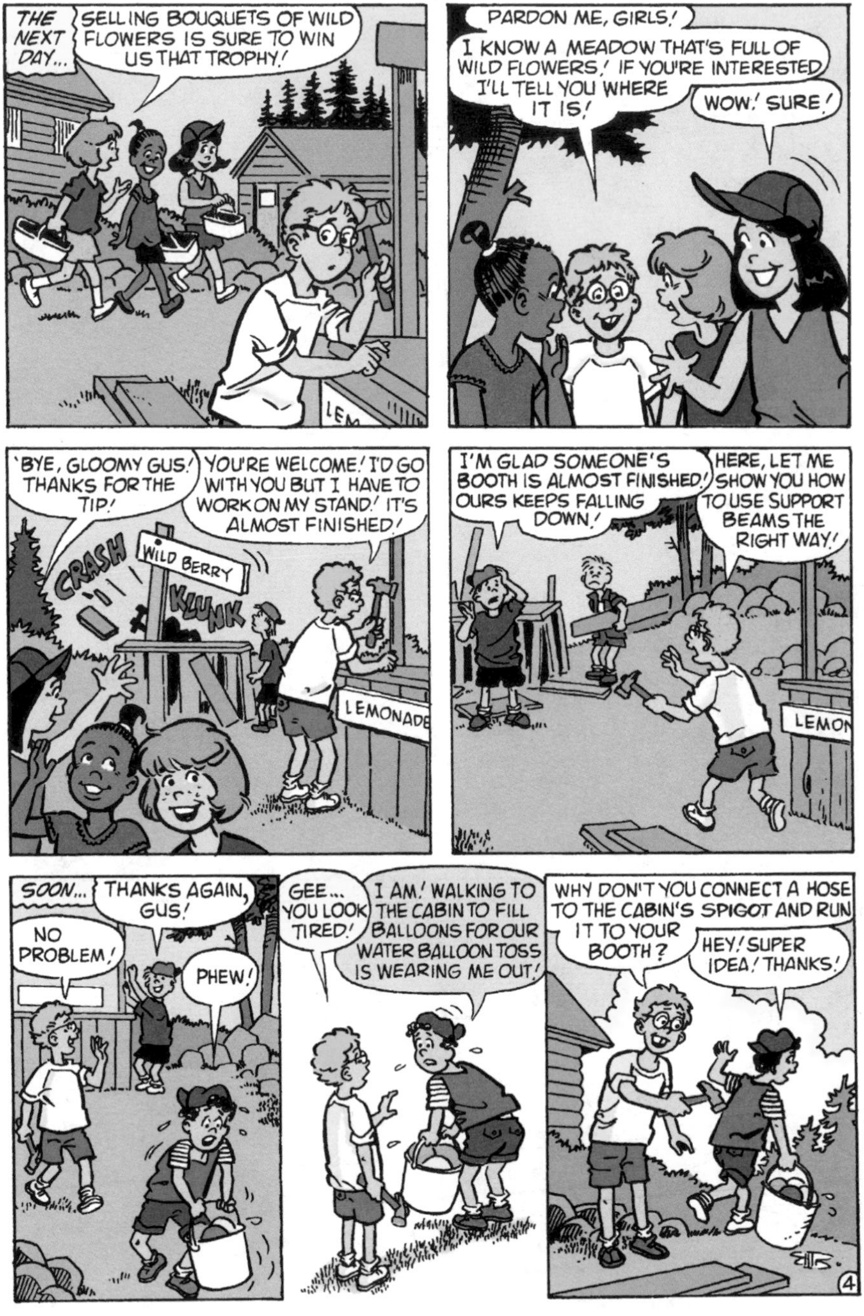
THE NEXT DAY...
SELLING BOUQUETS OF WILD FLOWERS IS SURE TO WIN US THAT TROPHY!
LEM
PARDON ME, GIRLS!
I KNOW A MEADOW THAT'S FULL OF WILD FLOWERS! IF YOU'RE INTERESTED I'LL TELL YOU WHERE IT IS!
WOW! SURE!
'BYE, GLOOMY GUS! THANKS FOR THE TIP!
YOU'RE WELCOME! I'D GO WITH YOU BUT I HAVE TO WORK ON MY STAND! IT'S ALMOST FINISHED!
CRASH
WILD BERRY
KLUNK
LEMONADE
I'M GLAD SOMEONE'S BOOTH IS ALMOST FINISHED! OURS KEEPS FALLING DOWN!
HERE, LET ME SHOW YOU HOW TO USE SUPPORT BEAMS THE RIGHT WAY!
LEMON
SOON...
THANKS AGAIN, GUS!
NO PROBLEM!
PHEW!
GEE... YOU LOOK TIRED!
I AM! WALKING TO THE CABIN TO FILL BALLOONS FOR OUR WATER BALLOON TOSS IS WEARING ME OUT!
WHY DON'T YOU CONNECT A HOSE TO THE CABIN'S SPIGOT AND RUN IT TO YOUR BOOTH?
HEY! SUPER IDEA! THANKS!
4

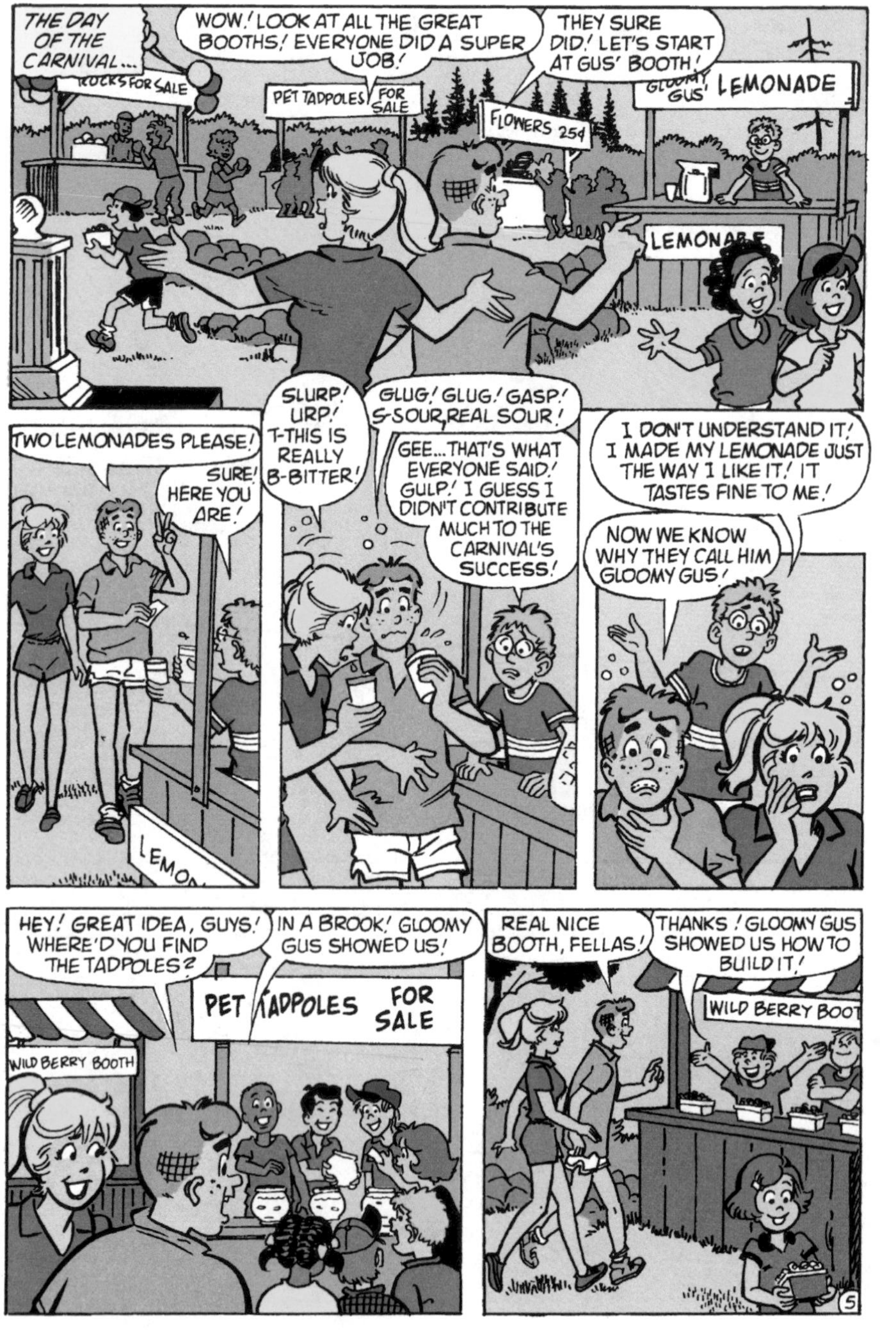
THE DAY OF THE CARNIVAL...
WOW! LOOK AT ALL THE GREAT BOOTHS! EVERYONE DID A SUPER JOB!
THEY SURE DID! LET'S START AT GUS' BOOTH!
ROCKS FOR SALE
PET TADPOLES FOR SALE
FLOWERS 25¢
GLOOMY GUS' LEMONADE
LEMONADE
TWO LEMONADES PLEASE!
SURE! HERE YOU ARE!
SLURP! URP! T-THIS IS REALLY B-BITTER!
GLUG! GLUG! GASP! S-SOUR, REAL SOUR!
GEE...THAT'S WHAT EVERYONE SAID! GULP! I GUESS I DIDN'T CONTRIBUTE MUCH TO THE CARNIVAL'S SUCCESS!
I DON'T UNDERSTAND IT! I MADE MY LEMONADE JUST THE WAY I LIKE IT! IT TASTES FINE TO ME!
NOW WE KNOW WHY THEY CALL HIM GLOOMY GUS!
HEY! GREAT IDEA, GUYS! WHERE'D YOU FIND THE TADPOLES?
IN A BROOK! GLOOMY GUS SHOWED US!
PET TADPOLES FOR SALE
WILD BERRY BOOTH
REAL NICE BOOTH, FELLAS!
THANKS! GLOOMY GUS SHOWED US HOW TO BUILD IT!
WILD BERRY BOOT

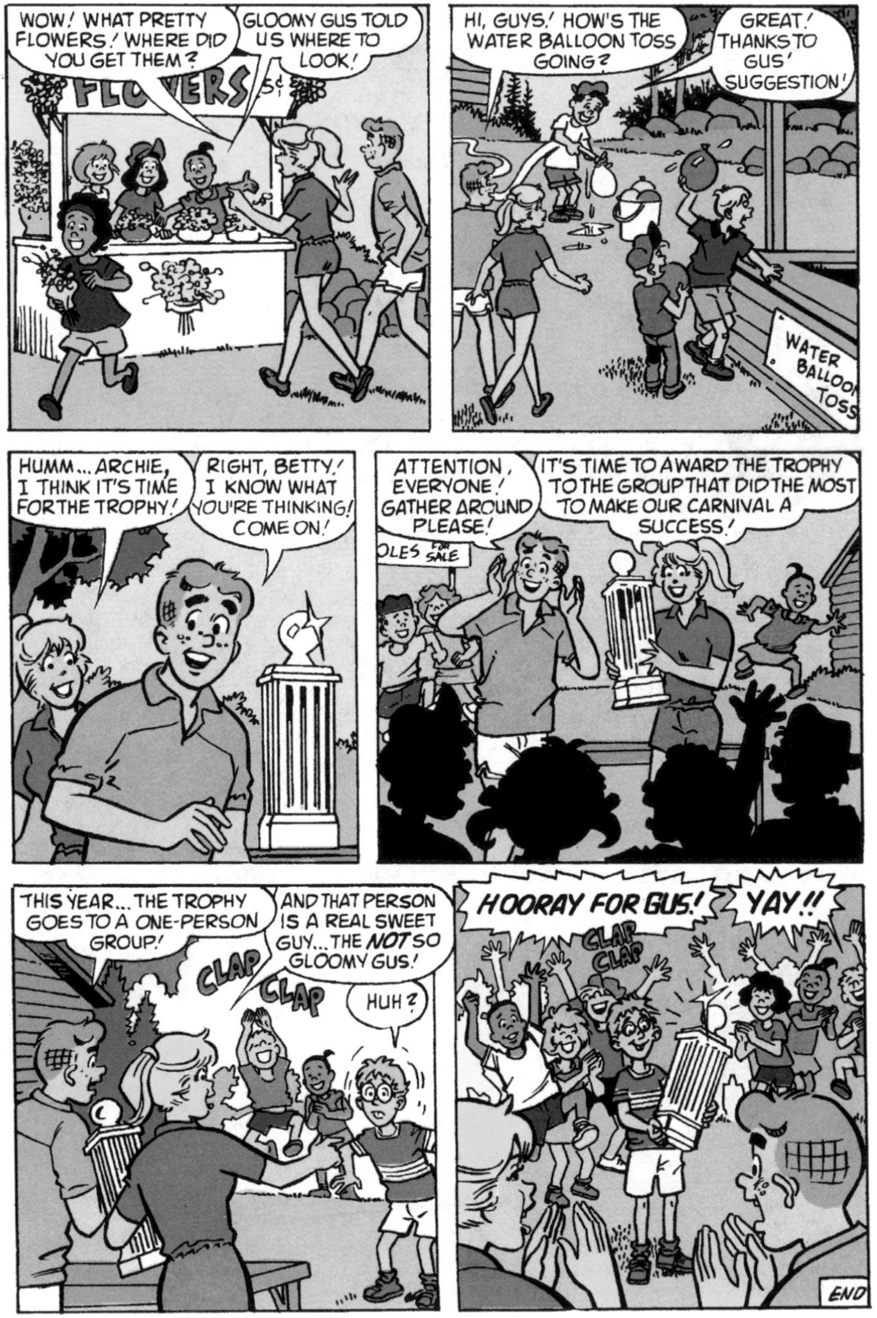
WOW! WHAT PRETTY FLOWERS! WHERE DID YOU GET THEM?
GLOOMY GUS TOLD US WHERE TO LOOK!
FLOWERS 5¢
HI, GUYS! HOW'S THE WATER BALLOON TOSS GOING?
GREAT! THANKS TO GUS' SUGGESTION!
WATER BALLOON TOSS
HUMM... ARCHIE, I THINK IT'S TIME FOR THE TROPHY!
RIGHT, BETTY! I KNOW WHAT YOU'RE THINKING! COME ON!
ATTENTION, EVERYONE! GATHER AROUND PLEASE!
IT'S TIME TO AWARD THE TROPHY TO THE GROUP THAT DID THE MOST TO MAKE OUR CARNIVAL A SUCCESS!
FOR SALE
THIS YEAR... THE TROPHY GOES TO A ONE-PERSON GROUP!
AND THAT PERSON IS A REAL SWEET GUY... THE NOT SO GLOOMY GUS!
CLAP
CLAP
HUH?
HOORAY FOR GUS!
YAY!!
CLAP
CLAP
END

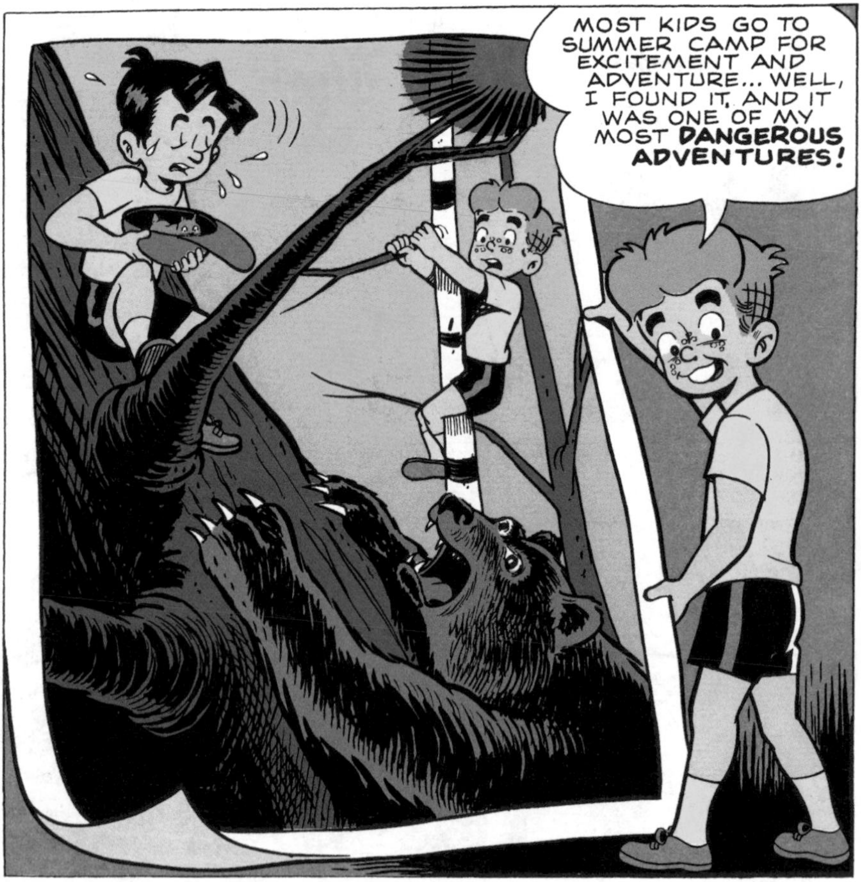
MOST KIDS GO TO SUMMER CAMP FOR EXCITEMENT AND ADVENTURE... WELL, I FOUND IT, AND IT WAS ONE OF MY MOST DANGEROUS ADVENTURES!

Little Archie in "GRIZZLY"

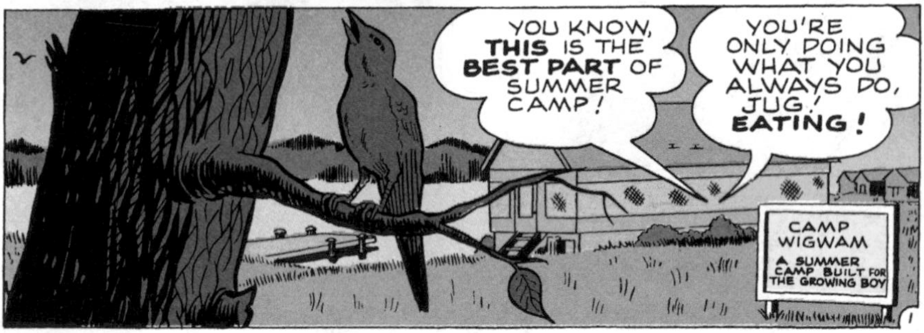
YOU KNOW, THIS IS THE BEST PART OF SUMMER CAMP!
YOU'RE ONLY DOING WHAT YOU ALWAYS DO, JUG! EATING!
CAMP WIGWAM
A SUMMER CAMP BUILT FOR THE GROWING BOY

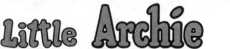

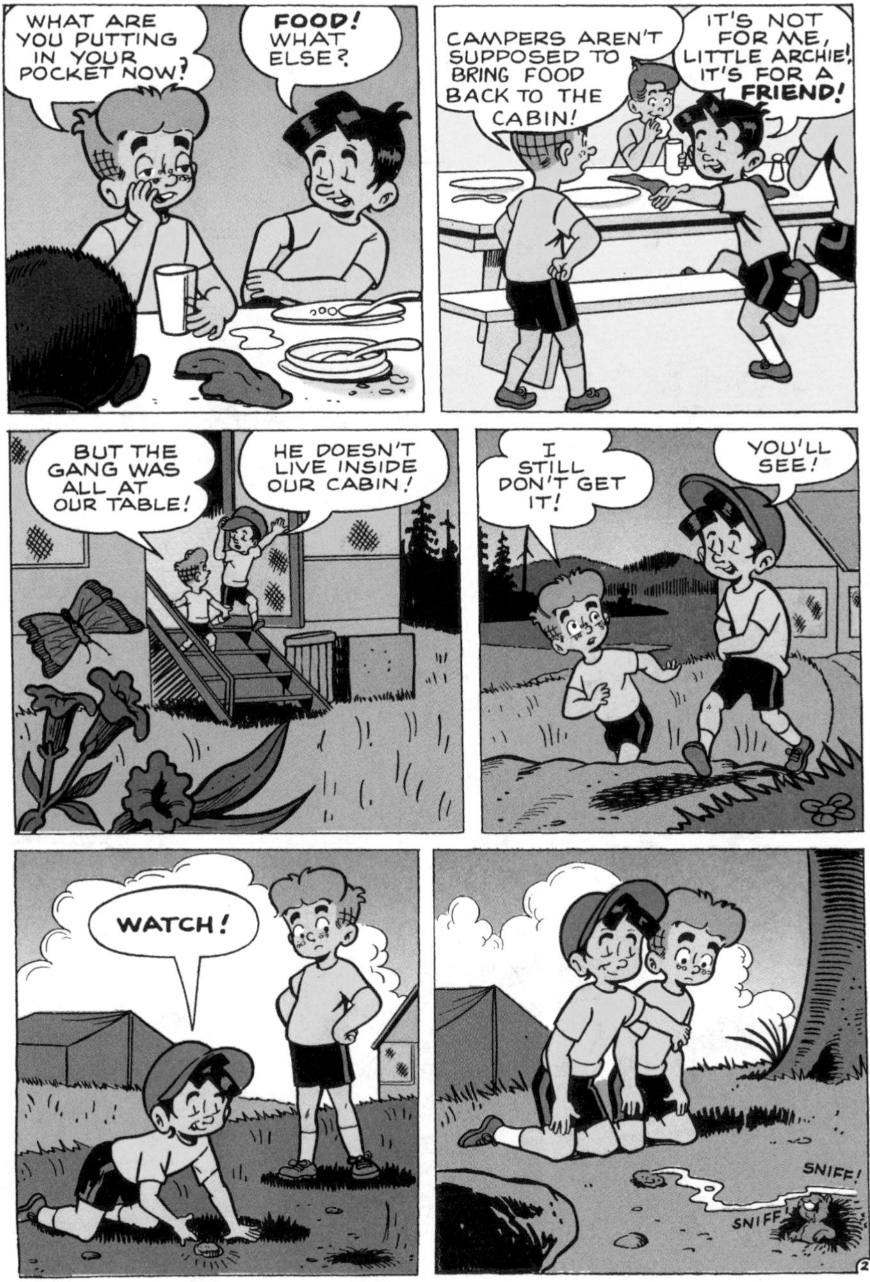
WHAT ARE YOU PUTTING IN YOUR POCKET NOW?
FOOD! WHAT ELSE?
CAMPERS AREN'T SUPPOSED TO BRING FOOD BACK TO THE CABIN!
IT'S NOT FOR ME, LITTLE ARCHIE! IT'S FOR A FRIEND!
BUT THE GANG WAS ALL AT OUR TABLE!
HE DOESN'T LIVE INSIDE OUR CABIN!
I STILL DON'T GET IT!
YOU'LL SEE!
WATCH!
SNIFF!
SNIFF!

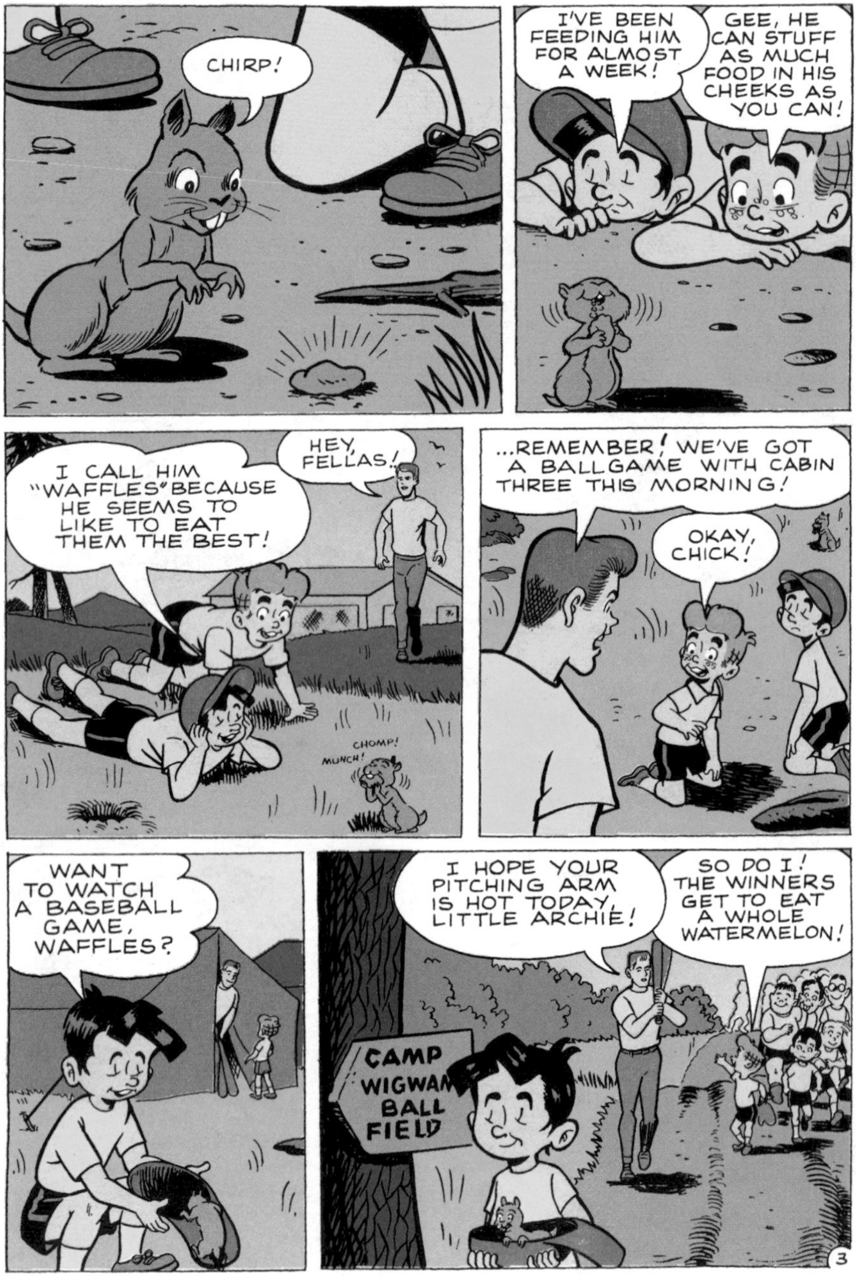
CHIRP!
I'VE BEEN FEEDING HIM FOR ALMOST A WEEK!
GEE, HE CAN STUFF AS MUCH FOOD IN HIS CHEEKS AS YOU CAN!
I CALL HIM "WAFFLES" BECAUSE HE SEEMS TO LIKE TO EAT THEM THE BEST!
HEY, FELLAS!
CHOMP!
MUNCH!
...REMEMBER! WE'VE GOT A BALLGAME WITH CABIN THREE THIS MORNING!
OKAY, CHICK!
WANT TO WATCH A BASEBALL GAME, WAFFLES?
I HOPE YOUR PITCHING ARM IS HOT TODAY, LITTLE ARCHIE!
SO DO I! THE WINNERS GET TO EAT A WHOLE WATERMELON!
CAMP WIGWAM BALL FIELD

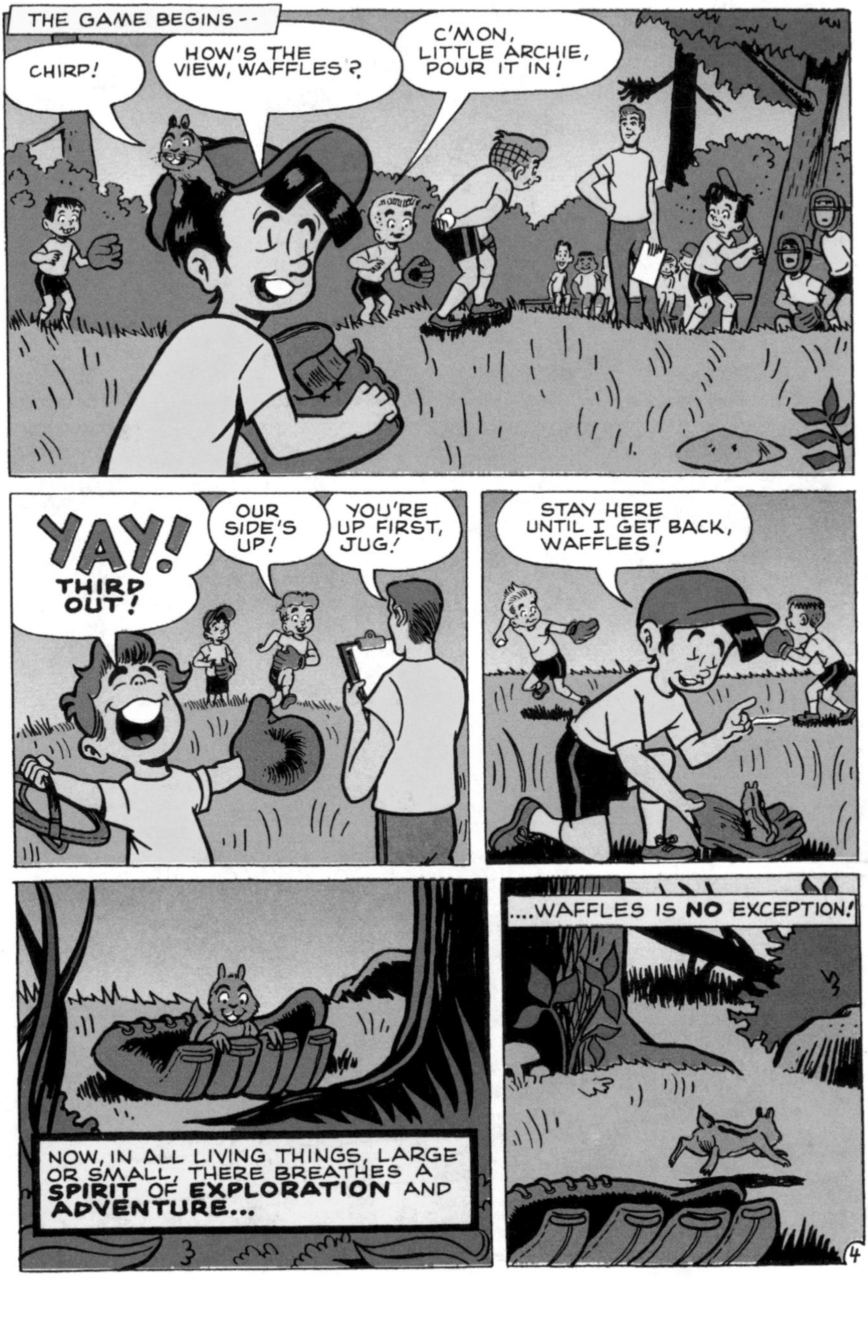
THE GAME BEGINS--
CHIRP!
HOW'S THE VIEW, WAFFLES?
C'MON, LITTLE ARCHIE, POUR IT IN!
YAY! THIRD OUT!
OUR SIDE'S UP!
YOU'RE UP FIRST, JUG!
STAY HERE UNTIL I GET BACK, WAFFLES!
NOW, IN ALL LIVING THINGS, LARGE OR SMALL, THERE BREATHES A SPIRIT OF EXPLORATION AND ADVENTURE...
....WAFFLES IS NO EXCEPTION!
4

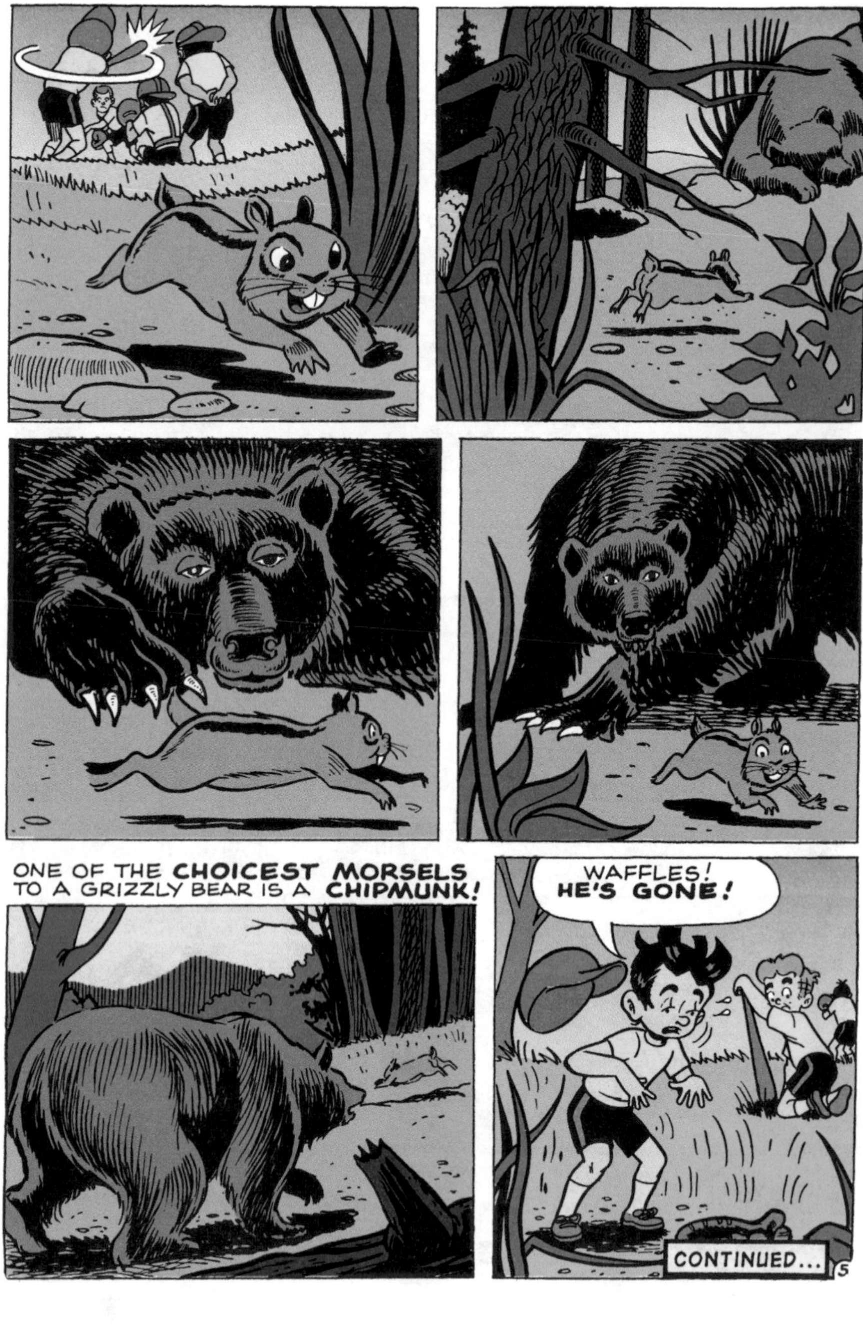
ONE OF THE CHOICEST MORSELS TO A GRIZZLY BEAR IS A CHIPMUNK!
WAFFLES! HE'S GONE!
CONTINUED...

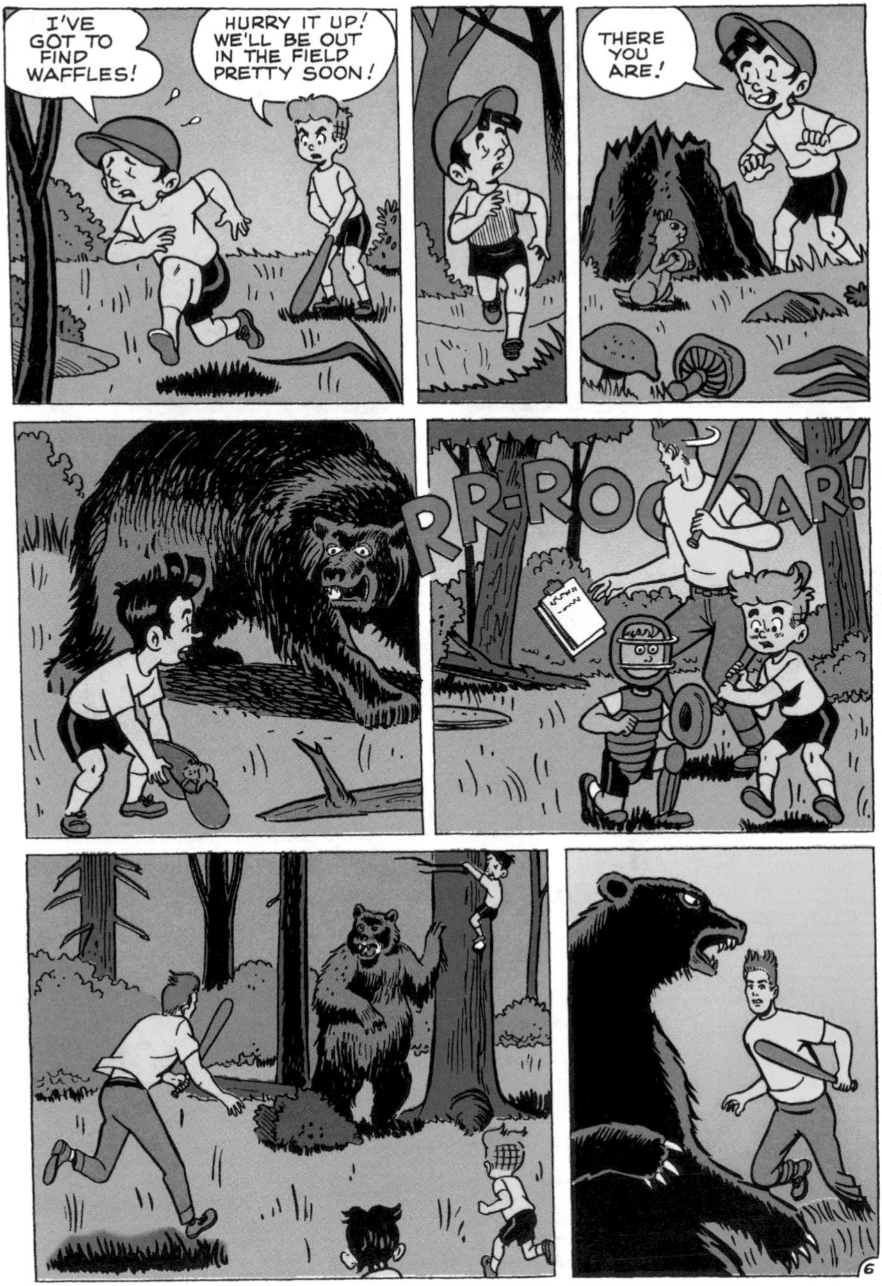
I'VE GOT TO FIND WAFFLES!
HURRY IT UP! WE'LL BE OUT IN THE FIELD PRETTY SOON!
THERE YOU ARE!
RR-ROOOAR!

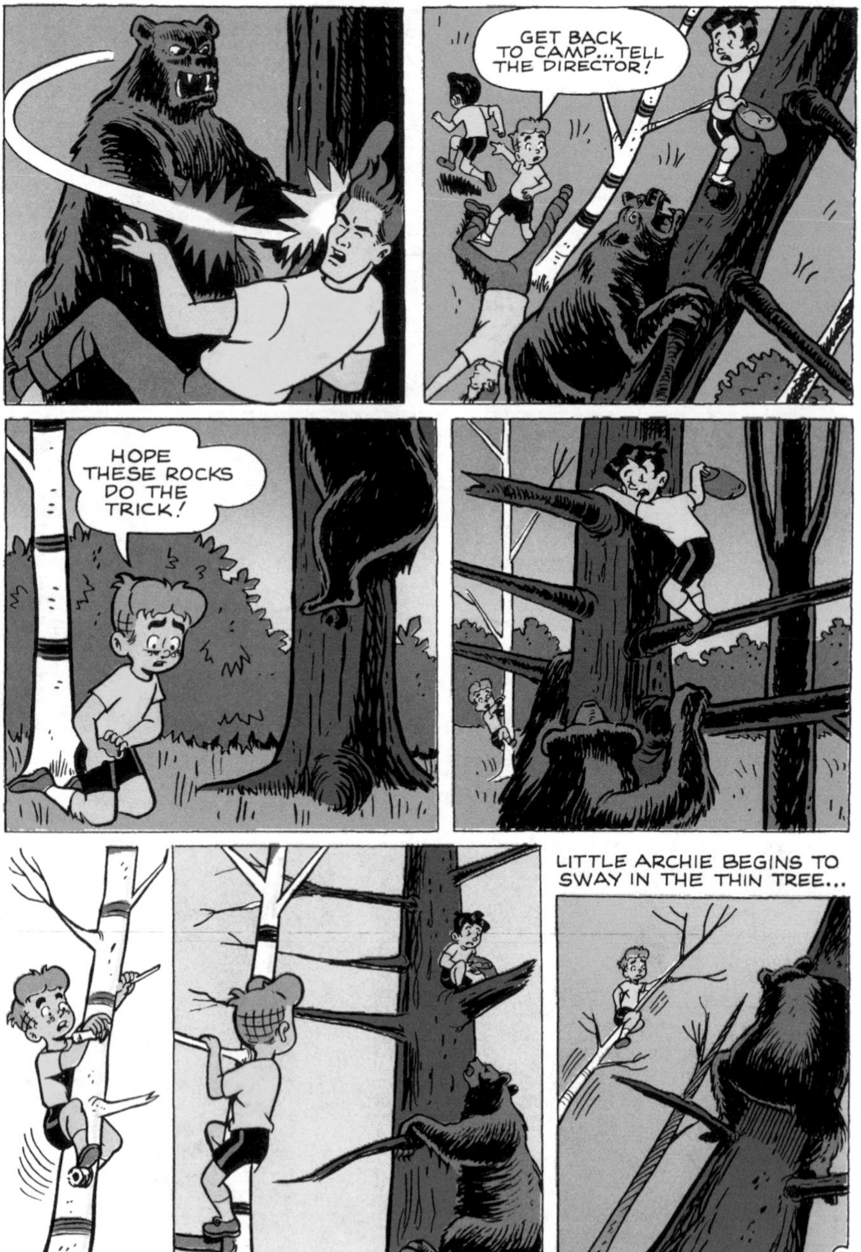
GET BACK TO CAMP...TELL THE DIRECTOR!
HOPE THESE ROCKS DO THE TRICK!
LITTLE ARCHIE BEGINS TO SWAY IN THE THIN TREE...

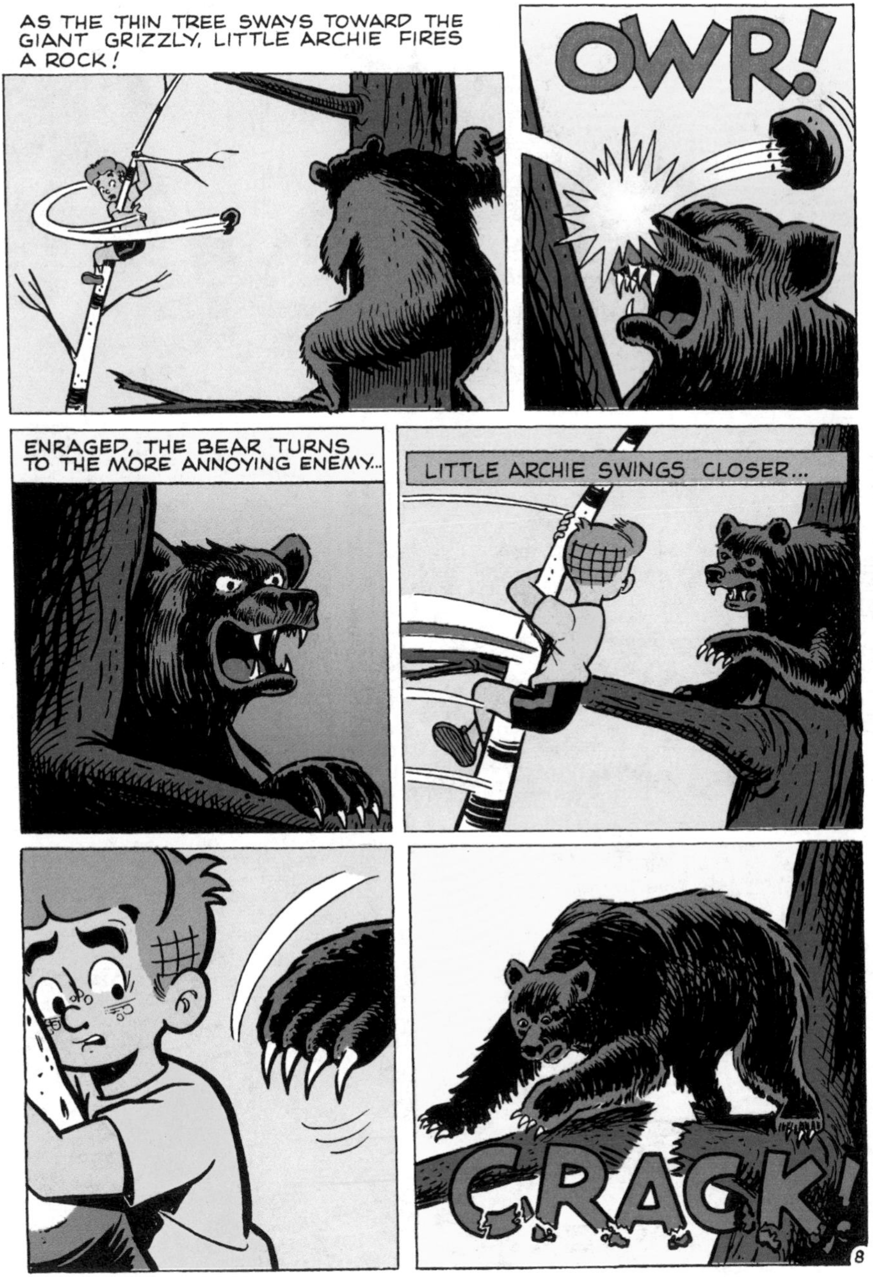
AS THE THIN TREE SWAYS TOWARD THE GIANT GRIZZLY, LITTLE ARCHIE FIRES A ROCK!
OWR!
ENRAGED, THE BEAR TURNS TO THE MORE ANNOYING ENEMY...
LITTLE ARCHIE SWINGS CLOSER...
CRACK!

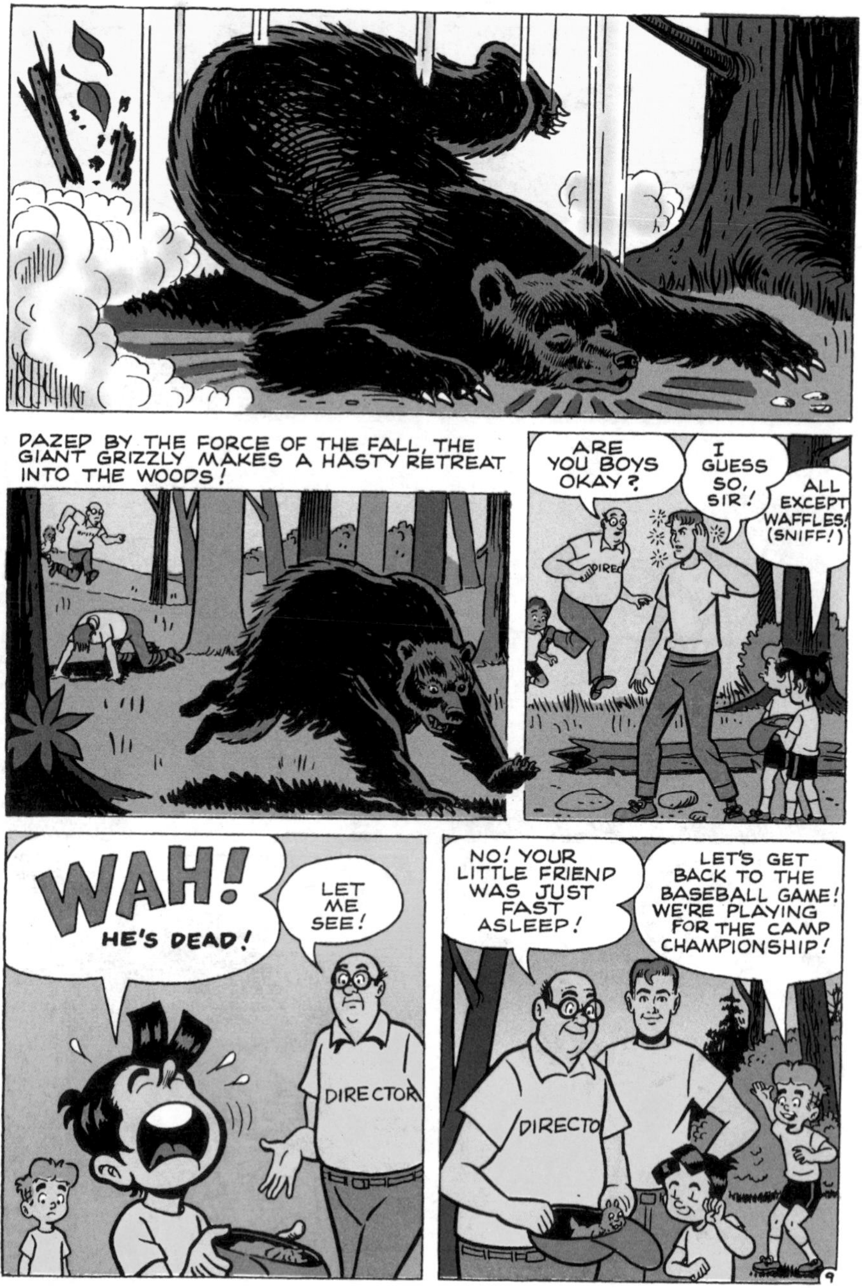

DAZED BY THE FORCE OF THE FALL, THE GIANT GRIZZLY MAKES A HASTY RETREAT INTO THE WOODS!
ARE YOU BOYS OKAY?
I GUESS SO, SIR!
ALL EXCEPT WAFFLES! (SNIFF!)
WAH!
HE'S DEAD!
LET ME SEE!
DIRECTOR
NO! YOUR LITTLE FRIEND WAS JUST FAST ASLEEP!
LET'S GET BACK TO THE BASEBALL GAME! WE'RE PLAYING FOR THE CAMP CHAMPIONSHIP!

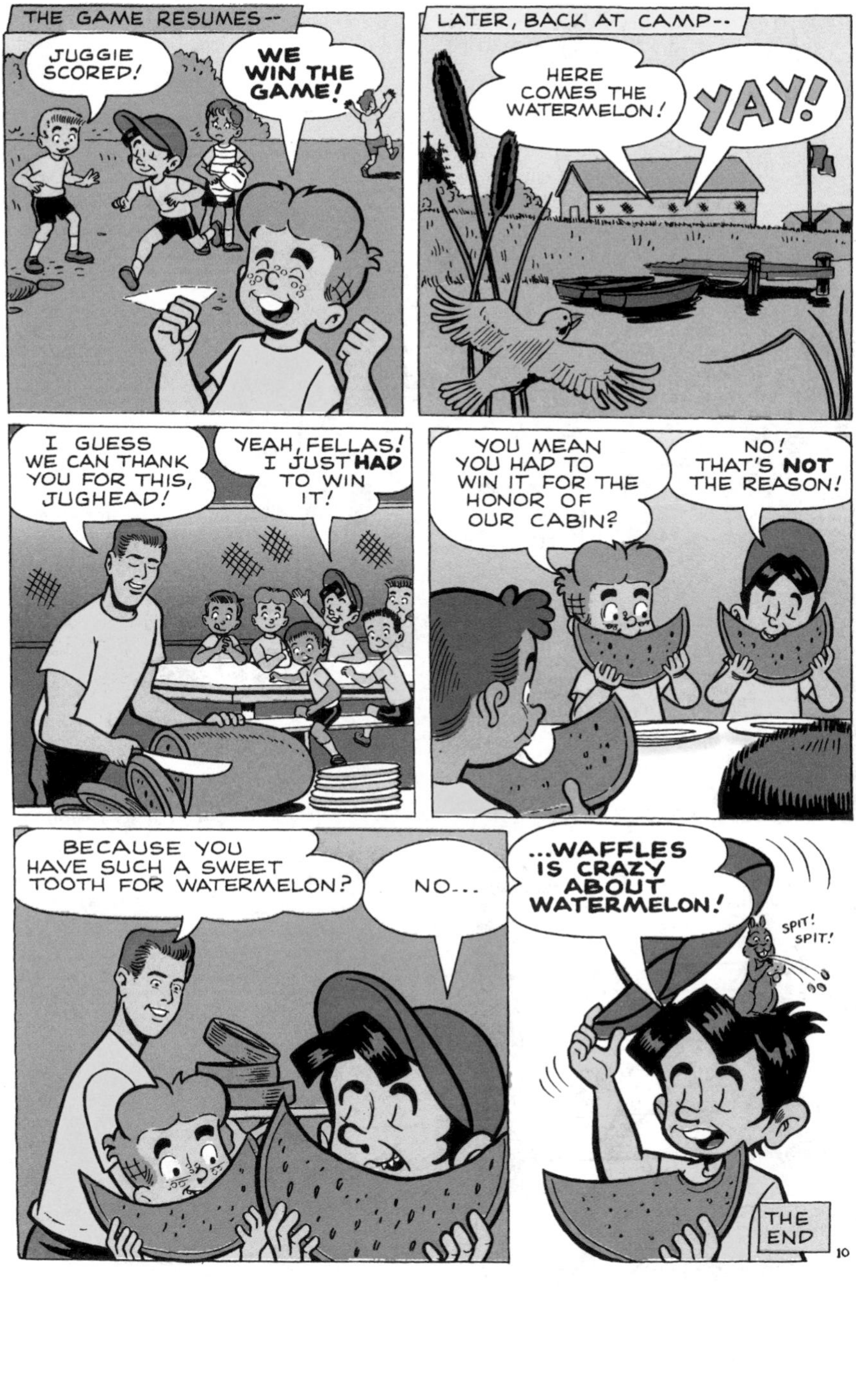
THE GAME RESUMES--
JUGGIE SCORED!
WE WIN THE GAME!
LATER, BACK AT CAMP--
HERE COMES THE WATERMELON!
YAY!
I GUESS WE CAN THANK YOU FOR THIS, JUGHEAD!
YEAH, FELLAS! I JUST HAD TO WIN IT!
YOU MEAN YOU HAD TO WIN IT FOR THE HONOR OF OUR CABIN?
NO! THAT'S NOT THE REASON!
BECAUSE YOU HAVE SUCH A SWEET TOOTH FOR WATERMELON?
NO...
...WAFFLES IS CRAZY ABOUT WATERMELON!
SPIT! SPIT!
THE END

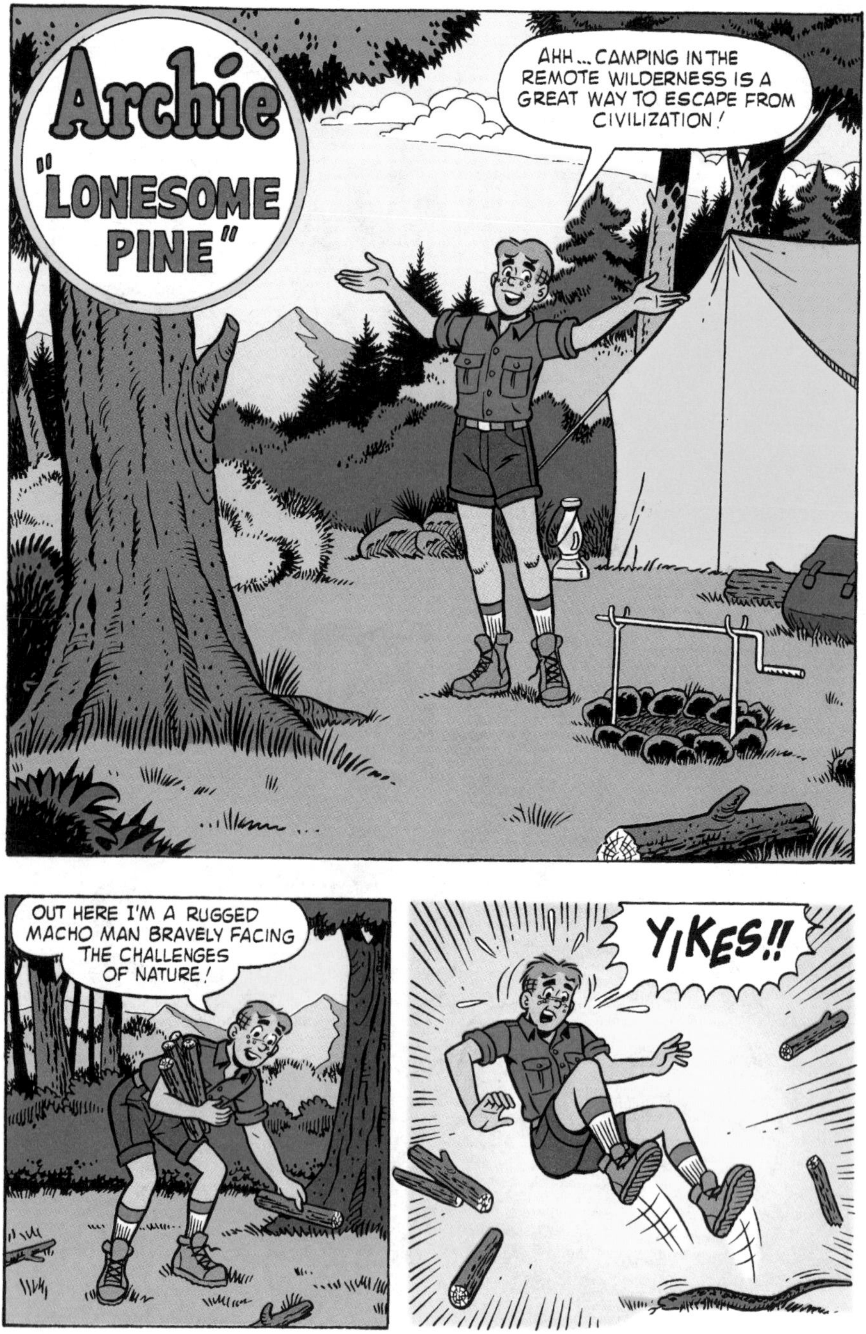
Archie
"LONESOME PINE"
AHH... CAMPING IN THE REMOTE WILDERNESS IS A GREAT WAY TO ESCAPE FROM CIVILIZATION!
OUT HERE I'M A RUGGED MACHO MAN BRAVELY FACING THE CHALLENGES OF NATURE!
YIKES!!

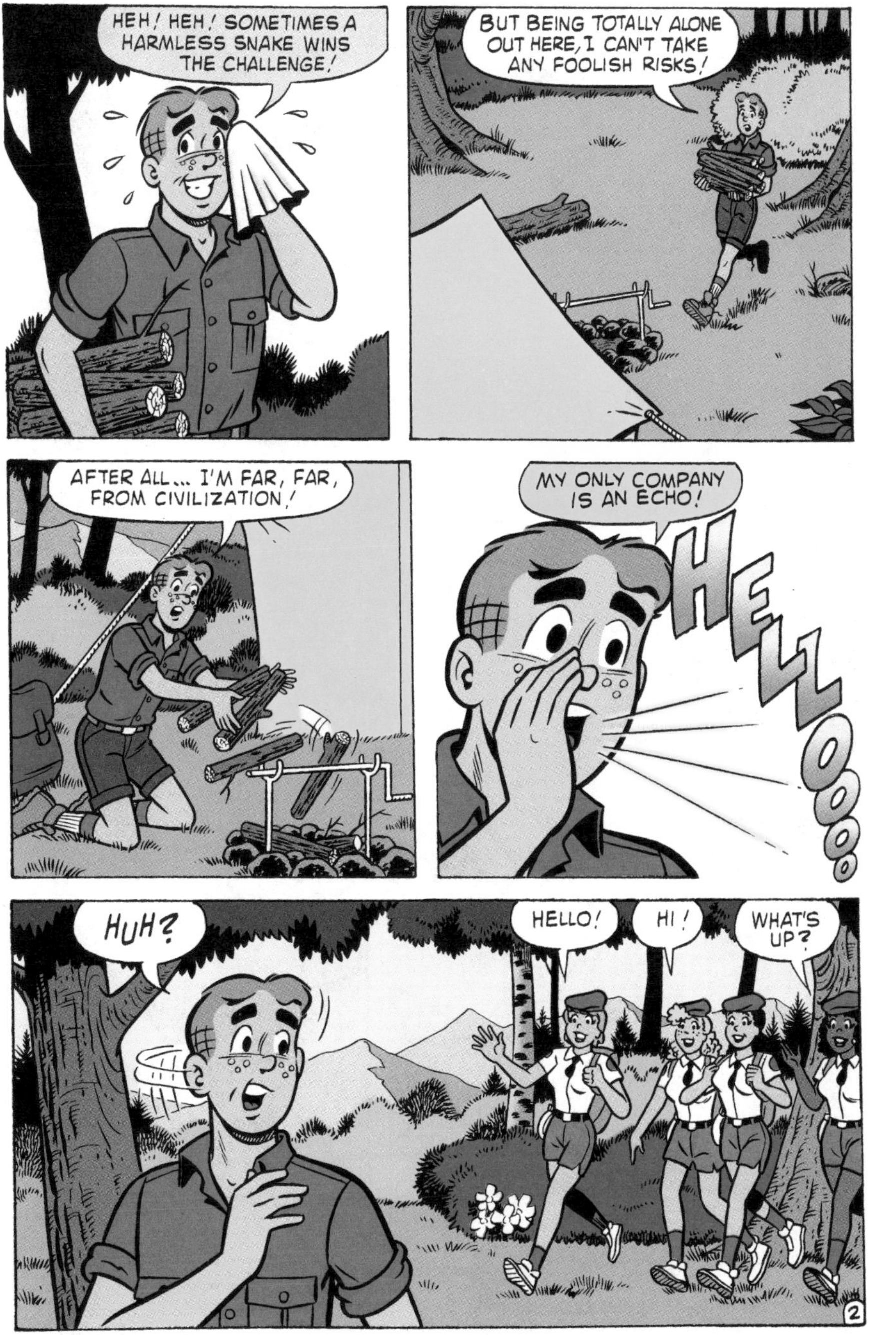
HEH! HEH! SOMETIMES A HARMLESS SNAKE WINS THE CHALLENGE!
BUT BEING TOTALLY ALONE OUT HERE, I CAN'T TAKE ANY FOOLISH RISKS!
AFTER ALL... I'M FAR, FAR, FROM CIVILIZATION!
MY ONLY COMPANY IS AN ECHO!
HELLOOOO
HUH?
HELLO!
HI!
WHAT'S UP?
2

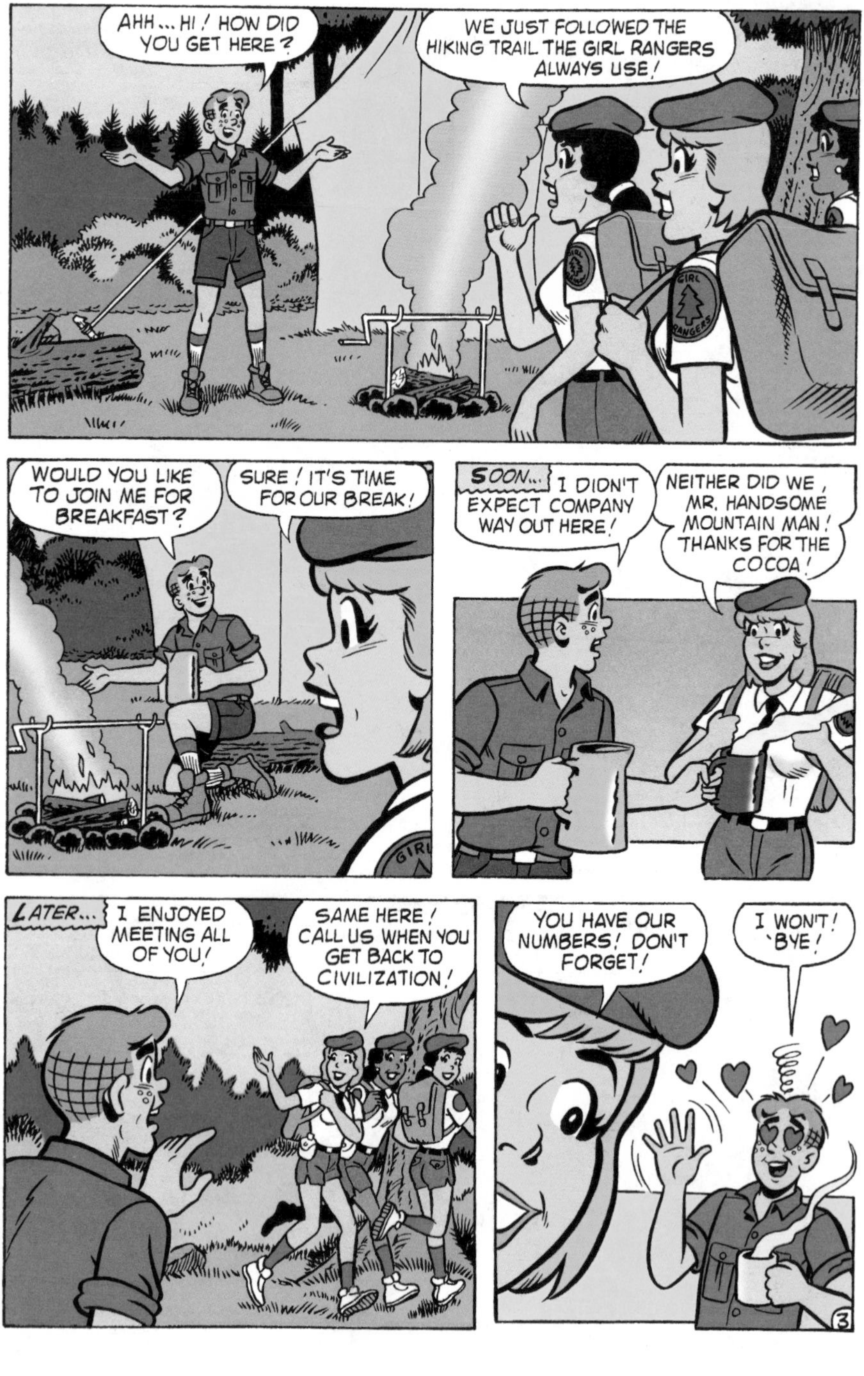
AHH... HI! HOW DID YOU GET HERE?
WE JUST FOLLOWED THE HIKING TRAIL THE GIRL RANGERS ALWAYS USE!
GIRL RANGERS
WOULD YOU LIKE TO JOIN ME FOR BREAKFAST?
SURE! IT'S TIME FOR OUR BREAK!
SOON...
I DIDN'T EXPECT COMPANY WAY OUT HERE!
NEITHER DID WE, MR. HANDSOME MOUNTAIN MAN! THANKS FOR THE COCOA!
LATER...
I ENJOYED MEETING ALL OF YOU!
SAME HERE! CALL US WHEN YOU GET BACK TO CIVILIZATION!
YOU HAVE OUR NUMBERS! DON'T FORGET!
I WON'T! 'BYE!
3

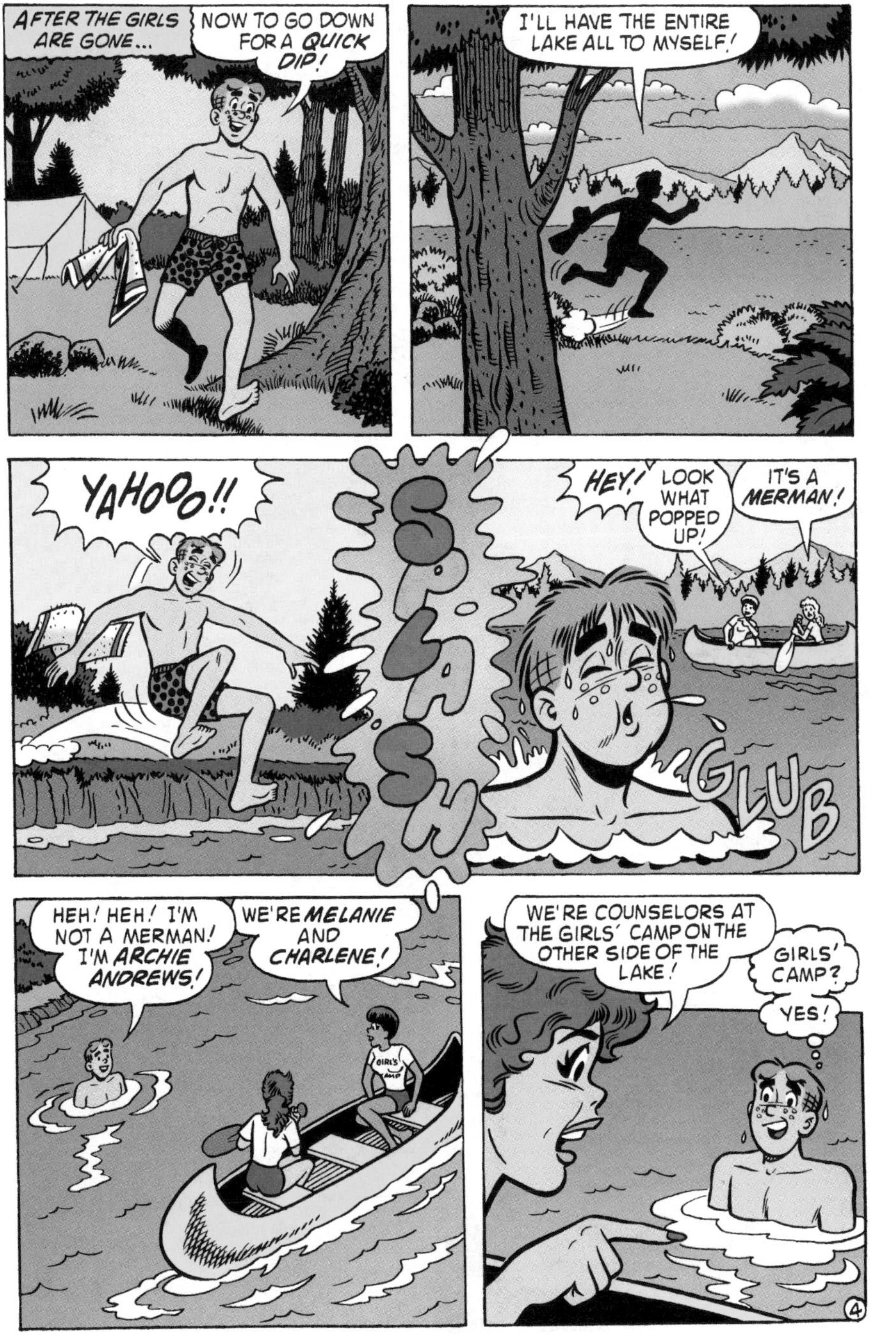
AFTER THE GIRLS ARE GONE...
NOW TO GO DOWN FOR A QUICK DIP!
I'LL HAVE THE ENTIRE LAKE ALL TO MYSELF!
YAHOOO!!
SPLASH
HEY!
LOOK WHAT POPPED UP!
IT'S A MERMAN!
GLUB
HEH! HEH! I'M NOT A MERMAN! I'M ARCHIE ANDREWS!
WE'RE MELANIE AND CHARLENE!
GIRL'S CAMP
WE'RE COUNSELORS AT THE GIRLS' CAMP ON THE OTHER SIDE OF THE LAKE!
GIRLS' CAMP?
YES!
4

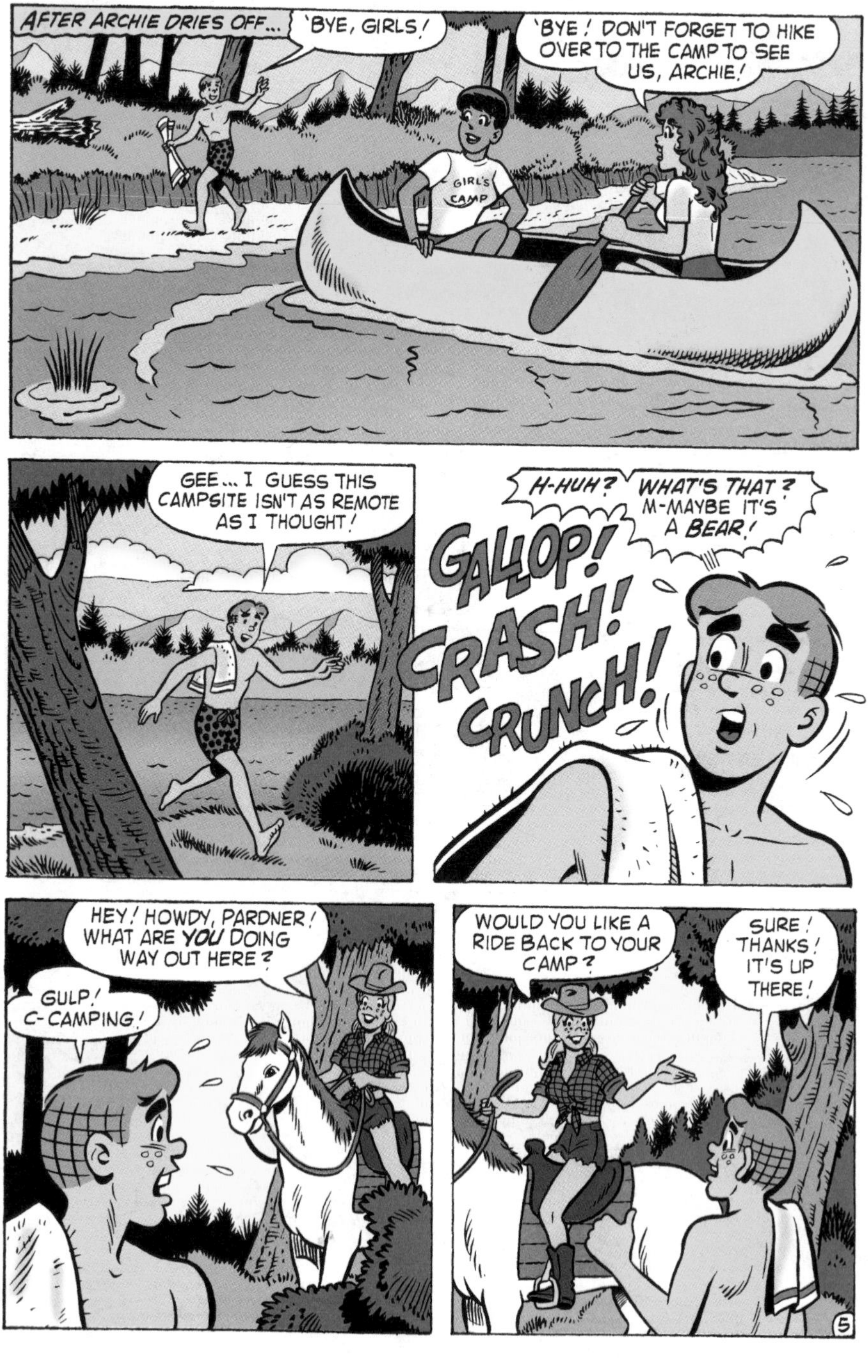

AFTER ARCHIE DRIES OFF...
'BYE, GIRLS!
'BYE! DON'T FORGET TO HIKE OVER TO THE CAMP TO SEE US, ARCHIE!
GIRL'S CAMP
GEE... I GUESS THIS CAMPSITE ISN'T AS REMOTE AS I THOUGHT!
GALLOP! CRASH! CRUNCH!
H-HUH?
WHAT'S THAT? M-MAYBE IT'S A BEAR!
HEY! HOWDY, PARDNER! WHAT ARE YOU DOING WAY OUT HERE?
GULP! C-CAMPING!
WOULD YOU LIKE A RIDE BACK TO YOUR CAMP?
SURE! THANKS! IT'S UP THERE!
5

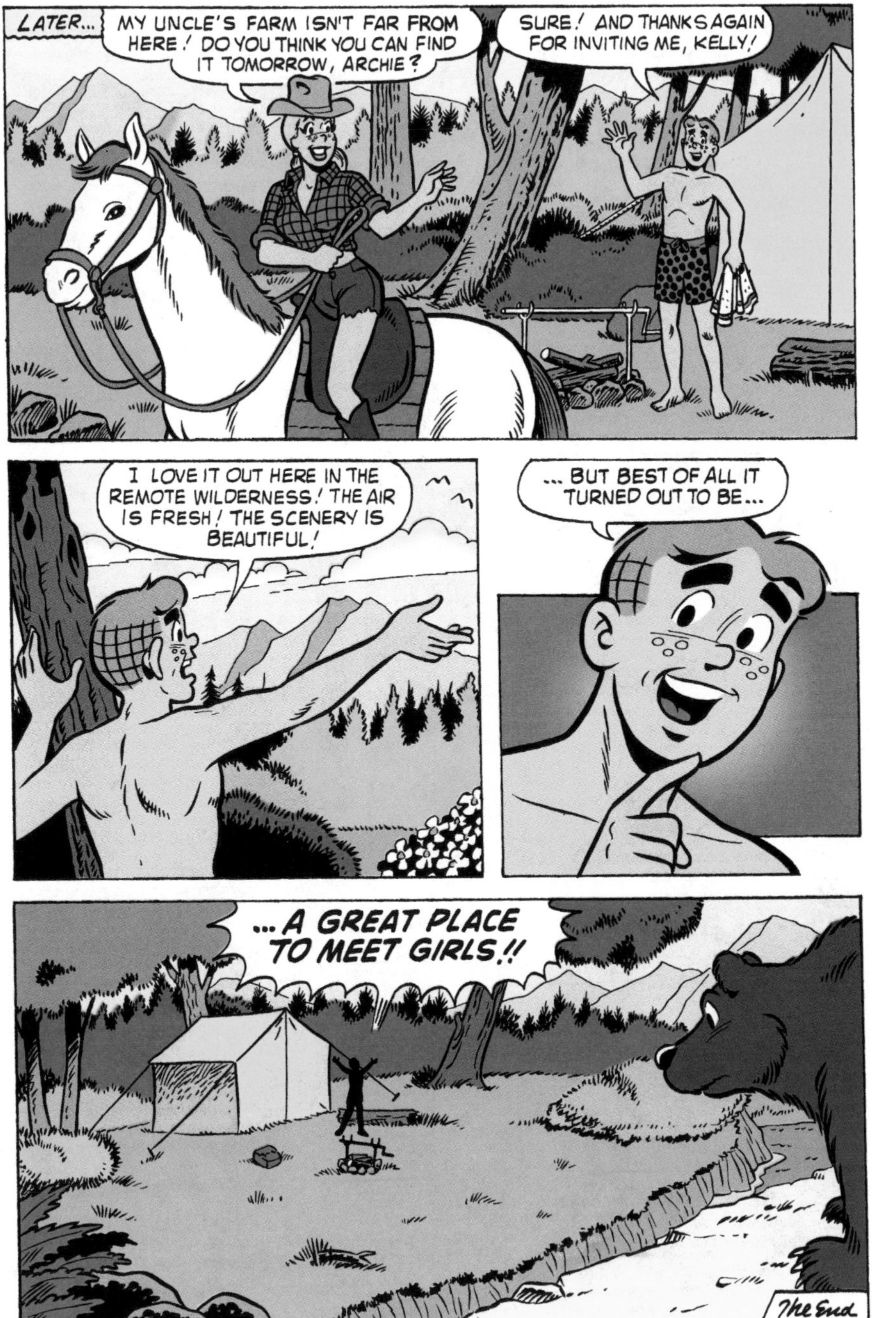
LATER...
MY UNCLE'S FARM ISN'T FAR FROM HERE! DO YOU THINK YOU CAN FIND IT TOMORROW, ARCHIE?
SURE! AND THANKS AGAIN FOR INVITING ME, KELLY!
I LOVE IT OUT HERE IN THE REMOTE WILDERNESS! THE AIR IS FRESH! THE SCENERY IS BEAUTIFUL!
... BUT BEST OF ALL IT TURNED OUT TO BE...
... A GREAT PLACE TO MEET GIRLS!!
The End

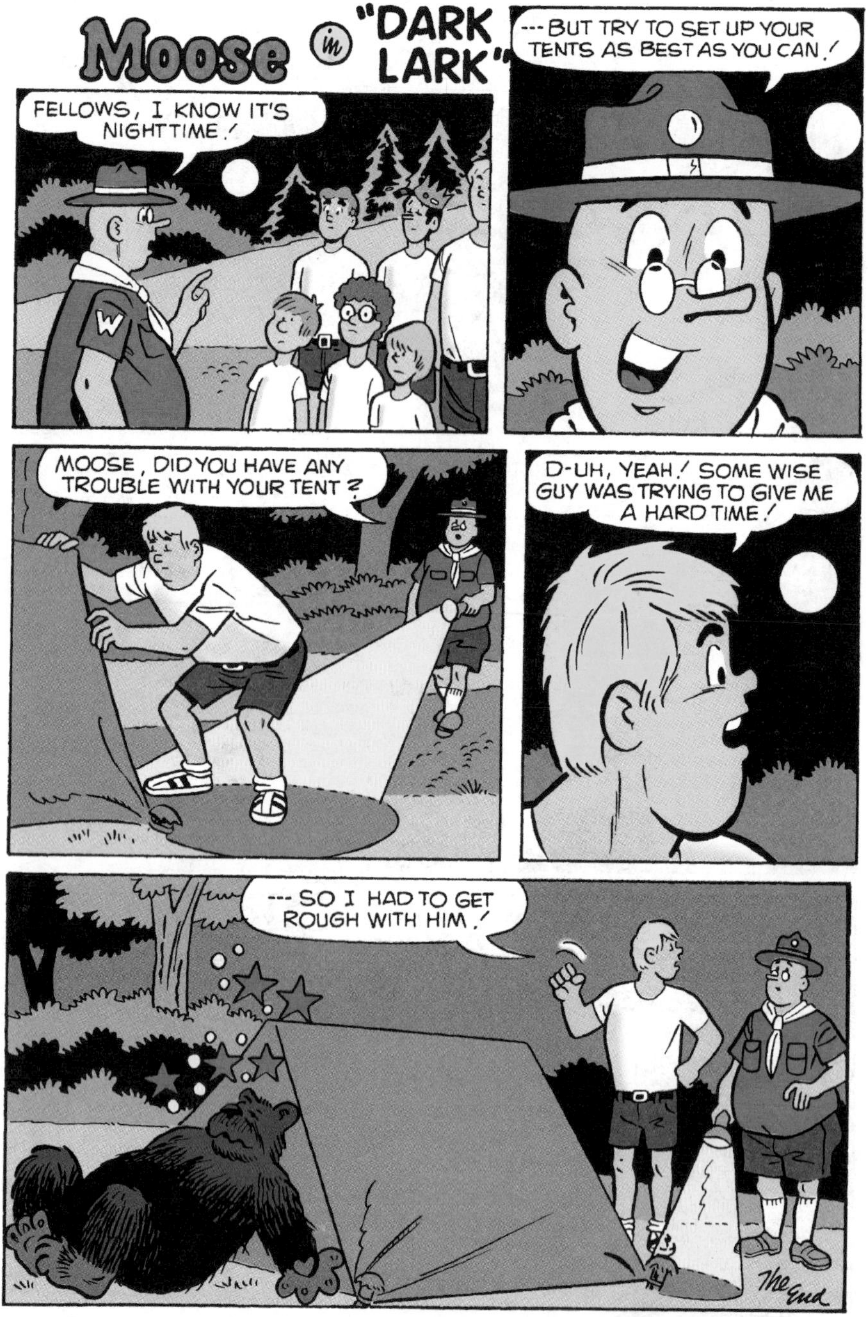
Moose in "DARK LARK"
FELLOWS, I KNOW IT'S NIGHTTIME!
W
--- BUT TRY TO SET UP YOUR TENTS AS BEST AS YOU CAN!
MOOSE, DID YOU HAVE ANY TROUBLE WITH YOUR TENT?
D-UH, YEAH! SOME WISE GUY WAS TRYING TO GIVE ME A HARD TIME!
--- SO I HAD TO GET ROUGH WITH HIM!
The End

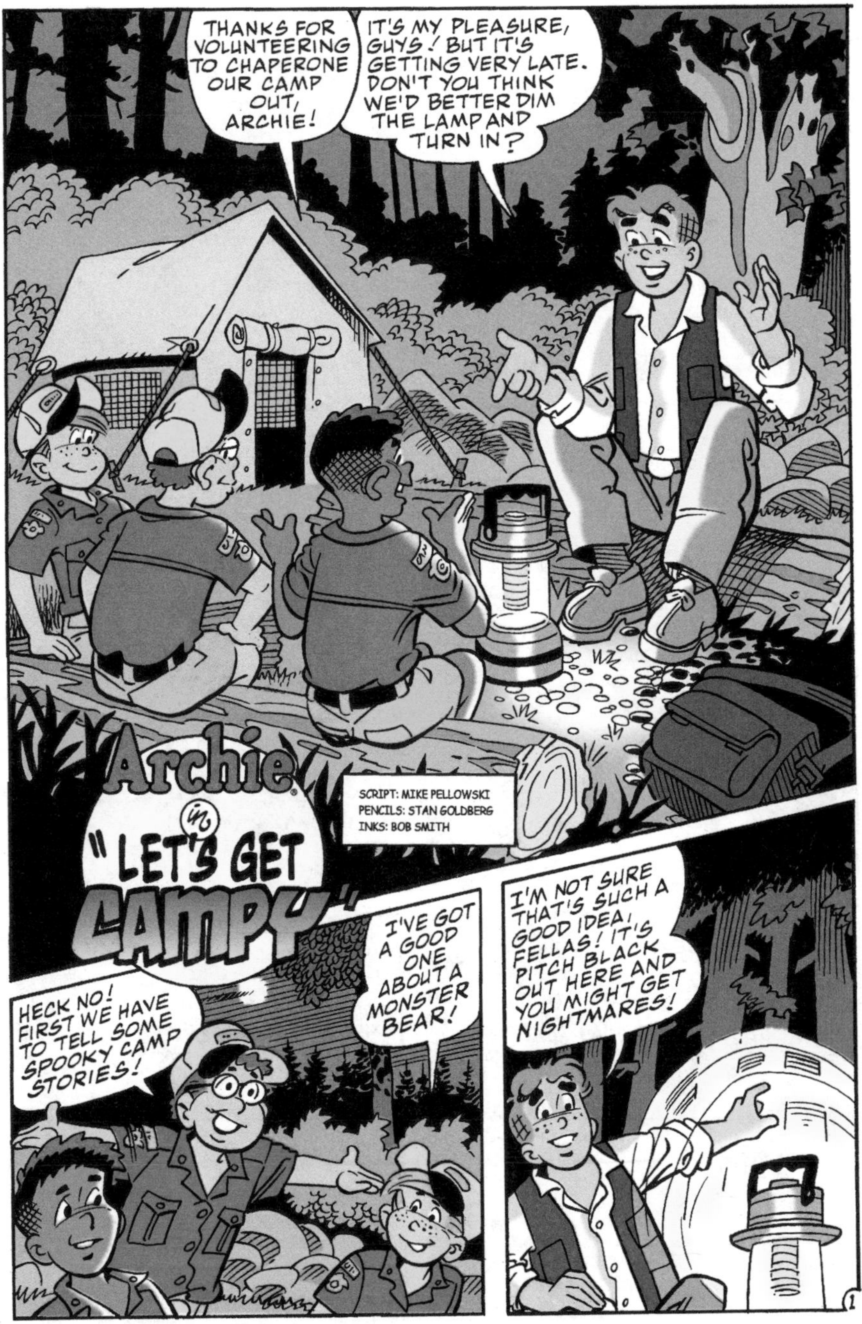

THANKS FOR VOLUNTEERING TO CHAPERONE OUR CAMP OUT, ARCHIE!
IT'S MY PLEASURE, GUYS! BUT IT'S GETTING VERY LATE. DON'T YOU THINK WE'D BETTER DIM THE LAMP AND TURN IN?
Archie® in "LET'S GET CAMPY"
SCRIPT: MIKE PELLOWSKI
PENCILS: STAN GOLDBERG
INKS: BOB SMITH
HECK NO! FIRST WE HAVE TO TELL SOME SPOOKY CAMP STORIES!
I'VE GOT A GOOD ONE ABOUT A MONSTER BEAR!
I'M NOT SURE THAT'S SUCH A GOOD IDEA, FELLAS! IT'S PITCH BLACK OUT HERE AND YOU MIGHT GET NIGHTMARES!
1

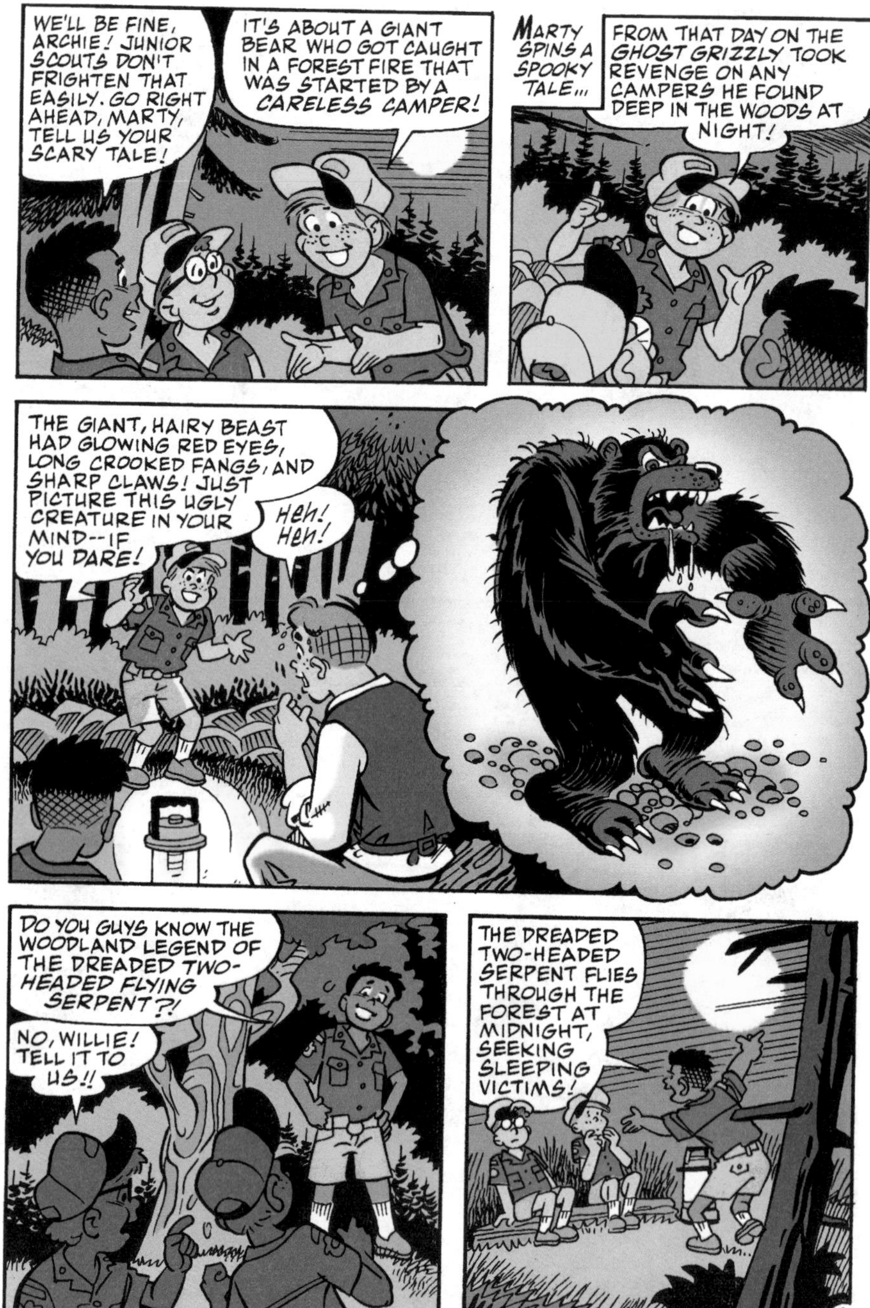

WE'LL BE FINE, ARCHIE! JUNIOR SCOUTS DON'T FRIGHTEN THAT EASILY. GO RIGHT AHEAD, MARTY, TELL US YOUR SCARY TALE!
IT'S ABOUT A GIANT BEAR WHO GOT CAUGHT IN A FOREST FIRE THAT WAS STARTED BY A CARELESS CAMPER!
MARTY SPINS A SPOOKY TALE...
FROM THAT DAY ON THE GHOST GRIZZLY TOOK REVENGE ON ANY CAMPERS HE FOUND DEEP IN THE WOODS AT NIGHT!
THE GIANT, HAIRY BEAST HAD GLOWING RED EYES, LONG CROOKED FANGS, AND SHARP CLAWS! JUST PICTURE THIS UGLY CREATURE IN YOUR MIND--IF YOU DARE!
Heh! Heh!
DO YOU GUYS KNOW THE WOODLAND LEGEND OF THE DREADED TWO-HEADED FLYING SERPENT?!
NO, WILLIE! TELL IT TO US!!
THE DREADED TWO-HEADED SERPENT FLIES THROUGH THE FOREST AT MIDNIGHT, SEEKING SLEEPING VICTIMS!
2

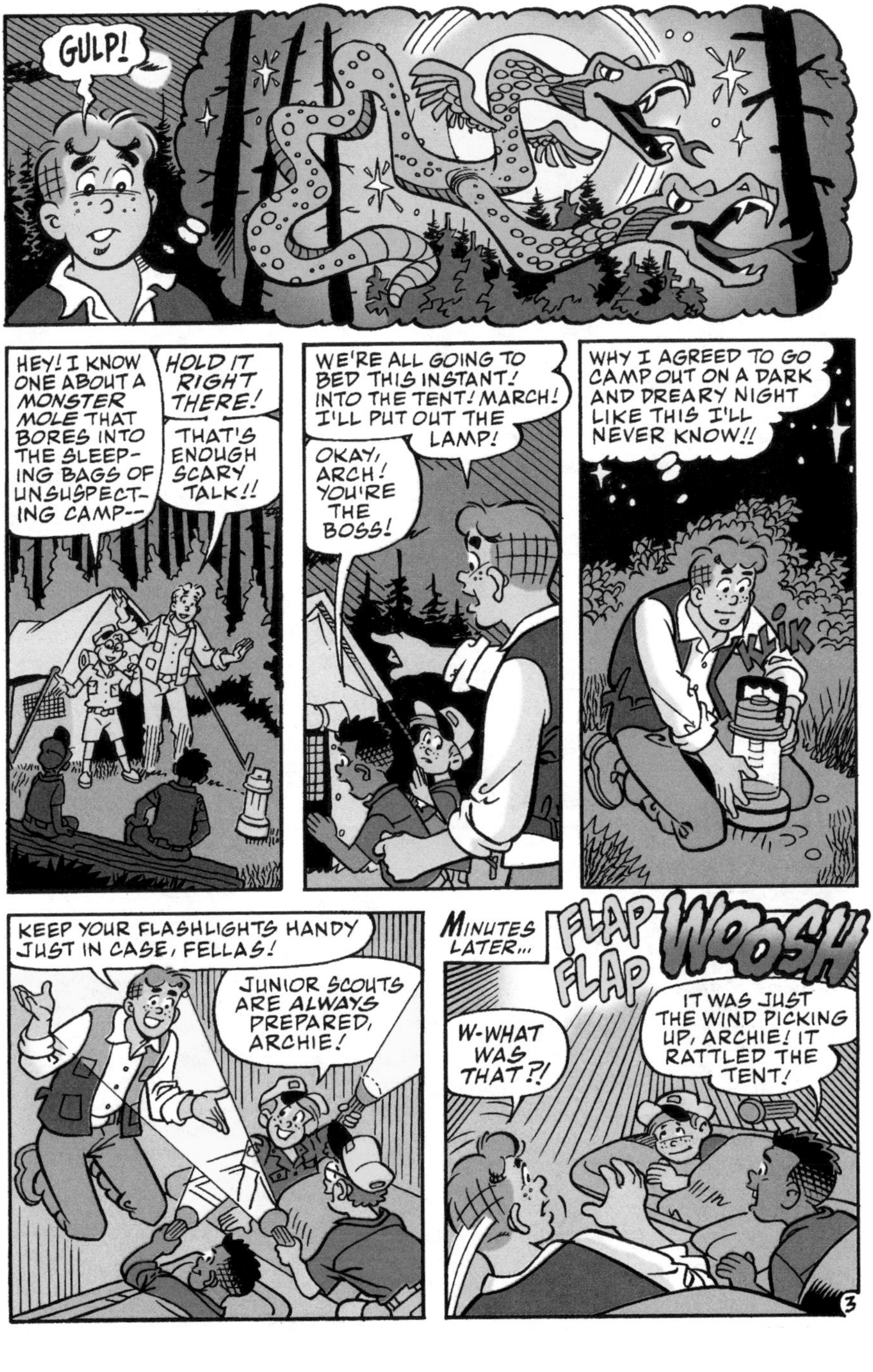
GULP!
HEY! I KNOW ONE ABOUT A MONSTER MOLE THAT BORES INTO THE SLEEPING BAGS OF UNSUSPECTING CAMP--
HOLD IT RIGHT THERE!
THAT'S ENOUGH SCARY TALK!!
WE'RE ALL GOING TO BED THIS INSTANT! INTO THE TENT! MARCH! I'LL PUT OUT THE LAMP!
OKAY, ARCH! YOU'RE THE BOSS!
WHY I AGREED TO GO CAMP OUT ON A DARK AND DREARY NIGHT LIKE THIS I'LL NEVER KNOW!!
KLIK
KEEP YOUR FLASHLIGHTS HANDY JUST IN CASE, FELLAS!
JUNIOR SCOUTS ARE ALWAYS PREPARED, ARCHIE!
MINUTES LATER...
FLAP FLAP
WOOSH
W-WHAT WAS THAT?!
IT WAS JUST THE WIND PICKING UP, ARCHIE! IT RATTLED THE TENT!
3

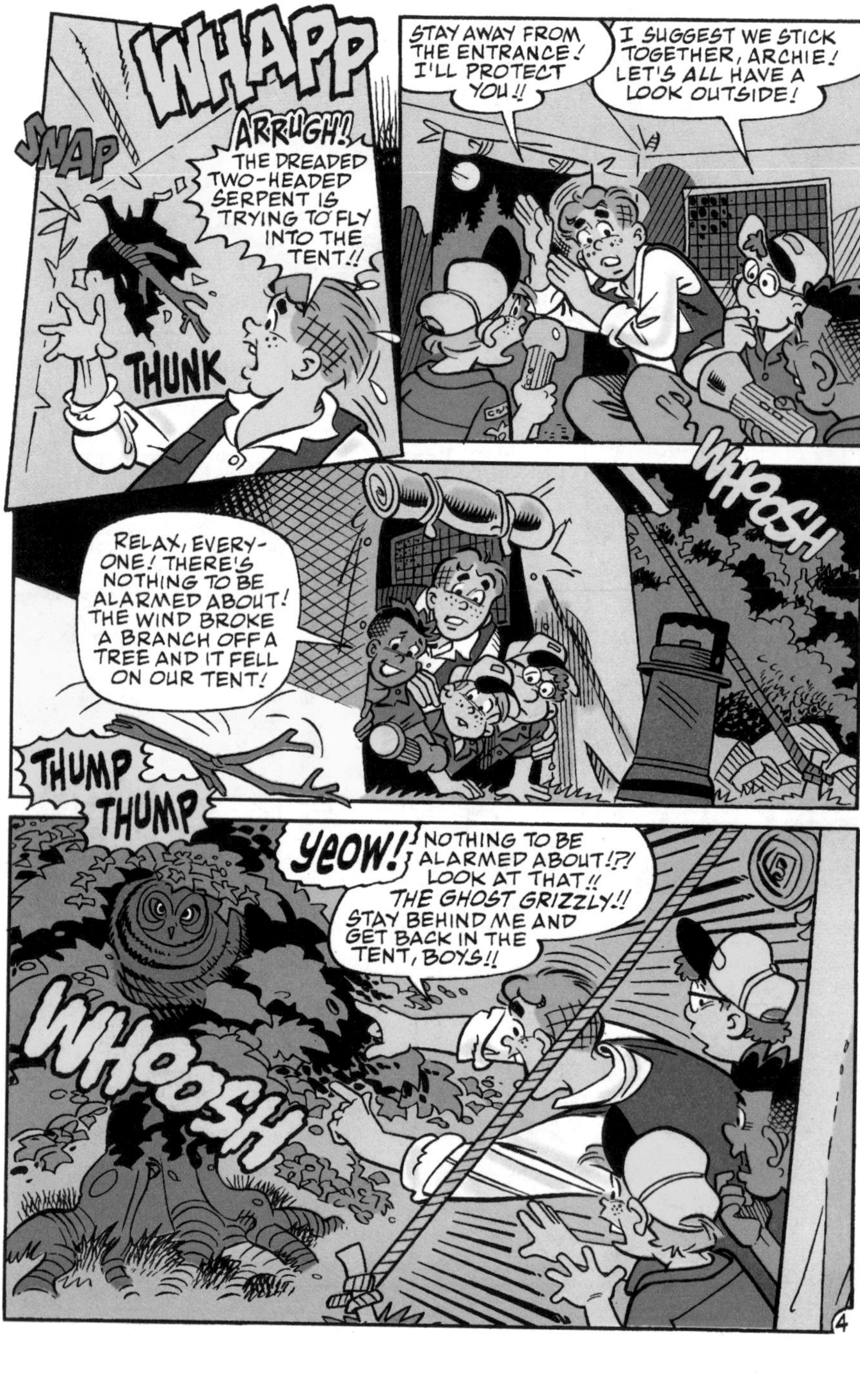

WHAPP
SNAP
ARRUGH!! THE DREADED TWO-HEADED SERPENT IS TRYING TO FLY INTO THE TENT!!
THUNK
STAY AWAY FROM THE ENTRANCE! I'LL PROTECT YOU!!
I SUGGEST WE STICK TOGETHER, ARCHIE! LET'S ALL HAVE A LOOK OUTSIDE!
WHOOSH
RELAX, EVERY-ONE! THERE'S NOTHING TO BE ALARMED ABOUT! THE WIND BROKE A BRANCH OFF A TREE AND IT FELL ON OUR TENT!
THUMP
THUMP
YEOW! NOTHING TO BE ALARMED ABOUT!?! LOOK AT THAT!! THE GHOST GRIZZLY!! STAY BEHIND ME AND GET BACK IN THE TENT, BOYS!!
WHOOSH

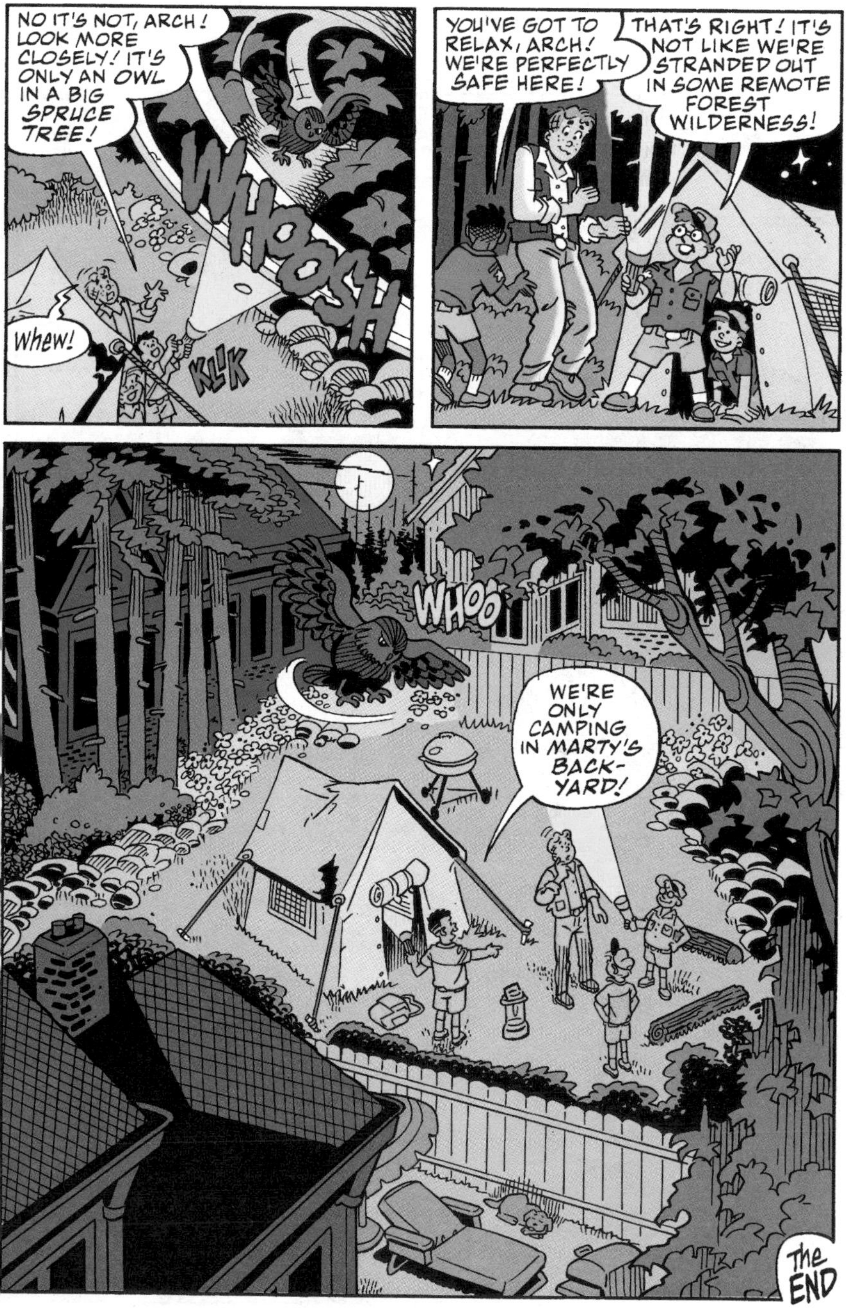
NO IT'S NOT, ARCH! LOOK MORE CLOSELY! IT'S ONLY AN OWL IN A BIG SPRUCE TREE!
WHOOSH
Whew!
KLIK
YOU'VE GOT TO RELAX, ARCH! WE'RE PERFECTLY SAFE HERE!
THAT'S RIGHT! IT'S NOT LIKE WE'RE STRANDED OUT IN SOME REMOTE FOREST WILDERNESS!
WHOO
WE'RE ONLY CAMPING IN MARTY'S BACK-YARD!
The END

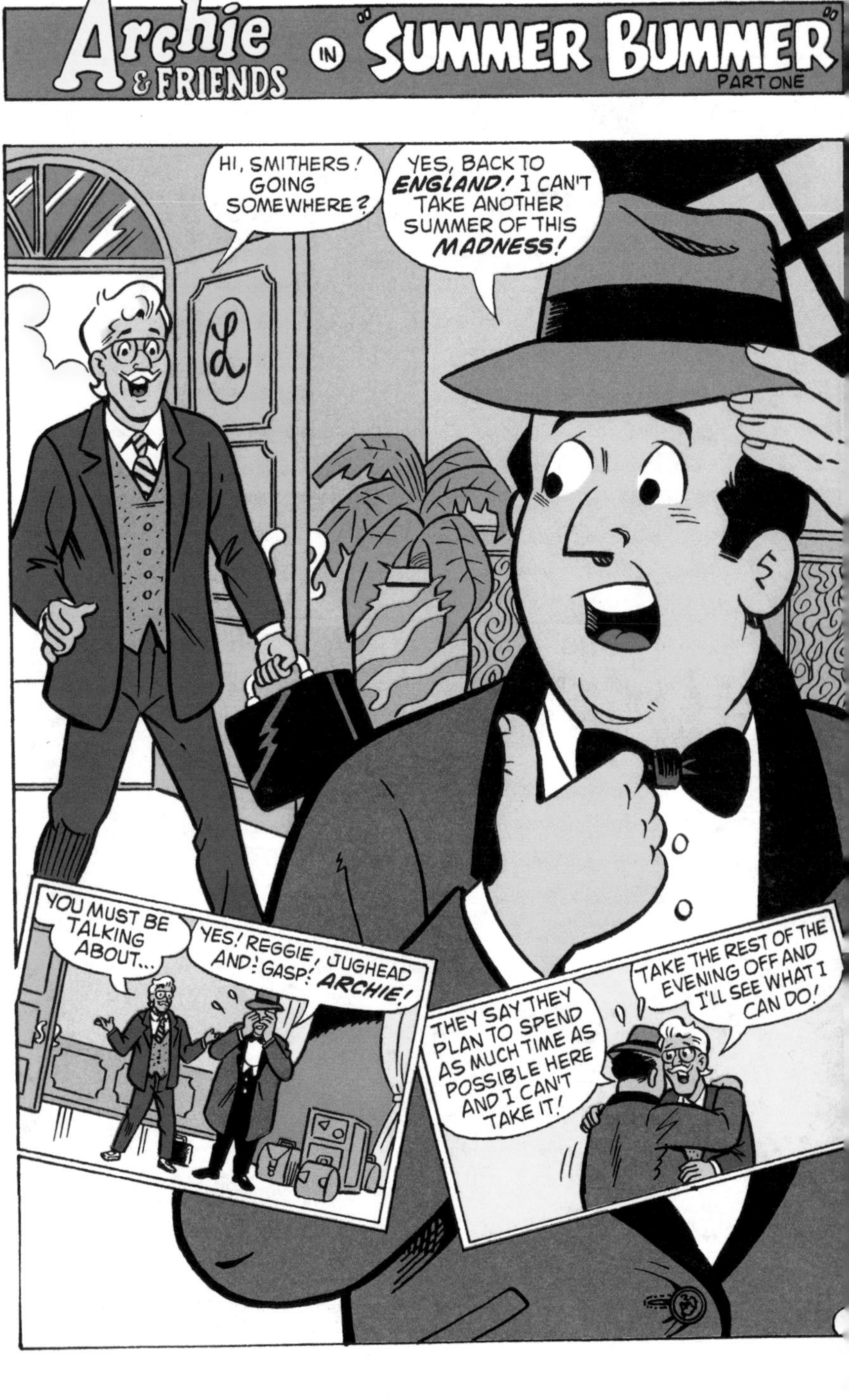
Archie & FRIENDS
IN "SUMMER BUMMER"
PART ONE
HI, SMITHERS! GOING SOMEWHERE?
YES, BACK TO ENGLAND! I CAN'T TAKE ANOTHER SUMMER OF THIS MADNESS!
YOU MUST BE TALKING ABOUT...
YES! REGGIE, JUGHEAD AND! GASP! ARCHIE!
THEY SAY THEY PLAN TO SPEND AS MUCH TIME AS POSSIBLE HERE AND I CAN'T TAKE IT!
TAKE THE REST OF THE EVENING OFF AND I'LL SEE WHAT I CAN DO!

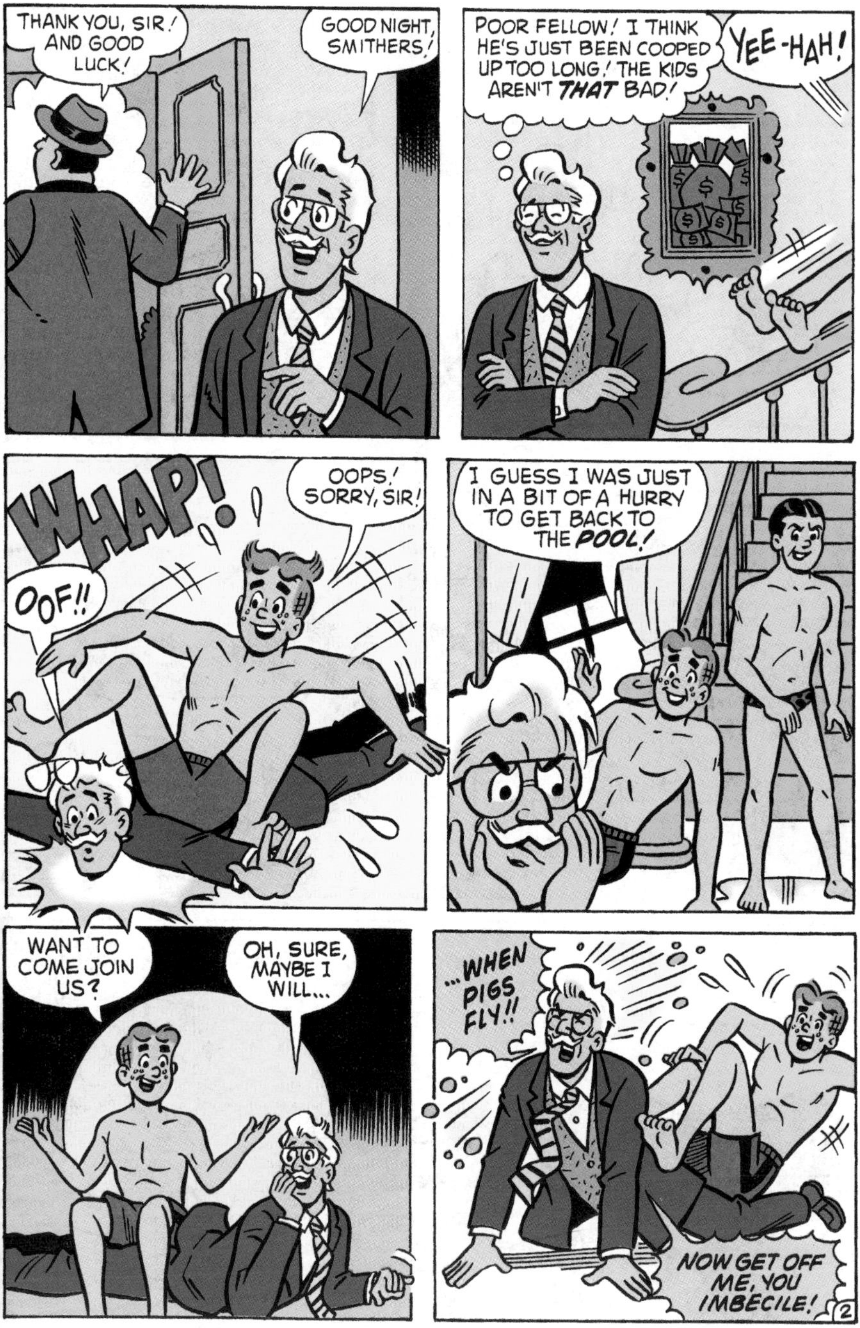

THANK YOU, SIR! AND GOOD LUCK!
GOOD NIGHT, SMITHERS!
POOR FELLOW! I THINK HE'S JUST BEEN COOPED UP TOO LONG! THE KIDS AREN'T THAT BAD!
YEE-HAH!
WHAP!
OOPS! SORRY, SIR!
OOF!!
I GUESS I WAS JUST IN A BIT OF A HURRY TO GET BACK TO THE POOL!
WANT TO COME JOIN US?
OH, SURE, MAYBE I WILL...
...WHEN PIGS FLY!!
NOW GET OFF ME, YOU IMBECILE!
2

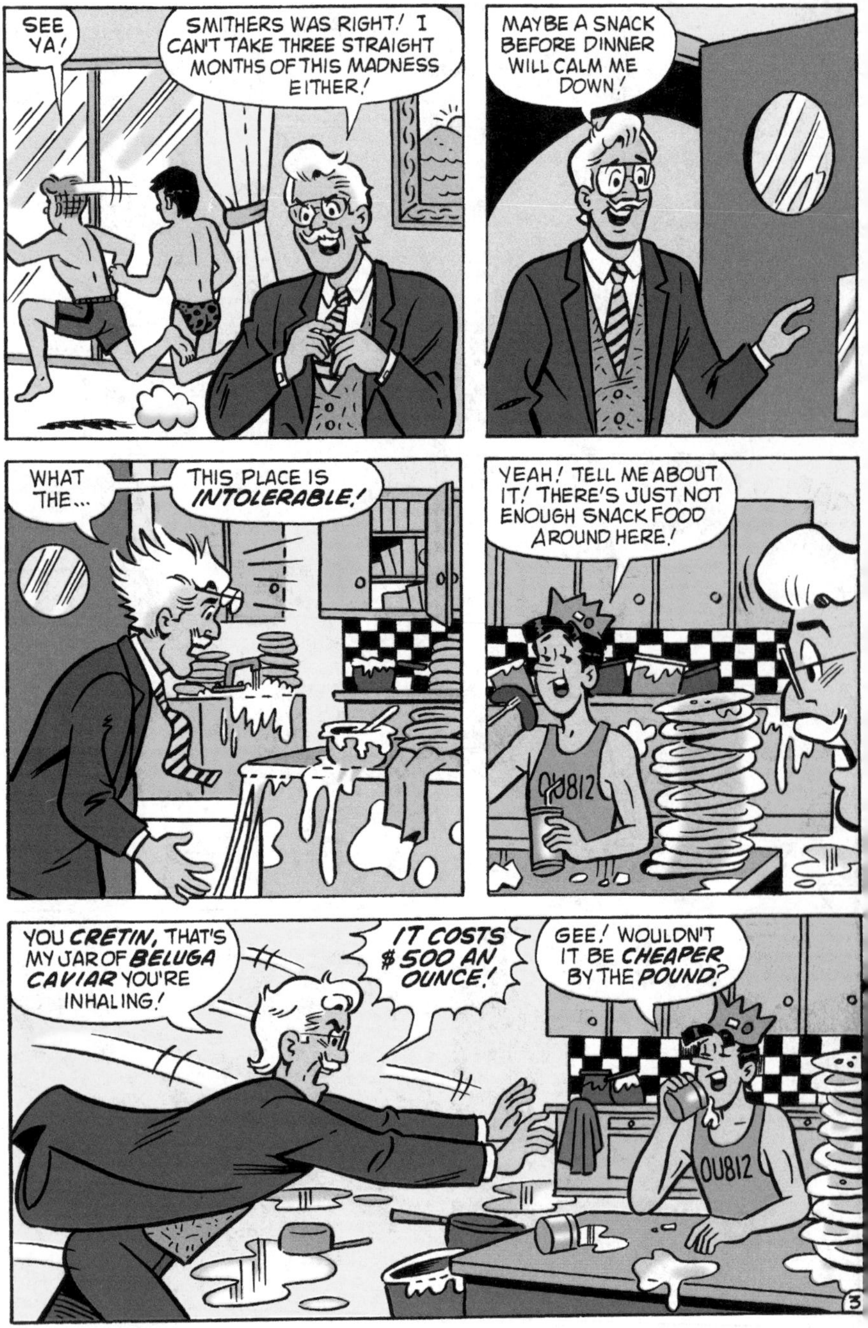

SEE YA!
SMITHERS WAS RIGHT! I CAN'T TAKE THREE STRAIGHT MONTHS OF THIS MADNESS EITHER!
MAYBE A SNACK BEFORE DINNER WILL CALM ME DOWN!
WHAT THE...
THIS PLACE IS *INTOLERABLE!*
YEAH! TELL ME ABOUT IT! THERE'S JUST NOT ENOUGH SNACK FOOD AROUND HERE!
OU812
YOU *CRETIN,* THAT'S MY JAR OF *BELUGA CAVIAR* YOU'RE INHALING!
IT COSTS $500 AN OUNCE!
GEE! WOULDN'T IT BE *CHEAPER* BY THE *POUND?*
OU812
3

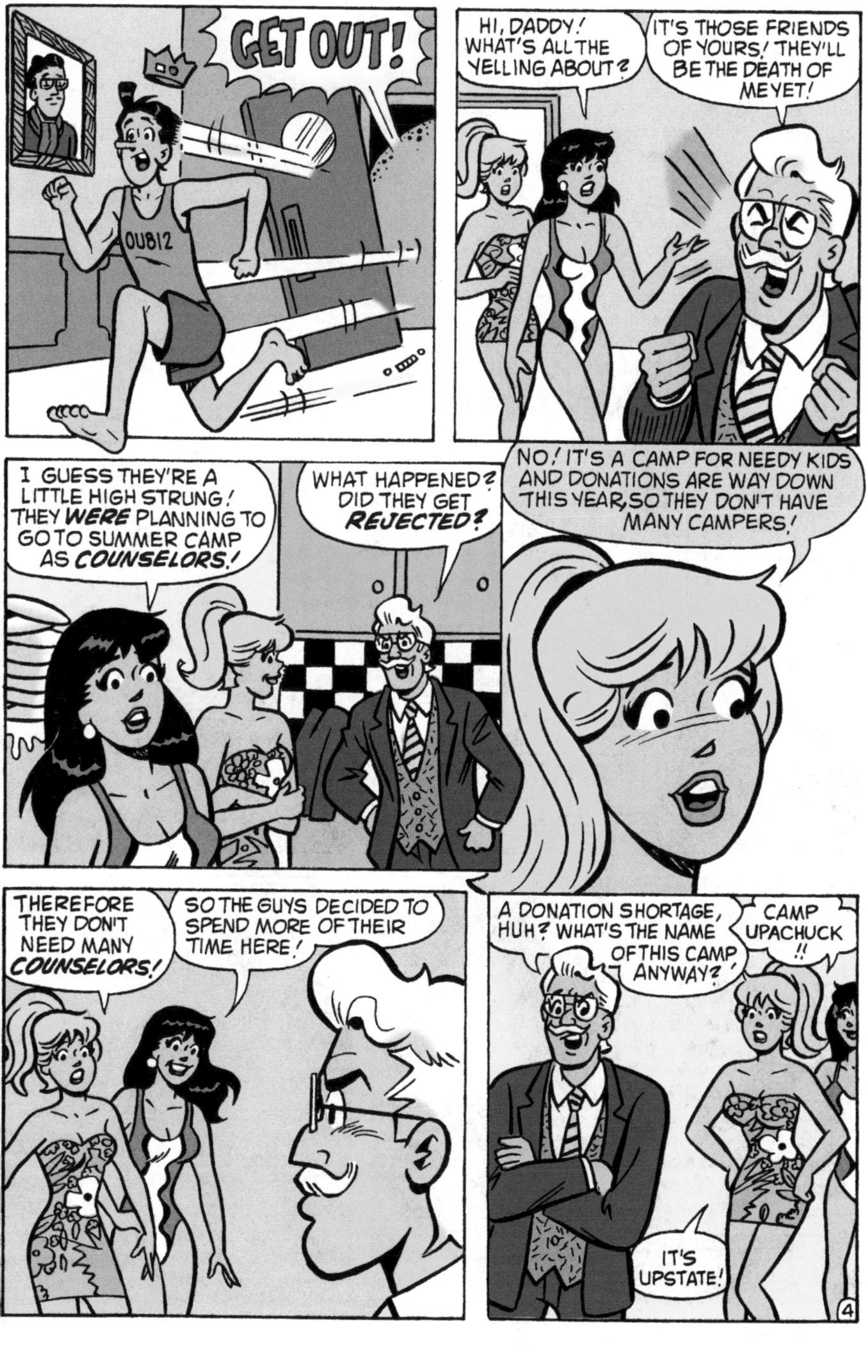
GET OUT!
OU812
HI, DADDY! WHAT'S ALL THE YELLING ABOUT?
IT'S THOSE FRIENDS OF YOURS! THEY'LL BE THE DEATH OF ME YET!
I GUESS THEY'RE A LITTLE HIGH STRUNG! THEY WERE PLANNING TO GO TO SUMMER CAMP AS COUNSELORS!
WHAT HAPPENED? DID THEY GET REJECTED?
NO! IT'S A CAMP FOR NEEDY KIDS AND DONATIONS ARE WAY DOWN THIS YEAR, SO THEY DON'T HAVE MANY CAMPERS!
THEREFORE THEY DON'T NEED MANY COUNSELORS!
SO THE GUYS DECIDED TO SPEND MORE OF THEIR TIME HERE!
A DONATION SHORTAGE, HUH? WHAT'S THE NAME OF THIS CAMP ANYWAY?
CAMP UPACHUCK!!
IT'S UPSTATE!
4

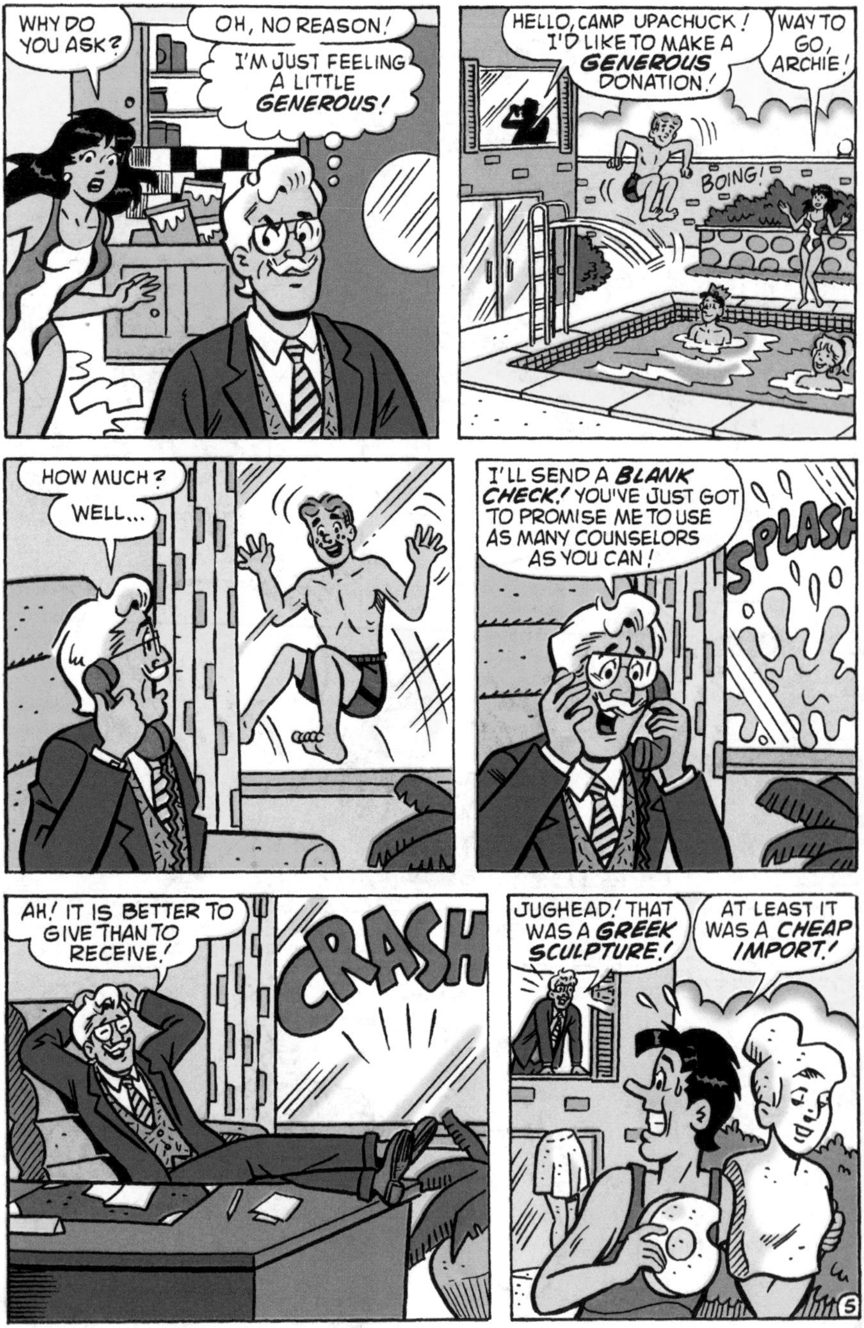

WHY DO YOU ASK?
OH, NO REASON!
I'M JUST FEELING A LITTLE GENEROUS!
HELLO, CAMP UPACHUCK! I'D LIKE TO MAKE A GENEROUS DONATION!
WAY TO GO, ARCHIE!
BOING!
HOW MUCH?
WELL...
I'LL SEND A BLANK CHECK! YOU'VE JUST GOT TO PROMISE ME TO USE AS MANY COUNSELORS AS YOU CAN!
SPLASH
AH! IT IS BETTER TO GIVE THAN TO RECEIVE!
CRASH
JUGHEAD! THAT WAS A GREEK SCULPTURE!
AT LEAST IT WAS A CHEAP IMPORT!
5

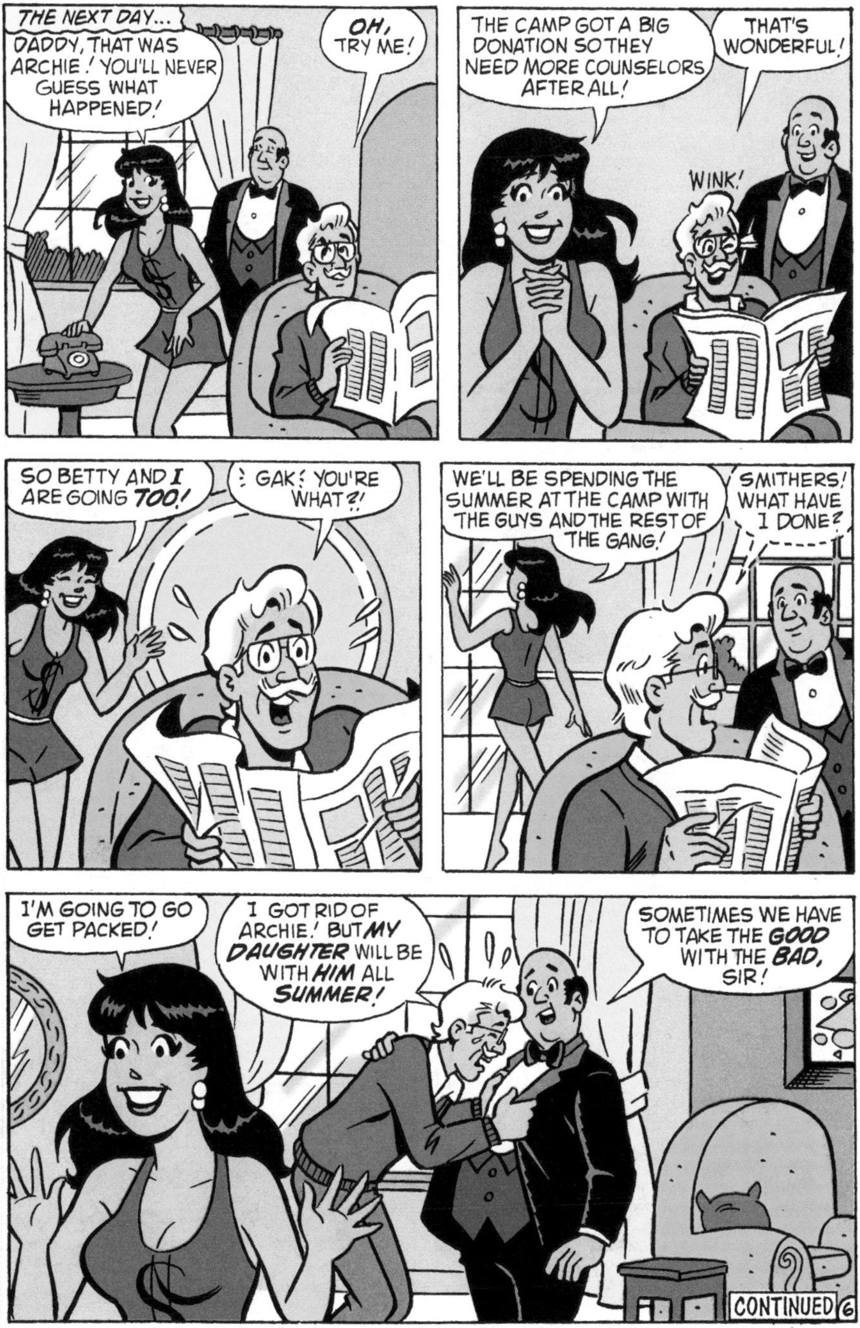
THE NEXT DAY...
DADDY, THAT WAS ARCHIE! YOU'LL NEVER GUESS WHAT HAPPENED!
OH, TRY ME!
THE CAMP GOT A BIG DONATION SO THEY NEED MORE COUNSELORS AFTER ALL!
THAT'S WONDERFUL!
WINK!
SO BETTY AND I ARE GOING TOO!
GAK! YOU'RE WHAT?!
WE'LL BE SPENDING THE SUMMER AT THE CAMP WITH THE GUYS AND THE REST OF THE GANG!
SMITHERS! WHAT HAVE I DONE?
I'M GOING TO GO GET PACKED!
I GOT RID OF ARCHIE! BUT MY DAUGHTER WILL BE WITH HIM ALL SUMMER!
SOMETIMES WE HAVE TO TAKE THE GOOD WITH THE BAD, SIR!
CONTINUED
6

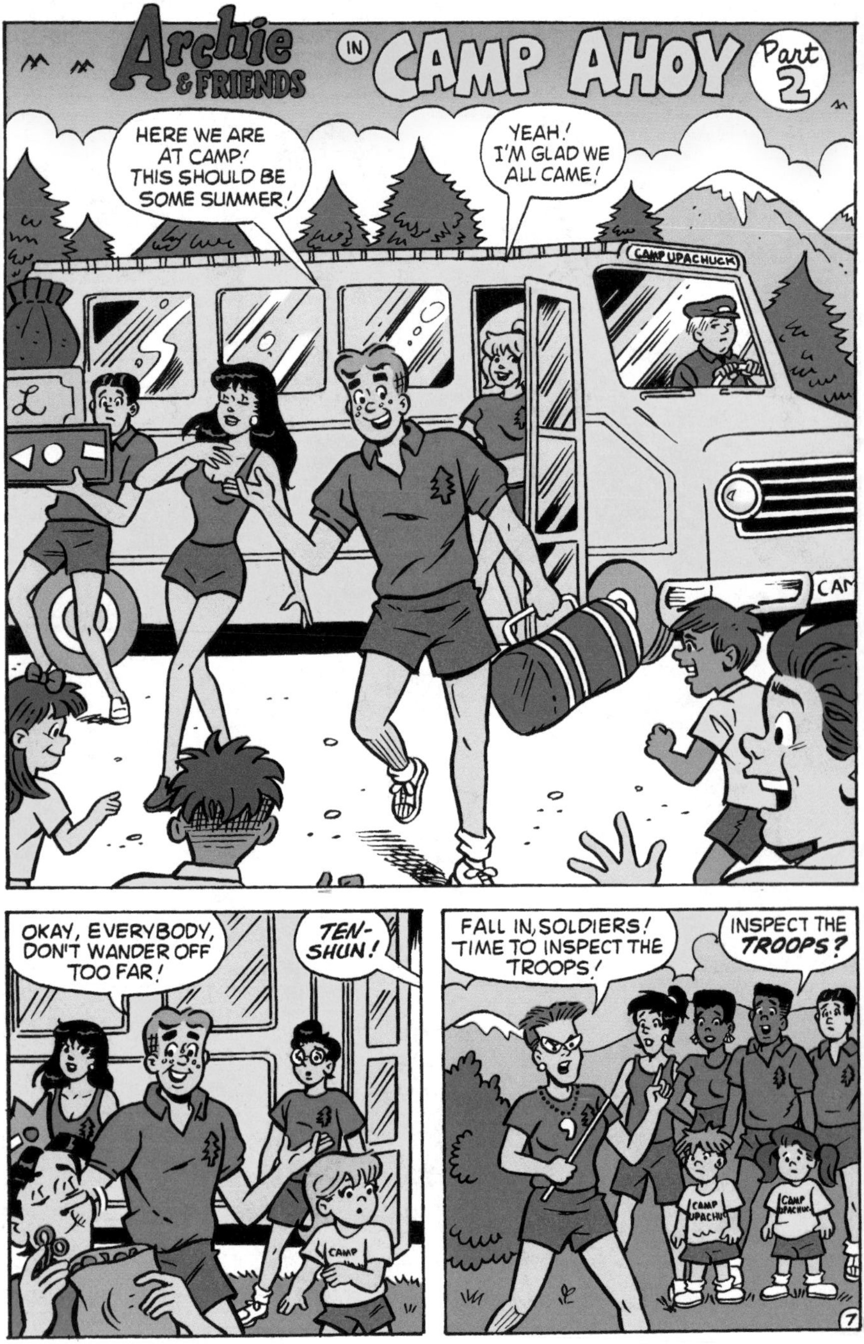
Archie & FRIENDS
IN
CAMP AHOY
Part 2
HERE WE ARE AT CAMP! THIS SHOULD BE SOME SUMMER!
YEAH! I'M GLAD WE ALL CAME!
CAMP UPACHUCK
CAM
OKAY, EVERYBODY, DON'T WANDER OFF TOO FAR!
TEN-SHUN!
CAMP
FALL IN, SOLDIERS! TIME TO INSPECT THE TROOPS!
INSPECT THE ***TROOPS?***
CAMP UPACHUCK
CAMP UPACHUCK
7

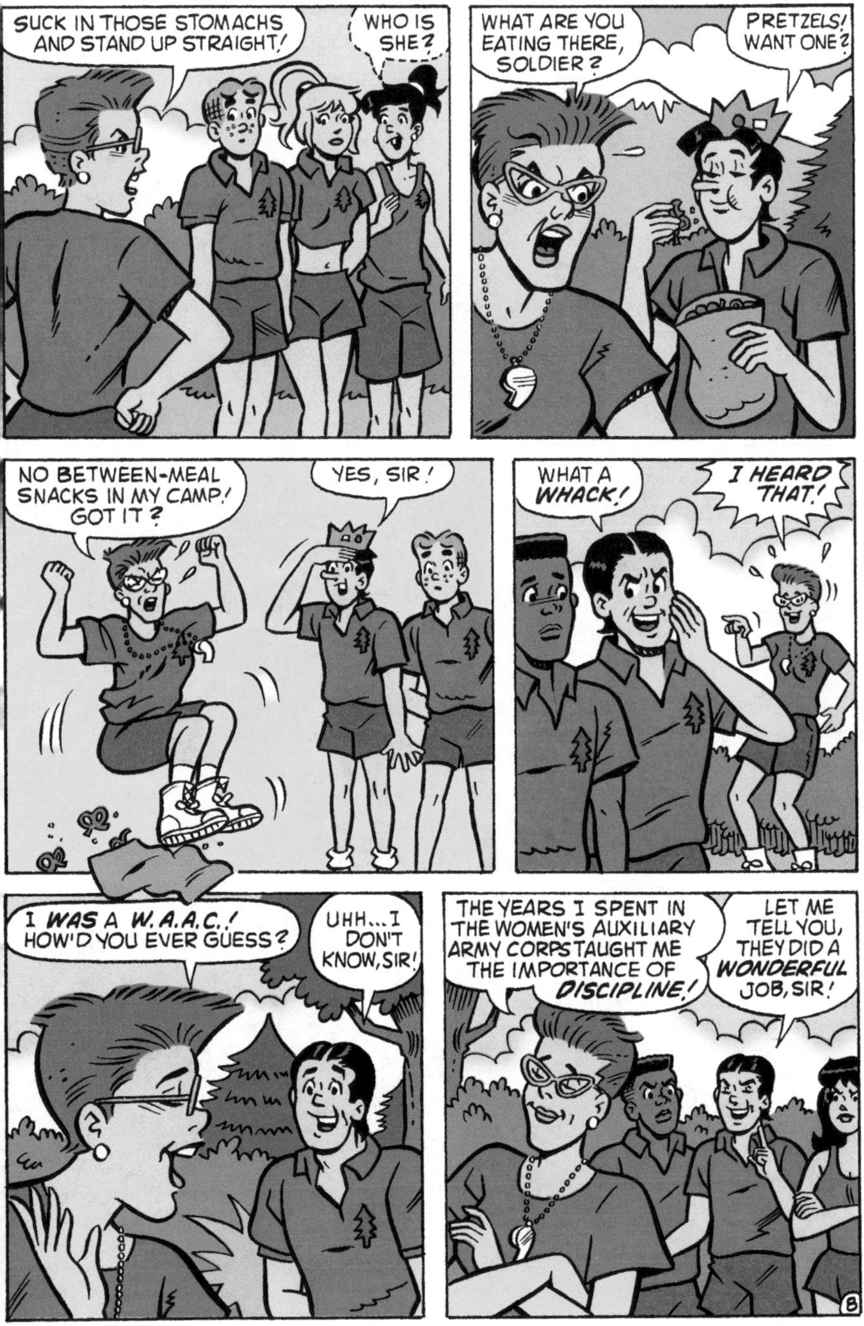
SUCK IN THOSE STOMACHS AND STAND UP STRAIGHT!
WHO IS SHE?
WHAT ARE YOU EATING THERE, SOLDIER?
PRETZELS! WANT ONE?
NO BETWEEN-MEAL SNACKS IN MY CAMP! GOT IT?
YES, SIR!
WHAT A WHACK!
I HEARD THAT!
I WAS A W.A.A.C.! HOW'D YOU EVER GUESS?
UHH...I DON'T KNOW, SIR!
THE YEARS I SPENT IN THE WOMEN'S AUXILIARY ARMY CORPS TAUGHT ME THE IMPORTANCE OF DISCIPLINE!
LET ME TELL YOU, THEY DID A WONDERFUL JOB, SIR!
8

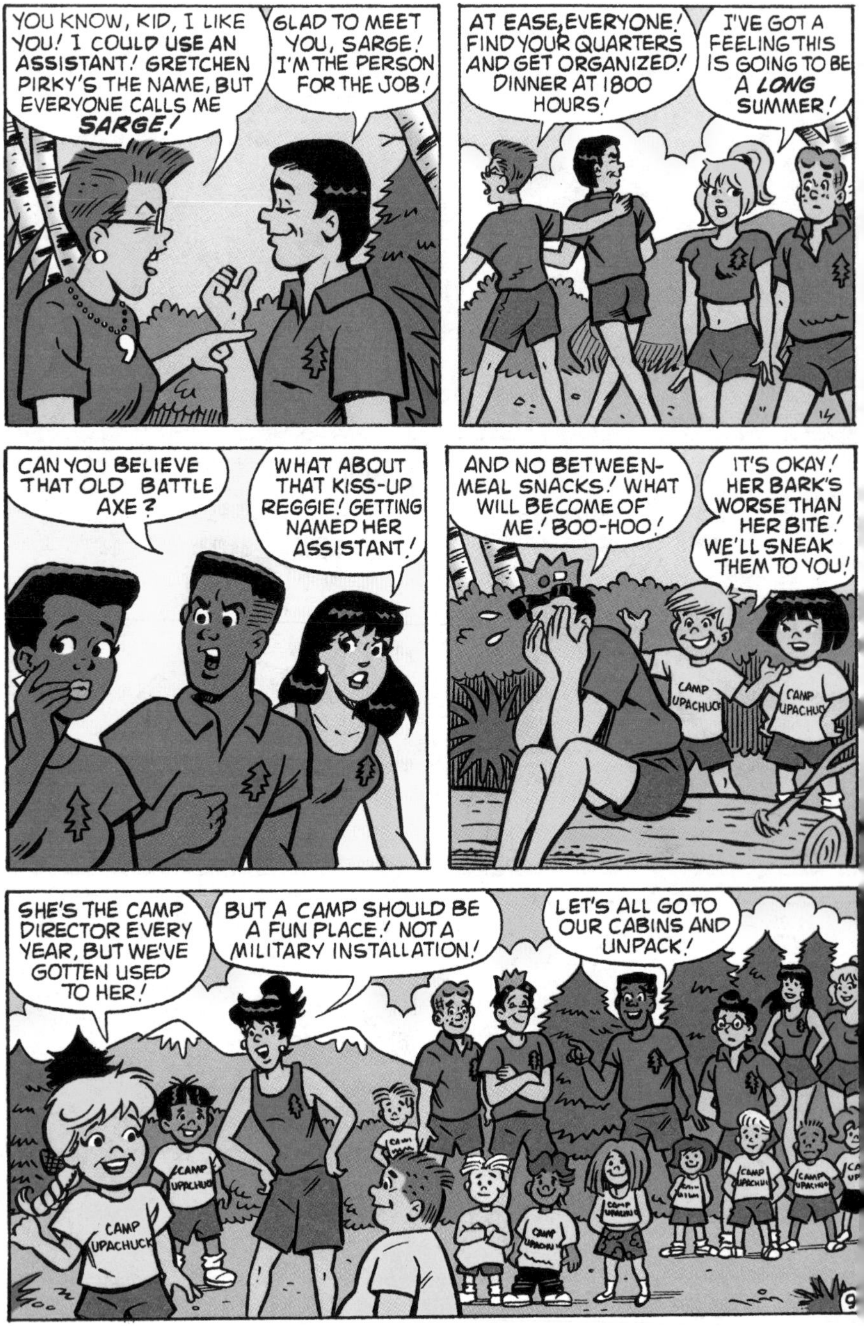
YOU KNOW, KID, I LIKE YOU! I COULD USE AN ASSISTANT! GRETCHEN PIRKY'S THE NAME, BUT EVERYONE CALLS ME SARGE!
GLAD TO MEET YOU, SARGE! I'M THE PERSON FOR THE JOB!
AT EASE, EVERYONE! FIND YOUR QUARTERS AND GET ORGANIZED! DINNER AT 1800 HOURS!
I'VE GOT A FEELING THIS IS GOING TO BE A LONG SUMMER!
CAN YOU BELIEVE THAT OLD BATTLE AXE?
WHAT ABOUT THAT KISS-UP REGGIE! GETTING NAMED HER ASSISTANT!
AND NO BETWEEN-MEAL SNACKS! WHAT WILL BECOME OF ME! BOO-HOO!
IT'S OKAY! HER BARK'S WORSE THAN HER BITE! WE'LL SNEAK THEM TO YOU!
CAMP UPACHUCK
CAMP UPACHUCK
SHE'S THE CAMP DIRECTOR EVERY YEAR, BUT WE'VE GOTTEN USED TO HER!
BUT A CAMP SHOULD BE A FUN PLACE! NOT A MILITARY INSTALLATION!
LET'S ALL GO TO OUR CABINS AND UNPACK!
CAMP UPACHUCK
CAMP UPACHUCK

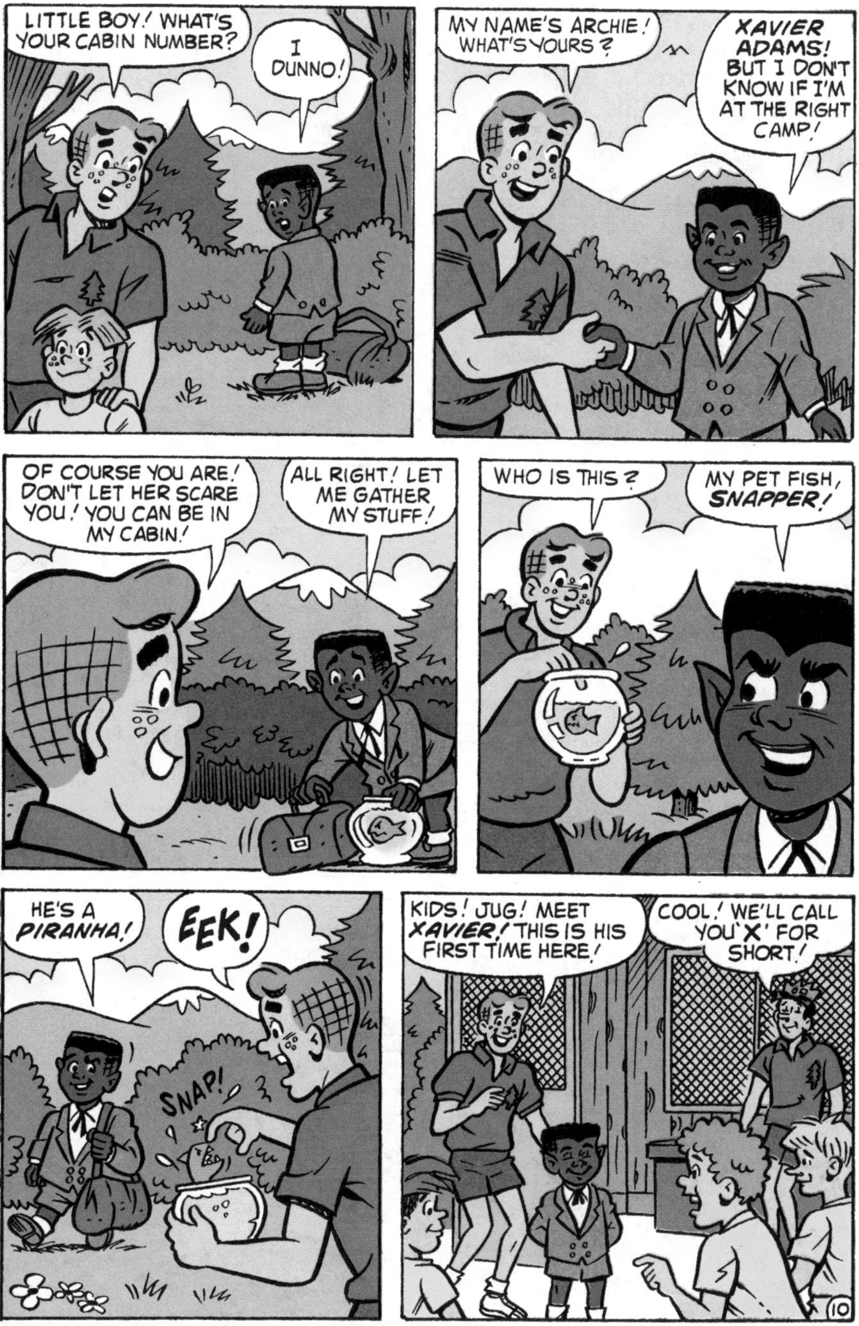
LITTLE BOY! WHAT'S YOUR CABIN NUMBER?
I DUNNO!
MY NAME'S ARCHIE! WHAT'S YOURS?
XAVIER ADAMS! BUT I DON'T KNOW IF I'M AT THE RIGHT CAMP!
OF COURSE YOU ARE! DON'T LET HER SCARE YOU! YOU CAN BE IN MY CABIN!
ALL RIGHT! LET ME GATHER MY STUFF!
WHO IS THIS?
MY PET FISH, SNAPPER!
HE'S A PIRANHA!
EEK!
SNAP!
KIDS! JUG! MEET XAVIER! THIS IS HIS FIRST TIME HERE!
COOL! WE'LL CALL YOU 'X' FOR SHORT!
10

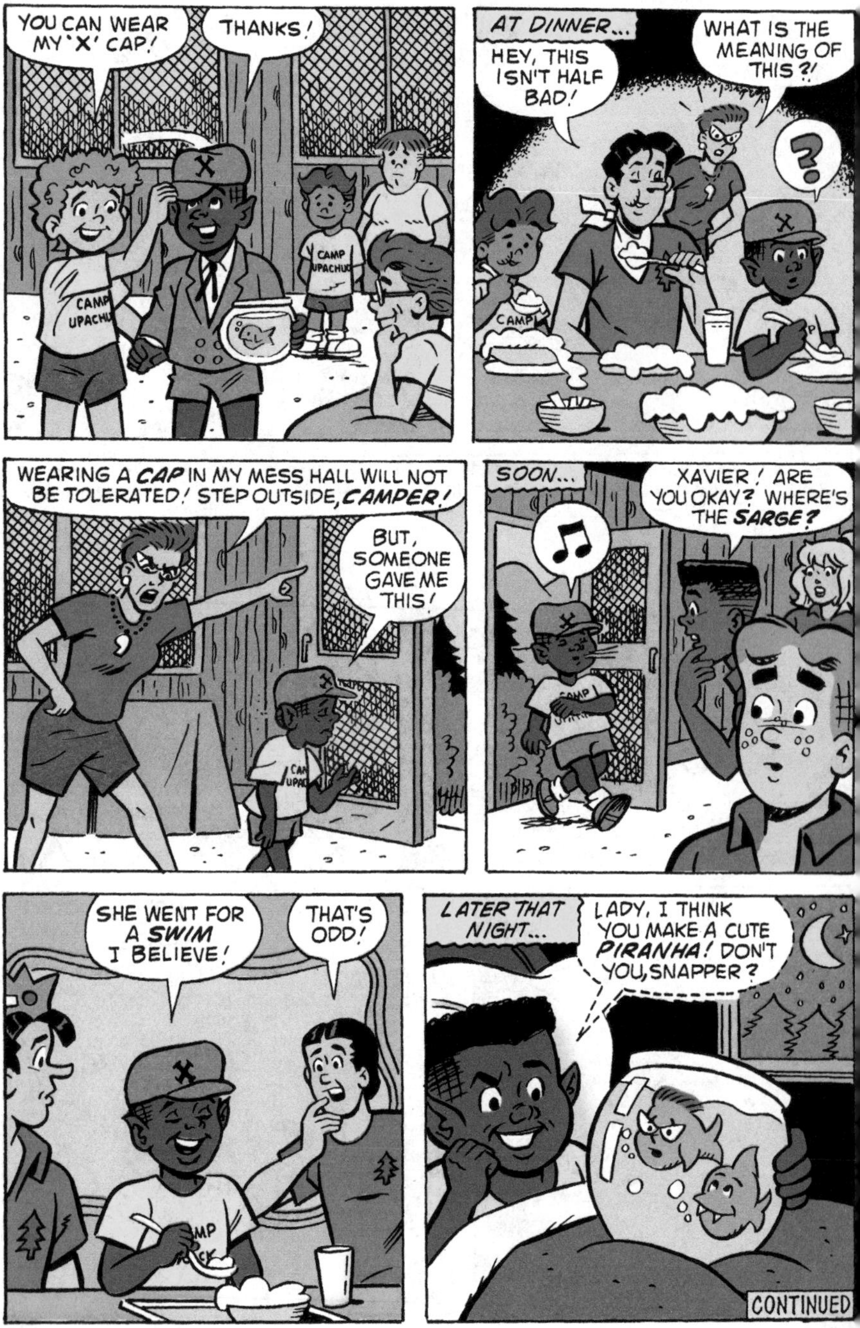
YOU CAN WEAR MY 'X' CAP!
THANKS!
AT DINNER...
HEY, THIS ISN'T HALF BAD!
WHAT IS THE MEANING OF THIS?!
?
WEARING A CAP IN MY MESS HALL WILL NOT BE TOLERATED! STEP OUTSIDE, CAMPER!
BUT, SOMEONE GAVE ME THIS!
SOON...
XAVIER! ARE YOU OKAY? WHERE'S THE SARGE?
SHE WENT FOR A SWIM I BELIEVE!
THAT'S ODD!
LATER THAT NIGHT...
LADY, I THINK YOU MAKE A CUTE PIRANHA! DON'T YOU, SNAPPER?
CONTINUED

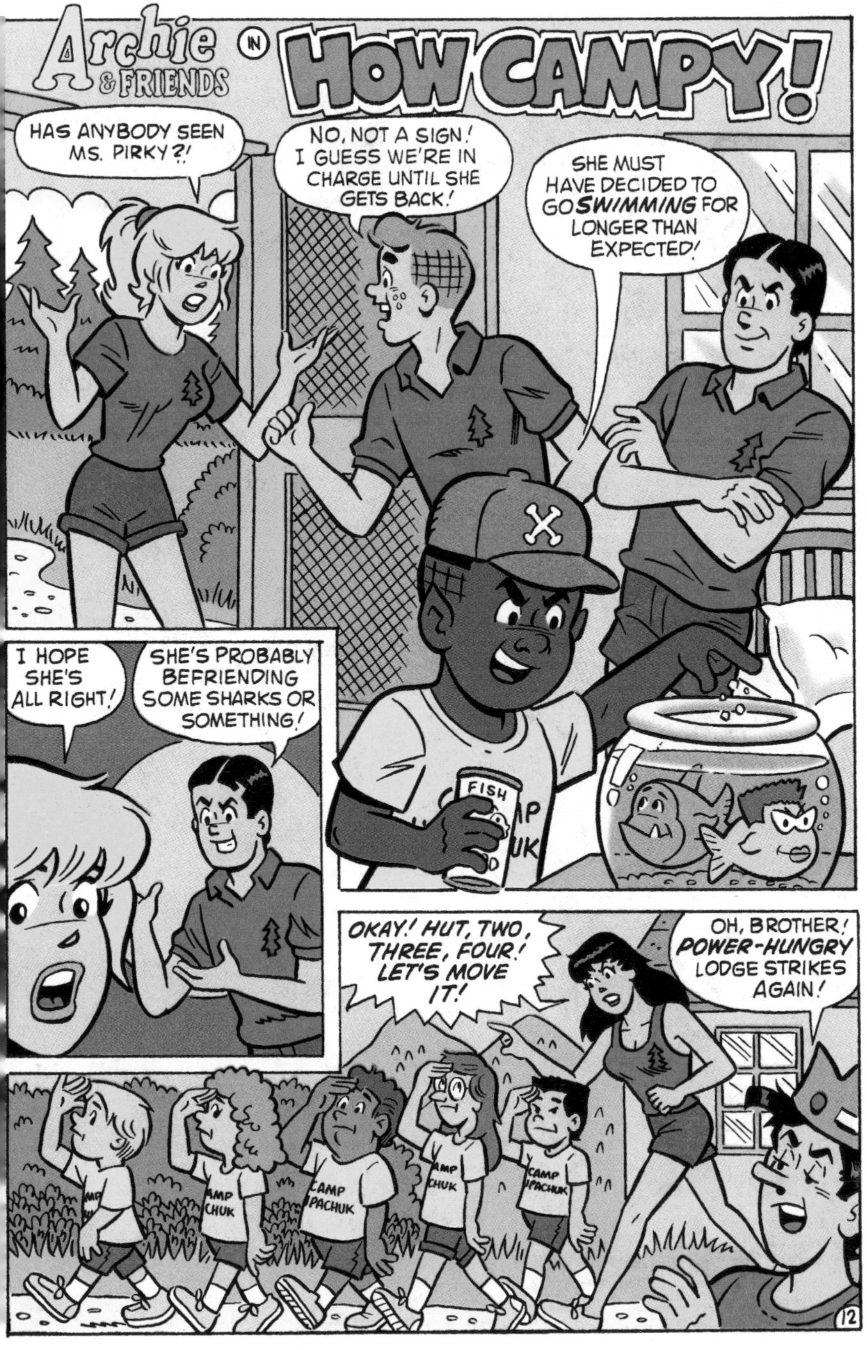
Archie & FRIENDS IN HOW CAMPY!
HAS ANYBODY SEEN MS. PIRKY?!
NO, NOT A SIGN! I GUESS WE'RE IN CHARGE UNTIL SHE GETS BACK!
SHE MUST HAVE DECIDED TO GO SWIMMING FOR LONGER THAN EXPECTED!
FISH
I HOPE SHE'S ALL RIGHT!
SHE'S PROBABLY BEFRIENDING SOME SHARKS OR SOMETHING!
OKAY! HUT, TWO, THREE, FOUR! LET'S MOVE IT!
OH, BROTHER! POWER-HUNGRY LODGE STRIKES AGAIN!
CAMP IPACHUK
12

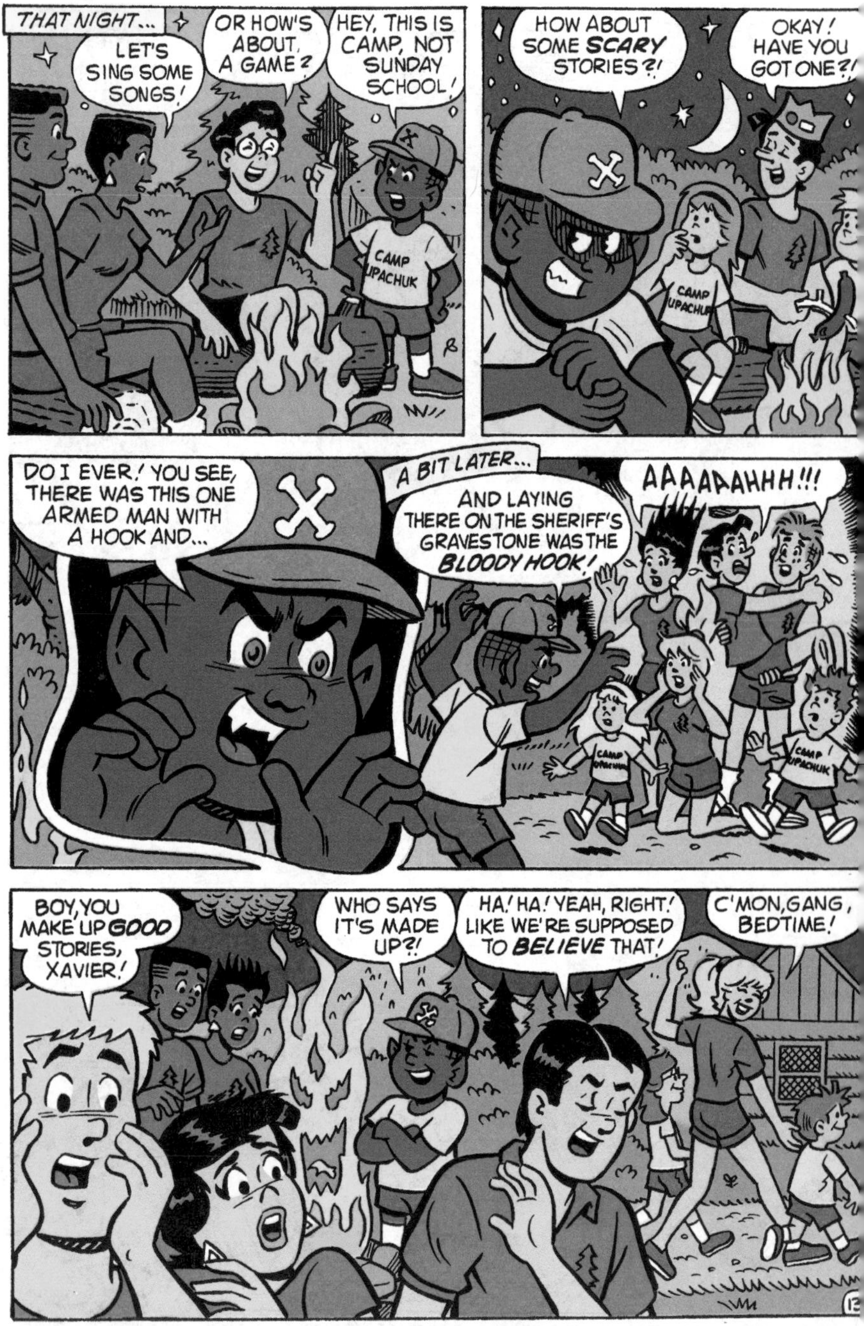
THAT NIGHT...
LET'S SING SOME SONGS!
OR HOW'S ABOUT A GAME?
HEY, THIS IS CAMP, NOT SUNDAY SCHOOL!
CAMP UPACHUK
HOW ABOUT SOME SCARY STORIES?!
OKAY! HAVE YOU GOT ONE?!
CAMP UPACHUK
DO I EVER! YOU SEE, THERE WAS THIS ONE ARMED MAN WITH A HOOK AND...
A BIT LATER...
AND LAYING THERE ON THE SHERIFF'S GRAVESTONE WAS THE BLOODY HOOK!
AAAAAAHHH!!!
CAMP UPACHUK
CAMP UPACHUK
BOY, YOU MAKE UP GOOD STORIES, XAVIER!
WHO SAYS IT'S MADE UP?!
HA! HA! YEAH, RIGHT! LIKE WE'RE SUPPOSED TO BELIEVE THAT!
C'MON, GANG, BEDTIME!

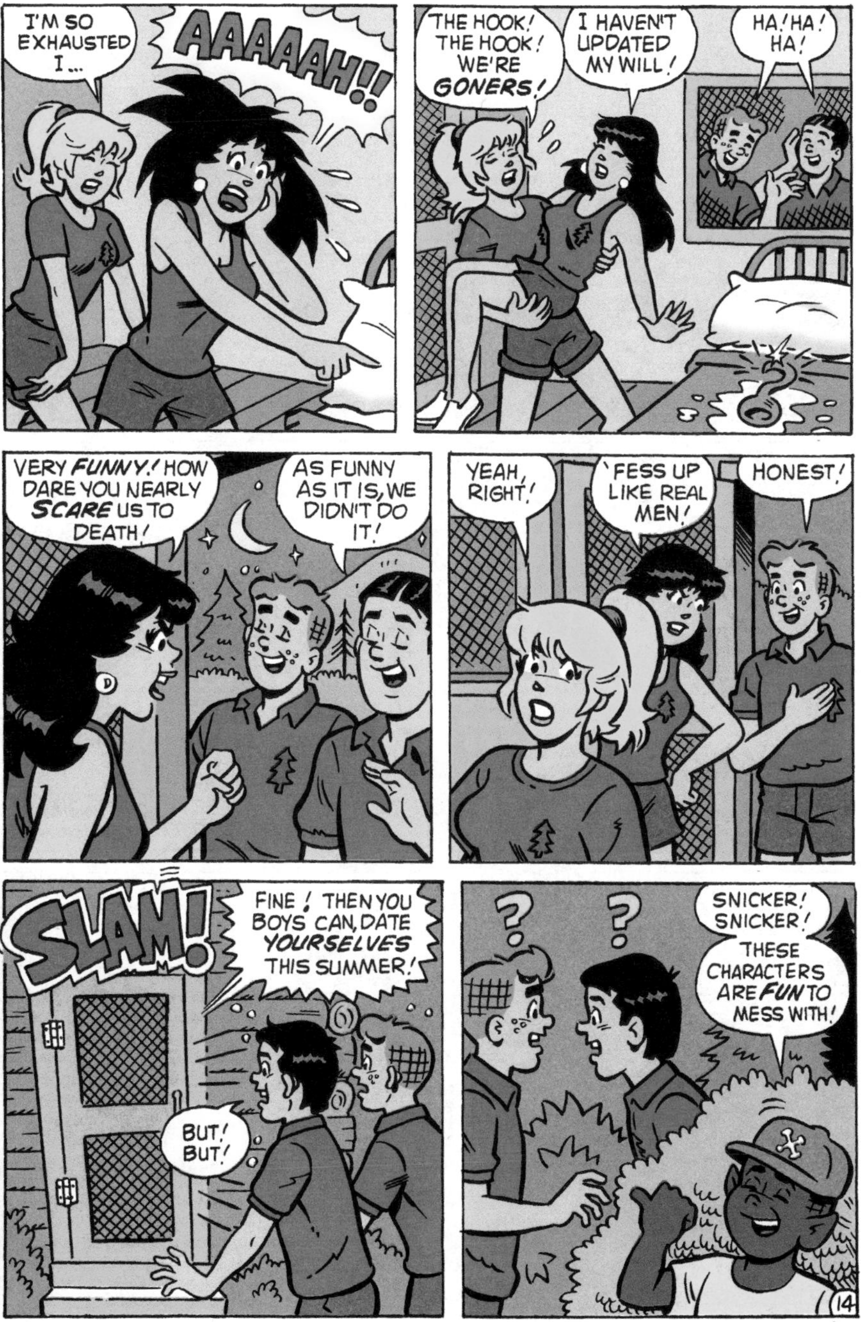
I'M SO EXHAUSTED I...
AAAAAH!!
THE HOOK! THE HOOK! WE'RE GONERS!
I HAVEN'T UPDATED MY WILL!
HA! HA! HA!
VERY FUNNY! HOW DARE YOU NEARLY SCARE US TO DEATH!
AS FUNNY AS IT IS, WE DIDN'T DO IT!
YEAH, RIGHT!
'FESS UP LIKE REAL MEN!
HONEST!
SLAM!
FINE! THEN YOU BOYS CAN DATE YOURSELVES THIS SUMMER!
BUT! BUT!
SNICKER! SNICKER!
THESE CHARACTERS ARE FUN TO MESS WITH!
14

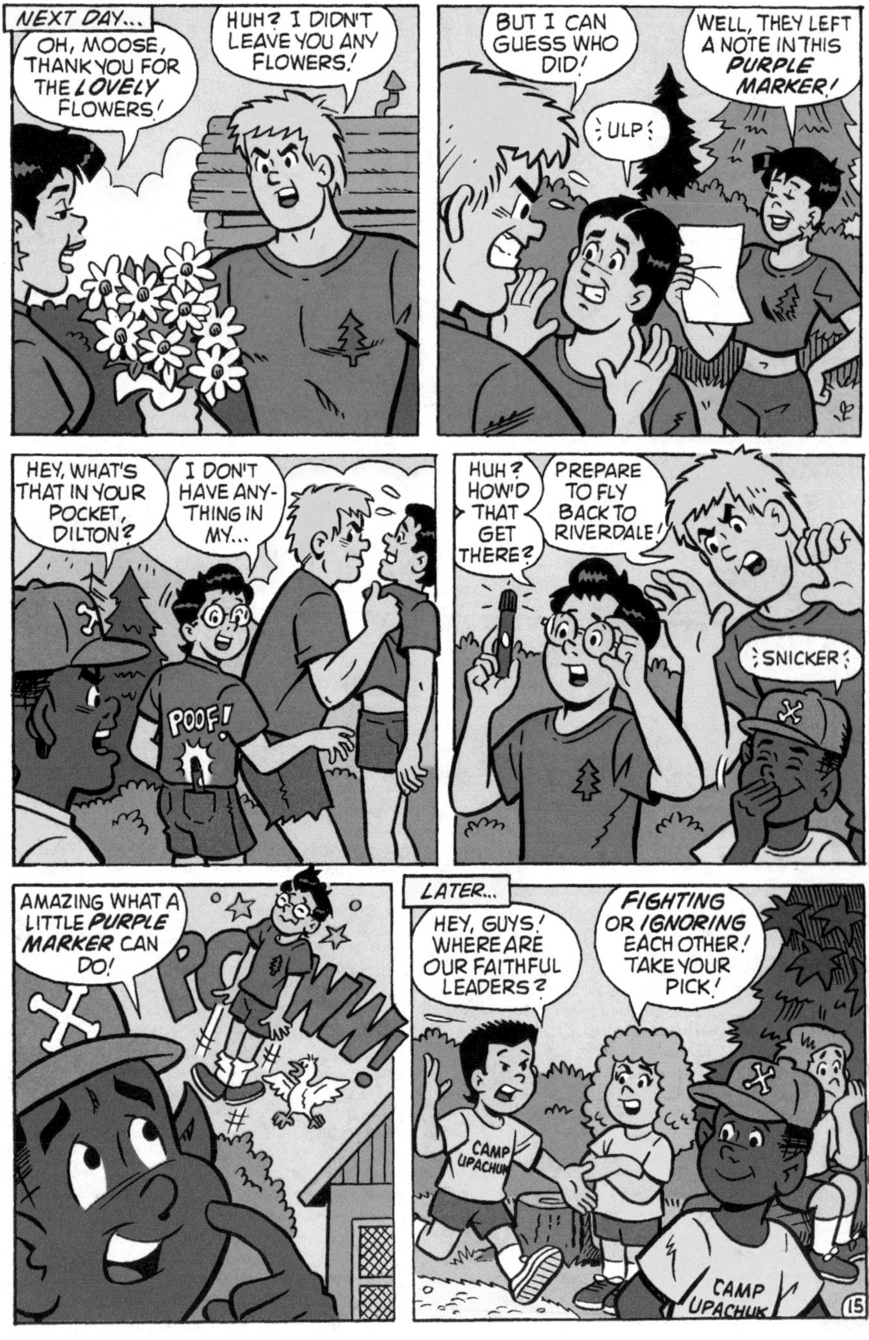

NEXT DAY...
OH, MOOSE, THANK YOU FOR THE LOVELY FLOWERS!
HUH? I DIDN'T LEAVE YOU ANY FLOWERS!
BUT I CAN GUESS WHO DID!
WELL, THEY LEFT A NOTE IN THIS PURPLE MARKER!
ULP
HEY, WHAT'S THAT IN YOUR POCKET, DILTON?
I DON'T HAVE ANY-THING IN MY...
POOF!
HUH? HOW'D THAT GET THERE?
PREPARE TO FLY BACK TO RIVERDALE!
SNICKER
AMAZING WHAT A LITTLE PURPLE MARKER CAN DO!
POWW!
LATER...
HEY, GUYS! WHERE ARE OUR FAITHFUL LEADERS?
FIGHTING OR IGNORING EACH OTHER! TAKE YOUR PICK!
CAMP UPACHUK
CAMP UPACHUK

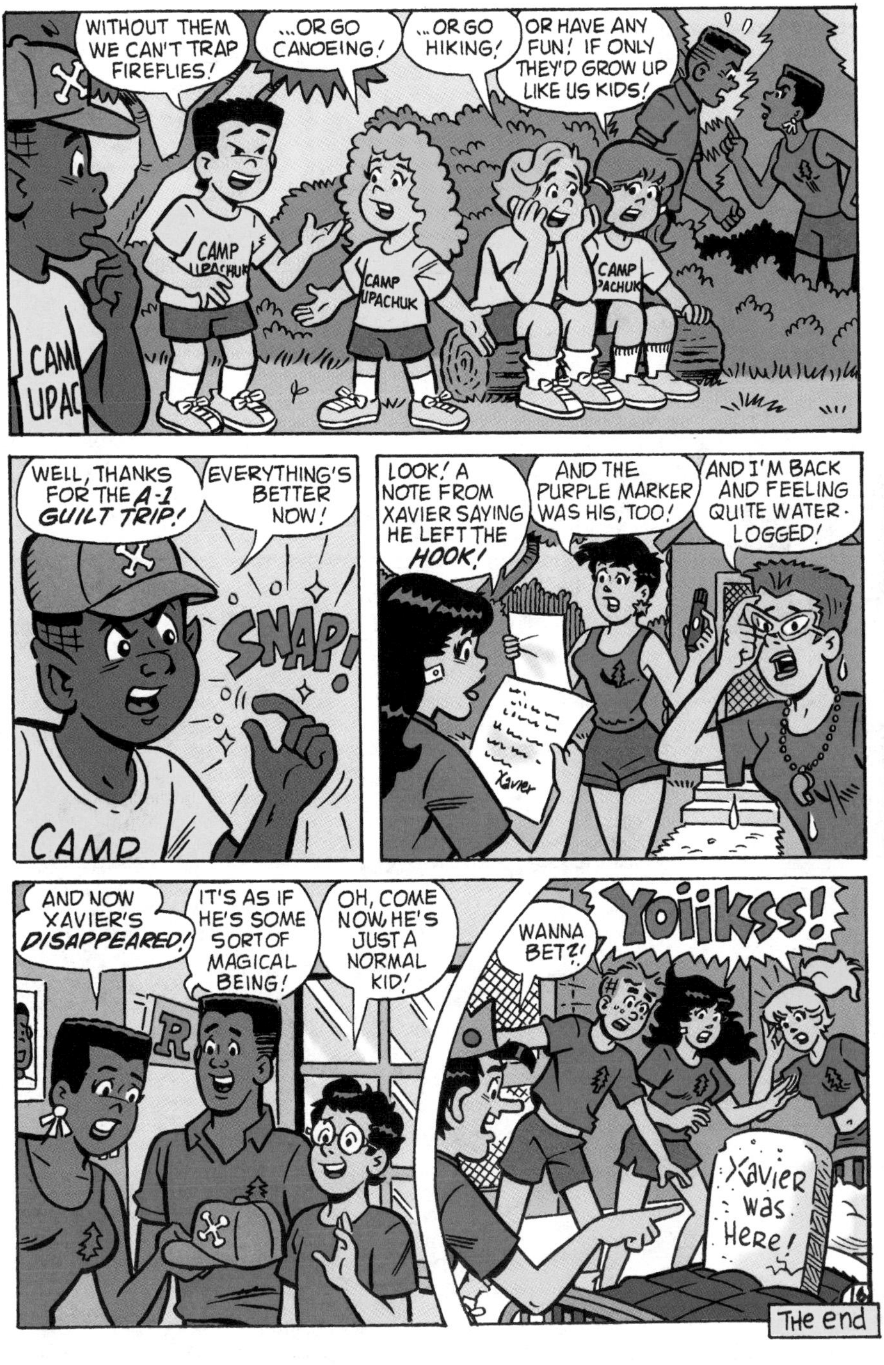
WITHOUT THEM WE CAN'T TRAP FIREFLIES!
...OR GO CANOEING!
...OR GO HIKING!
OR HAVE ANY FUN! IF ONLY THEY'D GROW UP LIKE US KIDS!
CAMP UPACHUK
CAMP UPACHUK
CAMP PACHUK
CAM UPAC
WELL, THANKS FOR THE *A-1 GUILT TRIP!*
EVERYTHING'S BETTER NOW!
SNAP!
CAMP
LOOK! A NOTE FROM XAVIER SAYING HE LEFT THE *HOOK!*
AND THE PURPLE MARKER WAS HIS, TOO!
AND I'M BACK AND FEELING QUITE WATER-LOGGED!
Xavier
AND NOW XAVIER'S *DISAPPEARED!*
IT'S AS IF HE'S SOME SORT OF MAGICAL BEING!
OH, COME NOW, HE'S JUST A NORMAL KID!
Yoiikss!
WANNA BET?!
Xavier was Here!
The end

16

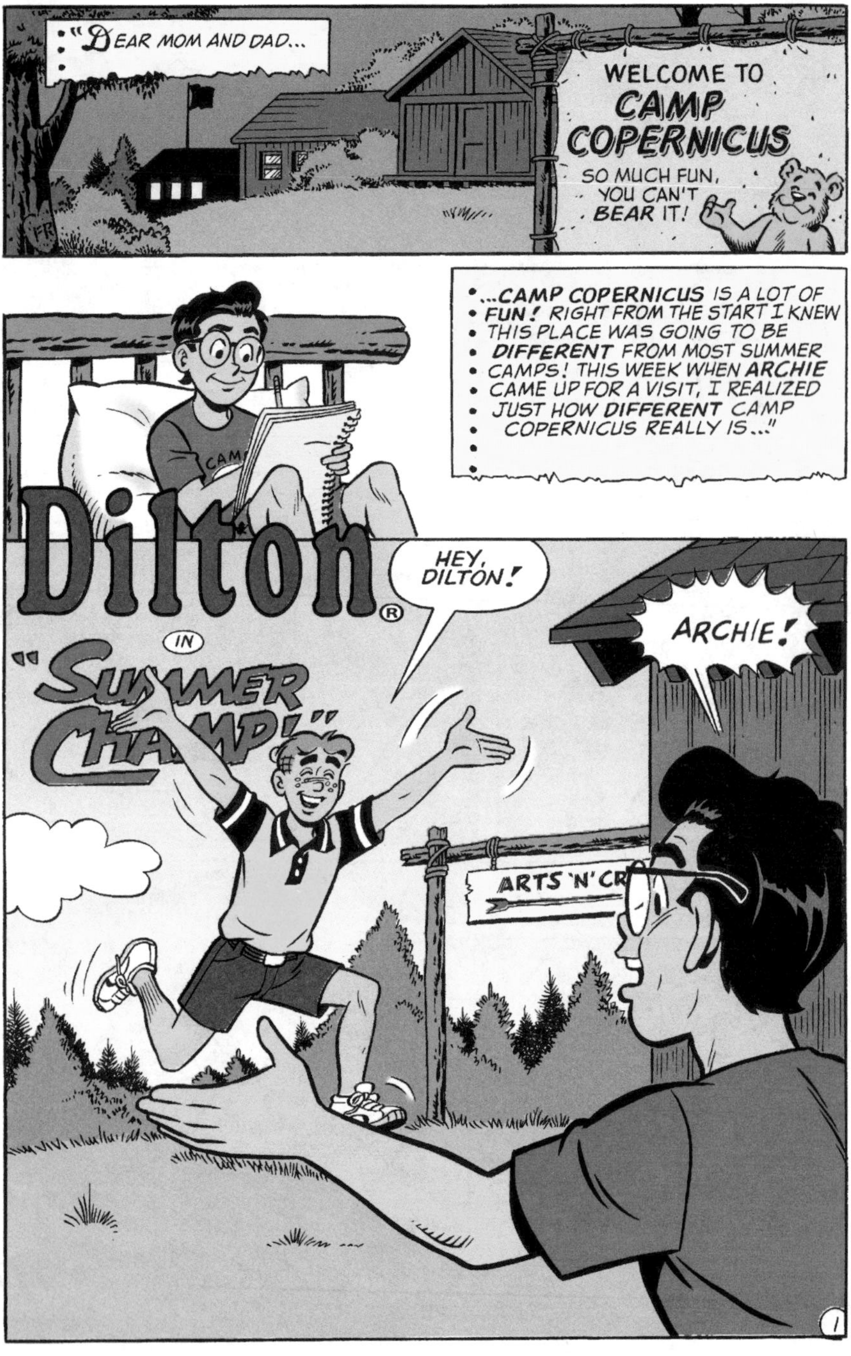
"DEAR MOM AND DAD...
WELCOME TO CAMP COPERNICUS
SO MUCH FUN, YOU CAN'T BEAR IT!
...CAMP COPERNICUS IS A LOT OF FUN! RIGHT FROM THE START I KNEW THIS PLACE WAS GOING TO BE DIFFERENT FROM MOST SUMMER CAMPS! THIS WEEK WHEN ARCHIE CAME UP FOR A VISIT, I REALIZED JUST HOW DIFFERENT CAMP COPERNICUS REALLY IS..."
Dilton®
IN
"SUMMER CHAMP!"
HEY, DILTON!
ARCHIE!
ARTS 'N' CR
1

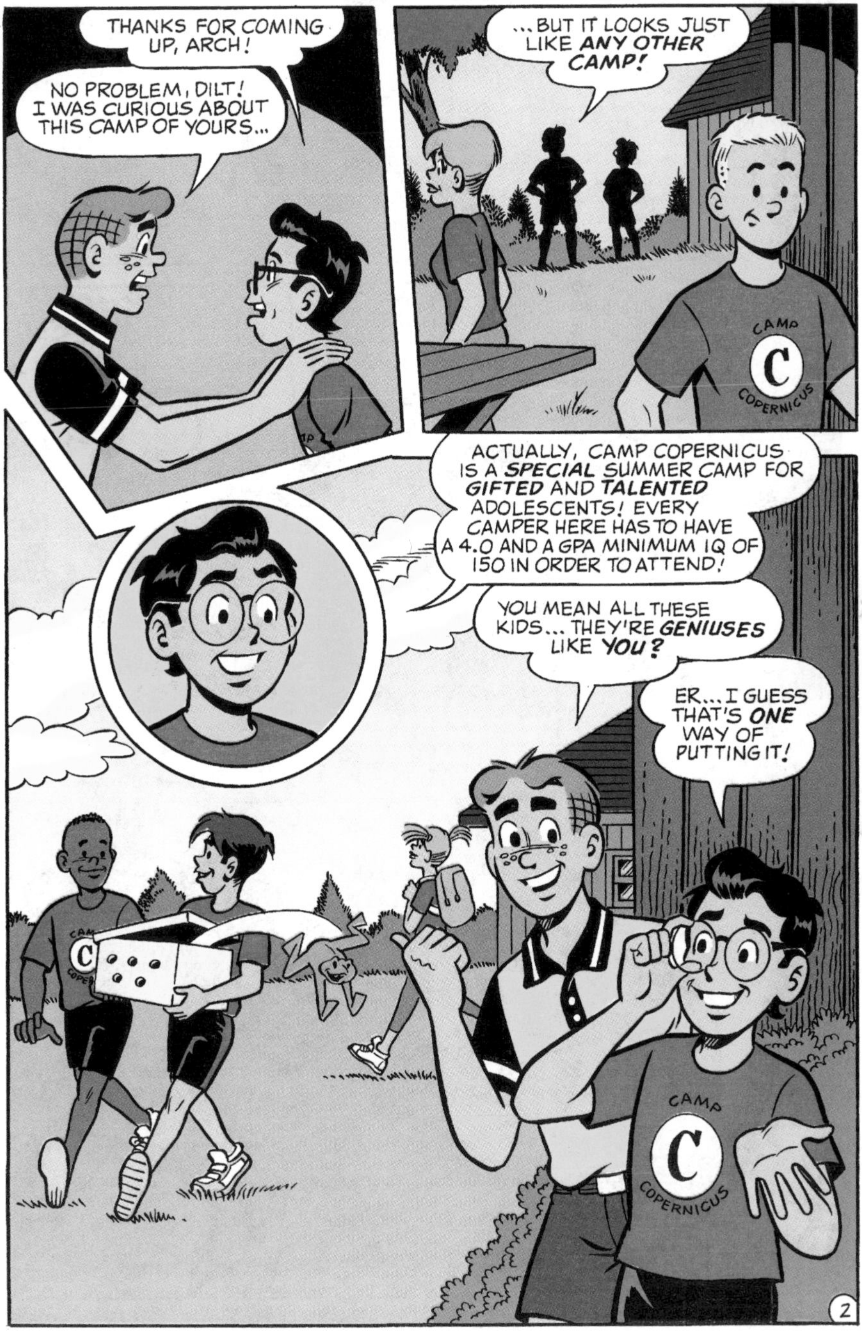

THANKS FOR COMING UP, ARCH!
NO PROBLEM, DILT! I WAS CURIOUS ABOUT THIS CAMP OF YOURS...
...BUT IT LOOKS JUST LIKE ANY OTHER CAMP!
CAMP C COPERNICUS
ACTUALLY, CAMP COPERNICUS IS A SPECIAL SUMMER CAMP FOR GIFTED AND TALENTED ADOLESCENTS! EVERY CAMPER HERE HAS TO HAVE A 4.0 AND A GPA MINIMUM IQ OF 150 IN ORDER TO ATTEND!
YOU MEAN ALL THESE KIDS... THEY'RE GENIUSES LIKE YOU?
ER... I GUESS THAT'S ONE WAY OF PUTTING IT!
CAMP C COPERNICUS

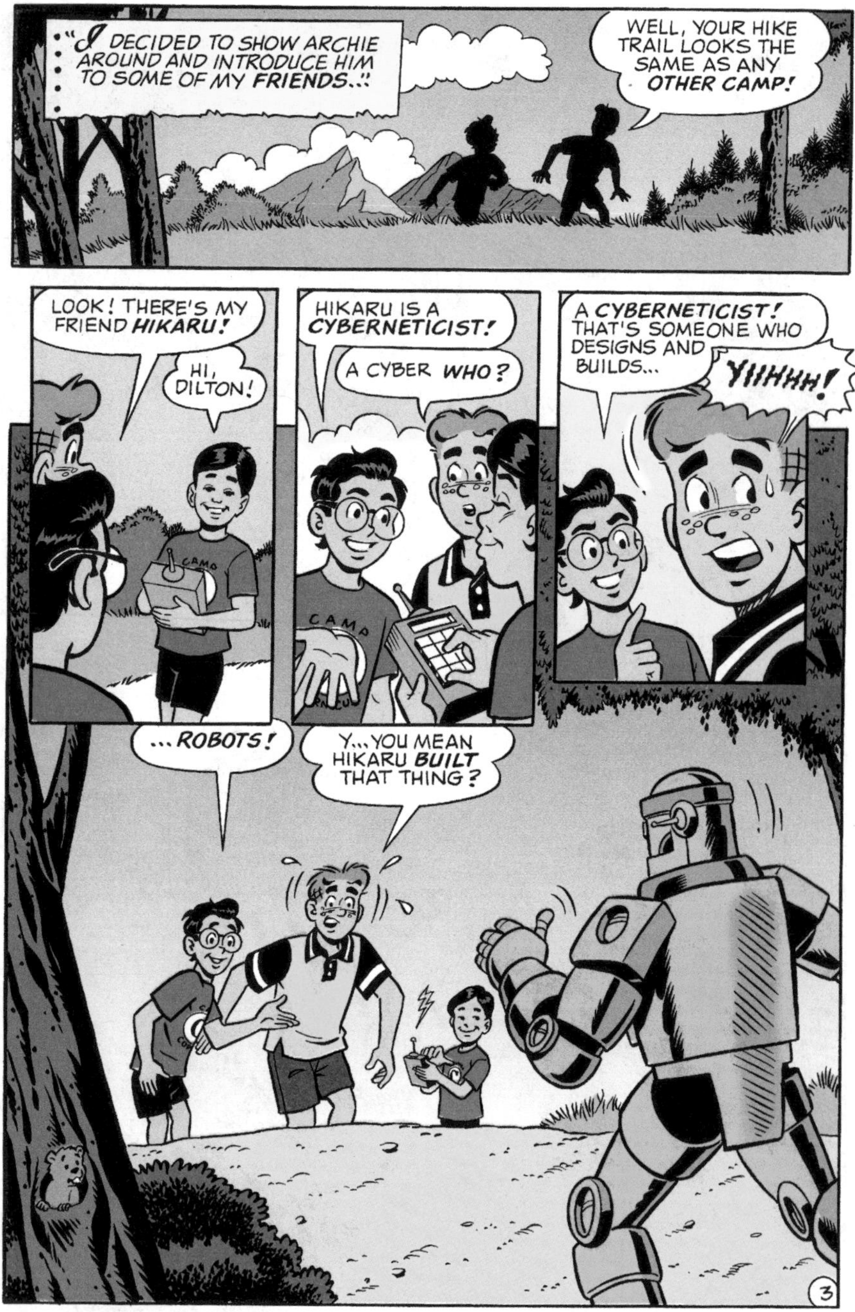

"I DECIDED TO SHOW ARCHIE AROUND AND INTRODUCE HIM TO SOME OF MY FRIENDS..."
WELL, YOUR HIKE TRAIL LOOKS THE SAME AS ANY OTHER CAMP!
LOOK! THERE'S MY FRIEND HIKARU!
HI, DILTON!
HIKARU IS A CYBERNETICIST!
A CYBER WHO?
A CYBERNETICIST! THAT'S SOMEONE WHO DESIGNS AND BUILDS...
YIIHHH!
...ROBOTS!
Y...YOU MEAN HIKARU BUILT THAT THING?
3

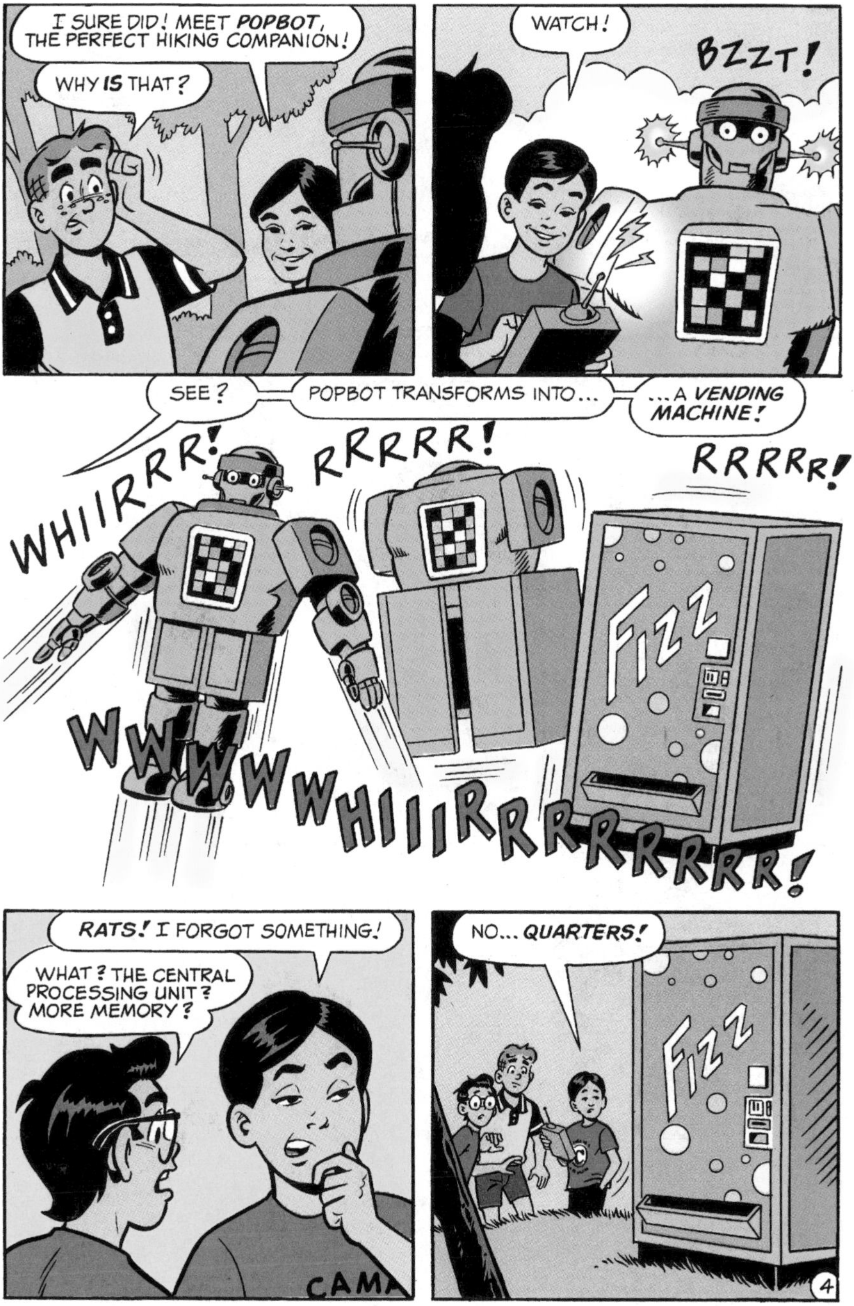
I SURE DID! MEET POPBOT, THE PERFECT HIKING COMPANION!
WHY IS THAT?
WATCH!
BZZT!
SEE?
POPBOT TRANSFORMS INTO...
...A VENDING MACHINE!
WHIIRRR!
RRRRR!
RRRRR!
FIZZ
WWWWWHIIIRRRRRRRRR!
RATS! I FORGOT SOMETHING!
WHAT? THE CENTRAL PROCESSING UNIT? MORE MEMORY?
CAMA
NO... QUARTERS!
FIZZ
4

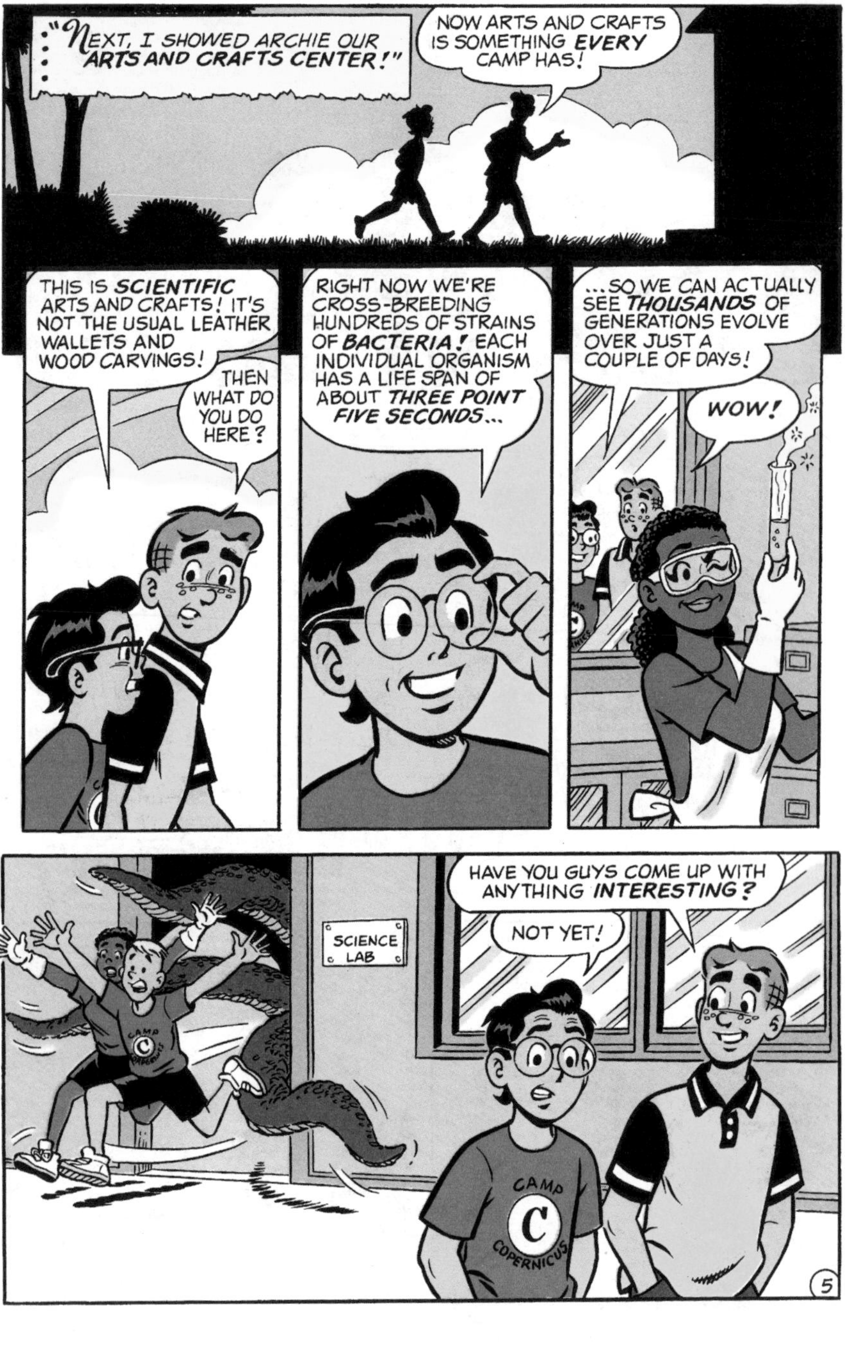

"NEXT, I SHOWED ARCHIE OUR ARTS AND CRAFTS CENTER!"
NOW ARTS AND CRAFTS IS SOMETHING EVERY CAMP HAS!
THIS IS SCIENTIFIC ARTS AND CRAFTS! IT'S NOT THE USUAL LEATHER WALLETS AND WOOD CARVINGS!
THEN WHAT DO YOU DO HERE?
RIGHT NOW WE'RE CROSS-BREEDING HUNDREDS OF STRAINS OF BACTERIA! EACH INDIVIDUAL ORGANISM HAS A LIFE SPAN OF ABOUT THREE POINT FIVE SECONDS...
...SO WE CAN ACTUALLY SEE THOUSANDS OF GENERATIONS EVOLVE OVER JUST A COUPLE OF DAYS!
WOW!
SCIENCE LAB
HAVE YOU GUYS COME UP WITH ANYTHING INTERESTING?
NOT YET!
CAMP C COPERNICUS

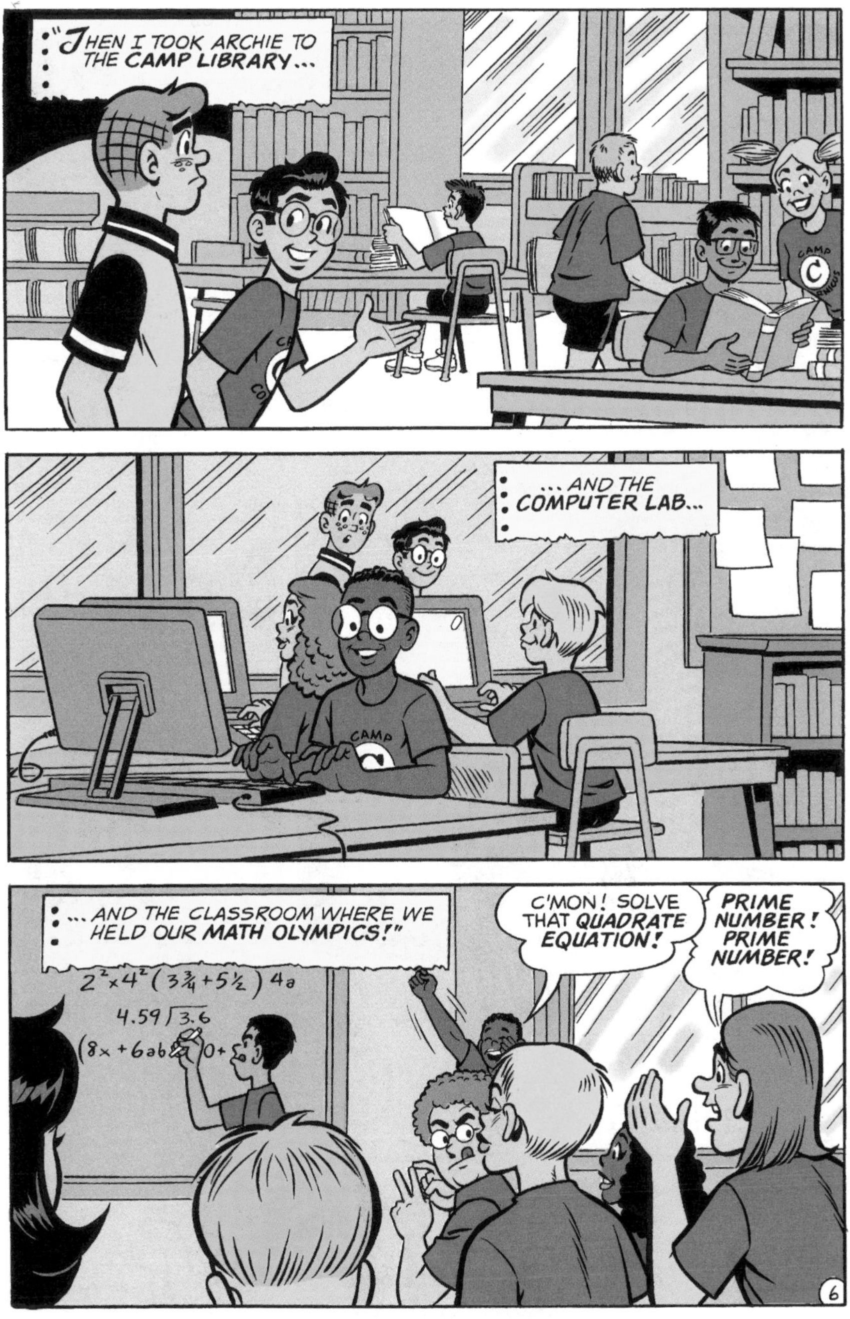
"THEN I TOOK ARCHIE TO THE CAMP LIBRARY...
... AND THE COMPUTER LAB...
... AND THE CLASSROOM WHERE WE HELD OUR MATH OLYMPICS!"
$2^2 \times 4^2 (3\frac{3}{4}+5\frac{1}{2})$ 4a
4.59 $\overline{)3.6}$
(8x + 6ab 0+
C'MON! SOLVE THAT QUADRATE EQUATION!
PRIME NUMBER! PRIME NUMBER!
6

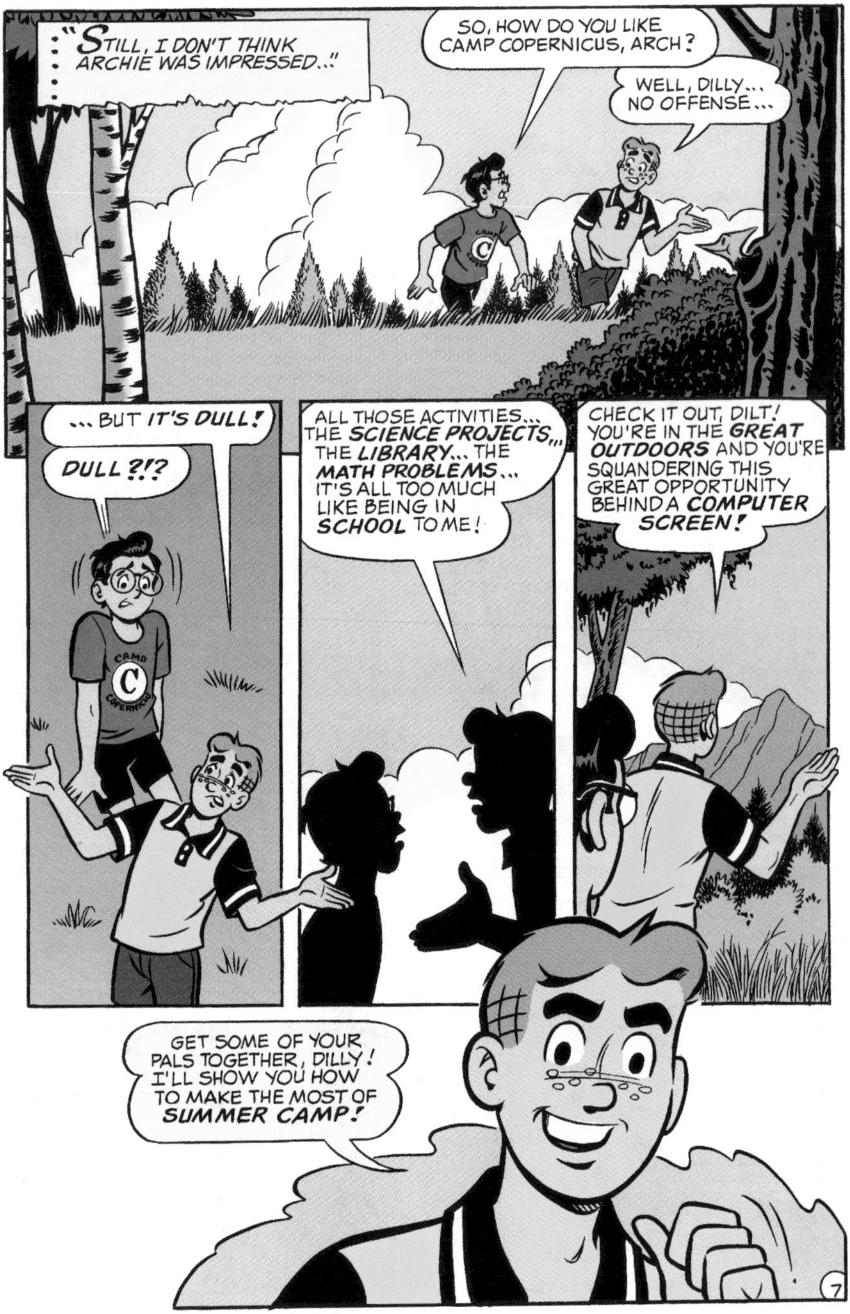

"STILL, I DON'T THINK ARCHIE WAS IMPRESSED..."
SO, HOW DO YOU LIKE CAMP COPERNICUS, ARCH?
WELL, DILLY... NO OFFENSE...
...BUT IT'S DULL!
DULL?!?
ALL THOSE ACTIVITIES... THE SCIENCE PROJECTS... THE LIBRARY... THE MATH PROBLEMS... IT'S ALL TOO MUCH LIKE BEING IN SCHOOL TO ME!
CHECK IT OUT, DILT! YOU'RE IN THE GREAT OUTDOORS AND YOU'RE SQUANDERING THIS GREAT OPPORTUNITY BEHIND A COMPUTER SCREEN!
GET SOME OF YOUR PALS TOGETHER, DILLY! I'LL SHOW YOU HOW TO MAKE THE MOST OF SUMMER CAMP!

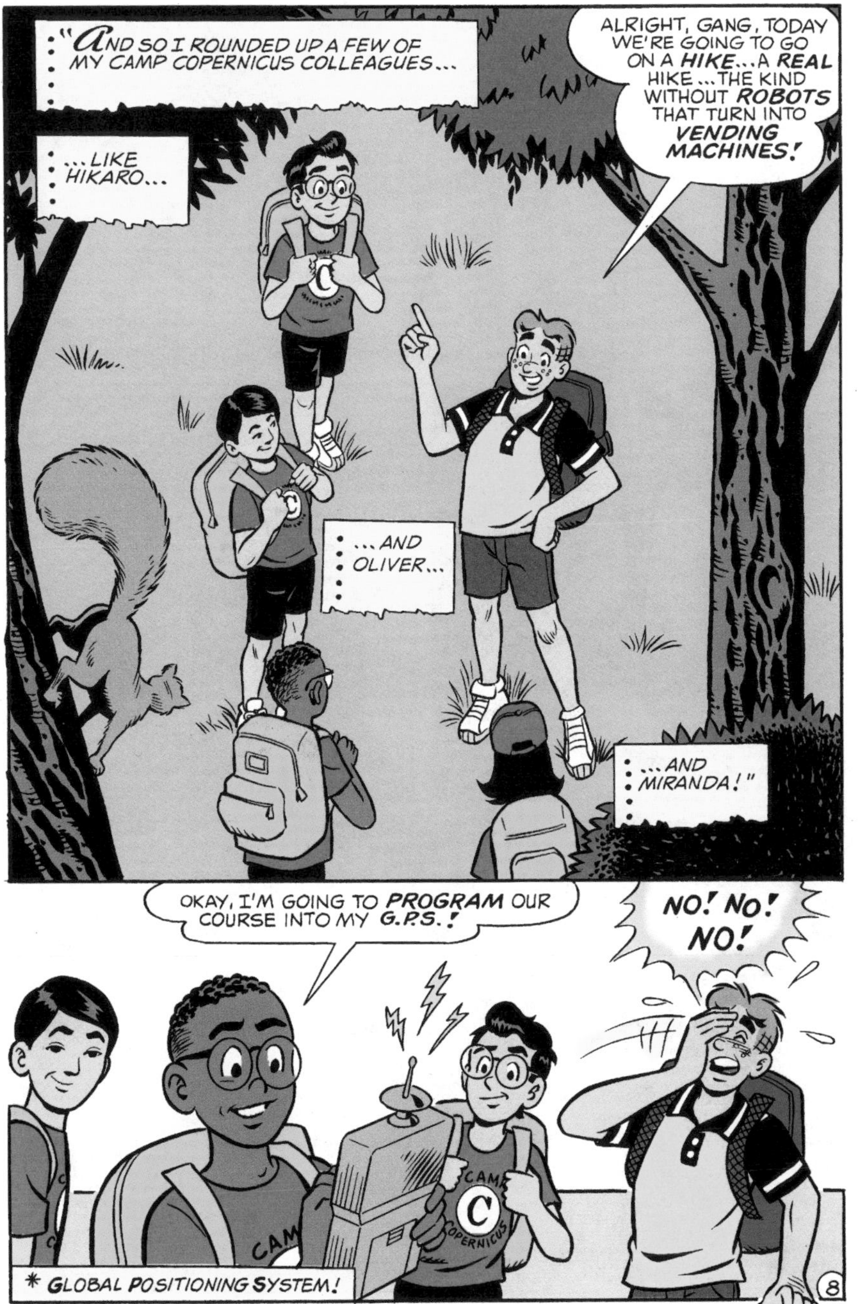
"AND SO I ROUNDED UP A FEW OF MY CAMP COPERNICUS COLLEAGUES...
ALRIGHT, GANG, TODAY WE'RE GOING TO GO ON A HIKE... A REAL HIKE... THE KIND WITHOUT ROBOTS THAT TURN INTO VENDING MACHINES!
...LIKE HIKARO...
...AND OLIVER...
...AND MIRANDA!"
OKAY, I'M GOING TO PROGRAM OUR COURSE INTO MY G.P.S.!
NO! NO! NO!
CAMP
COPERNICUS
* GLOBAL POSITIONING SYSTEM!
8

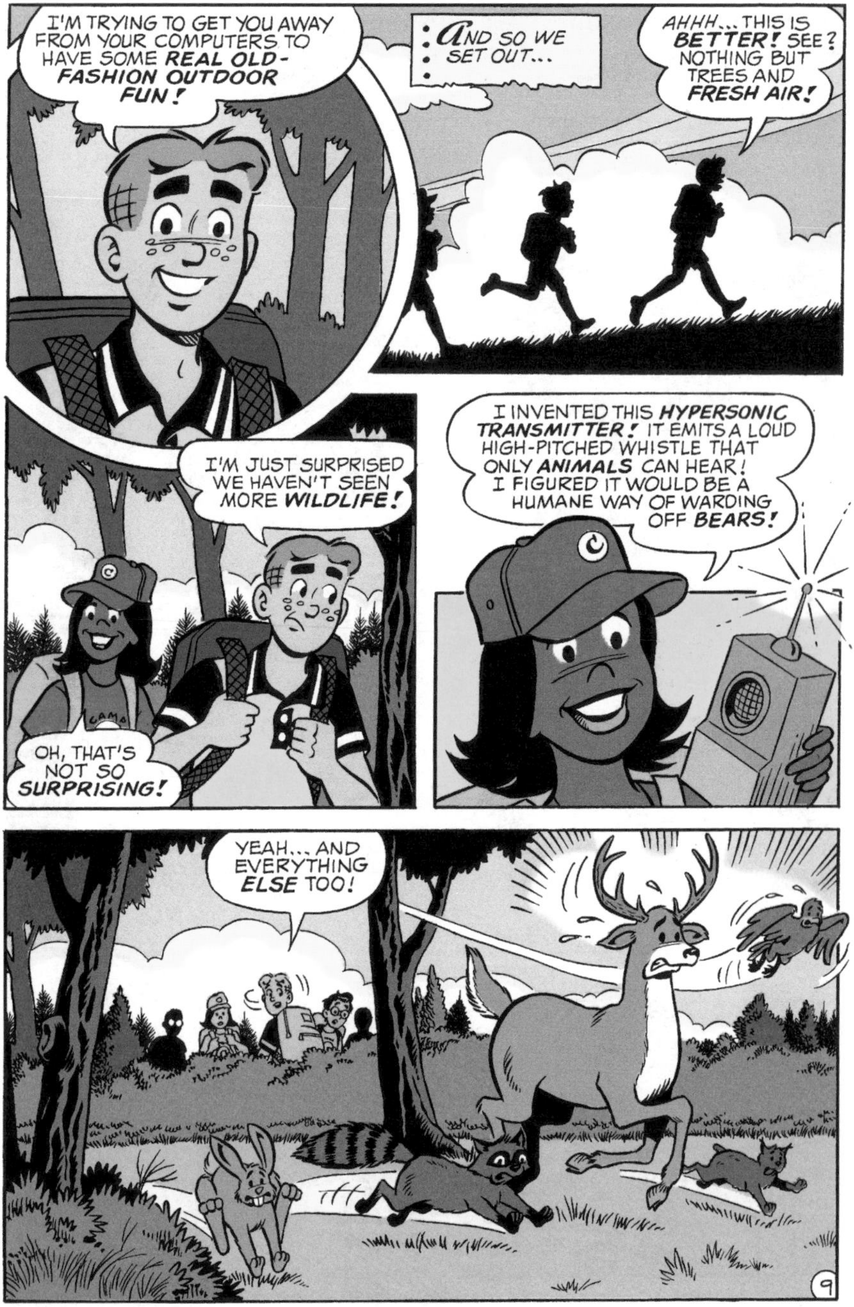
I'M TRYING TO GET YOU AWAY FROM YOUR COMPUTERS TO HAVE SOME **REAL OLD-FASHION OUTDOOR FUN!**
AND SO WE SET OUT...
AHHH... THIS IS **BETTER!** SEE? NOTHING BUT TREES AND **FRESH AIR!**
I'M JUST SURPRISED WE HAVEN'T SEEN MORE **WILDLIFE!**
OH, THAT'S NOT SO **SURPRISING!**
I INVENTED THIS **HYPERSONIC TRANSMITTER!** IT EMITS A LOUD HIGH-PITCHED WHISTLE THAT ONLY **ANIMALS** CAN HEAR! I FIGURED IT WOULD BE A HUMANE WAY OF WARDING OFF **BEARS!**
YEAH... AND EVERYTHING **ELSE** TOO!

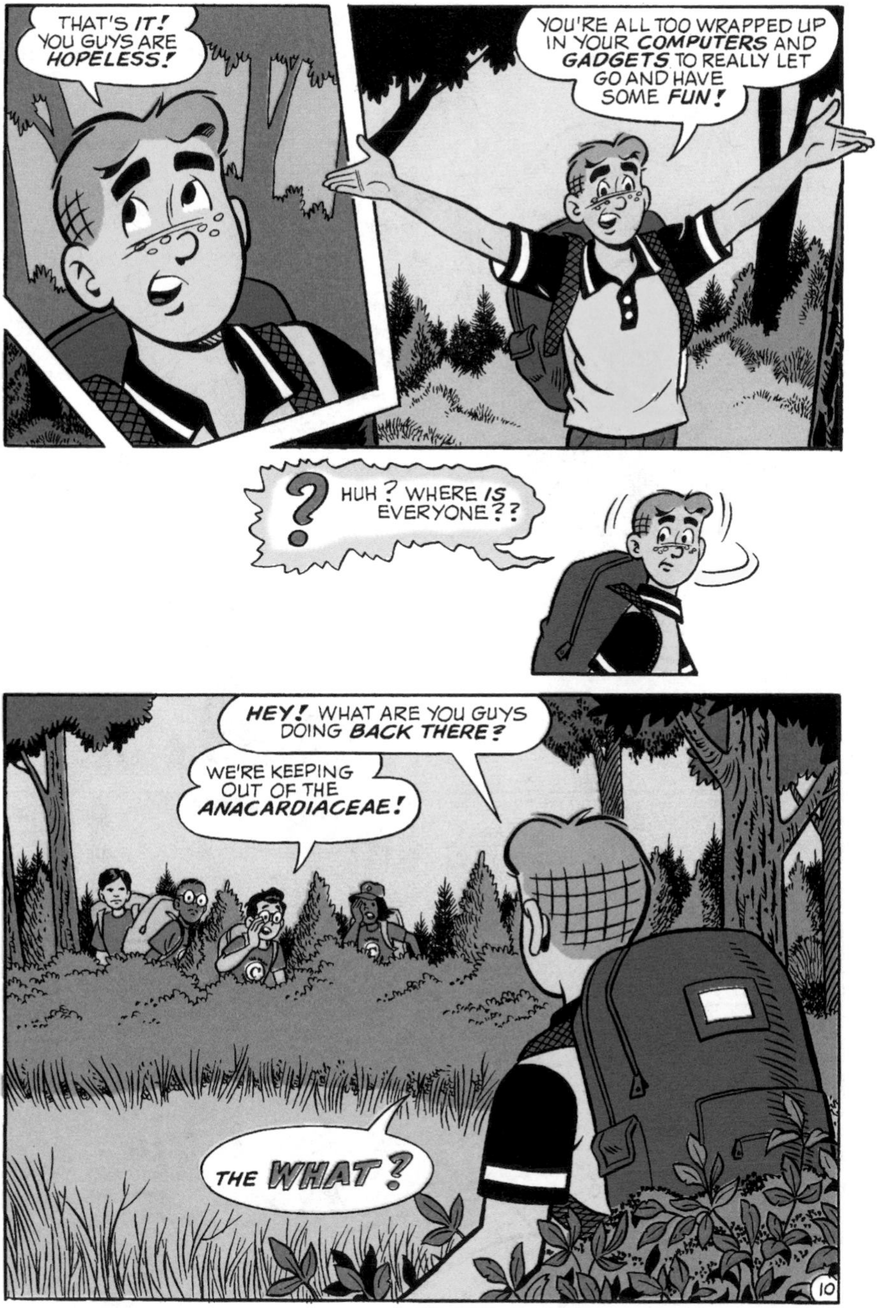

THAT'S IT! YOU GUYS ARE HOPELESS!
YOU'RE ALL TOO WRAPPED UP IN YOUR COMPUTERS AND GADGETS TO REALLY LET GO AND HAVE SOME FUN!
? HUH? WHERE IS EVERYONE??
HEY! WHAT ARE YOU GUYS DOING BACK THERE?
WE'RE KEEPING OUT OF THE ANACARDIACEAE!
THE WHAT?
10

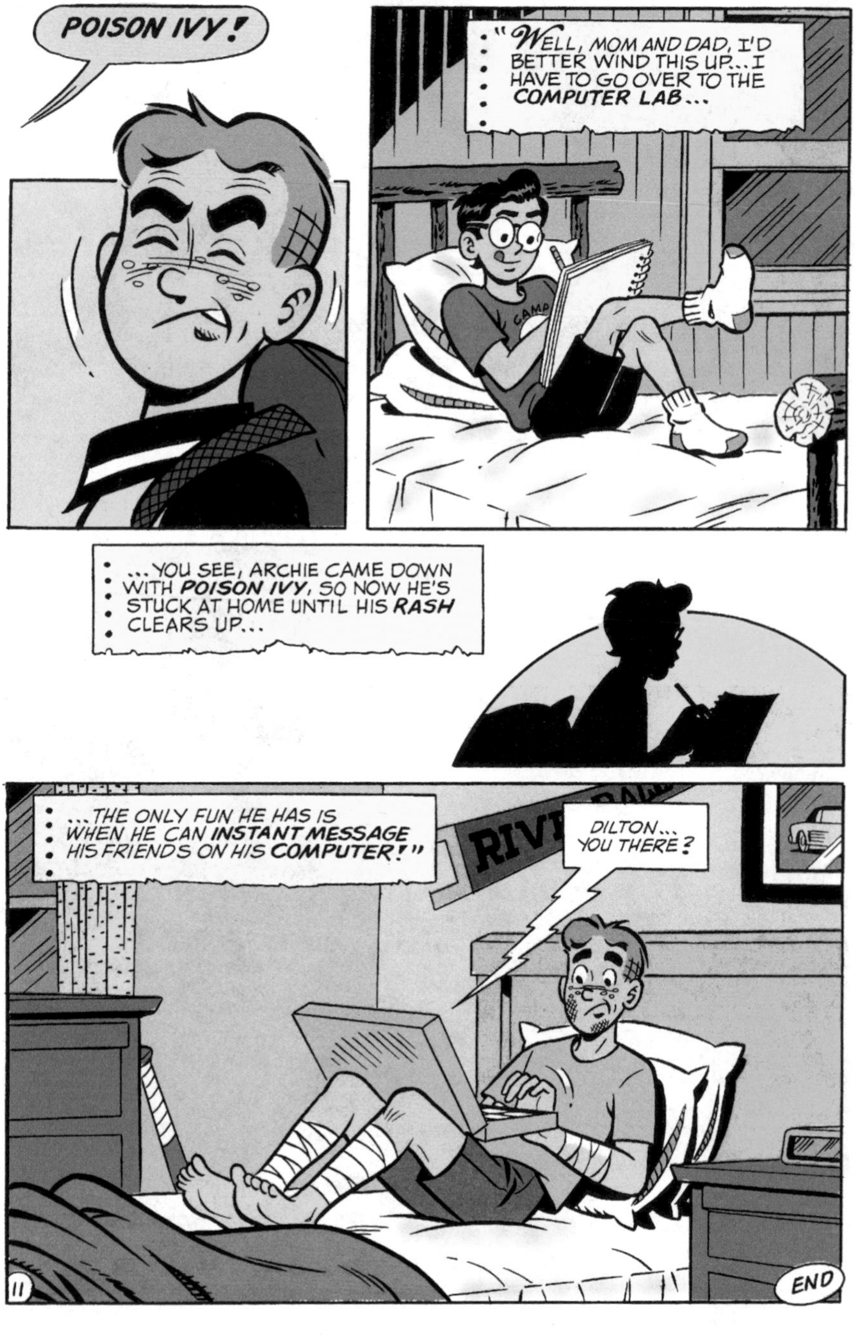
POISON IVY!
"WELL, MOM AND DAD, I'D BETTER WIND THIS UP...I HAVE TO GO OVER TO THE COMPUTER LAB...
CAMP
...YOU SEE, ARCHIE CAME DOWN WITH POISON IVY, SO NOW HE'S STUCK AT HOME UNTIL HIS RASH CLEARS UP...
...THE ONLY FUN HE HAS IS WHEN HE CAN INSTANT MESSAGE HIS FRIENDS ON HIS COMPUTER!"
RIV
DILTON... YOU THERE?
11
END

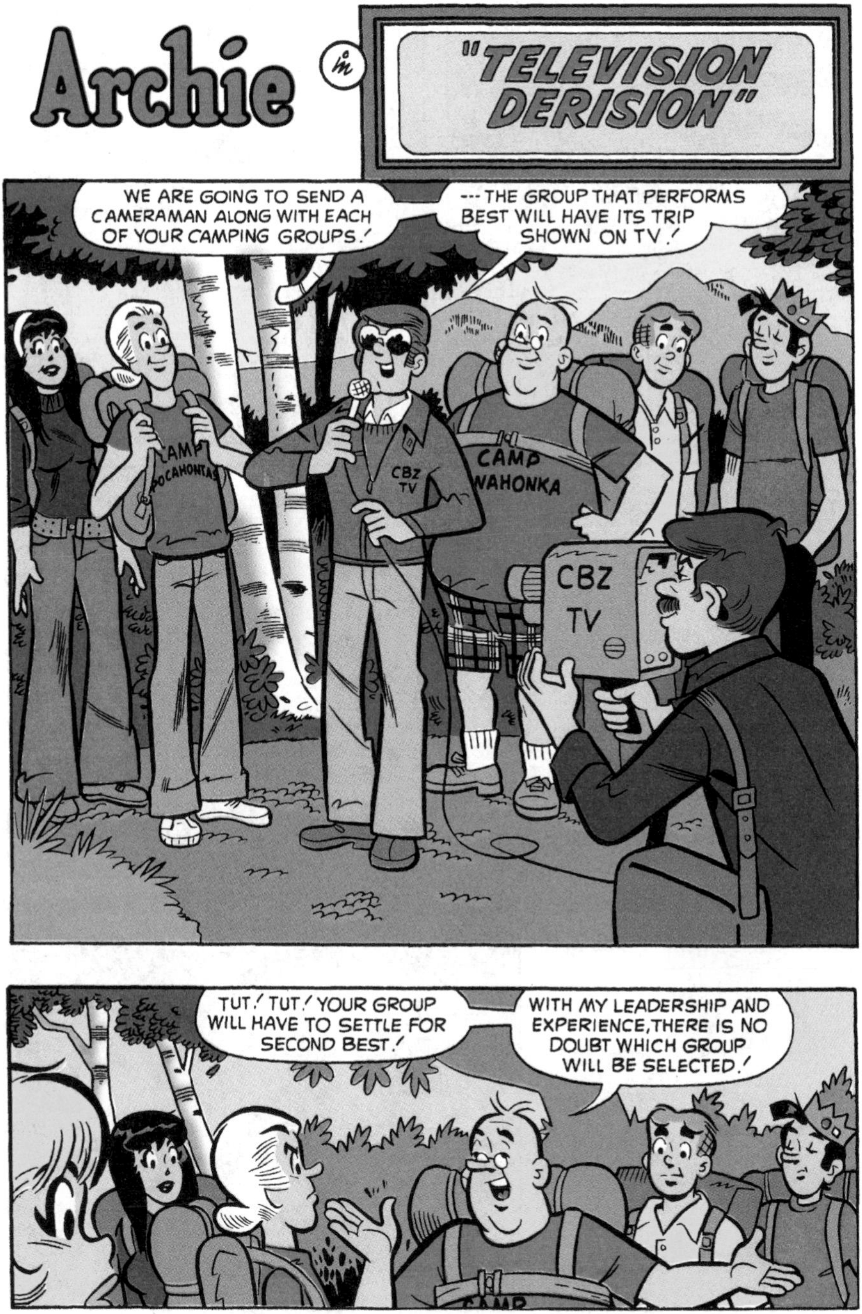
Archie in
"TELEVISION DERISION"
WE ARE GOING TO SEND A CAMERAMAN ALONG WITH EACH OF YOUR CAMPING GROUPS.!
--- THE GROUP THAT PERFORMS BEST WILL HAVE ITS TRIP SHOWN ON TV.!
CAMP POCAHONTAS
CBZ TV
CAMP WAHONKA
CBZ TV
TUT! TUT! YOUR GROUP WILL HAVE TO SETTLE FOR SECOND BEST!
WITH MY LEADERSHIP AND EXPERIENCE, THERE IS NO DOUBT WHICH GROUP WILL BE SELECTED!

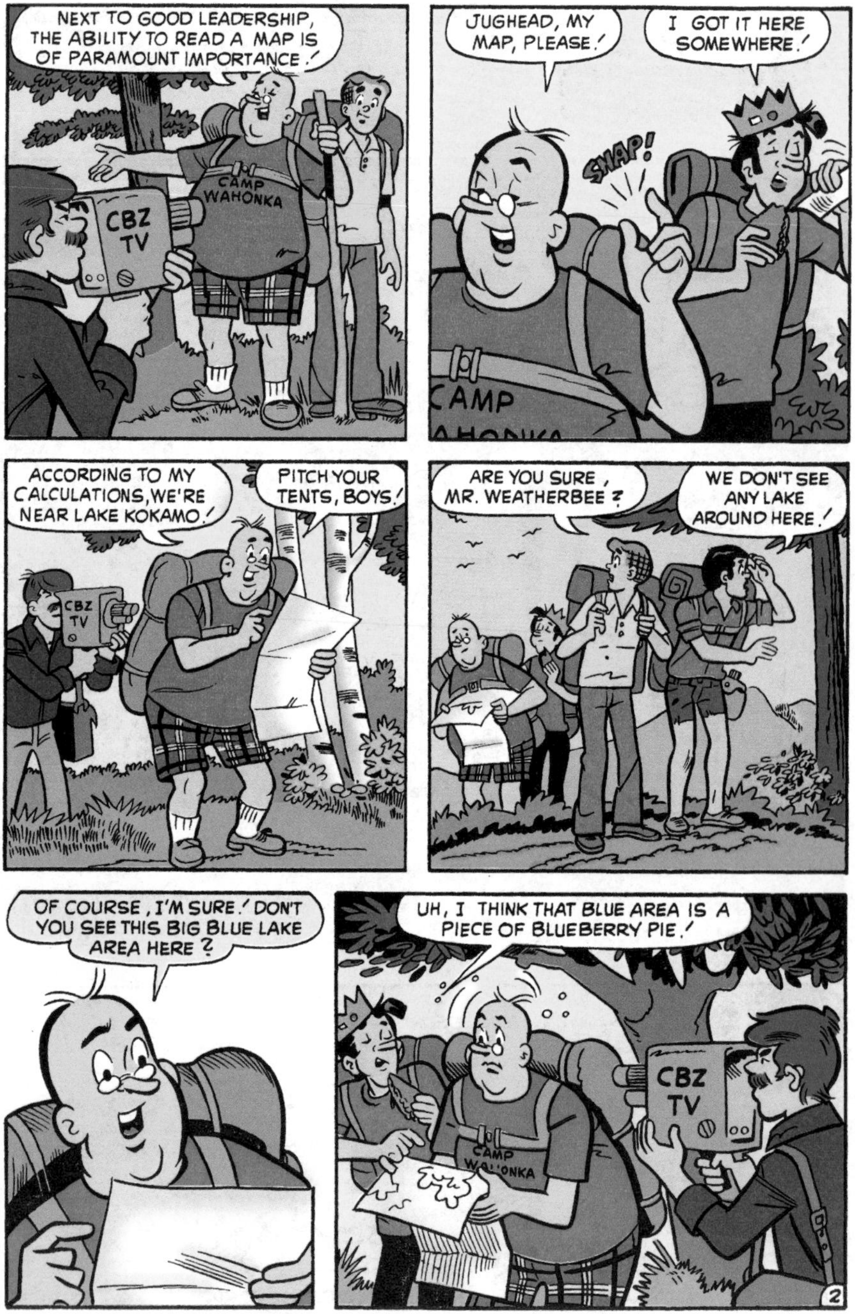
NEXT TO GOOD LEADERSHIP, THE ABILITY TO READ A MAP IS OF PARAMOUNT IMPORTANCE!
CAMP WAHONKA
CBZ TV
JUGHEAD, MY MAP, PLEASE!
I GOT IT HERE SOMEWHERE!
SNAP!
ACCORDING TO MY CALCULATIONS, WE'RE NEAR LAKE KOKAMO!
PITCH YOUR TENTS, BOYS!
CBZ TV
ARE YOU SURE, MR. WEATHERBEE?
WE DON'T SEE ANY LAKE AROUND HERE!
OF COURSE, I'M SURE! DON'T YOU SEE THIS BIG BLUE LAKE AREA HERE?
UH, I THINK THAT BLUE AREA IS A PIECE OF BLUEBERRY PIE!
CBZ TV
CAMP WAHONKA
2

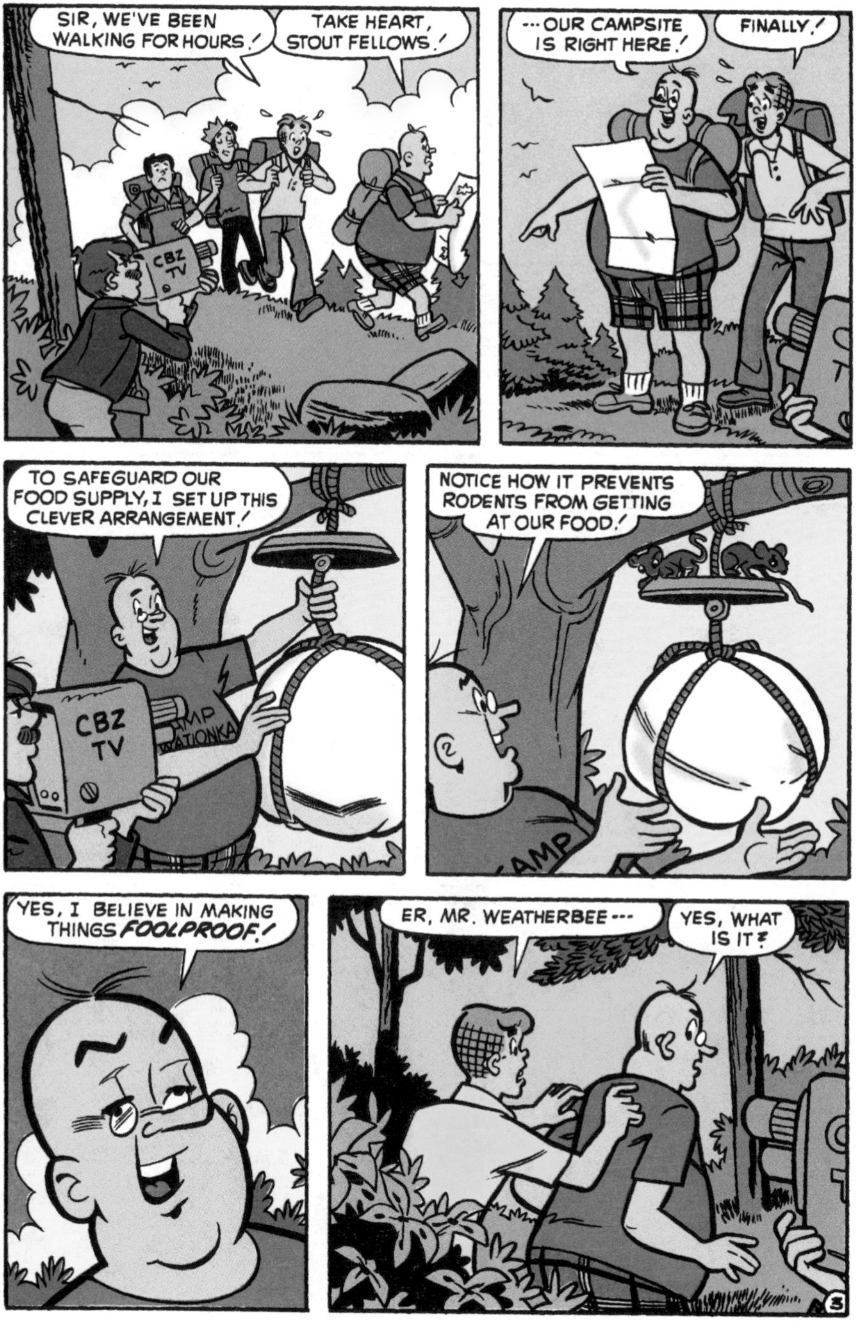
SIR, WE'VE BEEN WALKING FOR HOURS!
TAKE HEART, STOUT FELLOWS!
CBZ TV
--- OUR CAMPSITE IS RIGHT HERE!
FINALLY!
TO SAFEGUARD OUR FOOD SUPPLY, I SET UP THIS CLEVER ARRANGEMENT!
CBZ TV
NOTICE HOW IT PREVENTS RODENTS FROM GETTING AT OUR FOOD!
YES, I BELIEVE IN MAKING THINGS FOOLPROOF!
ER, MR. WEATHERBEE ---
YES, WHAT IS IT?
3

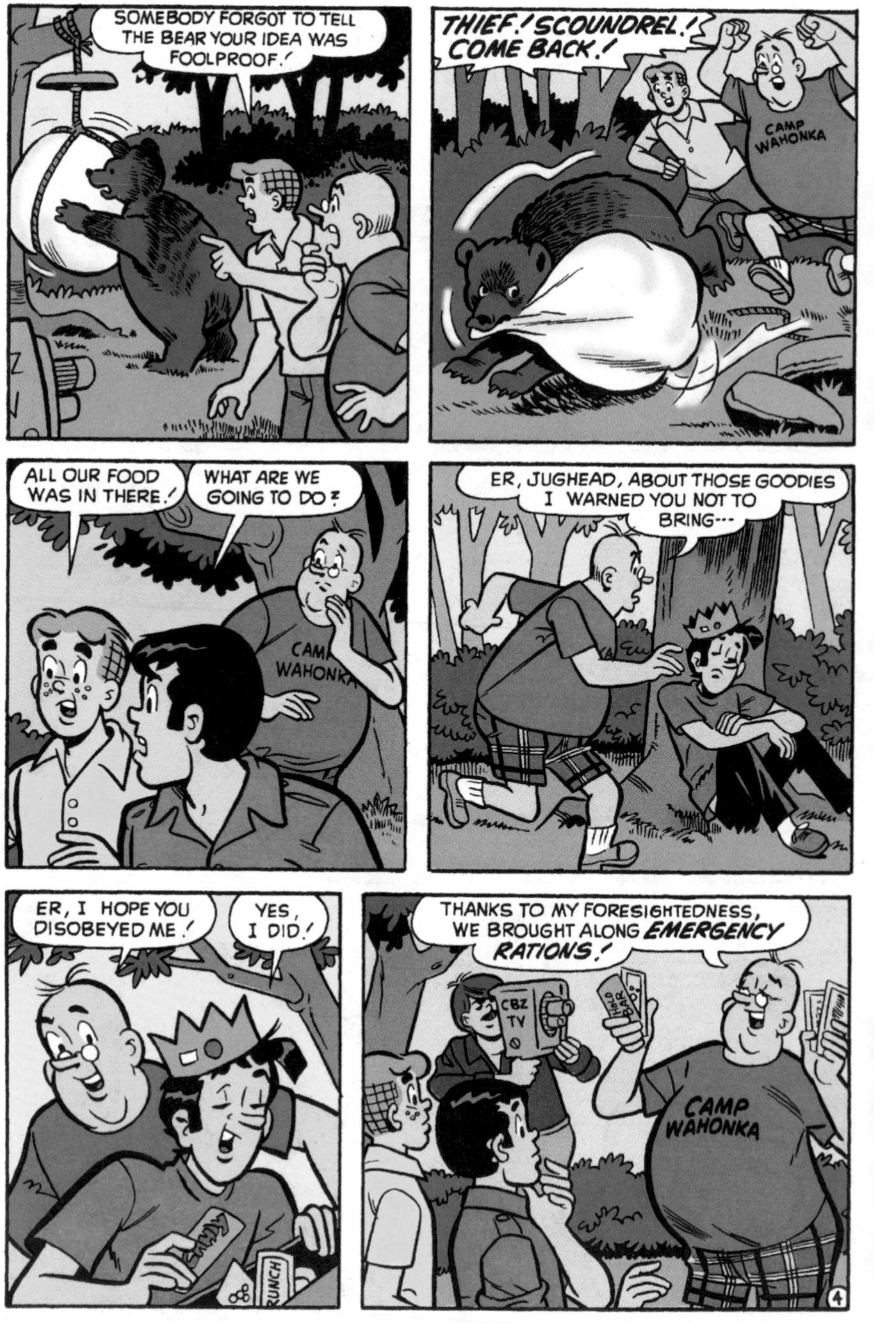
SOMEBODY FORGOT TO TELL THE BEAR YOUR IDEA WAS FOOLPROOF.!
THIEF.! SCOUNDREL.! COME BACK.!
CAMP WAHONKA
ALL OUR FOOD WAS IN THERE.!
WHAT ARE WE GOING TO DO?
CAMP WAHONKA
ER, JUGHEAD, ABOUT THOSE GOODIES I WARNED YOU NOT TO BRING---
ER, I HOPE YOU DISOBEYED ME.!
YES, I DID.!
CRUNCH
THANKS TO MY FORESIGHTEDNESS, WE BROUGHT ALONG *EMERGENCY RATIONS*.!
CBZ TV
CAMP WAHONKA
4

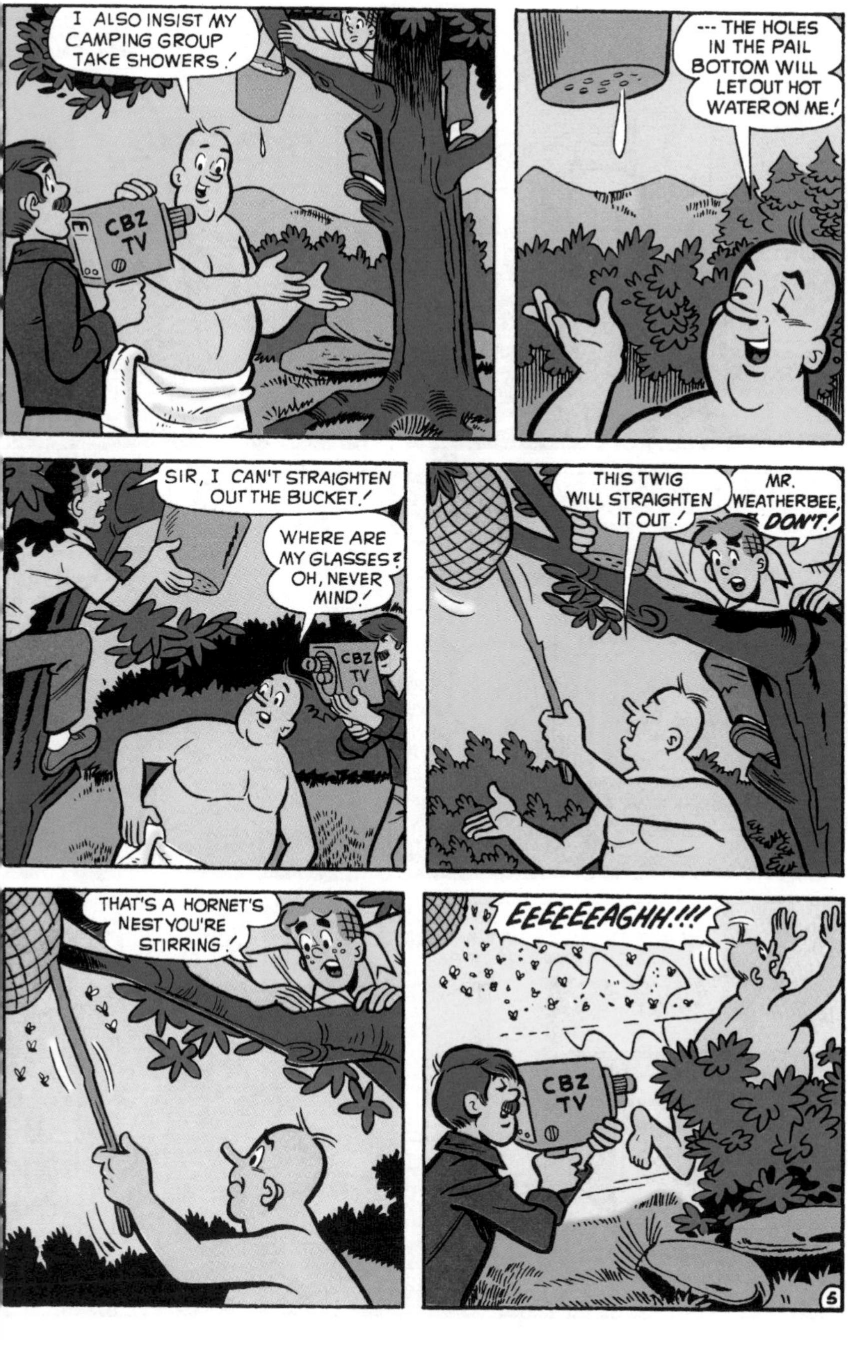
I ALSO INSIST MY CAMPING GROUP TAKE SHOWERS!
--- THE HOLES IN THE PAIL BOTTOM WILL LET OUT HOT WATER ON ME!
CBZ TV
SIR, I CAN'T STRAIGHTEN OUT THE BUCKET!
WHERE ARE MY GLASSES? OH, NEVER MIND!
CBZ TV
THIS TWIG WILL STRAIGHTEN IT OUT!
MR. WEATHERBEE, DON'T!
THAT'S A HORNET'S NEST YOU'RE STIRRING!
EEEEEEAGHH!!!
CBZ TV
5

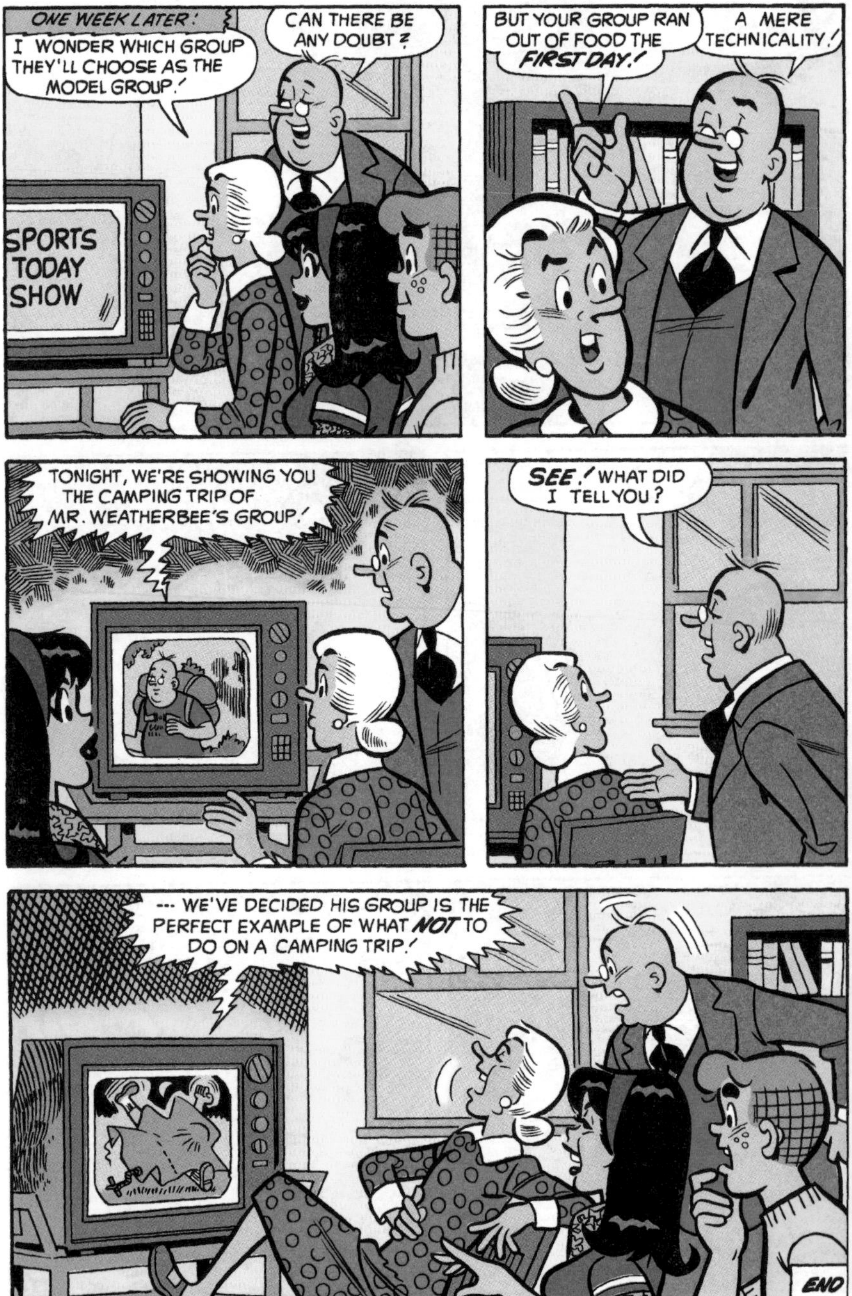
ONE WEEK LATER:
I WONDER WHICH GROUP THEY'LL CHOOSE AS THE MODEL GROUP!
CAN THERE BE ANY DOUBT?
SPORTS TODAY SHOW
BUT YOUR GROUP RAN OUT OF FOOD THE FIRST DAY!
A MERE TECHNICALITY!
TONIGHT, WE'RE SHOWING YOU THE CAMPING TRIP OF MR. WEATHERBEE'S GROUP!
SEE! WHAT DID I TELL YOU?
--- WE'VE DECIDED HIS GROUP IS THE PERFECT EXAMPLE OF WHAT NOT TO DO ON A CAMPING TRIP!
END

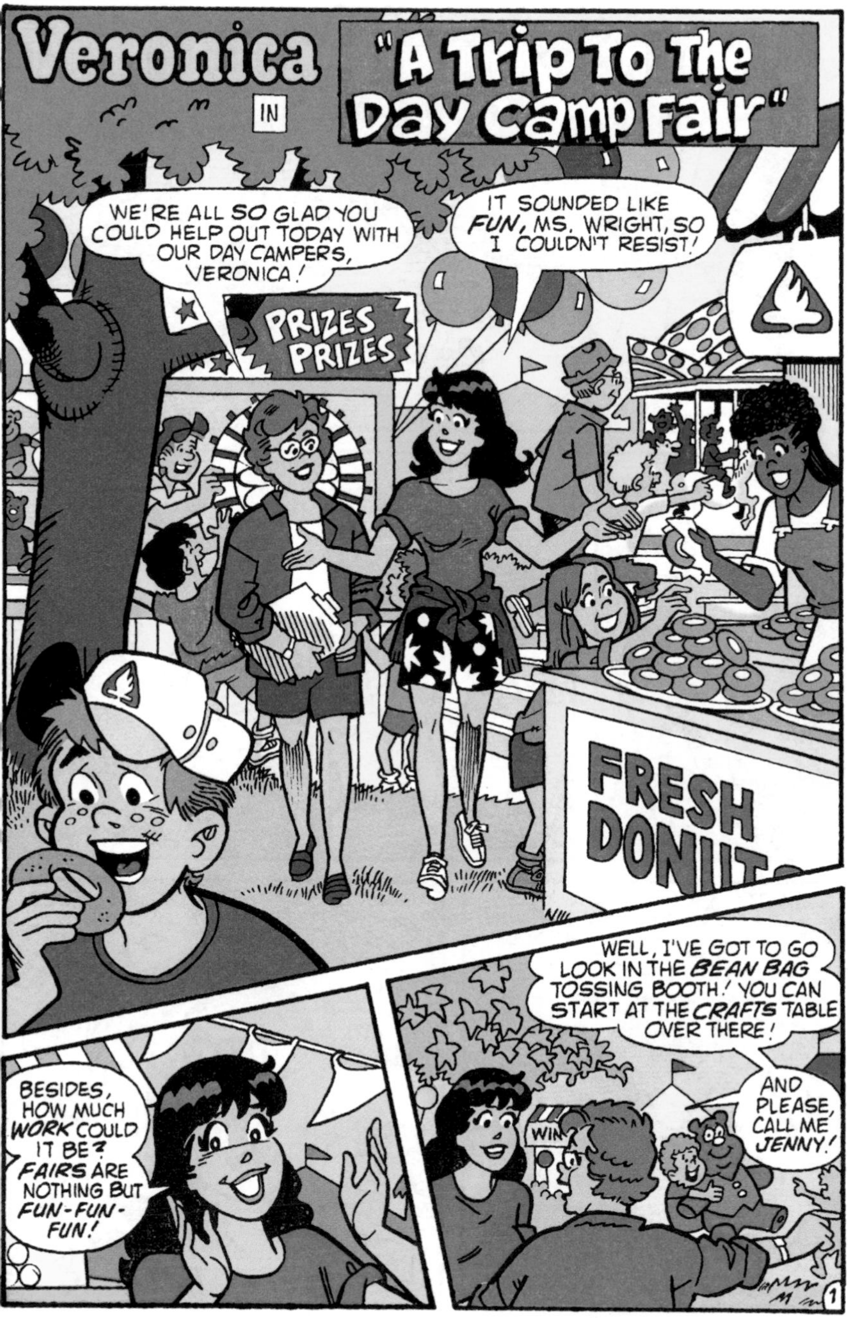
Veronica
IN
"A Trip To The Day Camp Fair"
WE'RE ALL SO GLAD YOU COULD HELP OUT TODAY WITH OUR DAY CAMPERS, VERONICA!
IT SOUNDED LIKE FUN, MS. WRIGHT, SO I COULDN'T RESIST!
PRIZES PRIZES
FRESH DONUTS
BESIDES, HOW MUCH WORK COULD IT BE? FAIRS ARE NOTHING BUT FUN-FUN-FUN!
WELL, I'VE GOT TO GO LOOK IN THE BEAN BAG TOSSING BOOTH! YOU CAN START AT THE CRAFTS TABLE OVER THERE!
AND PLEASE, CALL ME JENNY!
WIN
1

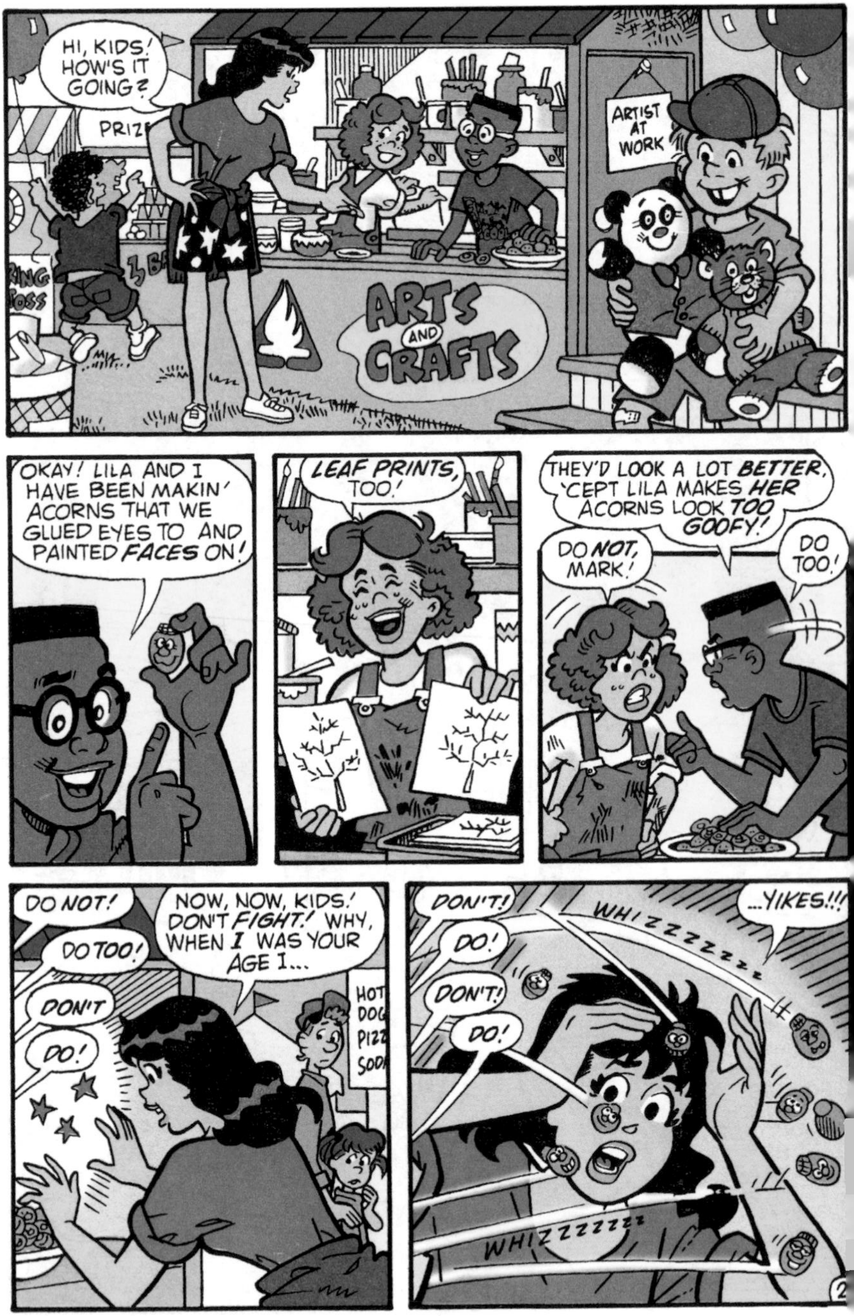
HI, KIDS! HOW'S IT GOING?
PRIZ
ARTIST AT WORK
ARTS AND CRAFTS
OKAY! LILA AND I HAVE BEEN MAKIN' ACORNS THAT WE GLUED EYES TO AND PAINTED FACES ON!
LEAF PRINTS, TOO!
THEY'D LOOK A LOT BETTER, 'CEPT LILA MAKES HER ACORNS LOOK TOO GOOFY!
DO NOT, MARK!
DO TOO!
DO NOT!
DO TOO!
DON'T
DO!
NOW, NOW, KIDS! DON'T FIGHT! WHY, WHEN I WAS YOUR AGE I...
HOT DOG PIZZ SOD
DON'T!
DO!
DON'T!
DO!
WHIZZZZZZZZ
...YIKES!!!
WHIZZZZZZZZ

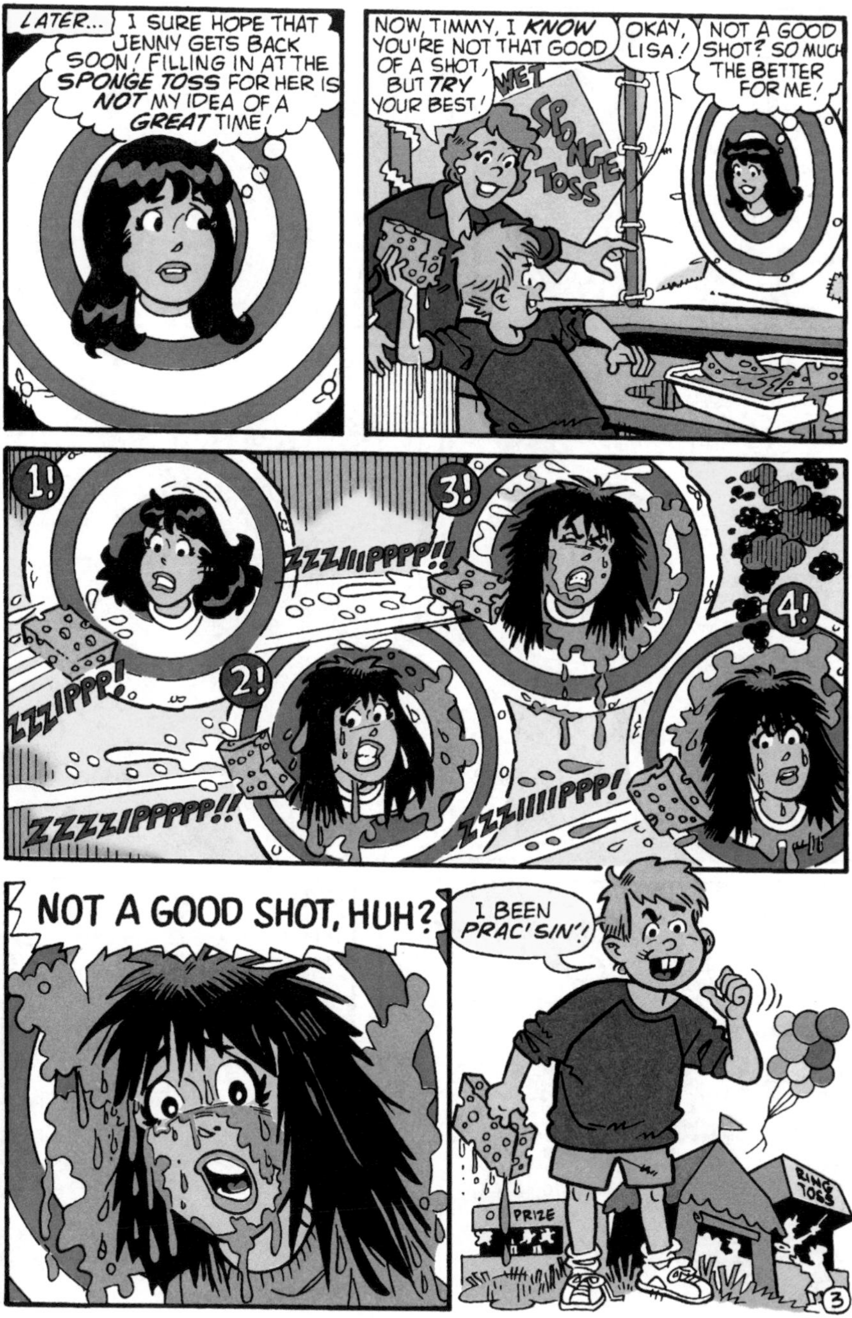

LATER...
I SURE HOPE THAT JENNY GETS BACK SOON! FILLING IN AT THE SPONGE TOSS FOR HER IS NOT MY IDEA OF A GREAT TIME!
NOW, TIMMY, I KNOW YOU'RE NOT THAT GOOD OF A SHOT, BUT TRY YOUR BEST!
OKAY, LISA!
NOT A GOOD SHOT? SO MUCH THE BETTER FOR ME!
WET SPONGE TOSS
1!
ZZZIIIPPPP!!
3!
ZZZIPPP!
2!
4!
ZZZZIPPPPP!!
ZZZIIIIPPP!
NOT A GOOD SHOT, HUH?
I BEEN PRAC'SIN'!
PRIZE
RING TOSS
3

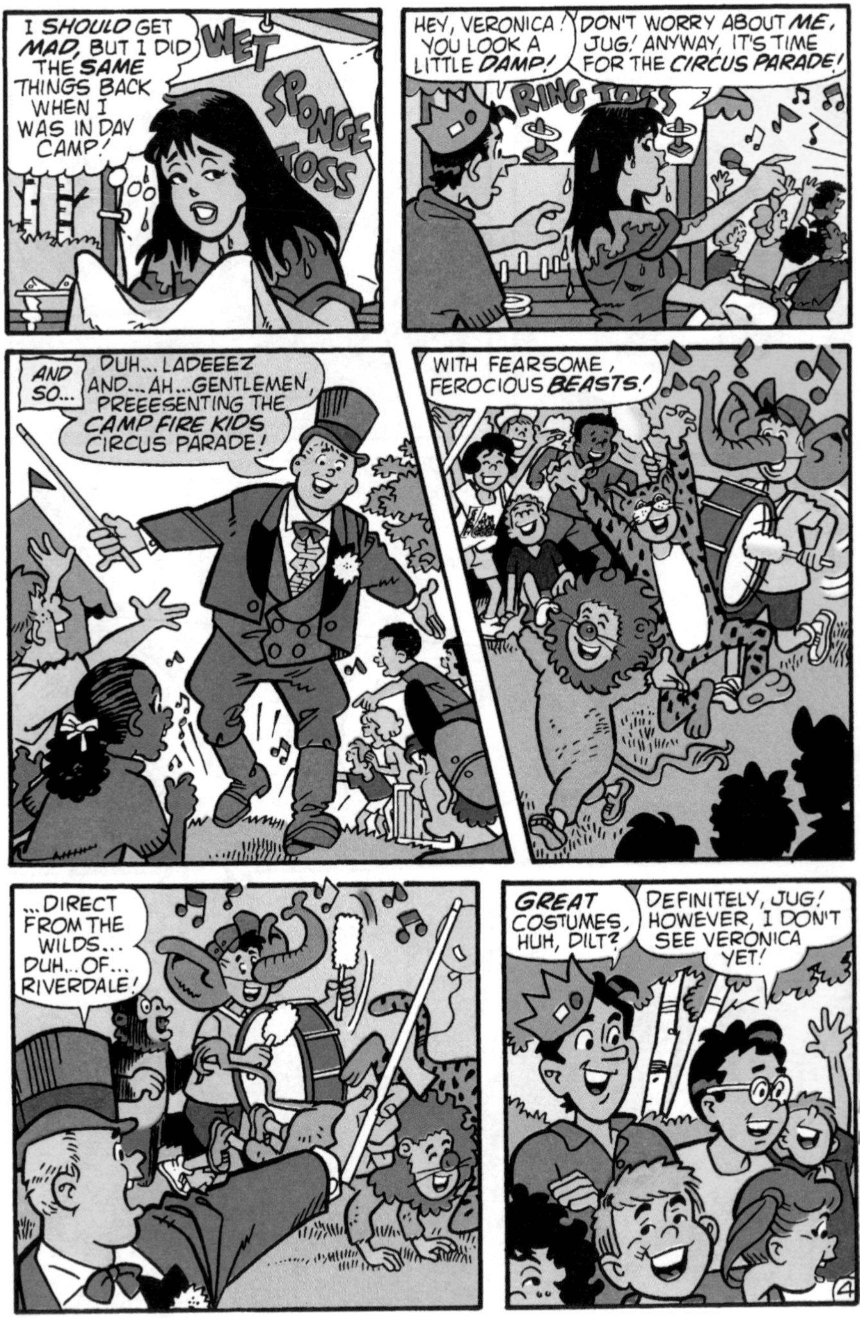
I SHOULD GET MAD, BUT I DID THE SAME THINGS BACK WHEN I WAS IN DAY CAMP!
WET SPONGE TOSS
HEY, VERONICA! YOU LOOK A LITTLE DAMP!
DON'T WORRY ABOUT ME, JUG! ANYWAY, IT'S TIME FOR THE CIRCUS PARADE!
RING TOSS
AND SO...
DUH... LADEEEZ AND... AH... GENTLEMEN, PREEESENTING THE CAMP FIRE KIDS CIRCUS PARADE!
WITH FEARSOME, FEROCIOUS BEASTS!
...DIRECT FROM THE WILDS... DUH... OF... RIVERDALE!
GREAT COSTUMES, HUH, DILT?
DEFINITELY, JUG! HOWEVER, I DON'T SEE VERONICA YET!
4

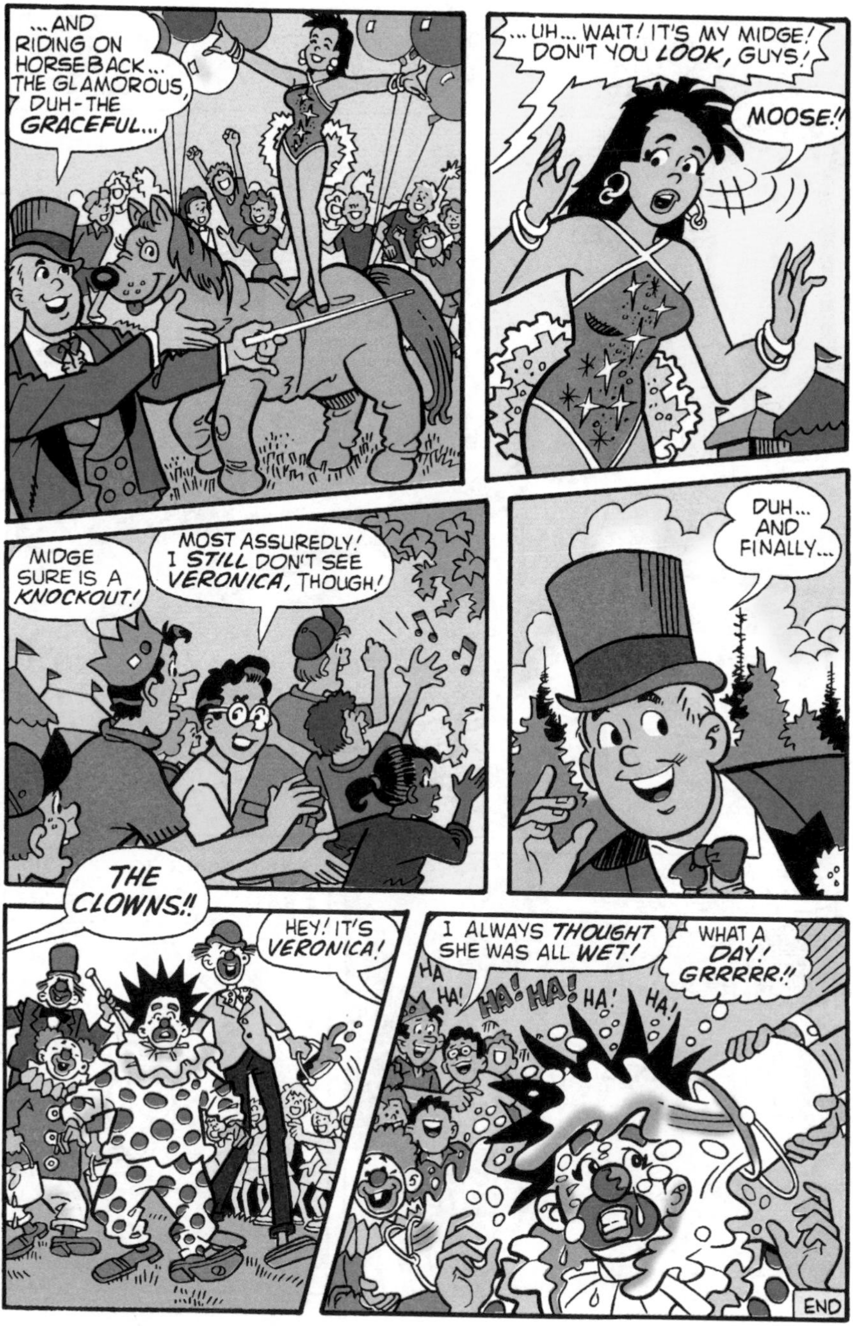
...AND RIDING ON HORSEBACK... THE GLAMOROUS, DUH-THE GRACEFUL...
...UH... WAIT! IT'S MY MIDGE! DON'T YOU LOOK, GUYS!
MOOSE!!
MIDGE SURE IS A KNOCKOUT!
MOST ASSUREDLY! I STILL DON'T SEE VERONICA, THOUGH!
DUH... AND FINALLY...
THE CLOWNS!!
HEY! IT'S VERONICA!
I ALWAYS THOUGHT SHE WAS ALL WET!
WHAT A DAY! GRRRRR!!
HA HA! HA! HA! HA! HA!
END

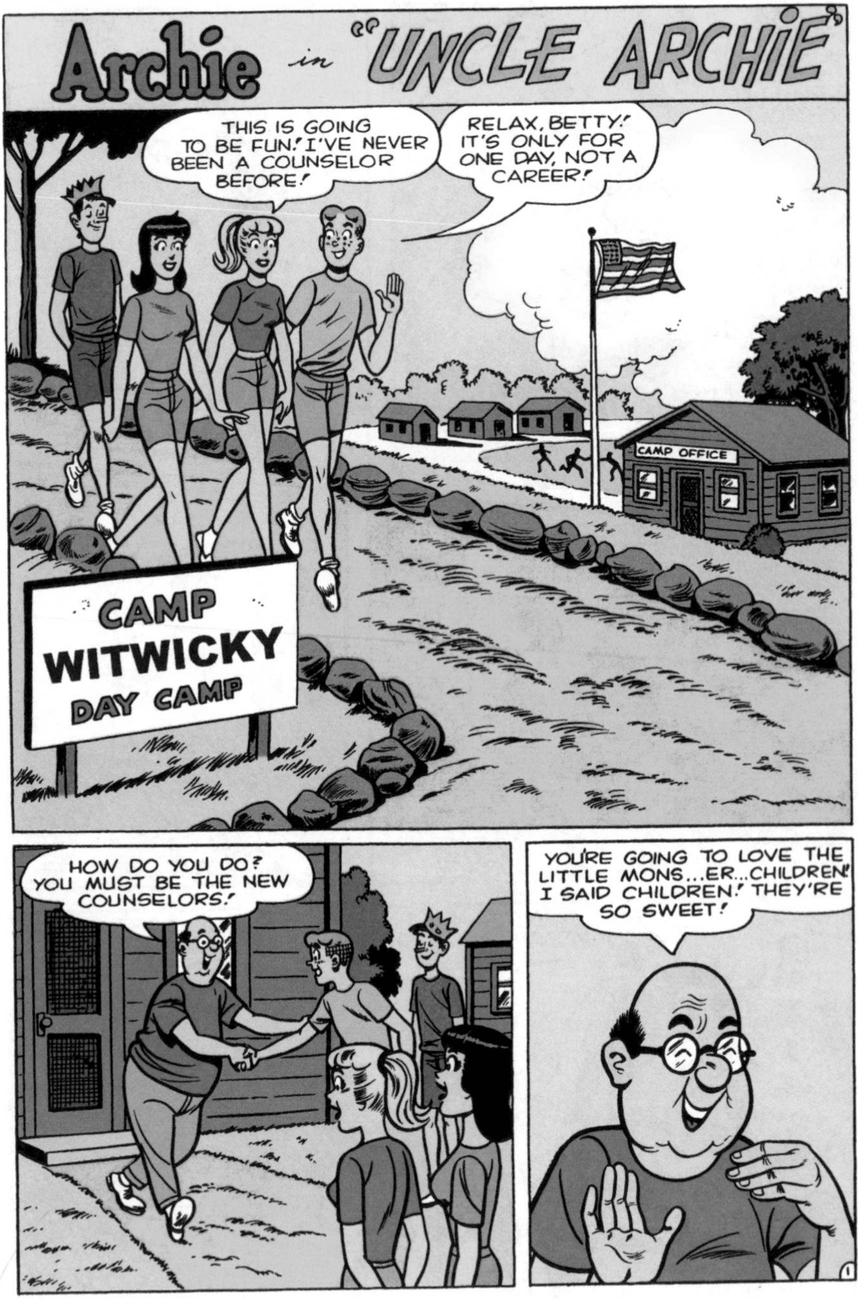

Archie in "UNCLE ARCHIE"
THIS IS GOING TO BE FUN! I'VE NEVER BEEN A COUNSELOR BEFORE!
RELAX, BETTY! IT'S ONLY FOR ONE DAY, NOT A CAREER!
CAMP OFFICE
CAMP WITWICKY DAY CAMP
HOW DO YOU DO? YOU MUST BE THE NEW COUNSELORS!
YOU'RE GOING TO LOVE THE LITTLE MONS...ER...CHILDREN! I SAID CHILDREN! THEY'RE SO SWEET!
1

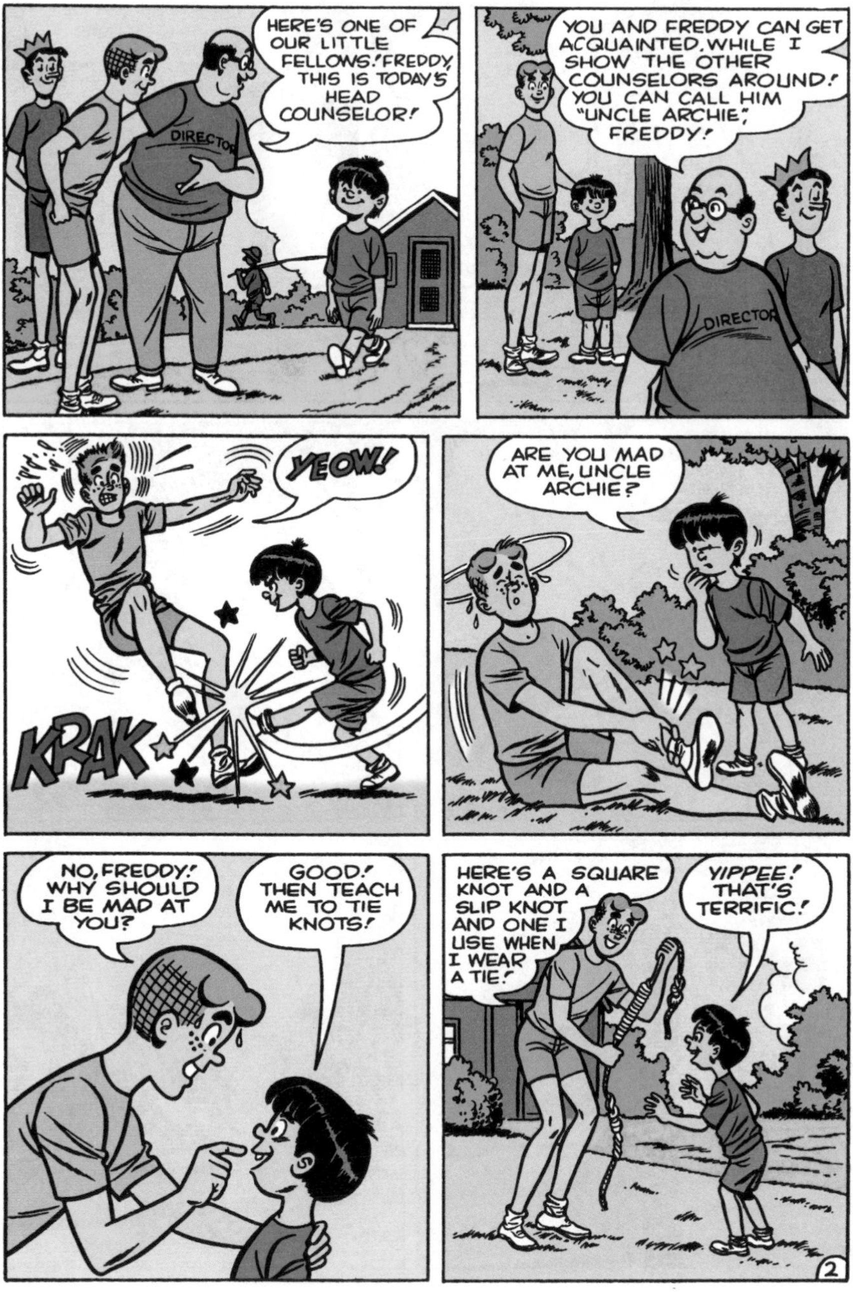
HERE'S ONE OF OUR LITTLE FELLOWS! FREDDY, THIS IS TODAY'S HEAD COUNSELOR!
DIRECTOR
YOU AND FREDDY CAN GET ACQUAINTED, WHILE I SHOW THE OTHER COUNSELORS AROUND! YOU CAN CALL HIM "UNCLE ARCHIE," FREDDY!
DIRECTOR
YEOW!
KRAK
ARE YOU MAD AT ME, UNCLE ARCHIE?
NO, FREDDY! WHY SHOULD I BE MAD AT YOU?
GOOD! THEN TEACH ME TO TIE KNOTS!
HERE'S A SQUARE KNOT AND A SLIP KNOT AND ONE I USE WHEN I WEAR A TIE!
YIPPEE! THAT'S TERRIFIC!
2

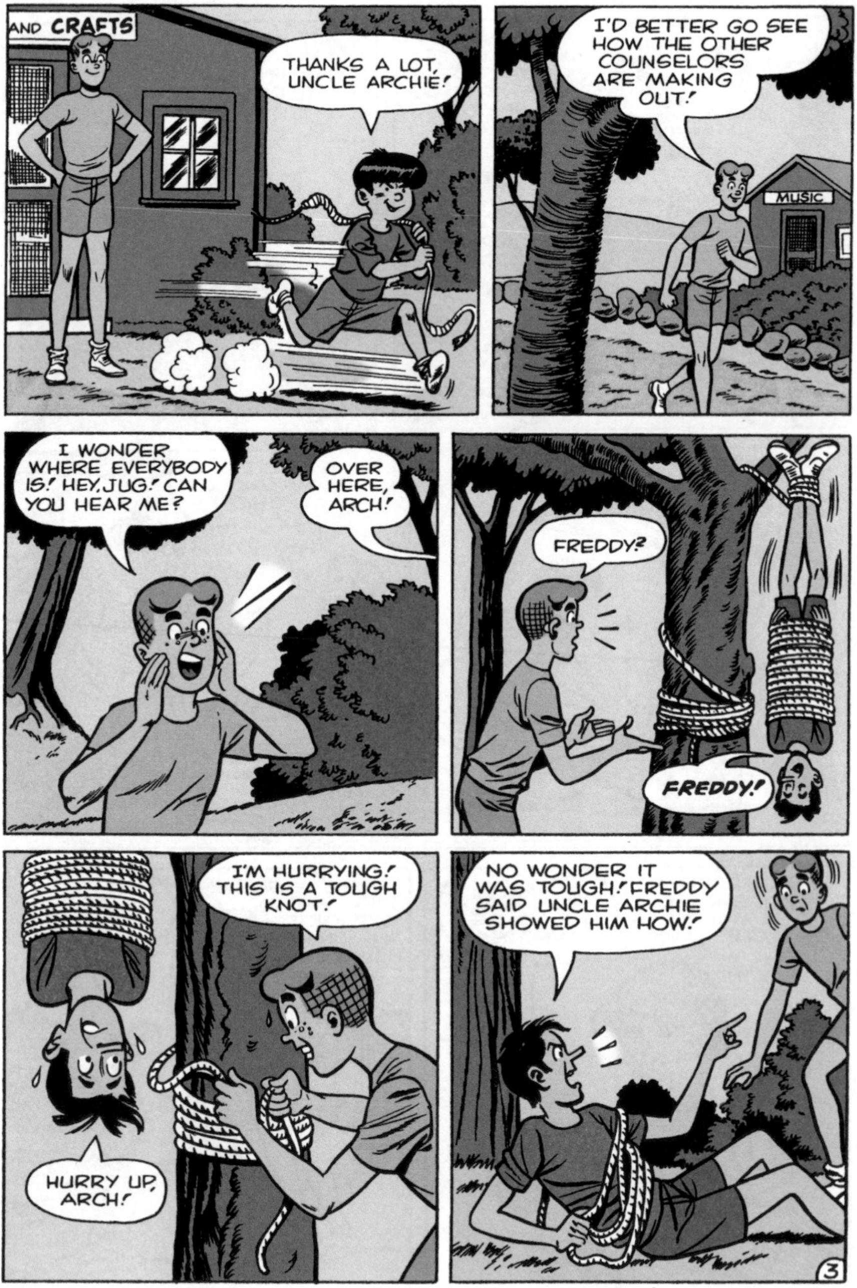
AND CRAFTS
THANKS A LOT, UNCLE ARCHIE!
I'D BETTER GO SEE HOW THE OTHER COUNSELORS ARE MAKING OUT!
MUSIC
I WONDER WHERE EVERYBODY IS! HEY, JUG! CAN YOU HEAR ME?
OVER HERE, ARCH!
FREDDY?
FREDDY!
I'M HURRYING! THIS IS A TOUGH KNOT!
HURRY UP, ARCH!
NO WONDER IT WAS TOUGH! FREDDY SAID UNCLE ARCHIE SHOWED HIM HOW!
3

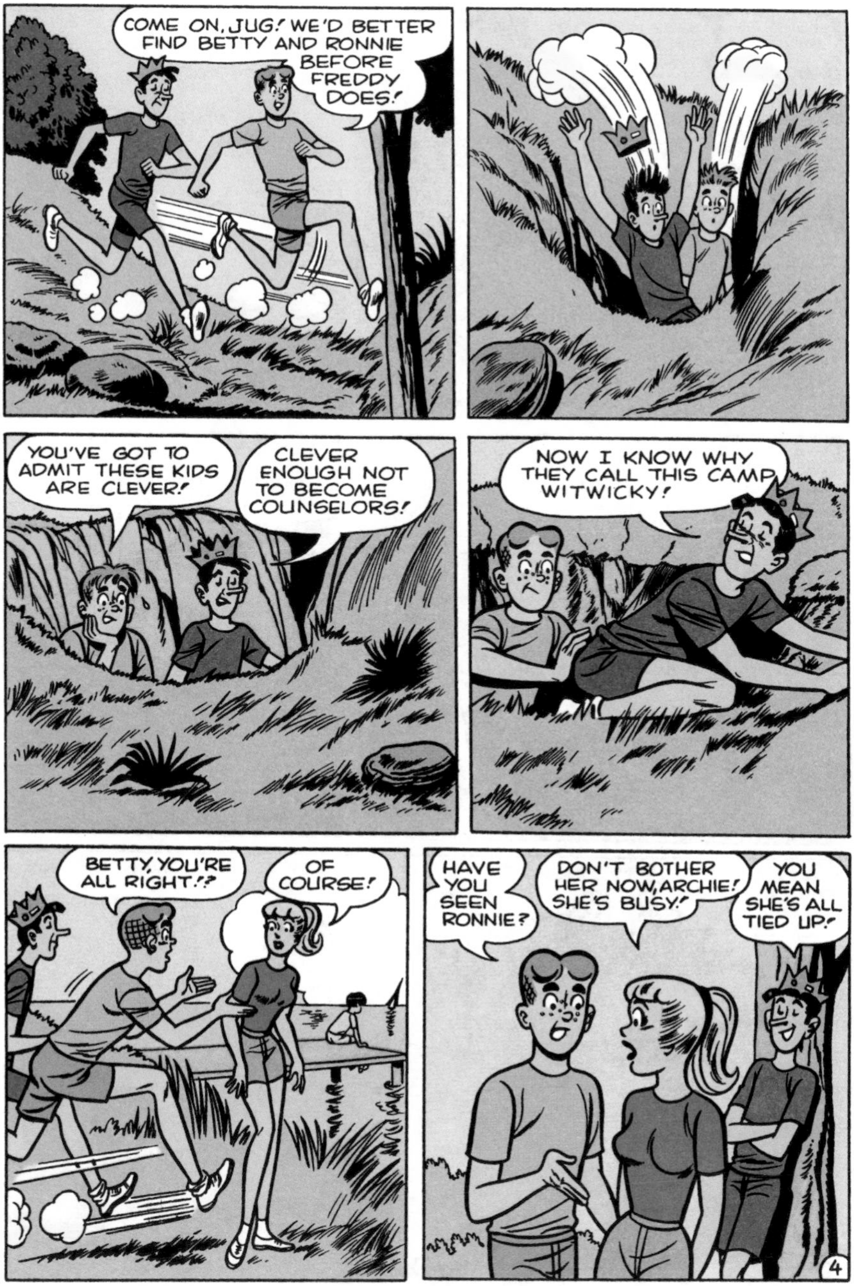
COME ON, JUG! WE'D BETTER FIND BETTY AND RONNIE BEFORE FREDDY DOES!
YOU'VE GOT TO ADMIT THESE KIDS ARE CLEVER!
CLEVER ENOUGH NOT TO BECOME COUNSELORS!
NOW I KNOW WHY THEY CALL THIS CAMP WITWICKY!
BETTY, YOU'RE ALL RIGHT!?
OF COURSE!
HAVE YOU SEEN RONNIE?
DON'T BOTHER HER NOW, ARCHIE! SHE'S BUSY!
YOU MEAN SHE'S ALL TIED UP!
4

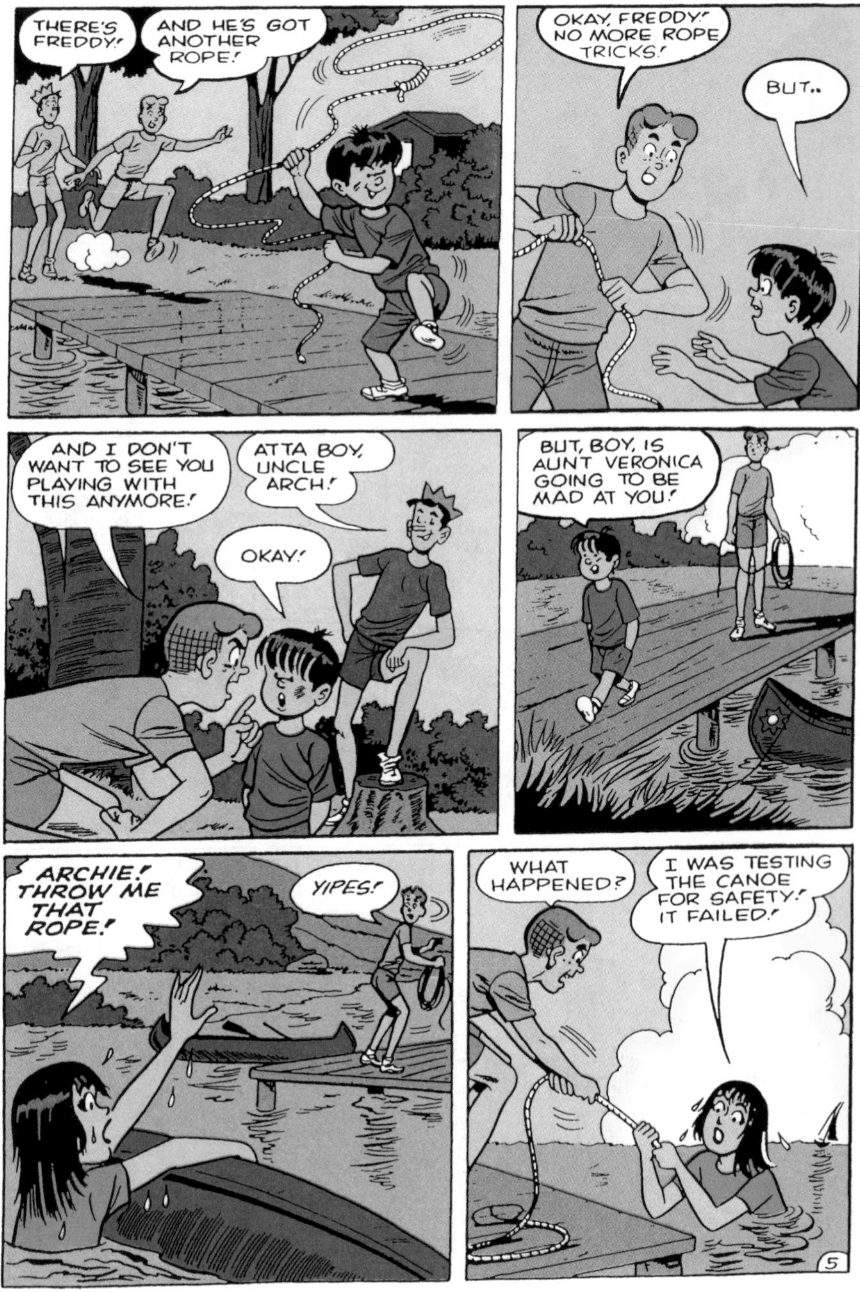
THERE'S FREDDY!
AND HE'S GOT ANOTHER ROPE!
OKAY, FREDDY! NO MORE ROPE TRICKS!
BUT..
AND I DON'T WANT TO SEE YOU PLAYING WITH THIS ANYMORE!
ATTA BOY, UNCLE ARCH!
OKAY!
BUT, BOY, IS AUNT VERONICA GOING TO BE MAD AT YOU!
ARCHIE! THROW ME THAT ROPE!
YIPES!
WHAT HAPPENED?
I WAS TESTING THE CANOE FOR SAFETY! IT FAILED!

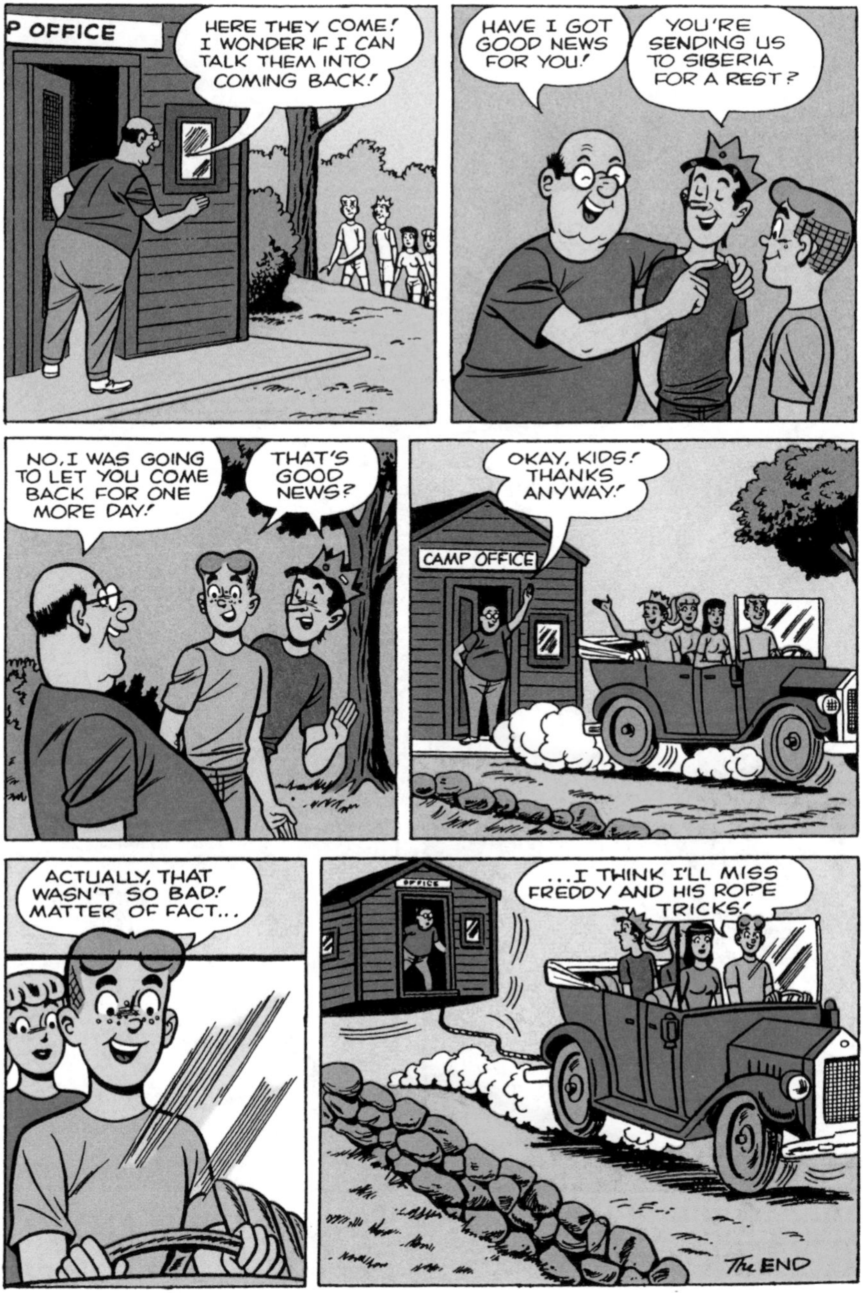
P OFFICE
HERE THEY COME! I WONDER IF I CAN TALK THEM INTO COMING BACK!
HAVE I GOT GOOD NEWS FOR YOU!
YOU'RE SENDING US TO SIBERIA FOR A REST?
NO, I WAS GOING TO LET YOU COME BACK FOR ONE MORE DAY!
THAT'S GOOD NEWS?
OKAY, KIDS! THANKS ANYWAY!
CAMP OFFICE
ACTUALLY, THAT WASN'T SO BAD! MATTER OF FACT...
OFFICE
...I THINK I'LL MISS FREDDY AND HIS ROPE TRICKS!
The END

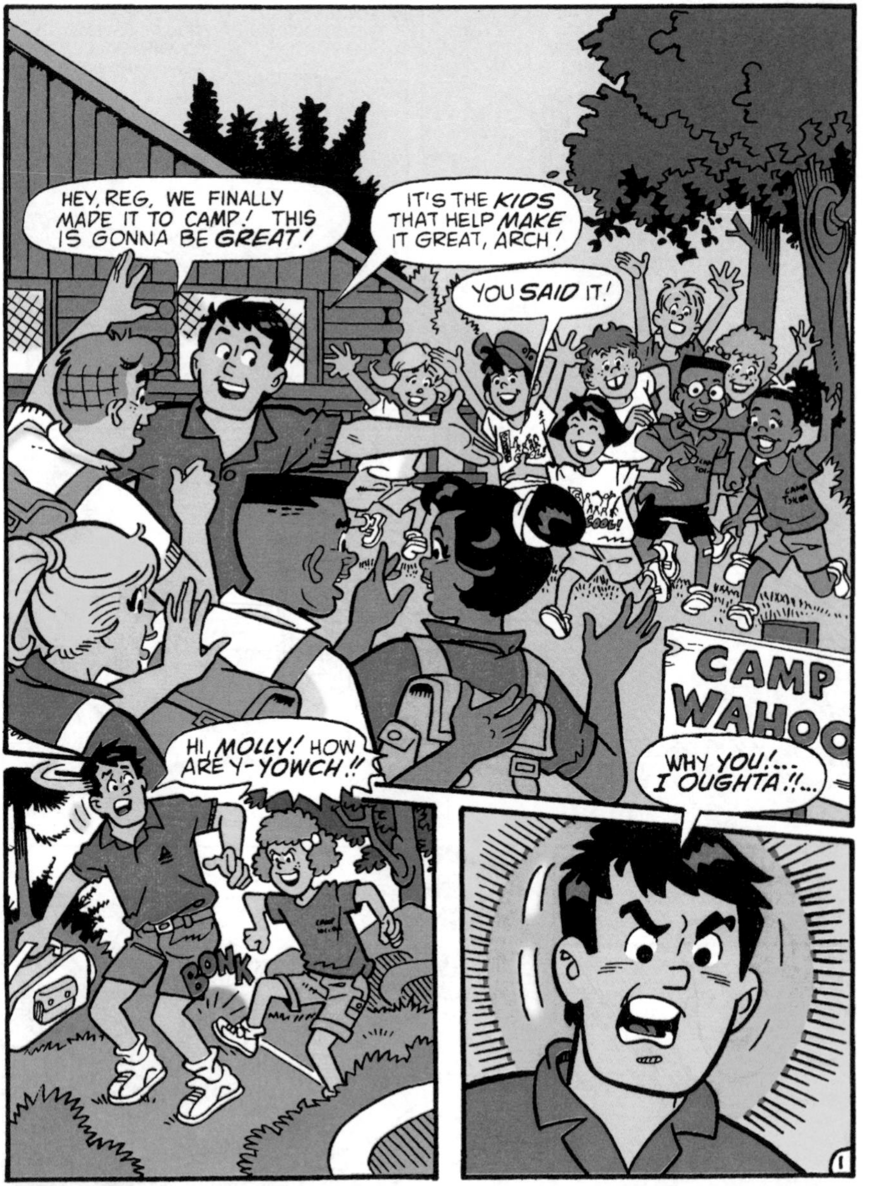
HEY, REG, WE FINALLY MADE IT TO CAMP! THIS IS GONNA BE GREAT!
IT'S THE KIDS THAT HELP MAKE IT GREAT, ARCH!
YOU SAID IT!
CAMP WAHOO
HI, MOLLY! HOW ARE Y-YOWCH!!
BONK
WHY YOU!... I OUGHTA!!...
1

Archie and the Gang in "CAMP FIRE DAYS"

PART I

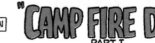

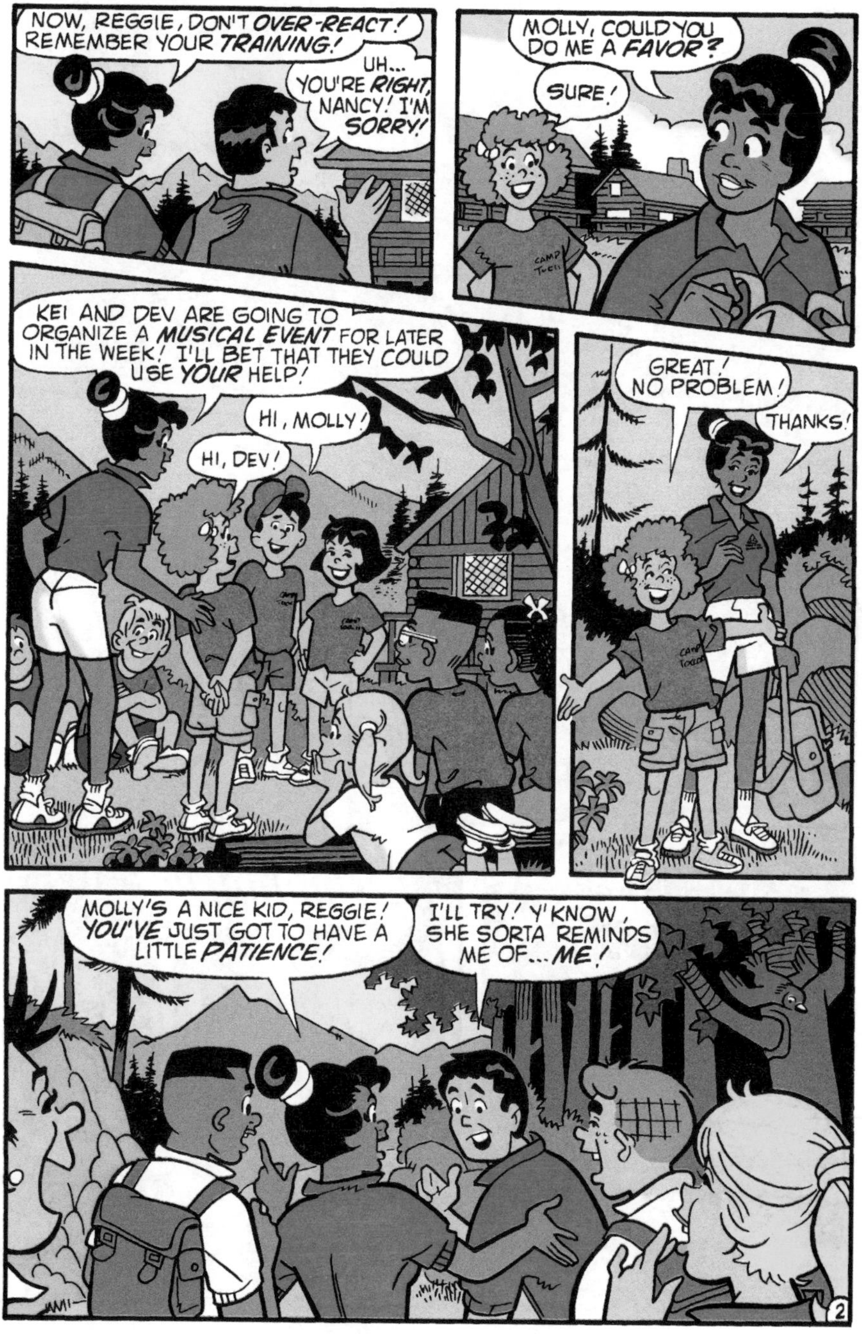

NOW, REGGIE, DON'T OVER-REACT! REMEMBER YOUR TRAINING!
UH... YOU'RE RIGHT, NANCY! I'M SORRY!
MOLLY, COULD YOU DO ME A FAVOR?
SURE!
CAMP TOCCI
KEI AND DEV ARE GOING TO ORGANIZE A MUSICAL EVENT FOR LATER IN THE WEEK! I'LL BET THAT THEY COULD USE YOUR HELP!
HI, MOLLY!
HI, DEV!
GREAT! NO PROBLEM!
THANKS!
MOLLY'S A NICE KID, REGGIE! YOU'VE JUST GOT TO HAVE A LITTLE PATIENCE!
I'LL TRY! Y'KNOW, SHE SORTA REMINDS ME OF... ME!
2

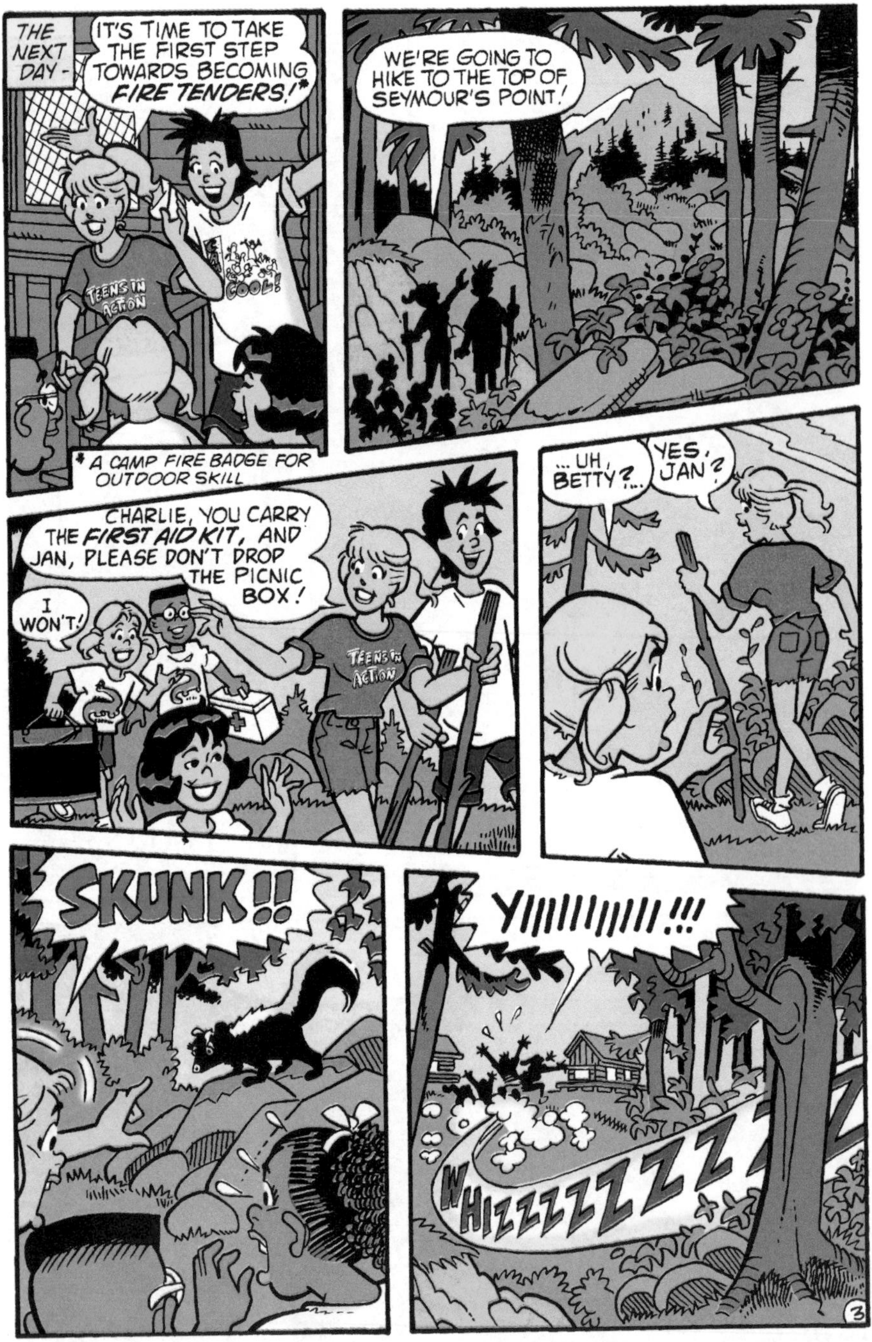
THE NEXT DAY -
IT'S TIME TO TAKE THE FIRST STEP TOWARDS BECOMING FIRE TENDERS!*
TEENS IN ACTION
COOL!
WE'RE GOING TO HIKE TO THE TOP OF SEYMOUR'S POINT!
* A CAMP FIRE BADGE FOR OUTDOOR SKILL
CHARLIE, YOU CARRY THE FIRST AID KIT, AND JAN, PLEASE DON'T DROP THE PICNIC BOX!
I WON'T!
TEENS IN ACTION
...UH, BETTY?...
YES, JAN?
SKUNK!!
YIIIIIIIIIII!!!
WHIZZZZZZZZ
3

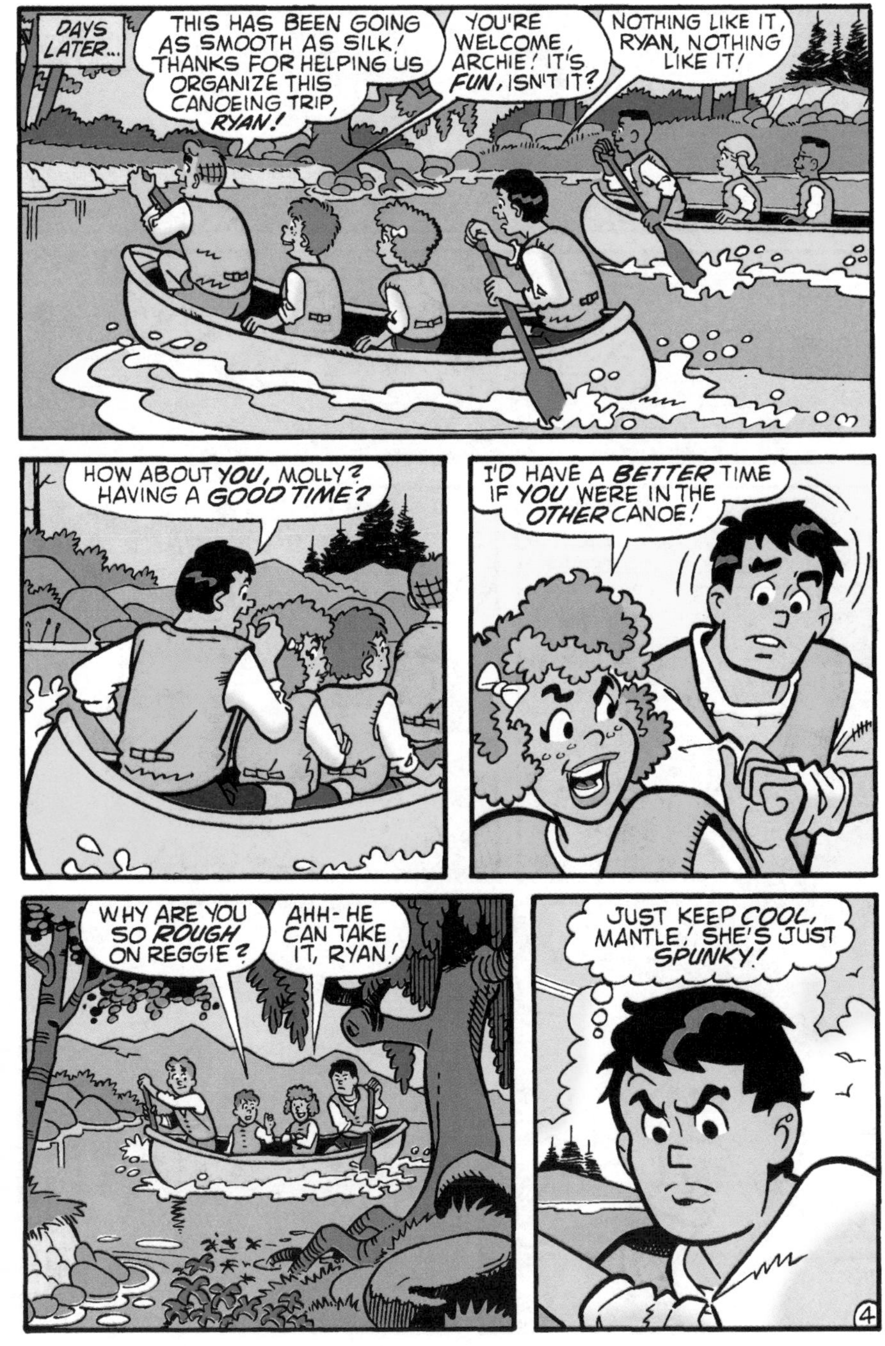
DAYS LATER...
THIS HAS BEEN GOING AS SMOOTH AS SILK! THANKS FOR HELPING US ORGANIZE THIS CANOEING TRIP, RYAN!
YOU'RE WELCOME, ARCHIE! IT'S FUN, ISN'T IT?
NOTHING LIKE IT, RYAN, NOTHING LIKE IT!
HOW ABOUT YOU, MOLLY? HAVING A GOOD TIME?
I'D HAVE A BETTER TIME IF YOU WERE IN THE OTHER CANOE!
WHY ARE YOU SO ROUGH ON REGGIE?
AHH- HE CAN TAKE IT, RYAN!
JUST KEEP COOL, MANTLE! SHE'S JUST SPUNKY!
4

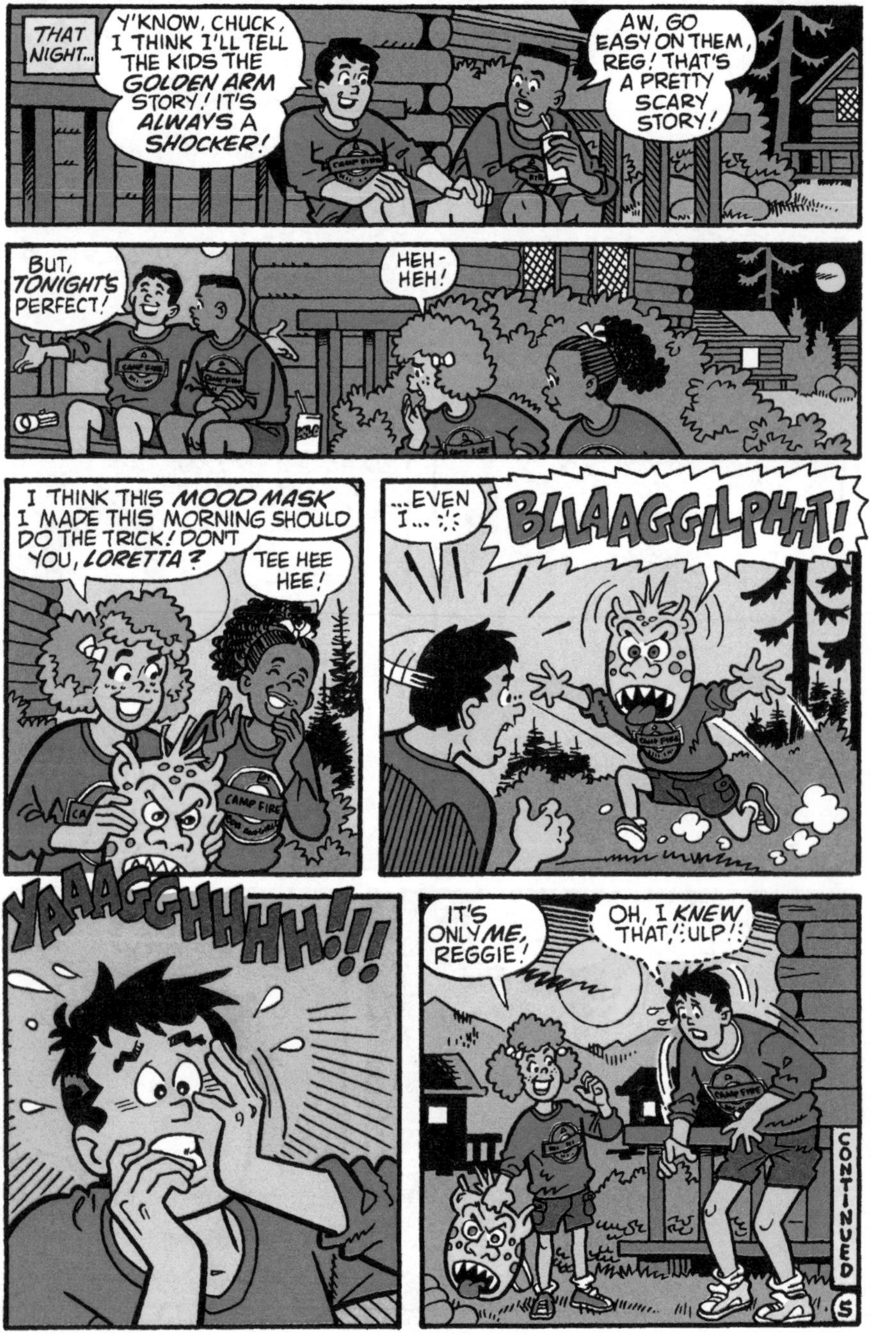
THAT NIGHT...
Y'KNOW, CHUCK, I THINK I'LL TELL THE KIDS THE GOLDEN ARM STORY! IT'S ALWAYS A SHOCKER!
AW, GO EASY ON THEM, REG! THAT'S A PRETTY SCARY STORY!
BUT, TONIGHT'S PERFECT!
HEH-HEH!
I THINK THIS MOOD MASK I MADE THIS MORNING SHOULD DO THE TRICK! DON'T YOU, LORETTA?
TEE HEE HEE!
...EVEN I...
BLLAAGGLLPHHT!
YAAAGGHHHHH!!!
IT'S ONLY ME, REGGIE!
OH, I KNEW THAT! ULP!
CONTINUED
5

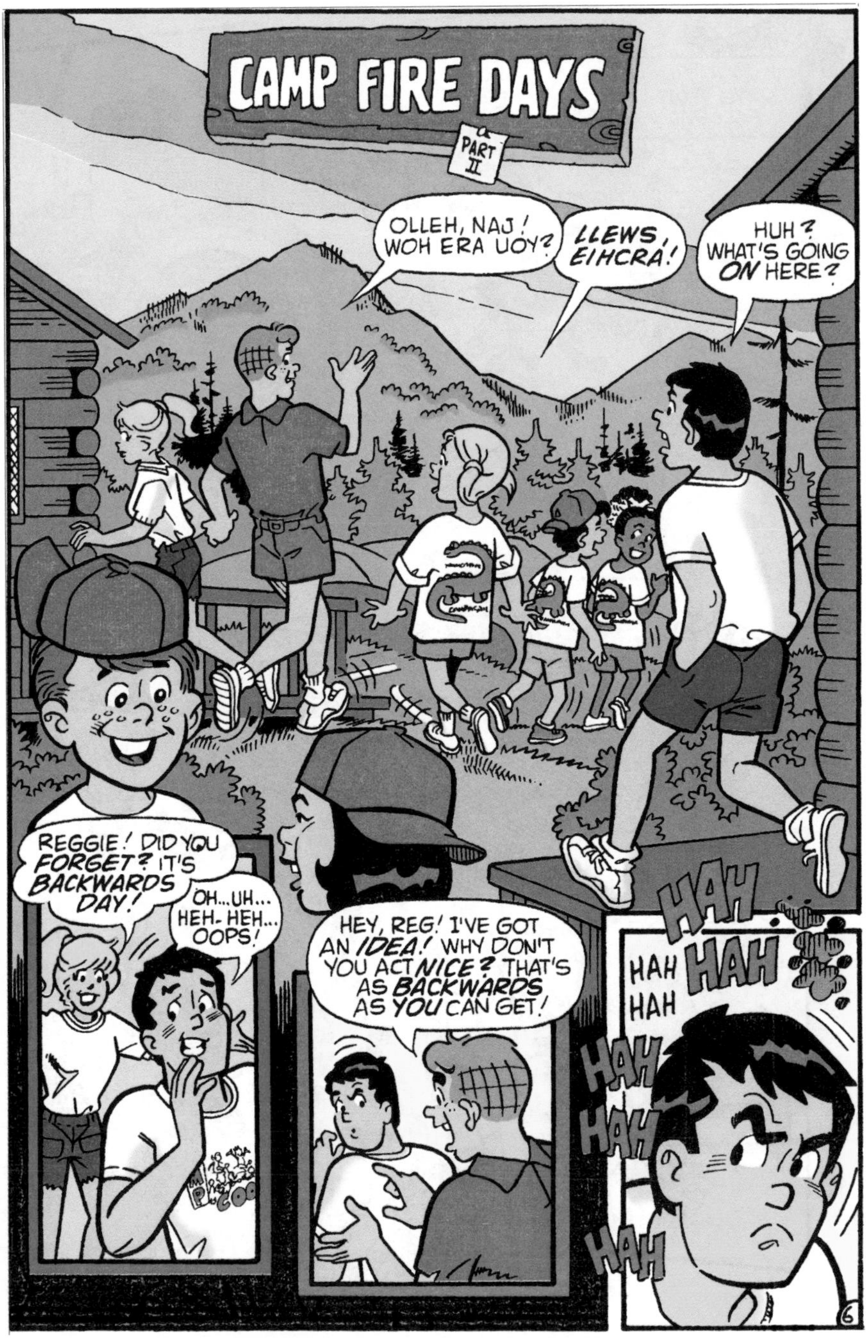
CAMP FIRE DAYS
PART II
OLLEH, NAJ! WOH ERA UOY?
LLEWS, EIHCRA!
HUH? WHAT'S GOING ON HERE?
REGGIE! DID YOU FORGET? IT'S BACKWARDS DAY!
OH...UH... HEH-HEH... OOPS!
HEY, REG! I'VE GOT AN IDEA! WHY DON'T YOU ACT NICE? THAT'S AS BACKWARDS AS YOU CAN GET!
HAH HAH HAH HAH
HAH HAH HAH
6

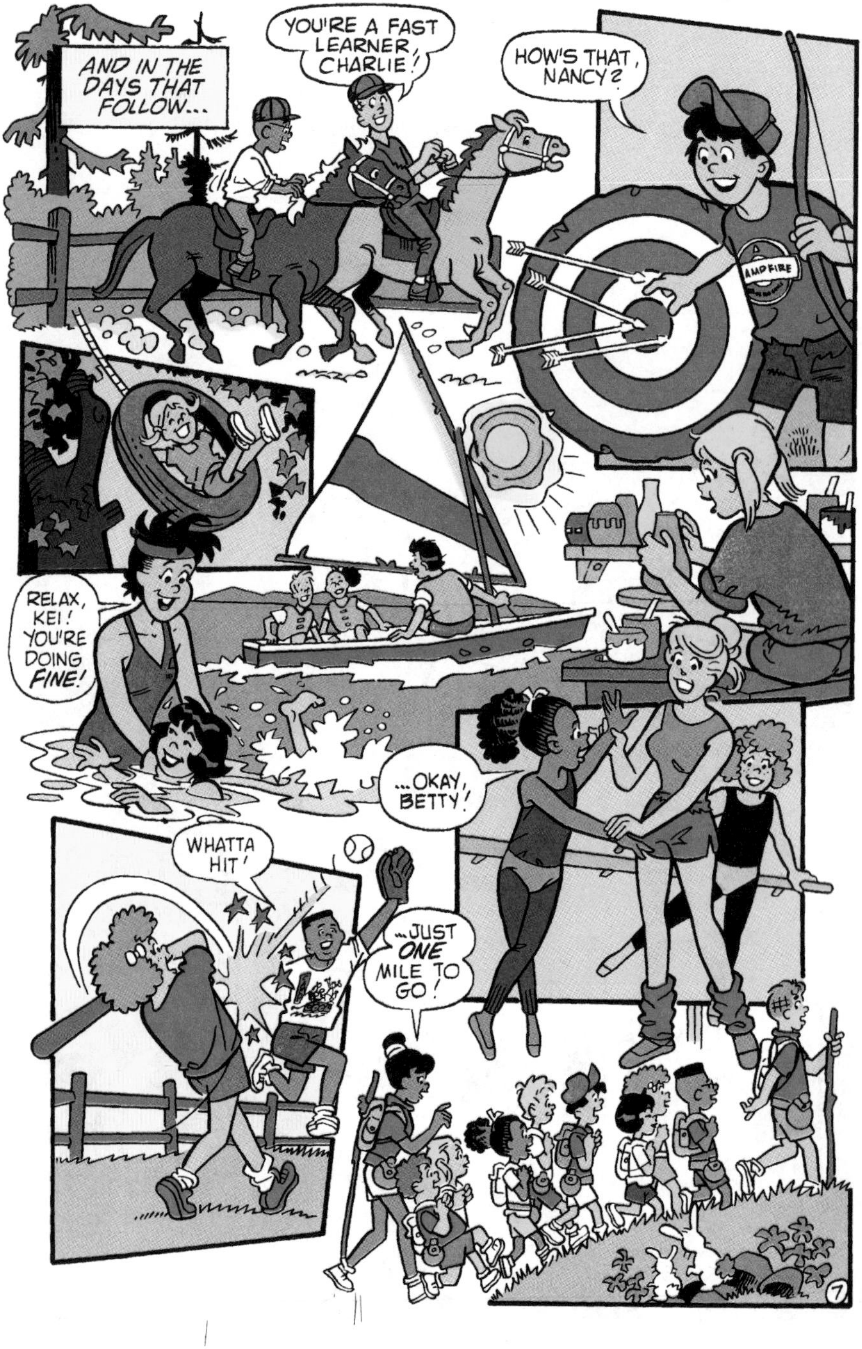
AND IN THE DAYS THAT FOLLOW...
YOU'RE A FAST LEARNER, CHARLIE!
HOW'S THAT, NANCY?
AMPFIRE
RELAX, KEI! YOU'RE DOING FINE!
...OKAY, BETTY!
WHATTA HIT!
...JUST ONE MILE TO GO!
7

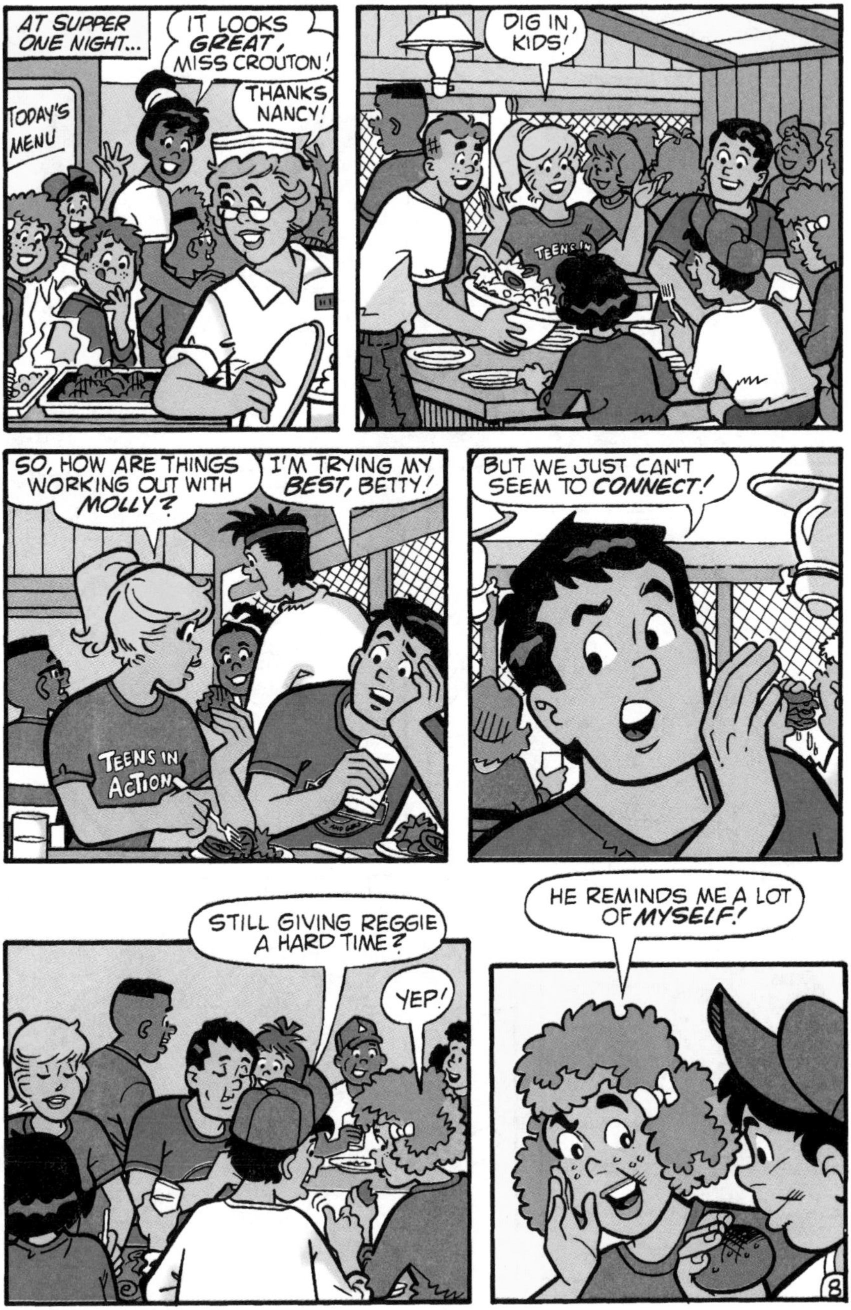
AT SUPPER ONE NIGHT...
IT LOOKS GREAT, MISS CROUTON!
THANKS, NANCY!
TODAY'S MENU
DIG IN, KIDS!
TEENS IN
SO, HOW ARE THINGS WORKING OUT WITH MOLLY?
I'M TRYING MY BEST, BETTY!
TEENS IN ACTION
BUT WE JUST CAN'T SEEM TO CONNECT!
STILL GIVING REGGIE A HARD TIME?
YEP!
HE REMINDS ME A LOT OF MYSELF!
8

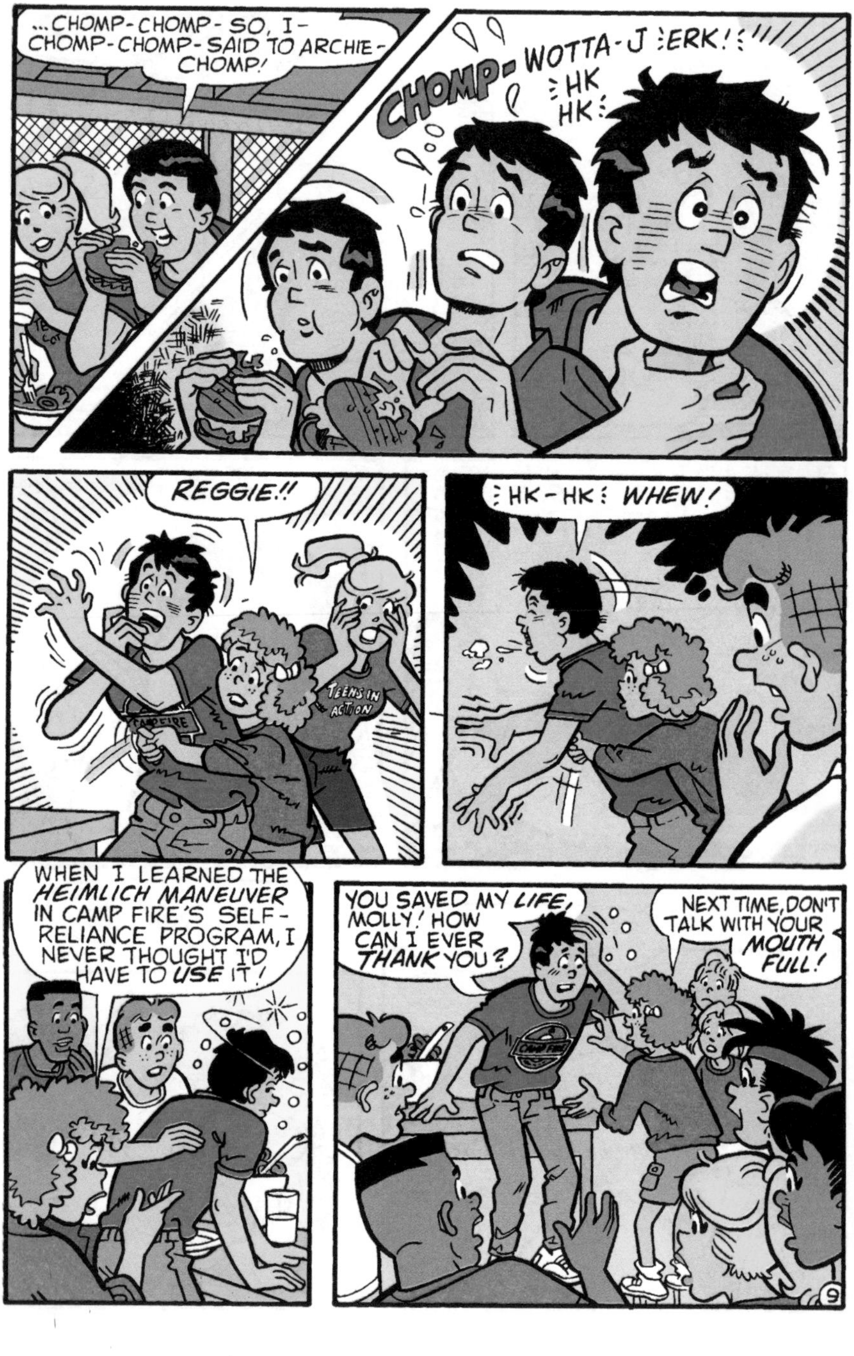
...CHOMP-CHOMP- SO, I- CHOMP-CHOMP- SAID TO ARCHIE- CHOMP!
CHOMP- WOTTA-J ERK!
HK HK
REGGIE!!
TEENS IN ACTION
HK-HK WHEW!
WHEN I LEARNED THE HEIMLICH MANEUVER IN CAMP FIRE'S SELF-RELIANCE PROGRAM, I NEVER THOUGHT I'D HAVE TO USE IT!
YOU SAVED MY LIFE, MOLLY! HOW CAN I EVER THANK YOU?
NEXT TIME, DON'T TALK WITH YOUR MOUTH FULL!
9

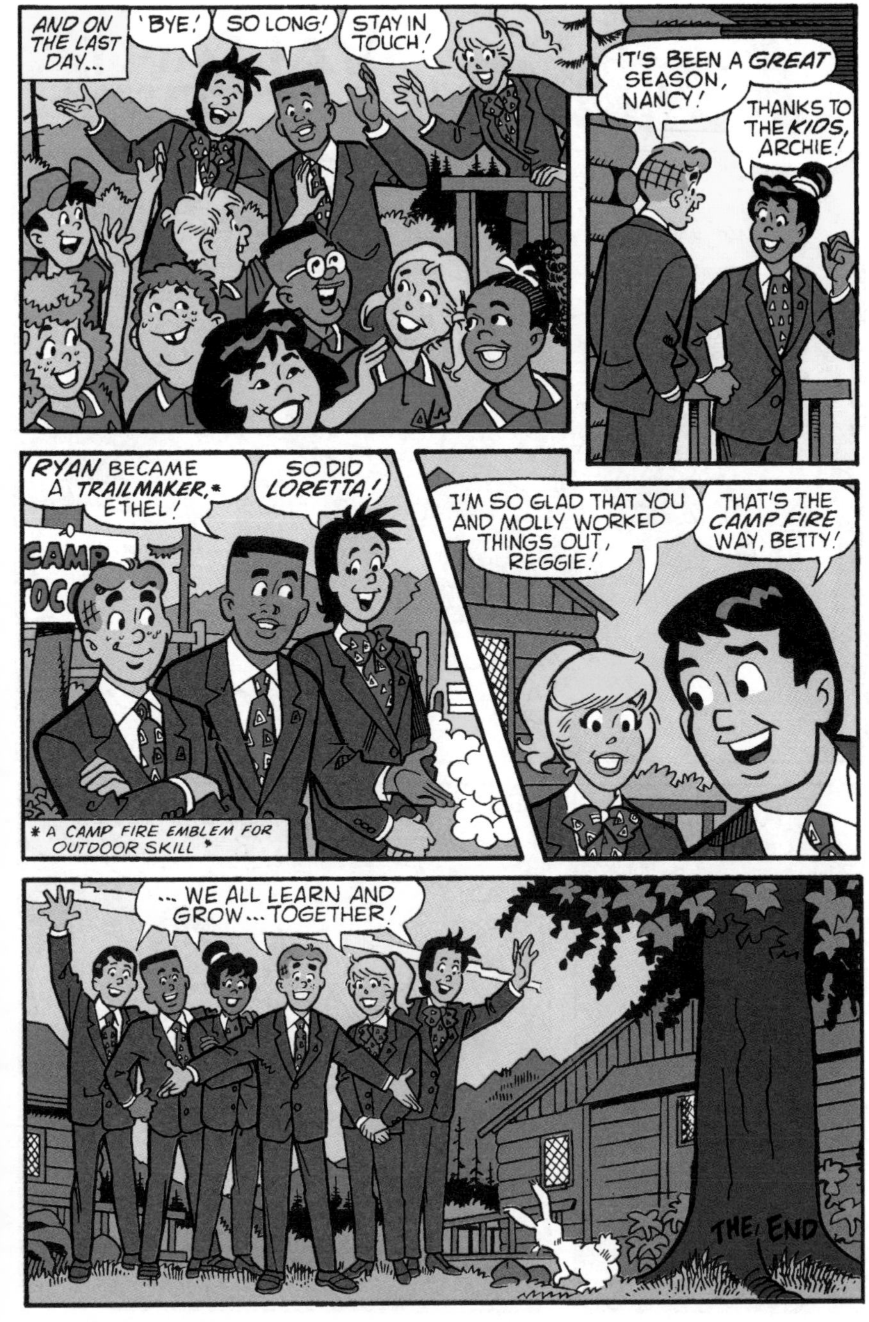
AND ON THE LAST DAY...
'BYE!
SO LONG!
STAY IN TOUCH!
IT'S BEEN A GREAT SEASON, NANCY!
THANKS TO THE KIDS, ARCHIE!
RYAN BECAME A TRAILMAKER,* ETHEL!
SO DID LORETTA!
CAMP
* A CAMP FIRE EMBLEM FOR OUTDOOR SKILL
I'M SO GLAD THAT YOU AND MOLLY WORKED THINGS OUT, REGGIE!
THAT'S THE CAMP FIRE WAY, BETTY!
... WE ALL LEARN AND GROW... TOGETHER!
THE END

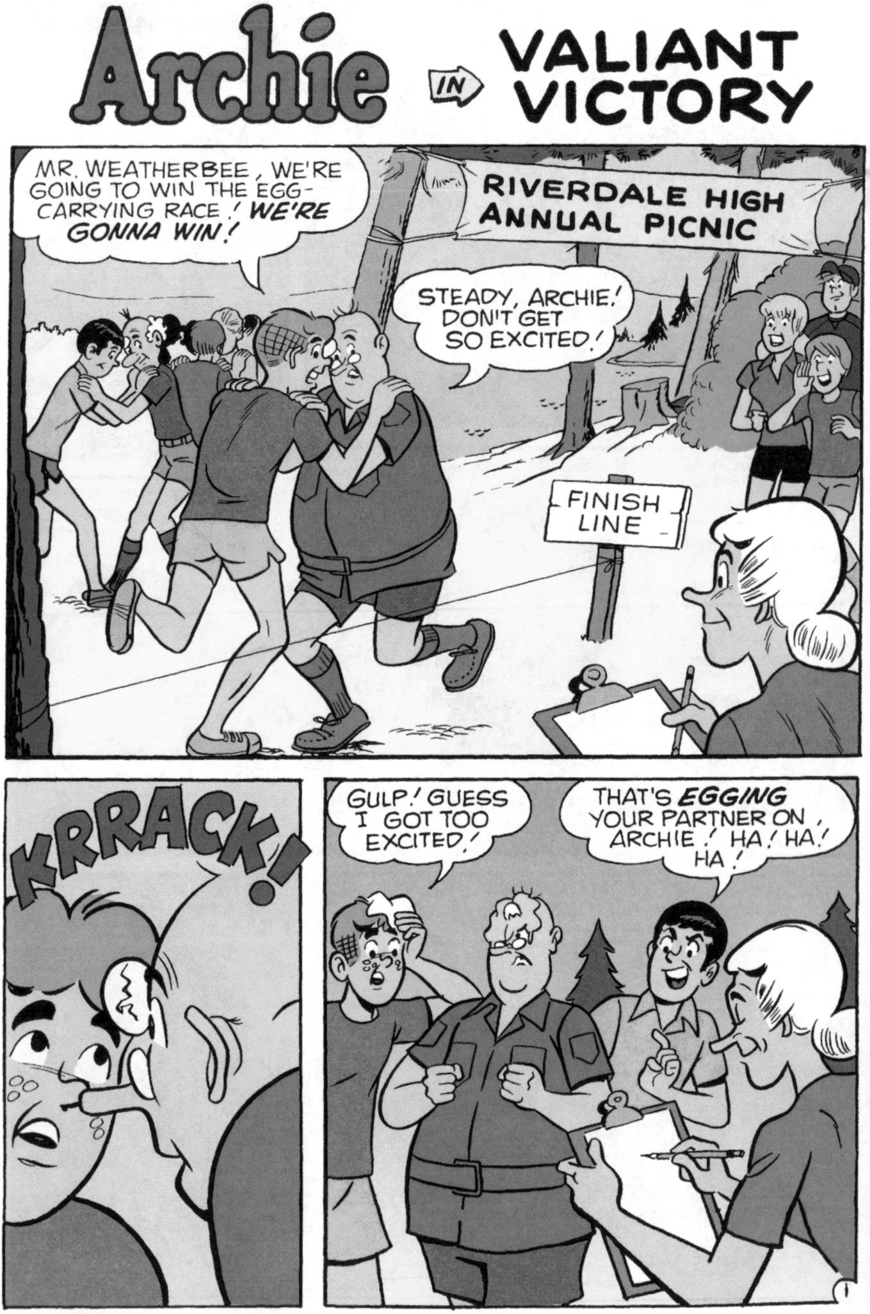

Archie IN VALIANT VICTORY
MR. WEATHERBEE, WE'RE GOING TO WIN THE EGG-CARRYING RACE! WE'RE GONNA WIN!
RIVERDALE HIGH ANNUAL PICNIC
STEADY, ARCHIE! DON'T GET SO EXCITED!
FINISH LINE
KRRACK!
GULP! GUESS I GOT TOO EXCITED!
THAT'S EGGING YOUR PARTNER ON, ARCHIE! HA! HA! HA!
1

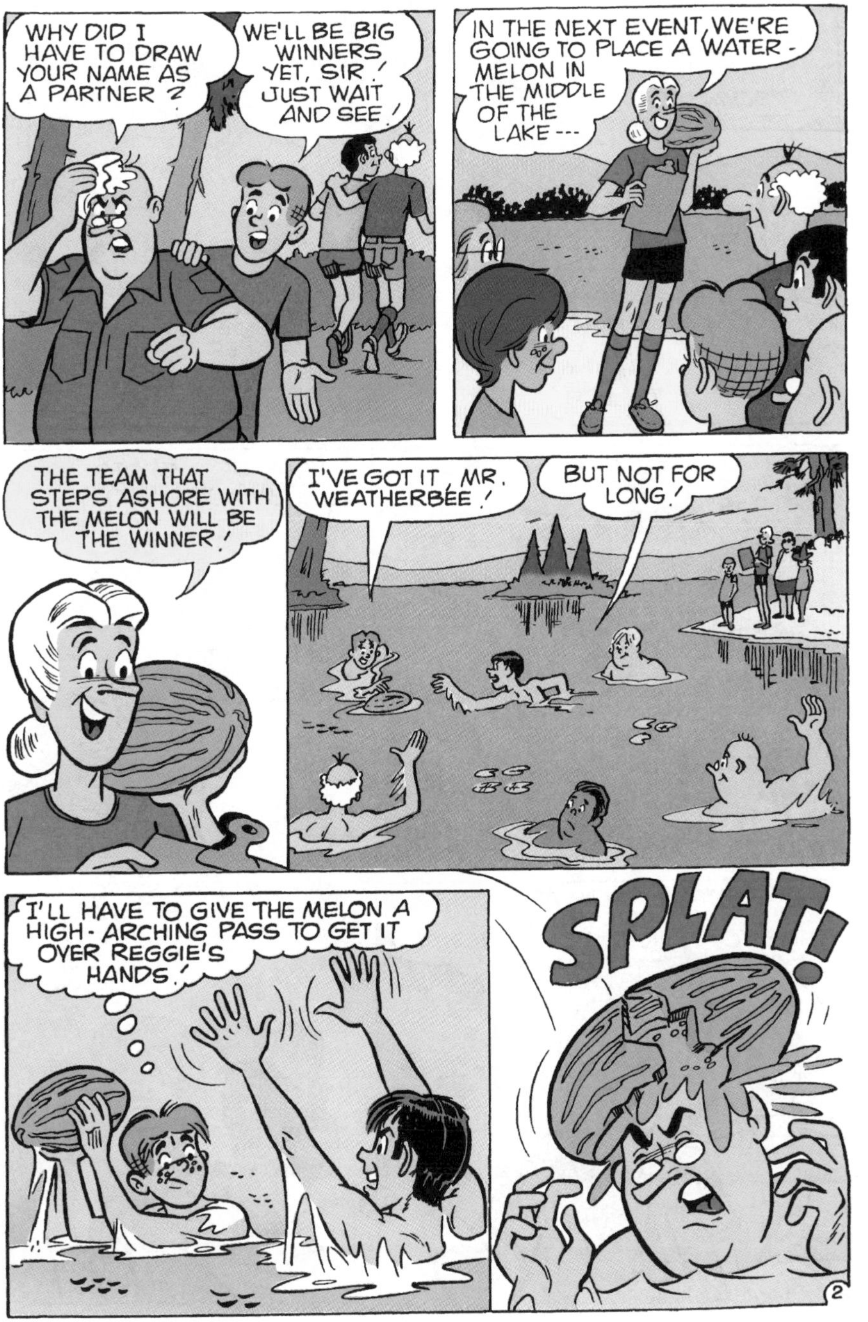

WHY DID I HAVE TO DRAW YOUR NAME AS A PARTNER ?
WE'LL BE BIG WINNERS YET, SIR ! JUST WAIT AND SEE !
IN THE NEXT EVENT, WE'RE GOING TO PLACE A WATER-MELON IN THE MIDDLE OF THE LAKE ---
THE TEAM THAT STEPS ASHORE WITH THE MELON WILL BE THE WINNER !
I'VE GOT IT, MR. WEATHERBEE !
BUT NOT FOR LONG !
I'LL HAVE TO GIVE THE MELON A HIGH-ARCHING PASS TO GET IT OVER REGGIE'S HANDS !
SPLAT!
2

HA! HA! YOU HAVE TO BRING *ALL* OF THE MELON ASHORE--- NOT JUST PART OF IT! YOU'RE *DISQUALIFIED!*

MY TEAM IS WAY AHEAD OF YOUR TEAM!

EVENT	WINNER
CANOE RACE	FLUTESNOOT-REGGIE
CARRY ON RACE	FLUTESNOOT-REGGIE
MELON CARRY	BENSON-MOOSE

ONLY BECAUSE YOU HAVE REGGIE FOR A PARTNER INSTEAD OF ARCHIE!

THE MAP-READING EVENT IS NEXT!

I'LL GIVE IT MY BEST SHOT, SIR!

NO! PLEASE DON'T!

YOUR BEST SHOTS ALWAYS WIND UP HITTING ME!

THAT'S NOT A NICE THING TO SAY!

I KNOW ARCHIE MEANS WELL, BUT GOOD INTENTIONS ARE NOT ENOUGH!

WE'RE SUPPOSED TO GO NORTH BY NORTHEAST FOR 300 PACES!

THAT'S THIS WAY, SIR!

START

③

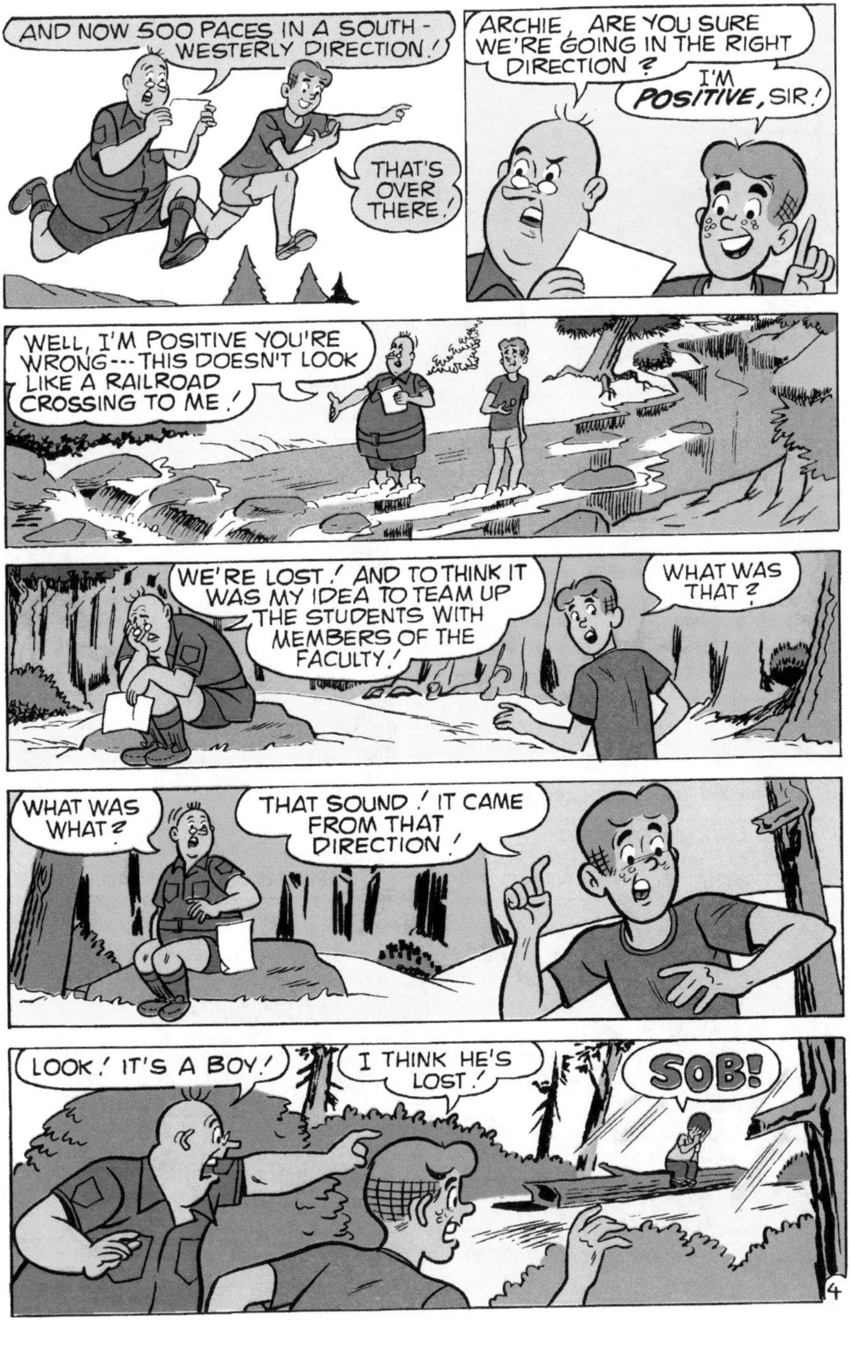
AND NOW 500 PACES IN A SOUTH-WESTERLY DIRECTION!
THAT'S OVER THERE!
ARCHIE, ARE YOU SURE WE'RE GOING IN THE RIGHT DIRECTION?
I'M POSITIVE, SIR!
WELL, I'M POSITIVE YOU'RE WRONG---THIS DOESN'T LOOK LIKE A RAILROAD CROSSING TO ME!
WE'RE LOST! AND TO THINK IT WAS MY IDEA TO TEAM UP THE STUDENTS WITH MEMBERS OF THE FACULTY!
WHAT WAS THAT?
WHAT WAS WHAT?
THAT SOUND! IT CAME FROM THAT DIRECTION!
LOOK! IT'S A BOY!
I THINK HE'S LOST!
SOB!
4

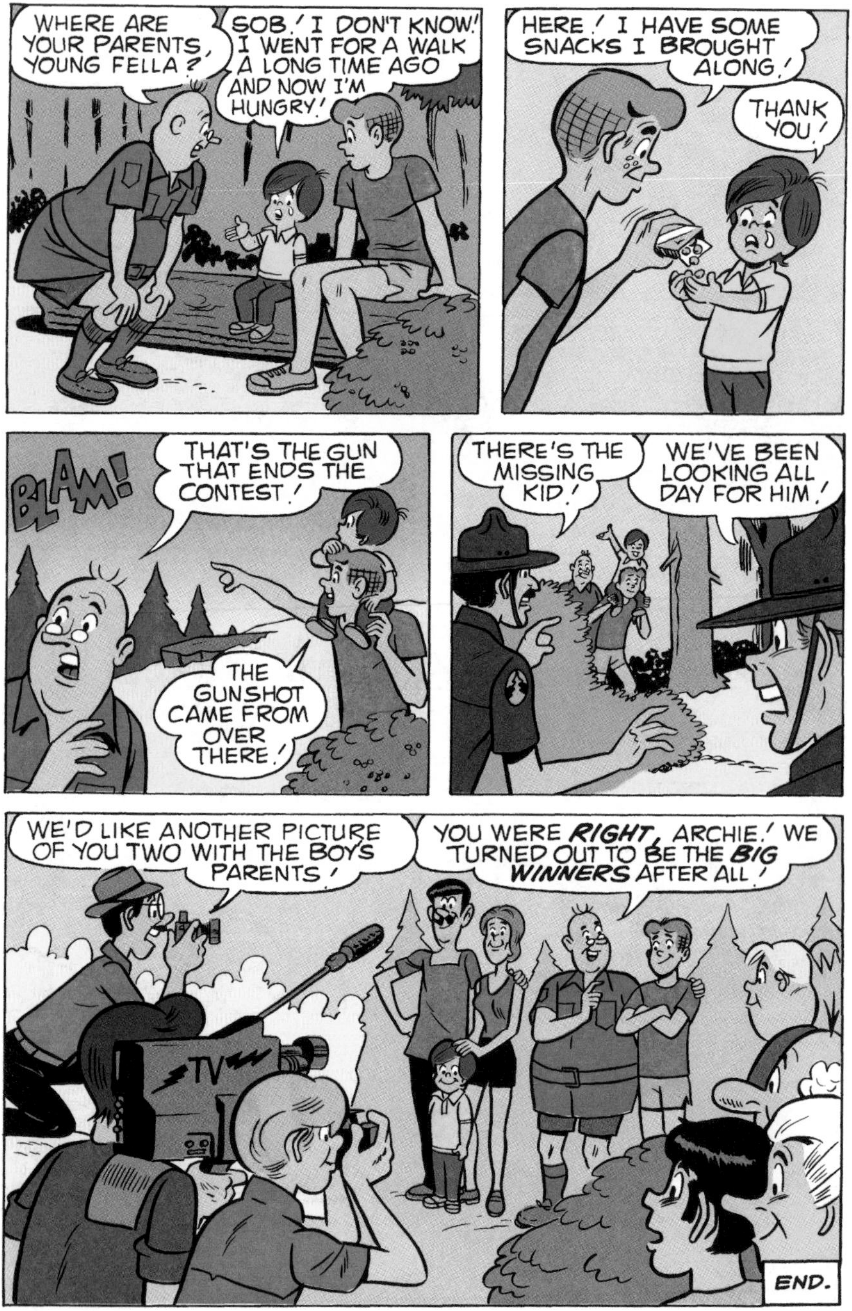
WHERE ARE YOUR PARENTS, YOUNG FELLA?
SOB.! I DON'T KNOW! I WENT FOR A WALK A LONG TIME AGO AND NOW I'M HUNGRY!
HERE! I HAVE SOME SNACKS I BROUGHT ALONG!
THANK YOU!
BLAM!
THAT'S THE GUN THAT ENDS THE CONTEST!
THE GUNSHOT CAME FROM OVER THERE!
THERE'S THE MISSING KID!
WE'VE BEEN LOOKING ALL DAY FOR HIM!
WE'D LIKE ANOTHER PICTURE OF YOU TWO WITH THE BOYS PARENTS!
YOU WERE RIGHT, ARCHIE! WE TURNED OUT TO BE THE BIG WINNERS AFTER ALL!
TV
END.

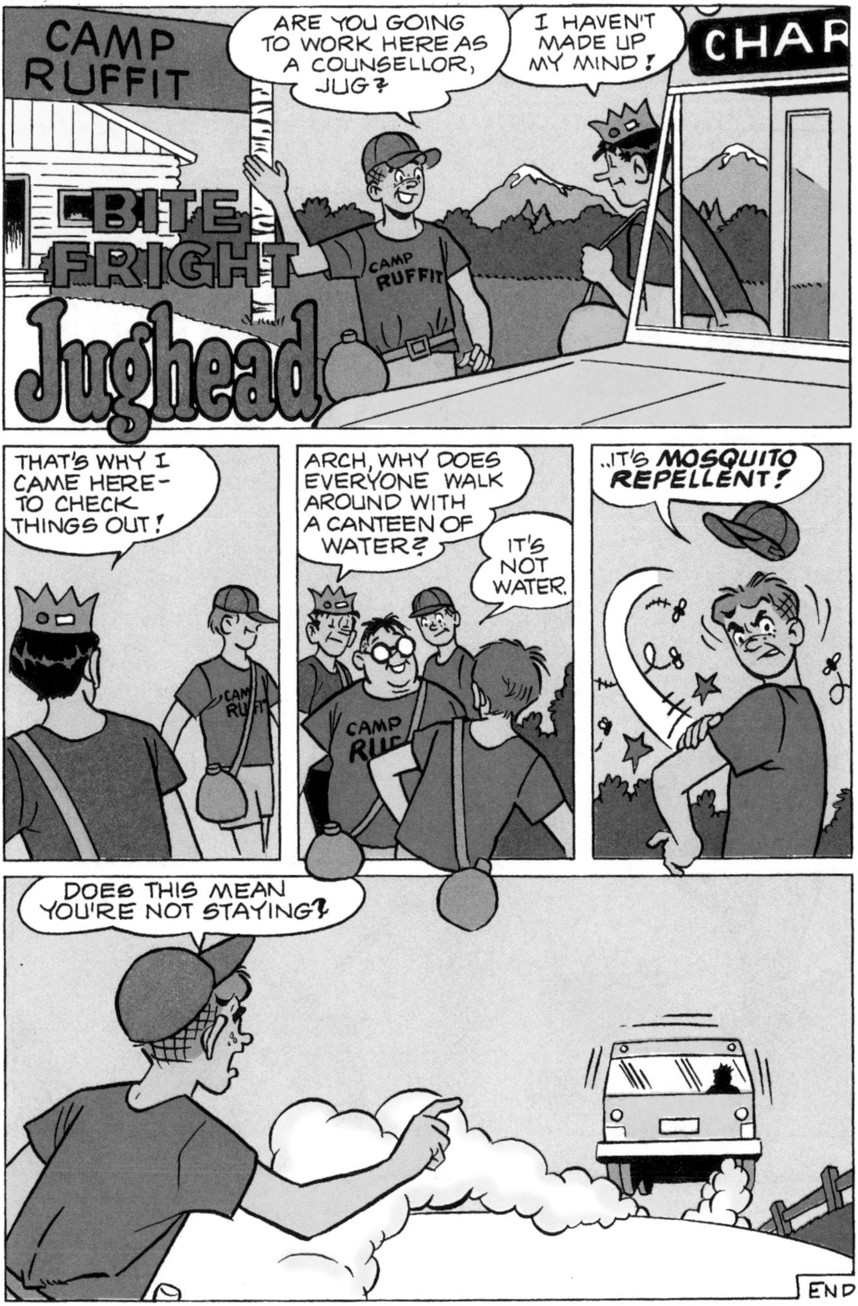
CAMP RUFFIT
ARE YOU GOING TO WORK HERE AS A COUNSELLOR, JUG?
I HAVEN'T MADE UP MY MIND!
CHAR
BITE FRIGHT
Jughead
CAMP RUFFIT
THAT'S WHY I CAME HERE-TO CHECK THINGS OUT!
ARCH, WHY DOES EVERYONE WALK AROUND WITH A CANTEEN OF WATER?
IT'S NOT WATER.
..IT'S MOSQUITO REPELLENT!
DOES THIS MEAN YOU'RE NOT STAYING?
END

Jughead CAMP SCAMP

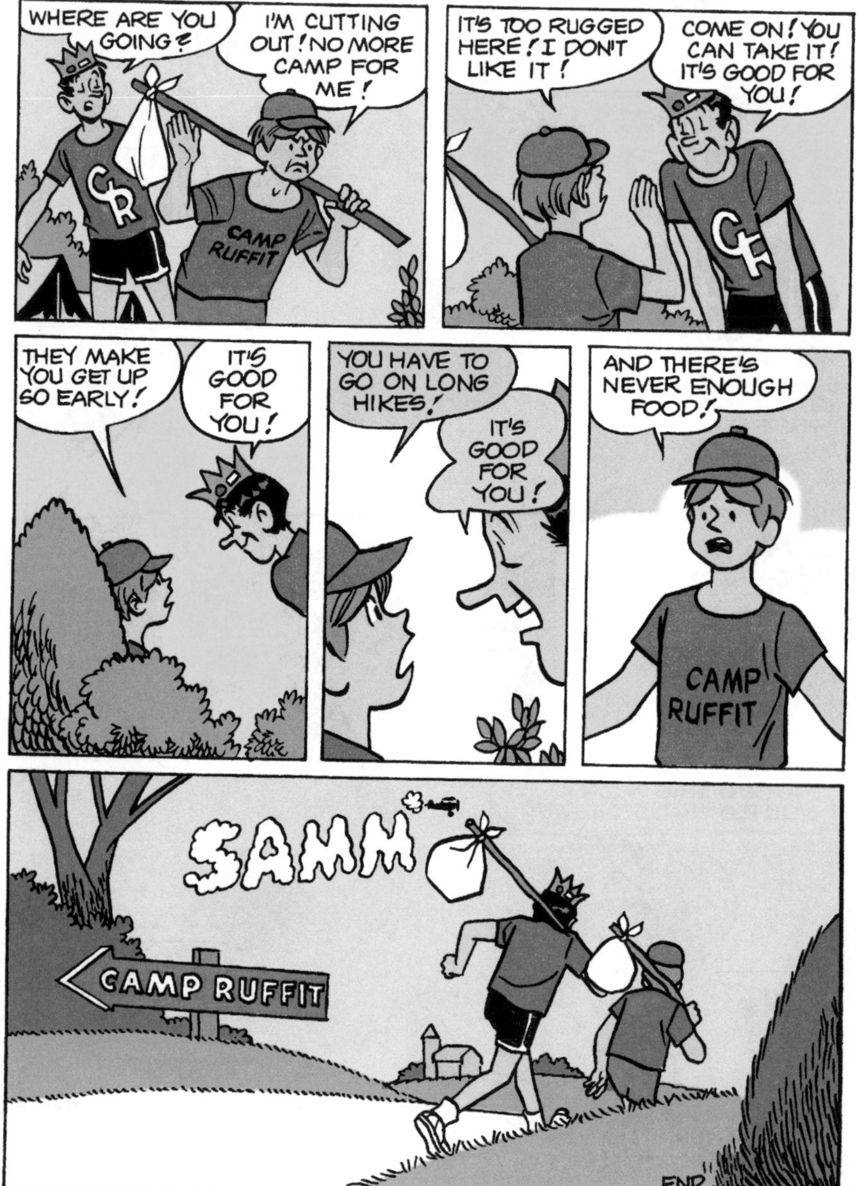

WHERE ARE YOU GOING?
I'M CUTTING OUT! NO MORE CAMP FOR ME!
CAMP RUFFIT
IT'S TOO RUGGED HERE! I DON'T LIKE IT!
COME ON! YOU CAN TAKE IT! IT'S GOOD FOR YOU!
THEY MAKE YOU GET UP SO EARLY!
IT'S GOOD FOR YOU!
YOU HAVE TO GO ON LONG HIKES!
IT'S GOOD FOR YOU!
AND THERE'S NEVER ENOUGH FOOD!
CAMP RUFFIT
SAMM
CAMP RUFFIT
END

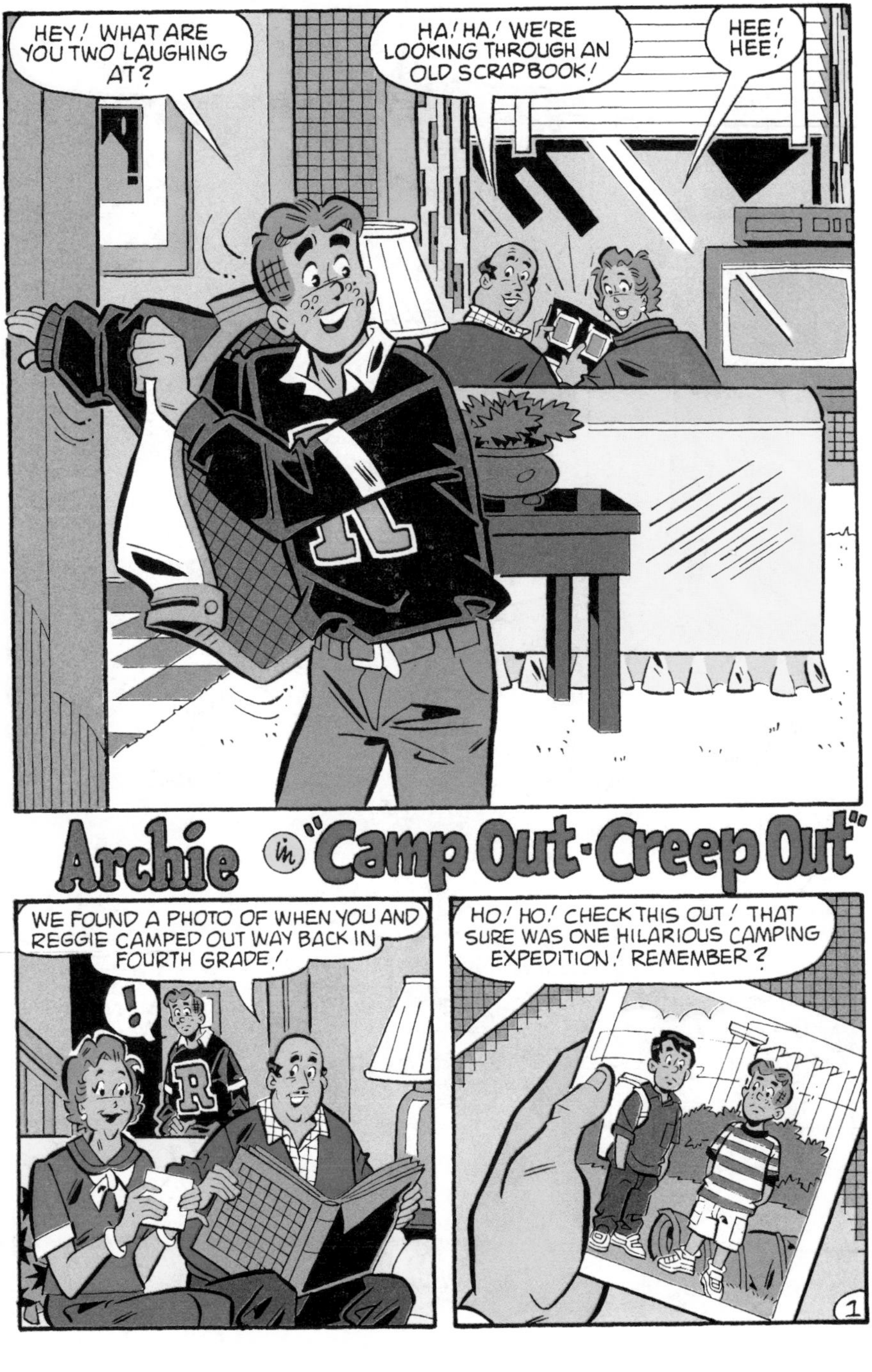
HEY! WHAT ARE YOU TWO LAUGHING AT?
HA! HA! WE'RE LOOKING THROUGH AN OLD SCRAPBOOK!
HEE! HEE!
Archie in "Camp Out-Creep Out"
WE FOUND A PHOTO OF WHEN YOU AND REGGIE CAMPED OUT WAY BACK IN FOURTH GRADE!
!
HO! HO! CHECK THIS OUT! THAT SURE WAS ONE HILARIOUS CAMPING EXPEDITION! REMEMBER?
1

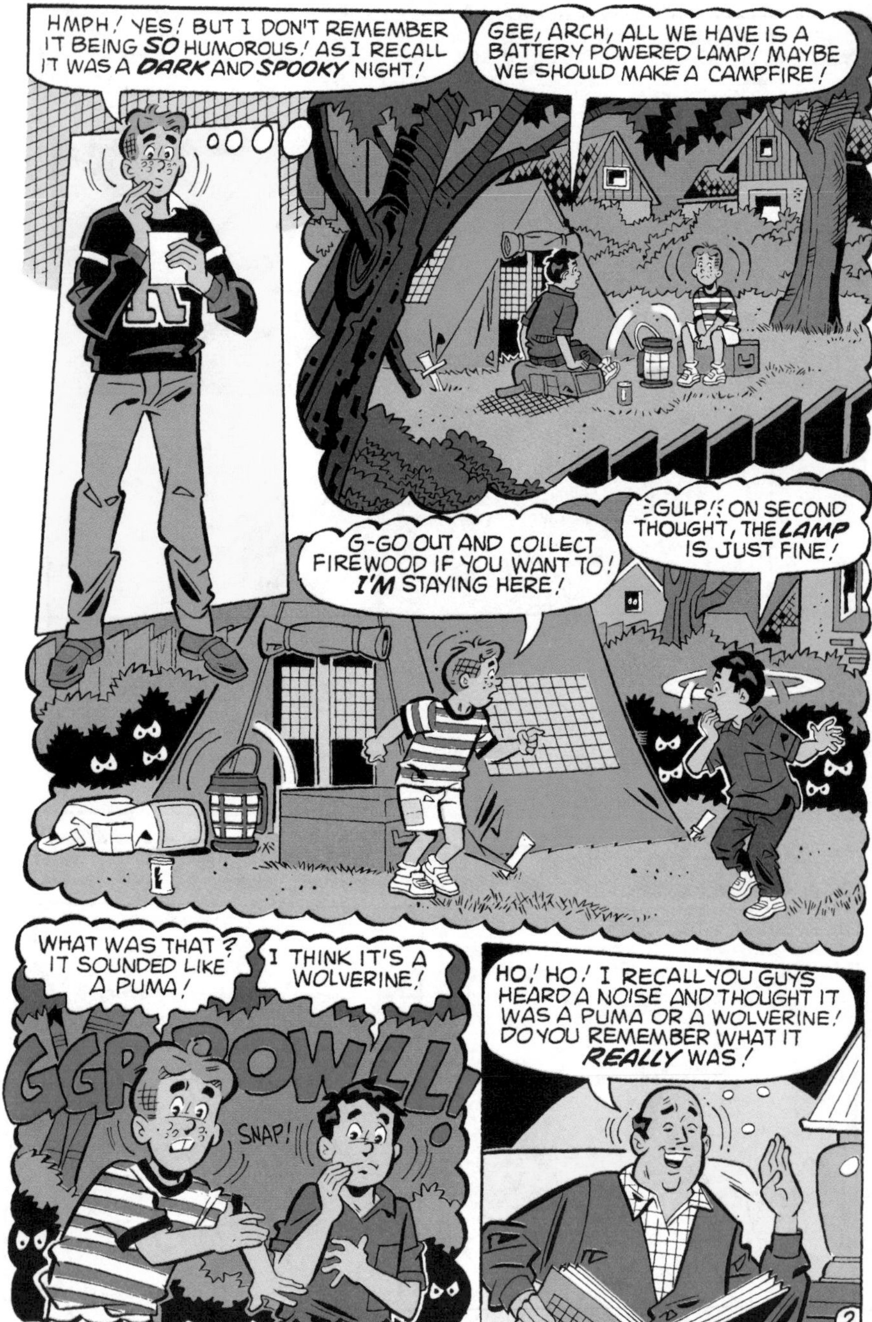
HMPH! YES! BUT I DON'T REMEMBER IT BEING SO HUMOROUS! AS I RECALL IT WAS A DARK AND SPOOKY NIGHT!
GEE, ARCH, ALL WE HAVE IS A BATTERY POWERED LAMP! MAYBE WE SHOULD MAKE A CAMPFIRE!
G-GO OUT AND COLLECT FIREWOOD IF YOU WANT TO! I'M STAYING HERE!
GULP! ON SECOND THOUGHT, THE LAMP IS JUST FINE!
WHAT WAS THAT? IT SOUNDED LIKE A PUMA!
I THINK IT'S A WOLVERINE!
GGROWLL!
SNAP!
HO! HO! I RECALL YOU GUYS HEARD A NOISE AND THOUGHT IT WAS A PUMA OR A WOLVERINE! DO YOU REMEMBER WHAT IT REALLY WAS!
2

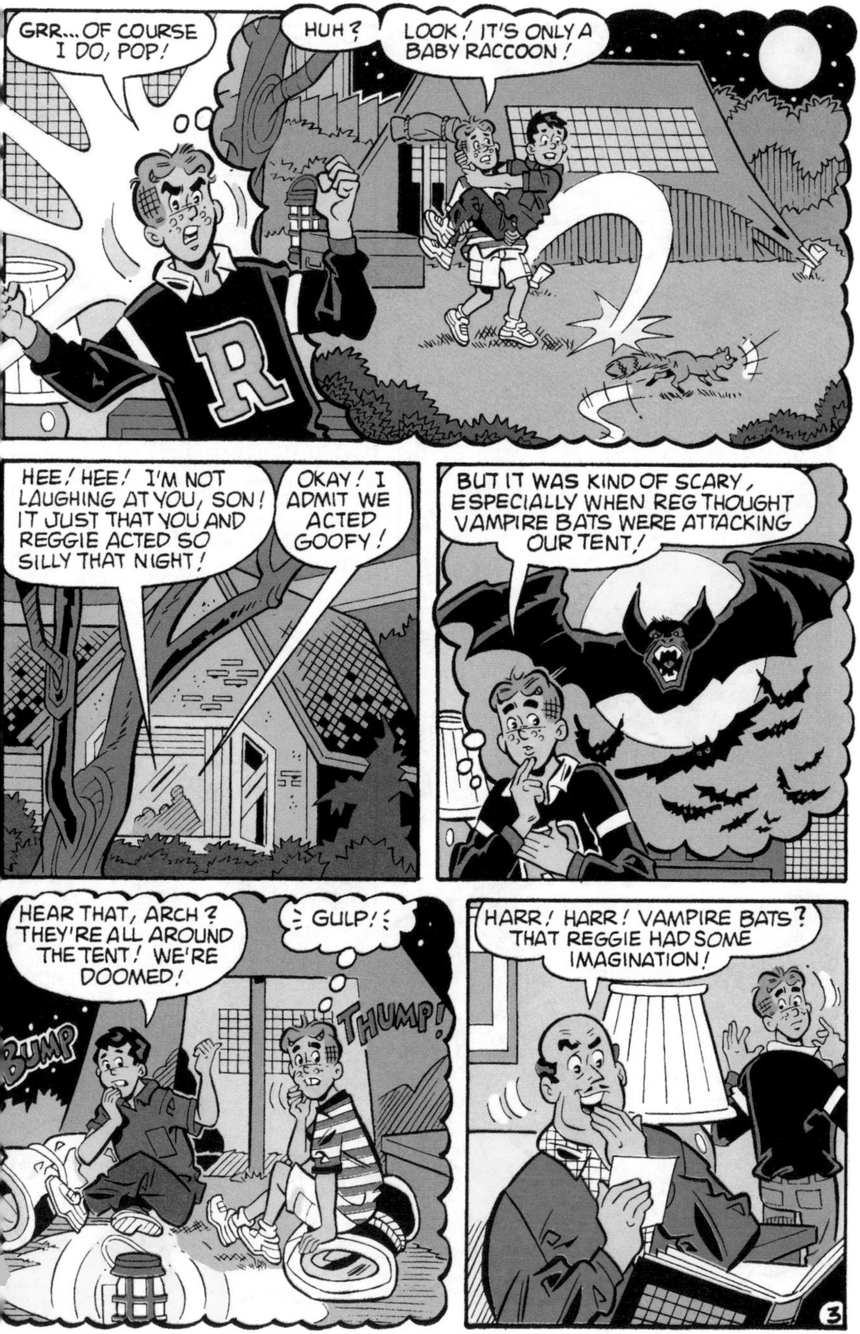
GRR... OF COURSE I DO, POP!
HUH?
LOOK! IT'S ONLY A BABY RACCOON!
HEE! HEE! I'M NOT LAUGHING AT YOU, SON! IT JUST THAT YOU AND REGGIE ACTED SO SILLY THAT NIGHT!
OKAY! I ADMIT WE ACTED GOOFY!
BUT IT WAS KIND OF SCARY, ESPECIALLY WHEN REG THOUGHT VAMPIRE BATS WERE ATTACKING OUR TENT!
HEAR THAT, ARCH? THEY'RE ALL AROUND THE TENT! WE'RE DOOMED!
GULP!
BUMP
THUMP!
HARR! HARR! VAMPIRE BATS? THAT REGGIE HAD SOME IMAGINATION!
3

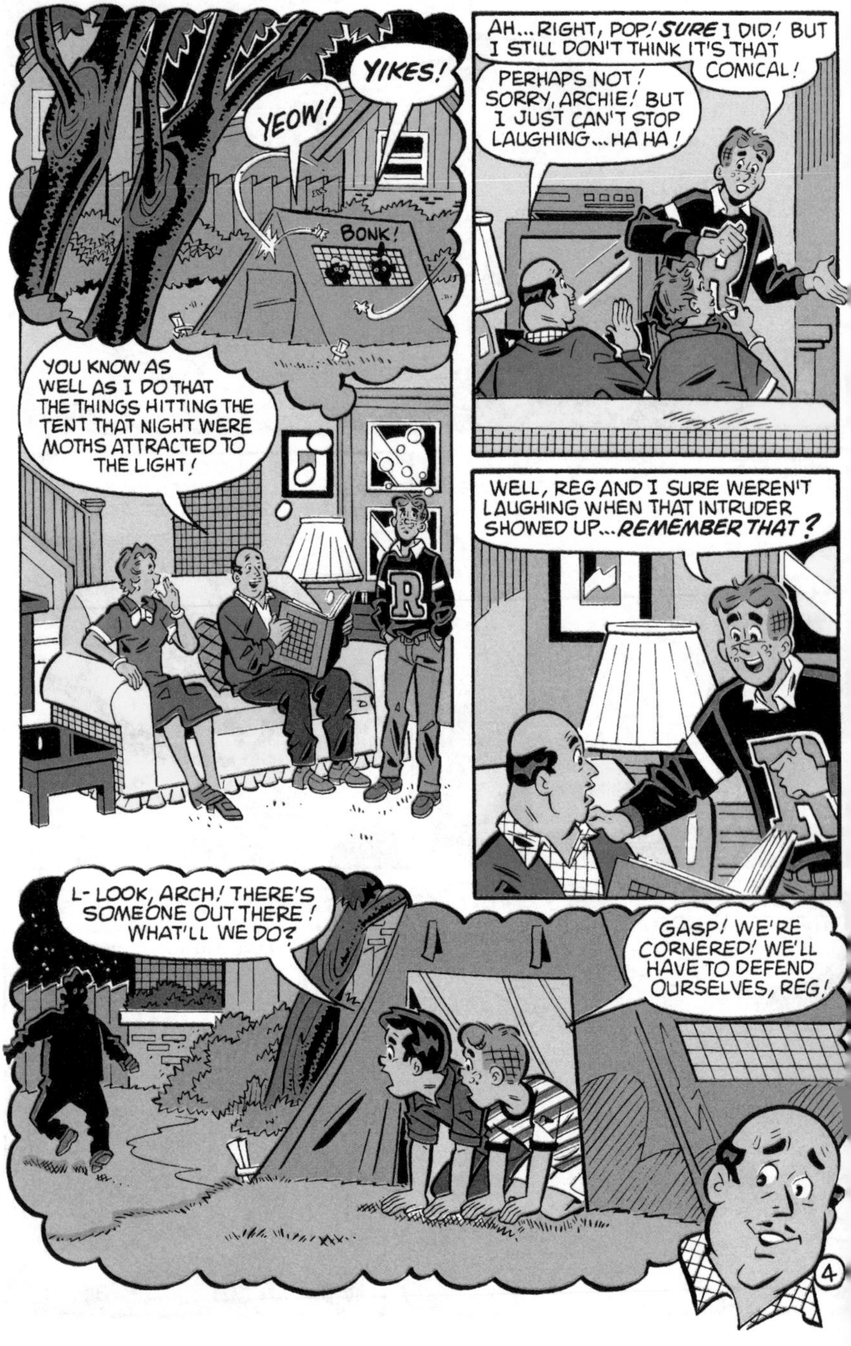

YEOW!
YIKES!
BONK!
AH... RIGHT, POP! SURE I DID! BUT I STILL DON'T THINK IT'S THAT COMICAL!
PERHAPS NOT! SORRY, ARCHIE! BUT I JUST CAN'T STOP LAUGHING... HA HA!
YOU KNOW AS WELL AS I DO THAT THE THINGS HITTING THE TENT THAT NIGHT WERE MOTHS ATTRACTED TO THE LIGHT!
WELL, REG AND I SURE WEREN'T LAUGHING WHEN THAT INTRUDER SHOWED UP... REMEMBER THAT?
L-LOOK, ARCH! THERE'S SOMEONE OUT THERE! WHAT'LL WE DO?
GASP! WE'RE CORNERED! WE'LL HAVE TO DEFEND OURSELVES, REG!
4

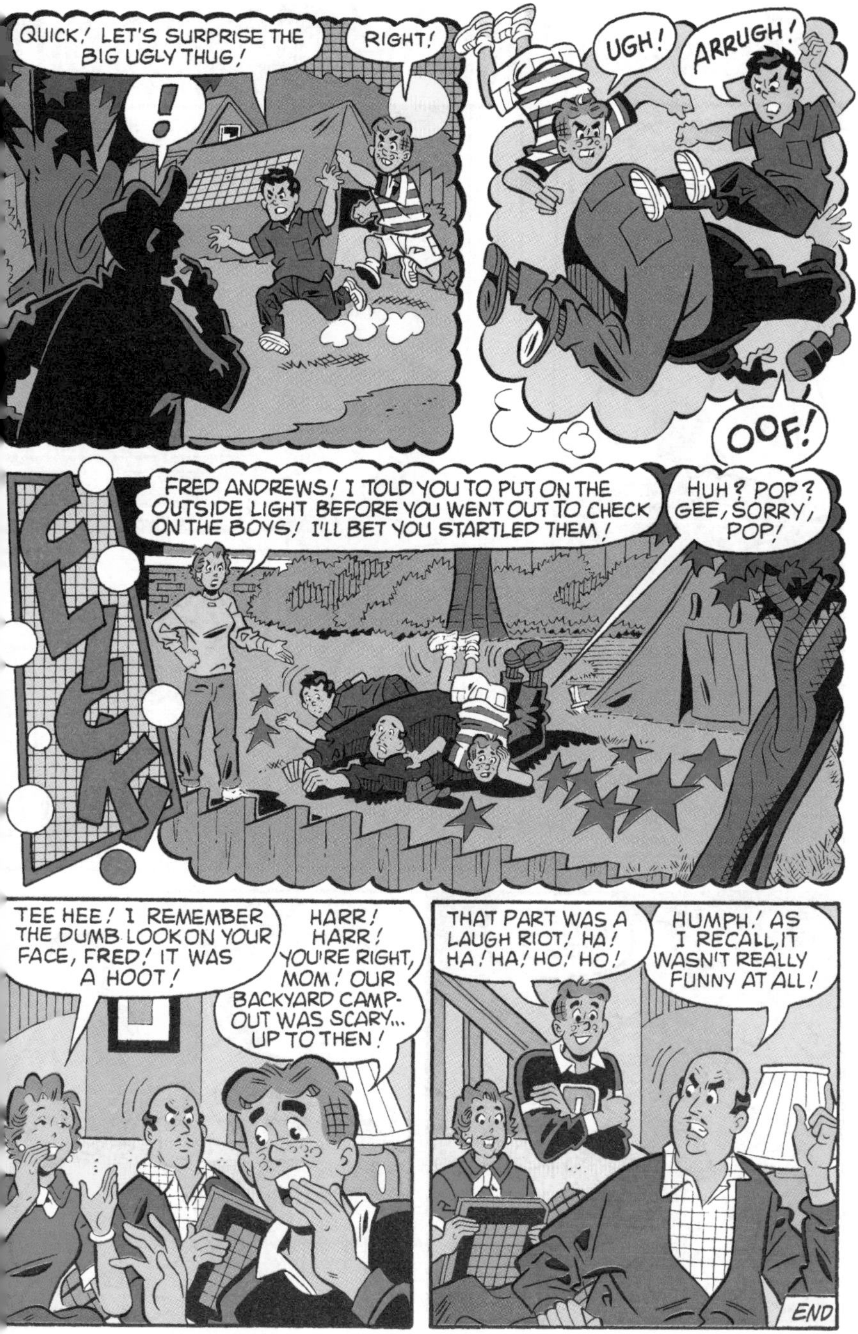
QUICK! LET'S SURPRISE THE BIG UGLY THUG!
RIGHT!
!
UGH!
ARRUGH!
OOF!
FRED ANDREWS! I TOLD YOU TO PUT ON THE OUTSIDE LIGHT BEFORE YOU WENT OUT TO CHECK ON THE BOYS! I'LL BET YOU STARTLED THEM!
HUH? POP? GEE, SORRY, POP!
CLICK!
TEE HEE! I REMEMBER THE DUMB LOOK ON YOUR FACE, FRED! IT WAS A HOOT!
HARR! HARR! YOU'RE RIGHT, MOM! OUR BACKYARD CAMP-OUT WAS SCARY... UP TO THEN!
THAT PART WAS A LAUGH RIOT! HA! HA! HA! HO! HO!
HUMPH! AS I RECALL, IT WASN'T REALLY FUNNY AT ALL!
END

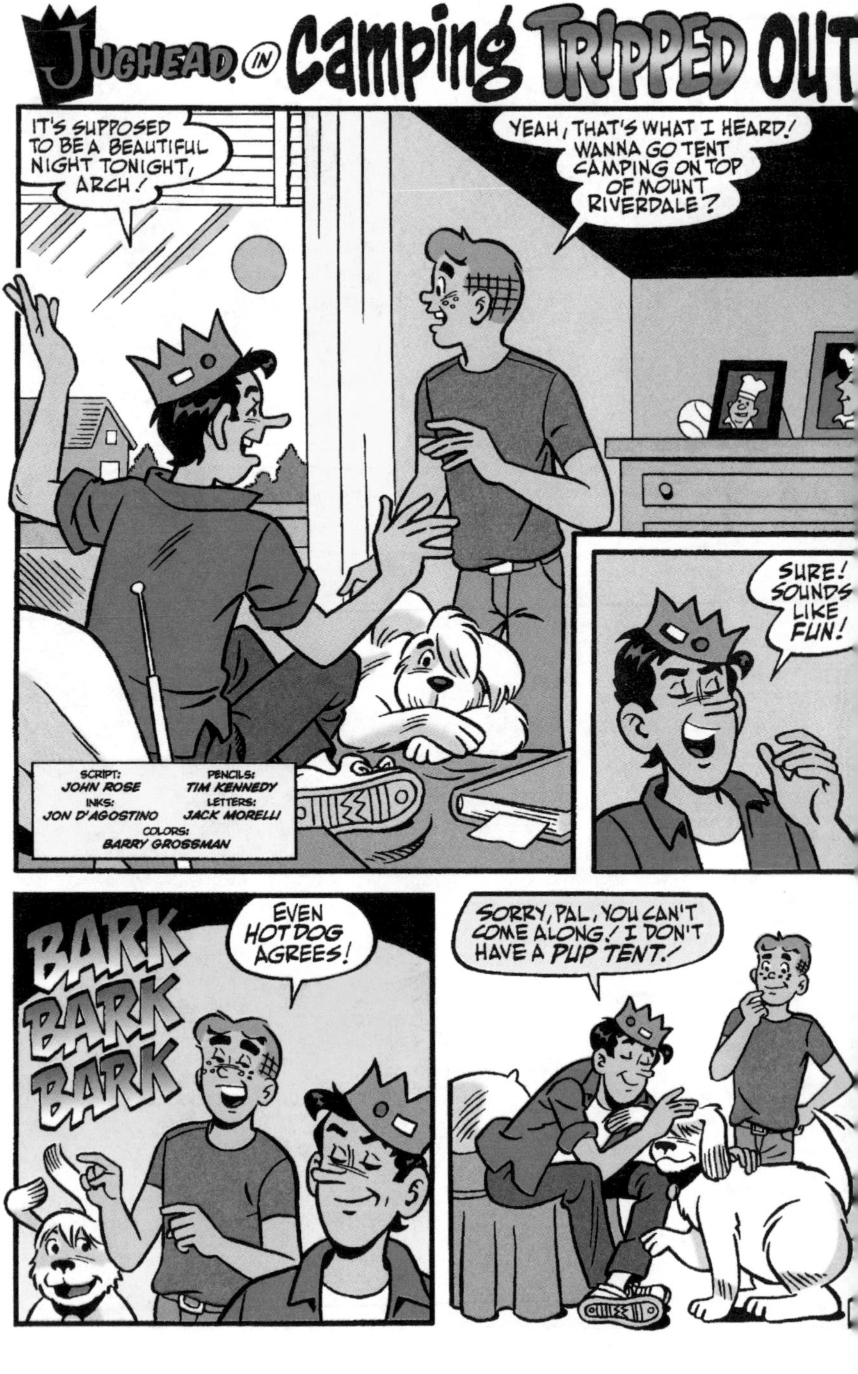
JUGHEAD IN Camping TRIPPED OUT
IT'S SUPPOSED TO BE A BEAUTIFUL NIGHT TONIGHT, ARCH!
YEAH, THAT'S WHAT I HEARD! WANNA GO TENT CAMPING ON TOP OF MOUNT RIVERDALE?
SCRIPT: JOHN ROSE
PENCILS: TIM KENNEDY
INKS: JON D'AGOSTINO
LETTERS: JACK MORELLI
COLORS: BARRY GROSSMAN
SURE! SOUNDS LIKE FUN!
BARK BARK BARK
EVEN HOT DOG AGREES!
SORRY, PAL, YOU CAN'T COME ALONG! I DON'T HAVE A PUP TENT!

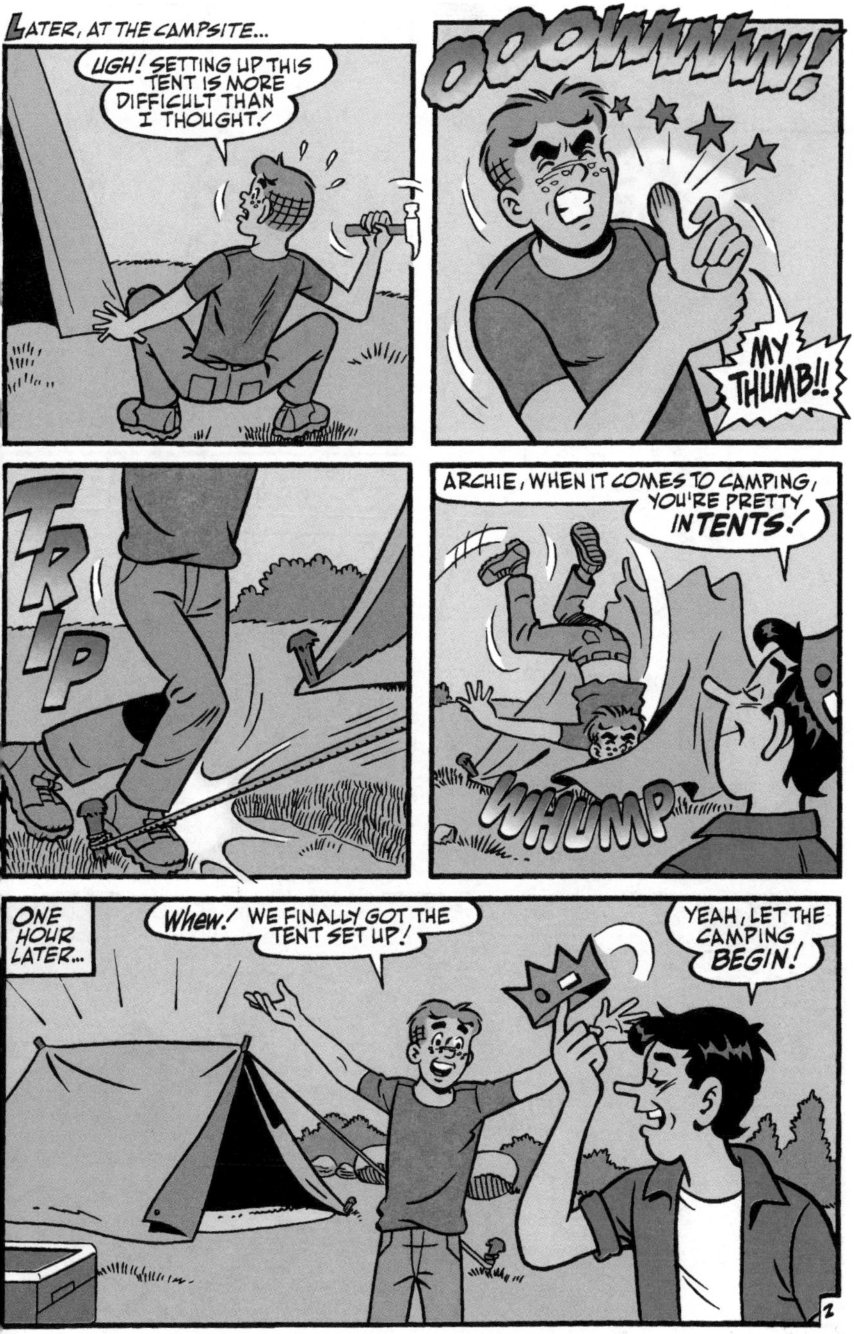
LATER, AT THE CAMPSITE...
UGH! SETTING UP THIS TENT IS MORE DIFFICULT THAN I THOUGHT!
OOOWWWW!
MY THUMB!!
TRIP
ARCHIE, WHEN IT COMES TO CAMPING, YOU'RE PRETTY INTENTS!
WHUMP
ONE HOUR LATER...
Whew! WE FINALLY GOT THE TENT SET UP!
YEAH, LET THE CAMPING BEGIN!
2

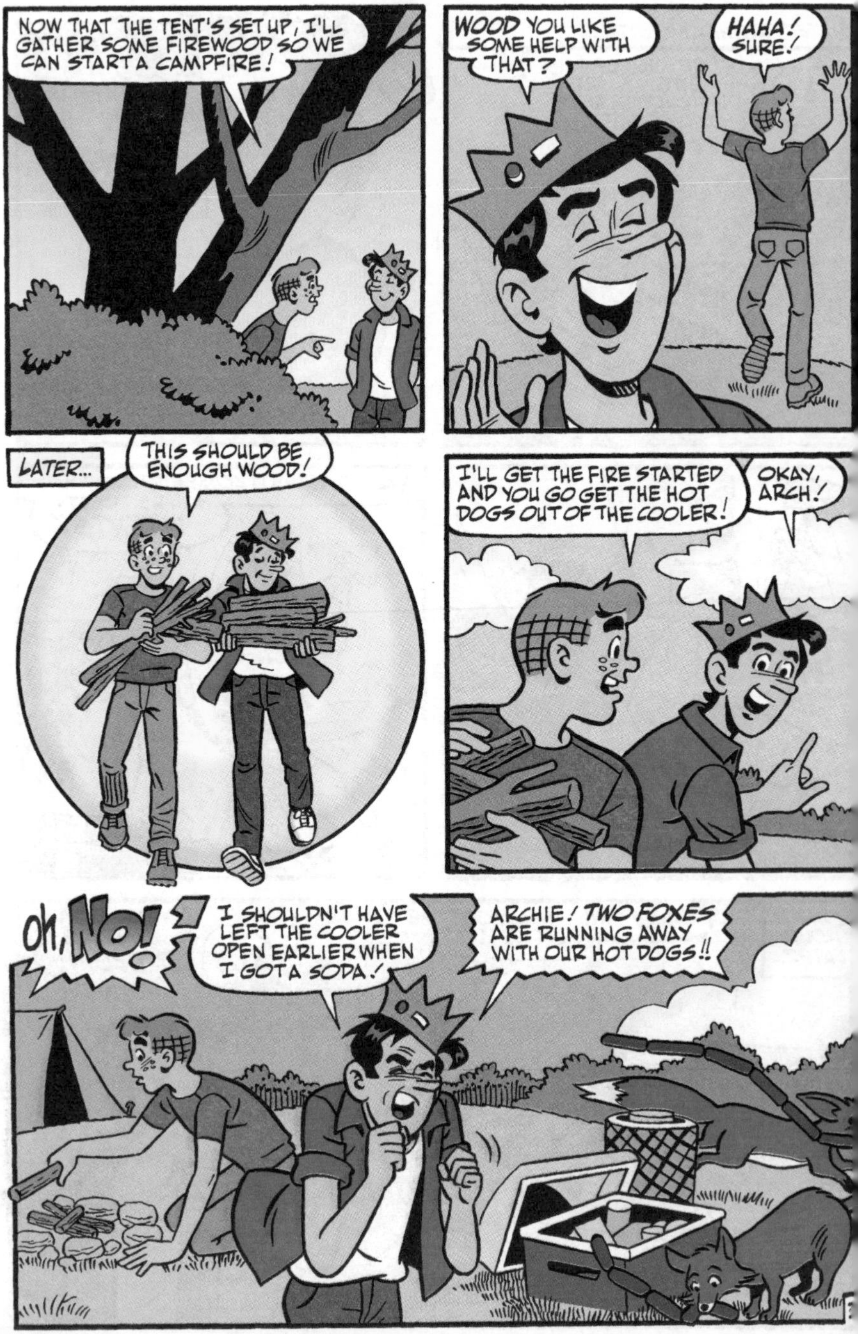
NOW THAT THE TENT'S SET UP, I'LL GATHER SOME FIREWOOD SO WE CAN START A CAMPFIRE!
WOOD YOU LIKE SOME HELP WITH THAT?
HAHA! SURE!
LATER...
THIS SHOULD BE ENOUGH WOOD!
I'LL GET THE FIRE STARTED AND YOU GO GET THE HOT DOGS OUT OF THE COOLER!
OKAY, ARCH!
Oh, NO!
I SHOULDN'T HAVE LEFT THE COOLER OPEN EARLIER WHEN I GOT A SODA!
ARCHIE! TWO FOXES ARE RUNNING AWAY WITH OUR HOT DOGS!!

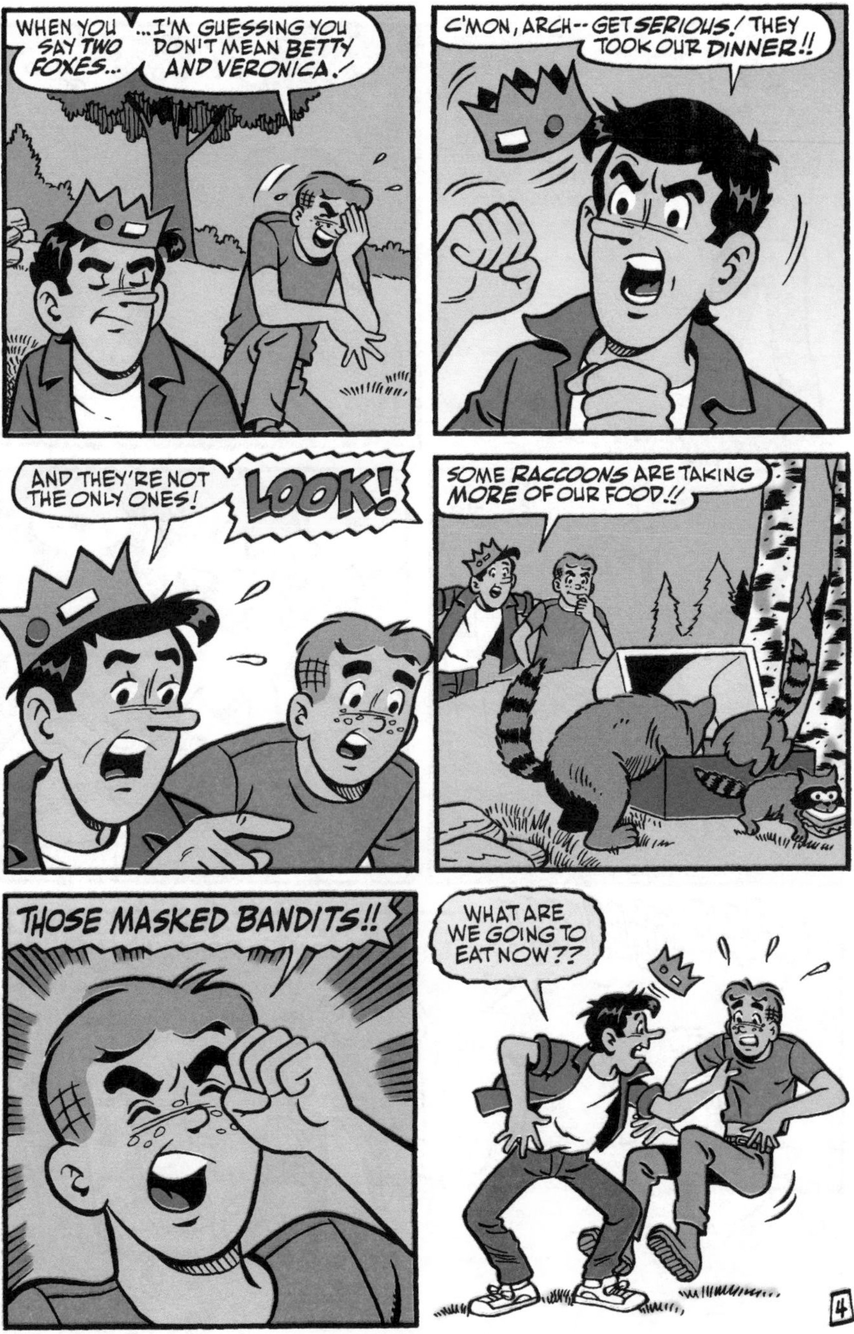
WHEN YOU SAY TWO FOXES...
...I'M GUESSING YOU DON'T MEAN BETTY AND VERONICA!
C'MON, ARCH-- GET SERIOUS! THEY TOOK OUR DINNER!!
AND THEY'RE NOT THE ONLY ONES!
LOOK!
SOME RACCOONS ARE TAKING MORE OF OUR FOOD!!
THOSE MASKED BANDITS!!
WHAT ARE WE GOING TO EAT NOW??
4

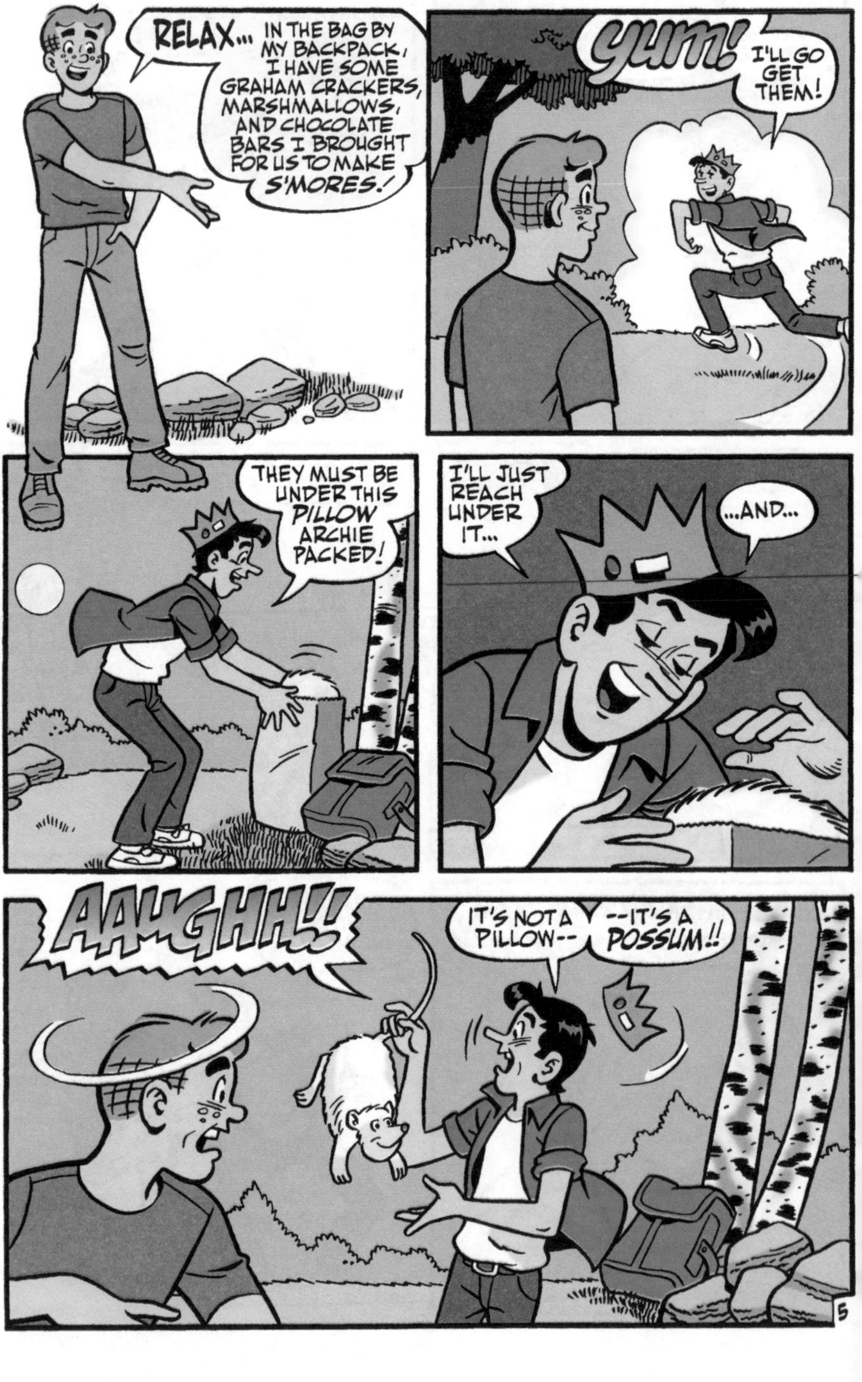
RELAX... IN THE BAG BY MY BACKPACK, I HAVE SOME GRAHAM CRACKERS, MARSHMALLOWS, AND CHOCOLATE BARS I BROUGHT FOR US TO MAKE S'MORES!
YUM!
I'LL GO GET THEM!
THEY MUST BE UNDER THIS PILLOW ARCHIE PACKED!
I'LL JUST REACH UNDER IT...
...AND...
AAUGHH!!
IT'S NOT A PILLOW--
--IT'S A POSSUM!!

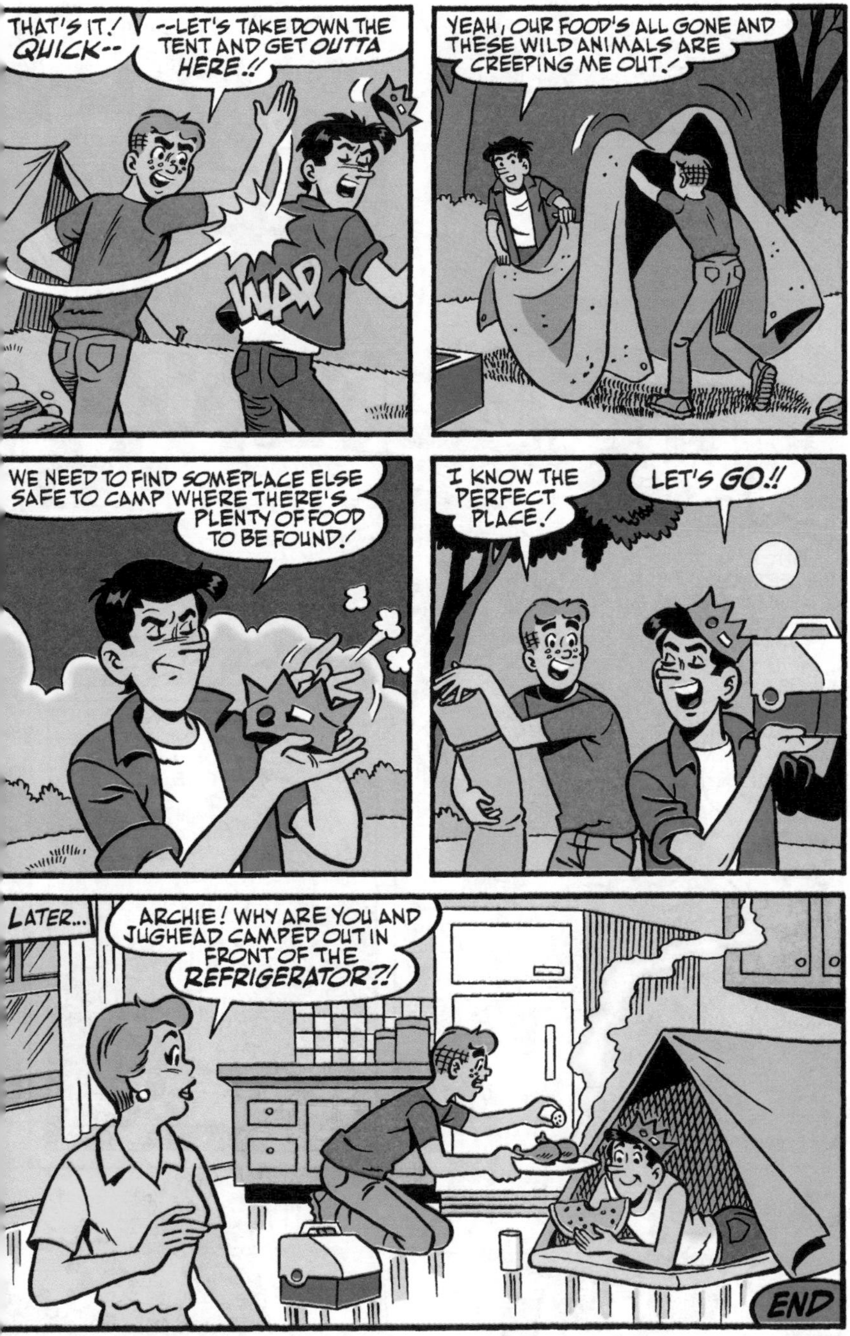

THAT'S IT! QUICK--
--LET'S TAKE DOWN THE TENT AND GET OUTTA HERE!!
WAP
YEAH, OUR FOOD'S ALL GONE AND THESE WILD ANIMALS ARE CREEPING ME OUT!
WE NEED TO FIND SOMEPLACE ELSE SAFE TO CAMP WHERE THERE'S PLENTY OF FOOD TO BE FOUND!
I KNOW THE PERFECT PLACE!
LET'S GO!!
LATER...
ARCHIE! WHY ARE YOU AND JUGHEAD CAMPED OUT IN FRONT OF THE REFRIGERATOR?!
END

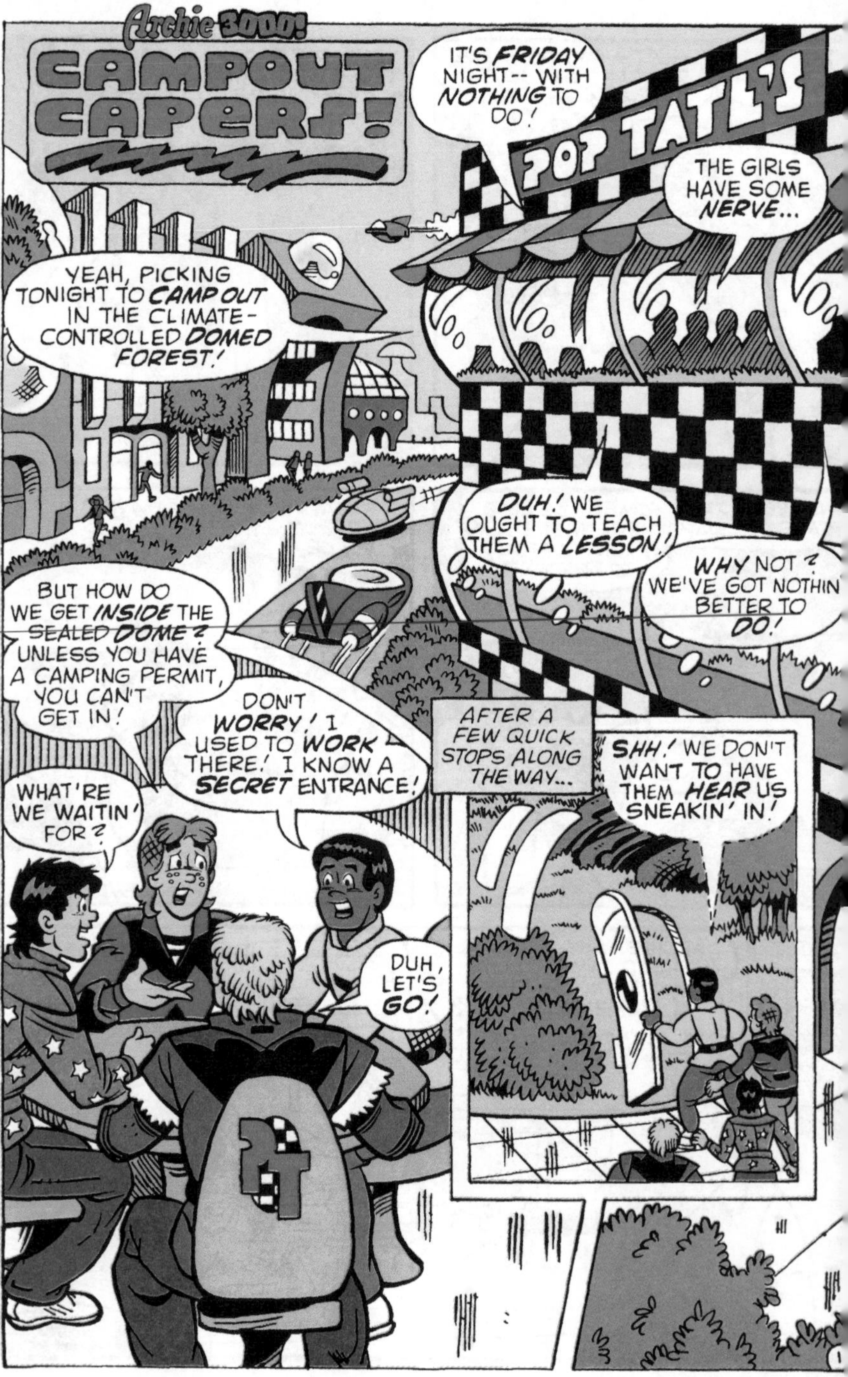
Archie 3000!
CAMPOUT CAPERS!
IT'S FRIDAY NIGHT-- WITH NOTHING TO DO!
POP TATE'S
THE GIRLS HAVE SOME NERVE...
YEAH, PICKING TONIGHT TO CAMP OUT IN THE CLIMATE-CONTROLLED DOMED FOREST!
DUH! WE OUGHT TO TEACH THEM A LESSON!
WHY NOT? WE'VE GOT NOTHIN BETTER TO DO!
BUT HOW DO WE GET INSIDE THE SEALED DOME? UNLESS YOU HAVE A CAMPING PERMIT, YOU CAN'T GET IN!
DON'T WORRY! I USED TO WORK THERE! I KNOW A SECRET ENTRANCE!
WHAT'RE WE WAITIN' FOR?
DUH, LET'S GO!
AFTER A FEW QUICK STOPS ALONG THE WAY...
SHH! WE DON'T WANT TO HAVE THEM HEAR US SNEAKIN' IN!

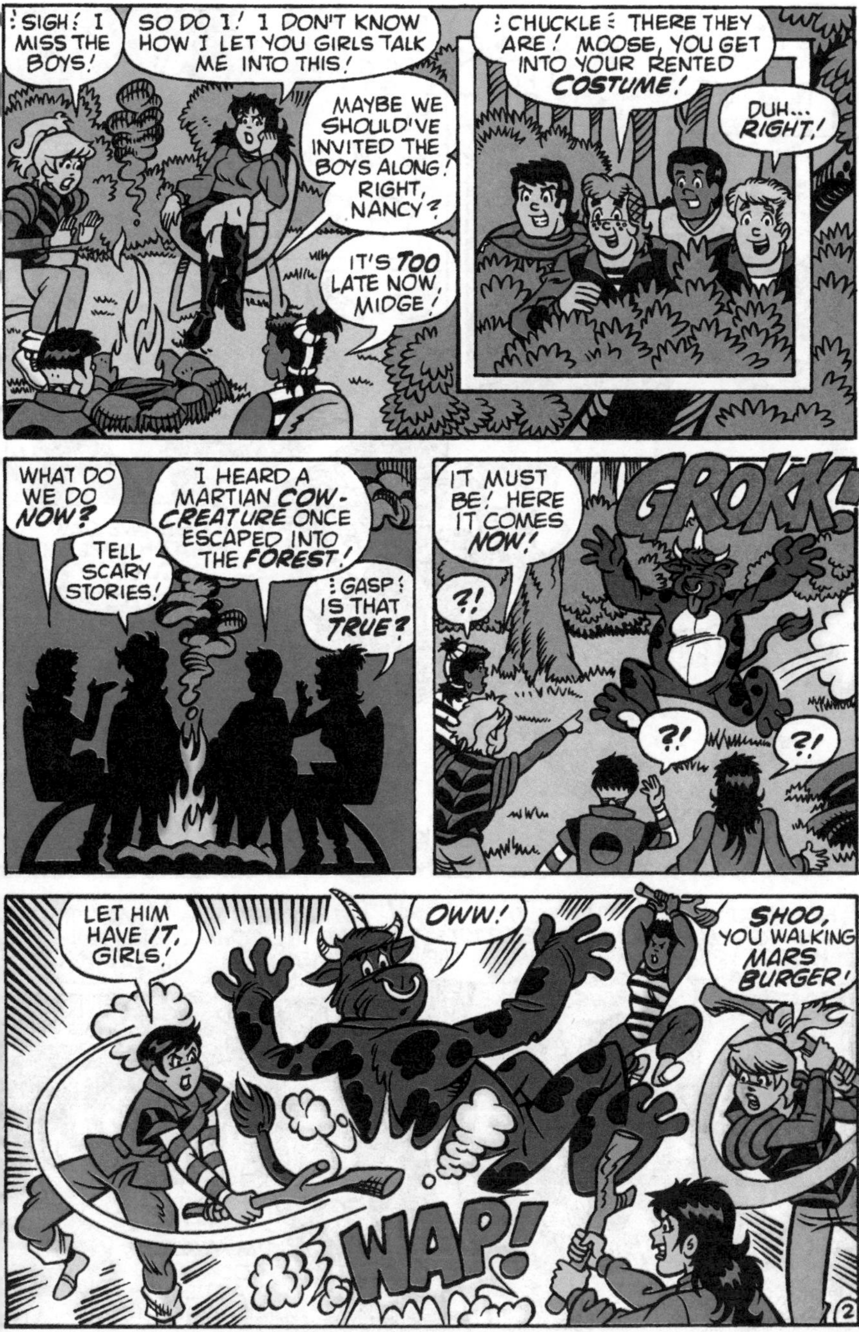
:SIGH: I MISS THE BOYS!
SO DO I! I DON'T KNOW HOW I LET YOU GIRLS TALK ME INTO THIS!
MAYBE WE SHOULD'VE INVITED THE BOYS ALONG! RIGHT, NANCY?
IT'S TOO LATE NOW, MIDGE!
:CHUCKLE: THERE THEY ARE! MOOSE, YOU GET INTO YOUR RENTED COSTUME!
DUH... RIGHT!
WHAT DO WE DO NOW?
TELL SCARY STORIES!
I HEARD A MARTIAN COW-CREATURE ONCE ESCAPED INTO THE FOREST!
:GASP: IS THAT TRUE?
IT MUST BE! HERE IT COMES NOW!
GROKK!
?!
?!
?!
LET HIM HAVE IT, GIRLS!
OWW!
SHOO, YOU WALKING MARS BURGER!
WAP!

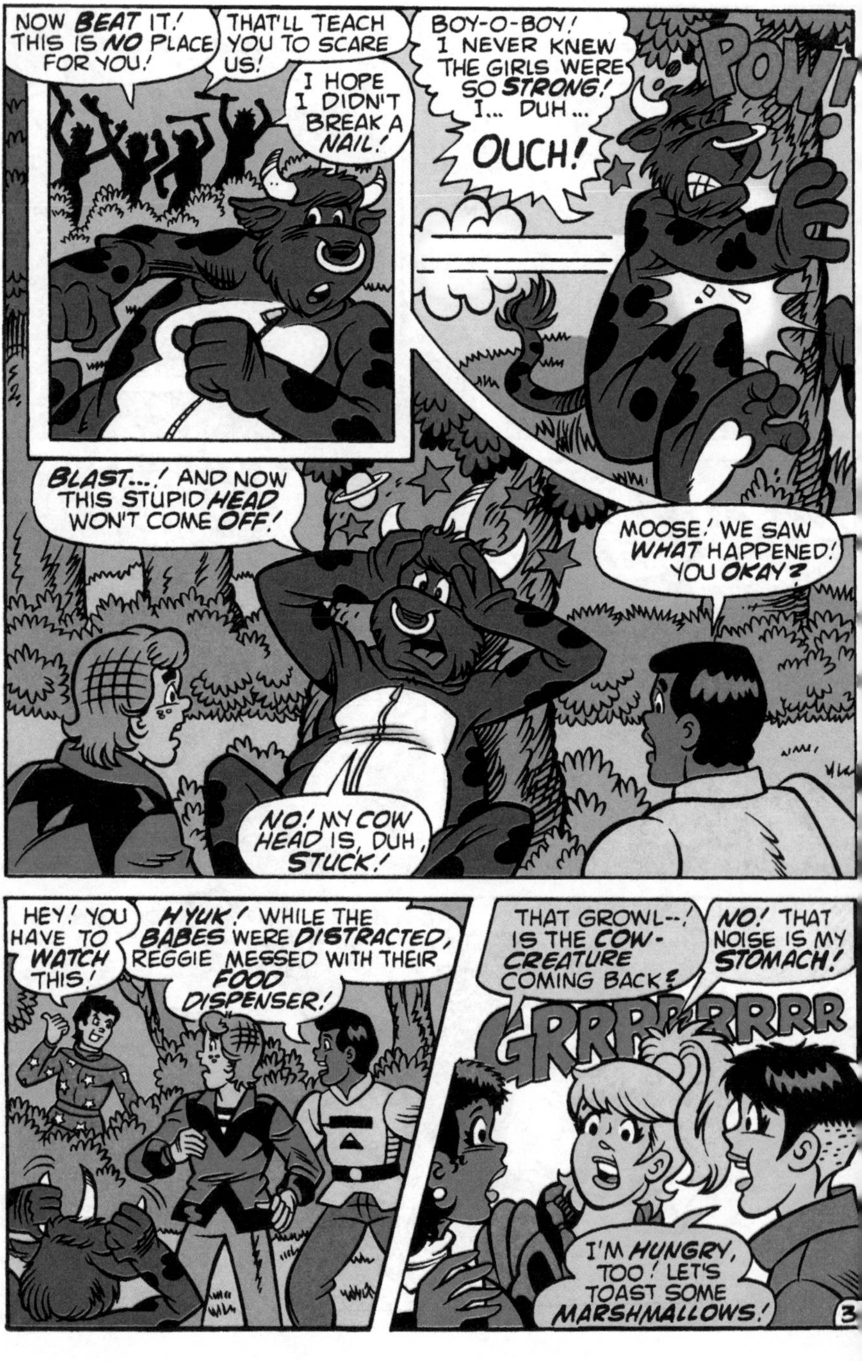
NOW BEAT IT! THIS IS NO PLACE FOR YOU!
THAT'LL TEACH YOU TO SCARE US!
I HOPE I DIDN'T BREAK A NAIL!
BOY-O-BOY! I NEVER KNEW THE GIRLS WERE SO STRONG! I... DUH ...
OUCH!
POW!
BLAST...! AND NOW THIS STUPID HEAD WON'T COME OFF!
MOOSE! WE SAW WHAT HAPPENED! YOU OKAY?
NO! MY COW HEAD IS, DUH, STUCK!
HEY! YOU HAVE TO WATCH THIS!
HYUK! WHILE THE BABES WERE DISTRACTED, REGGIE MESSED WITH THEIR FOOD DISPENSER!
THAT GROWL--! IS THE COW-CREATURE COMING BACK?
NO! THAT NOISE IS MY STOMACH!
GRRRRRRRR
I'M HUNGRY, TOO! LET'S TOAST SOME MARSHMALLOWS!

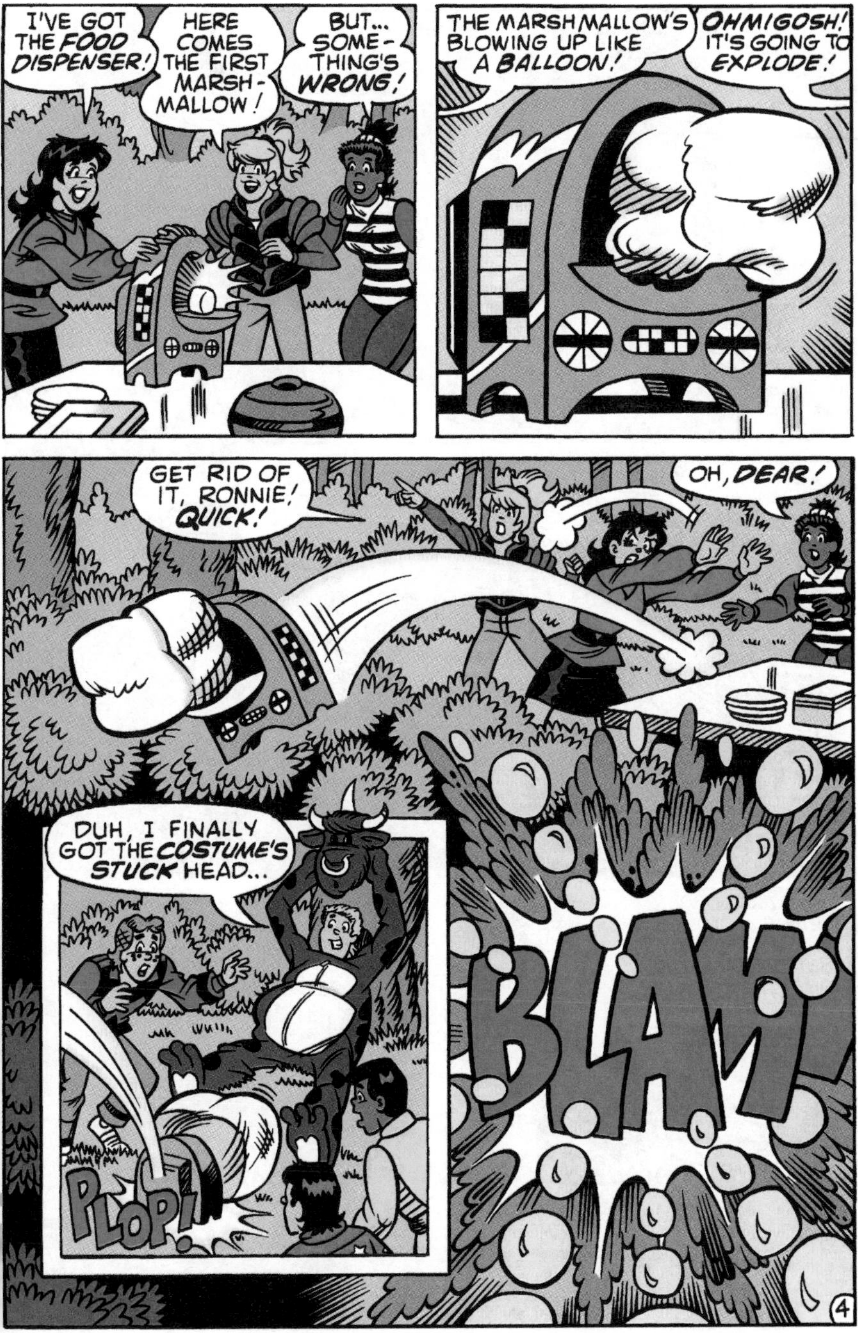
I'VE GOT THE FOOD DISPENSER!
HERE COMES THE FIRST MARSH-MALLOW!
BUT... SOME-THING'S WRONG!
THE MARSHMALLOW'S BLOWING UP LIKE A BALLOON!
OHMIGOSH! IT'S GOING TO EXPLODE!
GET RID OF IT, RONNIE! QUICK!
OH, DEAR!
DUH, I FINALLY GOT THE COSTUME'S STUCK HEAD...
PLOP!
BLAM!

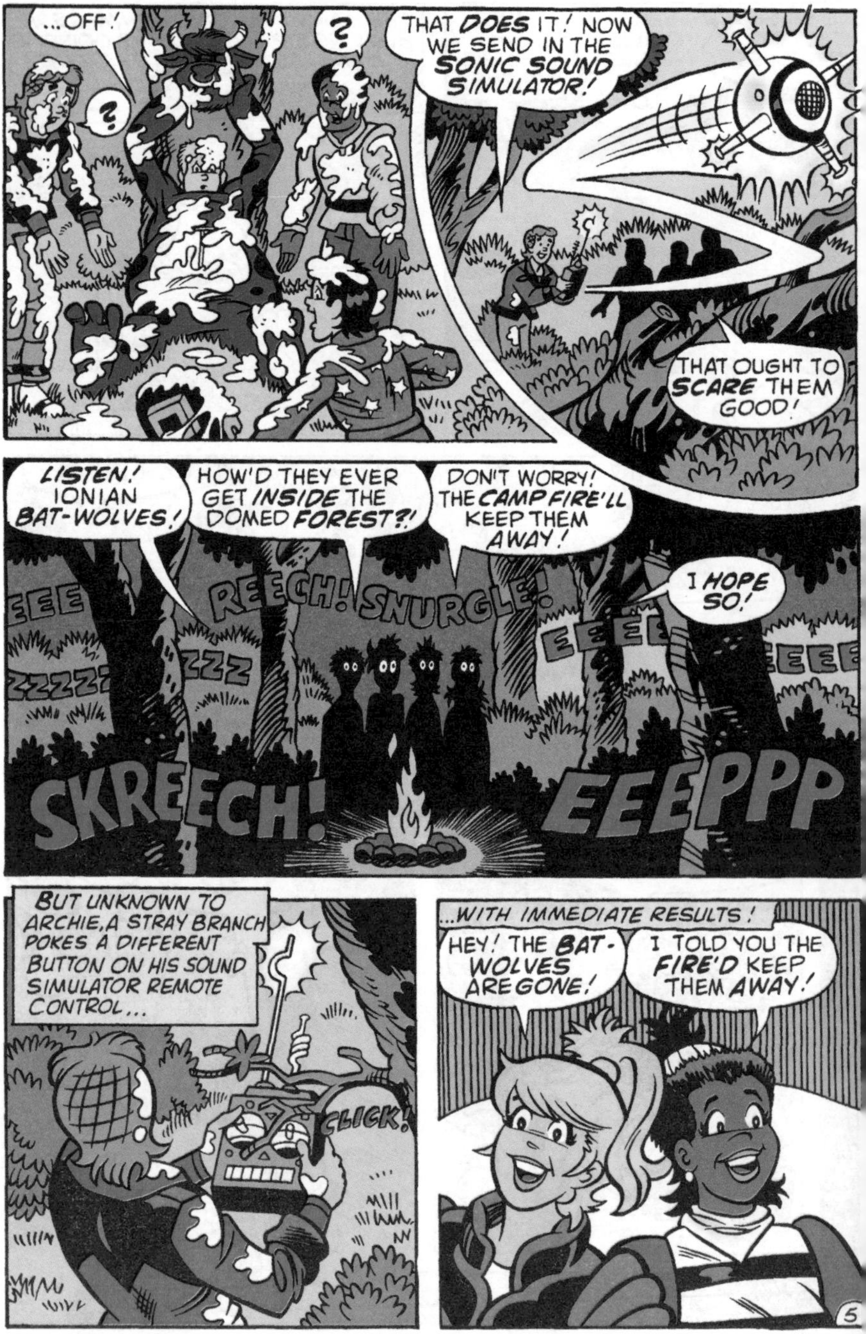
...OFF!
?
?
THAT DOES IT! NOW WE SEND IN THE SONIC SOUND SIMULATOR!
THAT OUGHT TO SCARE THEM GOOD!
LISTEN! IONIAN BAT-WOLVES!
HOW'D THEY EVER GET INSIDE THE DOMED FOREST?!
DON'T WORRY! THE CAMP FIRE'LL KEEP THEM AWAY!
I HOPE SO!
REECH! SNURGLE!
SKREECH!
EEEPPP
BUT UNKNOWN TO ARCHIE, A STRAY BRANCH POKES A DIFFERENT BUTTON ON HIS SOUND SIMULATOR REMOTE CONTROL...
CLICK!
...WITH IMMEDIATE RESULTS!
HEY! THE BAT-WOLVES ARE GONE!
I TOLD YOU THE FIRE'D KEEP THEM AWAY!
5

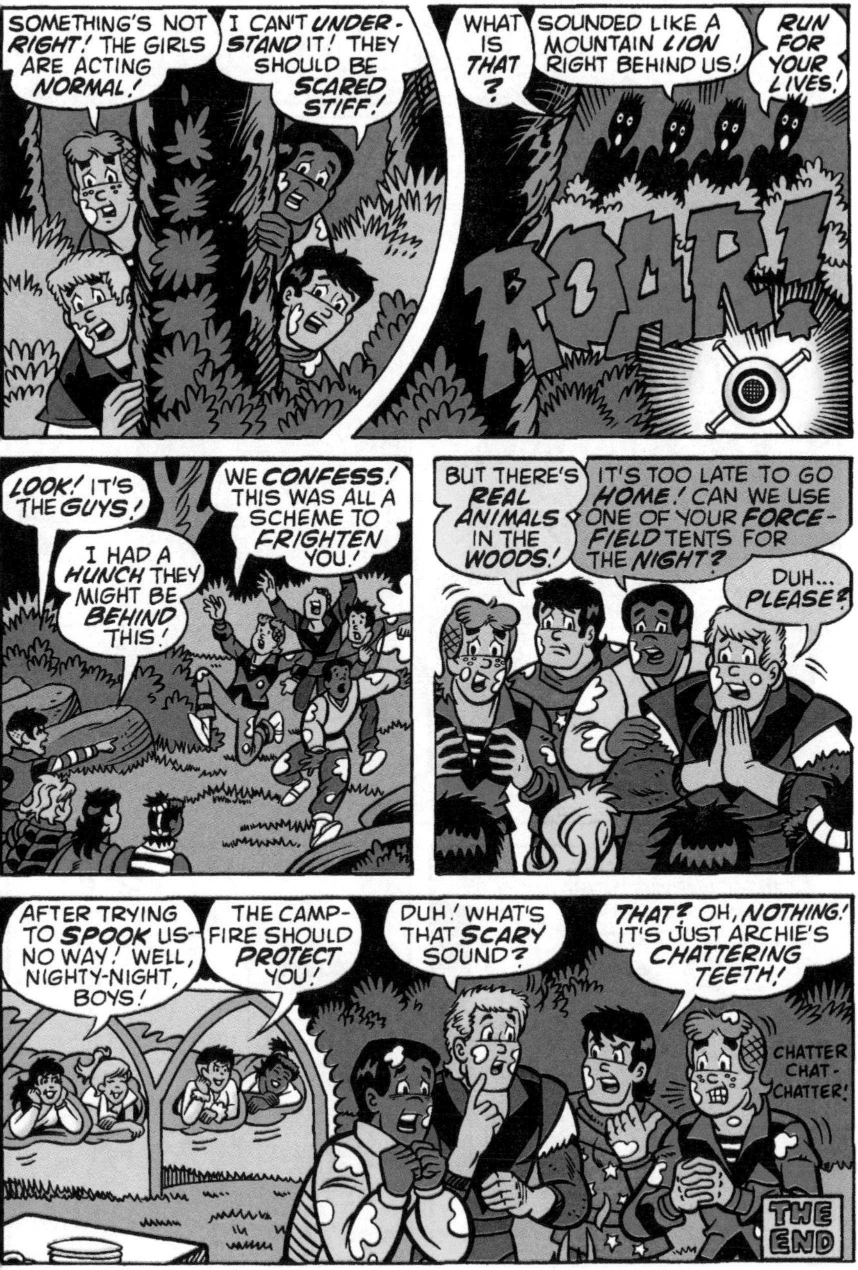

SOMETHING'S NOT RIGHT! THE GIRLS ARE ACTING NORMAL!
I CAN'T UNDERSTAND IT! THEY SHOULD BE SCARED STIFF!
WHAT IS THAT?
SOUNDED LIKE A MOUNTAIN LION RIGHT BEHIND US!
RUN FOR YOUR LIVES!
ROAR!
LOOK! IT'S THE GUYS!
I HAD A HUNCH THEY MIGHT BE BEHIND THIS!
WE CONFESS! THIS WAS ALL A SCHEME TO FRIGHTEN YOU!
BUT THERE'S REAL ANIMALS IN THE WOODS!
IT'S TOO LATE TO GO HOME! CAN WE USE ONE OF YOUR FORCE-FIELD TENTS FOR THE NIGHT?
DUH... PLEASE?
AFTER TRYING TO SPOOK US-- NO WAY! WELL, NIGHTY-NIGHT, BOYS!
THE CAMP-FIRE SHOULD PROTECT YOU!
DUH! WHAT'S THAT SCARY SOUND?
THAT? OH, NOTHING! IT'S JUST ARCHIE'S CHATTERING TEETH!
CHATTER CHAT-CHATTER!
THE END

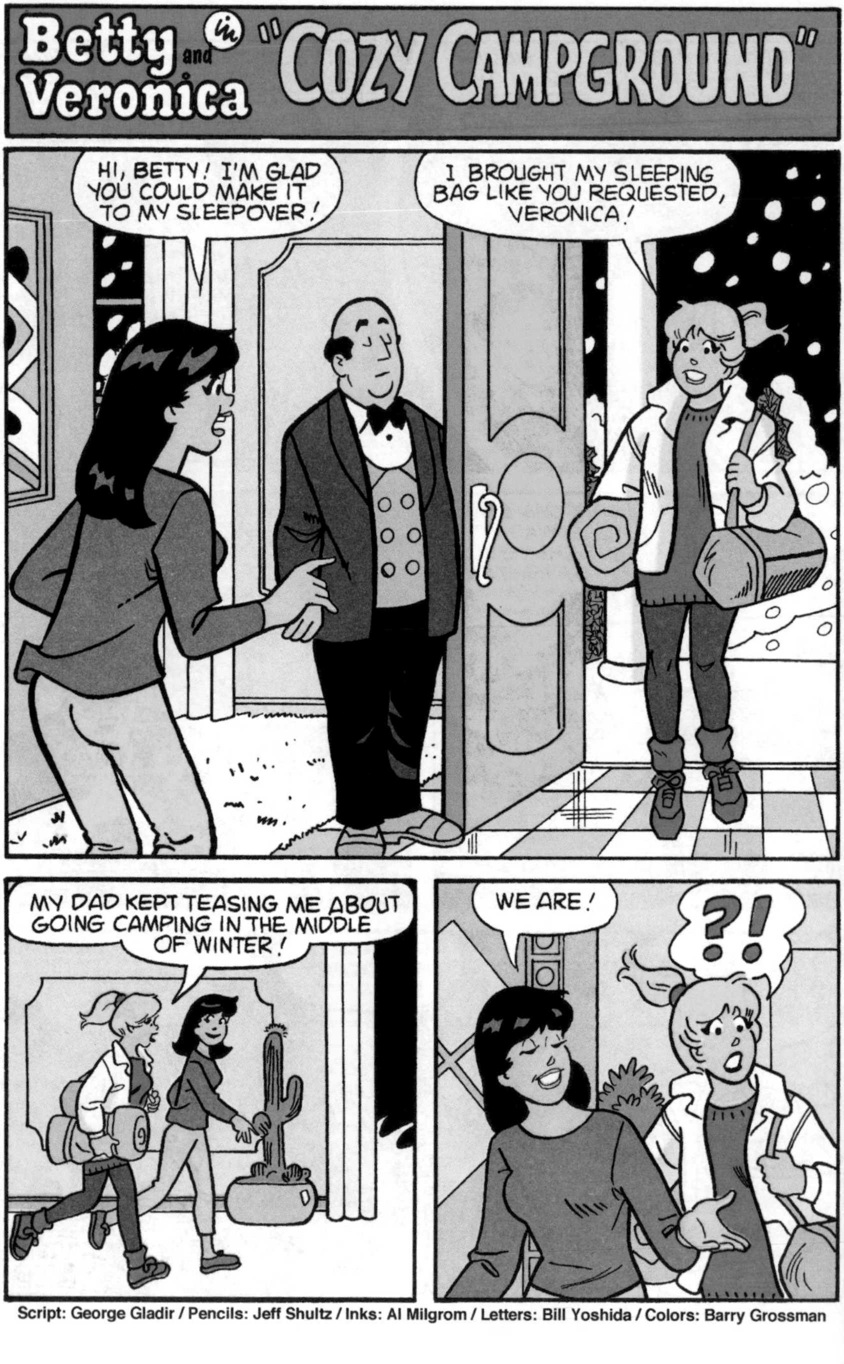
Betty and Veronica in "COZY CAMPGROUND"
HI, BETTY! I'M GLAD YOU COULD MAKE IT TO MY SLEEPOVER!
I BROUGHT MY SLEEPING BAG LIKE YOU REQUESTED, VERONICA!
MY DAD KEPT TEASING ME ABOUT GOING CAMPING IN THE MIDDLE OF WINTER!
WE ARE!
?!

Script: George Gladir / Pencils: Jeff Shultz / Inks: Al Milgrom / Letters: Bill Yoshida / Colors: Barry Grossman

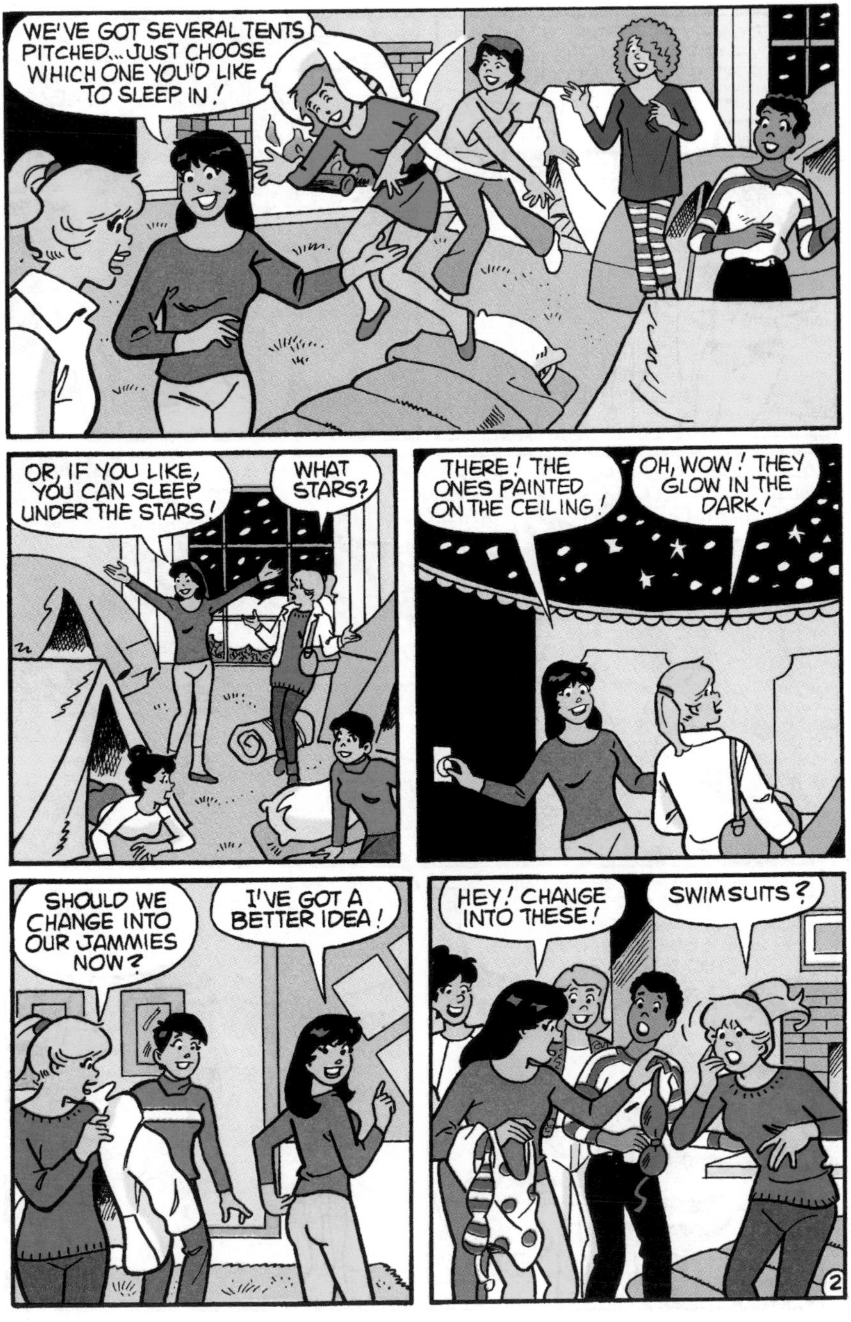

WE'VE GOT SEVERAL TENTS PITCHED... JUST CHOOSE WHICH ONE YOU'D LIKE TO SLEEP IN!
OR, IF YOU LIKE, YOU CAN SLEEP UNDER THE STARS!
WHAT STARS?
THERE! THE ONES PAINTED ON THE CEILING!
OH, WOW! THEY GLOW IN THE DARK!
SHOULD WE CHANGE INTO OUR JAMMIES NOW?
I'VE GOT A BETTER IDEA!
HEY! CHANGE INTO THESE!
SWIMSUITS?
2

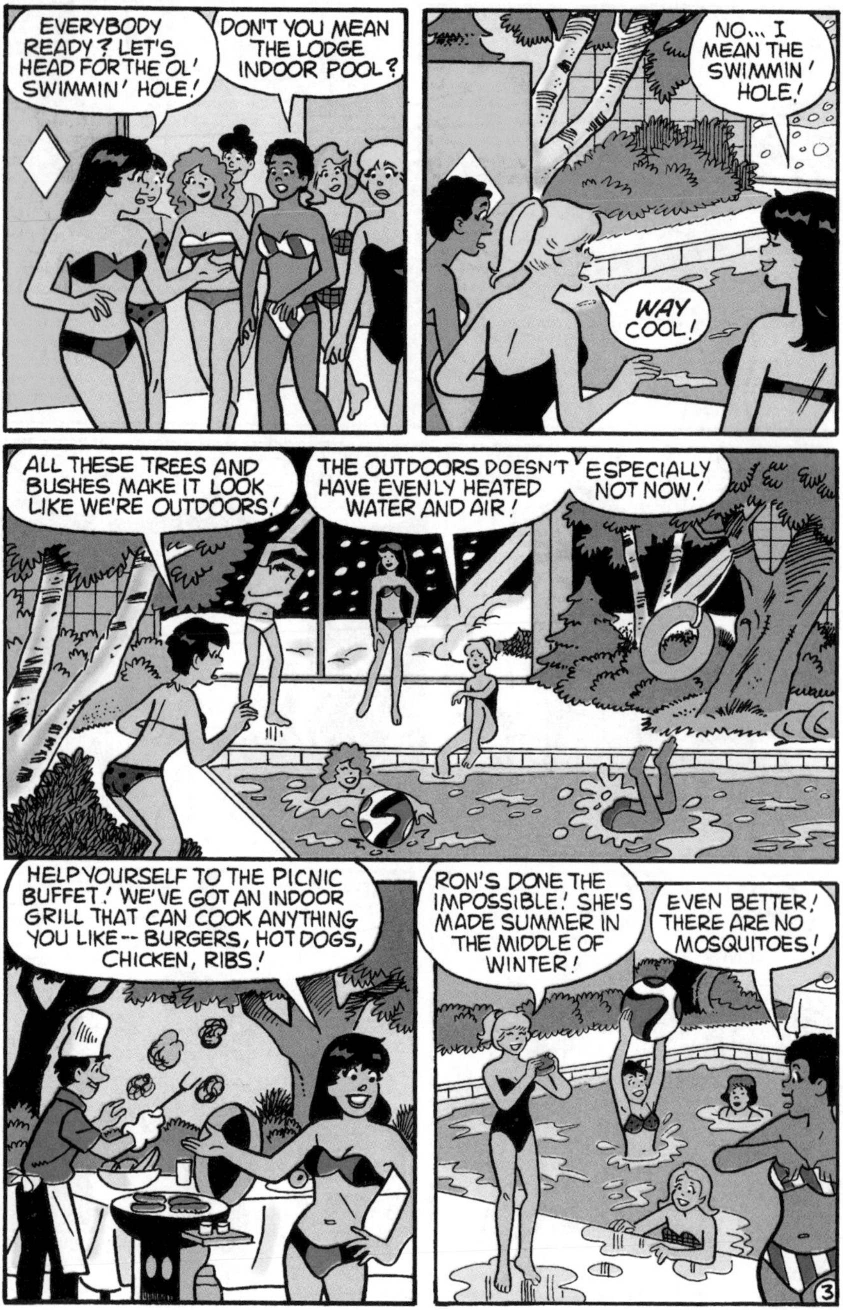
EVERYBODY READY? LET'S HEAD FOR THE OL' SWIMMIN' HOLE!
DON'T YOU MEAN THE LODGE INDOOR POOL?
NO... I MEAN THE SWIMMIN' HOLE!
WAY COOL!
ALL THESE TREES AND BUSHES MAKE IT LOOK LIKE WE'RE OUTDOORS!
THE OUTDOORS DOESN'T HAVE EVENLY HEATED WATER AND AIR!
ESPECIALLY NOT NOW!
HELP YOURSELF TO THE PICNIC BUFFET! WE'VE GOT AN INDOOR GRILL THAT CAN COOK ANYTHING YOU LIKE-- BURGERS, HOT DOGS, CHICKEN, RIBS!
RON'S DONE THE IMPOSSIBLE! SHE'S MADE SUMMER IN THE MIDDLE OF WINTER!
EVEN BETTER! THERE ARE NO MOSQUITOES!
3

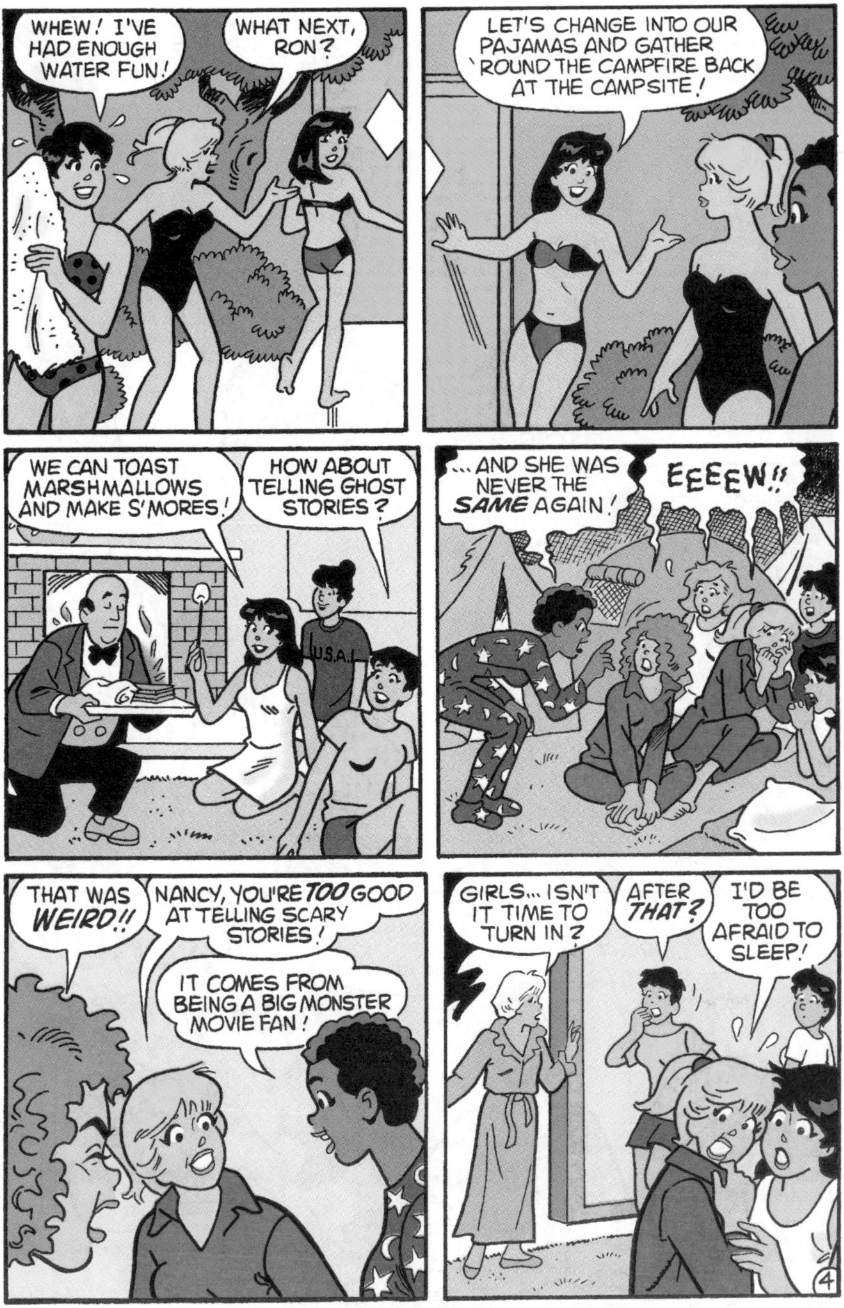
WHEW! I'VE HAD ENOUGH WATER FUN!
WHAT NEXT, RON?
LET'S CHANGE INTO OUR PAJAMAS AND GATHER 'ROUND THE CAMPFIRE BACK AT THE CAMPSITE!
WE CAN TOAST MARSHMALLOWS AND MAKE S'MORES!
HOW ABOUT TELLING GHOST STORIES?
...AND SHE WAS NEVER THE SAME AGAIN!
EEEEW!!
U.S.A.
THAT WAS WEIRD!!
NANCY, YOU'RE TOO GOOD AT TELLING SCARY STORIES!
IT COMES FROM BEING A BIG MONSTER MOVIE FAN!
GIRLS... ISN'T IT TIME TO TURN IN?
AFTER THAT?
I'D BE TOO AFRAID TO SLEEP!
4

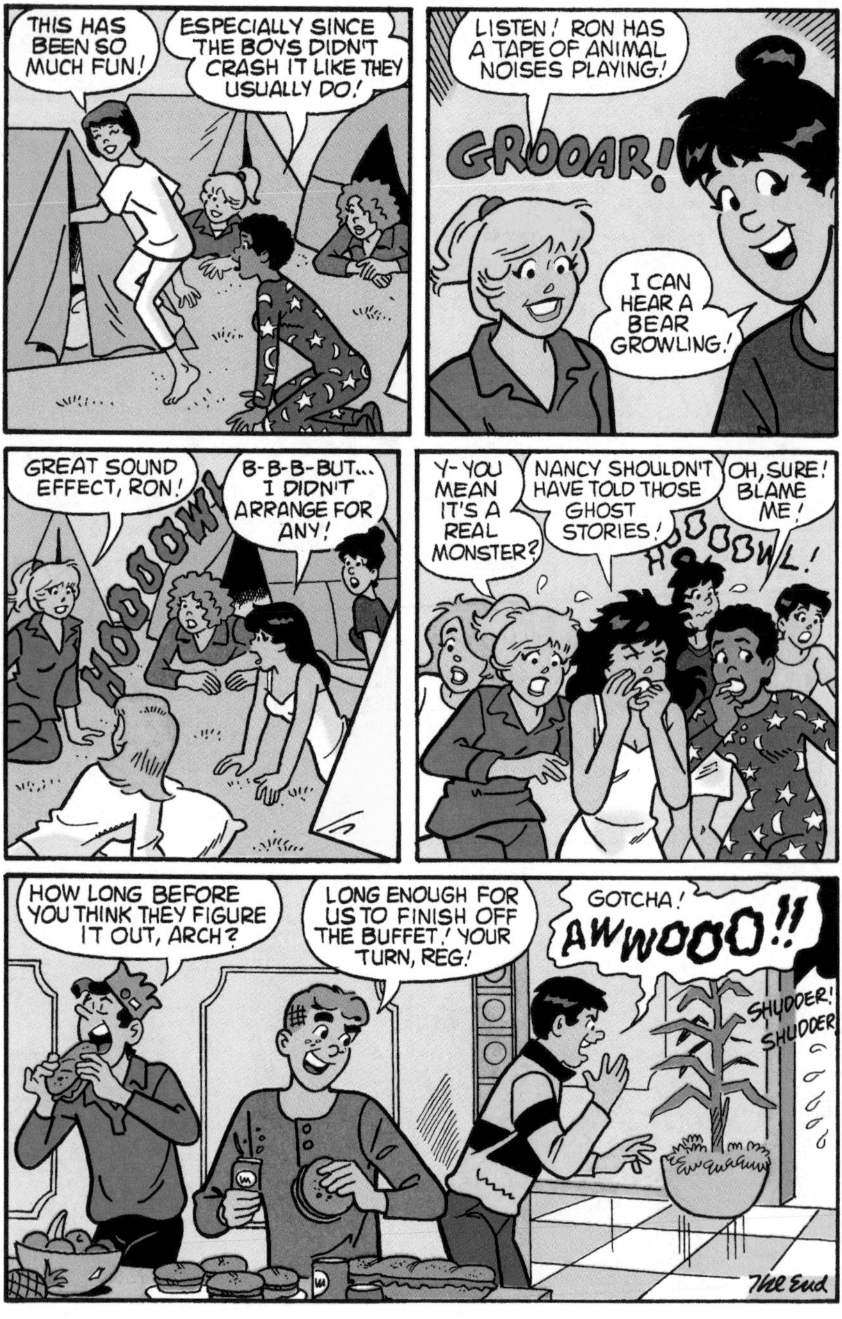
THIS HAS BEEN SO MUCH FUN!
ESPECIALLY SINCE THE BOYS DIDN'T CRASH IT LIKE THEY USUALLY DO!
LISTEN! RON HAS A TAPE OF ANIMAL NOISES PLAYING!
GROOAR!
I CAN HEAR A BEAR GROWLING!
GREAT SOUND EFFECT, RON!
HOOOOOW!
B-B-B-BUT... I DIDN'T ARRANGE FOR ANY!
Y-YOU MEAN IT'S A REAL MONSTER?
NANCY SHOULDN'T HAVE TOLD THOSE GHOST STORIES!
OH, SURE! BLAME ME!
HOOOOOWL!
HOW LONG BEFORE YOU THINK THEY FIGURE IT OUT, ARCH?
LONG ENOUGH FOR US TO FINISH OFF THE BUFFET! YOUR TURN, REG!
GOTCHA!
AWOOOO!!
SHUDDER! SHUDDER!
The End

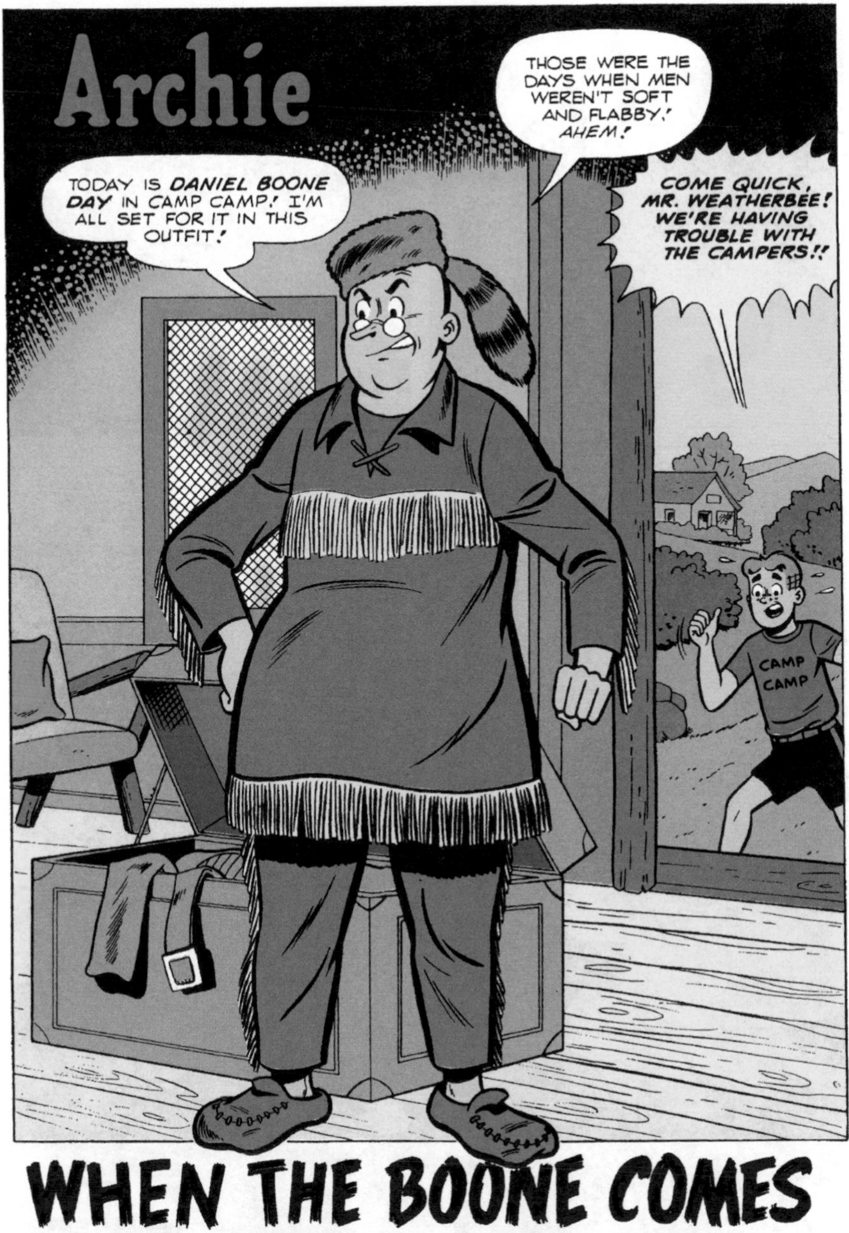
Archie
TODAY IS DANIEL BOONE DAY IN CAMP CAMP! I'M ALL SET FOR IT IN THIS OUTFIT!
THOSE WERE THE DAYS WHEN MEN WEREN'T SOFT AND FLABBY! AHEM!
COME QUICK, MR. WEATHERBEE! WE'RE HAVING TROUBLE WITH THE CAMPERS!!
CAMP CAMP

WHEN THE BOONE COMES OVER THE MOUNTAIN...

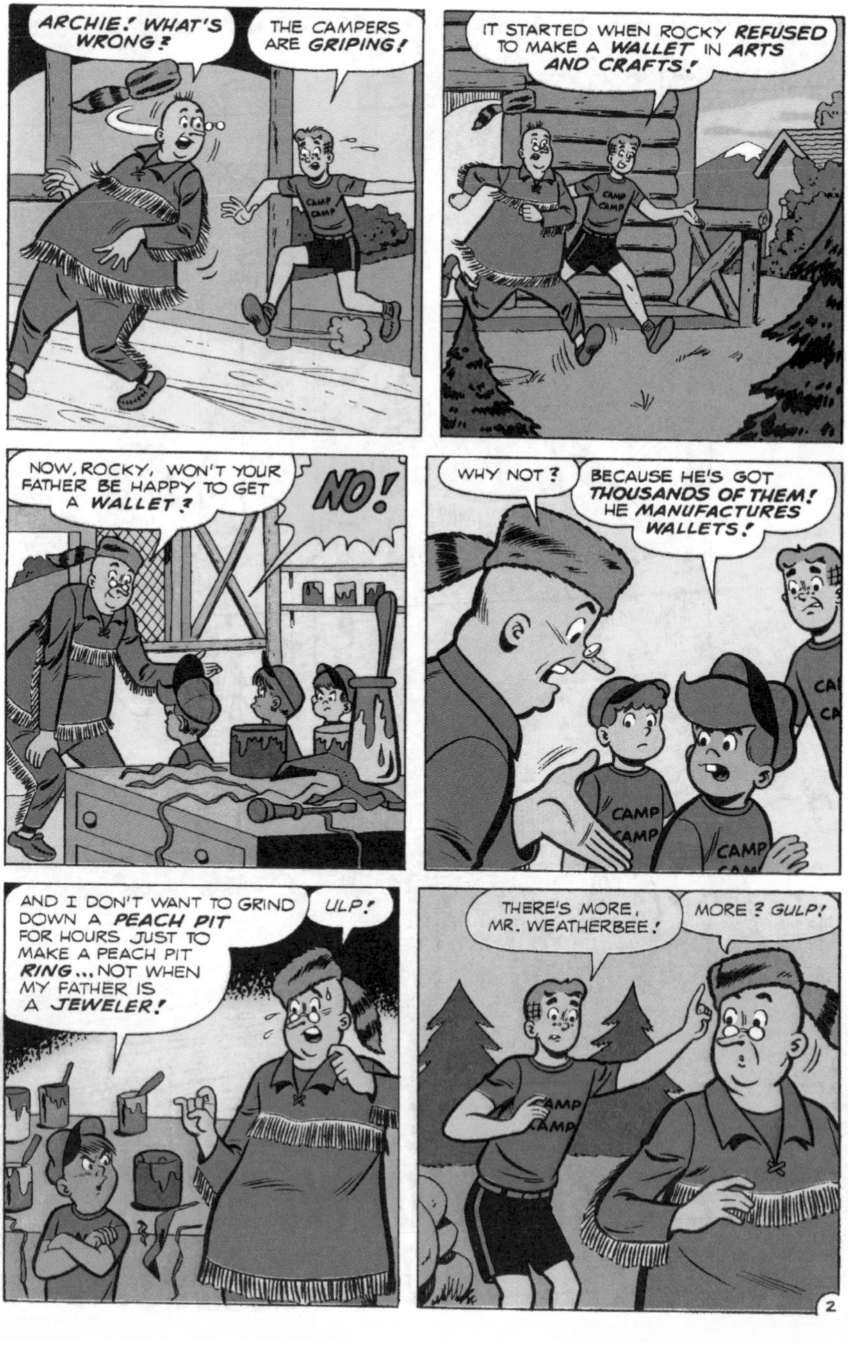
ARCHIE! WHAT'S WRONG?
THE CAMPERS ARE GRIPING!
IT STARTED WHEN ROCKY REFUSED TO MAKE A WALLET IN ARTS AND CRAFTS!
NOW, ROCKY, WON'T YOUR FATHER BE HAPPY TO GET A WALLET?
NO!
WHY NOT?
BECAUSE HE'S GOT THOUSANDS OF THEM! HE MANUFACTURES WALLETS!
AND I DON'T WANT TO GRIND DOWN A PEACH PIT FOR HOURS JUST TO MAKE A PEACH PIT RING... NOT WHEN MY FATHER IS A JEWELER!
ULP!
THERE'S MORE, MR. WEATHERBEE!
MORE? GULP!

THE CAMPERS IN MY GROUP ARE *COMPLAINING* ABOUT MAKING BEDS ... THEY SAY THEIR *MOTHERS DO IT FOR THEM* AT HOME!

MY GROUP DOESN'T LIKE *HIKES!* THEY SAY AT HOME THEY *RIDE* INSTEAD OF WALK ...

YES! THEY WANT AN *ESCALATOR* TO TAKE THEM *UP AND DOWN THE HILL* TO THE LAKE!

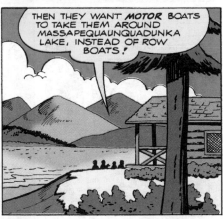

THEN THEY WANT *MOTOR* BOATS TO TAKE THEM AROUND MASSAPEQUAUNQUADUNKA LAKE, INSTEAD OF ROW BOATS!

HUMPH! IS THAT SO ?! WELL, I'M GOING TO HAVE A *TALK* WITH THEM!

CAMPERS!! I WANT YOU TO KNOW THAT YOUR *ATTITUDE* WILL HAVE TO *CHANGE* IN CAMP CAMP!

3

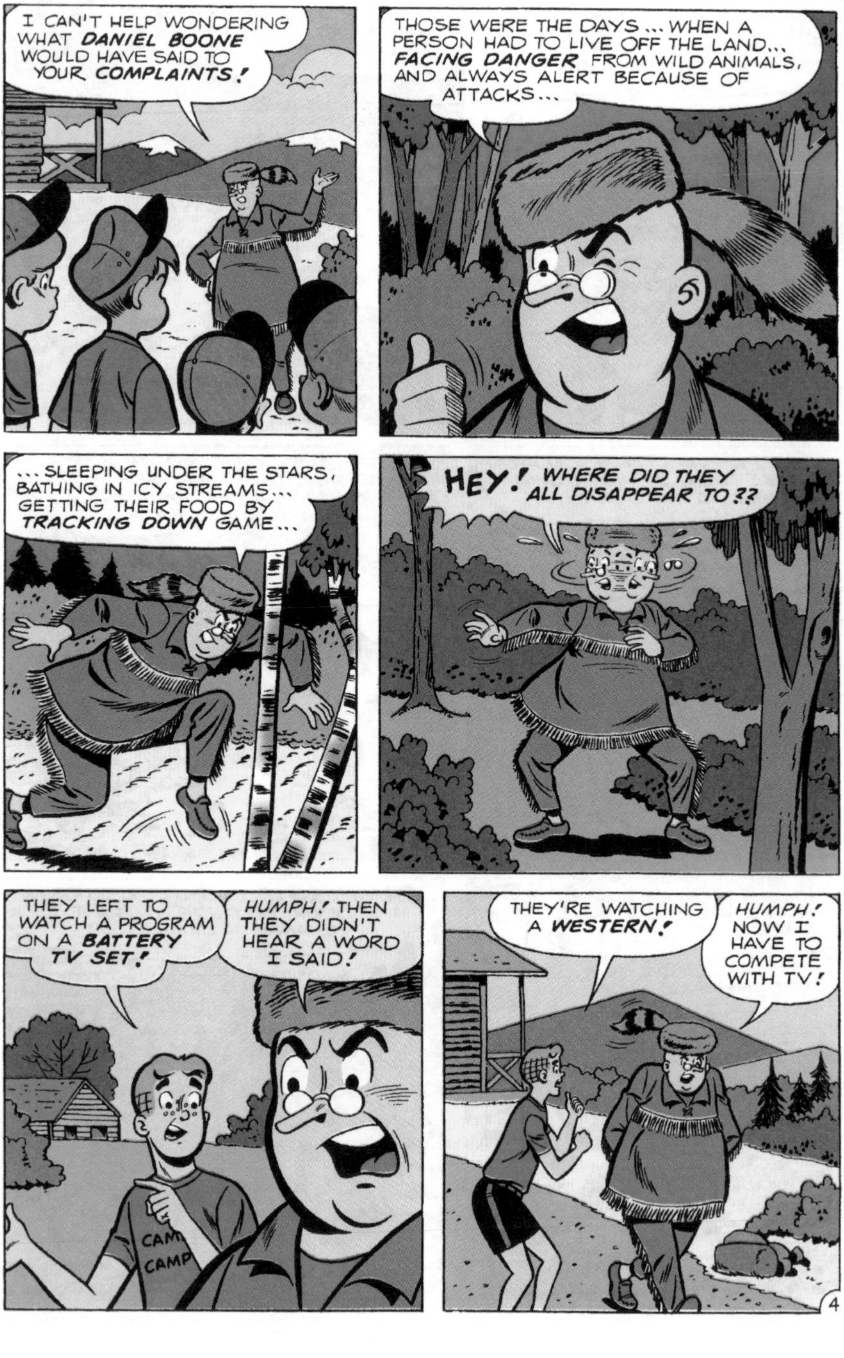
I CAN'T HELP WONDERING WHAT DANIEL BOONE WOULD HAVE SAID TO YOUR COMPLAINTS!
THOSE WERE THE DAYS ... WHEN A PERSON HAD TO LIVE OFF THE LAND... FACING DANGER FROM WILD ANIMALS, AND ALWAYS ALERT BECAUSE OF ATTACKS...
... SLEEPING UNDER THE STARS, BATHING IN ICY STREAMS... GETTING THEIR FOOD BY TRACKING DOWN GAME...
HEY! WHERE DID THEY ALL DISAPPEAR TO??
THEY LEFT TO WATCH A PROGRAM ON A BATTERY TV SET!
HUMPH! THEN THEY DIDN'T HEAR A WORD I SAID!
THEY'RE WATCHING A WESTERN!
HUMPH! NOW I HAVE TO COMPETE WITH TV!
CAMP
CAMP

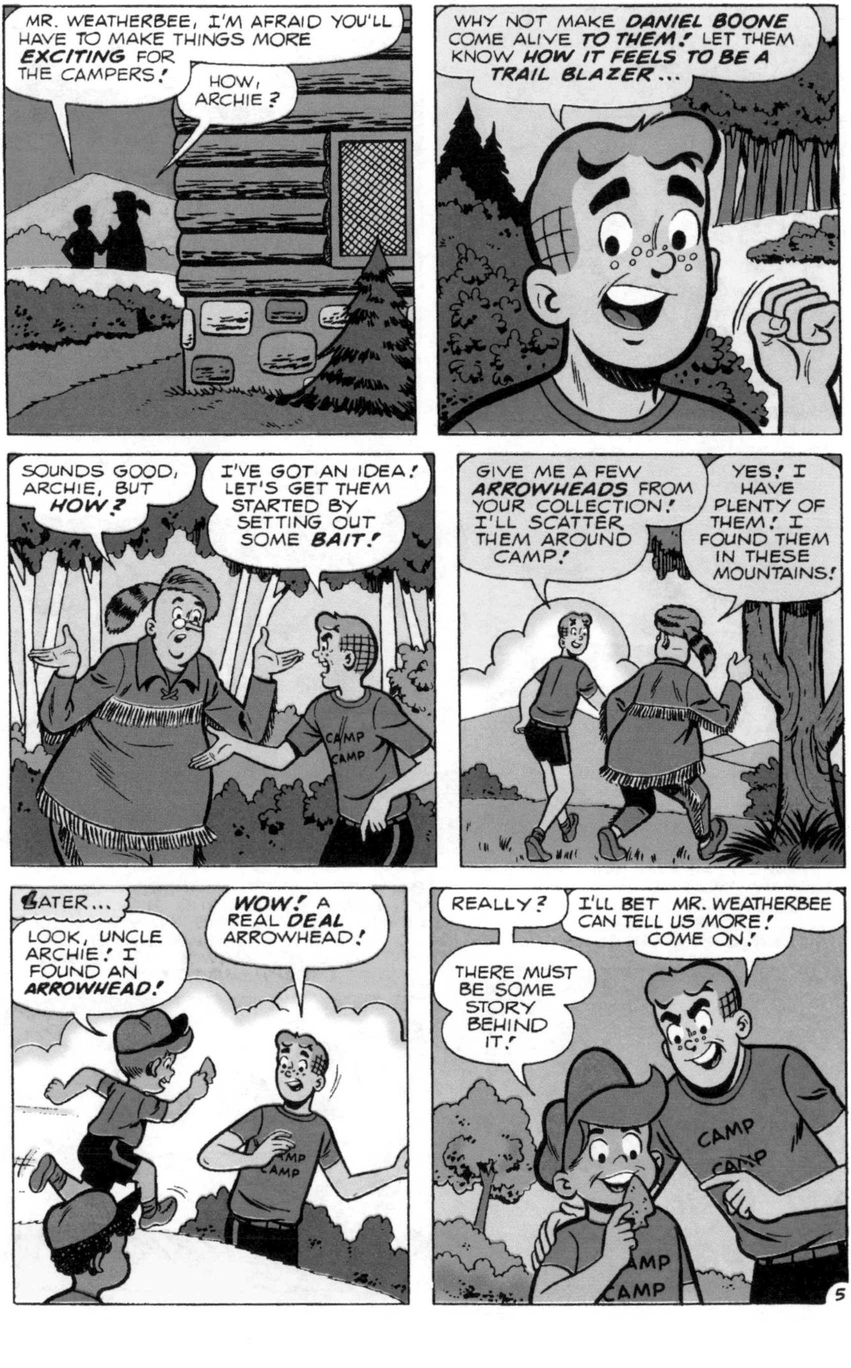
MR. WEATHERBEE, I'M AFRAID YOU'LL HAVE TO MAKE THINGS MORE EXCITING FOR THE CAMPERS!
HOW, ARCHIE?
WHY NOT MAKE DANIEL BOONE COME ALIVE TO THEM! LET THEM KNOW HOW IT FEELS TO BE A TRAIL BLAZER...
SOUNDS GOOD, ARCHIE, BUT HOW?
I'VE GOT AN IDEA! LET'S GET THEM STARTED BY SETTING OUT SOME BAIT!
GIVE ME A FEW ARROWHEADS FROM YOUR COLLECTION! I'LL SCATTER THEM AROUND CAMP!
YES! I HAVE PLENTY OF THEM! I FOUND THEM IN THESE MOUNTAINS!
LATER...
LOOK, UNCLE ARCHIE! I FOUND AN ARROWHEAD!
WOW! A REAL DEAL ARROWHEAD!
REALLY?
THERE MUST BE SOME STORY BEHIND IT!
I'LL BET MR. WEATHERBEE CAN TELL US MORE! COME ON!

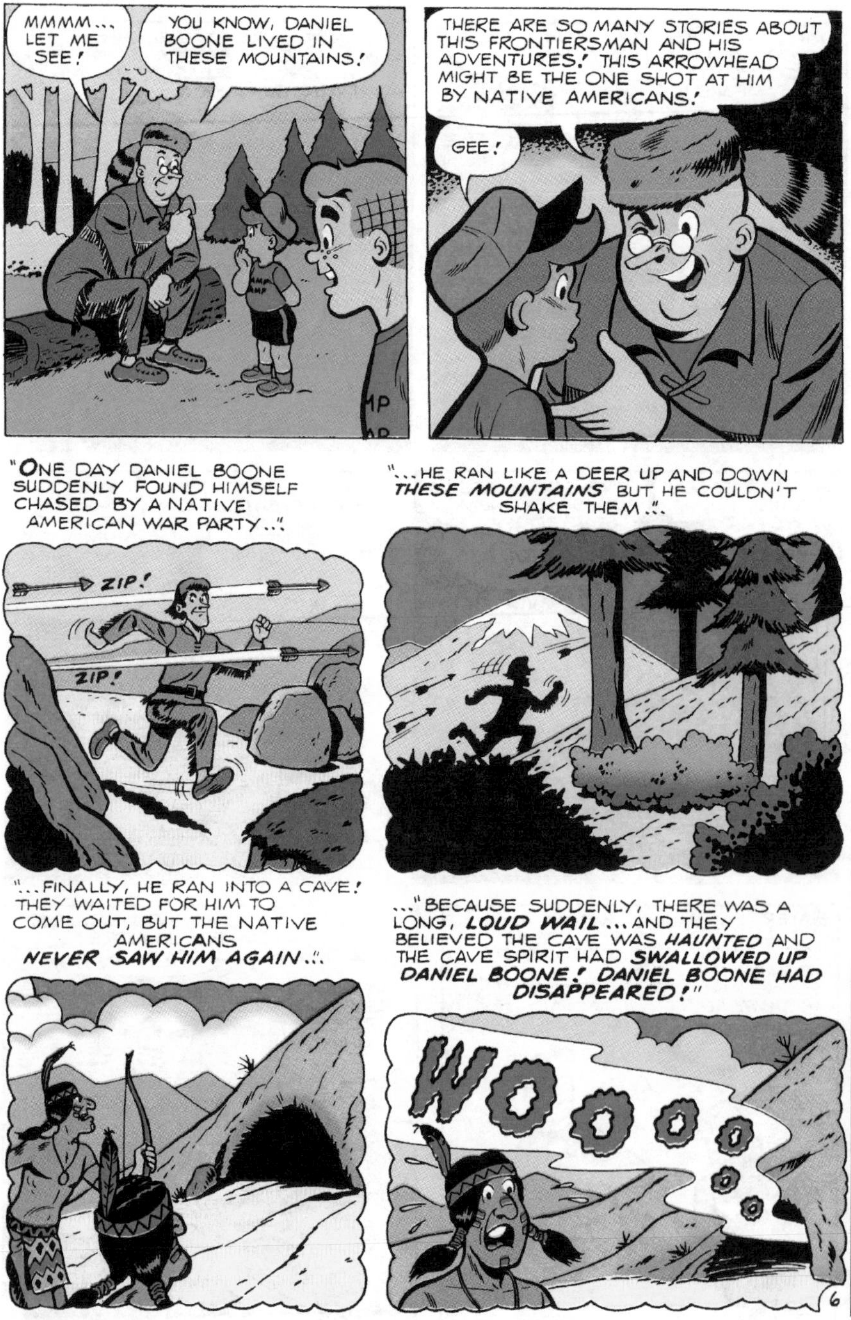
MMMM... LET ME SEE!
YOU KNOW, DANIEL BOONE LIVED IN THESE MOUNTAINS!
THERE ARE SO MANY STORIES ABOUT THIS FRONTIERSMAN AND HIS ADVENTURES! THIS ARROWHEAD MIGHT BE THE ONE SHOT AT HIM BY NATIVE AMERICANS!
GEE!
"ONE DAY DANIEL BOONE SUDDENLY FOUND HIMSELF CHASED BY A NATIVE AMERICAN WAR PARTY..."
ZIP!
ZIP!
"...HE RAN LIKE A DEER UP AND DOWN THESE MOUNTAINS BUT HE COULDN'T SHAKE THEM..."
"...FINALLY, HE RAN INTO A CAVE! THEY WAITED FOR HIM TO COME OUT, BUT THE NATIVE AMERICANS NEVER SAW HIM AGAIN..."
..."BECAUSE SUDDENLY, THERE WAS A LONG, LOUD WAIL... AND THEY BELIEVED THE CAVE WAS HAUNTED AND THE CAVE SPIRIT HAD SWALLOWED UP DANIEL BOONE! DANIEL BOONE HAD DISAPPEARED!"
WOOOOOO
6

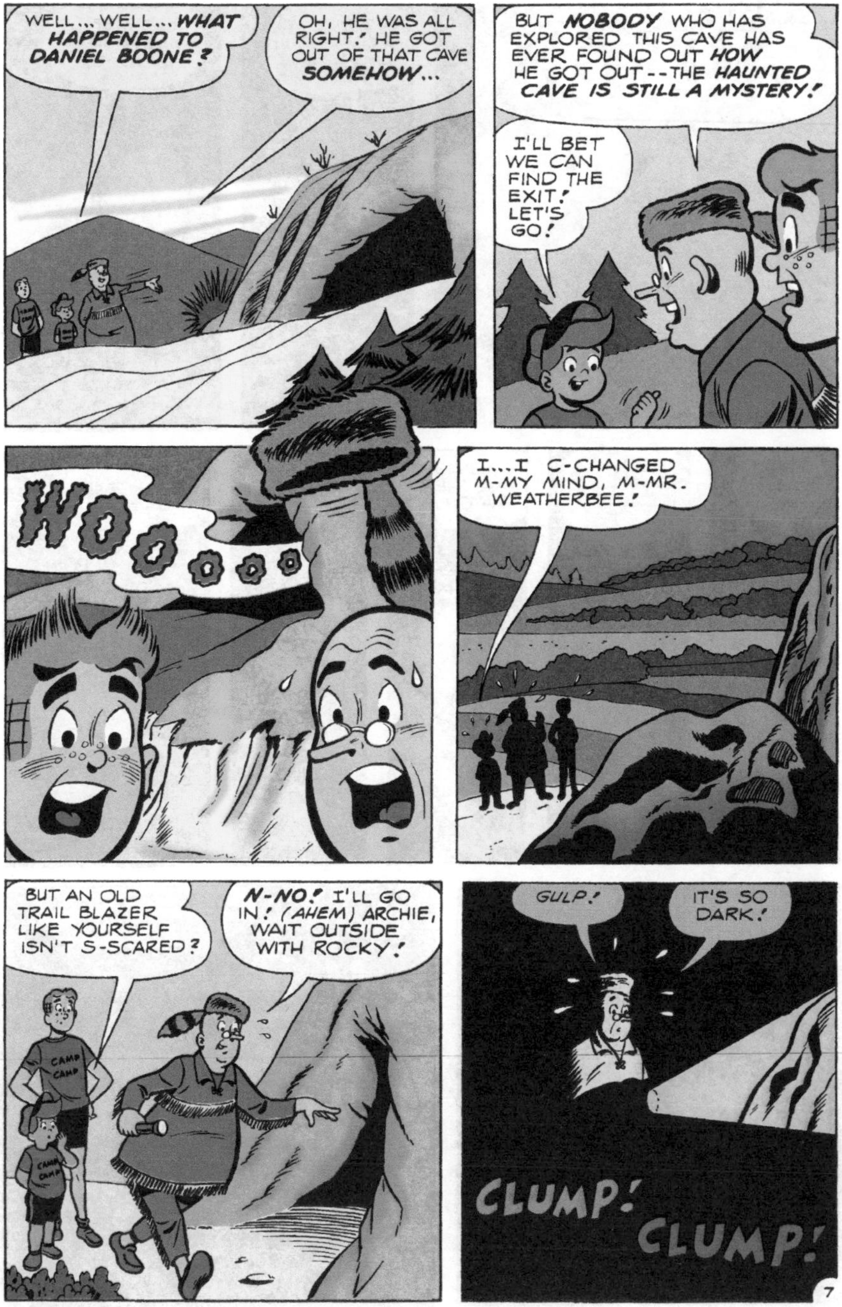
WELL... WELL... WHAT HAPPENED TO DANIEL BOONE?
OH, HE WAS ALL RIGHT! HE GOT OUT OF THAT CAVE SOMEHOW...
BUT NOBODY WHO HAS EXPLORED THIS CAVE HAS EVER FOUND OUT HOW HE GOT OUT--THE HAUNTED CAVE IS STILL A MYSTERY!
I'LL BET WE CAN FIND THE EXIT! LET'S GO!
WOOOOO
I...I C-CHANGED M-MY MIND, M-MR. WEATHERBEE!
BUT AN OLD TRAIL BLAZER LIKE YOURSELF ISN'T S-SCARED?
N-NO! I'LL GO IN! (AHEM) ARCHIE, WAIT OUTSIDE WITH ROCKY!
GULP!
IT'S SO DARK!
CLUMP! CLUMP!

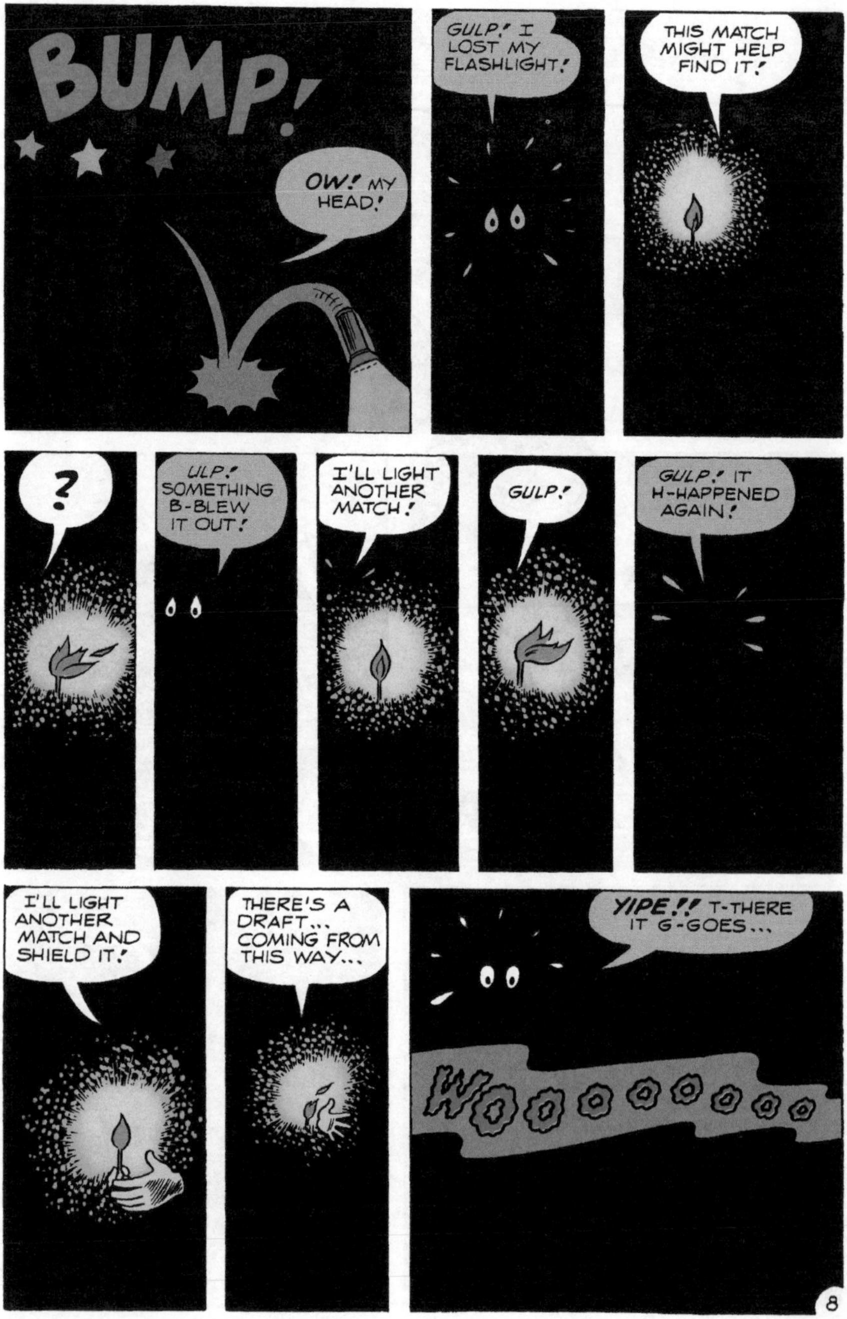
BUMP!
OW! MY HEAD!
GULP! I LOST MY FLASHLIGHT!
THIS MATCH MIGHT HELP FIND IT!
?
ULP! SOMETHING B-BLEW IT OUT!
I'LL LIGHT ANOTHER MATCH!
GULP!
GULP! IT H-HAPPENED AGAIN!
I'LL LIGHT ANOTHER MATCH AND SHIELD IT!
THERE'S A DRAFT... COMING FROM THIS WAY...
YIPE!!! T-THERE IT G-GOES...
WOOOOOOOOO

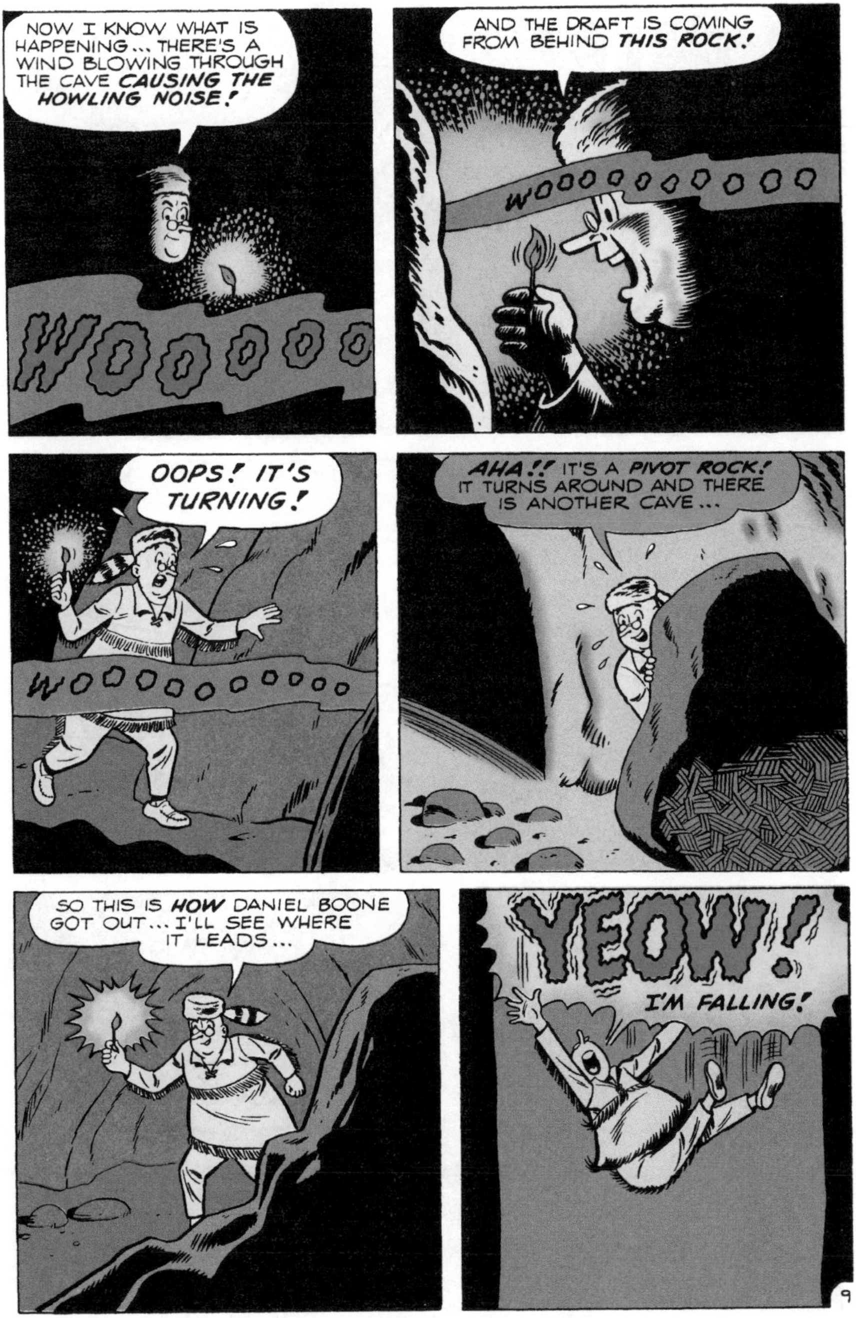
NOW I KNOW WHAT IS HAPPENING... THERE'S A WIND BLOWING THROUGH THE CAVE CAUSING THE HOWLING NOISE!
WOOOOO
AND THE DRAFT IS COMING FROM BEHIND THIS ROCK!
WOOOOOOOOOOO
OOPS! IT'S TURNING!
WOOOOOOOOOOO
AHA!! IT'S A PIVOT ROCK! IT TURNS AROUND AND THERE IS ANOTHER CAVE...
SO THIS IS HOW DANIEL BOONE GOT OUT... I'LL SEE WHERE IT LEADS...
YEOW!
I'M FALLING!

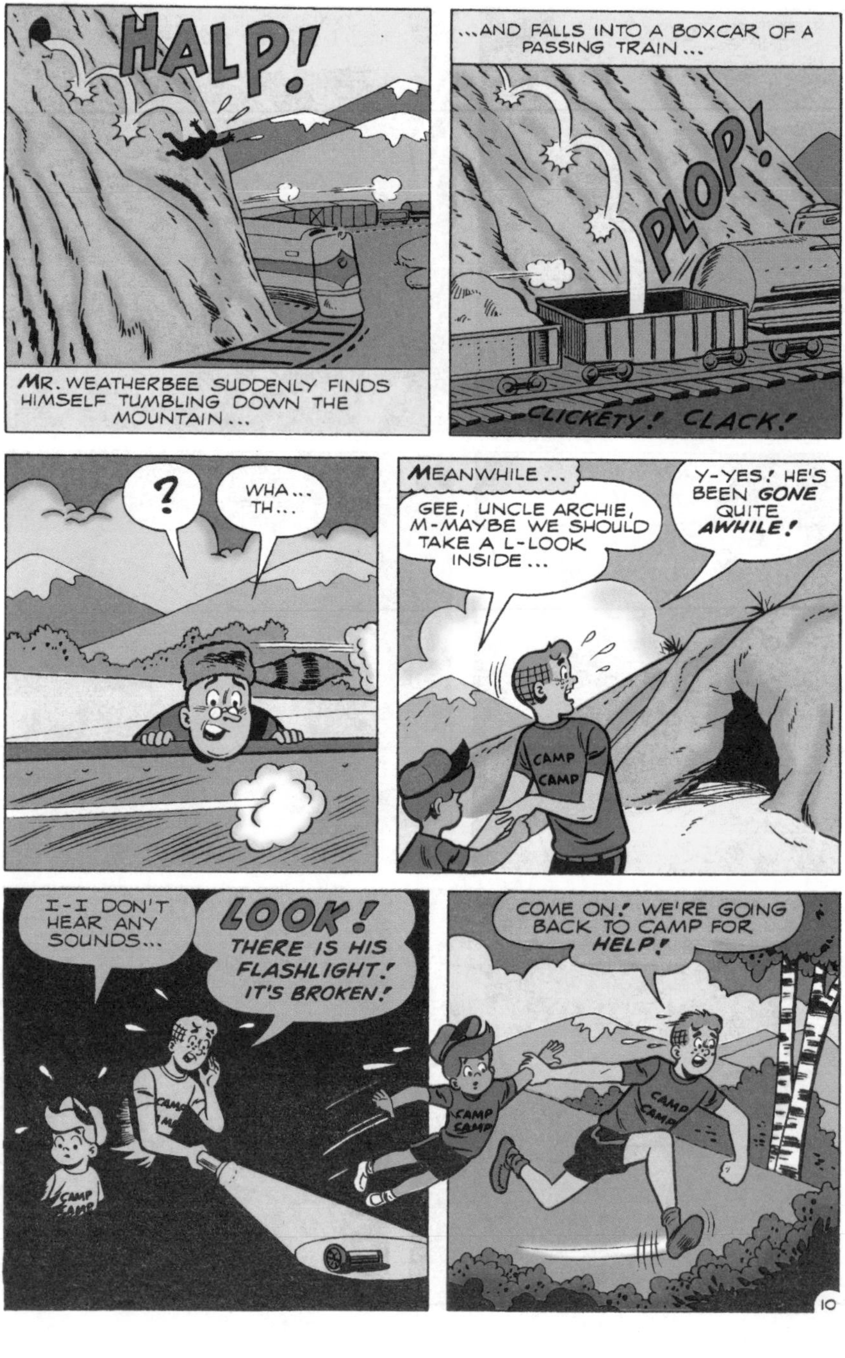
HALP!
MR. WEATHERBEE SUDDENLY FINDS HIMSELF TUMBLING DOWN THE MOUNTAIN...
...AND FALLS INTO A BOXCAR OF A PASSING TRAIN...
PLOP!
CLICKETY! CLACK!
?
WHA... TH...
MEANWHILE...
GEE, UNCLE ARCHIE, M-MAYBE WE SHOULD TAKE A L-LOOK INSIDE...
Y-YES! HE'S BEEN GONE QUITE AWHILE!
CAMP CAMP
I-I DON'T HEAR ANY SOUNDS...
LOOK! THERE IS HIS FLASHLIGHT! IT'S BROKEN!
COME ON! WE'RE GOING BACK TO CAMP FOR HELP!

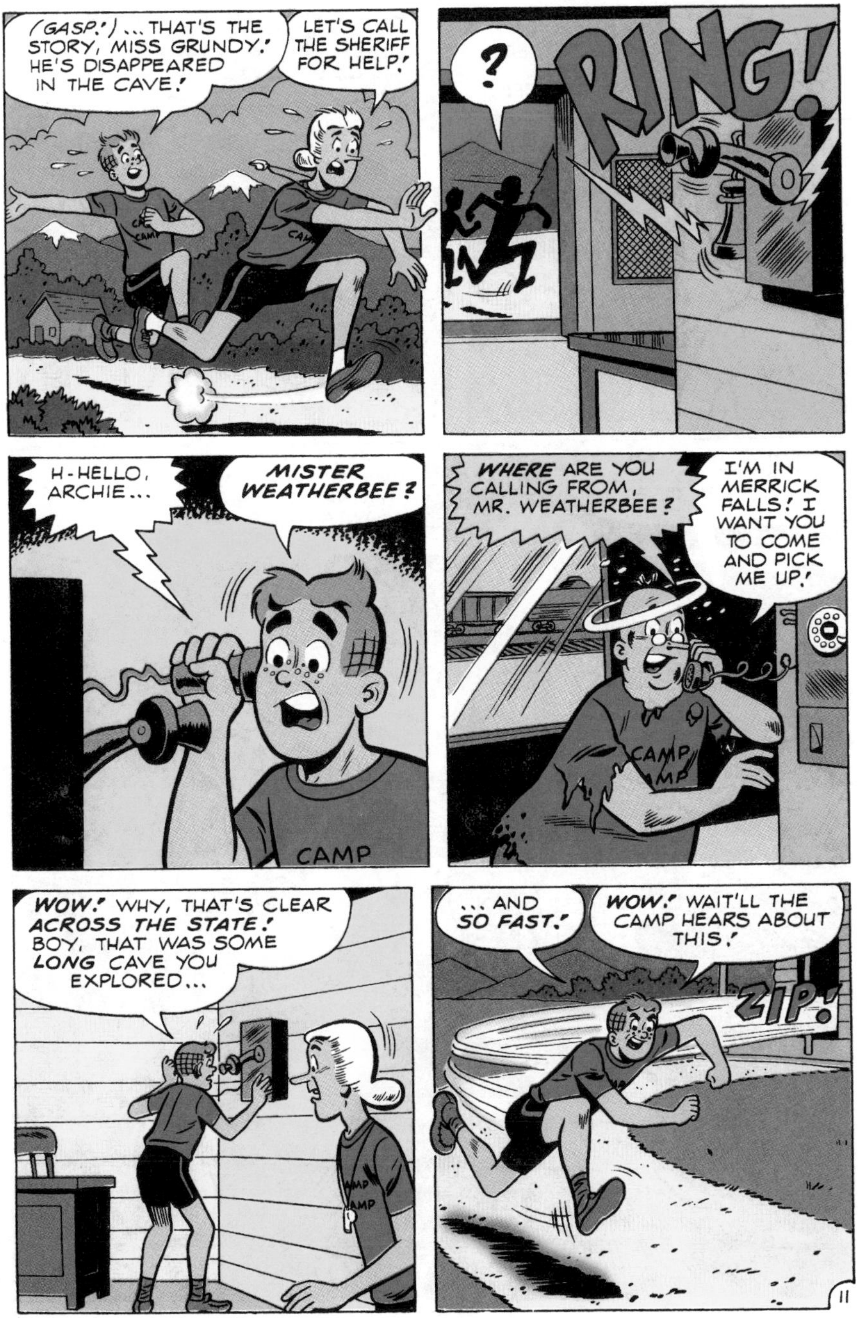
(GASP!) ... THAT'S THE STORY, MISS GRUNDY! HE'S DISAPPEARED IN THE CAVE!
LET'S CALL THE SHERIFF FOR HELP!
?
RING!
H-HELLO, ARCHIE...
MISTER WEATHERBEE?
WHERE ARE YOU CALLING FROM, MR. WEATHERBEE?
I'M IN MERRICK FALLS! I WANT YOU TO COME AND PICK ME UP!
CAMP
WOW! WHY, THAT'S CLEAR ACROSS THE STATE! BOY, THAT WAS SOME LONG CAVE YOU EXPLORED...
... AND SO FAST!
WOW! WAIT'LL THE CAMP HEARS ABOUT THIS!
ZIP!
11

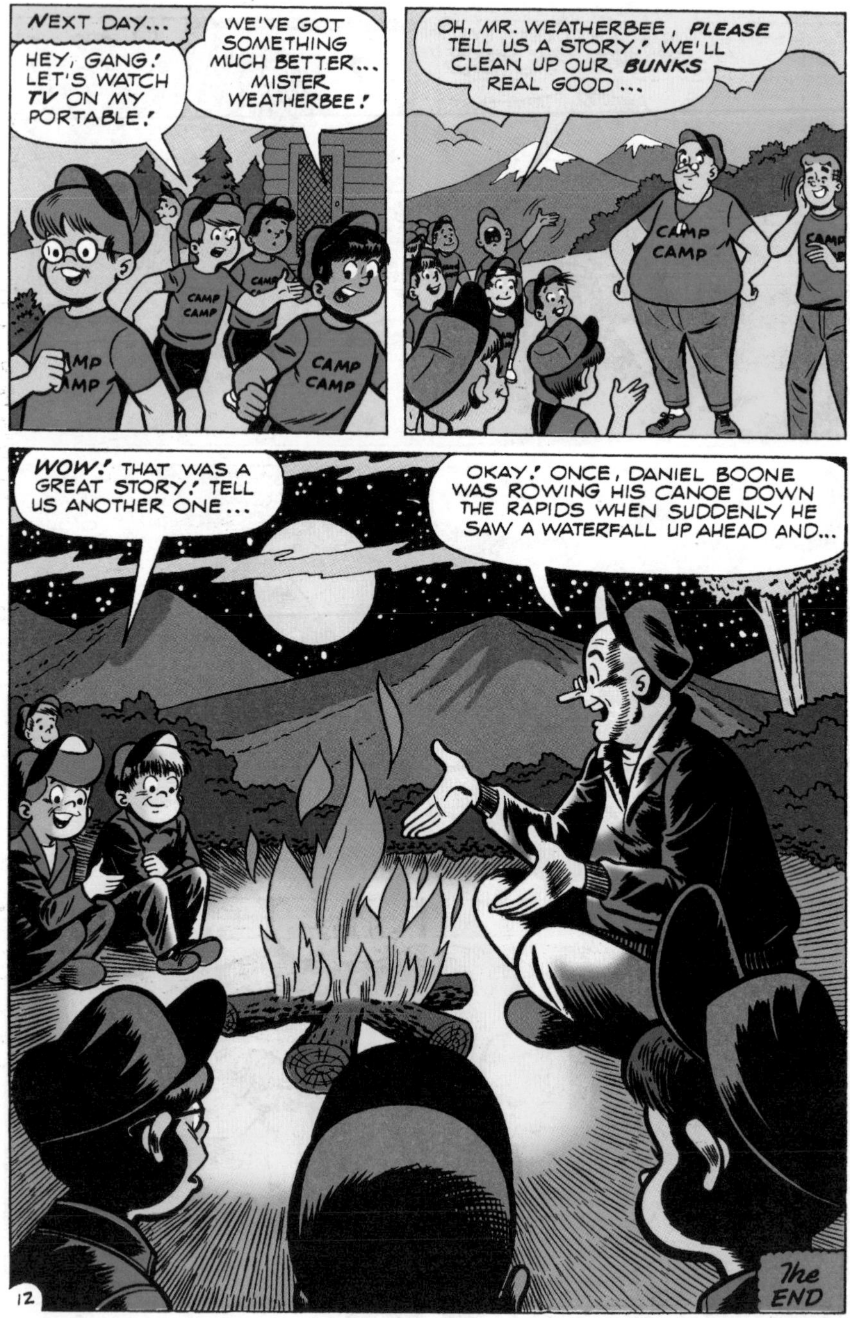
NEXT DAY...
HEY, GANG! LET'S WATCH TV ON MY PORTABLE!
WE'VE GOT SOMETHING MUCH BETTER... MISTER WEATHERBEE!
CAMP CAMP
OH, MR. WEATHERBEE, PLEASE TELL US A STORY! WE'LL CLEAN UP OUR BUNKS REAL GOOD...
CAMP CAMP
WOW! THAT WAS A GREAT STORY! TELL US ANOTHER ONE...
OKAY! ONCE, DANIEL BOONE WAS ROWING HIS CANOE DOWN THE RAPIDS WHEN SUDDENLY HE SAW A WATERFALL UP AHEAD AND...
12
The END